MW01088924

HEROES & HEROINES

MYTHS & TALES

ANTHOLOGY OF CLASSIC TALES

Foreword by Maria Tatar

FLAME TREE PUBLISHING

This is a FLAME TREE Book

Publisher & Creative Director: Nick Wells
Editorial Director: Catherine Taylor
Special thanks to Karen Fitzpatrick and Michael Kerrigan

FLAME TREE PUBLISHING
6 Melbray Mews, Fulham,
London SW6 3NS, United Kingdom
www.flametreepublishing.com

First published 2020

20 22 24 23 21
1 3 5 7 9 10 8 6 4 2

ISBN: 978-1-83964-166-4

The cover image is created by Flame Tree Studio
based on artwork by Vecster.

Incidental motif images by Shutterstock.com:
Alexander Ryabintsev and Trikona

A copy of the CIP data for this book is available from the British Library.

Printed and bound in China

EPIC TALES

HEROES & HEROINES

MYTHS & TALES

ANTHOLOGY OF CLASSIC TALES

Foreword by Maria Tatar

FLAME TREE PUBLISHING

Contents

Foreword ... 8
Publisher's Note ... 9

HEROES & HEROINES IN MYTH & FOLKLORE: INTRODUCTION ... 13
Hero Myths in Native American Culture ... 14
Quetzalcoatl and American Myths of the Discovery of Mexico ... 15
Celtic Gods and Heroes ... 15
The Legend of King Arthur ... 16
Gods and Heroes in Norse Mythology ... 16
Human Heroes and Demigods in Greek Mythology ... 18
Africa's Diverse Mythology ... 19
Egyptian Legends of the Gods ... 19
Mesopotamian Heroes: The Gilgamesh Epic ... 19
Classical Indian Literature ... 20
Chinese Cultural Gods and Heroes ... 21
Heroes, Warriors and Adventure in Japanese Mythology ... 22
Polynesian Parallels ... 23

TALES OF WARRIORS, TRAVEL & ADVENTURE
Introduction ... 25
The Legend of Scar-face ... 26
(From Native American Mythology)
The Legend of Hiawatha ... 30
(From Native American Mythology)
The Noble Tlascalan Leader Tlalhuicole ... 32
(From Mesoamerican Mythology)
Sargon, A Babylonian Conqueror ... 33
(From Mesopotamian Mythology)
The Gilgamesh Epic ... 33
(From Mesopotamian Mythology)
The Story of Sanehat ... 41
(From Egyptian Mythology)
The Story of the Educated Peasant Khuenanpu ... 48
(From Egyptian Mythology)

The Journey of the Priest Unu Amen into Syria 55
(From Egyptian Mythology)

The Wanderings of Odysseus 61
(From Greek Mythology)

Jason and the Argonauts 79
(From Greek Mythology)

The Calydonian Boar Hunt 89
(From Greek Mythology)

Adventures of Aeneas 91
(From Greco-Roman Mythology)

Yoshitsune and Benkei 106
(From Japanese Mythology)

Yorimasa 108
(From Japanese Mythology)

The Adventures of Prince Yamato Take 109
(From Japanese Mythology)

The Adventures of Momotaro 112
(From Japanese Mythology)

My Lord Bag of Rice 114
(From Japanese Mythology)

Kintaro, the Golden Boy 115
(From Japanese Mythology)

The Wonderful Adventures of Funakoshi Jiuyemon 117
(From Japanese Mythology)

Heroes & Heroines in Literature & Poetry

Introduction 129

Tales of Ramayana 130
(From Indian Mythology)

The Saga of Mahabharata 143
(From Indian Mythology)

Legends of Indra & Yama 204
(From Indian Mythology)

The 'Hadithi yar Liongo' 213
(From East African Mythology)

The Transformation of Arachne into a Spider 216
(From Greco-Roman Mythology)

The Story of Tereus, Procne and Philomela 221
(From Greco-Roman Mythology)

Stories of Cúchulainn of the Red Guard 231
(From Celtic Mythology)

Tales of Finn Mac Cumaill and the Fianna 244
(From Celtic Mythology)

The Legend of Tchi-Niu 260
(From Chinese Mythology)

Tales of King Arthur, from
Le Morte d'Arthur: Book I 264
(From British Mythology)

Extracts from the Sigurd Saga 268
(From Norse Mythology)

The Story of Frithiof the Bold 281
(From Norse Mythology)

Legends of the Gods, Demigods & Culture Heroes

Introduction 303

The Mexican Legend of Quetzalcoatl 304
(From Mesoamerican Mythology)

Viracocha 307
(From Incan Mythology)

Thonapa 307
(From Incan Mythology)

Anansi Obtains the Sky-God's Stories 308
(From West African Mythology)

The Legend of Ra and Isis 310
(From Egyptian Mythology)

The Legend of Horus of Behutet 312
(From Egyptian Mythology)

The Legend of Khnemu and
the Seven Years' Famine 314
(From Egyptian Mythology)

Perseus and the Gorgon 317
(From Greek Mythology)

Theseus 319
(From Greek Mythology)

Tales of Heracles 323
(From Greek Mythology)

Legends of Krishna 337
(From Indian Mythology)

The Ten Suns of Dijun and Xihe 343
(From Chinese Mythology)

Tales of the Five Emperors 345
(From Chinese Mythology)

Hou-Ji, the Ice-Child 353
(From Chinese Mythology)

Kuan Ti, the God of War 355
(From Chinese Mythology)

Legends of Thor 357
(From Norse Mythology)

Maui Snaring the Sun 375
(From Polynesian Mythology)

Leading Ladies & Affairs of the Heart

Introduction 379

A Thousand and One Nights:
Storyteller Heroine, Scheherazade 380
(From Middle Eastern Mythology)

The Princess of Babylon 382
(From Mesopotamian Mythology)

Wanjiru, Sacrificed by Her Family 418
(From Kenyan Mythology)

The End of Troy and the Saving of Helen 420
(From Greek Mythology)

The Story of Deirdre 422
(From Celtic Mythology)

Tales of the Goddess of Mercy 430
(From Chinese Mythology)

The Bamboo Cutter and the Moon Maiden 444
(From Japanese Mythology)

The Maiden with the Wooden Bowl 451
(From Japanese Mythology)

The Loves of Gompachi and Komurasaki 453
(From Japanese Mythology)

The Outcast Maiden and the Hatamoto 457
(From Japanese Mythology)

The Story of Princess Hase 467
(From Japanese Mythology)

Text Sources & Biographies 472

Foreword

J.R.R. TOLKIEN ONCE WROTE about the 'Great Cauldron of Story', a brew that includes myths, epics, fairy tales, legends, and all manner of other narratives. Bits and pieces, 'dainty' and 'undainty', are constantly added to that brew to enhance its aroma and flavour. The author of *The Lord of the Rings* also told us about how 'story-makers' become creators, building secondary worlds that we enter in our minds, all the while willingly suspending disbelief. Gods and heroes, villains and victims, tricksters and saints – these all populate the universe of Story, helping us to imagine perils and possibilities, anxieties and desires, terrors and fantasies. Conflict and conflagration, creation and destruction, suffering and redemption are *de rigueur* in tales that have served as charter narratives, foundational stories and cultural touchstones through the ages. There is *The Iliad*, which tells of the Trojan War, the Indian *Mahabharata* which plots the struggles between two kinship units, and the Egyptian account of the contest between Ra and Isis.

Evolutionary psychologists like Jonathan Gottschall have drawn our attention to storytelling as an adaptive behaviour. Anthropologists remind us that national epics foster cultural solidarity and enforce social norms. And folklorists assert that the stories we tell each other often clear a pathway to ethical behaviour, for they contain all manner of violence and oppression only to declare that injustice cannot and will not prevail. Like Odin's two ravens, Huginn and Muninn, they are carriers of thought and memory, helping us make sense of the world, consoling and comforting us, and teaching us survival skills by modelling wisdom, wit, courage, generosity and resilience. We have always needed the symbolic to help us discover what we need to navigate the real.

But beyond that, the stories we hear and read tug at our hearts and minds, teaching us about what could be, should be and might be, even as, and especially when, we resist their terms and rewrite them. Our new attentiveness to social injustices, gender identity, race and ethnicity, disability and alterity, along with an array of issues related to socio-economic status, makes some of the stories from times past shocking, not so much because of their violent turns but because they model behaviours that we can no longer embrace today. Nowhere is this more evident than in stories about heroic figures and the attributes, behaviours and traits that led to their social elevation and marked their rule.

It took nearly 300 years for the English language to invent a female counterpart to the male 'hero', first cited in the English language in 1387. The term was given in ancient times to men who possessed superhuman strength and performed great deeds. Occupying a liminal space between men and gods, heroes were often associated with military valour or Herculean abilities, as it were. It is no accident that a mythographer like Joseph Campbell focused on men in his landmark *Hero with a Thousand Faces*, with its one 'marvellously constant story' that follows the hero from the womb to the symbolic tomb, followed by resurrection and redemption in one form or another, often for all mankind. 'Women don't need to make the journey. In the whole mythological tradition the woman is *there*, waiting for the man to return,' he added.

Today we are reframing many stories from times past, recognizing that heroines were also able to carry out superhuman deeds, without ever leaving the house. Their quests may not take the form of journeys, but they require acts of courage and defiance. Like Scheherazade (see page 380), Philomela (page 221), Arachne (page 216) or Penelope (page 76), they use their homespun storytelling craft or draw on arts related to textile production (weaving tapestries that tell tales) to right wrongs and broadcast misdeeds, all in the service of changing the culture in which they live.

In this anthology, they can rise up and take their places in a new pantheon that is reshaping our notion of what constitutes courage and valour – what it means to be a hero today.

Recall Scheherazade's words: 'I will begin with a story and it will cause the king to stop his practice, save myself, and deliver the people.'[1] Scheherazade's triple project is ambitious and underscores the fact that there is nothing more powerful than a good story. She is seeking to put an end to Shahryar's[2] practice of beheading his wives, and she also wants to survive the tyrannical regime of her husband. The redemptive cliffhangers she crafts 'educate' the king by exposing him to the entire spectrum of human behaviour, arousing his desire to know not just 'what's next?' but also 'why?' and thereby creating a partnership in which there is much to talk about. Stories have been invented, not just to entertain and instruct, but also to get us talking and thinking about how to imagine a brighter and more colourful Elsewhere than the world in which we live today.

Maria Tatar
John L. Loeb Research Professor of
Germanic Languages & Literatures and Folklore & Mythology, Harvard University

Publisher's Note

AS TALES FROM MYTHOLOGY AND FOLKLORE are principally derived from an oral storytelling tradition, their written representation depends on the transcription, translation and interpretation by those who heard them and first put them to paper, and also on whether they are recently re-told versions or more directly sourced from original first-hand accounts. The stories in this book are a mixture, and you can learn more about the sources and authors at the back of the book. This collection presents a thoughtfully selected cross-section of stories from all over the world, though some countries may seem more heavily represented than others since their cultures more readily define characters with a heroic status. For the purposes of simplicity and consistency, most diacritical marks have been removed, since their usage in the original sources was sometimes inconsistent or would represent different pronunciation, depending on the original language of the story, not to mention that quite a sophisticated understanding of phonetic conventions would be required to understand how to pronounce them anyway.

We also ask the reader to remember that while the myths and tales are timeless, much of the factual information, opinions regarding the nature of countries and their peoples, as well as the style of writing in this anthology, are of the era during which they were written.

1 Muhsin Mahdi, ed. *The Arabian Nights*, trans. Husain Haddawy (New York: W.W. Norton, 1990), page 16.

2 Note the difference in spellings on page 380 from this standard English spelling – spellings vary enormously from one translation to the next.

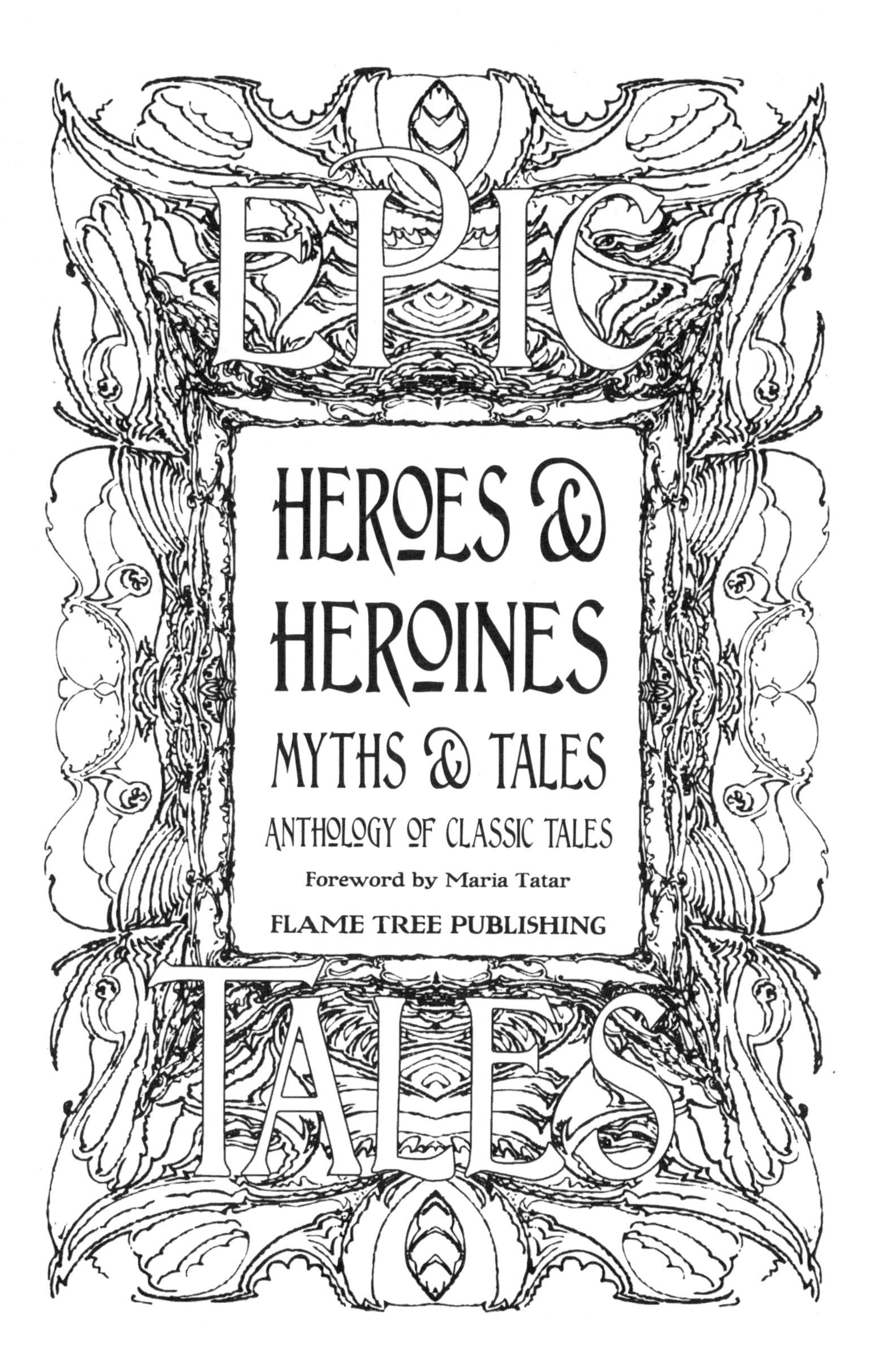
EPIC
HEROES & HEROINES
MYTHS & TALES
ANTHOLOGY OF CLASSIC TALES
Foreword by Maria Tatar
FLAME TREE PUBLISHING
TALES

Heroes & Heroines in Myth & Folklore

Introduction

EVERY CULTURE HAS had its heroes and heroines – men and women who are seen as perfectly personifying their civilization's highest principles and most cherished values.

Courage has typically topped the list of attributes – asked for a one-word definition of heroism to this day, most of us would have no hesitation in saying 'bravery'. Skill at arms and warlike prowess are also expected of the mythic hero. Rightly or wrongly, these qualities have been closely identified with social rank (the modern English word 'coward' comes from 'cowherd', a peasant's role). So too have gentleness (the origin of the modern English 'gentleman') and magnanimity – literally 'greatness of soul', and associated with the idea of 'nobility' – simultaneously status-markers and moral judgements.

No hero is an island, then: the idea encompasses an entire social vision. The same goes for the heroine as well. Traditionally, feminine virtue was very different from masculine valour: the heroine was patient, stoical, self-sacrificing ... an ancillary role, but just as vital to the social order.

Hero Myths in Native American Culture

We see the heroic qualities as defined by their social background in the hero myths of the Native Americans. Not only do these tales show the hero having to contend with trials of courage or tests of his abilities: they show him having to do so within the context of his society, on the terms of its tribal organization. He is, nevertheless, frequently defined by his difference from others. Lazy Boy in Plains Indian stories is derided because he spends his time sleeping, and refuses to engage in the industrious pursuits of war and the chase suitable to young Plains warriors. It is only when the entire tribe is threatened by man-eating buffaloes that he wakes up, sets out alone to defeat the buffalo and then returns and goes back to sleep that the people recognize his extraordinary skills.

Unpromising and reluctant heroes such as Lazy Boy are frequent in Plains tales, but also occur with regularity among tribes of the Plateau (the river-cut tablelands of central interior British Columbia, eastern Oregon and Washington) and among the Iroquois. Among the Okanagon on the Washington–British Columbia border he is Dirty Boy, who lives in a decrepit lodge of brush and bark at the edge of the camp and soils his bed. His only companion is his grandmother, whom the tales describe as a toothless old crone dressed in rags. Unknown to the people, the grandmother is Star and the boy is Sun. When the chief arranges a contest to select suitable marriage partners for his daughters, Dirty Boy wins all the contests but the chief and his elder daughter are reluctant to accept this filthy child as a son-in-law. The younger daughter, however, goes to Dirty Boy's lodge. In the morning, when a wealthy tribe arrive to celebrate the marriage ceremony of the pair, the grandmother emerges as a young woman in a skin dress sparkling with starlight and with stars in her hair, while so many stars shine around Dirty Boy that people are dazzled if they look at him. The younger daughter is bathed by the grandmother and also becomes covered in stars, but the jealous elder daughter has to go and live with the ravens (the myth does not specify why, but it is presumably due to the ravens' reputation for cheating, which becomes apparent in other tales).

Such tales define the nature of the hero and carry a moral that things should not always be judged by their appearance. In other stories the heroes are often twins who suffer adversity but support each other. In Apache stories one of the twins is lame, the other blind. The tales tell of how the blind brother carries the lame one to give him legs and of how the lame twin acts as his brother's eyes.

Elsewhere the world is formed by arguments that occur between the twin heroes. The famous tales of Manabozho from the Menominee (a Great Lakes tribe) are characteristic of these. Manabozho is helped by a good manitou (a spirit or power that influences life) and it is from him that many stories of the Noble Savage have passed into the popular imagination and from whom, according to the Menominee storytellers, the tales of Brer Rabbit derive. Manabozho had a twin, Naqpote, who could assume the form of a wolf, and whatever Manabozho did during the day, Naqpote would reverse at night. According to one tale, the twins decided to have a final contest. Manabozho called all his helpers – the thunderers (in Great Lakes mythology there was a division between the sky powers – represented by the thunderers – and the underwater powers – represented by the underwater panther).

Thunderers are mythological creatures, associated with the thunderbird, whose eyes flash lightning and whose wing claps are thunder; his earthly counterparts are the eagles, the geese, ducks and pigeons. Naqpote set his assistants – the under-ground bear, snakes, otters, fishes, deer and other beasts of the field – against them. The contest was undecided. Naqpote now lives in a stone canoe in the north of the world and has threatened to return; Manabozho appears to people frequently as a little white rabbit with trembling ears who anxiously awaits the return of his twin.

Hero tales often involve characters whose births are little short of miraculous. Among the Blackfoot, Blood-Clot Boy is born from a clot of buffalo blood and returns to rescue his aged parents from the tyrannical rule imposed on them by their son-in-law. The Crow Indians tell of Lodge Boy and Thrown-Away whose mother is killed by the evil Red Woman. Lodge Boy lives behind the curtain which lines his father's tipi, but Thrown-Away is cast into a spring where the animals succour him. When the two are finally reconciled with their father, they are found to have gained prodigious skills and perform magic to bring their mother back to life before setting out on adventures in which they overcome various giants and cannibals who threaten the people.

Quetzalcoatl and American Myths of the Discovery of Mexico

The ultimate hero-divinity was – by an extraordinary collision of myth and history – the Spanish conquistador Hernán Cortés (1485–1547), who arrived in Mexico in 1519. Immediately prior to the Europeans' discovery, it had been widely believed in Mesoamerica that, at a relatively remote period, strangers from the east had visited American soil, eventually returning to their own abodes in the Land of Sunrise. See, for example, the Mexican legend of Quetzalcoatl on page 304. He landed with several companions at Veracruz, and speedily brought to bear the power of a civilizing agency upon native opinion. In the ancient Mexican *pinturas*, or paintings, he is represented as being habited in a long black gown, fringed with white crosses.

After sojourning with the Mexicans for a number of years, during which time he initiated them into the arts of life and civilization, he departed from their land on a magic raft, promising, however, to return. His second advent was anxiously looked for, and when Cortés and his companions arrived at Vera Cruz, the identical spot at which Quetzalcoatl was supposed to have set out on his homeward journey, the Mexicans fully believed him to be the returned hero. Of course Montezuma, their monarch, was not altogether taken by surprise at the coming of the white man, as he had been informed of the arrival of mysterious strangers in Yucatán and elsewhere in Central America; but in the eyes of the commonalty the Spanish leader was a 'hero-god' indeed.

Celtic Gods and Heroes

The Celts had gods for all of the important aspects of their lives: warfare, hunting, fertility, healing, good harvests and so on. Much of the difficulty in classifying them arises from the fact that very few were recognized universally. In much greater numbers were local, tribal and possibly family deities. Our knowledge of the Celtic pantheon is based on the interpretations of contemporary observers, later vernacular literature (mainly from Ireland and Wales) and archaeological finds.

It is to Christian monks that we owe the survival of the ancient oral traditions of the pagan Celts and a more lucid insight into the nature of their deities – and indeed perhaps more specifically their *heroes*. Very little was committed to paper before the monks began writing down Irish tales in the sixth century AD. The earliest written Welsh material dates from the twelfth century. Informative though they might be, however, the stories are influenced by Romano-Christian thinking and no doubt the monks censored the worst excesses of heathenism. In other words their reluctance to characterize these figures in Celtic myths as deities is thought to be behind their demotion to the rank of heroes in subsequent tradition.

The stories are collected in sequences which follow the exploits of heroes, legendary kings and mythical characters from their unusual forms of conception and birth to their remarkable deaths. Along the way we learn of their expeditions to the otherworld, their loves and their battles. Many of the Irish legends are contained in three such collections. The first, known as the *Mythological Cycle* or *Book of Invasions*, records the imagined early history of Ireland. The second, the *Ulster Cycle*, tells of Cúchulainn, a hero with superhuman strength and magical powers. The third is the story of another hero, Finn mac Cumaill, his son Ossian and their warriors, the Fianna. This is known as the *Fenian Cycle*. The pagan character of the mythology found in Irish literature is very clear. The Welsh tales, collected mainly in the *Mabinogion*, are much later (fourteenth century) and are contaminated more by time and changing literary fashions.

The Legend of King Arthur

The legend of King Arthur and the Knights of the Round Table has captured the imagination of readers, writers, artists, and composers for more than a thousand years. From its first flourishing in the Middle Ages, through each successive era, it has been a touchstone for strong leadership and accord, speaking to an elusive 'golden age' that never existed and offering consolation when things fall apart. Even in our modern age, the phenomenal number of films, TV series, novels, history books, video games, comics, websites, tourist attractions, university courses, and merchandise drawing inspiration from the Arthurian legend reveals just how powerful Arthur's story continues to be, captivating people the world over.

Among the countless re-workings of King Arthur's reign *Le Morte d'Arthur*, completed in 1469–70 by Sir Thomas Malory, 'knight-prisoner', has been the most influential in shaping perceptions of Arthur and his companions across the ages. Written in England during the dynastic conflict known as The Wars of the Roses, the *Morte d'Arthur* draws on an impressive range of French and English sources, such as the Post-Vulgate Cycle, the *Prose Tristan*, the *Alliterative Morte Arthure*, and John Hardyng's *Chronicle*, weaving them into a single compelling narrative that captures a range of conflicting emotions and insights into the medieval world. Chivalry, friendship, love, jealousy, cowardice, bravery, loyalty, betrayal, sin, and redemption all have a part to play in this epic tale.

From Merlin and the sword in the stone, Excalibur and the Lady of the Lake, and the quest for the Holy Grail, to the tragic love affair of Sir Lancelot and Queen Guinevere, and the treachery of Sir Mordred, Malory uses the very best the Arthurian legend has to offer to navigate the mutability of the world and the uncertainty of the human condition.

Gods and Heroes in Norse Mythology

Thor

The best-loved of the Northern gods, the mighty figure of Thor might be considered a divine hero. He strode the cosmos, fighting the forces of evil: giants and trolls. He was the protector of Asgard and the gods could always call upon him if they were in trouble – as could mankind – and many relied on him.

Ordinary people put their trust in Thor, for Thor's concerns were with justice, order and the protection of gods and men. Ancient inscriptions on rune stones, such as 'may Thor bless these runes' or 'may Thor bless this memorial', or sometimes just 'may Thor bless' are common.

Sometimes Thor's protection was invoked merely with a carving of a hammer. Thor's hammer as a symbol of protection is also seen in miniature version in the form of little hammers of silver or other metals which were placed in graves alongside the buried bodies.

Thor's mighty strength excelled that of all other gods. He was huge, with red hair and beard and red eyebrows that sank down over his face when he was angry. Thunder was thought to be the sound of Thor's chariot driving across the sky, and his fierce, red, flashing eyes befitted the god of thunder and lightning. Thor also had an enormous appetite, regularly devouring more than a whole ox at one sitting.

Thor's most important possession was his hammer, Miolnir, which could never miss its mark, whether raised up or thrown, and would always return to Thor's hand. With this weapon Thor kept the forces of evil at bay, protecting the gods and mankind. Furthermore, Miolnir held the power to sanctify and could be raised for the purpose of blessing. As well as Miolnir, Thor owned a belt of strength which doubled his already formidable might when buckled on, and a pair of iron gloves, without which he could not wield Miolnir.

Thor's main occupation was destroying giants, a constant threat to the worlds of gods and men. Thor actively sought them out, with the express intention of their annihilation, and seldom hesitated to raise his hammer when he encountered one. If any gods were threatened, Thor would instantly appear. Famous stories tell how Thor defeated the giant Hrungnir, strongest of all giants, in a duel; and how he destroyed the giant Geirrod, in spite of Geirrod's attempts to attack him. The situation was not always clear-cut, however. Giants were occasionally helpful – although Geirrod and his two daughters made many attempts to defeat Thor, another giantess, Grid, chose to forewarn Thor and lent him a staff and some iron gloves. Thor even had two sons, Modi and Magni, with a giantess, Jarnsaxa. Nevertheless, Giants were usually Thor's hostile adversaries.

Many tales of Thor are affectionately humorous, attesting to the fondness the populace had for him. When Thor's hammer was stolen by a giant demanding Freyia as his wife, Thor, to his horror, had to agree to be dressed up as the bride and delivered to the giant in order to destroy the giant and thus reclaim his hammer. Gentle humour is also evident in the tale of Thor's encounter with a magical giant king, Utgard-Loki. Thor's brute strength is not enough when pitted against Utgard-Loki's magical wiles, but even so the giants have to retain a healthy respect for Thor for trying.

The Volsunga Saga and Sigurd

While the first part of the *Elder Edda* consists of a collection of alliterative poems describing the creation of the world, the adventures of the gods, their eventual downfall, and gives a complete exposition of the Northern code of ethics, the second part comprises a series of heroic lays describing the exploits of the Volsung family, and especially of their chief representative, Sigurd, the favourite hero of the North.

These lays form the basis of the great Scandinavian epic, the *Volsunga Saga*, and have supplied not only the materials for the *Nibelungenlied*, the German epic, and for countless folk tales, but also for Wagner's celebrated operas, *The Rhinegold*, *Valkyr*, *Siegfried*, and *The Dusk of the Gods*.

Frithiof the Bold

The story of Frithiof the Bold is from a legendary Icelandic saga originating in *c.* 1300. It follows on from *The Saga of Thorstein Vikingsson* and is set in eighth-century Norway. Frithiof was the son of Thorstein and was raised with King Beli's daughter. Everyone was jealous of Frithiof's strength and attributes and he was de-nied marriage to the women he loved. The saga is one of a hero who fights to marry the love of his life. The Saga has been translated into every European language and Kaiser Willhelm II of Germany had a statue of Frithiof erected in 1913. William Morris originally published his and Eirikr Magnusson's translation of this saga in two parts, in the March and April 1871 issues of *Dark Blue*, and following this it was included in *Three Northern Love Stories, and Other Tales.* It is extracts from this version that are used in this book, with some spellings altered and divided into two parts (as per the *Dark Blue*).

Human Heroes and Demigods in Greek Mythology

As we have seen, in Greek mythology the gods and goddesses often seem less than godly. Likewise, the distinction between demigods and heroes is unclear. While some heroes, like Jason and Oedipus, are sons of mortal parents, others, like Heracles, Perseus and Achilles, come from the union of gods or goddesses with mortals. Zeus and Alcmene produced Heracles (his name 'Glory to Hera' was meant to appease Zeus' wife, the goddess Hera); Zeus and Danae produced Perseus; Peleus and the sea-nymph Thetis were responsible for Achilles; while rumours of divine intervention surround both Theseus (Poseidon is his putative father) and Odysseus (the putative bastard son of Sisyphus, offspring of Aeolus, god of winds).

Many rival states claimed a hero as their founder and protector, no doubt embellishing their origins: Theseus of Athens, Jason of Iolcos, Ajax of Salamis. Noble families also asserted a hero as their ancestor. Alexander the Great, for example, claimed descent from both Achilles and the Egyptian god Amon (Ammon) and insisted that his own semi-divine status was recognized throughout Greece. The bards, including Homer and Hesiod, who sang for their living, often took care to extol the ancestors of their patrons and audiences.

The catalogue of ships in Homer's *Iliad* leaves no Greek state off the roll of ancient glory; the 50 Argonauts are each attributed to a noble Greek family.

The figure most akin to a national hero is Heracles. He never settled in any one city that could take full credit for his exploits, and his wanderings carried him beyond the bounds of Greece – far into Africa and Asia Minor. He was one of the earliest mythical heroes to be featured in Greek art (dating from the eighth century BC) and on the coins of city states (on which he is usually depicted strangling snakes while in his cradle). As a symbol of national patriotism he is the only hero to be revered throughout Greece; he is also the only hero to be granted immortality.

What makes Greek heroes particularly interesting is their depiction by bards as deeply complex characters. Typically, they follow a common pattern: unnatural birth, return home as prodigal sons after being separated at an early age, exploits against monsters to prove their manhood and subsequent kingship or glorious death. Super strong and courageous they may be, mostly noble and honourable, but all have to contend with a ruthless streak that often outweighs the good. Heracles, for example, hurls his wife and children into a fire in a fit of madness and his uncontrollable lust forces him on King Thespius' 50 daughters in a single night. Nor is he averse to homosexual affairs (with Hylas, for instance), though Greek pederasty is mostly excluded from the myths.

Despite recapturing the Golden Fleece for Greece, Jason never finds contentment; he deserts his wife Medea and dies when the *Argo*'s rotting prow falls on him. Theseus is also disloyal to his wife Ariadne, abandoning her on the island of Naxos; he kills his Amazon wife Antiope and causes the death both of his son Hippolytus and his father Aegeus. Even the noble and fearless Achilles, the Greek hero of the Trojan War, a man who cannot bear dishonourable conduct, violates the dead hero's code by desecrating Hector's corpse and refusing to hand it over to the Trojans.

Like the heroes, therefore, cities that turn their hero's burial places into shrines (and oracles) receive good fortune, but they also risk invoking the hero's unpredictable temper.

Africa's Diverse Mythology

No real unified mythology exists in Africa – the migration of its peoples, the political fragmentation, and the sheer size of the continent have resulted in a huge diversity of lifestyles and traditions. Literally thousands of completely different languages are spoken, 2,000 in West Africa alone between the Senegal River and the headwaters of the Congo River. A complete collection of all myths of the African peoples would fill countless volumes, even if we were to ignore the fact that the collection is being added to all the time by modern-day enthusiasts. The poem 'The Story of Liongo' is featured to tell the story of East African hero, warrior and poet of the Swahili people.

Egyptian Legends of the Gods

The Egyptians believed that at one time all the great gods and goddesses had lived upon earth, and that they had ruled Egypt in much the same way as the Pharoahs, with whom they were more or less acquainted. They went about among men and took a real personal interest in their affairs, and, according to tradition, they spared no pains in promoting their wishes and well-being. Their rule was on the whole beneficent, chiefly because in addition to their divine attributes they possessed natures, and apparently bodily constitutions, that were similar to those of men.

Like men also they were supposed to feel emotions and passions, and to be liable to the accidents that befell men, and to grow old, and even to die. The greatest of all the gods was Ra, and he reigned over Egypt for very many years. His reign was marked by justice and righteousness, and he was in all periods of Egyptian history regarded as the type of what a king should be. When men instead of gods reigned over Egypt they all delighted to call themselves sons of Ra, and every king believed that Ra was his true father, and regarded his mother's husband as his father only in name. This belief was always common in Egypt, and even Alexander the Great found it expedient to adopt it, for he made a journey to the sanctuary of Amen (Ammon) in the Oasis of Siwah in order to be officially acknowledged by the god. Having obtained this recognition, he became the rightful lord of Egypt.

Mesopotamian Heroes: The Gilgamesh Epic

The Gilgamesh epic ranks with the Babylonian myth of creation as one of the greatest literary productions of ancient Babylonia. The main element in its composition is a conglomeration of mythic matter, drawn from various sources, with perhaps a substratum of historic fact, the whole being woven into a continuous narrative around the central figure of Gilgamesh, prince of Erech. It is not possible at present to fix the date when the epic was first written. Our knowledge of it is gleaned chiefly from mutilated fragments belonging to the library of Assur-bani-pal, but from internal and other evidence we gather that some at least of the traditions embodied in the epic are of much greater antiquity than his reign. Thus a tablet dated 2100 BC contains a variant of the deluge story inserted in the eleventh tablet of the Gilgamesh epic. Probably this and other portions of the epic existed in oral tradition before they were committed to writing – that is, in the remote Sumerian period.

The epic, which centres round the ancient city of Erech, relates the adventures of a half-human, half-divine hero, Gilgamesh by name, who is king over Erech. Two other characters figure prominently in the narrative – Eabani, who evidently typifies primitive man (but also, according to certain authorities, a form of the sun-god, even as Gilgamesh himself), and Ut-Napishtim, the hero of the Babylonian deluge myth. Each of the three would seem to have been originally the hero of a separate group of traditions which in time became incorporated, more or less naturally, with the other two.

Gilgamesh may have been at one time a real personage, though nothing is known of him historically. Possibly the exploits of some ancient king of Erech furnished a basis for the narrative. His mythological character is more easily established. In this regard he is the personification of the sun. He represents, in fact, the fusion of a great national hero with a mythical being. Throughout the epic there are indications that Gilgamesh is partly divine by nature, though nothing specific is said on that head. His identity with the solar god is veiled in the popular narrative, but it is evident that he has some connection with the god Shamash, to whom he pays his devotions and who acts as his patron and protector.

Classical Indian Literature

The pantheon of Indian gods has been recorded in many forms and in many languages, but most importantly in the great Sanskrit epic of *Mahabharata*, a poem which is the longest in any language, at 200,000 lines, and written between 400 BC and AD 200. It consists of a huge mass of legendary material which has developed around one key heroic narrative – the struggle for power between two related families, the Pandavas and the Kauravas. At the centre of this work is the *Bhagavadgita*, which has become the national gospel of India, and the most significant religious text of Hinduism. The *Bhagavadgita* was written in the first or second century AD and comprises eighteen chapters. There is a philosophical discussion of the nature of God, and a compelling explanation of how he can be seen, and known.

The *Mahabharata* is a fascinating and extraordinarily vivid work, singing with a characterization that is so rare in old testaments. There is an exquisite blend of characters which create a drama that has enveloped thousands of tales, each of which relates a unique perception, lesson or belief. Most importantly, however, the *Mahabharata* is entertaining, serving to teach and to work the imagination in order to put forth the fundamental beliefs of the Hindu religion.

Other great works include the *Ramayana*, written about 300 BC. This details the story of Rama and his wife Sita – the perfect king and his wife, directly descended from the gods and the earth. This is a romantic work and less important in the development of the Indian mythology than its counterpart the *Mahabharata*, but it has nonetheless become one of the most popular scriptures of Hinduism, and acts as a gospel of purity and despair.

The *Harivamsa* (AD 400) was another important work in the combined religious and mythological structure of the Indian literature, and it was swiftly followed by the *Puranas* (AD 400 to 1000). The *Harivamsa* works as an afterword to the *Mahabharata*, explaining the ancestry and the exploits of Krishna, together with other Hindu legend. The *Puranas*, of which eighteen survive, are extensive works examining the mythology of Hinduism, the sagas of heroes, and the legends of saints. The most significant of them, the *Bhagavata-Purana*, celebrates the god Vishnu in his many incarnations, particularly as Krishna. The *Bhagavata-Purana* has had a profound influence on almost every aspect of Indian culture – her religion, art, music and literature, and many scholars consider it the greatest poem ever written.

The Sanskrit interpretation and record of Hindu and subsequent mythology is one of the most imaginative and luxuriant of any culture; indeed, there was a belief for many years that the folktale tradition originated in India. One of the greatest collections is the *Panchatantra*, a collection of animal fables which are some of the most famous in Europe.

The central part of classical Sanskrit literature is, however, the *Vedas*, which are sacred Hindu writings from about 1400 to 1200 BC. There are also commentaries on the *Vedas* in the *Brahmanas*, the *Aranyakas*, and the *Upanishads* (1000 to 500 BC), and the epic and wisdom literature (400 BC to AD 1000).

The oldest document is the *Rig-Veda*, which is a collection of more than a thousand hymns, composed about 1400 BC. This is the most important part of early Hinduism and later became known as the *Brahmanas*. These texts did not originally take a written form; they were carried across centuries of oral communication and have been preserved with all the embellishments presented by the many translations. Hindu literature both fed and fed from the *Rig-Veda*, and much of early mythology has become synonymous with it.

Chinese Cultural Gods and Heroes

In contrast to many other mythologies, Chinese mythology is quite rich in accounts of beings who introduced cultural innovations into the world. These beings are often ambivalent in nature, either being semi-divine humans or gods. This ambivalence between the divine and the mortal realms was to become characteristic of later Chinese concepts of sages and emperors. Whether they were deified humans or gods demoted to human status, the mythical ancestors of various dynasties and tribes in China are said to have played a key role in introducing cultural innovations into the world.

A series of ten divine or semi-divine kings are associated with the earliest phase of the Zhou people, according to their accounts. The first of these was Fu Xi, sometimes associated with the goddess Nu Wa, who appears in a number of myths but who is particularly associated with the invention of writing. According to this myth, Fu Xi was the ruler of the universe and observed the markings and patterns found on various creatures. Based on his observations, he devised the Eight Trigrams that form the basis of the divinatory manual, the *Yi-jing* (this is also known as *I Ching*, and means Book of Changes). He is credited with the invention of music and also, after watching spiders at work, made fishing nets for humans. His successor, Shen Nung, was the farmer god who invented the plough and taught humans the art of agriculture. He also discovered the medicinal qualities of plants by pounding them with his whip and evaluating them by their smell and taste.

A later divine king was the famous Yellow Emperor, Huang Ti, who had over twenty sons, each of whom went on to sire important families of the Zhou dynasty. To him goes the credit for many innovations, such as the invention of the fire drill, by means of which he was able to clear forests and drive away wild animals using fire. Though he sometimes was viewed as a warrior god he was generally seen as peace-loving and had an ancient connection with healing; the Yellow Emperors *Classic of Medicine*, which still forms the basis of traditional Chinese medical treatment, was attributed to him. One of Huang Ti's successors was Di Ku, who was married to the goddess Jiang Yuan. She became pregnant after accidentally treading on a footprint and gave birth to Hou-Ji. Thinking the child was unlucky, she tried on three occasions to rid herself of him by having him exposed to the elements, but each time he was saved. When the child grew up he made agricultural tools for the people and imparted the knowledge of crop cultivation, thereby guaranteeing the Chinese people a constant supply of food.

Hou-Ji was followed by the celebrated Yao, who was to be adopted in later times by the Confucians as the archetypal model of the sage – intelligent, accomplished, courteous and reverent. It was during his reign that the world was devastated by the catastrophic series of floods which required the intervention of Gun, as already mentioned. Yao wanted to appoint his chief minister as his successor but the latter refused so Yao turned his attention to Shun (Hibiscus), the low-class son of Gu Sou (Blind Man). Shun had come to the attention of Yao because Gu Sou was an obstinate reprobate who tried to kill Shun on three occasions. Shun had miraculously escaped each time. Through his filial piety, a virtue always esteemed by the Chinese, Shun eventually reforms his father's behaviour. After having put Shun through various tests, Yao retired and passed the throne to Shun. Shun, in his turn, was eventually replaced by Yu, the son of Gun.

Gender in Chinese Myths

Many scholars believe that the earliest human societies worldwide were matriarchal in organization, but with the advent of the Bronze and Iron Ages, if not earlier, a shift seems to have occurred in many cultures to a patriarchal system that down-graded the female status. There are a few goddesses mentioned in Chinese mythology that hint at the former importance of women in society, such as Nu Wa, Chang Xi and Chang E, but the later male writers who compiled collections of myths seem to have done their best to undervalue the significance of the female in tune with the orthodox Confucian views of society. Nevertheless, apart from those mentioned above, other goddesses were important in ancient times as founders of early dynasties. Jian Di (Bamboo-slip Maiden) is mentioned as the progenitor of the first person of the Shang Dynasty, while Jiang the Originator was said to have been the mother of the first of the Zhou people. Like Hariti and other goddesses in India, disease and disaster is sometimes attributed to a female source in Chinese myth in the form of the Queen Mother of the West, a fierce and cruel being with tangled hair, tiger's fangs and a panther's tail, who was accompanied by other ferocious felines.

Heroes, Warriors and Adventure in Japanese Mythology

Early heroes and warriors in Japanese mythology are always regarded as minor divinities, and the very nature of Shinto, associated with ancestor worship, has enriched those of Japan with many a fascinating legend. For strength, skill, endurance, and a happy knack of overcoming all manner of difficulties by a subtle form of quick-witted enterprise, the Japanese hero must necessarily take a high position among the famous warriors of other countries. There is something eminently chivalrous about the heroes of Japan. The most valiant men are those who champion the cause of the weak or redress evil and tyranny of every kind, and we trace in the Japanese hero, who is very far from being a crude swashbuckler, these most excellent qualities. He is not always above criticism, and sometimes we find in him a touch of cunning, but such a characteristic is extremely rare, and very far from being a national trait. An innate love of poetry and the beautiful has had its refining influence upon the Japanese hero, with the result that his strength is combined with gentleness.

Benkei is one of the most lovable of Japanese heroes. He possessed the strength of many men, his tact amounted to genius, his sense of humour was strongly developed, and the most loving of Japanese mothers could not have shown more gentleness when his master's wife gave birth to a child. We follow the two great warriors Yoshitsune and Benkei across the sea, over mountains, outwitting again and again their numerous enemies.

The Land of the Rising Sun has given us many more warriors worthy to rank with the Knights of King Arthur: Minamoto no Yorimasa, Minamoto no Yorimitsu (Raiko), Watanabe no Tsuna (or Isuna), Kintaro, Momotaro and Yamato Take(ru) to name but a few. More than one legend deals with the destruction of devils and goblins, and of the rescue of maidens who had the misfortune to be their captives. One hero slays a great monster that crouched upon the roof of the Emperor's palace, another despatches the Goblin of Oeyama, another thrusts his sword through a gigantic spider, and another slays a serpent.

Polynesian Parallels

The peoples of Polynesia are believed to have originated in offshore islands much closer to southern and southeast Asia, like today's Taiwan and Indonesia, setting off south- and westward from about 4,000 years ago. Coast-based communities, skilled in sailing by outrigger-canoe and in starlight navigation, they proceeded very gradually, hopping from island to island, over countless generations. (Hawaii doesn't appear to have been inhabited before the fourth century, whilst the Maori were not to reach New Zealand till the fourteenth.)

The figure of Maui is central to different cultures across the region and fascinates us now in many ways. For two main reasons in particular, however, he stands out. One is that so many of the stories in which he features have no equivalent in any of the other mythologies of the world. The other, paradoxically, is that so many do. (Maui is, for example, very obviously comparable with the various 'trickster' heroes of Native American tradition.)

The first is easily enough explained: the Polynesians' ancestors seem to have been island-dwellers to begin with, cut off from the mainstream culture of the Asian mainland. In their subsequent centuries of migration, they became more isolated still. The second is more contentious, but at the same time potentially more important. Do the stories Maui shares with other heroes suggest that there may be mythic foundations that underpin every civilization – and, perhaps, a 'collective unconscious' that unites all humankind?

Tales of Warriors, Travel & Adventure

Introduction

MIGHTY, COURAGEOUS AND SELF-CONFIDENT, the warrior is the archetypal hero. (For better or for worse, ours has been and remains a 'macho' world.) Conventionally royal or noble, the warrior protects his people from all those who would seek to harm them – whether they be monstrous serpents or rival kings. He is also the conqueror of his nation's foes, extending his authority and influence over other lands. Often undertaken by the self-same hero, mythic travel tends to do much the same: striking out, transcending existing limits; venturing beyond. Adventure is the very stuff of story, but whilst mythic narratives were obviously designed to entertain, they also serve to foster faith in the civilizations that fostered them. Every enemy defeated, every dragon slain, is a little victory for order, a little triumph of stability over change, a tactful reminder that things are right the way they are.

The Legend of Scar-face

IN A FAR-OFF TIME, there lived an Indian (Native American) who had a very beautiful daughter. Many young warriors desired to marry her, but at each request, she only shook her head and said she had no need of a husband.

'Why is this?' asked her father. A great many of these young men are rich and handsome, yet still you refuse them.'

'Why should I marry?' replied the girl, 'when I have all that I could possibly want here with you at our lodge.'

'It is a shame for us,' said her mother, 'that we should still have an unmarried daughter. People will begin to believe you keep a secret lover.'

At this, the girl bowed her head and addressed her parents solemnly: 'I have no secret lover, I promise you, but now hear the truth. The Sun-god above has decreed that I cannot marry and he has told me that I will live happily, to a great age, if I preserve myself for him alone.'

'Ah!' replied her father, 'if the Sun-god has spoken thus, then his wishes must be obeyed. It is not for us to question the ways of the gods.'

In a nearby village there dwelt a poor young warrior who had neither parents nor relatives. Left to fend for himself, he had become a mighty hunter with a brave and noble spirit. He would have been a very good-looking young man, but for a long scar on his cheek, left by the claw of a great grizzly bear he had slain in close combat. The other warriors of the village had ostracized the youth because of this disfigurement. They had given him the name of Scar-face and nothing pleased them more than to make a mockery of his appearance. Each of these young men had been unsuccessful in their attempt to win the hand of the beautiful young maiden and now, slightly embittered by failure, they made it an occasion to poke some fun at the poor, deformed youth.

'Why don't you ask that girl to marry you,' they taunted him. 'She could hardly refuse a man like you, so rich and handsome.'

They laughed a great deal to see that they had touched upon a sensitive nerve, for Scar-face blushed from ear to ear at their suggestion and stared longingly in the direction of the young woman's lodge.

'I will go and do as you say,' he suddenly replied and marched off defiantly towards the river to deliver his proposal.

He found the young woman stooping by the banks gathering rushes. Respectfully, he approached her, and as she gazed upon him with bright, enticing eyes, he shyly announced his purpose: 'I know that I am poor and shabbily dressed,' he told her, 'but I have seen you refuse rich men clothed in luxurious fur. I am not handsome either, but you have shunned men of the noblest features. Would you consider having me for your husband? I cannot promise you wealth, but I can promise you love, as much of it as you care to receive from me.'

The young girl lowered her eyes and stared silently into the shallow water. After a time she turned towards Scar-face and spoke softly: 'It little matters to me that you are poor. My father is wealthy and would happily provide for us both. I am glad that a man of courage has finally asked me to marry him. But wait! I cannot accept your offer, for the Sun-god has reserved me for himself and has declared that I may never take a mortal husband. Seek him out, if you truly care for me, and beg him to release me from this covenant. If he agrees to do this, ask him to remove that scar from your face and I will treat it as a sign of his blessing.'

Scar-face was sad at heart to hear these words. He had no idea where to begin his search for the Sun-god and felt that a deity so powerful would almost certainly refuse to surrender to him his intended bride. But the young warrior had never before recoiled from a challenge, no matter how difficult it appeared, and the prospect of such a glorious reward seemed well worth risking his life for. For many days and many nights he journeyed over the sweeping prairies and on through the dense forests, carrying a small sack of food, a spare pair of moccasins, and a simple bow and arrow. Every day his sack of food grew lighter, but he saved as much as he could, eating wild berries and roots and sometimes killing a small bird. At length, he came across a bear's cave and paused to ask directions to the lodge of the Sun-god.

'I have travelled far and wide,' the bear told him, 'but I have never come across the Sun-god's lodge. Stripe-face, who lives beyond in that hole, may be able to assist you. Go and ask him for his help.'

Scar-face moved towards the hole and stooping over it, called aloud to the animal within: 'O generous Stripe-face, O wise old badger, can you tell me the way to the lodge of the Sun-god?'

'I am old and frail and never journey very far,' replied the badger. 'I do not know where he lives. Over there, through the trees, you will find a wolverine. Go and speak with him.'

Scar-face obeyed the badger's instructions, but having called aloud for several minutes, he could find no trace of the wolverine. Wearily, he sat on the ground and began to examine what remained of his food: 'Pity me, wolverine,' he cried out despondently, 'my moccasins are worn through, my food is almost gone. Take pity on me, or I shall meet my death here.'

'How can I help you,' said a voice, and turning around, Scar-face came face to face with the wolverine.

'I have travelled a great distance in search of the Sun-god,' he told the animal, 'but no one can tell me where he lives.'

'I can show you where he lives,' replied the wolverine, 'but first you must rest, for the journey is long. Tomorrow, as soon as you awake, I will set you on the right path.'

Early the next morning, the wolverine took Scar-face to the edge of the forest and pointed out the trail he should follow. Scar-face set off and walked many miles until he came upon the shores of a vast lake whose waters stretched as far as the eye could see. His spirits fell at this sight, for the great lake presented him with a problem he could not hope to overcome.

'I cannot cross this black and fearful water,' he said to himself, 'and I do not have the strength to return home to my own people. The end has come and I must give up the fight.'

But help was not so very far away and soon two beautiful white swans advanced towards him on the water.

'You are not far from the object of your search,' they called to him. 'Lie on our backs and we will carry you to the other side.'

Scar-face rose up and waded into the water. Before long, he had safely reached dry land where he thanked the swans and began following once more the broad trail leading to the home of the Sun-god.

It was now past midday and still the young warrior had not reached his destination. But he refused to lose hope and before long his optimism was rewarded, for he soon stumbled upon an array of beautiful objects lying in the earth which he knew must be from another world. He had never seen such splendid, golden-tipped arrows, or a war shield so elaborately decorated with beads and precious stones. He felt tempted to remove these items from the earth, but decided that would be dishonourable of him, and tried to picture instead what the owner of such fine weapons might look like. He had moved a little further onwards when he observed quite the handsomest youth he had ever seen approaching in the distance. The young man wore clothing of the smoothest animal skin and moccasins sewn with brightly coloured feathers.

'I am searching for my bow and arrows, have you seen them?' the beautiful stranger inquired.

'Yes, I have seen them, back there, lying on the ground,' replied Scar-face.

'And you did not wish to seize these items for yourself?' the young man asked.

'No,' answered Scar-face, 'I felt that would be wrong of me. I knew that the owner would eventually return for them.'

'I admire your honesty, and you have saved me a tiring search,' said the stranger. 'Where is it you come from? You appear to be a very long way from home.'

'I am looking for the Sun-god,' Scar-face told him, 'and I believe I am not very far from his house.'

'You are right,' replied the handsome youth. 'The Sun-god is my father and I am Apisirahts, the Morning Star. Come, I will take you to my father's lodge. He will be pleased to meet a man of such honest character.'

They set off together and shortly afterwards Morning Star pointed to a great lodge, basked in glorious golden light, whose walls were covered with magnificent paintings of medicine animals and other rare and curious creatures. At the entrance to the lodge stood a beautiful woman, Morning Star's mother, Kikomikis, the Moon-goddess. She embraced her son and welcomed the footsore traveller into their home. Then, the great Sun-god made his appearance and he too greeted Scar-face kindly, inviting him to stay for as long as he needed and urging him to accept the guidance and friendship of his son, Apisirahts.

'He will show you the wonderful sights of our kingdom,' the Sun-god told Scar-face. 'Go with him wherever you please, but never hunt near the Great Water, for that is the home of the savage birds who bear talons as long as spears and bills as sharp as arrows. They have carried off many of our finest warriors and would not hesitate to kill you both.'

Scar-face listened carefully to all that was said and during the months which followed, he lived happily among his celestial friends, learning to love the Sun-god as a father and becoming more and more intimate with Apisirahts whom he came to regard as the brother he had always longed for in his earthly home.

One day, he set off with Apisirahts on a hunting excursion, but the two did not follow their usual route and soon they found themselves by the shores of the Great Water.

'We are the finest hunters in the kingdom,' said Morning Star, 'so let us wait no longer, but go and kill these savage birds that put terror into the hearts of our people.'

'Your father has already told us not to pursue them,' replied Scar-face, 'and I have promised to heed his warning.'

'Then I will go and hunt them alone,' said Morning Star and he jumped into the water, waving his spear and shouting his war-cry. Scar-face was forced to follow, for he did not wish to see his brother come to any harm. Soon he had overtaken Apisirahts and began lashing out boldly with his weapon, slaying the monstrous creatures that swooped down upon him, attempting to sink their barbed claws into his flesh. When he had slaughtered every last one of them, he severed their heads and the two young men carried these back towards the Sun-god's lodge, anxious to relate the details of their heroic conquest.

The Moon-goddess was shocked to see the carcasses of the savage birds and scolded her son for his foolishness. But at the same time, she was relieved that Morning Star had escaped unharmed and ran to inform the Sun-god of his safe return, instinctively aware that she had Scar-face to thank for her son's safe delivery.

'I will not forget what you have done for us this day,' the Sun-god told Scar-face. 'If I can ever repay you, you must let me know at once and whatever you request of me shall be brought to you.'

Scar-face hesitated only a moment and then began to explain to the god the reason for his long journey away from home.

'You have never greedily demanded anything of us,' said the god, 'and you have suffered patiently all these months a great burden of anxiety, knowing that I alone have the power to decide your future with a woman you love and admire so earnestly. Your kindness and your patience have earned the young maiden her freedom. Return home now and make her your wife.

'One thing I will ask of you, however, when you return to your home. Build a lodge in honour of me, shape it like the world, round with thick walls, and paint it red so that every day you will be reminded of your visit here. It shall be a great Medicine Lodge and if your wife remains pure and true I will always be there to help you in times of illness or hardship.'

Then the god explained to Scar-face many of the intricacies of Sun-medicine and rubbed a powerful remedy into the skin on his cheek which caused his unsightly scar to disappear instantly. The young warrior was now ready to return home and the Moon-goddess gave him many beautiful gifts to take to his people. The Sun-god pointed to a short route through the Milky Way and soon he had reached the earth, ready to enter his village in triumph.

It was a very hot day and the sun shone brilliantly in the sky, forcing the people to shed their clothing and sit in the shade. Towards midday, when the heat was at its fiercest, the chief of the village peered through the window of his lodge and caught sight of a figure, wrapped from head to foot in thick animal skins, sitting on a butte nearby.

'Who is that strange person sitting in winter clothing? The heat will certainly kill him, for I see that he has no food or water. Go and invite him to sit indoors with us.'

Some of the villages approached the stranger and called to him: 'Our chief is concerned for you. He wishes you to withdraw to the shade of his lodge.'

But they had no sooner spoken these words when the figure arose and flung his outer garments to the ground. The robe he wore underneath was of the most delicate, embroidered cloth and the weapons he carried were of an extraordinary, gleaming metal. Gazing upon the stranger's face, the villagers recognized in it something familiar, and at last, one of them cried out in surprise: 'It is Scar-face, the poor young warrior we thought had been lost forever. But look, the blemish on his face has disappeared.'

All the people rushed forward to examine the young man for themselves.

'Where have you been?' they asked excitedly. 'Who gave you all these beautiful things?'

But the handsome warrior did not answer. His eyes searched instead through the crowd until they fell upon the beautiful face of the maiden he had returned home to marry.

'The trail was long and tortuous,' he told her as he walked boldly forward, 'but I found the lodge of the Sun-god and I won his favour. He has taken away my scar and given me all these things as proof of his consent. Come with me now and be my wife for that is the Sun-god's greatest wish.'

The maiden ran towards him and fell upon his breast, tears of great joy flowing freely down her cheeks. That same day the young couple were married and before long they had raised a great Medicine Lodge to the Sun-god. During the long years ahead, they were never sick or troubled in any way and were blessed with two fine, strong children, a girl and a boy, whom they named Apisirahts and Kikomikis. This legend is attributed to the famous Blackfeet tribe of the western territories.

The Legend of Hiawatha

A GREAT MANY FANCIFUL MYTHS AND LEGENDS have sprung up around Hiawatha, the famous Iroquois warrior and chief. Such a tradition is demonstrated, for example, by H. W. Longfellow, whose poem, Hiawatha, combines historical fact and mythical invention to produce a highly colourful demi-god figure akin to the Algonquin deity, Michabo. The real Hiawatha, an actual historical figure, lived in the sixteenth century and was renowned for promoting a very down-to-earth policy of tribal union. His greatest achievement was the formation of the original Five Nations Confederacy of the Iroquois people. The legend chosen here, although it too reveres Hiawatha as a man of mystical qualities, is based on that historical accomplishment and has been adapted from a story told by a nineteenth-century Onondaga chief.

Along the banks of Tioto, or Cross Lake as it was often called, there lived an eminent young warrior named Hiawatha. Also known as the Wise Man throughout the district, he exerted a powerful influence over the people. No one knew exactly where Hiawatha had come from. They knew only that he was of a high and mysterious origin and investigated no further than this. He had a canoe, controlled by his will, which could move without the aid of paddles, but he did not use it for any common purpose and pushed it out into the water only when he attended the general council of the tribes.

It was from Hiawatha that the villagers sought advice when they attempted to raise corn and beans. As a direct result of his instruction, their crops flourished; even after they had harvested the corn, food was never in short supply for he taught them how to remove obstructions from watercourses and to clear their fishing grounds. The people listened to Hiawatha with ever-increasing respect, and as he continued to provide them with wise laws and proverbs for their development, they came to believe that he had been sent by the Great Spirit himself, for a short but precious stay amongst them.

After a time, Hiawatha elected to join the Onondagas tribe and it was not long before he had been elevated to a prime position of authority, next in line to its chief. The Onondagas enjoyed a long period of peace and prosperity under Hiawatha's guidance, and there was not one among the other tribes of the region that did not yield to their superiority.

But then, one day, a great alarm was suddenly raised among the entire people of the region. From north of the Great Lakes, a ferocious band of warriors advanced towards them [The Huron, ancient enemies of the Iroquois, although at one time part of the same race.], destroying whatever property they could lay their hands on and indiscriminately slaughtering men, women and children. Everyone looked to Hiawatha for comfort and advice and, as a first measure, he called together a council of all the tribes from the east to the west and appointed a time for a meeting to take place on the banks of the Onondaga Lake.

By midday, a great body of men, women and children had gathered together in anticipation that they would shortly experience some form of deliverance. But after they had waited several hours they became anxious to know what had become of Hiawatha, for he appeared to be nowhere in sight. Three days elapsed and still Hiawatha did not appear. The crowd, beginning to fear that he was not coming at all, despatched a group of messengers to his home and here they found him sitting on the ground, seized by a terrible misgiving that some form of tragedy would follow his attendance at the meeting. Such fear was hastily overruled by the messengers, whose main concern was to pacify their beleaguered tribesmen. Soon, they had persuaded Hiawatha to follow them and, taking his daughter with him, he pushed his wonderful canoe into the water and set out for the council.

As soon as the people saw him, they sent up shouts of welcome and relief. The venerated warrior climbed ashore and began ascending the steep banks of the lake leading to the place occupied by the council. As he walked, however, he became conscious of a loud, whirring noise overhead. He lifted his eyes upwards and perceived something which looked like a small cloud descending rapidly towards the earth. Filled with terror and alarm, the crowd scattered in confusion, but Hiawatha stood still, instructing his daughter to do the same, for he considered it cowardly to flee, and futile, in any event, to attempt to escape the designs of the Great Spirit. The object approached with greater speed and as it came nearer, it revealed the shape of a gigantic white heron, whose wings, pointed and outstretched, masked all light in the sky. The creature descended with ever-increasing velocity, until, with a mighty crash, it fell upon the girl, instantly crushing her to death.

Hiawatha stared at the spot where the prostrate bird lay and then, in silent anguish, he signalled to a group of warriors nearby to lift the carcass from the earth. They came forward and did as he requested, but when they had moved the bird, not a trace of Hiawatha's daughter was discovered. No word was spoken. The people waited in silence, until at length, Hiawatha stooped to the ground and selected a feather from the snow-white plumage. With this, he decorated his costume, and after he had ensured that other warriors followed his example, he walked in calm dignity to the head of the council. [Since this event, the plumage of the white heron was used by the Onondagas as a decoration while on the war-path.] During that first day, he listened gravely and attentively to the different plans of the various tribal chiefs and speakers. But on the second day he arose and with a voice of great authority and strength he began to address his people:

'My friends and brothers, listen to what I say to you. It would be a very foolish thing to challenge these northern invaders in individual tribes. Only by uniting in a common band of brotherhood may we hope to succeed. Let us do this, and we shall swiftly drive the enemy from our land.

'You, the Mohawks, sitting under the shadow of the great tree whose roots sink deep into the earth, you shall be the first nation, because you are warlike and mighty.

'You, the Oneidas, who recline your bodies against the impenetrable stone, you shall be the second nation, because you have never failed to give wise counsel.

'You, the Onondagas, who occupy the land at the foot of the great hills, because you are so gifted in speech, you shall be the third nation.

'You, the Senecas, who reside in the depths of the forest, you shall be the fourth nation, because of your cunning and speed in the hunt.

'And you, the Cayugas, who roam the prairies and possess great wisdom, you shall be the fifth nation, because you understand more than any of us how to raise corn and build lodges.

'Unite ye five nations, for if we form this powerful alliance, the Great Spirit will smile down on us and we shall remain free, prosperous and happy. But if we remain as we are, always at variance with each other, he will frown upon us and we shall be enslaved or left to perish in the war-storm.

'Brothers, these are the words of Hiawatha. I have said all that I have to say.'

On the following day, Hiawatha's great plan was considered and adopted by the council. Once more, he stood up and addressed the people with wise words of counsel, but even as his speech drew to a close he was being summoned back to the skies by the Great Spirit.

Hiawatha went down to the shore and assumed the seat in his canoe, satisfied within that his mission to the Iroquois had been accomplished. Strange music was heard on the air at that moment and while the wondering multitude stood gazing at their beloved chief, he was silently wafted from sight, and they never saw him again.

The Noble Tlascalan Leader Tlalhuicole

LESS THAN A YEAR before the Spaniards arrived in Mexico war broke out between the Huexotzincans and the Tlascalans, to the former of whom the Aztecs acted as allies. On the battlefield there was captured by guile a very valiant Tlascalan leader called Tlalhuicole, so renowned for his prowess that the mere mention of his name was generally sufficient to deter any Mexican hero from attempting his capture. He was brought to Mexico in a cage, and presented to the Emperor Montezuma, who, on learning of his name and renown, gave him his liberty and overwhelmed him with honours. He further granted him permission to return to his own country, a boon he had never before extended to any captive.

But Tlalhuicole refused his freedom, and replied that he would prefer to be sacrificed to the gods, according to the usual custom. Montezuma, who had the highest regard for him, and prized his life more than any sacrifice, would not consent to his immolation. At this juncture war broke out between Mexico and the Tarascans, and Montezuma announced the appointment of Tlalhuicole as chief of the expeditionary force. He accepted the command, marched against the Tarascans, and, having totally defeated them, returned to Mexico laden with an enormous booty and crowds of slaves. The city rang with his triumph. The emperor begged him to become a Mexican citizen, but he replied that on no account would he prove a traitor to his country.

Montezuma then once more offered him his liberty, but he strenuously refused to return to Tlascala, having undergone the disgrace of defeat and capture. He begged Montezuma to terminate his unhappy existence by sacrificing him to the gods, thus ending the dishonour he felt in living on after having undergone defeat, and at the same time fulfilling the highest aspiration of his life – to die the death of a warrior on the stone of combat. Montezuma, himself the noblest pattern of Aztec chivalry, touched at his request, could not but agree with him that he had chosen the most fitting fate for a hero, and ordered him to be chained to the stone of combat, the blood-stained *temalacatl*. The most renowned of the Aztec warriors were pitted against him, and the emperor himself graced the sanguinary tournament with his presence. Tlalhuicole bore himself in the combat like a lion, slew eight warriors of renown, and wounded more than twenty. But at last he fell, covered with wounds, and was haled by the exulting priests to the altar of the terrible war-god Huitzilopochtli, to whom his heart was offered up.

Sargon, A Babylonian Conqueror

THE FIRST GREAT SEMITIC EMPIRE in Babylonia was that founded by the famous Sargon of Akkad. As is the case with many popular heroes and monarchs whose deeds are remembered in song and story – for example, Perseus, OEdipus, Cyrus, Romulus, and our own King Arthur – the early years of Sargon were passed in obscurity.

Sargon is, in fact, one of the 'fatal children'. He was, legend stated, born in concealment and sent adrift, like Moses, in an ark of bulrushes on the waters of the Euphrates, whence he was rescued and brought up by one Akki, a husbandman. But the time of his recognition at length arrived, and he received the crown of Babylonia. His foreign conquests were extensive. On four successive occasions he invaded Syria and Palestine, which he succeeded in welding into a single empire with Babylonia. Pressing his victories to the margin of the Mediterranean, he erected upon its shores statues of himself as an earnest of his conquests. He also overcame Elam and northern Mesopotamia and quelled a rebellion of some magnitude in his own dominions. His son, Naram-Sin, claimed for himself the title of 'King of the Four Zones', and enlarged the empire left him by his father, penetrating even into Arabia. A monument unearthed by J. de Morgan at Susa depicts him triumphing over the conquered Elamites. He is seen passing his spear through the prostrate body of a warrior whose hands are upraised as if pleading for quarter. His head-dress is ornamented with the horns emblematic of divinity, for the early Babylonian kings were the direct vicegerents of the gods on earth.

Even at this comparatively early time (*c.* 3800 BC) the resources of the country had been well exploited by its Semitic conquerors, and their absorption of the Sumerian civilization had permitted them to make very considerable progress in the enlightened arts. Some of their work in bas-relief, and even in the lesser if equally difficult craft of gem-cutting, is among the finest efforts of Babylonian art. Nor were they deficient in more utilitarian fields. They constructed roads through the most important portions of the empire, along which a service of posts carried messages at stated intervals, the letters conveyed by these being stamped or franked by clay seals, bearing the name of Sargon.

The Gilgamesh Epic

The Birth of Gilgamesh

AMONG THE TRADITIONS concerning the birth of Gilgamesh is one related by Aelian (*Historia Animalium*, XII, 21) of Gilgamos (Gilgamesh), the grandson of Sokkaros – the first king to reign in Babylonia after the deluge.

Sokkaros was warned by means of divination that his daughter should bear a son who would deprive him of his throne. Thinking to frustrate the designs of fate he shut her up in a tower, where she was closely watched. But in time she bore a son, and her attendants, knowing how angry the King would be to learn of the event, flung the child from the tower. But before he reached the ground an eagle seized him up and bore him off to a certain garden, where he was duly found and cared for by a peasant. And when he grew to manhood he became King of the Babylonians, having, presumably, usurped the throne of his grandfather.

Here we have a myth obviously of solar significance, conforming in every particular to a definite type of sun-legend. It cannot have been by chance that it became attached to the person of Gilgamesh. Everything in the epic, too, is consonant with the belief that Gilgamesh is a sun-god – his connection with Shamash (who may have been his father in the tradition given by Aelian, as well as the eagle which saved him from death), the fact that no mention is made of his father in the poem, though his mother is brought in more than once, and the assumption throughout the epic that he is more than human.

Given the key to his mythical character it is not hard to perceive in his adventures the daily (or annual) course of the sun, rising to its full strength at noonday (or mid-summer), and sinking at length to the western horizon, to return in due time to the abode of men. Like all solar deities – like the sun itself – his birth and origin are wrapped in mystery. He is, indeed, one of the 'fatal children', like Sargon, Perseus, or Arthur. When he first appears in the narrative he is already a full-grown hero, the ruler and (it would seem) oppressor of Erech. His mother, Rimat-belit, is a priestess in the temple of Ishtar, and through her he is descended from Ut-Napishtim, a native of Shurippak, and the hero of the Babylonian flood-legend.

An Epic in Fragments

Let us examine in detail the Gilgamesh epic as we have it in the broken fragments which remain to us. The first and second tablets are much mutilated. A number of fragments are extant which belong to one or other of these two, but it is not easy to say where the first ends and the second begins.

One fragment would seem to contain the very beginning of the first tablet – a sort of general preface to the epic, comprising a list of the advantages to be derived from reading it. After this comes a fragment whose title to inclusion in the epic is doubtful. It describes a siege of the city of Erech, but makes no mention of Gilgamesh. The woeful condition of Erech under the siege is thus picturesquely detailed: 'She asses (tread down) their young, cows (turn upon) their calves. Men cry aloud like beasts, and maidens mourn like doves. The gods of strong-walled Erech are changed to flies, and buzz about the streets. The spirits of strong-walled Erech are changed to serpents, and glide into holes. For three years the enemy besieged Erech, and the doors were barred, and the bolts were shot, and Ishtar did not raise her head against the foe.' If this fragment be indeed a portion of the Gilgamesh epic, we have no means of ascertaining whether Gilgamesh was the besieger, or the raiser of the siege, or whether he was concerned in the affair at all.

Gilgamesh as Tyrant

Now we come to the real commencement of the poem, inscribed on a fragment which some authorities assign to the beginning of the second tablet, but which more probably forms a part of the first. In this portion we find Gilgamesh filling the double role of ruler and oppressor of Erech – the latter evidently not inconsistent with the character of a hero.

There is no mention here of a siege, nor is there any record of the coming of Gilgamesh, though, as has been indicated, he probably came as a conqueror. His intolerable tyranny towards the people of Erech lends colour to this view. He presses the young men into his service in the building of a great wall, and carries off the fairest maidens to his court. Finally his harshness constrained the people to appeal to the gods, and they prayed the goddess Aruru to create a mighty hero who would champion their cause, and through fear of whom Gilgamesh should be forced to temper his severity. The gods themselves added their prayers to those of the oppressed people, and Aruru at length agreed to create a champion against Gilgamesh. 'Upon hearing these words (so runs the narrative), Aruru conceived a man (in the image) of Anu in her mind. Aruru washed her hands, she broke off a piece of clay, she cast it on the ground. Thus she created Eabani, the hero.' When the creation of this champion was finished his appearance was that of a wild man of the mountains. 'The whole of his body was (covered) with hair, he was clothed with long hair like a woman. His hair was luxuriant, like that of the corn-god. He knew (not) the land and the inhabitants thereof, he was clothed with garments as the god of the field. With the gazelles he ate herbs, with the beasts he slaked his thirst, with the creatures of the water his heart rejoiced.' In pictorial representations on cylinder-seals and elsewhere Eabani is depicted as a sort of satyr, with the head, arms, and body of a man, and the horns, ears, and legs of a beast. As we have seen, he is a type of beast-man, a sort of Caliban, ranging with the beasts of the field, utterly ignorant of the things of civilization.

The Beguiling of Eabani

The poem goes on to introduce a new character, Tsaidu, the hunter, apparently designed by the gods to bring about the meeting of Gilgamesh and Eabani. How he first encounters Eabani is not quite clear from the mutilated text. One reading has it that the King of Erech, learning the plan of the gods for his overthrow, sent Tsaidu into the mountains in search of Eabani, with instructions to entrap him by whatever means and bring him to Erech.

Another reading describes the encounter as purely accidental. However this may be, Tsaidu returned to Erech and related to Gilgamesh the story of his encounter, telling him of the strength and fleetness of the wild man, and his exceeding shyness at the sight of a human being. By this time it is evident that Gilgamesh knows or conjectures the purpose for which Eabani is designed, and intends to frustrate the divine plans by anticipating the meeting between himself and the wild man. Accordingly he bids Tsaidu return to the mountains, taking with him Ukhut, one of the sacred women of the temple of Ishtar. His plan is that Ukhut with her wiles shall persuade Eabani to return with her to Erech. Thus the hunter and the girl set out. 'They took the straight road, and on the third day they reached the usual drinking-place of Eabani. Then Tsaidu and the woman placed themselves in hiding. For one day, for two days, they lurked by the drinking-place. With the beasts (Eabani) slaked his thirst, with the creatures of the waters his heart rejoiced. Then Eabani (approached) ...'

The scene which follows is described at some length. Ukhut had no difficulty in enthralling Eabani with the snares of her beauty. For six days and seven nights he remembered nothing because of his love for her. When at length he bethought him of his gazelles, his flocks and herds, he found that they would no longer follow him as before. So he sat at the feet of Ukhut while she told him of Erech and its king. 'Thou art handsome, O Eabani, thou art like a god. Why dost thou traverse the plain with the beasts? Come, I will take thee to strong-walled Erech, to the bright palace, the dwelling of Anu and Ishtar, to the palace of Gilgamesh, the perfect in strength, who, like a mountain-bull, wieldeth power over man.' Eabani found the prospect delightful. He longed for the friendship of Gilgamesh, and declared himself willing to follow the woman to the city of Erech. And so Ukhut, Eabani, and Tsaidu set out on their journey.

Gilgamesh meets Eabani

The feast of Ishtar was in progress when they reached Erech. Eabani had conceived the idea that he must do battle with Gilgamesh before he could claim that hero as a friend, but being warned (whether in a dream, or by Ukhut, is not clear) that Gilgamesh was stronger than he, and withal a favourite of the gods, he wisely refrained from combat. Meanwhile Gilgamesh also had dreamed a dream, which, interpreted by his mother, Rimat-belit, foretold the coming of Eabani. That part of the poem which deals with the meeting of Gilgamesh and Eabani is unfortunately no longer extant, but from the fragments which take up the broken narrative we gather that they met and became friends.

The portions of the epic next in order appear to belong to the second tablet. In these we find Eabani lamenting the loss of his former freedom and showering maledictions on the temple-maiden who has lured him thither. However, Shamash, the sun-god, intervenes (perhaps in another dream or vision; these play a prominent part in the narrative), and showing him the benefits he has derived from his sojourn in the haunts of civilization, endeavours with various promises and inducements to make him stay in Erech – 'Now Gilgamesh, thy friend and brother, shall give thee a great couch to sleep on, shall give thee a couch carefully prepared, shall give thee a seat at his left hand, and the kings of the earth shall kiss thy feet.' With this, apparently, Eabani is satisfied. He ceases to bewail his position at Erech and accepts his destiny with calmness.

In the remaining fragments of the tablet we find him concerned about another dream or vision; and before this portion of the epic closes the heroes have planned an expedition against the monster Khumbaba, guardian of the abode of the goddess Irnina (a form of Ishtar), in the Forest of Cedars.

In the very mutilated IIIrd tablet the two heroes go to consult the priestess Rimat-belit, the mother of Gilgamesh, and through her they ask protection from Shamash in the forthcoming expedition. The old priestess advises her son and his friend how to proceed, and after they have gone we see her alone in the temple, her hands raised to the sun-god, invoking his blessing on Gilgamesh: 'Why hast thou troubled the heart of my son Gilgamesh? Thou hast laid thy hand upon him, and he goeth away, on a far journey to the dwelling of Khumbaba; he entereth into a combat (whose issue) he knows not; he followeth a road unknown to him. Till he arrive and till he return, till he reach the Forest of Cedars, till he hath slain the terrible Khumbaba and rid the land of all the evil that thou hatest, till the day of his return – let Aya, thy betrothed, thy splendour, recall him to thee.' With this dignified and beautiful appeal the tablet comes to an end.

The Monster Khumbaba

The Fourth tablet is concerned with a description of the monster with whom the heroes are about to do battle. Khumbaba, whom Bel had appointed to guard the cedar (*i.e.*, one particular cedar which appears to be of greater height and sanctity than the others), is a creature of most terrifying aspect, the very presence of whom in the forest makes those who enter it grow weak and impotent.

As the heroes draw near, Eabani complains that his hands are feeble and his arms without strength, but Gilgamesh speaks words of encouragement to him.

The next fragments bring us into the fifth tablet. The heroes, having reached 'a verdant mountain', paused to survey the Forest of Cedars. When they entered the forest the death of Khumbaba was foretold to one or other, or both of them, in a dream, and they hastened forward to the combat. Unfortunately the text of the actual encounter has not been preserved, but we learn from the context that the heroes were successful in slaying Khumbaba.

Ishtar's Love for Gilgamesh

In the Sixth tablet, which relates the story of Ishtar's love for Gilgamesh, and the slaying of the sacred bull, victory again waits on the arms of the heroes, but here nevertheless we have the key to the misfortunes which later befall them.

On his return to Erech after the destruction of Khumbaba, Gilgamesh was loudly acclaimed. Doffing the soiled and bloodstained garments he had worn during the battle, he robed himself as befitted a monarch and a conqueror. Ishtar beheld the King in his regal splendour, the flowers of victory still fresh on his brow, and her heart went out to him in love. In moving and seductive terms she besought him to be her bridegroom, promising that if he would enter her house 'in the gloom of the cedar' all manner of good gifts should be his – his flocks and herds would increase, his horses and oxen would be without rival, the river Euphrates would kiss his feet, and kings and princes would bring tribute to him. But Gilgamesh, knowing something of the past history of this capricious goddess, rejected her advances with scorn, and began to revile her. He taunted her, too, with her treatment of former lovers – of Tammuz, the bridegroom of her youth, to whom she clung weepingly year after year; of Alalu the eagle; of a lion perfect in might and a horse glorious in battle; of the shepherd Tabulu and of Isullanu, the gardener of her father.

All these she had mocked and ill-treated in cruel fashion, and Gilgamesh perceived that like treatment would be meted out to him should he accept the proffered love of the goddess. The deity was greatly enraged at the repulse, and mounted up to heaven: 'Moreover Ishtar went before Anu (her father), before Anu she went and she (said): 'O my father, Gilgamesh has kept watch on me; Gilgamesh has counted my garlands, my garlands and my girdles.'

Underlying the story of Ishtar's love for Gilgamesh there is evidently a nature-myth of some sort, perhaps a spring-tide myth; Gilgamesh, the sun-god, or a hero who has taken over his attributes, is wooed by Ishtar, the goddess of fertility, the great mother-goddess who presides over spring vegetation. In the recital of her former love-affairs we find mention of the Tammuz myth, in which Ishtar slew her consort Tammuz, and other mythological fragments. It is possible also that there is an astrological significance in this part of the narrative.

The Bull of Anu

To resume the tale: In her wrath and humiliation Ishtar appealed to her father and mother, Anu and Anatu, and begged the former to create a mighty bull and send it against Gilgamesh. Anu at first demurred, declaring that if he did so it would result in seven years' sterility on the earth; but finally he consented, and a great bull, Alu, was sent to do battle with Gilgamesh. The portion of the text which deals with the combat is much mutilated, but it appears that the conflict was hot and sustained, the celestial animal finally succumbing to a sword-thrust from Gilgamesh. Ishtar looks on in impotent anger. 'Then Ishtar went up on to the wall of strong-walled Erech; she mounted to the top and she uttered a curse, (saying), "Cursed be Gilgamesh, who has provoked me to anger, and has slain the bull from heaven." Then Eabani incurs the anger of the deity – "When Eabani heard these words of Ishtar, he tore out the entrails of the bull, and he cast them before her, saying, 'As for thee, I will conquer thee, and I will do to thee even as I have done to him.' Ishtar was beside herself with rage. Gilgamesh and his companion dedicated the great horns of the bull to the sun-god, and having washed their hands in the river Euphrates, returned once more to Erech. As the triumphal procession passed through the city the people came out of their houses to do honour to the heroes. The remainder of the tablet is concerned with a great banquet given by Gilgamesh to celebrate his victory over the bull Alu, and with further visions of Eabani.

The seventh and eighth tablets are extremely fragmentary, and so much of the text as is preserved is open to various readings. It is possible that to the seventh tablet belongs a description of the underworld given to Eabani in a dream by the temple-maiden Ukhut, whom he had cursed in a previous tablet, and who had since died. The description answers to that given in another ancient text – the myth of Ishtar's descent into Hades – and evidently embodies the popular belief concerning the underworld. 'Come, descend with me to the house of darkness, the abode of Irkalla, to the house whence the enterer goes not forth, to the path whose way has no return, to the house whose dwellers are deprived of light, where dust is their nourishment and earth their good. They are clothed, like the birds, in a garment of feathers; they see not the light, they dwell in darkness.'

The Death of Eabani

This sinister vision appears to have been a presage of Eabani's death. Shortly afterwards he fell ill and died at the end of twelve days.

The manner of his death is uncertain. One reading of the mutilated text represents Eabani as being wounded, perhaps in battle, and succumbing to the effects of the wound. But another makes him say to his friend Gilgamesh, 'I have been cursed, my friend, I shall not die as one who has been slain in battle.' The breaks in the text are responsible for the divergence. The latter reading is probably the correct one; Eabani has grievously offended Ishtar, the all-powerful, and the curse which has smitten him to the earth is probably hers. In modern folk-lore phraseology he died of ju-ju. The death of the hero brings the eighth tablet to a close.

In the ninth tablet we find Gilgamesh mourning the loss of his friend.

The Quest of Gilgamesh

On the heart of Gilgamesh, likewise, the fear of death had taken hold, and he determined to go in search of his ancestor, Ut-Napishtim, who might be able to show him a way of escape. Straightway putting his determination into effect, Gilgamesh set out for the abode of Ut-Napishtim. On the way he had to pass through mountain gorges, made terrible by the presence of wild beasts. From the power of these he was delivered by Sin, the moon-god, who enabled him to traverse the mountain passes in safety.

At length he came to a mountain higher than the rest, the entrance to which was guarded by scorpion-men. This was Mashu, the Mountain of the Sunset, which lies on the western horizon, between the earth and the underworld. 'Then he came to the mountain of Mashu, the portals of which are guarded every day by monsters; their backs mount up to the ramparts of heaven, and their foreparts reach down beneath Aralu. Scorpion-men guard the gate (of Mashu); they strike terror into men, and it is death to behold them. Their splendour is great, for it overwhelms the mountains; from sunrise to sunset they guard the sun. Gilgamesh beheld them, and his face grew dark with fear and terror, and the wildness of their aspect robbed him of his senses.' On approaching the entrance to the mountain Gilgamesh found his way barred by these scorpion-men, who, perceiving the strain of divinity in him, did not blast him with their glance, but questioned him regarding his purpose in drawing near the mountain of Mashu. When Gilgamesh had replied to their queries, telling them how he wished to reach the abode of his ancestor, Ut-Napishtim, and there learn the secret of perpetual life and youthfulness, the scorpion-men advised him to turn back. Before him, they said, lay the region of thick darkness; for twelve *kasbu* (twenty-four hours) he would have to journey through the thick darkness ere he again emerged into the light of day. And so they refused to let him pass. But Gilgamesh implored, 'with tears,' says the narrative, and at length the monsters consented to admit him. Having passed the gate of the Mountain of the Sunset (by virtue of his character as a solar deity) Gilgamesh traversed the region of thick darkness during the space of twelve *kasbu*. Toward the end of that period the darkness became ever less pronounced; finally it was broad day, and Gilgamesh found himself in a beautiful garden or park studded with trees, among which was the tree of the gods, thus charmingly depicted in the text – 'Precious stones it bore as fruit, branches hung from it which were beautiful to behold. The top of the tree was lapis-lazuli, and it was laden with fruit which dazzled the eye of him that beheld.' Having paused to admire the beauty of the scene, Gilgamesh bent his steps shoreward.

The tenth tablet describes the hero's encounter with the sea-goddess Sabitu, who, on the approach of one 'who had the appearance of a god, in whose body was grief, and who looked as though he had made a long journey,' retired into her palace and fastened the door. But Gilgamesh, knowing that her help was necessary to bring him to the dwelling of Ut-Napishtim, told her of his quest, and in despair threatened to break down the door unless she opened to him. At last Sabitu consented to listen to him whilst he asked the way to Ut-Napishtim. Like the scorpion-men, the sea-goddess perceived that Gilgamesh was not to be turned aside from his quest, so at last she bade him go to Adad-Ea, Ut-Napishtim's ferryman, without whose aid, she said, it would be futile to persist further in his mission. Adad-Ea, likewise, being consulted by Gilgamesh, advised him to desist, but the hero, pursuing his plan of intimidation, began to smash the ferryman's boat with his axe, whereupon Adad-Ea was obliged to yield. He sent his would-be passenger into the forest for a new rudder, and after that the two sailed away.

Gilgamesh and Ut-Napishtim

Ut-Napishtim was indeed surprised when he beheld Gilgamesh approaching the strand. The hero had meanwhile contracted a grievous illness, so that he was unable to leave the boat; but he addressed his queries concerning perpetual life to the deified Ut-Napishtim, who stood on the shore. The hero of the flood was exceeding sorrowful, and explained that death is the common lot of mankind, 'nor is it given to man to know the hour when the hand of death will fall upon him – the Annunaki, the great gods, decree fate, and with them Mammetum, the maker of destiny, and they determine death and life, but the days of death are not known.'

The narrative is continued without interruption into the eleventh tablet. Gilgamesh listened with pardonable scepticism to the platitudes of his ancestor. 'I behold thee, Ut-Napishtim, thy appearance differs not from mine, thou art like unto me, thou art not otherwise than I am; thou art like unto me, thy heart is stout for the battle ... how hast thou entered the assembly of the gods; how hast thou found life?'

In reply Ut-Napishtim introduces the story of the Babylonian deluge, which, told as it is without interruption, forms a separate and complete narrative, and is in itself a myth of exceptional interest for another time.

The Quest Continues

To return to the epic: The recital of Ut-Napishtim served its primary purpose in the narrative by proving to Gilgamesh that his case was not that of his deified ancestor. Meanwhile the hero had remained in the boat, too ill to come ashore; now Ut-Napishtim took pity on him and promised to restore him to health, first of all bidding him sleep during six days and seven nights.

Gilgamesh listened to his ancestor's advice, and by and by 'sleep, like a tempest, breathed upon him.' Ut-Napishtim's wife, beholding the sleeping hero, was likewise moved with compassion, and asked her husband to send the traveller safely home. He in turn bade his wife compound a magic preparation, containing seven ingredients, and administer it to Gilgamesh while he slept. This was done, and an enchantment thus put upon the hero. When he awoke (on the seventh day) he renewed his importunate request for the secret of perpetual life. His host sent him to a spring of water where he might bathe his sores and be healed; and having tested the efficacy of the magic waters Gilgamesh returned once more to his ancestor's dwelling, doubtless to persist in his quest for life. Notwithstanding that Ut-Napishtim had already declared it impossible for Gilgamesh to attain immortality, he now directed him (apparently at the instance of his wife) to the place where he would find the plant of life, and instructed Adad-Ea to conduct him thither.

The magic plant, which bestowed immortality and eternal youth on him who ate of it, appears to have been a weed, a creeping plant, with thorns which pricked the hands of the gatherer; and, curiously enough, Gilgamesh seems to have sought it at the bottom of the sea. At length the plant was found, and the hero declared his intention of carrying it with him to Erech. And so he set out on the return journey, accompanied by the faithful ferryman not only on the first, and watery, stage of his travels, but also overland to the city of Erech itself. When they had journeyed twenty *kasbu* they left an offering (presumably for the dead), and when they had journeyed thirty *kasbu*, they repeated a funeral chant. The narrative goes on: 'Gilgamesh saw a well of fresh water, he went down to it and offered a libation. A serpent smelled the odour of the plant, advanced ... and carried off the plant. Gilgamesh sat down and wept, the tears ran down his cheeks.' He lamented bitterly the loss of the precious plant, seemingly predicted to him when he made his offering at the end of twenty *kasbu*. At length they reached Erech, when Gilgamesh sent Adad-Ea to enquire concerning the building of the city walls, a proceeding which has possibly some mythological significance.

The twelfth tablet opens with the lament of Gilgamesh for his friend Eabani, whose loss he has not ceased to deplore. 'Thou canst no longer stretch thy bow upon the earth; and those who were slain with the bow are round about thee. Thou canst no longer bear a sceptre in thy hand; and the spirits of the dead have taken thee captive. Thou canst no longer wear shoes upon thy feet; thou canst no longer raise thy war-cry on the earth. No more dost thou kiss thy wife whom thou didst love; no more dost thou smite thy wife whom thou didst hate. No more dost thou kiss thy daughter whom thou didst love; no more dost thou smite thy daughter whom thou didst hate. The sorrow of the underworld hath taken hold upon thee.' Gilgamesh went from temple to temple, making offerings and desiring the gods to restore Eabani to him; to Ninsum he went, to Bel, and to Sin, the moon-god, but they heeded him not. At length he cried to Ea, who took compassion on him and persuaded Nergal to bring the shade of Eabani from the underworld. A hole was opened in the earth and the spirit of the dead man issued therefrom like a breath of wind. Gilgamesh addressed Eabani thus: 'Tell me, my friend, tell me, my friend; the law of the earth which thou hast seen, tell me.' Eabani answered him: 'I cannot tell thee, my friend, I cannot tell thee.' But afterwards, having bidden Gilgamesh 'sit down and weep,' he proceeded to tell him of the conditions which prevailed in the underworld, contrasting the lot of the warrior duly buried with that of a person whose corpse is cast uncared for into the fields. 'On a couch he lies, and drinks pure water, the man who was slain in battle – thou and I have oft seen such a one – his father and his mother (support) his head, and his wife (kneels) at his side. But the man whose corpse is cast upon the field – thou and I have oft seen such a one – his spirit rests not in the earth. The man whose spirit has none to care for it – thou and I have oft seen such a one – the dregs of the vessel, the leavings of the feast, and that which is cast out upon the streets, are his food.' Upon this solemn note the epic closes.

The Story of Sanehat

THE EGYPTIAN HERO IS HIMSELF supposed to relate his own adventures thus:

The Erpa, the Duke, the Chancellor of the King of the North, the *smer uati*, the judge, the Antchmer of the marches, the King in the lands of the Nubians, the veritable royal kinsman loving him, the member of the royal bodyguard, Sanehat, says: I am a member of the bodyguard of his lord, the servant of the King, and of the house of Neferit, the feudal chieftainess, the Erpat princess, the highly favoured lady, the royal wife of Usertsen, whose word is truth in Khnemetast, the royal daughter of Amenemhat, whose word is truth in Qanefer. On the seventh day of the third month of the season Akhet, in the thirtieth year [of his reign], the god drew nigh to his horizon, and the King of the South, the King of the North, SehetepabRa (i.e. Amenemhat II), ascended into heaven, and was invited to the Disk, and his divine members mingled with those of him that made him. The King's House was in silence, hearts were bowed down in sorrow, the two Great Gates were shut fast, the officials sat motionless, and the people mourned.

Now behold, [before his death] His Majesty had despatched an army to the Land of the Themehu, under the command of his eldest son, the beautiful god Usertsen. And he went and raided the desert lands in the south, and captured slaves from the Thehenu (Libyans), and he was at that moment returning and bringing back Libyan slaves and innumerable beasts of every kind. And the high officers of the Palace sent messengers into the western country to inform the King's son concerning what had taken place in the royal abode. And the messengers found him on the road, and they came to him by night and asked him if it was not the proper time for him to hasten his return, and to set out with his bodyguard without letting his army in general know of his departure. They also told him that a message had been sent to the princes who were in command of the soldiers in his train not to proclaim [the matter of the King's death] to anyone else.

Sanehat continues: When I heard his voice speaking I rose up and fled. My heart was cleft in twain, my arms dropped by my side, and trembling seized all my limbs. I ran about distractedly, hither and thither, seeking a hiding-place. I went into the thickets in order to find a place wherein I could travel without being seen. I made my way upstream, and I decided not to appear in the Palace, for I did not know but that deeds of violence were taking place there. And I did not say, 'Let life follow it', but I went on my way to the district of the Sycamore. Then I came to the Lake (or Island) of Seneferu, and I passed the whole day there on the edge of the plain. On the following morning I continued my journey, and a man rose up immediately in front of me on the road, and he cried for mercy; he was afraid of me. When the night fell I walked into the village of Nekau, and I crossed the river in an *usekht* boat without a rudder, by the help of the wind from the west. And I travelled eastwards of the district of Aku, by the pass of the goddess Herit, the Lady of the Red Mountain. Then I allowed my feet to take the road downstream, and I travelled on to Anebuheq, the fortress that had been built to drive back the Satiu (nomad marauders), and to hold in check the tribes that roamed the desert. I crouched down in the scrub during the day to avoid being seen by the watchmen on the top of the fortress. I set out again on the march, when the night fell, and when daylight fell on the earth I arrived at Peten, and I rested myself by the Lake of Kamur. Then thirst came upon me and overwhelmed me. I suffered torture. My throat was burnt up, and I said, 'This indeed is the taste of death.' But I took courage, and collected my members (i.e.

myself), for I heard the sounds that are made by flocks and herds. Then the Satiu of the desert saw me, and the master of the caravan who had been in Egypt recognised me. And he rose up and gave me some water, and he warmed milk [for me], and I travelled with the men of his caravan, and thus I passed through one country after the other [in safety]. I avoided the land of Sunu and I journeyed to the land of Qetem, where I stayed for a year and a half.

And Ammuiansha, the Shekh of Upper Thennu, took me aside and said to me, 'You will be happy with me, for you will hear the language of Egypt.' Now he said this because he knew what manner of man I was, for he had heard the people of Egypt who were there with him bear testimony concerning my character. And he said to me, 'Why and wherefore have you come here? Is it because the departure of King SehetepabRa from the Palace to the horizon has taken place, and you did not know what would be the result of it?' Then I spoke to him with words of deceit, saying, 'I was among the soldiers who had gone to the land of Themeh. My heart cried out, my courage failed me utterly, it made me follow the ways over which I fled. I hesitated, but felt no regret. I did not listen to any evil counsel, and my name was not heard on the mouth of the herald. How I came to be brought into this country I know not; it was, perhaps, by the Providence of God.'

And Ammuiansha said to me, 'What will become of the land without that beneficent god the terror of whom passed through the lands like the goddess Sekhmet in a year of pestilence?' Then I made answer to him, saying, 'His son shall save us. He has entered the Palace, and has taken possession of the heritage of his father. Moreover, he is the god who has no equal, and no other can exist beside him, the lord of wisdom, perfect in his plans, of good will when he passes decrees, and one comes forth and goes in according to his ordinance. He reduced foreign lands to submission whilst his father [sat] in the Palace directing him in the matters which had to be carried out. He is mighty of valour, he slays with his sword, and in bravery he has no compeer. One should see him attacking the nomads of the desert, and pouncing upon the robbers of the highway! He beats down opposition, he smites arms helpless, his enemies cannot be made to resist him. He takes vengeance, he cleaves skulls, none can stand up before him. His strides are long, he slays him that flees, and he who turns his back upon him in flight never reaches his goal. When attacked his courage stands firm. He attacks again and again, and he never yields. His heart is bold when he sees the battle array, he permits none to sit down behind. His face is fierce [as] he rushes on the attacker. He rejoices when he takes captive the chief of a band of desert robbers. He seizes his shield, he rains blows upon him, but he has no need to repeat his attack, for he slays his foe before he can hurl his spear at him. Before he draws his bow the nomads have fled, his arms are like the souls of the Great Goddess. He fights, and if he reaches his object of attack he spars not, and he leaves no remnant. He is beloved, his pleasantness is great, he is the conqueror, and his town loves him more than herself; she rejoices in him more than in her god, and men throng about him with rejoicings. He was king and conqueror before his birth, and he has worn his crowns since he was born. He has multiplied births, and he it is whom God has made to be the joy of this land, which he has ruled, and the boundaries of which he has enlarged. He has conquered the Lands of the South, shall he not conquer the Lands of the North? He has been created to smite the hunters of the desert, and to crush the tribes that roam the sandy waste....' Then the Shekh of Upper Thennu said to me, 'Assuredly Egypt is a happy country in that it knows his vigour. Verily, as long as you tarry with me I will do good to you.'

And he set me before his children, and he gave me his eldest daughter as wife, and he made me to choose for myself a very fine territory which belonged to him, and which lay on the border of a neighbouring country, and this beautiful region was called Aa. In it there are figs, and wine is more abundant than water. Honey is plentiful, oil exists in large quantities, and fruits of every kind are on the trees thereof. Wheat, barley, herds of cattle, and flocks of sheep and goats are there in untold numbers. And the Shekh showed me very great favour, and his affection for me was so great that he made me Shekh of one of the best tribes in his country. Bread-cakes were made for me each day, and each day wine was brought to me with roasted flesh and wild fowl, and the wild creatures of the plain that were caught were laid before me, in addition to the game which my hunting dogs brought in. Food of all kinds was made for me, and milk was prepared for me in various ways. I passed many years in this manner, and my children grew up into fine strong men, and each one of them ruled his tribe. Every ambassador on his journey to and from Egypt visited me. I was kind to people of every class. I gave water to the thirsty man. I suppressed the highway robber. I directed the operations of the bowmen of the desert, who marched long distances to suppress the hostile Shekhs, and to reduce their power, for the Shekh of Thennu had appointed me General of his soldiers many years before this. Every country against which I marched I terrified into submission. I seized the crops by the wells, I looted the flocks and herds, I carried away the people and their slaves who ate their bread, I slew the men there. Through my sword and bow, and through my well-organised campaigns, I was highly esteemed in the mind of the Shekh, and he loved me, for he knew my bravery, and he set me before his children when he saw the bravery of my arms.

Then a certain mighty man of valour of Thennu came and reviled me in my tent; he was greatly renowned as a man of war, and he was unequalled in the whole country, which he had conquered. He challenged me to combat, being urged to fight by the men of his tribe, and he believed that he could conquer me, and he determined to take my flocks and herds as spoil. And the Shekh took counsel with me about the challenge, and I said, 'I am not an acquaintance of his, and I am by no means a friend of his. Have I ever visited him in his domain or entered his door, or passed through his compound? [Never!] He is a man whose heart becomes full of evil thoughts, whensoever he ses me, and he wishs to carry out his fell design and plunder me. He is like a wild bull seeking to slay the bull of a herd of tame cattle so that he may make the cows his own. Or rather he is a mere braggart who wishs to seize the property which I have collected by my prudence, and not an experienced warrior. Or rather he is a bull that loves to fight, and that loves to make attacks repeatedly, fearing that otherwise some other animal will prove to be his equal. If, however, his heart be set upon fighting, let him declare [to me] his intention. Is God, Who knows everything, ignorant of what he has decided to do?'

And I passed the night in stringing my bow, I made ready my arrows of war, I unsheathed my dagger, and I put all my weapons in order. At daybreak the tribes of the land of Thennu came, and the people who lived on both sides of it gathered themselves together, for they were greatly concerned about the combat, and they came and stood up round about me where I stood. Every heart burned for my success, and both men and women uttered cries (or exclamations), and every heart suffered anxiety on my behalf, saying, 'Can there exist possibly any man who is a mightier fighter and more doughty a man of war than he?' Then my adversary grasped his shield, and his battle-axe, and his spears, and after he had hurled his weapons at me, and I had succeeded in avoiding his short spears, which arrived harmlessly one after the other, he became filled with fury, and making up his mind to attack me at close quarters he threw himself upon me. And I hurled my javelin at him, which remained fast in his neck, and he uttered a long cry and fell on his face, and I slew him with his own weapons. And as I stood upon his back I shouted the cry of victory, and every Aamu man (i.e. Asiatic) applauded me, and I gave thanks to Menthu (the War-god of Thebes); and the slaves of my opponent mourned for their lord. And the Shekh Ammuiansha took me in his arms and embraced me. I carried off his (i.e. the opponent's) property. I seized his cattle as spoil, and what he meditated doing to me I did to him. I took possession of the contents of his tent, I stripped his compound, I became rich, I increased my store of goods, and I added greatly to the number of my cattle.

Thus did God prosper the man who made Him his support. Thus that day was washed (i.e. satisfied) the heart of the man who was compelled to make his escape from his own into another country. Thus that day the integrity of the man who was once obliged to take to flight as a miserable fugitive was proven in the sight of all the Court. Once I was a wanderer wandering about hungry, and now I can give bread to my neighbours. Once I had to flee naked from my country, and now I am the possessor of splendid raiment, and of apparel made of the finest byssus. Once I was obliged to do my own errands and to fetch and carry for myself, and now I am the master of troops of servants. My house is beautiful, my estate is spacious, and my name is repeated in the Great House. Oh Lord of the gods, who has ordered my goings, I will offer propitiatory offerings to you: I beseech you to restore me to Egypt, and Oh be You pleased most graciously to let me once again look upon the spot where my mind dwells for hours [at a time]! How great a boon would it be for me to cleanse my body in the land of my birth! Let, I pray, a period of happiness attend me, and may God give me peace. May He dispose events in such a way that the close of the career of the man who has suffered misery, whose heart has seen sorrow, who has wandered into a strange land, may be happy. Is He not at peace with me this day? Surely He shall hearken to him that is afar off.... Let the King of Egypt be at peace with me, and may I live upon his offerings. Let me salute the Mistress of the Land (i.e. the Queen) who is in his palace, and let me hear the greetings of her children. Oh would that my members could become young again! For now old age is stealing on me. Infirmity overtakes me. Mine eyes refuse to see, my hands fall helpless, my knees shake, my heart stands still, the funerary mourners approach and they will bear me away to the City of Eternity, wherein I shall become a follower of Nebertcher. She will declare to me the beauties of her children, and they shall traverse it with me.

Behold now, the Majesty of the King of Egypt, KheperkaRa, whose word is truth, having spoken concerning the various things that had happened to me, sent a messenger to me bearing royal gifts, such as he would send to the king of a foreign land, with the intention of making glad the heart of your servant now [speaking], and the princes of his palace made me to hear their salutations. And here is a copy of the document, which was brought to your servant [from the King] instructing him to return to Egypt:

'The royal command of the Horus, Ankh-mestu, Lord of Nekhebet and Uatchet, Ankh-mestu, King of the South, King of the North, KheperkaRa, the son of Ra, Amenemhat, the everliving, to my follower Sanehat. This royal order is despatched to you to inform you. You have travelled about everywhere, in one country after another, having set out from Qetem and reached Thennu, and you have journeyed from place to place at your own will and pleasure. Observe now, what you have done [to others, making them obey you], shall be done to you. Make no excuses, for they shall be set aside; argue not with [my] officials, for your arguments shall be refuted. Your heart shall not reject the plans which your mind has formulated. Your Heaven (i.e. the Queen), who is in the Palace, is stable and flourishing at this present time, her head is crowned with the sovereignty of the earth, and her children are in the royal chambers of the Palace. Lay aside the honours which you have, and your life of abundance (or luxury), and journey to Egypt. Come and look upon your native land, the land where you were born, smell the earth (i.e. do homage) before the Great Gate, and associate with the nobles thereof. For at this time you are beginning to be an old man, and you can no longer produce sons, and you have [ever] in your mind the day of [your] burial, when you will assume the form of a servant [of Osiris]. The unguents for your embalmment on the night [of mummification] have been set apart for you, together with your mummy swathings, which are the work of the hands of the goddess Tait. Your funerary procession, which will march on the day of your union with the earth, has been arranged, and there are prepared for you a gilded mummy-case, the head whereof is painted blue, and a canopy made of *mesket* wood. Oxen shall draw you [to the tomb], the wailing women shall precede you, the funerary dances shall be performed, those who mourn you shall be at the door of your tomb, the funerary offerings dedicated to you shall be proclaimed, sacrifices shall be offered for you with your oblations, and your funerary edifice shall be built in white stone, side by side with those of the princes and princesses. Your death must not take place in a foreign land, the Aamu folk shall not escort you [to your grave], you shall not be placed in the skin of a ram when your burial is effected; but at your burial there shall be ... and the smiting of the earth, and when you departest lamentations shall be made over your body.'

When this royal letter reached me, I was standing among the people of my tribe, and when it had been read to me I threw myself face downwards on the ground, and bowed until my head touched the dust, and I clasped the document reverently to my breast. Then [I rose up] and walked to and fro in my abode, rejoicing and saying, 'How can these things possibly be done to your servant who is now speaking, whose heart made him to fly into foreign lands [where dwell] peoples who stammer in their speech? Assuredly it is a good and gracious thought [of the King] to deliver me from death [here], for your Ka (i.e. double) will make my body end [its existence] in my native land.'

Here is a copy of the reply that was made by the servant of the Palace, Sanehat, to the above royal document:

'In peace the most beautiful and greatest! your Ka knows of the flight which your servant, who is now speaking, made when he was in a state of ignorance, Oh you beautiful god, Lord of Egypt, beloved of Ra, favoured of Menthu, the Lord of Thebes. May Amen-Ra, lord of the thrones of the Two Lands, and Sebek, and Ra, and Horus, and Hathor, and Tem and his Company of the Gods, and Neferbaiu, and Semsuu, and Horus of the East, and Nebt-Amehet, the goddess who is joined to your head, and the Tchatchau gods who preside over the Nile flood, and Menu, and Heru-khenti-semti, and Urrit, the Lady of Punt, and Nut, and Heru-ur (Haroeris), and Ra, and all the gods of Tamera (Egypt), and of the Islands of the Great Green Sea (i.e. Mediterranean), bestow upon you a full measure of their good gifts, and grant life and serenity to your nostrils, and may they grant to you an eternity which has no limit, and everlastingness which has no bounds! May your fear penetrate and extend into all countries and mountains, and mayest you be the possessor of all the region which the sun encircles in his course. This is the prayer which your servant who now speaks makes on behalf of his lord who has delivered him from Ament.

'The lord of knowledge who knows men, the Majesty of the Setepsa abode (i.e. the Palace), knows well that his servant who is now speaking was afraid to declare the matter, and that to repeat it was a great thing. The great god (i.e. the King), who is the counterpart of Ra, has done wisely in what he has done, and your servant who now speaks has meditated upon it in his mind, and has made himself to conform to his plans. Your Majesty is like Horus, and the victorious might of your arms has conquered the whole world. Let your Majesty command that Maka [chief of] the country of Qetma, and Khentiaaush [chief of] Khent-Keshu, and Menus [chief of] the lands of the Fenkhu, be brought hither, and these Governors will testify that these things have come to pass at the desire of your Ka (i.e. double), and that Thenu does not speak words of overboldness to you, and that she is as [obedient as] your hunting dogs. Behold, the flight, which your servant who is now speaking made, was made by him as the result of ignorance; it was not wilful, and I did not decide upon it after careful meditation. I cannot understand how I could ever have separated myself from my country. It seems to me now to have been the product of a dream wherein a man who is in the swamps of the Delta imagins himself to be in Abu (Elephantine, or Syene), or of a man who whilst standing in fertile fields imagines himself to be in the deserts of the Sudan. I fear nothing and no man can make with truth [accusations] against me. I have never turned my ear to disloyal plottings, and my name has never been in the mouth of the crier [of the names of proscribed folk]; though my members quaked, and my legs shook, my heart guided me, and the God who ordained this flight of mine led me on. Behold, I am not a stiff-necked man (or rebel), nay, I held in honour [the King], for I knew the land of Egypt and that Ra has made your fear to exist everywhere in Egypt, and the awe of you to permeate every foreign land. I beseech you to let me enter my native land. I beseech you to let me return to Egypt. You are the apparel of the horizon. The Disk (i.e. the Sun) shines at your wish. One drinks the water of the river Nile at your pleasure. One breathes the air of heaven when you give the word of command. Your servant who now speaks will transfer the possessions which he has gotten in this land to his kinsfolk. And as for the embassy of your Majesty which has been despatched to the servant who now speaks, I will do according to your Majesty's desire, for I live by the breath which you give, Oh you beloved of Ra, Horus, and Hathor, and your holy nostrils are beloved of Menthu, Lord of Thebes; may you live forever!'

And I tarried one day in the country of Aa in order to transfer my possessions to my children. My eldest son attended to the affairs of the people of my settlement, and the men and women thereof (i.e. the slaves), and all my possessions were in his hand, and all my children, and all my cattle, and all my fruit trees, and all my palm plantations and groves.

Then your servant who is now speaking set out on his journey and travelled towards the South. When I arrived at Heruuatu, the captain of the frontier patrol sent a messenger to inform the Court of my arrival. His Majesty sent a courteous overseer of the servants of the Palace, and following him came large boats laden with gifts from the King for the soldiers of the desert who had escorted me and guided me to the town of Heruuatu. I addressed each man among them by name and every toiler had that which belonged to him.

I continued my journey, the wind bore me along, food was prepared for me and drink made ready for me, and the best of apparel (?), until I arrived at Athettaui. On the morning of the day following my arrival, five officials came to me, and they bore me to the Great House, and I bowed low until my forehead touched the ground before him. And the princes and princesses were standing waiting for me in the *umtet* chamber, and they advanced to meet me and to receive me, and the *smeru* officials conducted me into the hall, and led me to the privy chamber of the King, where I found His Majesty [seated] upon the Great Throne in the *umtet* chamber of silver-gold. I arrived there, I raised myself up after my prostrations, and I knew not that I was in his presence. Then this god (i.e. the King) spoke to me harshly, and I became like a man who is confounded in the darkness; my intelligence left me, my limbs quaked, my heart was no longer in my body, and I knew not whether I was dead or alive. Then His Majesty said to one of his high officials, 'Raise him, and let him speak to me.' And His Majesty said to me, 'You have come then! You have smitten foreign lands and you have travelled, but now weakness has vanquished you, you have become old, and the infirmities of your body are many. The warriors of the desert shall not escort you [to your grave] ... will you not speak and declare your name?' And I was afraid to contradict him, and I answered him about these matters like a man who was stricken with fear. Thus did my Lord speak to me.

And I answered and said, 'The matter was not of my doing, for, behold, it was done by the hand of God; bodily terror made me to flee according to what was ordained. But, behold, I am here in your presence! You are life. Your Majesty does as you please.' And the King dismissed the royal children, and His Majesty said to the Queen, 'Look now, this is Sanehat who comes in the guise of an Asiatic, and who has turned himself into a nomad warrior of the desert.' And the Queen laughed a loud hearty laugh, and the royal children cried out with one voice before His Majesty, saying, 'Oh Lord King, this man cannot really be Sanehat'; and His Majesty said, 'It is indeed!'

Then the royal children brought their instruments of music, their *menats* and their sistra, and they rattled their sistra, and they passed backwards and forwards before His Majesty, saying, 'Thy hands perform beneficent acts, Oh King. The graces of the Lady of Heaven rest [upon you]. The goddess Nubt gives life to your nostrils, and the Lady of the Stars joins herself to you, as you sail to the South wearing the Crown of the North, and to the North wearing the Crown of the South. Wisdom is established in the mouth of your Majesty, and health is on your brow. You strike terror into the miserable wretches who entreat your mercy. Men propitiate you, Oh Lord of Egypt, [as they do] Ra, and you are acclaimed with cries of joy like Nebertcher. Your horn conquers, your arrow slays, [but] you give breath to him that is afflicted. For our sakes graciously give a boon to this traveller Sanehat, this desert warrior who was born in Tamera (Egypt). He fled through fear of you, and he departed to a far country because of his terror of you. Does not the face that gazes on your blench? Does not the eye that gazes into your feel terrified?'

Then His Majesty said, 'Let him fear not, and let him not utter a sound of fear. He shall be a *smer* official among the princes of the palace, he shall be a member of the company of the *shenit* officials. Get gone to the refectory of the palace, and see to it that rations are provided for him.'

Thereupon I came forth from the privy chamber of the King, and the royal children clasped my hands, and we passed on to the Great Door, and I was lodged in the house of one of the King's sons, which was beautifully furnished. In it there was a bath, and it contained representations of the heavens and objects from the Treasury. And there [I found] apparel made of royal linen, and myrrh of the finest quality which was used by the King, and every chamber was in charge of officials who were favourites of the King, and every officer had his own appointed duties. And [there] the years were made to slide off my members. I cut and combed my hair, I cast from me the dirt of a foreign land, together with the apparel of the nomads who live in the desert. I arrayed myself in apparel made of fine linen, I anointed my body with costly ointments, I slept upon a bedstead [instead of on the ground], I left the sand to those who dwelt on it, and the crude oil of wood wherewith they anoint themselves.

I was allotted the house of a nobleman who had the title of *smer*, and many workmen laboured upon it, and its garden and its groves of trees were replanted with plants and trees. Rations were brought to me from the palace three or four times each day, in additions to the gifts which the royal children gave me unceasingly. And the site of a stone pyramid among the pyramids was marked out for me. The surveyor-in-chief to His Majesty chose the site for it, the director of the funerary designers drafted the designs and inscriptions which were to be cut upon it, the chief of the masons of the necropolis cut the inscriptions, and the clerk of the works in the necropolis went about the country collecting the necessary funerary furniture.

I made the building flourish, and provided everything that was necessary for its upkeep. I acquired land round about it. I made a lake for the performance of funerary ceremonies, and the land about it contained gardens, and groves of trees, and I provided a place where the people on the estate might dwell similar to that which is provided for a *smeru* nobleman of the first rank. My statue, which was made for me by His Majesty, was plated with gold, and the tunic thereof was of silver-gold. Not for any ordinary person did he do such things. May I enjoy the favour of the King until the day of my death shall come!

Here ends the book; [given] from its beginning to its end, as it has been found in writing.

The Story of the Educated Peasant Khuenanpu

ONCE UPON A TIME there lived a man whose name was Khuenanpu, a peasant of Sekhet-hemat (a district to the west of Cairo now known as Wadi an-Natrun), and he had a wife whose name was Nefert. This peasant said to this wife of his, 'Behold, I am going down into Egypt in order to bring back food for my children. Go you and measure up the grain which remains in the granary, [and see how many] measures [there are].' Then she measured it, and there were eight measures. Then this peasant said to this wife of his, 'Behold, two measures of grain shall be for the support of yourself and your children, but of the other six you shall make bread and beer whereon I am to live during the days on which I shall be travelling.'

And this peasant went down into Egypt, having laden his asses with *aaa* plants, and *retmet* plants, and soda and salt, and wood of the district of ..., and *aunt* wood of the Land of Oxen (the Oasis of Farafrah), and skins of panthers and wolves, and *neshau* plants, and *anu* stones, and *tenem* plants, and *kheperur* plants, and *sahut*, and *saksut* seeds (?), and *masut* plants, and *sent* and *abu* stones, and *absa* and *anba* plants, and doves and *naru* and *ukes* birds, and *tebu, uben* and *tebsu* plants, and *kenkent* seeds, and the plant 'hair of the earth', and *anset* seeds, and all kinds of beautiful products of the land of Sekhet-hemat.

And when this peasant had marched to the south, to Hensu (the Khanes of the Hebrews and Herakleopolis of the Greeks, the modern Ahnas al-Madinah), and had arrived at the region of Perfefa, to the north of Metnat, he found a man standing on the river bank whose name was Tehutinekht, who was the son of a man whose name was Asri; both father and son were serfs of Rensi, the son of Meru the steward. When this man Tehutinekht saw the asses of this peasant, of which his heart approved greatly, he said, 'Would that I had any kind of god with me to help me to seize for myself the goods of this peasant!'

Now the house of this Tehutinekht stood upon the upper edge of a sloping path along the river bank, which was narrow and not wide. It was about as wide as a sheet of linen cloth, and upon one side of it was the water of the stream, and on the other was a growing crop. Then this Tehutinekht said to his slave, 'Run and bring me a sheet of linen out of my house'; and it was brought to him immediately. Then he shook out the sheet of linen over the narrow sloping path in such a way that its upper edge touched the water, and the fringed edge the growing crop. And when this peasant was going along the public path, this Tehutinekht said to him, 'Be careful, peasant, would you walk upon my clothes?' And this peasant said, 'I will do as you please; my way is good.' And when he turned to the upper part of the path, this Tehutinekht said, 'Is my corn to serve as a road for you, Oh peasant?' Then this peasant said, 'My way is good. The river-bank is steep, and the road is covered up with your corn, and you have blocked up the path with your linen garment. Do you really intend not to let us pass? Has it come to pass that he dares to say such a thing?'

[At that moment] one of the asses bit off a large mouthful of the growing corn, and this Tehutinekht said, 'Behold, your ass is eating my corn! Behold, he shall come and tread it out.' Then this peasant said, 'My way is good. Because one side of the road was made impassable [by you], I led my ass to the other side (?), and now you have seized my ass because he bit off a large mouthful of the growing corn. However, I know the master of this estate, which belongs to Rensi, the son of Meru. There is no doubt that he has driven every robber out of the whole country, and shall I be robbed on his estate?' And this Tehutinekht said, 'Is not this an illustration of the proverb which the people use, "The name of the poor man is only mentioned because of his master?" It is I who speak to you, but it is the steward [Rensi, the son of Meru] of whom you are thinking.'

Then Tehutinekht seized a cudgel of green tamarisk wood, and beat cruelly with it every part of the peasant's body, and took his asses from him and carried them off into his compound. And this peasant wept and uttered loud shrieks of pain because of what was done to him. And this Tehutinekht said, 'Howl not so loudly, peasant, or verily [you shall depart] to the domain of the Lord of Silence.' Then this peasant said, 'You have beaten me, and robbed me of my possessions, and now you wish to steal even the very complaint that comes out of my mouth! Lord of Silence indeed! Give me back my goods. Do not make me utter complaints about your fearsome character.'

And this peasant spent ten whole days in making entreaties to this Tehutinekht [for the restoration of his goods], but Tehutinekht paid no attention to them whatsoever. At the end of this time this peasant set out on a journey to the south, to the city of Hensu, in order to lay his complaint before Rensi, the son of Meru, the steward, and he found him just as he was coming forth from the door in the courtyard of his house which opened on the river bank, to embark in his official boat on the river. And this peasant said, 'I earnestly wish that it may happen that I may make glad your heart with the words which I am going to say! Perhaps you will allow someone to call your confidential servant to me, in order that I may send him back to you thoroughly well informed as to my business.' Then Rensi, the son of Meru, the steward, caused his confidential servant to go to this peasant, who sent him back to him thoroughly well informed as to his business. And Rensi, the son of Meru, the steward, made inquiries about this Tehutinekht from the officials who were immediately connected with him, and they said to him, 'Lord, the matter is indeed only one that concerns one of the peasants of Tehutinekht who went [to do business] with another man near him instead of with him. And, as a matter of fact, [officials like Tehutinekht] always treat their peasants in this manner whenever they go to do business with other people instead of with them. Would you trouble yourself to inflict punishment upon Tehutinekht for the sake of a little soda and a little salt? [It is unthinkable.] Just let Tehutinekht be ordered to restore the soda and the salt and he will do so [immediately].' And Rensi, the son of Meru, the steward, held his peace; he made no answer to the words of these officials, and to this peasant he made no reply whatsoever.

And this peasant came to make his complaint to Rensi, the son of Meru, the steward, and on the first occasion he said, 'Oh my lord steward, greatest one of the great ones, guide of the things that are not and of these that are, when you go down into the Sea of Truth (the name of a lake in the Other World), and sail thereon, may the attachment (?) of your sail not tear away, may your boat not drift (?), may no accident befall your mast, may the poles of your boat not be broken, may you not run aground when you would walk on the land, may the current not carry you away, may you not taste the calamities of the stream, may you never see a face of fear, may the timid fish come to you, and mayest you obtain fine, fat waterfowl. Oh you who are the father of the orphan, the husband of the widow, the brother of the woman who has been put away by her husband, and the clother of the motherless, grant that I may place your name in this land in connection with all good law. Guide in whom there is no avarice, great man in whom there is no meanness, who destroys falsehood and make what is true exist, who come to the word of my mouth, I speak that you may hear. Perform justice, Oh you who are praised, to whom those who are most worthy of praise give praise. Do away the oppression that weighs me down. Behold, I am weighted with sorrow, behold, I am sorely wronged. Try me, for behold, I suffer greatly.'

Now this peasant spoke these words in the time of the King of the South, the King of the North, NebkauRa, whose word is truth. And Rensi, the son of Meru, the steward, went into the presence of His Majesty, and said, 'My Lord, I have found one of these peasants who can really speak with true eloquence. His goods have been stolen from him by an official who is in my service, and behold, he has come to lay before me a complaint concerning this.' His Majesty said to Rensi, the son of Meru, the steward, 'If you would see me in a good state of health, keep him here, and do not make any answer at all to anything which he shall say, so that he may continue to speak. Then let that which he shall say be written down, and brought to us, so that we may hear it. Take care that his wife and his children have food to live on, and see that one of these peasants goes to remove want from his house. Provide food for the peasant himself to live on, but you shall make the provision in such a way that the food may be given to him without letting him know that it is you who have given it to him. Let the food be given to his friends and let them give it to him.' So there were given to him four bread-cakes and two pots of beer daily. These were provided by Rensi, the son of Meru, the steward, and he gave them to a friend, and it was this friend who gave them to the peasant. And Rensi, the son of Meru, the steward, sent instructions to the governor of [the Oasis of] Sekhet-hemat to supply the wife of the peasant with daily rations, and there were given to her regularly the bread-cakes that were made from three measures of corn.

Then this peasant came a second time to lay his complaint [before Rensi], and he found him as he was coming out from the ..., and he said, 'Oh steward, my lord, the greatest of the great, you richest of the rich, whose greatness is true greatness, whose riches are true riches, you rudder of heaven, you pole of the earth, you measuring rope for heavy weights (?)! Oh rudder, slip not, Oh pole, topple not, Oh measuring rope, make no mistake in measuring! The great lord takes away from her that has no master (or owner), and steals from him that is alone [in the world]. Your rations are in your house – a pot of beer and three bread-cakes. What do you spend in satisfying those who depend upon you? Shall he who must die die with his people? Will you be a man of eternity (i.e. will you live forever?) Behold, are not these things evils, namely, the balance that leans side-ways, the pointer of the balance that does not show the correct weight, and an upright and just man who departs from his path of integrity? Observe! The truth goes badly with you, being driven out of her proper place, and the officials commit acts of injustice. He who ought to estimate a case correctly gives a wrong decision. He who ought to keep himself from stealing commits an act of robbery. He who should be strenuous to arrest the man who breaks the word (i.e. law) in its smallest point, is himself guilty of departing therefrom. He who should give breath stifles him that could breathe. The land that ought to give repose drives repose away. He who should divide in fairness has become a robber. He who should blot out the oppressor gives him the command to turn the town into a waste of water. He who should drive away evil himself commits acts of injustice.'

Then Rensi, the son of Meru, the steward, said [to the peasant], 'Does your case appear in your heart so serious that I must have my servant [Tchutinekht] seized on your account?' This peasant said, 'He who measures the heaps of corn filches from them for himself, and he who fills [the measure] for others robs his neighbours. Since he who should carry out the behests of the law gives the order to rob, who is to repress crime? He who should do away with offences against the law himself commits them. He who should act with integrity behaves crookedly. He who does acts of injustice is applauded. When will you find yourself able to resist and to put down acts of injustice? [When] the ... comes to his place of yesterday the command comes: 'Do a [good] deed in order that one may do a [good] deed [to you]', that is to say, 'Give thanks to everyone for what he does'. This is to drive back the bolt before it is shot, and to give a command to the man who is already overburdened with orders. Would that a moment of destruction might come, wherein your vines should be laid low, and your geese diminished, and your waterfowl be made few in number! [Thus] it comes that the man who ought to see clearly has become blind, and he who ought to hear distinctly has become deaf, and he who ought to be a just guide has become one who leads into error.

'Observe! You are strong and powerful. Your arm is able to do deeds of might, and [yet] your heart is avaricious. Compassion has removed itself from you. The wretched man whom you have destroyed cries aloud in his anguish. You are like the messenger of the god Henti (the Crocodile-god). Set not out [to do evil] for the Lady of the Plague (i.e. Sekhmet).... As there is nothing between you and her for a certain purpose, so there is nothing against you and her. If you will not do it [then] she will not show compassion. The beggar has the powerful owner of possessions (or revenues) robbed, and the man who has nothing has the man who has secreted [much] stolen goods. To steal anything at all from the beggar is an absolute crime on the part of the man who is not in want, and [if he does this] shall his action not be inquired into? You are filled full with your bread, and are drunken with your beer, and you are rich [beyond count]. When the face of the steersman is directed to what is in front of him, the boat falls out of its course, and sails wherever it pleases. When the King [remains] in his house, and when you work the rudder, acts of injustice take place round about you, complaints are widespread, and the loss (?) is very serious. And one says, 'What is taking place?' You should make yourself a place of refuge [for the needy]. Your quay should be safe. But observe! your town is in commotion. Your tongue is righteous, make no mistake [in judgment]. The abominable behaviour of a man is, as it were, [one of] his members. Speak no lies yourself, and take good heed that your high officials do not do so. Those who assess the dues on the crops are like a ..., and to tell lies is very dear to their hearts. You who have knowledge of the affairs of all the people, do you not understand my circumstances? Observe, you who relieves the wants of all who have suffered by water, I am on the path of him that has no boat. Oh you who bring every drowning man to land, and who saves the man whose boat has foundered, are you going to let me perish?'

And this peasant came a third time to lay his complaint [before Rensi], and he said, 'Oh my Lord Rensi, the steward! You are Ra, the lord of heaven with your great chiefs. The affairs of all men [are ruled by you]. You are like the water-flood. You are Hep (the Nile-god) who makes green the fields, and who makes the islands that are deserts become productive. Exterminate the robber, be you the advocate of those who are in misery, and be not towards the petitioner like the water-flood that sweeps him away. Take heed to yourself likewise, for eternity comes, and behave in such a way that the proverb, 'Righteousness (or truth) is the breath of the nostrils', may be applicable to you. Punish those who are deserving of punishment, and then these shall be like you in dispensing justice. Do not the small scales weigh incorrectly? Does not the large balance incline to one side? In such cases is not Thoth merciful? When you do acts of injustice you become the second of these three, and if these be merciful you also may be merciful. Answer not good with evil, and do not set one thing in the place of another. Speech flourishes more than the *senmit* plants, and grows stronger than the smell of the same. Make no answer to it whilst you pour out acts of injustice, to make grow apparel, which three ... will cause him to make. [If] you work the steering pole against the sail (?), the flood shall gather strength against the doing of what is right. Take good heed to yourself and set yourself on the mat (?) on the look-out place. The equilibrium of the earth is maintained by the doing of what is right. Tell not lies, for you are a great man. Act not in a light manner, for you are a man of solid worth. Tell not lies, for you are a pair of scales. Make no mistake [in your weighing], for you are a correct reckoner (?). Observe! You are all of a piece with the pair of scales. If they weigh incorrectly, you also shall act falsely. Let not the boat run aground when you are working the steering pole ... the look-out place. When you have to proceed against one who has carried off something, take you nothing, for behold, the great man ceases to be a great man when he is avaricious. Your tongue is the pointer of the scales; your heart is the weight; your lips are the two arms of the scales. If you cover your face so as not to see the doer of violent deeds, who is there [left] to repress lawless deeds? Observe! You are like a poor man for the man who washes clothes, who is avaricious and destroys kindly feeling (?). He who forsakes the friend who endows him for the sake of his client is his brother, who has come and brought him a gift. Observe! You are a ferryman who ferries over the stream only the man who possesses the proper fare, whose integrity is well attested (?). Observe! You are like the overseer of a granary who does not at once permit to pass him that comes empty. Observe! You are among men like a bird of prey that lives upon weak little birds. Observe! You are like the cook whose sole joy is to kill, whom no creature escapes. Observe! You are like a shepherd who is careless about the loss of his sheep through the rapacious crocodile; you never count [your sheep]. Would that you would make evil and rapacious men be fewer! Safety has departed from [every] town throughout the land. You should hear, but most assuredly you hear not! Why have you not heard that I have this day driven back the rapacious man? When the crocodile pursues.... How long is this condition of yours to last? Truth which is concealed shall be found, and falsehood shall perish. Do not imagine that you are master of tomorrow, which has not yet come, for the evils which it may bring with it are unknown.'

And behold, when this peasant had said these things to Rensi, the son of Meru, the steward, at the entrance to the hall of the palace, Rensi caused two men with leather whips to seize him, and they beat him in every member of his body. Then this peasant said: 'The son of Meru has made a mistake. His face is blind in respect of what he sees, he is deaf in respect of what he hears, and he is forgetting that which he ought to remember. Observe! You are like a town that has no governor, and a community that has no chief, and a ship that has no captain, and a body of men who have no guide. Observe! You are like a high official who is a thief, a governor of a town who takes [bribes], and the overseer of a province who has been appointed to suppress robbery, but who has become the captain of those who practise it.'

And this peasant came a fourth time to lay his complaint before Rensi, and he met him as he was coming out from the door of the temple of the god Herushefit, and said, 'Oh you who are praised, the god Herushefit, from whose house you come forth, praises you. When well-doing perishes, and there is none who seeks to prevent its destruction, falsehood makes itself seen boldly in the land. If it happens that the ferry-boat is not brought for you to cross the stream in, how will you be able to cross the stream? If you have to cross the stream in your sandals, is your crossing pleasant? Assuredly it is not! What man is there who continues to sleep until it is broad daylight? [This habit] destroys the marching by night, and the travelling by day, and the possibility of a man profiting by his good luck, in very truth. Observe! One cannot tell you sufficiently often that 'Compassion has departed from you.' And behold, how the oppressed man whom you have destroyed complains! Observe! You are like a man of the chase who would satisfy his craving for bold deeds, who determines to do what he wishes, to spear the hippopotamus, to shoot the wild bull, to catch fish, and to catch birds in his nets. He who is without hastiness will not speak without due thought. He whose habit is to ponder deeply will not be light-minded. Apply your heart earnestly and you shall know the truth. Pursue diligently the course which you have chosen, and let him that hears the plaintiff act rightly. He who follows a right course of action will not treat a plaintiff wrongly. When the arm is brought, and when the two eyes see, and when the heart is of good courage, boast not loudly in proportion to your strength, in order that calamity may not come to you. He who passes by [his] fate halts between two opinions. The man who eats tastes [his food], the man who is spoken to answers, the man who sleeps sees visions, but nothing can resist the presiding judge when he is the pilot of the doer [of evil]. Observe, Oh stupid man, you are apprehended. Observe, Oh ignorant man, you are freely discussed. Observe, too, that men intrude upon your most private moments. Steersman, let not your boat run aground. Nourisher [of men], let not men die. Destroyer [of men], let not men perish. Shadow, let not men perish through the burning heat. Place of refuge, let not the crocodile commit ravages. It is now four times that I have laid my complaint before you. How much more time shall I spend in doing this?'

This peasant came a fifth time to make his complaint, and said, 'Oh my lord steward, the fisherman with a *khut* instrument ..., the fisherman with a ... kills *i*-fish, the fisherman with a harpoon spears the *aubbu* fish, the fisherman with a *tchabhu* instrument catches the *paqru* fish, and the common fishermen are always drawing fish from the river. Observe! You are even as they. Wrest not the goods of the poor man from him. The helpless man you know him. The goods of the poor man are the breath of his life; to seize them and carry them off from him is to block up his nostrils. You are committed to the hearing of a case and to the judging between two parties at law, so that you may suppress the robber; but, verily, what you do is to support the thief. The people love you, and yet you are a law-breaker. You have been set as a dam before the man of misery, take heed that he is not drowned. Verily, you are like a lake to him, Oh you who flows quickly.'

This peasant came the sixth time to lay his complaint [before Rensi], and said, 'Oh my lord steward ... who makes truth, who makes happiness (or, what is good), who destroys [all evil]; you are like the satiety that comes to put an end to hunger, you are like the raiment that comes to do away nakedness; you are like the heavens that become calm after a violent storm and refresh with warmth those who are cold; you are like the fire that cooks that which is raw, and you are like the water that quenches the thirst. Yet look round about you! He who ought to make a division fairly is a robber. He who ought to make everyone satisfied has been the cause of the trouble. He who ought to be the source of healing is one of those who cause sicknesses. The transgressor diminishes the truth. He who fills well the right measure acts rightly, provided that he gives neither too little nor too much. If an offering be brought to you, do you share it with your brother (or neighbour), for that which is given in charity is free from after-thought (?). The man who is dissatisfied induces separation, and the man who has been condemned brings on schisms, even before one can know what is in his mind. When you have arrived at a decision delay not in declaring it. Who keeps within him that which he can eject?... When a boat comes into port it is unloaded, and the freight thereof is landed everywhere on the quay. It is [well] known that you have been educated, and trained, and experienced, but behold, it is not that you may rob [the people]. Nevertheless, you do [rob them] just as other people do, and those who are found about you are thieves (?). You who should be the most upright man of all the people are the greatest transgressor in the whole country. [You are] the wicked gardener who waters his plot of ground with evil deeds in order to make his plot tell lies, so that he may flood the town (or estate) with evil deeds (or calamities).'

This peasant came the seventh time in order to lay his complaint [before Rensi], and said, 'Oh my lord steward, you are the steering pole of the whole land, and the land sails according to your command. You are the second (or counterpart) of Thoth, who judges impartially. My lord, permit you a man to appeal to you in respect of his cause which is righteous. Let not your heart fight against it, for it is unseemly for you to do so; [if you do this] you of the broad face will become evil-hearted. Curse not the thing that has not yet taken place, and rejoice not over that which has not yet come to pass. The tolerant judge rejoices in showing kindness, and he withholds all action concerning a decision that has been given, when he knows not what plan was in the heart. In the case of the judge who breaks the law, and overthrows uprightness, the poor man cannot live [before him], for the judge plunders him, and the truth salutes him not. But my body is full, and my heart is overloaded, and the expression thereof comes forth from my body by reason of the condition of the same. [When] there is a breach in the dam the water pours out through it: even so is my mouth opened and it utters speech. I have now emptied myself, I have poured out what I had to pour out, I have unburdened my body, I have finished washing my linen. What I had to say before you is said, my misery has been fully set out before you; now what have you to say in excuse (or apology)? your lazy cowardice has been the cause of your sin, your avarice has rendered you stupid, and your gluttony has been your enemy. Do you think that you will never find another peasant like me? If he has a complaint to make do you think that he will not stand, if he is a lazy man, at the door of his house? He whom you force to speak will not remain silent. He whom you force to wake up will not remain asleep. The faces which you make keen will not remain stupid. The mouth which you open will not remain closed. He whom you make intelligent will not remain ignorant. He whom you instruct will not remain a fool. These are they who destroy evils. These are the officials, the lords of what is good. These are the crafts-folk who make what exists. These are they who put on their bodies again the heads that have been cut off.'

This peasant came the eighth time to lay his complaint [before Rensi], and said, 'Oh my lord steward, a man falls because of covetousness. The avaricious man has no aim, for his aim is frustrated. Your heart is avaricious, which befitt you not. You plunder, and your plunder is no use to you. And yet formerly you did permit a man to enjoy that to which he had good right! your daily bread is in your house, your belly is filled, grain overflows [in your granaries], and the overflow perishes and is wasted. The officials who have been appointed to suppress acts of injustice have been rapacious robbers, and the officials who have been appointed to stamp out falsehood have become hiding-places for those who work iniquity. It is not fear of you that has driven me to make my complaint to you, for you do not understand my mind (or heart). The man who is silent and who turns back in order to bring his miserable state [before you] is not afraid to place it before you, and his brother does not bring [gifts] from the interior of [his quarter]. Your estates are in the fields, your food is on [your] territory, and your bread is in the storehouse, yet the officials make gifts to you and you seize them. Are you not then a robber? Will not the men who plunder hasten with you to the divisions of the fields? Perform the truth for the Lord of Truth, who possesses the real truth. You writing reed, you roll of papyrus, you palette, you Thoth, you are remote from acts of justice. Oh Good One, you are still goodness. Oh Good One, you are truly good. Truth endures forever. It goes down to the grave with those who perform truth, it is laid in the coffin and is buried in the earth; its name is never removed from the earth, and its name is remembered on earth for good (or blessing). That is the ordinance of the word of God. If it be a matter of a hand-balance it never goes askew; if it be a matter of a large pair of scales, the standard thereof never inclines to one side. Whether it be I who come, or another, verily you must make speech, but do not answer whether you speak to one who ought to hold his peace, or whether you seize one who cannot seize you. You are not merciful, you are not considerate. You have not withdrawn yourself, you have not gone afar off. But you have not in any way given in respect of me any judgment in accordance with the command, which came forth from the mouth of Ra himself, saying, 'Speak the truth, perform the truth, for truth is great, mighty, and everlasting. When you perform the truth you will find its virtues (?), and it will lead you to the state of being blessed (?). If the hand-balance is askew, the pans of the balance, which perform the weighing, hang crookedly, and a correct weighing cannot be carried out, and the result is a false one; even so the result of wickedness is wickedness.'

This peasant came the ninth time to lay his complaint [before Rensi], and said, 'The great balance of men is their tongues, and all the rest is put to the test by the hand balance. When you punish the man who ought to be punished, the act tells in your favour. [When he does not this] falsehood becomes his possession, truth turns away from before him, his goods are falsehood, truth forsakes him, and supports him not. If falsehood advances, she makes a mistake, and goes not over with the ferry-boat [to the Island of Osiris]. The man with whom falsehood prevails has no children and no heirs upon the earth. The man in whose boat falsehood sails never reaches land, and his boat never comes into port. Be not heavy, but at the same time do not be too light. Be not slow, but at the same time be not too quick. Rage not at the man who is listening to you. Cover not over your face before the man with whom you are acquainted. Make not blind your face towards the man who is looking at you. Thrust not aside the suppliant as you go down. Be not indolent in making known your decision. Do [good] to him that will do [good] to you. Do not listen to the cry of the mob, who say, 'A man will assuredly cry out when his case is really righteous.' There is no yesterday for the indolent man, there is no friend for the man who is deaf to [the words of] truth, and there is no day of rejoicing for the avaricious man. The informer becomes a poor man, and the poor man becomes a beggar, and the unfriendly man becomes a dead person. Observe now, I have laid my complaint before you, but you will not listen to it; I shall now depart, and make my complaint against you to Anubis.'

Then Rensi, the son of Meru, the steward, caused two of his servants to go and bring back the peasant. Now this peasant was afraid, for he believed that he would be beaten severely because of the words which he had spoken to him. And this peasant said, 'This is [like] the coming of the thirsty man to salt tears, and the taking of the mouth of the suckling child to the breast of the woman that is dry. That the sight of which is longed for comes not, and only death approaches.'

Then Rensi, the son of Meru, the steward, said, 'Be not afraid, Oh peasant, for behold, you shall dwell with me.' Then this peasant swore an oath, saying, 'Assuredly I will eat of your bread, and drink of your beer forever.' Then Rensi, the son of Meru, the steward, said, 'Come here, however, so that you may hear your petitions'; and he caused to be [written] on a roll of new papyrus all the complaints which this peasant had made, each complaint according to its day. And Rensi, the son of Meru, the steward, sent the papyrus to the King of the South, the King of the North, NebkauRa, whose word is truth, and it pleased the heart of His Majesty more than anything else in the whole land. And His Majesty said, 'Pass judgment on yourself, Oh son of Meru.' And Rensi, the son of Meru, the steward, despatched two men to bring him back. And he was brought back, and an embassy was despatched to Sekhet Hemat.... Six persons, besides ... his grain, and his millet, and his asses, and his dogs.... [The remaining lines are mutilated, but the words which are visible make it certain that Tehutinekht the thief was punished, and that he was made to restore to the peasant everything which he had stolen from him.]

The Journey of the Priest Unu Amen into Syria

ON THE EIGHTEENTH DAY of the third month of the season of the Inundation, of the fifth year, Unu-Amen, the senior priest of the Hait chamber of the house of Amen, the Lord of the thrones of the Two Lands, set out on his journey to bring back wood for the great and holy Boat of Amen-Ra, the King of the Gods, which is called 'User-hat', and floats on the canal of Amen.

On the day wherein I arrived at Tchan (Tanis or Zoan), the territory of Nessubanebtet (i.e. King Smendes) and Thent-Amen, I delivered to them the credentials which I had received from Amen-Ra, the King of the Gods, and when they had had my letters read before them, they said, 'We will certainly do whatsoever Amen-Ra, the King of the Gods, our Lord, commands.' And I lived in that place until the fourth month of the season of the Inundation, and I abode in the palace at Zoan. Then Nessubanebtet and Thent-Amen despatched me with the captain of the large ship called Menkabuta, and I set sail on the sea of Kharu (Syria) on the first day of the fourth month of the Season of the Inundation. I arrived at Dhir, a city of Tchakaru, and Badhilu, its prince, made his servants bring me bread-cakes by the ten thousand, and a large jar of wine, and a leg of beef. And a man who belonged to the crew of my boat ran away, having stolen vessels of gold that weighed five *teben*, and four vessels of silver that weighed twenty *teben*, and silver in a leather bag that weighed eleven *teben*; thus he stole five *teben* of gold and thirty-one *teben* of silver.

On the following morning I rose up, and I went to the place where the prince of the country was, and I said to him, 'I have been robbed in your port. Since you are the prince of this land, and the leader thereof, you must make search and find out what has become of my money. I swear to you that the money [once] belonged to Amen-Ra, King of the Gods, the Lord of the Two Lands; it belonged to Nessubanebtet, it belonged to my lord Her-Heru, and to the other great kings of Egypt, but it now belongs to Uartha, and to Makamaru, and to Tchakar-Bal, Prince of Kepuna (Byblos).' And he said to me, 'Be angry or be pleased, [as you like], but, behold, I know absolutely nothing about the matter of which you speak to me. Had the thief been a man who was a subject of mine, who had gone down into your ship and stolen your money, I would in that case have made good your loss from the moneys in my own treasury, until such time as it had been found out who it was that robbed you, and what his name was, but the thief who has robbed you belongs to your own ship. Yet tarry here for a few days, and stay with me, so that I may seek him out.' So I tarried there for nine days, and my ship lay at anchor in his port. And I went to him and I said to him, 'Verily you have not found my money, [but I must depart] with the captain of the ship and with those who are travelling with him.' ...

[The text here is mutilated, but from the fragments of the lines that remain it seems clear that Unu-Amen left the port of Dhir, and proceeded in his ship to Tyre. After a short stay there he left Tyre very early one morning and sailed to Kepuna (Byblos), so that he might have an interview with the governor of that town, who was called Tchakar-Bal. During his interview with Tchakar-Bal the governor of Tyre produced a bag containing thirty *teben* of silver, and Unu-Amen promptly seized it, and declared that he intended to keep it until his own money which had been stolen was returned to him. Whilst Unu-Amen was at Byblos he buried in some secret place the image of the god Amen and the amulets belonging to it, which he had brought with him to protect him and to guide him on his way. The name of this image was 'Amen-ta-mat'. The text then proceeds in a connected form thus:]

And I passed nineteen days in the port of Byblos, and the governor passed his days in sending messages to me each day, saying, 'Get you gone out of my harbour.' Now on one occasion when he was making an offering to his gods, the god took possession of a certain young chief of his chiefs, and he caused him to fall into a fit of frenzy, and the young man said, 'Bring up the god (i.e. the figure of Amen-ta-mat). Bring the messenger who has possession of him. Make him set out on his way. Make him depart immediately.' Now the man who had been seized with the fit of divine frenzy continued to be moved by the same during the night. And I found a certain ship, which was bound for Egypt, and when I had transferred to it all my property, I cast a glance at the darkness, saying, 'If the darkness increases I will transfer the god to the ship also, and not permit any other eye whatsoever to look upon him.' Then the superintendent of the harbour came to me, saying, 'Tarry you here until tomorrow morning, according to the orders of the governor.' And I said to him, 'Are not you yourself he who has passed his days in coming to me daily and saying, "Get you gone out of my harbour?" Do you not say, 'Tarry here,' so that I may let the ship which I have found [bound for Egypt] depart, when you will again come and say, 'Haste you to be gone'?'

And the superintendent of the harbour turned away and departed, and told the governor what I had said. And the governor sent a message to the captain of the ship bound for Egypt, saying, 'Tarry till the morning; these are the orders of the governor.' And when the morning had come, the governor sent a messenger, who took me to the place where offerings were being made to the god in the fortress wherein the governor lived on the sea coast. And I found him seated in his upper chamber, and he was reclining with his back towards an opening in the wall, and the waves of the great Syrian sea were rolling in from seawards and breaking on the shore behind him. And I said to him, 'The grace of Amen [be with you]!' And he said to me, 'Including this day, how long is it since you came from the place where Amen is?' And I said to him, 'Five months and one day, including today.' And he said to me, 'Verily if that which you sayest is true, where are the letters of Amen which ought to be in your hand? Where are the letters of the high priest of Amen which ought to be in your hand?'

And I said to him, 'I gave them to Nessubanebtet and Thent-Amen.' Then was he very angry indeed, and he said to me, 'Verily, there are neither letters nor writings in your hands for us! Where is the ship made of acacia wood which Nessubanebtet gave to you? Where are his Syrian sailors? Did he not hand you over to the captain of the ship so that after you had started on your journey they might kill you and cast you into the sea? Whose permission did they seek to attack the god? And indeed whose permission were they seeking before they attacked you?' This is what he said to me.

And I said to him, 'The ship [wherein I sailed] was in very truth an Egyptian ship, and it had a crew of Egyptian sailors who sailed it on behalf of Nessubanebtet. There were no Syrian sailors placed on board of it by him.' He said to me, 'I swear that there are twenty ships lying in my harbour, the captains of which are in partnership with Nessubanebtet. And as for the city of Sidon, to where you wish to travel, I swear that there are there ten thousand other ships, the captains of which are in partnership with Uarkathar, and they are sailed for the benefit of his house.' At this grave moment I held my peace. And he answered and said to me, 'On what matter of business have you come hither?' And I said to him, 'The matter concerning which I have come is wood for the great and holy Boat of Amen-Ra, the King of the Gods. What your father did [for the god], and what your father's father did for him, do you also.' That was what I said to him. And he said to me, 'They certainly did do work for it (i.e. the boat). Give me a gift for my work for the boat, and then I also will work for it. Assuredly my father and my grandfather did do the work that was demanded of them, and Pharaoh, life, strength, and health be to him! caused six ships laden with the products of Egypt to come here, and the contents thereof were unloaded into their storehouses. Now, you must most certainly cause some goods to be brought and given to me for myself.'

Then he caused to be brought the books which his father had kept day by day, and he had them read out before me, and it was found that one thousand *teben* of silver of all kinds were [entered] in his books. And he said to me, 'If the Ruler of Egypt had been the lord of my possessions, and if I had indeed been his servant, he would never have had silver and gold brought [to pay my father and my father's father] when he told them to carry out the commands of Amen. The instructions which they (i.e. Pharaoh) gave to my father were by no means the command of one who was their king. As for me, I am assuredly not your servant, and indeed I am not the servant of him that made you to set out on your way. If I were to cry out now, and to shout to the cedars of Lebanon, the heavens would open, and the trees would be lying spread out on the sea-shore. I ask you now to show me the sails which you have brought to carry your ships which shall be loaded with your timber to Egypt. And show me also the tackle with which you will transfer to your ships the trees which I shall cut down for you for.... [Unless I make for you the tackle] and the sails of your ships, the tops will be too heavy, and they will snap off, and you will perish in the midst of the sea, [especially if] Amen utters his voice in the sky (i.e. if there is thunder), and he unfetters Sutekh (the Storm-god) at the moment when he rages. Now Amen has assumed the overlordship of all lands, and he has made himself their master, but first and foremost he is the overlord of Egypt, whence you have come. Excellent things have come forth from Egypt, and have reached even to this place wherein I am; and moreover, knowledge (or learning) has come forth therefrom, and has reached even this place where I am. But of what use is this beggarly journey of yours which you have been made to take?'

And I said to him, 'What a shameful thing [to say]! It is not a beggarly journey on which I have been despatched by those among whom I live. And besides, assuredly there is not a single boat that floats that does not belong to Amen. To him belong the sea and the cedars of Lebanon, concerning which you say, 'They are my property.' In Lebanon grows [the wood] for the Boat Amen-userhat, the lord of boats. Amen-Ra, the King of the Gods, spoke and told Her-Heru, my lord, to send me forth; and therefore he caused me to set out on my journey together with this great god (i.e. the figure of Amen). Now behold, you have caused this great god to pass nine and twenty days here in a boat that is lying at anchor in your harbour, for most assuredly you did know that he was resting here. Amen is now what he has always been, and yet you would dare to stand up and haggle about the [cedars of] Lebanon with the god who is their lord! And as concerning what you have spoken, saying, 'The kings of Egypt in former times caused silver and gold to be brought [to my father and father's father', you are mistaken], since they had bestowed upon them life and health, they would never have caused gold and silver to be brought to them; but they might have caused gold and silver to be brought to your fathers instead of life and health. And Amen-Ra, the King of the Gods, is the Lord of life and health. He was the god of your fathers, and they served him all their lives, and made offerings to him, and indeed you yourself are a servant of Amen. If now you will say to Amen, 'I will perform your commands, I will perform your commands', and will bring this business to a prosperous ending, you shall live, you shall be strong, you shall be healthy, and you shall rule your country to its uttermost limits wisely and well, and you shall do good to your people. But take good heed that you love not the possessions of Amen-Ra, the King of the Gods, for the lion loves the things that belong to him. And now, I pray you to allow my scribe to be summoned to me, and I will send him to Nessubanebtet and Thent-Amen, the local governors whom Amen has appointed to rule the northern portion of his land, and they will send to me everything which I shall tell them to send to me, saying, 'Let such and such a thing be brought', until such time as I can make the journey to the South (i.e. to Egypt), when I will have your miserable dross brought to you, even to the uttermost portion thereof, in very truth.' That was what I said to him.

And he gave my letter into the hand of his ambassador. And he loaded up on a ship wood for the fore part and wood for the hind part [of the Boat of Amen], and four other trunks of cedar trees which had been cut down, in all seven trunks, and he despatched them to Egypt. And his ambassador departed to Egypt, and he returned to me in Syria in the first month of the winter season (November-December). And Nessubanebtet and Thent-Amen sent to me five vessels of gold, five vessels of silver, ten pieces of byssus, each sufficiently large to make a suit of raiment, five hundred rolls of fine papyrus, five hundred hides of oxen, five hundred ropes, twenty sacks of lentils, and thirty vessels full of dried fish. And for my personal use they sent to me five pieces of byssus, each sufficiently large to make a suit of raiment, a sack of lentils, and five vessels full of dried fish. Then the Governor was exceedingly glad and rejoiced greatly, and he sent three hundred men and three hundred oxen [to Lebanon] to cut down the cedar trees, and he appointed overseers to direct them. And they cut down the trees, the trunks of which lay there during the whole of the winter season. And when the third month of the summer season had come, they dragged the tree trunks down to the sea-shore. And the Governor came out of his palace, and took up his stand before the trunks, and he sent a message to me, saying, 'Come.' Now as I was passing close by him, the shadow of his umbrella fell upon me, whereupon Pen-Amen, an officer of his bodyguard, placed himself between him and me, saying, 'The shadow of Pharaoh, life, strength, and health, be to him! your Lord, falls upon you.' And the Governor was angry with Pen-Amen, and he said, 'Let him alone.' Therefore I walked close to him.

And the Governor answered and said to me, 'Behold, the orders [of Pharaoh] which my fathers carried out in times of old, I also have carried out, notwithstanding the fact that you have not done for me what your fathers were wont to do for me. However, look for yourself, and take note that the last of the cedar trunks has arrived, and here it lies. Do now whatsoever you please with them, and take steps to load them into ships, for assuredly they are given to you as a gift. I beg you to pay no heed to the terror of the sea voyage, but if you persist in contemplating [with fear] the sea voyage, you must also contemplate [with fear] the terror of me [if you tarry here]. Certainly I have not treated you as the envoys of Kha-em-Uast (Rameses IX) were treated here, for they were made to pass seventeen (or fifteen) years in this country, and they died here.'

Then the Governor spoke to the officer of his bodyguard, saying, 'Lay hands on him, and take him to see the tombs wherein they lie.' And I said to him, 'Far be it from me to look upon such [ill-omened] things! As concerning the messengers of Kha-em-Uast, the men whom he sent to you as ambassadors were merely [officials] of his, and there was no god with his ambassadors, and so you say, 'Hasten to look upon your colleagues.' Behold, would you not have greater pleasure, and should you not [instead of saying such things] cause to be made a stele whereon should be said by you:

'Amen-Ra, the King of the Gods, sent to me Amen-ta-mat, his divine ambassador, together with Unu-Amen, his human ambassador, in quest of trunks of cedar wood for the Great and Holy Boat of Amen-Ra, the King of the Gods. And I cut down cedar trees, and I loaded them into ships. I provided the ships myself, and I manned them with my own sailors, and I made them to arrive in Egypt that they might bespeak [from the god for me] ten thousand years of life, in addition to the span of life which was decreed for me. And this petition has been granted.

'[And would you not rather] that, after the lapse of time, when another ambassador came from the land of Egypt who understood this writing, he should utter your name which should be on the stele, and pray that you should receive water in Amentet, even like the gods who subsist?'

And he said to me, 'These words which you have spoken to me are of a certainty a great testimony.' And I said to him, 'Now, as concerning the multitude of words which you have spoken to me: As soon as I arrive at the place where the First Prophet (i.e. Her-Heru) of Amen dwells, and he knows [how you have] performed the commands of the God [Amen], he will cause to be conveyed to you [a gift of] certain things.' Then I walked down to the beach, to the place where the trunks of cedar had been lying, and I saw eleven ships [ready] to put out to sea; and they belonged to Tchakar-Bal. [And the governor sent out an order] saying, 'Stop him, and do not let any ship with him on board [depart] to the land of Egypt.' Then I sat myself down and wept. And the scribe of the Governor came out to me, and said to me, 'What ails you?' And I said to him, 'Consider the ***kashu*** birds that fly to Egypt again and again! And consider how they flock to the cool water brooks! Until the coming of whom must I remain cast aside hither? Assuredly you see those who have come to prevent my departure a second time.'

Then [the scribe] went away and told the Governor what I had said; and the Governor shed tears because of the words that had been repeated to him, for they were full of pain. And he caused the scribe to come out to me again, and he brought with him two skins [full] of wine and a goat. And he caused to be brought out to me Thentmut, an Egyptian singing woman who lived in his house, and he said to her, 'Sing to him, and let not the cares of his business lay hold upon his heart.' And to me he sent a message, saying, 'Eat and drink, and let not business lay hold upon your heart. You shall hear everything which I have to say to you tomorrow morning.'

And when the morning had come, he caused [the inhabitants of the town] to be assembled on the quay, and having stood up in their midst, he said to the Tchakaru, 'For what purpose have you come here?' And they said to him, 'We have come here seeking for the ships which have been broken and dashed to pieces, that is to say, the ships which you did despatch to Egypt, with our unfortunate fellow-sailors in them.' And he said to them, 'I know not how to detain the ambassador of Amen in my country any longer. I beg of you to let me send him away, and then do pursue him, and prevent him [from escaping].' And he made me embark in a ship, and sent me forth from the sea-coast, and the winds drove me ashore to the land of Alasu (Cyprus?). And the people of the city came forth to slay me, and I was dragged along in their midst to the place where their queen Hathaba lived; and I met her when she was coming forth from one house to go into another. Then I cried out in entreaty to her, and I said to the people who were standing about her, 'Surely there must be among you someone who understands the language of Egypt.' And one of them said, 'I understand the speech [of Egypt].' Then I said to him, 'Tell my Lady these words: I have heard it said far from here, even in the city of [Thebes], the place where Amen dwells that wrong is done in every city, and that only in the land of Alasu (Cyprus?) is right done. And yet wrong is done here every day!' And she said, 'What is it that you really wish to say?' I said to her, 'Now that the angry sea and the winds have cast me up on the land wherein you dwell, you will surely not permit these men who have received me to slay me! Moreover, I am an ambassador of Amen. And consider carefully, for I am a man who will be searched for every day. And as for the sailors of Byblos whom they wish to kill, if their lord finds ten of your sailors he will assuredly slay them.' Then she caused her people to be called off me, and they were made to stand still, and she said to me, 'Lie down and sleep....' [The rest of the narrative is missing].

The Wanderings of Odysseus

FLUSHED WITH THE GLORY of his victory at Troy, the brave and clever Odysseus gathered together the men of Ithaca into twelve ships, and headed across the perilous seas to their homeland. Odysseus was the grandson of the Autolycus, a thief of great artfulness and notoriety. That same cunning lay deep within the breast of Odysseus and it would, said the Oracle before Odysseus set off for Troy, bring about his solitary survival. For Odysseus alone would return from Troy, beaten and infinitely weary, having battled the great gods of the sea and sky and winds, having faced temptations and fears which would bring about the certain death of a lesser man. The journey would take ten years, and its cost would be Odysseus's men and very nearly his soul. r

The Cicones

Ten years had passed since brave Odysseus had last set eyes on his faithful wife Penelope, and their son Telemachus. The victory at Troy had been a sweet one, and sated by the triumph, the lean and weathered warrior made plans to return his men to their homeland. Twelve ships were prepared for the voyage, laden with the spoils of their warfare and leaving the wretched and burning city of Troy a blazing beacon behind them.

Odysseus and his men were filled with rumbustuous excitement at the prospect of seeing home once more; they leapt and frolicked aboard the mighty vessels, unable to leave behind the boisterous energy nurtured in them by ten years' war. The sea lay calm and welcoming. The journey had begun, and the ships groaned with booty.

But greed is a fatal human trait, and not content with the plunder they had foraged at Troy, Odysseus and his men sought new bounty, landing first on the island of the Cicones. A mass of carousing warriors, they swept onshore, taking the city of Ismarus, sending its inhabitants to their deaths, and feasting on the carcasses of their sheep and cattle. Only the priest of Apollo was spared from the carnage.

This priest was a clever man, and he sank to his knees in gratitude, bowing his head in respectful silence as he supplied the marauders with skins of powerful wine. While the men feasted and celebrated the newest of their victories, Odysseus grew increasingly uneasy. Although he shared the piratical spirit of his men, he had an ingrown prudence which argued against the excesses of their plundering. He implored his men to return to their ships, doubting now the wisdom of their attack. Soon enough his worries were confirmed.

As the men of Ithaca lay spent and drunk on wine and rich foods, the Cicones appeared on the hilltops, eager for revenge and accompanied by troops they had rallied from the islands around their country. Odysseus tried to rouse his men, but his efforts were futile. The Cicones attacked, driving the disoriented travellers back to their ship, mercilessly slaying those who lagged behind. The carnage took tremendous toll on the crews of each ship, and lamed by defeat they limped out of the harbour and back to sea. Back aboard ship, the surviving men worked quietly, bewildered by the proof of their humanity, their weakness. Home lay just round the Cape at the point of the Peloponnese. But as anticipation rose within them, so did the savage gales of the north-east winds. Zeus, king of the gods, would wreak his vengeance.

The Lotus-Eaters

The powerful winds wrenched and buffeted the wretched ships, carrying them and their dispirited crew far from the point of the Cape, ever further from the welcoming shores of Ithaca. The sails were torn, and desperation clung to the men as they struggled against the most powerful of enemies – the sea and the winds themselves. And then, on the tenth day, there was peace. Just beyond the curve of the gentle waves lay land, a southern island from which a pervading and sweet perfume rose languorously into the air.

Ever watchful, Odysseus dared send ashore only three men from his depleted crew, and the men prepared the boat, their hearts beating. As their oars cut softly through the waves, an eerie and disquieting lassitude overwhelmed the men. Their trembling hands were warmed and stilled, their hearts were calmed in their breasts. And there, in front of them, appeared a remarkable being, whose serenity and stillness relaxed the anxious sailors, With a smile the creature beckoned them forth, holding out to them as he signalled, a large and purple flower.

The perfume of the flower snaked around the men, entrancing them and drawing them forth.

'The lotus flower,' the creature whispered softly. 'Sip its nectar. It is our food and drink here on the island of the lotus-eaters. It brings peace.' With that the lotus-eater raised the flower to the mouths of the men, who one by one drank deeply from its cup. Expressions of pure joy crossed their faces and their minds and memories were cleared of all but the rich and overwhelming pleasures of the nectar.

'It is the food of forgetfulness,' smiled the lotus-eater. 'Come, join us in the land of indolence. We have no worries here.'

Odysseus stood on the prow of his ship, a shadow of concern crossing his noble brow. 'Remain here,' he ordered his men, his voice unusually curt. His senses were buzzing with anticipation. He could feel an uneasy melancholy touching at the corners of his mind, and he angrily shrugged it away. All was not well on the island. He could sense no violence here, but danger lurked in a different cloak. He made his way to shore.

There was no sign of his sailors, and he strode purposefully in the direction he'd seen them take. He fought the growing ease which threatened to fill his mind, the strength of his character, his cunning forcefully keeping the invading sensations at bay. His men lolled by the fire of a group of beautiful beings. There was no anger or fear among them. They smiled a beatific welcome and signalled that he was to join them.

A lotus flower was held up for him to drink, and as he softened, a bell of fear rang in his brain. He curled back his lips and with renewed resolve, thrust the flower away. He drew from his pocket a length of rope, and hastily tied it to the scabbards of his men. He ignored their weak protests, and with his sword in their bags, forced them back to shore, and to the ship.

Their eyes were vague, their smiles bloodless. Odysseus and his men were as strangers to them, but they went aboard ship where they were lashed to the masts until the ship could sail on. The enchantment raised the heads of every man aboard Odysseus's ships. He roared at them to keep their heads down, to pierce their longing with good clean thoughts.

'Think of home, men,' he shouted. 'Forget it not, for it is what fires us onwards.'

And so they were to escape the fruit of the lotus-eaters, and the life of ease that threatened to overcome them. Odysseus and his men, weakened but still alive, sailed on.

The Cyclopes

Odysseus and his men sailed until they were forced to stop for food and fresh water. A small island appeared in the distance, and as they drew nigh, they saw that it was inhabited only by goats, who fed on the succulent, sweet grass which grew plentifully across the terrain. Fresh water cascaded from moss-carpeted rocks, and tumbled through the leafy country. The men's lips grew wet in anticipation of its cold purity.

As they clambered aboard shore, the fresh air filling their lungs, the men felt whole once more, and when they discovered, in their travels, an inviting cave filled with goats' milk and cheese, they settled down to feast. Their bellies groaning, and faces pink with pleasure, Odysseus and his men settled back to sleep on the smooth face of the cave, warmed by the hot spring that pooled in its centre, and sated by their sumptuous meal.

They were woken abruptly by heavy footfall, which shook the ground with each step. Eyeing one another warily, the tired men stayed silent, barely alert, but overwhelmingly fearful. Into the cave burst a flock of snow-white sheep and behind them the frightful giant Polyphemus, a Cyclops with one eye in the centre of his face. Polyphemus was the son of Poseidon, and he lived on the island with his fellow Cyclopes, existing peacefully in seclusion. He had not seen man for many years, and his single eyebrow raised in anticipation when he came upon his visitors. Odysseus took charge.

'Sire, in the name of Zeus, I beg your hospitality for the night. I've weary men who ...'

His words were cut off. The Cyclops laughed with outrage and reaching over, plucked up several of Odysseus's men and ate them whole. The others cowered in fear, but Odysseus stood firm, his stance betraying none of the fear that surged through his noble blood.

'I ask you again,' he began. But Polyphemus merely grunted and turned to roll a boulder across the opening to the cave. He settled down to sleep, his snores lifting the men from the stone floor of the cave, and forbidding them sleep. They huddled round Odysseus, who pondered their plight.

When he woke, Polyphemus ate two more men, and with his sheep, left the cave, carefully closing the door on the anxious men. They moved around their prison with agitation, wretched with fear. It was many hours before the Cyclops returned, but the men could not sleep. They waited for the sound of footsteps, they sickened at the thought of their inescapable death.

But the brave Odysseus feared not. His cunning led him through the maze of their predicament, and carefully and calmly he formed a plan. He was waiting when Polyphemus returned, and sidled up to the weary Cyclops with his goatskin of wine.

'Have a drink, ease your fatigue,' he said quietly, and with surprise the giant accepted. Unused to wine, he fell quickly into confusion, and laid himself unsteadily on the floor of the cave.

'Who are you, generous benefactor,' he slurred, clutching at the goatskin.

'My name is No one,' said Odysseus, a satisfied smile fleeting across his face.

'No one ...' the giant repeated the name and slipped into a deep slumber, his snores jolting the men once more.

Odysseus leapt into action. Reaching for a heavy bough of olive-wood, he plunged in into the fire and moulded its end to a barbed point. He lifted it from the fire, and with every ounce of strength and versatility left in his depleted body, he thrust it into Polyphemus' single eye, and stepped back, out of harm's way.

The Cyclops' roar propelled him through the air, momentarily deafening him. The men shuddered in the corner, shrieking with terror as the giant fumbled wildly for his torturers, grunting and shrieking with the intense pain. Soon his friends came running, and when they enquired the nature of his troubles, he could only cry, 'No one has blinded me' at which they returned, perplexed to their homes.

The morning came, cool and inviting, and hearing his sheep scrabbling at the door to get out to pasture, Polyphemus rose, and feeling along the walls, he found his boulder, and moved it. A smug look crossed his tortured features, and he stood outside the cave, his hands moving across the sheep as they left.

'You cannot leave this cave,' he taunted. 'You cannot escape me now.' He giggled with mirth at his cleverness, but his smile faded to confusion and then anger when he realized that the sheep had exited, and the cave was now empty. The men were gone.

Odysseus and his men laughed out loud as they unstrapped themselves from the bellies of the sheep, and racing towards their ships, Odysseus called out, 'Cyclops. It was not No one who blinded you. It was Odysseus of Ithaca,' and with that he lifted their mooring and set out for sea.

The torment of the giant rose in a deluge of sound and fury, echoing across the island and wakening his friends. Tearing off slabs of the mountainside, Polyphemus hurled them towards the escaping voice, which continued to taunt him. He roared a prayer to his father Poseidon, begging for vengeance, and struggled across the grass towards the sea.

But Odysseus had left, his ship surging across the sea to join with the rest of the fleet. Odysseus had escaped once more, and the sea opened up to him and his men, and they continued homewards, unaware that Poseidon had heard the cries of his son, and had answered them. Vengeance would be his.

The Island of Aeolus

Odysseus and the rest of his fleet were carried out to sea by the swell of water which spread from the rocks which Polyphemus had plunged into the waters. His cries echoed across the waters, growing louder as he realized the full measure of Odysseus's treachery, for as he and his men left they had robbed him of most of his flock, which they now cooked on spits over roaring fires in the galley.

They sailed to the Island of Aeolus, the guardian of winds, who lived with his six sons and six daughters in great comfort. Here, Odysseus and his men were entertained and feted, fed with sumptuous buffets which boasted unusual delicacies, their thirst slaked by fine wines and exotic nectars. They remained there for thirty days, convincing Aeolus that the gods must detest these men for unfounded reasons., for they were perfect guests, and Odysseus was a fair man, and an eloquent spokesman and orator.

But at last Odysseus grew restless, eager once more to set sail for Ithaca. The generosity of Aeolus had calmed his men, and well-nourished they were ready to do battle with the elements which were bound to hamper their return. But Aeolus had a gift for Odysseus, which he presented as the men prepared to leave the island. With great solemnity he passed to the warrior a bag, carefully bound with golden lace, and knotted many times over. In it were secured all the winds, except the gentle winds of the west, which would blow them to Ithaca. It was a sacred gift, and a token of Aeolus's regard for his visitor.

The men set off at last, their bellies filled, their minds alert, all maladies relieved. They sailed, blown by the west wind, for nine days, until the bright shores of Ithaca shone, a brilliant beacon in the distance. And so it was that Odysseus, greatly fatigued by the journey, and by the excitement of reaching his native shores once more, allowed himself to rest, to fall into a deep slumber that would prepare him for the festivities about to greet him.

But several of the men who sailed under his command begrudged their gracious leader, and envious of his favour with Aeolus, decided to take for themselves some of the gift presented to Odysseus. It must contain treasure, they thought, so large and unwieldy a parcel it was, and the men encouraged one another, fantasizing about what that bag might contain.

And so it was that the men tiptoed to Odysseus's chambers, and eased the bag from his side, careful not to disturb his slumber. And it was with greedy smiles, and anxious, fumbling hands that the bag was opened and the fierce winds released. They swirled around them, tossing and plunging the ships into waves higher than the mountains of the gods. In no time they were returned to the Island of Aeolus, helpless and frightened by nature's angry howls.

Odysseus was roughly awakened, and pushed forward to greet the displeased Aeolus. Aeolus cursed himself for humouring such foolish men, and understood at last the antipathy felt towards them by the great powers of Greece.

'Be gone, ill-starred wretch,' he snarled, and turned away from the unhappy seamen, towards the confines of his palace.

And so there was nothing for it but to return to the merciless seas, where the winds played havoc in their renewed freedom, where Poseidon waited for his chance to strike.

The Laestrygonians

The ships of Odysseus and his men were buffeted for many days before the winds exhausted their breath. And so they abandoned the ill-fated travellers, and left them in a dreadful calm. The ships sat still, mired in the stagnant waters, sunburnt and parched by the fiery sun. For a week they struggled with the heavy oars, seeming to move no further across the waveless sea. And then, on the eighth day, their ships limped into the rocky harbour of the Laestrygonians, where they moored themselves in an untidy row and made their way to shore. Odysseus was more cautious. Their travels had made him wiser than ever, and he tied his boat beyond the others, to a rocky outcrop in the open water. He signalled the men aboard to hold back, and climbed up the mast to get a better view.

Three of his men had rowed ashore, and Odysseus watched them as they spoke to two lovely young maidens, drawing water from a clear spring. The men stopped to take a drink before pressing on in the direction pointed out to them by the maidens. They looked calm and assured. Odysseus felt no such conviction, and he remained where he was, chewing his lower lip with concern. His men could see the others, and pestered Odysseus to allow them ashore, to drink of the cool fresh water, but he bade them to be silent and returned to his look-out.

The three men were easily visible from his post and Odysseus could see them reaching the walls of a magnificent castle, gilded and festooned with jewels. They hesitated at the gates. And it was then that the Laestrygonians attacked. Great, heaving giants plummeted through the gates on to the hapless men, racing towards shore and wailing a terrible cry, a battle song that tweaked at Odysseus's memory. These were the the evil cannibals who brought overwhelming fear to the heart of every traveller. Their shores were the most dangerous in Greece, their fearsome appetite for violence and unwitting seamen legendary.

They stampeded to shore, flocking in crowds to crush the ships under a deluge of rocks and spears. The sailors were skewered like lambs, and plucked from the waters, swallowed whole or sectioned and dipped into a bath of melted sheep's fat which lay bubbling in a cauldron beside the shores. The Laestrygonians had received word of Odysseus's ships and were prepared for the feast. They splashed and howled, laughing and eating until every one of Odysseus's comrade's ships was destroyed, emptied of its human cargo which presented such a cruel breakfast.

Odysseus had long since cut the ropes which anchored him to the rocks, and he and his crew raced for the deep sea, rowing faster than any mortal before them. Flushed with fear, their hearts pounding, they rowed for two days, one single crew saved from the tortures of the Laestrygonians by the wit of their captain. They rowed until they reached the shores of another island, where they collapsed, unable to lift their weary heads, caring not if in their refuge they courted danger.

Circe and the Island of Aeaea

For nearly two days the men slept on the shores of the unknown island, drinking in the peacefulness which covered them like a blanket, coming to terms with the loss of their comrades in their dreams. They woke freshened, but wary, eager to explore the land, but made prudent by their misadventures. In the distance, smoke curled lethargically into the windless sky. The island was inhabited, but by whom?

Odysseus divided the group into two camps, one taken by himself, the other led by his lieutenant, the courageous and loyal warrior Eurylochus. They drew lots from a helmet, and so it was decreed that Eurylochus would lead his party into the forest, towards the signs of life. His men gathered themselves up, and brushed off their clothes, trembling with anticipation and fear. They moved off.

The path wound its way through the tree-clad island, drawing the men into the bosom of the hills. There, at its centre, was a roughly hewn cottage, chimney smoking, and no sign of danger. Its fine stone walls were guarded by wolves and lions, but they leapt playfully towards the explorers, licking them and wagging their tails. Confused but comforted by the welcome, the men drew forward, and soon were enticed by the exquisite melody which drifted from the cottage. A woman's voice rang out, pure and sweet, calming their hearts, and drying the sweat on their brows. They moved forward confidently, only Eurylochus hanging back in caution.

They were greeted by the figure of a beautiful woman, whose hair tumbled to her heels, whose eyes were two green jewels in an ivory facade. Her smile was benevolent, welcoming, her arms outstretched. The men stumbled over one another to greet her, and were led into the cavernous depths of the cottage, where tables groaned with luxurious morsels of food – candied fruits, roasted spiced meats, plump vegetables and glazed breads, tumbling from platters of silver and gold. Wines and juices glistened in frosted glasses, and a barrel of fine brandy dripped into platinum goblets. It was a feast beyond compare, and the aroma enveloped the men, drawing them forward. They ate and drank while Eurylochus waited uncomfortably, outside the gates. And after many hours, when the men had taken their fill, they sat back with smiles of contentment, of satisfied gluttony, and raised their eyes in gratitude to their hostess.

'Who are you, fine woman?' slurred one of the crewman, made bold by the spirits.

'I am Circe,' she whispered back. And with a broad sweep of her hand, and a cry of laughter which startled her guests, drawing them from their stupor, she shouted, ' And you are but swine, like all men.'

Circe was a great and beautiful enchantress, living alone on this magical island where all visitors were pampered and fed with a charmed repast until Circe grew bored with them. And then, stroking their stupid heads, Circe would make them beasts. Now, she raised her mighty hands and laid them down upon the heads of Eurylochus's men and turned them to swine, corralling them snuffling and grunting through the door. Eurylochus peered round a tree in dismay. Ten men had entered, and now ten pigs left. The enchantress followed them, penning them in sties and stopping to speak gently to the other beasts, who had once been men. Happily she returned to her cottage and took up her loom once more.

Eurylochus sprinted through the forest, breathless with fear and disbelief as he rejoined Odysseus and the crew. Odysseus drew himself up, and a determined look transformed his distinguished features. He reached for his sword, and thrusting a dagger in his belt he set off to rescue his men, turning his head heavenwards and praying for assistance from the very gods who had spurned him. Odysseus had suffered the insults of war, and the tortures of their perilous journey. He would fight for his men, for his depleted crew. No woman, enchantress or not, would outwit him, would take from him his few remaining men.

As he struggled through the forest, a youth stumbled across his path.

'Here,' he whispered. 'Take this.' And he thrust into the hands of Odysseus a divine herb known as Moly, a plant with black roots and a snow white flower so beautiful that only those with celestial hands had the strength to pluck it. Moly was an antidote against the spells of Circe, and with this in his possession, Odysseus would be safe. The boy, who was really the god Hermes, sent by the goddess Athene, warned Odysseus of Circe's magical powers, and offered him a plan.

And so it was that Odysseus reached the cottage of Circe, and entered its welcoming gates. There the same feast greeted him, and he partook of the food until he lay sleepy and sated. Circe could hardly disguise her glee at the ease with which she had trapped this new traveller, and as she waved her wand to change him into a pig, Odysseus rose and spoke.

'Your magic has no power over me,' he said, and he thrust her to the ground at the point of his sword. She trembled with fear, and with longing.

'You,' she breathed, 'you must be the brave Odysseus, come from far to be my loving friend.' And she threw down her wand and took the soldier into her warm embrace. They lay together for a night of love, and in the morning, spent yet invigorated by their carnal feast they rose to set free Odysseus's men.

And there, on the enchanted island of Circe, Odysseus and his men spent days which stretched into golden weeks and then years, fed from the platters laden with food, their glasses poured over with drink, resting and growing fat, until they had forgotten the tortures of their journey. Odysseus was charmed by the lovely Circe, and all thoughts of Penelope and Telemachus were chased from his mind. His body was numbed by the pleasures inflicted upon it.

But the great Odysseus was a supreme leader, and even pure indulgence could not blunt his keen mind forever. As his senses gradually cleared, as Circe's powers over his body, over his soul began to wane, he felt the first rush of homesickness, of longing for Ithaca and his family. And in his heart he began to feel the weight of his responsibilities, the burden of his obligations to his country, to his men and to the gods.

With that, he made secret plans for their escape, and as the enchantment began also to wear at the sanity of his men, as they grew tired of the hedonism which filled their every waking hour, they became party to his strategy. With that, he went in search of Circe.

The House of Hades

Odysseus found the enchantress Circe in a calm and equable mood. She loved Odysseus, who had warmed her heart and her bed, but she had known since first setting eyes on the great warrior that he could never be completely hers. This day had been long in coming, but now that it was upon her, she gave him her blessing.

There were, however, tasks to be undertaken before Odysseus could be freed. He and his men could not voyage to Ithaca until they had met with the ghost of the blind prophet Tiresias, wiser than any dead or alive. They must travel to him at Hades, bringing gifts to sacrifice to the powers of the Underworld. Whitened by fear the men agreed to journey with Odysseus, to learn their fate and to receive instructions for their return to Ithaca.

All his men, spare one, prepared themselves for the voyage, but Elpenor, the youngest of the crew, lay sleeping on the roof of the cottage, where he'd stumbled in a drunken stupor the previous night. He woke to see the ship and his comrades setting sail from the island of Circe, and forgetting himself, he tumbled to the ground where he met an instant and silent death.

The men pressed on, unaware that one of their lot was missing. They sailed through a fair wind, raised by Circe, and as darkness drew itself around them, they entered the deep waters of Oceanus, where the Cimmerians lived in eternal night. There the rivers Phlegethon, Cocytus and Styx converged beneath a great rock, and Odysseus and his men drew aground. Following Circe's instructions, they dug a deep well in the earth beside the rock, then they cut the throats of a ram and a ewe, allowing their virgin blood to fill the trough.

The ghosts of the departed began to gather round the blood, some in battle-stained garb, others lost and confused; they struggled up to the pit and fought for a drink. Odysseus drew his sword to hold back the swelling crowd, startled as Elpenor, pale and blood-spattered, greeted his former master. He pressed forward, moaning and reaching greedily for the mortals.

'I have no grave,' he uttered. 'I cannot rest.' He clung to Odysseus whose cold stare belied the anxiety that pressed down on his heart. He was too close to the wretched creatures of the Underworld, near enough to be dragged down with them. He shook Elpenor loose.

'I will build you a grave,' he said gruffly. 'A fine grave with a tomb. There your ashes will lay and you shall have peace.'

Elpenor pulled back at once, a bemused expression crossing his pale face. He slid away, as reaching arms grappled into the space he left. Faces blended together in a grotesque dance of the macabre, writhing bodies struggling to catch a glimpse of mortals, of the other side. Familiar features appeared and then disappeared, as Odysseus fought to keep control of his senses.

'Odysseus,' the voice was soft, crooning. How often he'd heard it, sheltered in the tender arms of its bearer, rocked, adored. Mother.

Anticleia had been alive when he'd sailed for Troy and until this moment he knew not of her death. He longed to reach out for her, to take her pale and withered body against his own, to provide her with the comfort she had so tenderly invested in him.

But his duties prodded at his conscience, and he pricked his sword at her, edging her away from him, searching the tumultuous mass for Tiresias. At last he appeared from the shadowy depths, stopping to drink deeply from the bloody sacrifice. He leaned against his golden staff, and spoke slowly, in a language mellowed with age.

'Odysseus,' Tiresias said. 'Thy homecoming will not be easy. Poseidon bears spite against thee for blinding his Cyclops son Polyphemus. Yet you have guardians, and all may go well still, if, when you reach the hallowed shores of Trinacrian, ye harm not the herds of the Sun that pasture there. Control thy men, Odysseus. Allow not the greed that has tainted their hearts, that has led you astray, to shadow your journey.'

He paused, drinking again from the trenches and shrugging aside the groping arms of his comrades. He spat into the pool of blood.

'If you slay them, Odysseus, you will bring death upon your men, wreckage to your ships, and if you do escape, you will find thy house in trouble, no glory in your homecoming. And in the end, death will come to thee from the sea, from the great Poseidon.' With that, Tiresias leaned heavily on his staff and stumbled away, calling out as he left, 'Mark my words, brave Odysseus. My sight is not hampered by the darkness.'

Odysseus sat down and pondered the blind man's words. Anticleia appeared once again and he beckoned her closer, coaxed her to drink, and with the power invested in her by the blood, she drew a deep breath and spoke. She asked eagerly of his news, and told of her own, how she had died of grief thinking him dead at Troy. But his father, Laertes, she said, was still alive, though weakened by despair and feeble in his old age. Penelope his wife waited for him, loyal despite the attentions of many suitors. And Telemachus had become a man, grown tall and strong like his father.

Odysseus was torn by the sight of his mother, knowing not when he would set eyes on her again. He reached out to touch her, but she shrank from his embrace, a vision only, no substance, no warm blood coursing through her veins. He stood abruptly and was thronged by the clambering dead, as his mother drifted from his sight. He called after her, but she had gone.

Many of his comrades from Troy appeared now, eager to see the fine Odysseus, curious about his presence in Hades without having suffered the indignity of death. There was Agamemnon, and again, Achilles, whose stature was diminished, whose glory had tarnished. Ajax was there, and Tantalus and Sisyphus reached out to him, howling with anguish. And then there was Minos, and Orion, and Heracles, great men once, ghostly spectres now. They circled him and he felt chilled by their emptiness, by their singleness, by their determination to possess him. He turned away and strode from the group, shaking with the effort.

And his men joined him there, as they rowed away from that perilous island, down the Ocean river and back to the open sea. The friendly winds tossed them back to Circe's island, where the enchantress awaited them. Their belongings were ready, and she had resigned herself to the loss of her great love. She pulled Odysseus to one side, stroking him until he stiffened with pleasure, tempted as always to remain with her, enjoyed and enjoying. She whispered in his ear, warning him of the hazards which stood between Aeaea and Ithaca, the perils of his course. And he kissed her deeply and with a great surge of confidence, pushed her aside and went to meet his men.

Together they uncovered the body of poor Elpenor, and burned it with great ceremony, placing his ashes in a grand and sturdy tomb. Their duty done, they looked towards home.

And so it was that Odysseus escaped the fires of Hades, and the clutches of the shrewd Circe, and found himself heading once more towards Ithaca and home, the warnings of Circe and Tiresias echoing in his ears. As chance would have it, the first of the dangers lay just across the shimmering sea.

The Sirens

The air was hot and heavy around the vessel; the sunlight glinted on her bow as she cut through the silent sea. The men were restless. The silence held the threat of ill fate and they looked to Odysseus with wary eyes, seeking his wisdom, begging him wordlessly for comfort.

Odysseus stood tall alongside the mast, his noble profile chiselled against the airless horizon. He looked troubled, his head cocked to one side as he heard the first whispers of a beautiful melody.

It stung and tore at his sanity, dredging up a memory, a warning, but lulling him somehow away from his men, from his responsibilities, from the course of his voyage. He struggled against the growing sound, alert to the knowledge that his men had not yet heard its seductive strains but every fibre of his being ached to find its source, to touch its creator.

The Sirens. The words leapt to his troubled mind, and with great effort he drew himself from the reverie.

'Lash me to the mast,' he cried suddenly. Something in his voice caused his astonished men to obey.

'But captain, sir ...' one of the younger seamen ventured to express his amazement.

'Now!' Odysseus felt the bewildered hurt of his men. He also heard the growing symphony of the Sirens. He felt himself being drawn back, their melody licking at his mind like the hottest of fires, burning his resolve and his sanity.

'The candles,' he mouthed groggily. 'Melt the candles.' He could barely choke out the words. 'The wax ... in your ears.'

A startled silence was filled by the roaring of Odysseus's first mate: 'Do as he says, men. We have never had cause to question the wisdom of Odysseus. He has the strength and the cunning of ten men. He sees what we cannot see. We must put our faith in him.'

The ears of each man were carefully plugged by the wax of forty candles. As the last man turned his head, a swell of sound filled the air. Odysseus gave himself to it, wrestling with the lashings that restrained his strong frame. The sweet song of death called him, beckoned him from his lofty post.

The Sirens. The birds of death, temptresses of darkness – their sensuous melody played on the chords of his mind, calling him to a blackness which would envelope him forever. They appeared around him, luxuriant hair tumbling about angelic faces. He was trapped in a swarm of soaring wings and resplendent feathers. Women of the birds, with voices to lull even the hardiest warrior to certain death.

The deafened crew of his ship watched in amazement as the elegant creatures swooped among them, their eyes gleaming with secret knowledge, their voices capturing Odysseus in a cloud of passionate yearning.

Befuddled by the play on his senses, Odysseus signalled to his men to begin to row, then he sank back against the mast, spent and sickened by longing. The mighty vessel collected speed, ploughing through the sea that rippled with the thrust of the Sirens and the power of their music.

The sound increased, their music tortuously alluring as the Sirens fought for the spirit of Odysseus. The men battled with their oars, churning the water aside, sensing the danger that had hewn such fear on the face of their leader.

The music of the Sirens took on a rising note of mirth, and then, as the ship surged away from their grips, they laughed aloud.

'You will be ours again,' they sang together, laughing and diving around the fallen man. 'Ours to the end.'

They rose in a cluster of discord and light and disappeared, a painful silence filling the cacophony of sound that was no more. Odysseus rose again. He looked to the east, to the island of the Sirens, and he signalled to his men to clear their ears. He'd had to hear it. Circe had warned him of the Sirens, and although he trusted not the weak natures of his men, he had relished the chance to tempt his own resolve. But it was a bitter triumph, for he'd very nearly been lost to them, tugged so close to the edge of his mind, to madness and the darkness beneath.

A sweet wind caught the main sail and the ship plunged forward. Their small victory raised a smile on the weather-beaten faces of the seamen, and then they turned their faces to waters new.

Scylla and Charybdis

Circe had warned Odysseus of the dangers that would beset him and his crew should they choose to ignore the words of wise Tiresias. The next part of their journey would take them though a narrow strait, peopled by some of the most fearsome monsters in all the lands. Odysseus was to guide the ship through the narrow passage, through fierce and rolling waters, looking neither up nor down, embodying all humility.

But the pride of Odysseus was more deeply rooted than his fear, and ignoring Circe's words, he took a stand on the prow of his ship, heavily armoured and emboldened by the support of his men. Here he stood as they passed the rocks of Charybdis, the hateful daughter of Poseidon, who came to the surface three times each day in order to belch out a powerful whirlpool, drawing into her frothing gut all that came back with it. There was no sign of her now, the waters suspiciously stilled. Ahead lay an island, drenched in warm sunlight, beckoning to the weary sailors. They must just make it through.

Odysseus had kept the details of this fearsome strait from his men. They had been weakened by battle, and by the horrific sights which had met their eyes since leaving Troy. They were so close to Ithaca, he dared not cast their hopes and anticipation into shadow. And so it was that only Odysseus knew of the next monster who was to be thrust upon them in that dangerous channel, only Odysseus who knew that she was capable of tasks more gruesome than any of them had seen in all their travels.

For Scylla was a gluttonous and evil creature that haunted the strait, making her home in a gore-splattered den where she feasted on the remains of luckless sailors. She was, they said, a nymph who had been the object of Glaucus's attentions. Glaucus was a sea-god who had been turned into a merman by a strange herb he had unwittingly swallowed. And as much as he adored Scylla, so he was loved by Circe who, in a jealous rage, had turned Scylla into a terrible sea-monster with six dog's heads around her waist. She lived there in the cliff face in the straits of Messina, and devoured sailors who passed. She moved silently. Odysseus was loath to admit it, but the silent danger she represented placed more fear in his heart than the bravest of enemies.

Odysseus and his men passed further into the quiet strait, their mouths dry with fear. A silence hung over them like a shroud. And then it was broken by a tiny splash, and tinkle of water dripping, and up, with a mighty roar, came Scylla, the mouths on each head gaping open, their lethal jaws sprung for one purpose alone. Smoothly she leaned forward and in a flash of colour, of torn clothing and hellish screams, six of his best men were plucked from their posts aboard ship and drawn into the mouth of her cave. Their cries rent at the heart, at the conscience of Odysseus, and he turned helplessly to his remaining crew who looked at him with genuine fear, distrust and anger. A mutinous fever bubbled at the edges of their loyalty, and Odysseus knew he had lost them. He looked back at the cave where Scylla had silenced his hapless men, and signalled the others to row faster. A repeat of her attack would leave him with too few men to carry on. They rowed towards the shores of the great three-cornered island, Thrinacie, where the herds of the Sun-god Helios grazed peacefully on the hilltops.

The Flock of Helios

Shaken by the torture of his men, Odysseus proclaimed that they would make no further stops until they reached the shores of Ithaca. But the mutiny that had been brooding was thrust forward in the form of an insolent Eurylochus, who insisted that they set down their anchors, and have a night of rest. Tiresias and Circe had warned him of this flock of sheep, and Odysseus ordered his men to touch them not, to ignore their bleatings, their succulent fat which spoke of years of grazing on tender grasses, nurtured by Helios himself. The sailors took a solemn oath and Odysseus grudgingly allowed them to moor the ship to the rocky coast. They set about preparing a fire, and after a silent meal, fell into a deep sleep.

When morning broke, the skyline was littered with heavy clouds, tugging on the reins of a prevailing wind. And with it came a tempest which blew over the island for thirty days, prohibiting the safe voyage of the men, trapping them on an island that was empty of nourishment. And so it was that for thirty days the crew dined meagrely on corn and wine which the lovely Circe had provided, and when that was devoured, they took up their harpoons and fished the swirling waters for sustenance. And as hunger grew wild within their bodies, so did their minds wander a seditious path, along which their loyalty was cast and their oaths forgotten.

One night as Odysseus slept, weakened by hunger like his men, the errant sailors slaughtered several of Helios's sacred cows, dedicating some to the god, but gorging themselves on the carcasses of many more, till they sat, fattened and slovenly, rebelliously content. The cows were enchanted, and lowed while impaled on a spit over the fire, their empty carcasses rising to trample the ground around the men, but they repented not and continued to eat until soon their treachery was brought to the attention of Helios himself. Odysseus woke to discover the travesty and corralled his men aboard ship, urging them to escape before vengeance could be sprung upon them. But it was too late.

As Helios cried out to Zeus, imploring the king of gods to take divine retribution, Poseidon reached up his powerful staff and stirred up a tempest so violent that the ship was immediately cast to pieces in the furious waters. And Zeus sent storms and thunderbolts which broke the ship and its men into tiny pieces, crashing down the mast upon the sailors and killing them all. Only Odysseus who had remained true to the gods, was saved, and he clung to the wreckage, which formed a makeshift raft. For nine days he tumbled across waves that were larger than the fist of Poseidon himself, but his resolve was strong, his will to live was greater than the anger of the gods.

His men were drowned. Thoughts of Penelope and Telemachus kept him afloat as he fought the turbulent seas, escaping the grasp of an angry Poseidon. He was battered by the storm which drove him back to Charybdis, and as her great whirlpool was spat out, his raft was sucked into the waters that were drawn into her greedy belly. Faint with hunger, with fear, he reached out and held on to the spreading branches of a great fig tree and there he hung, perilously close to the vortex of water, until his raft was thrown out again. And Odysseus dropped into the sea, and paddled and drifted until he spied land once again. And only then did he allow himself to lay down his head, secure in the knowledge that help was at hand. So the noble Odysseus slept, and was washed towards the shores of this secluded island of Ogygia.

Calypso's Island

Odysseus could see land and in the distance a beautiful nymph, the most beautiful woman on whom he had ever laid eyes. Her milk-white skin was gleaming in the moonlight, and the wrathful winds tossed her silken hair. Her voice was soft, inviting above the raging storms.

'Come to me, Odysseus,' she whispered. 'Here you will find love, and eternal life.'

Odysseus struggled for breath, filled with longing and wonder. She reached a slender hand towards him, across the expanse of water, and lifted him from its depths, the strength of her grip, the length of her reach inhuman. He shuddered at her touch.

'You have come to join me,' she said calmly, as Odysseus laid restless and dripping beneath her.

Odysseus nodded, his passion spent. He was alive. The others had been clutched by the revengeful Poseidon. He was grateful to this nymph. He would plan his escape later.

'I have asked for you, and you have come,' she intoned quietly, settling herself at his side. Odysseus felt the first stirring of fear, but dismissed it as the lovely maiden smiled down on him.

She was Calypso, the lovely daughter of Thetis, and like Circe she was an enchantress. She lived alone on the island, in a comfortable cavern overhung by vines and fragrant foliage. She was gentle, and quiet, tending to Odysseus's every need, feeding him with morsels of delicious foods, warming him with handspun garments which clung to his body like a new skin, and she welcomed him in her bed, running his body over with hot hands that explored and relaxed the beaten hero until he grew to love her, and to build his life with her on the idyllic island.

For seven years he lived with Calypso, drunk with luxury and love. She was more beautiful than any he had seen before, and her island was dripping with pleasures. And as his happiness grew deeper, his fire and fervour spent to become a peaceful equilibrium, he felt the jab of conscience, of something untoward eating at the corners of his idyll, and he realized that he was living in a numb oblivion, that his passion to return home, to see his family, to take up the responsibilities of his leadership, were as strong in him as they had ever been and that he must allow them to surge forth, to fill him again with fiery ambition.

And in that seventh year he spent more and more time seated on the banks of the island, gazing towards his own land where time did not stand still and where his wife's suitors were threatening to take over his country, his rule. He came eventually to the notice of Athene, whose favour he had kept despite the outrage of the other gods, and she went at once to Zeus on his behalf. Zeus was fair and kind, and he balanced the sins of Odysseus against his innate good will, and the struggles to keep in check his unruly crews, all of which were lost to him now. Poseidon was away from Olympus and the time seemed right to set Odysseus free, for he had lived long enough in an enchanted purgatory.

Calypso reluctantly agreed to allow him his freedom, and she provided him with the tools to create a sturdy boat, and with provisions of food and drink enough to last the entire journey. She bathed him, dressed him in fine silks and jewels, as befitted a returning warrior, and kissing him gently but with all the fire of her love for him, she bade him go, with a tear-stained farewell. She had provided him with instructions which would see him round the dangers, across the perils that could beset him. He set sail for Ithaca.

Nausicaa and the Phaeacians

With the stars of the Great Bear twinkling on his left, Odysseus sailed for eighteen days, tossed gently on a calm sea with a favourable wind breathing on the sails which were pulled tight. And then Poseidon, returning to Olympus, noticed this solitary sailor, and filled with all the fury of a wronged god, produced a calamitous wave which struck out at Odysseus and thrust him overboard. And there ensued a storm of gigantic proportions which stirred the sea into a feverish pitch which threatened with each motion to drown the terrified sailor.

But despite his many wrongs, his well-publicized shortcomings, Odysseus had made friends, and inspired awe and respect among many in Greece. And so it was that the sea-goddess Ino-Leucothea took pity on him, and swimming easily to him in the tempestuous sea, cast off his clothes and hung around his waist a magic veil, which would carry him safely to shore. She lingered before swimming away, her eyes lighting on his strong body which splashed powerfully in the waters, and she laid her hand briefly on his skin, warming him through and filling him with a deep and new energy.

Odysseus swam on, the sea calmed by Athene, and landed, exhausted on the shores of the island of the Phaeacians, where he fell into a profound slumber. Athene moved inland, into the chamber of Nausicaa, the lovely daughter of King Alcinous, and into her dreams, urging her to visit the shores of the island, to wash her clothes in the stream that tumbled by the body of the sleeping warrior. And when she woke, Nausicaa encouraged her friends to come with her to the stream, to play there, and to make clean her soiled garments.

Their cries of frivolity woke the sleepy Odysseus and he crawled from under a bush, naked and unruly. His wild appearance sent the friends of Nausicaa running for help, but she stood still, her virgin heart beating with anticipation. His untamed beauty inspired a carnal longing that was new to her, and from that moment she was devoted to him. She listened carefully to his words and taking his hand, led him to see her father.

Now Athene knew that King Alcinous would be less affected by Odysseus's beauty than his daughter, and prepared a healing mist which enshrouded Odysseus, who had been hastily dressed by Nausicaa.

Alcinous lived in a splendid palace, filled with glittering treasures and elegant furnishings. His table was renowned across the lands, delicious fruits soaked in fine liquors, breads veined with rich nuts, succulent meats which swirled in fine juices, glazed vegetables and herbs from the most remote gardens across the world. There were jellies and sweets, baked goods, cheeses and pâtes, fresh figs and luscious olives, all available every day to whomever visited the kind and generous leader. His women were well-versed in the vocabulary of caring for their men, and the palace gleamed with every luxury, with every necessity, to make an intelligent man content.

He listened to Odysseus now, and was struck by the power of his words. Odysseus had the appearance of a stray, but the demeanour of greatness. Alcinous wondered curiously if he was a god in disguise, so eloquent and masterful was their unknown visitor. But Odysseus kept from them his identity knowing not the reception he would receive, and careful not to destroy his chances of borrowing a ship and some men to take him to Ithaca.

And Odysseus was warmly welcomed in the palace, and fed such marvellous foods and drinks, living in such comfortable splendour, that he considered at length the request by King Alcinous and his lovely wife that he stay on to take Nausicaa as his bride. But he was too close to home to give up, and Alcinous, too polite and kind to keep Odysseus against his will, agreed to let him pass on, aided by the Phaeacian ships and hardy sailors.

So it was that on the final night of his stay with the Phaeacians he was made the guest of honour at a luxuriant feast, where the conversation turned to travels, and to war, and finally, to the victory of Troy. Inspired by their talk, a minstrel took up his lute and began to sing of the wars, of the clear skies of Ithaca, the valour of Achilles, and the skill of Odysseus and Epius. So loudly did he extol the virtues of the brave son of Laertes that Odysseus was forced to lower his head in despair, and the tears fell freely to his plate where they glinted and caught the attention of the king and his men.

'Why do you suffer such dismay?' asked Alcinous gently, for he had grown fond of the elegant stranger in their midst.

Odysseus' reply was choked. The burden of the last ten years now threatened to envelope him. He had never pondered long the nature of the trials that had faced him, but as he ordered them in his mind, preparing his story to tell the King, their enormity swamped him, frightened him, made him weak.

'I am Odysseus,' he said quietly, 'son of Laertes.'

The room filled with excited joy – glasses were lifted, toasts offered, Odysseus was carried to the king where he received a long and honourable blessing. Then silence overcame them and they listened to the tales of the illustrious Odysseus who had suffered such misadventure, and overcome all with his cunning and mastery. They gazed in wonderment on the hero. He had long been thought dead, but everyone knew of the devotion, the loyalty of his wife Penelope, who refused to contemplate the idea. They encouraged him to return home. And if the unknown castaway received such glory in their generous household, a warrior of such note received the very bounty of the gods.

Ships were prepared and laden with gifts. The strongest and bravest of the Phaeacians were chosen to set sail with him, and warmed by the love and admiration of his new friends, Odysseus was placed in fine robes at the helm of a new ship, and sent towards home.

Odysseus, worn by troubles, and the relief of reaching his shores, slept deeply on board the ship, and loathe to wake him, the awe-struck sailors lifted him gently to the sands of Ithaca, where they piled his body with all the glorious gifts provided by the King, and then they retreated through the bay of Phorcys. Poseidon had been smouldering with rage at the disloyalty of Athene and Zeus, but realizing that Odysseus had been charmed, and had friends who would not allow his destruction, he allowed the hero to be placed on the sands, turning his wrath instead on the sailors. As they passed from the harbour into the seas, he struck a blow with his mighty staff and turned them all to stone, their ship frozen forever on the silent waters that led to Ithaca. It remained there as a warning to all who thought they could betray Poseidon and his mighty powers.

And so the mighty Odysseus lay once again on the shores of Ithaca, knowing not that ten years' journey had brought him at last to his promised land, or that the glory predicted by the Phaeacians would not yet be his. Battles new lined themselves on the horizon, but Odysseus was home, and from that secure base, could take on all.

Penelope and Telemachus

When brave Odysseus was laid, deep in slumber, on the shores of Ithaca, he knew nothing of the dangers which faced his country. Loyal Penelope was ensconced in their palace, at the mercy of over a hundred suitors, rulers from neighbouring islands who wished to annex Ithaca. Telemachus had left the island in search of his father, and many of the suitors were involved in a plot to murder him upon his return. Laertes was alive, but old and troubled. When Odysseus woke, he knew not where he was. He was visited by Athene, who briefed him on the ills of his homeland, and who dressed him in the guise of a beggar, and led him to the hut of the faithful swineherd Eumaeus. Here Odysseus could plot, and plan, prepare the tools of battle to make Ithaca his once more.

When Odysseus awoke on the sands of Ithaca, a mist had fallen over the majestic land and he knew not where he was. The Phaeacians had vanished from his sight, and he had only a groggy but pleasant memory of his visit to them. He should be at Ithaca now, he thought, but he could see nothing in the steamy air that enshrouded him. From the mists he heard a soft voice – familiar to Odysseus, but he no longer trusted in anything, and he sat back cautiously.

'You are in the land of the great warrior and traveller Odysseus,' said the voice, which belonged to a young and comely shepherd. 'How do you not know it?'

Odysseus lied glibly about his reasons for being there, inventing a fantastic story that was quite different from his actual voyage. At this the shepherd laughed, and changing shape, became Athene.

'So, crafty Odysseus,' she smiled. 'What a rogue you are. The greatest gods would have trouble inventing such tricks.' With that she held out a hand to the weary traveller, and led him across the sands.

'I've hidden you from your countrymen,' she explained, indicating the mists which surrounded them. 'Things are not as you would have hoped. It is not safe for you now. You must tread slowly.'

She helped Odysseus to hide away his treasures, and sat him down to explain to him the matters of his homeland. Penelope was still faithful to him, but time was running out, and she knew that if he did not appear to her within the next months, Penelope would have little recourse but to join herself with another. Telemachus was greatly angered by the insolent suitors who banded themselves at the palace, taking as their own everything that had belonged to his father, and gorging themselves on the food meant for the people of Ithaca. It was an untidy situation, and Telemachus struggled to believe that his father was still alive.

He had left the island for the mainland, desperate for news of Odysseus, never believing that his father could be dead. He'd vowed to allow one year for news, failing which he would agree to the wishes of a stepfather and stand aside.

In Greece Telemachus was greeted with little interest, and his attempts to uncover the whereabouts of his father were useless. Old Nestor, who knew everything about the war at Troy, and had followed the lives of the great men who had made the victory there, had heard nothing of Odysseus. He had disappeared, he said sadly, shaking his head. Determined, Telemachus pressed on to Sparta where Helen welcomed the son of Odysseus, but had little news to impart. Telemachus began to feel the first stirrings of despair, and sat with his head pressed into his hands. When Menelaus returned to his home that evening, he found Telemachus like this, and leaning over the youth, whispered words of comfort.

'I too have wandered,' he said gently.' And news of your father has reached me through the minions of Poseidon.' He went on to warn Telemachus of Poseidon's rage, explaining how Odysseus had blinded his one-eyed son Polyphemus. Menelaus told how Odysseus had been cast upon the shores of Calypso, where he lived a life that was half enchantment and half longing for his past.

Telemachus moved swiftly. His father was alive. A rescue must be planned at once, but most importantly he must warn his mother. The suitors had moved in too closely. They must be disposed of immediately.

At home in Ithaca, Penelope was also filled with a despair that threatened to destroy her. Her loyalty to Odysseus had kept her sane, and filled her with a kind of clever glee which made possible the machinations of keeping the suitors at bay. She'd held her head low with humility, and explained to the suitors who continued to arrive, to take roost in her home, that she must complete work on a cloth she was weaving, before she could contemplate giving herself to another. She worked hours on end in the days, performing for the suitors at her loom, giving them every belief in her excuses for not receiving their attentions. And yet at night she returned to her lonely bedroom and there she sat by torchlight, unpicking the work of the day. And as the years went by, it became established knowledge that Penelope was not free to marry until she had finished her web.

But Penelope was aware that her excuse was wearing thin, that the seeds of suspicion had been sown in the minds of her suitors, and that they were paying inordinate interest in the mechanics of the loom itself. It was only a question of time before they would insist on her hand and she would be forced to make a choice. Her property was being wasted, her lands falling to ruin, her stocks emptied by their marauding parties. She longed for the firm hand of Odysseus to oust them from their adopted home, to renew the sense of vigour that was required by her workers to make things right again. Most importantly, however, she longed for the warm embrace of her husband, the nights of passion, of sweet love. She had resisted the attentions of her suitors, but her body was afire with longing, and she burned at a single look, at a fleeting touch. Penelope was ready for her husband's return. Soon it would be too late.

At the cottage of Eumaeus, Odysseus had been presented with a fine feast of suckling pig by the swineherd, who spoke sadly of his master's absence. He bemoaned the state of the island and explained to Odysseus in his disguise that the suitors visited his cottage regularly, taking their pick of the pigs so that his herd was sorely depleted. He said kindly that a beggarman was as entitled to a feast as were these inappropriate suitors, and he gave Odysseus his own cloak in which to warm himself by the fire. Odysseus told the loyal subject a wild story, but did say that he had heard news of Odysseus and that the great warrior would return to set his house in order within the next year. At this, the swineherd was filled with joy, and produced more food and wine for this bearer of good news. Odysseus settled in for the night.

By this time Telemachus had returned to the island, aided by Athene who had set out to greet him. He was taken to the cottage in darkness, so as not to arouse the suspicions of the suitors, who were plotting his death. Here a tearful reunion was made, away from the eyes of the swineherd who had been sent to the palace for more drink. Odysseus was transformed once more into his old self by Athene, and Telemachus drank in the sight of his father, who he'd hardly known as a child.

They sat together, heads touching, occasionally reaching over to reassure themselves of the other's presence, and the plans were made to restore Ithaca to her former glory, to rid it of the unruly suitors, to reinstate Odysseus and Telemachus at their rightful places at her helm.

The Battle for Ithaca

Odysseus and Telemachus were ready to set their plans into action. Just before Eumaeus returned to his cottage, Odysseus resumed the form of a beggarman and Telemachus slipped away into the night. The following morning dawned cool and clear, and Odysseus felt a renewed vigour coursing through his veins. He longed to appear in his battle garb, the strong and mighty Odysseus returned from the dead to reclaim his palace, but there was too much at stake to set a wrong foot and he knew the plans he had fixed with Telemachus must be followed to the tiniest detail.

Eumaeus accompanied Odysseus to the palace, to see if there was any work available for a willing but poverty-stricken beggar. He was greeted first by the rude and arrogant Antinous, the leader of Penelope's suitors, who had long considered himself the rightful heir to Odysseus's position within Ithaca. He gazed scathingly at Odysseus as he entered the room where the suitors lolled about on cushions, calling out to the over-burdened servants for refreshment and ever greater feasts of food.

'Who dares to trouble us?' he said lazily.

Odysseus introduced himself as a poor traveller, down on his luck after a long voyage in which his crew members had been struck down by Poseidon. To test them, Odysseus begged them for alms, but he was met by a barrage of rotten fruit, after which several of the younger suitors took turns beating him. Bruised and angry, Odysseus stood his ground, requesting menial work of any nature. And it was then that the young local beggar Irus stepped into the fray. Resenting the competition offered by Odysseus, he challenged him to a fight, at which the lazy suitors leapt to their feet, roaring at the impending carnage. For Odysseus had taken the form of an old man, and Irus was young and strong, a beggar only because of his slothful nature.

But the roars turned to silence as Odysseus lifted his robes to show legs as muscular and powerful as the greatest of warriors, and a prowess with a sword that belonged only to the master of the house. He slayed Irus with one fell of his sword. Odysseus was cheered not by the suitors, who suspected a rival for the attentions of Penelope, and they cast him out, kicking and beating him until he howled with pain and restrained anger. He could not show his true colours yet. The time was not ripe for battle. Odysseus made his way from the waiting rooms, into the kitchen where word of his ill-treatment reached Penelope. Knowing well that gods often travelled in disguise, she sent a message that she wished this sailor to be fed and made comfortable for the night. Penelope herself wished to speak to him, for a traveller might have word of the long-lost Odysseus and she yearned for news of him.

But Odysseus claimed to be too weak to see the mistress of the house, and it was agreed that they would speak later that evening. And so it was that Odysseus slipped from his bed in the kitchen and met with his son in the great hall. Quietly they removed the armour and weapons that the suitors had idly laid to one side, piling them outside the palace gates where they were snatched away by village boys. And now, in the darkened hall, Odysseus agreed to see Penelope, who felt a surge of excitement at their meeting which startled and concerned her. Odysseus had been gone too long, she was losing control.

They met by candlelight, and safe in his disguise, Odysseus wove for Penelope a fanciful story about his travels, which had little in common with the true nature of his voyages, but left her with no doubt that the brave Odysseus was on his way home, and would soon return to set things to right. And then Odysseus heard from Penelope the trials of the last twenty years, and hung his head in shame at the thought of his many years with Calypso, and the time lost through the greed and indolence of his men.

Penelope told of the suitors who had been first quietened by her insistence that the Oracle had promised Odysseus's return, but as the years had passed, they had grown insolent and arrogant, demanding her attentions, her hand in marriage. She had fought them off, she said, by claiming to weave the cloth that would shroud Laertes upon his death, and each night she had spent many hours unpicking the day's work. And then, when this trick had been discovered, she could delay her decision no longer and had feigned illness for many months. The next day was the Feast of Apollo and it was on this day that she had agreed to choose a husband. Penelope wept with misery, her fair face more beautiful with age and distress. Odysseus longed to take her in his arms, to warm her body and to ease her pain, but he held himself back from her, knowing that he must use his anger to feed his resolve, to rid his home of these suitors once and for all.

Penelope was grateful for the reassurance and calm understanding of this stranger, and she urged him to take a chamber for the night, sending the aged nurse Eurycleia to bathe his feet and weary legs. Eurycleia had been Odysseus's own nurse as a child, and when she saw his familiar scar, received in a youthful skirmish with a wild boar, she cried out. Odysseus grabbed her throat.

'Speak not, wise woman,' he whispered harshly, 'all will be set right at the dawn of the feast.' Eurycleia nodded, her eyes bulging with fear and concern and she gathered her skirts around her, heading for the servant's quarters.

The next day was the Feast, and the household was abuzz with activity and preparations. Odysseus took a seat amongst the suitors, strategically placed by the door, but he was jeered at and heckled until he was forced to move to a small stool. Penelope eventually appeared in their midst. Then Agelaus gave her an ultimatum. Today a choice must be made. Penelope turned pleadingly to Telemachus, but he nodded his grudging consent, and she announced that a competition would take place. With that she fled to a table, and shut her eyes in despair.

Telemachus took over, producing Odysseus's great bow, and gently explaining that his mother could only consider marriage to someone the equal of his father, someone who could string the bow and shoot an arrow through the rings of twelve axes set in a row. And one by one, the suitors failed to bend the stiff bow, and disgruntled, cast it aside and sat sullenly along the walls of the hall. So it was that the beggarman was the only remaining man, and he begged a chance to test his strength against the bow. He was taunted, and insults fired at him, but he stood his ground and with the permission of Penelope, who nodded a sympathetic assent, he took the bow.

Like a man born to the act, he deftly wired the bow, and taking an arrow, he fired it straight through the rings of the axes. The room was silent. Telemachus rose and strode across to stand by his father.

'The die is cast,' said Odysseus, thrusting aside his disguise. 'And another target presents itself. Prepare to pay for your treachery.' With that he lifted his arrow and shot Antinous clear through the neck. The suitors searched with amazement for their arms and armour, and finding them gone, tried to make due with the short daggers in their belts. They launched themselves on Odysseus and his son, but the two great men fought valiantly, sending arrow after arrow, spear after spear, to their fatal mark. And when Odysseus and Telemachus grew tired, Athene flew across them in the shape of a swallow and filled them with a surge of energy, a new life that saw them through the battle to victory.

The battle won, the suitors dead, the household was now scourged for those who had befriended the suitors, maids who had shared their beds, porters and shepherds who had made available the stocks and stores of Odysseus's palace. And these maids and men were beheaded and burnt in a fire that was seen for many miles.

Finally Odysseus could pause, and greet properly his long-lost wife, who sat wearily by his side, hardly daring to believe that he had returned. And yet, one look at his time and journey-lined face told her it was all true, and she was overwhelmed once again by her love for this brave man who was so long apart from her. With tears of joy they clutched one another, and their union was sweet and tender. And soon afterwards came Laertes, the veil of madness lifted by news of his son's return.

The courageous Odysseus was home at last, his cunning a match for all that the fates had set in his path. There would be more skirmishes before he could call Ithaca his own once more, and Poseidon must be appeased before he could live fearlessly surrounded by that great god's kingdom, but in time all was undertaken. Some say that Odysseus lived to a ripe old age, dying eventually and suitably on the sea. Others say that he died at the hand of his own son, Telegonus, by the enchantress Circe. All agree that Odysseus was beloved by his subjects, the tales of his journey becoming the food for legends which spread around the world.

Jason and the Argonauts

IT IS FORETOLD, 'Beware of a man with one sandal.' At first glance, hardly the most chilling of prophecies. Yet in an age circumscribed by gods and heroes, when the divine and human intertwined, any such prediction had to be viewed with respect. In this case doubly so, for the prophecy referred to none other than the hero Jason, son of Aeson of Iolcus, whose deeds in pursuit of the famous Golden Fleece would ripple throughout time and legend.

Aeson

Aeson, king of Iolcus, was forced to fly from his dominions, which had been usurped by his younger brother, Pelias, and with difficulty succeeded in saving the life of his young son, Jason, who was at that time only ten years of age. He entrusted him to the care of the Centaur Chiron, by whom he was carefully trained in company with other noble youths, who, like himself, afterwards signalized themselves by their bravery and heroic exploits. For ten years Jason remained in the cave of the Centaur, by whom he was instructed in all useful and warlike arts. But as he approached manhood he became filled with an unconquerable desire to regain his paternal inheritance. He therefore took leave of his kind friend and preceptor, and set out for Iolcus to demand from his uncle Pelias the kingdom which he had so unjustly usurped.

In the course of his journey he came to a broad and foaming river, on the banks of which he perceived an old woman, who implored him to help her across. At first he hesitated, knowing that even alone he would find some difficulty in stemming the fierce torrent; but, pitying her forlorn condition, he raised her in his arms, and succeeded, with a great effort, in reaching the opposite shore. But as soon as her feet had touched the earth she became transformed into a beautiful woman, who, looking kindly at the bewildered youth, informed him that she was the goddess Hera, and that she would henceforth guide and protect him throughout his career. She then disappeared, and, full of hope and courage at this divine manifestation, Jason pursued his journey. He now perceived that in crossing the river he had lost one of his sandals, but as it could not be recovered he was obliged to proceed without it.

On his arrival at Iolcus he found his uncle in the market-place, offering up a public sacrifice to Poseidon. When the king had concluded his offering, his eye fell upon the distinguished stranger, whose manly beauty and heroic bearing had already attracted the attention of his people. Observing that one foot was unshod, he was reminded of an oracular prediction which foretold to him the loss of his kingdom by a man wearing only one sandal. He, however, disguised his fears, conversed kindly with the youth, and drew from him his name and errand. Then pretending to be highly pleased with his nephew, Pelias entertained him sumptuously for five days, during which time all was festivity and rejoicing. On the sixth, Jason appeared before his uncle, and with manly firmness demanded from him the throne and kingdom which were his by right. Pelias, dissembling his true feelings, smilingly consented to grant his request, provided that, in return, Jason would undertake an expedition for him, which his advanced age prevented him from accomplishing himself. He informed his nephew that the shade of Phryxus had appeared to him in his dreams, and entreated him to bring back from Colchis his mortal remains and the Golden Fleece; and added that if Jason succeeded in obtaining for him these sacred relics, throne, kingdom, and sceptre should be his.

The Golden Fleece

Athamas, king of Boeotia, had married Nephele, a cloud-nymph, and their children were Helle and Phryxus. The restless and wandering nature of Nephele, however, soon wearied her husband, who, being a mortal, had little sympathy with his ethereal consort; so he divorced her, and married the beautiful but wicked Ino (sister of Semele), who hated her step-children, and even planned their destruction. But the watchful Nephele contrived to circumvent her cruel designs, and succeeded in getting the children out of the palace. She then placed them both on the back of a winged ram, with a fleece of pure gold, which had been given to her by Hermes; and on this wonderful animal brother and sister rode through the air over land and sea; but on the way Helle, becoming seized with giddiness, fell into the sea (called after her the Hellespont) and was drowned.

Phryxus arrived safely at Colchis, where he was hospitably received by king Aëtes, who gave him one of his daughters in marriage. In gratitude to Zeus for the protection accorded him during his flight, Phryxus sacrificed to him the golden ram, whilst the fleece he presented to Aëtes, who nailed it up in the Grove of Ares, and dedicated it to the god of War. An oracle having declared that the life of Aëtes depended on the safe-keeping of the fleece, he carefully guarded the entrance to the grove by placing before it an immense dragon, which never slept.

The Argo Launches

We will now return to Jason, who eagerly undertook the perilous expedition proposed to him by his uncle, who, well aware of the dangers attending such an enterprise, hoped by this means to rid himself for ever of the unwelcome intruder.

Jason accordingly began to arrange his plans without delay, and invited the young heroes whose friendship he had formed whilst under the care of Chiron, to join him in the perilous expedition. None refused the invitation, all feeling honoured at being allowed the privilege of taking part in so noble and heroic an undertaking.

Jason now applied to Argos, one of the cleverest ship-builders of his time, who, under the guidance of Pallas-Athene, built for him a splendid fifty-oared galley, which was called the Argo, after the builder. In the upper deck of the vessel the goddess had imbedded a board from the speaking oak of the oracle of Zeus at Dodona, which ever retained its powers of prophecy. The exterior of the ship was ornamented with magnificent carvings, and the whole vessel was so strongly built that it defied the power of the winds and waves, and was, nevertheless, so light that the heroes, when necessary, were able to carry it on their shoulders. When the vessel was completed, the Argonauts (so called after their ship) assembled, and their places were distributed by lot.

Jason was appointed commander-in-chief of the expedition, Tiphys acted as steersman, Lynceus as pilot. In the bow of the vessel sat the renowned hero Heracles; in the stern, Peleus (father of Achilles) and Telamon (the father of Ajax the Great). In the inner space were Castor and Pollux, Neleus (the father of Nestor), Admetus (the husband of Alcestes), Meleager (the slayer of the Calydonian boar), Orpheus (the renowned singer), Menoctius (the father of Patroclus), Theseus (afterwards king of Athens) and his friend Pirithöus (the son of Ixion), Hylas (the adopted son of Heracles), Euphemus (the son of Poseidon), Oileus (father of Ajax the Lesser), Zetes and Calais (the winged sons of Boreas), Idmon the Seer (the son of Apollo), Mopsus (the Thessalian prophet).

Before their departure Jason offered a solemn sacrifice to Poseidon and all the other sea-deities; he also invoked the protection of Zeus and the Fates, and then, Mopsus having taken the auguries, and found them auspicious, the heroes stepped on board. And now a favourable breeze having sprung up, they take their allotted places, the anchor is weighed, and the ship glides like a bird out of the harbour into the waters of the great sea.

The Argo, with her brave crew of fifty heroes, was soon out of sight, and the sea-breeze only wafted to the shore a faint echo of the sweet strains of Orpheus.

For a time all went smoothly, but the vessel was soon driven, by stress of weather, to take refuge in a harbour in the island of Lemnos. This island was inhabited by women only, who, the year before, in a fit of mad jealousy, had killed all the male population of the island, with the exception of the father of their queen, Hypsipyle. As the protection of their island now devolved upon themselves they were always on the look-out for danger. When, therefore, they sighted the Argo from afar they armed themselves and rushed to the shore, determined to repel any invasion of their territory.

On arriving in port the Argonauts, astonished at beholding an armed crowd of women, despatched a herald in one of their boats, bearing the staff of peace and friendship. Hypsipyle, the queen, proposed that food and presents should be sent to the strangers, in order to prevent their landing; but her old nurse, who stood beside her, suggested that this would be a good opportunity to provide themselves with noble husbands, who would act as their defenders, and thus put an end to their constant fears. Hypsipyle listened attentively to the advice of her nurse, and after some consultation, decided to invite the strangers into the city. Robed in his purple mantle, the gift of Pallas-Athene, Jason, accompanied by some of his companions, stepped on shore, where he was met by a deputation consisting of the most beautiful of the Lemnian women, and, as commander of the expedition, was invited into the palace of the queen.

When he appeared before Hypsipyle, she was so struck with his godlike and heroic presence that she presented him with her father's sceptre, and invited him to seat himself on the throne beside her. Jason thereupon took up his residence in the royal castle, whilst his companions scattered themselves through the town, spending their time in feasting and pleasure. Heracles, with a few chosen comrades, alone remained on board.

From day to day their departure was delayed, and the Argonauts, in their new life of dissipation, had almost forgotten the object of the expedition, when Heracles suddenly appeared amongst them, and at last recalled them to a sense of their duty.

Giants and Doliones

The Argonauts now pursued their voyage, till contrary winds drove them towards an island, inhabited by the Doliones, whose king Cyzicus received them with great kindness and hospitality. The Doliones were descendants of Poseidon, who protected them against the frequent attacks of their fierce and formidable neighbours, the earth-born Giants – monsters with six arms.

Whilst his companions were attending a banquet given by king Cyzicus, Heracles, who, as usual, had remained behind to guard the ship, observed that these Giants were busy blocking up the harbour with huge rocks. He at once realized the danger, and, attacking them with his arrows, succeeded in considerably thinning their numbers; then, assisted by the heroes, who at length came to his aid, he effectually destroyed the remainder.

The Argo now steered out of the harbour and set sail; but in consequence of a severe storm which arose at night, was driven back once more to the shores of the kindly Doliones. Unfortunately, however, owing to the darkness of the night, the inhabitants failed to recognize their former guests, and, mistaking them for enemies, commenced to attack them. Those who had so recently parted as friends were now engaged in mortal combat, and in the battle which ensued, Jason himself pierced to the heart his friend king Cyzicus; whereupon the Doliones, being deprived of their leader, fled to their city and closed the gates. When morning dawned, and both sides perceived their error, they were filled with the deepest sorrow and remorse; and for three days the heroes remained with the Doliones, celebrating the funereal rites of the slain, with every demonstration of mourning and solemnity.

The Argonauts once more set sail, and after a stormy voyage arrived at Mysia, where they were hospitably received by the inhabitants, who spread before them plentiful banquets and sumptuously regaled them.

While his friends were feasting, Heracles, who had declined to join them, went into the forest to seek a fir-tree which he required for an oar, and was missed by his adopted son Hylas, who set out to seek him. When the youth arrived at a spring, in the most secluded part of the forest, the nymph of the fountain was so struck by his beauty that she drew him down beneath the waters, and he was seen no more. Polyphemus, one of the heroes, who happened to be also in the forest, heard his cry for help, and on meeting Heracles informed him of the circumstance. They at once set out in search of the missing youth, no traces of whom were to be found, and whilst they were engaged looking for him, the Argo set sail and left them behind.

The ship had proceeded some distance before the absence of Heracles was observed. Some of the heroes were in favour of returning for him, others wished to proceed on their journey, when, in the midst of the dispute, the sea-god Glaucus arose from the waves, and informed them that it was the will of Zeus that Heracles, having another mission to perform, should remain behind. The Argonauts continued their voyage without their companions; Heracles returned to Argos, whilst Polyphemus remained with the Mysians, where he founded a city and became its king.

Next morning the Argo touched at the country of the Bebrycians, whose king Amycus was a famous pugilist, and permitted no strangers to leave his shores without matching their strength with his. When the heroes, therefore, demanded permission to land, they were informed that they could only do so provided that one of their number should engage in a boxing-match with the king. Pollux, who was the best pugilist in Greece, was selected as their champion, and a contest took place, which, after a tremendous struggle, proved fatal to Amycus, who had hitherto been victorious in all similar encounters.

Harpies and Stymphalides

They now proceeded towards Bithynia, where reigned the blind old prophet-king Phineus, son of Agenor. Phineus had been punished by the gods with premature old age and blindness for having abused the gift of prophecy. He was also tormented by the Harpies, who swooped down upon his food, which they either devoured or so defiled as to render it unfit to be eaten. This poor old man, trembling with the weakness of age, and faint with hunger, appeared before the Argonauts, and implored their assistance against his fiendish tormentors, whereupon Zetes and Calais, the winged sons of Boreas, recognizing in him the husband of their sister Cleopatra, affectionately embraced him, and promised to rescue him from his painful position.

The heroes prepared a banquet on the sea-shore, to which they invited Phineus; but no sooner had he taken his place, than the Harpies appeared and devoured all the viands. Zetes and Calais now rose up into the air, drove the Harpies away, and were pursuing them with drawn swords, when Iris, the swift-footed messenger of the gods, appeared, and desired them to desist from their work of vengeance, promising that Phineus should be no longer molested.

Freed at length from his tormentors the old man sat down and enjoyed a plentiful repast with his kind friends the Argonauts, who now informed him of the object of their voyage. In gratitude for his deliverance Phineus gave them much useful information concerning their journey, and not only warned them of the manifold dangers awaiting them, but also instructed them how they might be overcome.

After a fortnight's sojourn in Bithynia the Argonauts once more set sail, but had not proceeded far on their course, when they heard a fearful and tremendous crash. This was caused by the meeting of two great rocky islands, called the Symplegades, which floated about in the sea, and constantly met and separated.

Before leaving Bithynia, the blind old seer, Phineus, had informed them that they would be compelled to pass between these terrible rocks, and he instructed them how to do so with safety. As they now approached the scene of danger they remembered his advice, and acted upon it. Typhus, the steersman, stood at the helm, whilst Euphemus held in his hand a dove ready to be let loose; for Phineus had told them that if the dove ventured to fly through, they might safely follow. Euphemus now despatched the bird, which passed swiftly through the islands, yet not without losing some of the feathers of her tail, so speedily did they reunite. Seizing the moment when the rocks once more separated, the Argonauts worked at their oars with all their might, and achieved the perilous passage in safety.

After the miraculous passage of the Argo, the Symplegades became permanently united, and attached to the bottom of the sea.

The Argo pursued her course along the southern coast of the Pontus, and arrived at the island of Aretias, which was inhabited by birds, who, as they flew through the air, discharged from their wings feathers sharp as arrows.

As the ship was gliding along, Oileus was wounded by one of these birds, whereupon the Argonauts held a council, and by the advice of Amphidamas, an experienced hero, all put on their helmets, and held up their glittering shields, uttering, at the same time, such fearful cries that the birds flew away in terror, and the Argonauts were enabled to land with safety on the island.

Here they found four shipwrecked youths, who proved to be the sons of Phryxus, and were greeted by Jason as his cousins. On ascertaining the object of the expedition they volunteered to accompany the Argo, and to show the heroes the way to Colchis. They also informed them that the Golden Fleece was guarded by a fearful dragon, that king Aëtes was extremely cruel, and, as the son of Apollo, was possessed of superhuman strength.

Arrival at Colchis

Taking with them the four new-comers they journeyed on, and soon came in sight of the snow-capped peaks of the Caucasus, when, towards evening, the loud flapping of wings was heard overhead. It was the giant eagle of Prometheus on his way to torture the noble and long-suffering Titan, whose fearful groans soon afterwards fell upon their ears. That night they reached their journey's end, and anchored in the smooth waters of the river Phases. On the left bank of this river they beheld Ceuta, the capital of Colchis; and on their right a wide field, and the sacred grove of Ares, where the Golden Fleece, suspended from a magnificent oak-tree, was glittering in the sun. Jason now filled a golden cup with wine, and offered a libation to mother-earth, the gods of the country, and the shades of those of the heroes who had died on the voyage.

Next morning a council was held, in which it was decided, that before resorting to forcible measures kind and conciliatory overtures should first be made to king Aëtes in order to induce him to resign the Golden Fleece. It was arranged that Jason, with a few chosen companions, should proceed to the royal castle, leaving the remainder of the crew to guard the Argo. Accompanied, therefore, by Telamon and Augeas, and the four sons of Phryxus, he set out for the palace.

When they arrived in sight of the castle they were struck by the vastness and massiveness of the building, at the entrance to which sparkling fountains played in the midst of luxuriant and park-like gardens. Here the king's daughters, Chalciope and Medea, who were walking in the grounds of the palace, met them. The former, to her great joy, recognized in the youths who accompanied the hero her own long-lost sons, whom she had mourned as dead, whilst the young and lovely Medea was struck with the noble and manly form of Jason.

The news of the return of the sons of Phryxus soon spread through the palace, and brought Aëtes himself to the scene, whereupon the strangers were presented to him, and were invited to a banquet which the king ordered to be prepared in their honour. All the most beautiful ladies of the court were present at this entertainment; but in the eyes of Jason none could compare with the king's daughter, the young and lovely Medea.

When the banquet was ended, Jason related to the king his various adventures, and also the object of his expedition, with the circumstances which had led to his undertaking it. Aëtes listened, in silent indignation, to this recital, and then burst out into a torrent of invectives against the Argonauts and his grand-children, declaring that the Fleece was his rightful property, and that on no consideration would he consent to relinquish it. Jason, however, with mild and persuasive words, contrived so far to conciliate him, that he was induced to promise that if the heroes could succeed in demonstrating their divine origin by the performance of some task requiring superhuman power, the Fleece should be theirs.

The task proposed by Aëtes to Jason was that he should yoke the two brazen-footed, fire-breathing oxen of the king (which had been made for him by Hephaestus) to his ponderous iron plough. Having done this he must till with them the stony field of Ares, and then sow in the furrows the poisonous teeth of a dragon, from which armed men would arise. These he must destroy to a man, or he himself would perish at their hands.

When Jason heard what was expected of him, his heart for a moment sank within him; but he determined, nevertheless, not to flinch from his task, but to trust to the assistance of the gods, and to his own courage and energy.

The Field of Ares

Accompanied by his two friends, Telamon and Augeas, and also by Argus, the son of Chalciope, Jason returned to the vessel for the purpose of holding a consultation as to the best means of accomplishing these perilous feats.

Argus explained to Jason all the difficulties of the superhuman task which lay before him, and pronounced it as his opinion that the only means by which success was possible was to enlist the assistance of the Princess Medea, who was a priestess of Hecate, and a great enchantress. His suggestion meeting with approval, he returned to the palace, and by the aid of his mother an interview was arranged between Jason and Medea, which took place, at an early hour next morning, in the temple of Hecate.

A confession of mutual attachment took place, and Medea, trembling for her lover's safety, presented him with a magic salve, which possessed the property of rendering any person anointed with it invulnerable for the space of one day against fire and steel, and invincible against any adversary however powerful. With this salve she instructed him to anoint his spear and shield on the day of his great undertaking. She further added that when, after having ploughed the field and sown the teeth, armed men should arise from the furrows, he must on no account lose heart, but remember to throw among them a huge rock, over the possession of which they would fight among themselves, and their attention being thus diverted he would find it an easy task to destroy them. Overwhelmed with gratitude, Jason thanked her, in the most earnest manner, for her wise counsel and timely aid; at the same time he offered her his hand, and promised her he would not return to Greece without taking her with him as his wife.

Next morning Aëtes, in all the pomp of state, surrounded by his family and the members of his court, repaired to a spot whence a full view of the approaching spectacle could be obtained. Soon Jason appeared in the field of Ares, looking as noble and majestic as the god of war himself. In a distant part of the field the brazen yokes and the massive plough met his view, but as yet the dread animals themselves were nowhere to be seen. He was about to go in quest of them, when they suddenly rushed out from a subterranean cave, breathing flames of fire, and enveloped in a thick smoke.

The friends of Jason trembled; but the undaunted hero, relying on the magic powers with which he was imbued by Medea, seized the oxen, one after the other, by the horns, and forced them to the yoke. Near the plough was a helmet full of dragon's teeth, which he sowed as he ploughed the field, whilst with sharp pricks from his lance he compelled the monstrous creatures to draw the plough over the stony ground, which was thus speedily tilled.

While Jason was engaged sowing the dragon's teeth in the deep furrows of the field, he kept a cautious look-out lest the germinating giant brood might grow too quickly for him, and as soon as the four acres of land had been tilled he unyoked the oxen, and succeeded in frightening them so effectually with his weapons, that they rushed back in terror to their subterranean stables. Meanwhile armed men had sprung up out of the furrows, and the whole field now bristled with lances; but Jason, remembering the instructions of Medea, seized an immense rock and hurled it into the midst of these earth-born warriors, who immediately began to attack each other. Jason then rushed furiously upon them, and after a terrible struggle not one of the giants remained alive.

Furious at seeing his murderous schemes thus defeated, Aëtes not only perfidiously refused to give Jason the Fleece which he had so bravely earned, but, in his anger, determined to destroy all the Argonauts, and to burn their vessel.

Jason Secures the Golden Fleece

Becoming aware of the treacherous designs of her father, Medea at once took measures to baffle them. In the darkness of night she went on board the Argo, and warned the heroes of their approaching danger. She then advised Jason to accompany her without loss of time to the sacred grove, in order to possess himself of the long-coveted treasure. They set out together, and Medea, followed by Jason, led the way, and advanced boldly into the grove. The tall oak-tree was soon discovered, from the topmost boughs of which hung the beautiful Golden Fleece. At the foot of this tree, keeping his ever-wakeful watch, lay the dreadful, sleepless dragon, who at sight of them bounded forward, opening his huge jaws.

Medea now called into play her magic powers, and quietly approaching the monster, threw over him a few drops of a potion, which soon took effect, and sent him into a deep sleep; whereupon Jason, seizing the opportunity, climbed the tree and secured the Fleece. Their perilous task being now accomplished, Jason and Medea quitted the grove, and hastened on board the Argo, which immediately put to sea.

Meanwhile Aëtes, having discovered the loss of his daughter and the Golden Fleece, despatched a large fleet, under the command of his son Absyrtus, in pursuit of the fugitives. After some days' sail they arrived at an island at the mouth of the river Ister, where they found the Argo at anchor, and surrounded her with their numerous ships. They then despatched a herald on board of her, demanding the surrender of Medea and the Fleece.

Medea now consulted Jason, and, with his consent, carried out the following stratagem. She sent a message to her brother Absyrtus, to the effect that she had been carried off against her will, and promised that if he would meet her, in the darkness of night, in the temple of Artemis, she would assist him in regaining possession of the Golden Fleece. Relying on the good faith of his sister, Absyrtus fell into the snare, and duly appeared at the appointed trysting-place; and whilst Medea kept her brother engaged in conversation, Jason rushed forward and slew him. Then, according to a preconcerted signal, he held aloft a lighted torch, whereupon the Argonauts attacked the Colchians, put them to flight, and entirely defeated them.

The Argonauts now returned to their ship, when the prophetic board from the Dodonean oak thus addressed them: 'The cruel murder of Absyrtus was witnessed by the Erinyes, and you will not escape the wrath of Zeus until the goddess Circe has purified you from your crime. Let Castor and Pollux pray to the gods that you may be enabled to find the abode of the sorceress.' In obedience to the voice, the twin-brothers invoked divine assistance, and the heroes set out in search of the isle of Circe.

The good ship Argo sped on her way, and, after passing safely through the foaming waters of the river Eridanus, at length arrived in the harbour of the island of Circe, where she cast anchor.

Commanding his companions to remain on board, Jason landed with Medea, and conducted her to the palace of the sorceress. The goddess of charms and magic arts received them kindly, and invited them to be seated; but instead of doing so they assumed a supplicating attitude, and humbly besought her protection. They then informed her of the dreadful crime which they had committed, and implored her to purify them from it. This Circe promised to do. She forthwith commanded her attendant Naiads to kindle the fire on the altar, and to prepare everything necessary for the performance of the mystic rites, after which a dog was sacrificed, and the sacred cakes were burned. Having thus duly purified the criminals, she severely reprimanded them for the horrible murder of which they had been guilty; whereupon Medea, with veiled head, and weeping bitterly, was reconducted by Jason to the Argo.

The Voyage Home

Having left the island of Circe they were wafted by gentle zephyrs towards the abode of the Sirens, whose enticing strains soon fell upon their ears. The Argonauts, powerfully affected by the melody, were making ready to land, when Orpheus perceived the danger, and, to the accompaniment of his magic lyre, commenced one of his enchanting songs, which so completely absorbed his listeners that they passed the island in safety; but not before Butes, one of their number, lured by the seductive music of the Sirens, had sprung from the vessel into the waves below. Aphrodite, however, in pity for his youth, landed him gently on the island of Libibaon before the Sirens could reach him, and there he remained for many years.

And now the Argonauts approached new dangers, for on one side of them seethed and foamed the whirlpool of Charybdis, whilst on the other towered the mighty rock whence the monster Scylla swooped down upon unfortunate mariners; but here the goddess Hera came to their assistance, and sent to them the sea-nymph Thetis, who guided them safely through these dangerous straits.

The Argo next arrived at the island of the Phaeaces, where they were hospitably entertained by King Alcinous and his queen Arete. But the banquet prepared for them by their kind host was unexpectedly interrupted by the appearance of a large army of Colchians, sent by Aëtes to demand the restoration of his daughter.

Medea threw herself at the feet of the queen, and implored her to save her from the anger of her father, and Arete, in her kindness of heart, promised her her protection. Next morning, in an assembly of the people at which the Colchians were invited to be present, the latter were informed that as Medea was the lawful wife of Jason they could not consent to deliver her up; whereupon the Colchians, seeing that the resolution of the king was not to be shaken, and fearing to face the anger of Aëtes should they return to Colchis without her, sought permission of Alcinous to settle in his kingdom, which request was accorded them.

After these events the Argonauts once more set sail, and steered for Iolcus; but, in the course of a terrible and fearful night, a mighty storm arose, and in the morning they found themselves stranded on the treacherous quicksands of Syrtes, on the shores of Libya. Here all was a waste and barren desert, untenanted by any living creature, save the venomous snakes which had sprung from the blood of the Medusa when borne by Perseus over these arid plains.

They had already passed several days in this abode of desolation, beneath the rays of the scorching sun, and had abandoned themselves to the deepest despair, when the Libyan queen, who was a prophetess of divine origin, appeared to Jason, and informed him that a sea-horse would be sent by the gods to act as his guide.

Scarcely had she departed when a gigantic hippocamp was seen in the distance, making its way towards the Argo. Jason now related to his companions the particulars of his interview with the Libyan prophetess, and after some deliberation it was decided to carry the Argo on their shoulders, and to follow wherever the sea-horse should lead them. They then commenced a long and weary journey through the desert, and at last, after twelve days of severe toil and terrible suffering, the welcome sight of the sea greeted their view. In gratitude for having been saved from their manifold dangers they offered up sacrifices to the gods, and launched their ship once more into the deep waters of the ocean.

With heartfelt joy and gladness they proceeded on their homeward voyage, and after some days arrived at the island of Crete, where they purposed to furnish themselves with fresh provisions and water. Their landing, however, was opposed by a terrible giant who guarded the island against all intruders. This giant, whose name was Talus, was the last of the Brazen race, and being formed of brass, was invulnerable, except in his right ankle, where there was a sinew of flesh and a vein of blood. As he saw the Argo nearing the coast, he hurled huge rocks at her, which would inevitably have sunk the vessel had not the crew beat a hasty retreat. Although sadly in want of food and water, the Argonauts had decided to proceed on their journey rather than face so powerful an opponent, when Medea came forward and assured them that if they would trust to her she would destroy the giant.

Enveloped in the folds of a rich purple mantle, she stepped on deck, and after invoking the aid of the Fates, uttered a magic incantation, which had the effect of throwing Talus into a deep sleep. He stretched himself at full length upon the ground, and in doing so grazed his vulnerable ankle against the point of a sharp rock, whereupon a mighty stream of blood gushed forth from the wound. Awakened by the pain, he tried to rise, but in vain, and with a mighty groan of anguish the giant fell dead, and his enormous body rolled heavily over into the deep. The heroes being now able to land, provisioned their vessel, after which they resumed their homeward voyage.

After a terrible night of storm and darkness they passed the island of Aegina, and at length reached in safety the port of Iolcus, where the recital of their numerous adventures and hair-breadth escapes was listened to with wondering admiration by their fellow-countrymen.

The Argo was consecrated to Poseidon, and was carefully preserved for many generations till no vestige of it remained, when it was placed in the heavens as a brilliant constellation.

On his arrival at Iolcus, Jason conducted his beautiful bride to the palace of his uncle Pelias, taking with him the Golden Fleece, for the sake of which this perilous expedition had been undertaken. But the old king, who had never expected that Jason would return alive, basely refused to fulfil his part of the compact, and declined to abdicate the throne.

Indignant at the wrongs of her husband, Medea avenged them in a most shocking manner. She made friends with the daughters of the king, and feigned great interest in all their concerns. Having gained their confidence, she informed them, that among her numerous magic arts, she possessed the power of restoring to the aged all the vigour and strength of youth, and in order to give them a convincing proof of the truth of her assertion, she cut up an old ram, which she boiled in a cauldron, whereupon, after uttering various mystic incantations, there came forth from the vessel a beautiful young lamb. She then assured them, that in a similar manner they could restore to their old father his former youthful frame and vigour. The fond and credulous daughters of Pelias lent an all too willing ear to the wicked sorceress, and thus the old king perished at the hands of his innocent children.

Medea and Jason now fled to Corinth, where at length they found, for a time, peace and tranquillity, their happiness being completed by the birth of three children.

As time passed on, however, and Medea began to lose the beauty which had won the love of her husband, he grew weary of her, and became attracted by the youthful charms of Glauce, the beautiful daughter of Creon, king of Corinth. Jason had obtained her father's consent to their union, and the wedding-day was already fixed, before he disclosed to Medea the treachery which he meditated against her. He used all his persuasive powers in order to induce her to consent to his union with Glauce, assuring her that his affection had in no way diminished, but that for the sake of the advantages which would thereby accrue to their children, he had decided on forming this alliance with the royal house. Though justly enraged at his deceitful conduct, Medea dissembled her wrath, and, feigning to be satisfied with this explanation, sent, as a wedding-gift to her rival, a magnificent robe of cloth-of-gold. This robe was imbued with a deadly poison which penetrated to the flesh and bone of the wearer, and burned them as though with a consuming fire. Pleased with the beauty and costliness of the garment, the unsuspecting Glauce lost no time in donning it; but no sooner had she done so than the fell poison began to take effect. In vain she tried to tear the robe away; it defied all efforts to be removed, and after horrible and protracted sufferings, she expired.

Maddened at the loss of her husband's love Medea next put to death her three sons, and when Jason, thirsting for revenge, left the chamber of his dead bride, and flew to his own house in search of Medea, the ghastly spectacle of his murdered children met his view. He rushed frantically to seek the murderess, but nowhere could she be found. At length, hearing a sound above his head, he looked up, and beheld Medea gliding through the air in a golden chariot drawn by dragons.

In a fit of despair Jason threw himself on his own sword, and perished on the threshold of his desolate and deserted home.

The Calydonian Boar Hunt

ARTEMIS RESENTED any disregard or neglect of her worship; a remarkable instance of this is shown in the story of the Calydonian boar hunt, which is as follows:

Oeneus, king of Calydon in Aetolia, had incurred the displeasure of Artemis by neglecting to include her in a general sacrifice to the gods which he had offered up, out of gratitude for a bountiful harvest. The goddess, enraged at this neglect, sent a wild boar of extraordinary size and prodigious strength, which destroyed the sprouting grain, laid waste the fields, and threatened the inhabitants with famine and death. At this juncture, Meleager, the brave son of Oeneus, returned from the Argonautic expedition, and finding his country ravaged by this dreadful scourge, entreated the assistance of all the celebrated heroes of the age to join him in hunting the ferocious monster. Among the most famous of those who responded to his call were Jason, Castor and Polydeuces, Idas and Lynceus, Peleus, Telamon, Admetus, Perithous, and Theseus. The brothers of Althea, wife of Oeneus, joined the hunters, and Meleager also enlisted into his service the fleet-footed huntress Atalanta.

The father of this maiden was Schoeneus, an Arcadian, who, disappointed at the birth of a daughter when he had particularly desired a son, had exposed her on the Parthenian Hill, where he left her to perish. Here she was nursed by a she-bear, and at last found by some hunters, who reared her, and gave her the name of Atalanta. As the maiden grew up, she became an ardent lover of the chase, and was alike distinguished for her beauty and courage. Though often wooed, she led a life of strict celibacy, an oracle having predicted that inevitable misfortune awaited her, should she give herself in marriage to any of her numerous suitors.

Many of the heroes objected to hunt in company with a maiden; but Meleager, who loved Atalanta, overcame their opposition, and the valiant band set out on their expedition. Atalanta was the first to wound the boar with her spear, but not before two of the heroes had met their death from his fierce tusks. After a long and desperate encounter, Meleager succeeded in killing the monster, and presented the head and hide to Atalanta, as trophies of the victory. The uncles of Meleager, however, forcibly took the hide from the maiden, claiming their right to the spoil as next of kin, if Meleager resigned it. Artemis, whose anger was still unappeased, caused a violent quarrel to arise between uncles and nephew, and, in the struggle which ensued, Meleager killed his mother's brothers, and then restored the hide to Atalanta. When Althea beheld the dead bodies of the slain heroes, her grief and anger knew no bounds. She swore to revenge the death of her brothers on her own son, and unfortunately for him, the instrument of vengeance lay ready to her hand.

At the birth of Meleager, the Moirae, or Fates, entered the house of Oeneus, and pointing to a piece of wood then burning on the hearth, declared that as soon as it was consumed the babe would surely die. On hearing this, Althea seized the brand, laid it up carefully in a chest, and henceforth preserved it as her most precious possession. But now, love for her son giving place to the resentment she felt against the murderer of her brothers, she threw the fatal brand into the devouring flames. As it consumed, the vigour of Meleager wasted away, and when it was reduced to ashes, he expired. Repenting too late the terrible effects of her rash deed, Althea, in remorse and despair, took away her own life.

The news of the courage and intrepidity displayed by Atalanta in the famous boar hunt, being carried to the ears of her father, caused him to acknowledge his long-lost child. Urged by him to choose one of her numerous suitors, she consented to do so, but made it a condition that he alone, who could outstrip her in the race, should become her husband, whilst those she defeated should be put to death by her, with the lance which she bore in her hand. Thus many suitors had perished, for the maiden was unequalled for swiftness of foot, but at last a beautiful youth, named Hippomenes, who had vainly endeavoured to win her love by his assiduous attentions in the chase, ventured to enter the fatal lists. Knowing that only by stratagem could he hope to be successful, he obtained, by the help of Aphrodite, three golden apples from the garden of the Hesperides, which he threw down at intervals during his course. Atalanta, secure of victory, stooped to pick up the tempting fruit, and, in the meantime, Hippomenes arrived at the goal. He became the husband of the lovely Atalanta, but forgot, in his newly found happiness, the gratitude which he owed to Aphrodite, and the goddess withdrew her favour from the pair. Not long after, the prediction which foretold misfortune to Atalanta, in the event of her marriage, was verified, for she and her husband, having strayed unsanctioned into a sacred grove of Zeus, were both transformed into lions.

The trophies of the ever-memorable boar hunt had been carried by Atalanta into Arcadia, and, for many centuries, the identical hide and enormous tusks of the Calydonian boar hung in the temple of Athene at Tegea. The tusks were afterwards conveyed to Rome, and shown there among other curiosities.

A similar forcible instance of the manner in which Artemis resented any intrusion on her retirement, is seen in the fate which befell the famous hunter Actaeon, who happening one day to see Artemis and her attendants bathing, imprudently ventured to approach the spot. The goddess, incensed at his audacity, sprinkled him with water, and transformed him into a stag, whereupon he was torn in pieces and devoured by his own dogs.

Adventures of Aeneas

THE FOLLOWING IS A SELECTION of extracts from Virgil's Aeneid, which totals twelve books in its entirety, written in the time of emperor Augustus to explain how his ancestor Aeneas led a group of Trojans from the ruins of the city the Greeks had destroyed to find a new home in Italy.

The Sack of Troy

In the first book Aeneas' fleet has been blown to North Africa due to Juno's meddling. Those of the Trojans who have made it safely ashore come upon the great city of Carthage, whose queen is Dido. Aeneas' mother Venus intervenes by making Dido fall in love with Aeneas, and as the second book begins, Dido has encouraged the Trojan hero to describe the escape from Troy. In the following extract from Book Two the ghost of Hector appears to Aeneas to encourage him to flee from Troy, whereupon he wakes and goes out to see the destruction of his city:

'It was the time when by the gift of God rest comes stealing first and sweetest on unhappy men. In slumber, lo! before mine eyes Hector seemed to stand by, deep in grief and shedding abundant tears; torn by the chariot, as once of old, and black with gory dust, his swoln feet pierced with the thongs. Ah me! in what guise was he! how changed from the Hector who returns from putting on Achilles' spoils, or launching the fires of Phrygia on the Grecian ships! with ragged beard and tresses clotted with blood, and all the many wounds upon him that he received around his ancestral walls. Myself too weeping I seemed to accost him ere he spoke, and utter forth mournful accents: 'O light of Dardania, O surest hope of the Trojans, what long delay is this hath held thee? from what borders comest thou, Hector our desire? with what weary eyes we see thee, after many deaths of thy kin, after divers woes of people and city! What indignity hath marred thy serene visage? or why discern I these wounds?'

'He replies naught, nor regards my idle questioning; but heavily drawing a heart-deep groan, 'Ah, fly, goddess-born,' he says, 'and rescue thyself from these flames. The foe holds our walls; from her high ridges Troy is toppling down. Thy country and Priam ask no more. If Troy towers might be defended by strength of hand, this hand too had been their defence. Troy commends to thee her holy things and household gods; take them to accompany thy fate; seek for them a city, which, after all the seas have known thy wanderings, thou shalt at last establish in might.' So speaks he, and carries forth in his hands from their inner shrine the chaplets and strength of Vesta, and the everlasting fire.

'Meanwhile the city is stirred with mingled agony; and more and more, though my father Anchises' house lay deep withdrawn and screened by trees, the noises grow clearer and the clash of armour swells. I shake myself from sleep and mount over the sloping roof, and stand there with ears attent: even as when flame catches a corn-field while south winds are furious, or the racing torrent of a mountain stream sweeps the fields, sweeps the smiling crops and labours of the oxen, and hurls the forest with it headlong; the shepherd in witless amaze hears the roar from the cliff-top.

'Then indeed proof is clear, and the treachery of the Grecians opens out. Already the house of Deïphobus hath crashed down in wide ruin amid the overpowering flames; already our neighbour

Ucalegon is ablaze: the broad Sigean bay is lit with the fire. Cries of men and blare of trumpets rise up. Madly I seize my arms, nor is there so much purpose in arms; but my spirit is on fire to gather a band for fighting and charge for the citadel with my comrades. Fury and wrath drive me headlong, and I think how noble is death in arms.

'And lo! Panthus, eluding the Achaean weapons, Panthus son of Othrys, priest of Phoebus in the citadel, comes hurrying with the sacred vessels and conquered gods and his little grandchild in his hand, and runs distractedly towards my gates. 'How stands the state, O Panthus? what stronghold are we to occupy?' Scarcely had I said so, when groaning he thus returns: 'The crowning day is come, the irreversible time of the Dardanian land. No more are we a Trojan people; Ilium and the great glory of the Teucrians is no more. Angry Jupiter hath cast all into the scale of Argos. The Grecians are lords of the burning town. The horse, standing high amid the city, pours forth armed men, and Sinon scatters fire, insolent in victory. Some are at the wide-flung gates, all the thousands that ever came from populous Mycenae. Others have beset the narrow streets with lowered weapons; edge and glittering point of steel stand drawn, ready for the slaughter; scarcely at the entry do the guards of the gates essay battle, and hold out in the blind fight.'

'Heaven's will thus declared by the son of Othrys drives me amid flames and arms, where the baleful Fury calls, and tumult of shouting rises up. Rhipeus and Epytus, most mighty in arms, join company with me; Hypanis and Dymas meet us in the moonlight and attach themselves to our side, and young Coroebus son of Mygdon. In those days it was he had come to Troy, fired with mad passion for Cassandra, and bore a son's aid to Priam and the Phrygians: hapless, that he listened not to his raving bride's counsels. . . . Seeing them close-ranked and daring for battle, I therewith began thus: 'Men, hearts of supreme and useless bravery, if your desire be fixed to follow one who dares the utmost; you see what is the fortune of our state: all the gods by whom this empire was upheld have gone forth, abandoning shrine and altar; your aid comes to a burning city. Let us die, and rush on their encircling weapons. The conquered have one safety, to hope for none.'

'So their spirit is heightened to fury. Then, like wolves ravening in a black fog, whom mad malice of hunger hath driven blindly forth, and their cubs left behind await with throats unslaked; through the weapons of the enemy we march to certain death, and hold our way straight into the town. Night's sheltering shadow flutters dark around us. Who may unfold in speech that night's horror and death-agony, or measure its woes in weeping? The ancient city falls with her long years of sovereignty; corpses lie stretched stiff all about the streets and houses and awful courts of the gods. Nor do Teucrians alone pay forfeit of their blood; once and again valour returns even in conquered hearts, and the victorious Grecians fall. Everywhere is cruel agony, everywhere terror, and the sight of death at every turn.

'First, with a great troop of Grecians attending him, Androgeus meets us, taking us in ignorance for an allied band, and opens on us with friendly words: 'Hasten, my men; why idly linger so late? others plunder and harry the burning citadel; are you but now on your march from the tall ships?' He spoke, and immediately (for no answer of any assurance was offered) knew he was fallen among the foe. In amazement, he checked foot and voice; even as one who struggling through rough briers hath trodden a snake on the ground unwarned, and suddenly shrinks fluttering back as it rises in anger and puffs its green throat out; even thus Androgeus drew away, startled at the sight. We rush in and encircle them with serried arms, and cut them down dispersedly in their ignorance of the ground and seizure of panic. Fortune speeds our first labour. And here Coroebus, flushed with success and spirit, cries: 'O comrades, follow me where fortune points before us the path of safety, and shews her favour. Let us exchange shields, and accoutre ourselves in Grecian suits; whether craft or courage, who will ask of an enemy? the foe shall arm our hands.'

'Thus speaking, he next dons the plumed helmet and beautifully blazoned shield of Androgeus, and fits the Argive sword to his side. So does Rhipeus, so Dymas in like wise, and all our men in delight arm themselves one by one in the fresh spoils. We advance, mingling with the Grecians, under a protection not our own, and join many a battle with those we meet amid the blind night; many a Greek we send down to hell. Some scatter to the ships and run for the safety of the shore; some in craven fear again climb the huge horse, and hide in the belly they knew. Alas that none may trust at all to estranged gods!

'Lo! Cassandra, maiden daughter of Priam, was being dragged with disordered tresses from the temple and sanctuary of Minerva, straining to heaven her blazing eyes in vain; her eyes, for fetters locked her delicate hands. At this sight Coroebus burst forth infuriate, and flung himself on death amid their columns. We all follow him up, and charge with massed arms. Here first from the high temple roof we are overwhelmed with our own people's weapons, and a most pitiful slaughter begins through the fashion of our armour and the mistaken Greek crests; then the Grecians, with angry cries at the maiden's rescue, gather from every side and fall on us; Ajax in all his valour, and the two sons of Atreus, and the whole Dolopian army: as oft when bursting in whirlwind West and South clash with adverse blasts, and the East wind exultant on the coursers of the Dawn; the forests cry, and fierce in foam Nereus with his trident stirs the seas from their lowest depth. Those too appear, whom our stratagem routed through the darkness of dim night and drove all about the town; at once they know the shields and lying weapons, and mark the alien tone on our lips.

'We go down, overwhelmed by numbers. First Coroebus is stretched by Peneleus' hand at the altar of the goddess armipotent; and Rhipeus falls, the one man who was most righteous and steadfast in justice among the Teucrians: the gods' ways are not as ours: Hypanis and Dymas perish, pierced by friendly hands; nor did all thy goodness, O Panthus, nor Apollo's fillet protect thy fall. O ashes of Ilium and death flames of my people! you I call to witness that in your ruin I shunned no Grecian weapon or encounter, and my hand earned my fall, had destiny been thus. We tear ourselves away, I and Iphitus and Pelias, Iphitus now stricken in age, Pelias halting too under the wound of Ulysses, called forward by the clamour to Priam's house.

'Here indeed the battle is fiercest, as if all the rest of the fighting were nowhere, and no slaughter but here throughout the city, so do we descry the war in full fury, the Grecians rushing on the building, and their shielded column driving up against the beleaguered threshold. Ladders cling to the walls; and hard by the doors and planted on the rungs they hold up their shields in the left hand to ward off our weapons, and with their right clutch the battlements. The Dardanians tear down turrets and the covering of the house roof against them; with these for weapons, since they see the end is come, they prepare to defend themselves even in death's extremity: and hurl down gilded beams, the stately decorations of their fathers of old. Others with drawn swords have beset the doorway below and keep it in crowded column. We renew our courage, to aid the royal dwelling, to support them with our succour, and swell the force of the conquered.

Dido and Aeneas

Aeneas relates how he managed to lead a group of Trojans away from their burning city and the swords of the Greeks, including his father – who dies before they arrive at Carthage – and his young son, but sadly his wife did not make it out of Troy. Thinking that Crete might be the location of their new home, the Trojans sail there, however Aeneas receives a vision which shows him that the Italian shores and not Crete are where they should be heading. Book Four then takes us back to the present, where Aeneas is at Dido's court. Aeneas spends a year with the Carthaginian queen, until the gods remind him of his duty. To avoid Dido's tears and recriminations, he keeps his preparations for departure a complete secret, and finally sets sail whilst Dido is asleep. Dido is grief-stricken and ultimately commits suicide as seen in the following extract from Book Four.

But the Queen – who may delude a lover? – foreknew his devices, and at once caught the presaging stir. Safety's self was fear; to her likewise had evil Rumour borne the maddening news that they equip the fleet and prepare for passage. Helpless at heart, she reels aflame with rage throughout the city, even as the startled Thyiad in her frenzied triennial orgies, when the holy vessels move forth and the cry of Bacchus re-echoes, and Cithaeron calls her with nightlong din. Thus at last she opens out upon Aeneas:

'And thou didst hope, traitor, to mask the crime, and slip away in silence from my land? Our love holds thee not, nor the hand thou once gavest, nor the bitter death that is left for Dido's portion? Nay, under the wintry star thou labourest on thy fleet, and hastenest to launch into the deep amid northern gales; ah, cruel! Why, were thy quest not of alien fields and unknown dwellings, did thine ancient Troy remain, should Troy be sought in voyages over tossing seas?

'Fliest thou from me? me who by these tears and thine own hand beseech thee, since naught else, alas! have I kept mine own – by our union and the marriage rites preparing; if I have done thee any grace, or aught of mine hath once been sweet in thy sight, – pity our sinking house, and if there yet be room for prayers, put off this purpose of thine. For thy sake Libyan tribes and Nomad kings are hostile; my Tyrians are estranged; for thy sake, thine, is mine honour perished, and the former fame, my one title to the skies. How leavest thou me to die, O my guest? since to this the name of husband is dwindled down. For what do I wait? till Pygmalion overthrow his sister's city, or Gaetulian Iarbas lead me to captivity? At least if before thy flight a child of thine had been clasped in my arms, – if a tiny Aeneas were playing in my hall, whose face might yet image thine, – I would not think myself ensnared and deserted utterly.'

She ended; he by counsel of Jove held his gaze unstirred, and kept his distress hard down in his heart. At last he briefly answers:

'Never, O Queen, will I deny that thy goodness hath gone high as thy words can swell the reckoning; nor will my memory of Elissa be ungracious while I remember myself, and breath sways this body. Little will I say in this. I never hoped to slip away in stealthy flight; fancy not that; nor did I ever hold out the marriage torch or enter thus into alliance. Did fate allow me to guide my life by mine own government, and calm my sorrows as I would, my first duty were to the Trojan city and the dear remnant of my kindred; the high house of Priam should abide, and my hand had set up Troy towers anew for a conquered people. But now for broad Italy hath Apollo of Grynos bidden me steer, for Italy the oracles of Lycia. Here is my desire; this is my native country. If thy Phoenician eyes are stayed on Carthage towers and thy Libyan city, what wrong is it, I pray, that we Trojans find our rest on Ausonian land? We too may seek a foreign realm unforbidden. In my sleep, often as the dank shades of night veil the earth, often as the stars lift their fires, the troubled phantom of my father Anchises comes in warning and dread; my boy Ascanius, how I wrong one so dear in cheating him of an Hesperian kingdom and destined fields. Now even the gods' interpreter, sent straight from Jove – I call both to witness – hath borne down his commands through the fleet air. Myself in broad daylight I saw the deity passing within the walls, and these ears drank his utterance. Cease to madden me and thyself alike with plaints. Not of my will do I follow Italy. . . .'

Long ere he ended she gazes on him askance, turning her eyes from side to side and perusing him with silent glances; then thus wrathfully speaks:

'No goddess was thy mother, nor Dardanus founder of thy line, traitor! but rough Caucasus bore thee on his iron crags, and Hyrcanian tigresses gave thee suck. For why do I conceal it? For what further outrage do I wait? Hath our weeping cost him a sigh, or a lowered glance? Hath he broken into tears, or had pity on his lover? Where, where shall I begin? Now neither doth Queen

Juno nor our Saturnian lord regard us with righteous eyes. Nowhere is trust safe. Cast ashore and destitute I welcomed him, and madly gave him place and portion in my kingdom; I found him his lost fleet and drew his crews from death.

Alas, the fire of madness speeds me on. Now prophetic Apollo, now oracles of Lycia, now the very gods' interpreter sent straight from Jove through the air carries these rude commands! Truly that is work for the gods, that a care to vex their peace! I detain thee not, nor gainsay thy words: go, follow thine Italy down the wind; seek thy realm overseas. Yet midway my hope is, if righteous gods can do aught at all, thou wilt drain the cup of vengeance on the rocks, and re-echo calls on Dido's name. In murky fires I will follow far away, and when chill death hath severed body from soul, my ghost will haunt thee in every region. Wretch, thou shalt repay! I will hear; and the rumour of it shall reach me deep in the under world.'

Even on these words she breaks off her speech unfinished, and, sick at heart, escapes out of the air and sweeps round and away out of sight, leaving him in fear and much hesitance, and with much on his mind to say. Her women catch her in their arms, and carry her swooning to her marble chamber and lay her on her bed.

But good Aeneas, though he would fain soothe and comfort her grief, and talk away her distress, with many a sigh, and melted in soul by his great love, yet fulfils the divine commands and returns to his fleet. Then indeed the Teucrians set to work, and haul down their tall ships all along the shore. The hulls are oiled and afloat; they carry from the woodland green boughs for oars and massy logs unhewn, in hot haste to go. . . . One might descry them shifting their quarters and pouring out of all the town: even as ants, mindful of winter, plunder a great heap of wheat and store it in their house; a black column advances on the plain as they carry home their spoil on a narrow track through the grass.

Some shove and strain with their shoulders at big grains, some marshal the ranks and chastise delay; all the path is aswarm with work. What then were thy thoughts, O Dido, as thou sawest it? What sighs didst thou utter, viewing from the fortress roof the broad beach aswarm, and seeing before thine eyes the whole sea stirred with their noisy din? Injurious Love, to what dost thou not compel mortal hearts! Again, she must needs break into tears, again essay entreaty, and bow her spirit down to love, not to leave aught untried and go to death in vain.

'Anna, thou seest the bustle that fills the shore. They have gathered round from every quarter; already their canvas woos the breezes, and the merry sailors have garlanded the sterns. This great pain, my sister, I shall have strength to bear, as I have had strength to foresee. Yet this one thing, Anna, for love and pity's sake – for of thee alone was the traitor fain, to thee even his secret thoughts were confided, alone thou knewest his moods and tender fits – go, my sister, and humbly accost the haughty stranger: I did not take the Grecian oath in Aulis to root out the race of Troy; I sent no fleet against her fortresses; neither have I disentombed his father Anchises' ashes and ghost, that he should refuse my words entrance to his stubborn ears. Whither does he run? let him grant this grace – alas, the last! – to his lover, and await fair winds and an easy passage. No more do I pray for the old delusive marriage, nor that he give up fair Latium and abandon a kingdom. A breathing-space I ask, to give my madness rest and room, till my very fortune teach my grief submission. This last favour I implore: sister, be pitiful; grant this to me, and I will restore it in full measure when I die.'

So she pleaded, and so her sister carries and recarries the piteous tale of weeping. But by no weeping is he stirred, inflexible to all the words he hears. Fate withstands, and lays divine bars on unmoved mortal ears. Even as when the eddying blasts of northern Alpine winds are emulous to uproot the secular strength of a mighty oak, it wails on, and the trunk quivers and the high foliage strews the ground; the tree clings fast on the rocks, and high as her top soars into heaven, so deep strike her roots to hell; even thus is the hero buffeted with changeful perpetual accents, and distress thrills his mighty breast, while his purpose stays unstirred, and tears fall in vain.

Then indeed, hapless and dismayed by doom, Dido prays for death, and is weary of gazing on the arch of heaven. The more to make her fulfil her purpose and quit the light, she saw, when she laid her gifts on the altars alight with incense, awful to tell, the holy streams blacken, and the wine turn as it poured into ghastly blood. Of this sight she spoke to none – no, not to her sister.

Likewise there was within the house a marble temple of her ancient lord, kept of her in marvellous honour, and fastened with snowy fleeces and festal boughs. Forth of it she seemed to hear her husband's voice crying and calling when night was dim upon earth, and alone on the house-tops the screech-owl often made moan with funeral note and long-drawn sobbing cry. Therewithal many a warning of wizards of old terrifies her with appalling presage. In her sleep fierce Aeneas drives her wildly, and ever she seems being left by herself alone, ever going uncompanioned on a weary way, and seeking her Tyrians in a solitary land: even as frantic Pentheus sees the arrayed Furies and a double sun, and Thebes shows herself twofold to his eyes: or Agamemnonian Orestes, renowned in tragedy, when his mother pursues him armed with torches and dark serpents, and the Fatal Sisters crouch avenging in the doorway.

So when, overcome by her pangs, she caught the madness and resolved to die, she works out secretly the time and fashion, and accosts her sorrowing sister with mien hiding her design and hope calm on her brow.

'I have found a way, mine own – wish me joy, sisterlike – to restore him to me or release me of my love for him. Hard by the ocean limit and the set of sun is the extreme Aethiopian land, where ancient Atlas turns on his shoulders the starred burning axletree of heaven. Out of it hath been shown to me a priestess of Massylian race, warder of the temple of the Hesperides, even she who gave the dragon his food, and kept the holy boughs on the tree, sprinkling clammy honey and slumberous poppy-seed. She professes with her spells to relax the purposes of whom she will, but on others to bring passion and pain; to stay the river-waters and turn the stars backward: she calls up ghosts by night; thou shalt see earth moaning under foot and mountain-ashes descending from the hills. I take heaven, sweet, to witness, and thee, mine own darling sister, I do not willingly arm myself with the arts of magic.

Do thou secretly raise a pyre in the inner court, and let them lay on it the arms that the accursed one left hanging in our chamber, and all the dress he wore, and the bridal bed where I fell. It is good to wipe out all the wretch's traces, and the priestess orders thus.' So speaks she, and is silent, while pallor overruns her face. Yet Anna deems not her sister veils death behind these strange rites, and grasps not her wild purpose, nor fears aught deeper than at Sychaeus' death. So she makes ready as bidden. . . .

The Underworld

Book 6 of the Aeneid recounts how the Trojans make it to Cumae in Italy, where there is a famous Sibyl. She tells Aeneas of the many trials he has yet to face, but urges him to continue. He makes known his wish to visit Hades, and entreats her to serve as his guide in that perilous journey. She consents, but at the same time informs him that he must first obtain a golden twig, which grows in a dark forest. Having done so, Aeneas descends into the Underworld where he sees Dido on the way to finding his father Anchises. In this extract from Book 6 Anchises points out the future heroes of Rome waiting to be born, who include amongst them Romulus and the emperor Augustus:

But lord Anchises, deep in the green valley, was musing in earnest survey over the imprisoned souls destined to the daylight above, and haply reviewing his beloved children and all the tale of his people, them and their fates and fortunes, their works and ways. And he, when he saw Aeneas advancing to meet him over the greensward, stretched forth both hands eagerly, while tears rolled over his cheeks, and his lips parted in a cry: 'Art thou come at last, and hath thy love, O child of my desire, conquered the difficult road? Is it granted, O my son, to gaze on thy face and hear and answer in familiar tones? Thus indeed I forecast in spirit, counting the days between; nor hath my care misled me. What lands, what space of seas hast thou traversed to reach me, through what surge of perils, O my son! How I dreaded the realm of Libya might work thee harm!'

And he: 'Thy melancholy phantom, thine, O my father, came before me often and often, and drove me to steer to these portals. My fleet is anchored on the Tyrrhenian brine. Give thine hand to clasp, O my father, give it, and withdraw not from our embrace.'

So spoke he, his face wet with abundant weeping. Thrice there did he essay to fling his arms about his neck; thrice the phantom vainly grasped fled out of his hands even as light wind, and most like to fluttering sleep.

Meanwhile Aeneas sees deep withdrawn in the covert of the vale a woodland and rustling forest thickets, and the river of Lethe that floats past their peaceful dwellings. Around it flitted nations and peoples innumerable; even as in the meadows when in clear summer weather bees settle on the variegated flowers and stream round the snow-white lilies, all the plain is murmurous with their humming. Aeneas starts at the sudden view, and asks the reason he knows not; what are those spreading streams, or who are they whose vast train fills the banks?

Then lord Anchises: 'Souls, for whom second bodies are destined and due, drink at the wave of the Lethean stream the heedless water of long forgetfulness. These of a truth have I long desired to tell and shew thee face to face, and number all the generation of thy children, that so thou mayest the more rejoice with me in finding Italy.' – 'O father, must we think that any souls travel hence into upper air, and return again to bodily fetters? why this their strange sad longing for the light?' 'I will tell,' rejoins Anchises, 'nor will I hold thee in suspense, my son.' And he unfolds all things in order one by one.

'First of all, heaven and earth and the liquid fields, the shining orb of the moon and the Titanian star, doth a spirit sustain inly, and a soul shed abroad in them sways all their members and mingles in the mighty frame. Thence is the generation of man and beast, the life of winged things, and the monstrous forms that ocean breeds under his glittering floor. Those seeds have fiery force and divine birth, so far as they are not clogged by taint of the body and dulled by earthy frames and limbs ready to die. Hence is it they fear and desire, sorrow and rejoice; nor can they pierce the air while barred in the blind darkness of their prison-house. Nay, and when the last ray of life is gone, not yet, alas! does all their woe, nor do all the plagues of the body wholly leave them free; and needs must be that many a long ingrained evil should take root marvellously deep.

Therefore they are schooled in punishment, and pay all the forfeit of a lifelong ill; some are hung stretched to the viewless winds; some have the taint of guilt washed out beneath the dreary deep, or burned away in fire. We suffer, each a several ghost; thereafter we are sent to the broad spaces of Elysium, some few of us to possess the happy fields; till length of days completing time's circle takes out the ingrained soilure and leaves untainted the ethereal sense and pure spiritual flame. All these before thee, when the wheel of a thousand years hath come fully round, a God summons in vast train to the river of Lethe, that so they may regain in forgetfulness the slopes of upper earth, and begin to desire to return again into the body.'

Anchises ceased, and leads his son and the Sibyl likewise amid the assembled murmurous throng, and mounts a hillock whence he might scan all the long ranks and learn their countenances as they came.

'Now come, the glory hereafter to follow our Dardanian progeny, the posterity to abide in our Italian people, illustrious souls and inheritors of our name to be, these will I rehearse, and instruct thee of thy destinies. He yonder, seest thou? the warrior leaning on his pointless spear, holds the nearest place allotted in our groves, and shall rise first into the air of heaven from the mingling blood of Italy, Silvius of Alban name, the child of thine age, whom late in thy length of days thy wife Lavinia shall nurture in the woodland, king and father of kings; from him in Alba the Long shall our house have dominion. He next him is Procas, glory of the Trojan race; and Capys and Numitor; and he who shall renew thy name, Silvius Aeneas, eminent alike in goodness or in arms, if ever he shall receive his kingdom in Alba. Men of men! see what strength they display, and wear the civic oak shading their brows.

'They shall establish Nomentum and Gabii and Fidena city, they the Collatine hill-fortress, Pometii and the Fort of Inuus, Bola and Cora: these shall be names that are now nameless lands. Nay, Romulus likewise, seed of Mavors, shall join his grandsire's company, from his mother Ilia's nurture and Assaracus' blood. Seest thou how the twin plumes straighten on his crest, and his father's own emblazonment already marks him for upper air? Behold, O son! by his augury shall Rome the renowned fill earth with her empire and heaven with her pride, and gird about seven fortresses with her single wall, prosperous mother of men; even as our lady of Berecyntus rides in her chariot turret-crowned through the Phrygian cities, glad in the gods she hath borne, clasping an hundred of her children's children, all habitants of heaven, all dwellers on the upper heights.

'Hither now bend thy twin-eyed gaze; behold this people, the Romans that are thine. Here is Caesar and all Iülus' posterity that shall arise under the mighty cope of heaven. Here is he, he of whose promise once and again thou hearest, Caesar Augustus, a god's son, who shall again establish the ages of gold in Latium over the fields that once were Saturn's realm, and carry his empire afar to Garamant and Indian, to the land that lies beyond our stars, beyond the sun's yearlong ways, where Atlas the sky-bearer wheels on his shoulder the glittering star-spangled pole. Before his coming even now the kingdoms of the Caspian shudder at oracular answers, and the Maeotic land and the mouths of sevenfold Nile flutter in alarm. Nor indeed did Alcides traverse such spaces of earth, though he pierced the brazen-footed deer, or though he stilled the Erymanthian woodlands and made Lerna tremble at his bow: nor he who sways his team with reins of vine, Liber the conqueror, when he drives his tigers from Nysa's lofty crest. And do we yet hesitate to give valour scope in deeds, or shrink in fear from setting foot on Ausonian land?

'Ah, and who is he apart, marked out with sprays of olive, offering sacrifice? I know the locks and hoary chin of the king of Rome who shall establish the infant city in his laws, sent from little Cures' sterile land to the majesty of empire. To him Tullus shall next succeed, who shall break the peace of his country and stir to arms men rusted from war and armies now disused to triumphs; and hard on him over-vaunting Ancus follows, even now too elate in popular breath. Wilt thou see also the Tarquin kings, and the haughty soul of Brutus the Avenger, and the fasces regained? He shall first receive a consul's power and the merciless axes, and when his children would stir fresh war, the father, for fair freedom's sake, shall summon them to doom. Unhappy! yet howsoever posterity shall take the deed, love of country and limitless passion for honour shall prevail.

'Nay, behold apart the Decii and the Drusi, Torquatus with his cruel axe, and Camillus returning with the standards. Yonder souls likewise, whom thou discernest gleaming in equal arms, at one now, while shut in Night, ah me! what mutual war, what battle-lines and bloodshed shall they arouse, so they attain the light of the living! father-in-law descending from the Alpine barriers and the fortress of the Dweller Alone, son-in-law facing him with the embattled East. Nay, O my children, harden not your hearts to such warfare, neither turn upon her own heart the mastering might of your country; and thou, be thou first to forgive, who drawest thy descent from heaven;

cast down the weapons from thy hand, O blood of mine. . . . He shall drive his conquering chariot to the Capitoline height triumphant over Corinth, glorious in Achaean slaughter. He shall uproot Argos and Agamemnonian Mycenae, and the Aeacid's own heir, the seed of Achilles mighty in arms, avenging his ancestors in Troy and Minerva's polluted temple.

'Who might leave thee, lordly Cato, or thee, Cossus, to silence? who the Gracchan family, or these two sons of the Scipios, a double thunderbolt of war, Libya's bale? and Fabricius potent in poverty, or thee, Serranus, sowing in the furrow? Whither whirl you me all breathless, O Fabii? thou art he, the most mighty, the one man whose lingering retrieves our State. Others shall beat out the breathing bronze to softer lines, I believe it well; shall draw living lineaments from the marble; the cause shall be more eloquent on their lips; their pencil shall portray the pathways of heaven, and tell the stars in their arising: be thy charge, O Roman, to rule the nations in thine empire; this shall be thine art, to lay down the law of peace, to be merciful to the conquered and beat the haughty down.'

Thus lord Anchises, and as they marvel, he so pursues: 'Look how Marcellus the conqueror marches glorious in the splendid spoils, towering high above them all! He shall stay the Roman State, reeling beneath the invading shock, shall ride down Carthaginian and insurgent Gaul, and a third time hang up the captured armour before lord Quirinus.'

And at this Aeneas, for he saw going by his side one excellent in beauty and glittering in arms, but his brow had little cheer, and his eyes looked down:

'Who, O my father, is he who thus attends him on his way? son, or other of his children's princely race? How his comrades murmur around him! how goodly of presence he is! but dark Night flutters round his head with melancholy shade.'

Then lord Anchises with welling tears began: 'O my son, ask not of the great sorrow of thy people. Him shall fate but shew to earth, and suffer not to stay further. Too mighty, lords of heaven, did you deem the brood of Rome, had this your gift been abiding. What moaning of men shall arise from the Field of Mavors by the imperial city! what a funeral train shalt thou see, O Tiber, as thou flowest by the new-made grave! Neither shall the boyhood of any of Ilian race raise his Latin forefathers' hope so high; nor shall the land of Romulus ever boast of any fosterling like this.

'Alas his goodness, alas his antique honour, and right hand invincible in war! none had faced him unscathed in armed shock, whether he met the foe on foot, or ran his spurs into the flanks of his foaming horse. Ah me, the pity of thee, O boy! if in any wise thou breakest the grim bar of fate, thou shalt be Marcellus. Give me lilies in full hands; let me strew bright blossoms, and these gifts at least let me lavish on my descendant's soul, and do the unavailing service.'

Thus they wander up and down over the whole region of broad vaporous plains, and scan all the scene. And when Anchises had led his son over it, each point by each, and kindled his spirit with passion for the glories on their way, he tells him thereafter of the war he next must wage, and instructs him of the Laurentine peoples and the city of Latinus, and in what wise each task may be turned aside or borne.

Embassy to Evander

After a prolonged conversation with his father, Aeneas returned to his companions, and led them to the mouth of the Tiber, whose course they followed until they reached Latium, where their wanderings were to cease. Latinus, king of the country, received them hospitably, and promised the hand of his daughter Lavinia in marriage to Aeneas. Lavinia was very beautiful, and had already had many suitors, among whom Turnus, a prince, boasted of the most exalted rank. The queen, Amata, specially favoured this youth's suit; and the king would gladly have received him for a son-in-law, had he not twice been warned by the gods to reserve his daughter for a foreign prince, who had now appeared. Juno had not yet forgotten her hatred of the Trojan race, and conspired to meddle once more, stirring up Turnus' hostility against Aeneas and his men. In this extract from Book Eight, Aeneas seeks help from Evander, who has a settlement on the future site of Rome:

When Turnus ran up the flag of war on the towers of Laurentum, and the trumpets blared with harsh music, when he spurred his fiery steeds and clashed his armour, straightway men's hearts are in tumult; all Latium at once flutters in banded uprisal, and her warriors rage furiously. Their chiefs, Messapus, and Ufens, and Mezentius, scorner of the gods, begin to enrol forces on all sides, and dispeople the wide fields of husbandmen.

Venulus too is sent to the town of mighty Diomede to seek succour, to instruct him that Teucrians set foot in Latium; that Aeneas in his fleet invades them with the vanquished gods of his home, and proclaims himself the King summoned of fate; that many tribes join the Dardanian, and his name swells high in Latium. What he will rear on these foundations, what issue of battle he desires, if Fortune attend him, lies clearer to his own sight than to King Turnus or King Latinus.

Thus was it in Latium. And the hero of Laomedon's blood, seeing it all, tosses on a heavy surge of care, and throws his mind rapidly this way and that, and turns it on all hands in swift change of thought: even as when the quivering light of water brimming in brass, struck back from the sunlight or the moon's glittering reflection, flickers abroad over all the room, and now mounts aloft and strikes the high panelled roof. Night fell, and over all lands weary creatures were fast in deep slumber, the race of fowl and of cattle; when lord Aeneas, sick at heart of the dismal warfare, stretched him on the river bank under the cope of the cold sky, and let sleep, though late, overspread his limbs. To him the very god of the ground, the pleasant Tiber stream, seemed to raise his aged form among the poplar boughs; thin lawn veiled him with its gray covering, and shadowy reeds hid his hair. Thereon he addressed him thus, and with these words allayed his distresses:

'O born of the family of the gods, thou who bearest back our Trojan city from hostile hands, and keepest Troy towers in eternal life; O long looked for on Laurentine ground and Latin fields! here is thine assured home, thine home's assured gods. Draw not thou back, nor be alarmed by menace of war. All the anger and wrath of the gods is passed away . . . And even now for thine assurance, that thou think not this the idle fashioning of sleep, a great sow shall be found lying under the oaks on the shore, with her new-born litter of thirty head: white she couches on the ground, and the brood about her teats is white. By this token in thirty revolving years shall Ascanius found a city, Alba of bright name. My prophecy is sure.

'Now hearken, and I will briefly instruct thee how thou mayest unravel and overcome thy present task. An Arcadian people sprung of Pallas, following in their king Evander's company beneath his banners, have chosen a place in these coasts, and set a city on the hills, called Pallanteum after Pallas their forefather. These wage perpetual war with the Latin race; these do thou take to thy camp's alliance, and join with them in league. Myself I will lead thee by my banks and straight along my stream, that thou mayest oar thy way upward against the river. Up and arise, goddess-born, and even with the setting stars address thy prayers to Juno as is meet, and vanquish her wrath and menaces with humble vows. To me thou shalt pay a conqueror's sacrifice. I am he whom thou seest washing the banks with full flood and severing the rich tilth, glassy Tiber, best beloved by heaven of rivers. Here is my stately home; my fountain-head is among high cities.'

Thus spoke the River, and sank in the depth of the pool: night and sleep left Aeneas. He arises, and, looking towards the radiant sky of the sunrising, holds up water from the river in fitly-hollowed palms, and pours to heaven these accents:

'Nymphs, Laurentine Nymphs, from whom is the generation of rivers, and thou, O father Tiber, with thine holy flood, receive Aeneas and deign to save him out of danger. What pool soever holds thy source, who pitiest our discomforts, from whatsoever soil thou dost spring excellent in beauty, ever shall my worship, ever my gifts frequent thee, the hornèd river lord of Hesperian waters. Ah, be thou only by me, and graciously confirm thy will.' So speaks he, and chooses two galleys from his fleet, and mans them with rowers, and withal equips a crew with arms.

And lo! suddenly, ominous and wonderful to tell, the milk-white sow, of one colour with her white brood, is espied through the forest couched on the green brink; whom to thee, yes to thee, queenly Juno, good Aeneas offers in sacrifice, and sets with her offspring before thine altar. All that night long Tiber assuaged his swelling stream, and silently stayed his refluent wave, smoothing the surface of his waters to the fashion of still pool and quiet mere, to spare labour to the oar.

So they set out and speed on their way with prosperous cries; the painted fir slides along the waterway; the waves and unwonted woods marvel at their far-gleaming shields, and the gay hulls afloat on the river. They outwear a night and a day in rowing, ascend the long reaches, and pass under the chequered shadows of the trees, and cut through the green woodland in the calm water. The fiery sun had climbed midway in the circle of the sky when they see afar fortress walls and scattered house roofs, where now the might of Rome hath risen high as heaven; then Evander held a slender state. Quickly they turn their prows to land and draw near the town.

It chanced on that day the Arcadian king paid his accustomed sacrifice to the great son of Amphitryon and all the gods in a grove before the city. With him his son Pallas, with him all the chief of his people and his poor senate were offering incense, and the blood steamed warm at their altars. When they saw the high ships, saw them glide up between the shady woodlands and rest on their silent oars, the sudden sight appals them, and all at once they rise and stop the banquet. Pallas courageously forbids them to break off the rites; snatching up a spear, he flies forward, and from a hillock cries afar: 'O men, what cause hath driven you to explore these unknown ways? or whither do you steer? What is your kin, whence your habitation? Is it peace or arms you carry hither?' Then from the lofty stern lord Aeneas thus speaks, stretching forth in his hand an olive bough of peace-bearing:

'Thou seest men born of Troy and arms hostile to the Latins, who have driven us to flight in insolent warfare. We seek Evander; carry this message, and tell him that chosen men of the Dardanian captains are come pleading for an armed alliance.'

Pallas stood amazed at the august name. 'Descend,' he cries, 'whoso thou art, and speak with my father face to face, and enter our home and hospitality.' And giving him the grasp of welcome, he caught and clung to his hand. Advancing, they enter the grove and leave the river. Then Aeneas in courteous words addresses the King:

'Best of the Grecian race, thou whom fortune hath willed that I supplicate, holding before me boughs dressed in fillets, no fear stayed me because thou wert a Grecian chief and an Arcadian, or allied by descent to the twin sons of Atreus. Nay, mine own prowess and the sanctity of divine oracles, our ancestral kinship, and the fame of thee that is spread abroad over the earth, have allied me to thee and led me willingly on the path of fate. Dardanus, who sailed to the Teucrian land, the first father and founder of the Ilian city, was born, as Greeks relate, of Electra the Atlantid; Electra's sire is ancient Atlas, whose shoulder sustains the heavenly spheres. Your father is Mercury, whom white Maia conceived and bore on the cold summit of Cyllene; but Maia, if we give any credence to report, is daughter of Atlas, that same Atlas who bears up the starry heavens; so both our families branch from a single blood.

'In this confidence I sent no embassy, I framed no crafty overtures; myself I have presented mine own person, and come a suppliant to thy courts. The same Daunian race pursues us and thee in merciless warfare; we once expelled, they trust nothing will withhold them from laying all Hesperia wholly beneath their yoke, and holding the seas that wash it above and below. Accept and return our friendship. We can give brave hearts in war, high souls and men approved in deeds.'

Aeneas ended. The other ere now scanned in a long gaze the face and eyes and all the form of the speaker; then thus briefly returns:

'How gladly, bravest of the Teucrians, do I hail and own thee! how I recall thy father's words and the very tone and glance of great Anchises! For I remember how Priam son of Laomedon, when he sought Salamis on his way to the realm of his sister Hesione, went on to visit the cold borders of Arcadia. Then early youth clad my cheeks with bloom. I admired the Teucrian captains, admired their lord, the son of Laomedon; but Anchises moved high above them all. My heart burned with youthful passion to accost him and clasp hand in hand; I made my way to him, and led him eagerly to Pheneus' high town.

'Departing he gave me an adorned quiver and Lycian arrows, a scarf inwoven with gold, and a pair of golden bits that now my Pallas possesses. Therefore my hand is already joined in the alliance you seek, and soon as to-morrow's dawn rises again over earth, I will send you away rejoicing in mine aid, and supply you from my store. Meanwhile, since you are come hither in friendship, solemnise with us these yearly rites which we may not defer, and even now learn to be familiar at your comrades' board.'

The Death of Pallas

Aeneas and his Tuscan allies arrive on the battle scene just in time to give the necessary support to the almost exhausted Trojans; and now the fight rages more fiercely than ever, with deeds of great valour accomplished on both sides. Finally Evander's brave young son Pallas is killed by Turnus, who grabs his sword belt as spoils. When aware of the death of this promising young prince, Aeneas' heart is filled with grief, as he imagines the sorrow of Evander when he brings his son's body home for burial. Aeneas then and there registers a solemn vow to avenge Pallas' death by slaying Turnus, and immediately hastens forth to keep his word. It is foreshadowed in the extract from Book 10 below that Turnus will come to rue taking Pallas' sword belt, as from this point his destiny is sealed:

Meanwhile Turnus' gracious sister bids him take Lausus' room, and his fleet chariot parts the ranks. When he saw his comrades, 'It is time,' he cried, 'to stay from battle. I alone must assail Pallas; to me and none other Pallas is due; I would his father himself were here to see.' So speaks he, and his Rutulians draw back from a level space at his bidding. But then as they withdrew, he, wondering at the haughty command, stands in amaze at Turnus, his eyes scanning the vast frame, and his fierce glance perusing him from afar. And with these words he returns the words of the monarch: 'For me, my praise shall even now be in the lordly spoils I win, or in illustrious death: my father will bear calmly either lot: away with menaces.' He speaks, and advances into the level ring.

The Arcadians' blood gathers chill about their hearts. Turnus leaps from his chariot and prepares to close with him. And as a lion sees from some lofty outlook a bull stand far off on the plain revolving battle, and flies at him, even such to see is Turnus' coming. When Pallas deemed him within reach of a spear-throw, he advances, if so chance may assist the daring of his overmatched strength, and thus cries into the depth of sky: 'By my father's hospitality and the board whereto thou camest a wanderer, on thee I call, Alcides; be favourable to my high emprise; let Turnus even in death discern me stripping his blood-stained armour, and his swooning eyes endure the sight of his conqueror.'

Alcides heard him, and deep in his heart he stifled a heavy sigh, and let idle tears fall. Then with kindly words the father accosts his son: 'Each hath his own appointed day; short and irrecoverable is the span of life for all: but to spread renown by deeds is the task of valour. Under high Troy town many and many a god's son fell; nay, mine own child Sarpedon likewise perished. Turnus too his own fate summons, and his allotted period hath reached the goal.' So speaks he, and turns his eyes away from the Rutulian fields. But Pallas hurls his spear with all his strength, and pulls his sword flashing out of the hollow scabbard.

The flying spear lights where the armour rises high above the shoulder, and, forcing a way through the shield's rim, ceased not till it drew blood from mighty Turnus. At this Turnus long poises the spear-shaft with its sharp steel head, and hurls it on Pallas with these words: See thou if our weapon have not a keener point. He ended; but for all the shield's plating of iron and brass, for all the bull-hide that covers it round about, the quivering spear-head smashes it fair through and through, passes the guard of the corslet, and pierces the breast with a gaping hole. He tears the warm weapon from the wound; in vain; together and at once life-blood and sense follow it. He falls heavily on the ground, his armour clashes over him, and his bloodstained face sinks in death on the hostile soil. And Turnus standing over him . . .: 'Arcadians,' he cries, 'remember these my words, and bear them to Evander. I send him back his Pallas as was due. All the meed of the tomb, all the solace of sepulture, I give freely. Dearly must he pay his welcome to Aeneas.'

And with these words, planting his left foot on the dead, he tore away the broad heavy sword-belt engraven with a tale of crime, the array of grooms foully slain together on their bridal night, and the nuptial chambers dabbled with blood, which Clonus, son of Eurytus, had wrought richly in gold. Now Turnus exults in spoiling him of it, and rejoices at his prize. Ah spirit of man, ignorant of fate and the allotted future, or to keep bounds when elate with prosperity! – the day will come when Turnus shall desire to have bought Pallas' safety at a great ransom, and curse the spoils of this fatal day. But with many moans and tears Pallas' comrades lay him on his shield and bear him away amid their ranks. O grief and glory and grace of the father to whom thou shalt return! This one day sent thee first to war, this one day takes thee away, while yet thou leavest heaped high thy Rutulian dead.

And now no rumour of the dreadful loss, but a surer messenger flies to Aeneas, telling him his troops are on the thin edge of doom; it is time to succour the routed Teucrians. He mows down all that meets him, and hews a broad path through their columns with furious sword, as he seeks thee, O Turnus, in thy fresh pride of slaughter. Pallas, Evander, all flash before his eyes; the board whereto but then he had first come a wanderer, and the clasped hands. Here four of Sulmo's children, as many more of Ufens' nurture, are taken by him alive to slaughter in sacrifice to the shade below, and slake the flames of the pyre with captive blood.

Next he levelled his spear full on Magus from far. He stoops cunningly; the spear flies quivering over him; and, clasping his knees, he speaks thus beseechingly: 'By thy father's ghost, by Iülus thy growing hope, I entreat thee, save this life for a child and a parent. My house is stately; deep in it lies buried wealth of engraven silver; I have masses of wrought and unwrought gold. The victory of Troy does not turn on this, nor will a single life make so great a difference.' He ended; to him Aeneas thus returns answer: 'All the wealth of silver and gold thou tellest of, spare thou for thy children. Turnus hath broken off this thy trafficking in war, even then when Pallas fell. Thus judges the ghost of my father Anchises, thus Iülus.' So speaking, he grasps his helmet with his left hand, and, bending back his neck, drives his sword up to the hilt in the suppliant.

The Slaying of Turnus

As we come to the last book of the Aeneid, there have been losses on both sides. We know that Pallas has been slain by Turnus and Aeneas has vowed to avenge him. In his grief-stricken rage

Aeneas slays many warriors, among others Lausus and his aged father Mezentius, two allies of Latinus, who had specially distinguished themselves by their great bravery. In Book 12 Aeneas and Turnus finally meet on the battlefield and Turnus is defeated. With the death of Turnus the war comes to an end. A lasting peace is made with Latinus; and the brave Trojan hero, whose woes are now over, is united in marriage with Lavinia.

In concert with Latinus, Aeneas goes on to rule the Latins, and found a city, which he calls Lavinia in honour of his bride, and which becomes for a time the capital of Latium. Aeneas, as the gods had predicted, becomes the father of a son named Aeneas Silvia, who founds Alba Longa, where his descendants reign for many a year, and where one of his race, the Vestal Virgin Ilia, after marrying Mars, gives birth to Remus and Romulus, the founders of Rome. But let us return now to the climactic end of Book 12:

Meanwhile the King of Heaven's omnipotence accosts Juno as she gazes on the battle from a sunlit cloud. 'What yet shall be the end, O wife? what remains at the last? Heaven claims Aeneas as his country's god, thou thyself knowest and avowest to know, and fate lifts him to the stars. With what device or in what hope hangest thou chill in cloudland? Was it well that a deity should be sullied by a mortal's wound? or that the lost sword – for what without thee could Juturna avail? – should be restored to Turnus and swell the force of the vanquished? Forbear now, I pray, and bend to our entreaties; let not the pain thus devour thee in silence, and distress so often flood back on me from thy sweet lips. The end is come. Thou hast had power to hunt the Trojans over land or wave, to kindle accursed war, to put the house in mourning, and plunge the bridal in grief: further attempt I forbid thee.' Thus Jupiter began: thus the goddess, daughter of Saturn, returned with looks cast down:

'Even because this thy will, great Jupiter, is known to me for thine, have I left, though loth, Turnus alone on earth; nor else wouldst thou see mc now, alone on this skyey seat, enduring good and bad; but girt in flame I were standing by their very lines, and dragging the Teucrians into the deadly battle. I counselled Juturna, I confess it, to succour her hapless brother, and for his life's sake favoured a greater daring; yet not the arrow-shot, not the bending of the bow, I swear by the merciless well-head of the Stygian spring, the single ordained dread of the gods in heaven. And now I retire, and leave the battle in loathing.

This thing I beseech thee, that is bound by no fatal law, for Latium and for the majesty of thy kindred. When now they shall plight peace with prosperous marriages (be it so!), when now they shall join in laws and treaties, bid thou not the native Latins change their name of old, nor become Trojans and take the Teucrian name, or change their language, or alter their attire: let Latium be, let Alban kings endure through ages, let Italian valour be potent in the race of Rome. Troy is fallen; let her and her name lie where they fell.'

To her smilingly the designer of men and things:

'Jove's own sister thou art, and second seed of Saturn, such surge of wrath tosses within thy breast! But come, allay this madness so vainly stirred. I give thee thy will, and yield thee ungrudged victory. Ausonia shall keep her native speech and usage, and as her name is, it shall be. The Trojans shall sink mingling into their blood; I will add their sacred law and ritual, and make all Latins and of a single speech. Hence shall spring a race of tempered Ausonian blood, whom thou shalt see outdo men and gods in duty; nor shall any nation so observe thy worship.' To this Juno assented, and in gladness withdrew her purpose; meanwhile she quits her cloud, and retires out of the sky.

This done, the Father revolves inly another counsel, and prepares to separate Juturna from her brother's arms. Twin monsters there are, called the Dirae by their name, whom with infernal Megaera the dead of night bore at one single birth, and wreathed them in like serpent coils, and clothed them in windy wings. They appear at Jove's throne and in the courts of the grim king, and quicken the terrors of wretched men whensoever the lord of heaven deals sicknesses and dreadful death, or sends terror of war upon guilty cities. One of these Jupiter sent swiftly down from heaven's height, and bade her meet Juturna for a sign. She wings her way, and darts in a whirlwind to earth. Even as an arrow through a cloud, darting from the string when Parthian hath poisoned it with bitter gall, Parthian or Cydonian, and sped the immedicable shaft, leaps through the swift shadow whistling and unknown; so sprung and swept to earth the daughter of Night.

When she espies the Ilian ranks and Turnus' columns, suddenly shrinking to the shape of a small bird that often sits late by night on tombs or ruinous roofs, and vexes the darkness with her cry, in such change of likeness the monster shrilly passes and repasses before Turnus' face, and her wings beat restlessly on his shield. A strange numbing terror unnerves his limbs, his hair thrills up, and the accents falter on his tongue. But when his hapless sister knew afar the whistling wings of the Fury, Juturna unbinds and tears her tresses, with rent face and smitten bosom. 'How, O Turnus, can thine own sister help thee now? or what more is there if I break not under this? What art of mine can lengthen out thy day? can I contend with this ominous thing? Now, now I quit the field. Dismay not my terrors, disastrous birds; I know these beating wings, and the sound of death, nor do I miss high-hearted Jove's haughty ordinance. Is this his repayment for my maidenhood? what good is his gift of life for ever? why have I forfeited a mortal's lot? Now assuredly could I make all this pain cease, and go with my unhappy brother side by side into the dark. Alas mine immortality! will aught of mine be sweet to me without thee, my brother? Ah, how may Earth yawn deep enough for me, and plunge my godhead in the under world!'

So spoke she, and wrapping her head in her gray vesture, the goddess moaning sore sank in the river depth.

But Aeneas presses on, brandishing his vast tree-like spear, and fiercely speaks thus: 'What more delay is there now? or why, Turnus, dost thou yet shrink away? Not in speed of foot, in grim arms, hand to hand, must be the conflict. Transform thyself as thou wilt, and collect what strength of courage or skill is thine; pray that thou mayest wing thy flight to the stars on high, or that sheltering earth may shut thee in.' The other, shaking his head: 'Thy fierce words dismay me not, insolent! the gods dismay me, and Jupiter's enmity.'

And no more said, his eyes light on a vast stone, a stone ancient and vast that haply lay upon the plain, set for a landmark to divide contested fields: scarcely might twelve chosen men lift it on their shoulders, of such frame as now earth brings to birth: then the hero caught it up with trembling hand and whirled it at the foe, rising higher and quickening his speed. But he knows not his own self running nor going nor lifting his hands or moving the mighty stone; his knees totter, his blood freezes cold; the very stone he hurls, spinning through the empty void, neither wholly reached its distance nor carried its blow home. And as in sleep, when nightly rest weighs down our languorous eyes, we seem vainly to will to run eagerly on, and sink faint amidst our struggles; the tongue is powerless, the familiar strength fails the body, nor will words or utterance follow: so the disastrous goddess brings to naught all Turnus' valour as he presses on. His heart wavers in shifting emotion; he gazes on his Rutulians and on the city, and falters in terror, and shudders at the imminent spear; neither sees he whither he may escape nor how rush violently on the enemy, and nowhere his chariot or his sister at the reins.

As he wavers Aeneas poises the deadly weapon, and, marking his chance, hurls it in from afar with all his strength of body. Never with such a roar are stones hurled from some engine on ramparts, nor does the thunder burst in so loud a peal. Carrying grim death with it, the spear flies in fashion of some dark whirlwind, and opens the rim of the corslet and the utmost circles of the sevenfold shield. Right through the thigh it passes hurtling on; under the blow Turnus falls huge to earth with his leg doubled under him. The Rutulians start up with a groan, and all the hill echoes round about, and the width of high woodland returns their cry. Lifting up beseechingly his humbled eyes and suppliant hand: 'I have deserved it,' he says, 'nor do I ask for mercy; use thy fortune. If an unhappy parent's distress may at all touch thee, this I pray; even such a father was Anchises to thee; pity Daunus' old age, and restore to my kindred which thou wilt, me or my body bereft of day. Thou art conqueror, and Ausonia hath seen me stretch conquered hands. Lavinia is thine in marriage; press not thy hatred farther.'

Aeneas stood wrathful in arms, with rolling eyes, and lowered his hand; and now and now yet more the speech began to bend him to waver: when high on his shoulder appeared the sword-belt with the shining bosses that he knew, the luckless belt of the boy Pallas, whom Turnus had struck down with mastering wound, and wore on his shoulders the fatal ornament. The other, as his eyes drank in the plundered record of his fierce grief, kindles to fury, and cries terrible in anger: 'Mayest thou, thou clad in the spoils of my dearest, escape mine hands? Pallas it is, Pallas who now strikes the sacrifice, and exacts vengeance in thy guilty blood.' So saying, he fiercely plunges the steel full in his breast. But his limbs grow slack and chill, and the life with a moan flies indignantly into the dark

Yoshitsune and Benkei

YOSHITSUNE'S FATHER, YOSHITOMO, had been killed in a great battle with the Taira. At that time the Taira clan was all-powerful, and its cruel leader, Kiyomori, did all he could to destroy Yoshitomo's children. But the mother of these children, Tokiwa, fled into hiding, taking her little ones with her. With characteristic Japanese fortitude, she finally consented to become the wife of the hated Kiyomori. She did so because it was the only way to save the lives of her children. She was allowed to keep Yoshitsune with her, and she daily whispered to him: 'Remember thy father, Minamoto Yoshitomo! Grow strong and avenge his death, for he died at the hands of the Taira!'

When Yoshitsune was seven years of age he was sent to a monastery to be brought up as a monk. Though diligent in his studies, the young boy ever treasured in his heart the dauntless words of his brave, self-sacrificing mother. They stirred and quickened him to action. He used to go to a certain valley, where he would flourish his little wooden sword, and, singing fragments of war-songs, hit out at rocks and stones, desiring that he might one day become a great warrior, and right the wrongs so heavily heaped upon his family by the Taira clan.

One night, while thus engaged, he was startled by a great thunderstorm, and saw before him a mighty giant with a long red nose and enormous glaring eyes, bird-like claws, and feathered wings. Bravely standing his ground, Yoshitsune inquired who this giant might be, and was informed that he was King of the Tengu – that is, King of the elves of the mountains, sprightly little beings who were frequently engaged in all manner of fantastic tricks.

The King of the Tengu was very kindly disposed towards Yoshitsune. He explained that he admired his perseverance, and told him that he had appeared upon the scene with the meritorious intention of teaching him all that was to be learnt in the art of swordsmanship. The lessons progressed in a most satisfactory manner, and it was not long before Yoshitsune could vanquish as many as twenty small *tengu*, and this extreme agility stood Yoshitsune in very good stead, as we shall see later on in the story.

Now when Yoshitsune was fifteen years old he heard that there lived on Mount Hiei a very wild *bonze* (priest) by the name of Benkei. Benkei had for some time waylaid knights who happened to cross the Gojo Bridge of Kyoto. His idea was to obtain a thousand swords, and he was so brave, although such a rascal, that he had won from knights no less than nine hundred and ninety-nine swords by his lawless behaviour. When the news of these doings reached the ears of Yoshitsune he determined to put the teaching of the King of the Tengu to good use and slay this Benkei, and so put an end to one who had become a terror in the land.

One evening Yoshitsune started out, and, in order to establish the manner and bearing of absolute indifference, he played upon his flute till he came to the Gojo Bridge. Presently he saw coming towards him a gigantic man clad in black armour, who was none other than Benkei. When Benkei saw the youth he considered it to be beneath his dignity to attack what appeared to him to be a mere weakling, a dreamer who could play excellently, and no doubt write a pretty poem about the moon, which was then shining in the sky, but one who was in no way a warrior. This affront naturally angered Yoshitsune, and he suddenly kicked Benkei's halberd out of his hand.

Yoshitsune and Benkei Fight

Benkei gave a growl of rage, and cut about indiscriminately with his weapon. But the sprightliness of the *tengu* teaching favoured Yoshitsune. He jumped from side to side, from the front to the rear, and from the rear to the front again, mocking the giant with many a jest and many a peal of ringing laughter. Round and round went Benkei's weapon, always striking either the air or the ground, and ever missing its adversary.

At last Benkei grew weary, and once again Yoshitsune knocked the halberd out of the giant's hand. In trying to regain his weapon Yoshitsune tripped him up, so that he stumbled upon his hands and knees, and the hero, with a cry of triumph, mounted upon the now four-legged Benkei. The giant was utterly amazed at his defeat, and when he was told that the victor was none other than the son of Lord Yoshitomo he not only took his defeat in a manly fashion, but begged that he might henceforth become a retainer of the young conqueror.

From this time we find the names of Yoshitsune and Benkei linked together, and in all the stories of warriors, whether in Japan or elsewhere, never was there a more valiant and harmonious union of strength and friendship. We hear of them winning numerous victories over the Taira, finally driving them to the sea, where they perished at Dan-no-ura.

We get one more glimpse of Dan-no-ura from a legendary point of view. Yoshitsune and his faithful henchman arranged to cross in a ship from the province of Settsu to Saikoku. When they reached Dan-no-ura a great storm arose. Mysterious noises came from the towering waves, a far-away echo of the din of battle, of the rushing of ships and the whirling of arrows, of the footfall of a thousand men. Louder and louder the noise grew, and from the lashing crests of the waves there arose a ghostly company of the Taira clan. Their armour was torn and blood-stained, and they thrust out their vaporous arms and tried to stop the boat in which Yoshitsune and Benkei sailed. It was a ghostly reminiscence of the battle of Dan-no-ura, when the Taira had suffered a terrible and permanent defeat. Yoshitsune, when he saw this great phantom host, cried out for revenge even upon the ghosts of the Taira dead; but Benkei, always shrewd and circumspect, bade his master lay aside the sword, and took out a rosary and recited a number of Buddhist prayers. Peace came to the great company of ghosts, the wailing ceased, and gradually they faded into the sea which now became calm.

Legend tells us that fishermen still see from time to time ghostly armies come out of the sea and wail and shake their long arms. They explain that the crabs with dorsal markings are the wraiths of the Taira warriors. Later on we shall introduce another legend relating to these unfortunate ghosts, who seem never to tire of haunting the scene of their defeat.

Yorimasa

A LONG TIME AGO a certain Emperor became seriously ill. He was unable to sleep at night owing to a most horrible and unaccountable noise he heard proceeding from the roof of the palace, called the Purple Hall of the North Star. A number of his courtiers decided to lie in wait for this strange nocturnal visitor. As soon as the sun set they noticed that a dark cloud crept from the eastern horizon, and alighted on the roof of the august palace. Those who waited in the imperial bed-chamber heard extraordinary scratching sounds, as if what had at first appeared to be a cloud had suddenly changed into a beast with gigantic and powerful claws.

Night after night this terrible visitant came, and night after night the Emperor grew worse. He at last became so ill that it was obvious to all those in attendance upon him that unless something could be done to destroy this monster the Emperor would certainly die.

At last it was decided that Yorimasa was the one knight in the kingdom valiant enough to relieve his Majesty of these terrible hauntings. Yorimasa accordingly made elaborate preparations for the fray. He took his best bow and steel-headed arrows, donned his armour, over which he wore a hunting-dress, and a ceremonial cap instead of his usual helmet.

At sunset he lay in concealment outside the palace. While he thus waited thunder crashed overhead, lightning blazed in the sky, and the wind shrieked like a pack of wild demons. But Yorimasa was a brave man, and the fury of the elements in no way daunted him. When midnight came he saw a black cloud rush through the sky and rest upon the roof of the palace. At the north-east corner it stopped. Once more the lightning flashed in the sky, and this time he saw the gleaming eyes of a large animal. Noting the exact position of this strange monster, he pulled at his bow till it became as round as the full moon. In another moment his steel-headed arrow hit its mark. There was an awful roar of anger, and then a heavy thud as the huge monster rolled from the palace roof to the ground.

Yorimasa and his retainer ran forward and despatched the fearful creature they saw before them. This evil monster of the night was as large as a horse. It had the head of an ape, and the body and claws were like those of a tiger, with a serpent's tail, wings of a bird, and the scales of a dragon.

It was no wonder that the Emperor gave orders that the skin of this monster should be kept for all time as a curiosity in the Imperial treasure-house. From the very moment the creature died the Emperor's health rapidly improved, and Yorimasa was rewarded for his services by being presented with a sword called Shishi-wo, which means 'the King of Lions.' He was also promoted at Court, and finally married the Lady Ayame, the most beautiful of ladies-in-waiting at the Imperial Court.

The Adventures of Prince Yamato Take

KING KEIKO BADE HIS YOUNGEST SON, Prince Yamato, go forth and slay a number of brigands. Before his departure the Prince prayed at the shrines of Ise, and begged that Amaterasu, the Sun Goddess, would bless his enterprise. Prince Yamato's aunt was high-priestess of one of the Ise temples, and he told her about the task his father had entrusted to him. This good lady was much pleased to hear the news, and presented her nephew with a rich silk robe, saying that it would bring him luck, and perhaps be of service to him later on.

When Prince Yamato had returned to the palace and taken leave of his father, he left the court accompanied by his wife, the Princess Ototachibana, and a number of staunch followers, and proceeded to the Southern Island of Kiushiu, which was infested by brigands. The country was so rough and impassable that Prince Yamato saw at once that he must devise some cunning scheme by which he might take the enemy unawares.

Having come to this conclusion, he bade the Princess Ototachibana bring him the rich silk robe his aunt had given him. This he put on under the direction, no doubt, of his wife. He let down his hair, stuck a comb in it, and adorned himself with jewels. When he looked into a mirror he saw that the disguise was perfect, and that he made quite a handsome woman.

Thus gorgeously apparelled, he entered the enemy's tent, where Kumaso and Takeru were sitting. It happened that they were discussing the King's son and his efforts to exterminate their band. When they chanced to look up they saw a fair woman coming towards them.

Kumaso was so delighted that he beckoned to the disguised Prince and bade him serve wine as quickly as possible. Yamato was only too delighted to do so. He affected feminine shyness. He walked with very minute steps, and glanced out of the corner of his eyes with all the timidity of a bashful maiden.

Kumaso drank far more wine than was good for him. He still went on drinking just to have the pleasure of seeing this lovely creature pouring it out for him.

When Kumaso became drunk Prince Yamato flung down the wine-jar, whipped out his dagger, and stabbed him to death.

Takeru, when he saw what had happened to his brother, attempted to escape, but Prince Yamato leapt upon him. Once more his dagger gleamed in the air, and Takeru fell to the earth.

'Stay your hand a moment,' gasped the dying brigand. 'I would fain know who you are and whence you have come. Hitherto I thought that my brother and I were the strongest men in the kingdom. I am indeed mistaken.'

'I am Yamato,' said the Prince, 'and son of the King who bade me kill such rebels as you!'

'Permit me to give you a new name,' said the brigand politely. 'From henceforth you shall be called Yamato Take, because you are the bravest man in the land.'

Having thus spoken Takeru fell back dead.

The Wooden Sword

When the Prince was on his way to the capital he encountered another outlaw named Idzumo Takeru. Again resorting to strategy, he professed to be extremely friendly with this fellow. He cut a sword of wood and rammed it tightly into the sheath of his own steel weapon. He wore this whenever he expected to meet Takeru.

On one occasion Prince Yamato invited Takeru to swim with him in the river Hinokawa. While the brigand was swimming down-stream the Prince secretly landed, and, going to Takeru's clothes, lying on the bank, he managed to change swords, putting his wooden one in place of the keen steel sword of Takeru.

When Takeru came out of the water and put on his clothes the Prince asked him to show his skill with the sword. 'We will prove,' said he, 'which is the better swordsman of the two.'

Nothing loath, Takeru tried to unsheath his sword. It stuck fast, and as it happened to be of wood it was, of course, useless in any case. While the brigand was thus struggling Yamato cut off his head. Once again cunning had served him, and when he had returned to the palace he was feasted, and received many costly gifts from the King his father.

The 'Grass-Cleaving-Sword'

Prince Yamato did not long remain idle in the palace, for his father commanded him to go forth and quell an Ainu rising in the eastern provinces.

When the Prince was ready to depart the King gave him a spear made from a holly-tree called the 'Eight-Arms-Length-Spear'. With this precious gift Prince Yamato visited the temples of Ise. His aunt, the high-priestess, again greeted him. She listened with interest to all her nephew told her, and was especially delighted to know how well the robe she had given him had served in his adventures.

When she had listened to his story she went into the temple and brought forth a sword and a bag containing flints. These she gave to Yamato as a parting gift.

The sword was the sword of Murakumo, belonging to the insignia of the Imperial House of Japan. The Prince could not have received a more auspicious gift. This sword, it will be remembered, once belonged to the Gods, and was discovered by Susanoo.

After a long march Prince Yamato and his men found themselves in the province of Suruga. The governor hospitably received him, and by way of entertainment organised a deer-hunt. Our hero for once in a way was utterly deceived, and joined the hunt without the least misgiving.

The Prince was taken to a great and wild plain covered with high grass. While he was engaged in hunting down the deer he suddenly became aware of fire. In another moment he saw flames and clouds of smoke shooting up in every direction. He was surrounded by fire, from which there was, apparently, no escape. Too late the guileless warrior realised that he had fallen into a trap, and a very warm trap too!

Our hero opened the bag his aunt had given him, set fire to the grass near him, and with the sword of Murakumo he cut down the tall green blades on either side as quickly as possible. No sooner had he done so than the wind suddenly changed and blew the flames away from him, so that eventually the Prince made good his escape without the slightest burn of any kind. And thus it was that the sword of Murakumo came to be known as the 'Grass-Cleaving-Sword'.

The Sacrifice of Ototachibana

In all these adventures the Prince had been followed by his faithful wife, the Princess Ototachibana. Sad to say, our hero, so praiseworthy in battle, was not nearly so estimable in his love. He looked down on his wife and treated her with indifference. She, poor loyal soul, had lost her beauty in serving her lord. Her skin was burnt with the sun, and her garments were soiled and torn. Yet she never complained, and though her face became sad she made a brave effort to maintain her usual sweetness of manner.

Now Prince Yamato happened to meet the fascinating Princess Miyadzu. Her robes were charming, her skin delicate as cherry-blossom. It was not long before he fell desperately in love with her. When the time came for him to depart he swore that he would return again and make the beautiful Princess Miyadzu his wife. He had scarcely made this promise when he looked up and saw Ototachibana, and on her face was a look of intense sadness. But Prince Yamato hardened his heart, and rode away, secretly determined to keep his promise.

When Prince Yamato, his wife and men, reached the sea-shore of Idzu, his followers desired to secure a number of boats in order that they might cross the Straits of Kadzusa.

The Prince cried haughtily: 'Bah! this is only a brook! Why so many boats? I could jump across it!'

When they had all embarked and started on their journey a great storm arose. The waves turned into water-mountains, the wind shrieked, the lightning blazed in the dark clouds, and the thunder roared. It seemed that the boat that carried the Prince and his wife must needs sink, for this storm was the work of Rin-Jin, King of the Sea, who was angry with the proud and foolish words of Prince Yamato.

When the crew had taken down the sails in the hope of steadying the vessel the storm grew worse instead of better. At last Ototachibana arose, and, forgiving all the sorrow her lord had caused her, she resolved to sacrifice her life in order to save her much-loved husband.

Thus spoke the loyal Ototachibana: 'Oh, Rin-Jin, the Prince, my husband, has angered you with his boasting. I, Ototachibana, give you my poor life in the place of Yamato Take. I now cast myself into your great surging kingdom, and do you in return bring my lord safely to the shore.'

Having uttered these words, Ototachibana leapt into the seething waves, and in a moment they dragged that brave woman out of sight. No sooner had this sacrifice been made than the storm abated and the sun shone forth in a cloudless sky.

Yamato Take safely reached his destination, and succeeded in quelling the Ainu rising.

Our hero had certainly erred in his treatment of his faithful wife. Too late he learnt to appreciate her goodness; but let it be said to his credit that she remained a loving memory till his death, while the Princess Miyadzu was entirely forgotten.

The Slaying of the Serpent

Now that Yamato Take had carried out his father's instructions, he passed through the province of Owari until he came to the province of Omi.

The province of Omi was afflicted with a great trouble. Many were in mourning, and many wept and cried aloud in their sorrow. The Prince, on making inquiries, was informed that a great serpent every day came down from the mountains and entered the villages, making a meal of many of the unfortunate inhabitants.

Prince Yamato at once started to climb up Mount Ibaki, where the great serpent was said to live. About half-way up he encountered the awful creature. The Prince was so strong that he killed the serpent by twisting his bare arms about it. He had no sooner done so than sudden darkness came over the land, and rain fell heavily. However, eventually the weather improved, and our hero was able to climb down the mountain.

When he reached home he found that his feet burned with a strange pain, and, moreover, that he felt very ill. He realised that the serpent had stung him, and, as he was too ill to move, he was carried to a famous mineral spring. Here he finally regained his accustomed health and strength, and for these blessings gave thanks to Amaterasu, the Sun Goddess.

The Adventures of Momotaro

ONE DAY, while an old woman stood by a stream washing her clothes, she chanced to see an enormous peach floating on the water. It was quite the largest she had ever seen, and as this old woman and her husband were extremely poor she immediately thought what an excellent meal this extraordinary peach would make. As she could find no stick with which to draw the fruit to the bank, she suddenly remembered the following verse:

'Distant water is bitter,
The near water is sweet;
Pass by the distant water
And come into the sweet.'

This little song had the desired effect. The peach came nearer and nearer till it stopped at the old woman's feet. She stooped down and picked it up. So delighted was she with her discovery that she could not stay to do any more washing, but hurried home as quickly as possible.

When her husband arrived in the evening, with a bundle of grass upon his back, the old woman excitedly took the peach out of a cupboard and showed it to him.

The old man, who was tired and hungry, was equally delighted at the thought of so delicious a meal. He speedily brought a knife and was about to cut the fruit open, when it suddenly opened of its own accord, and the prettiest child imaginable tumbled out with a merry laugh.

'Don't be afraid,' said the little fellow. 'The Gods have heard how much you desired a child, and have sent me to be a solace and a comfort in your old age.'

The old couple were so overcome with joy that they scarcely knew what to do with themselves. Each in turn nursed the child, caressed him, and murmured many sweet and affectionate words. They called him Momotaro, or 'Son of a Peach'.

When Momotaro was fifteen years old he was a lad far taller and stronger than boys of his own age. The making of a great hero stirred in his veins, and it was a knightly heroism that desired to right the wrong.

One day Momotaro came to his foster-father and asked him if he would allow him to take a long journey to a certain island in the North-Eastern Sea where dwelt a number of devils, who had captured a great company of innocent people, many of whom they ate. Their wickedness was beyond description, and Momotaro desired to kill them, rescue the unfortunate captives, and bring back the plunder of the island that he might share it with his foster-parents.

The old man was not a little surprised to hear this daring scheme. He knew that Momotaro was no common child. He had been sent from heaven, and he believed that all the devils in the world could not harm him. So at length the old man gave his consent, saying: 'Go, Momotaro, slay the devils and bring peace to the land.'

When the old woman had given Momotaro a number of rice-cakes the youth bade his foster-parents farewell, and started out upon his journey.

The Triumph of Momotaro

While Momotaro was resting under a hedge eating one of the rice-cakes, a great dog came up to him, growled, and showed his teeth. The dog, moreover, could speak, and threateningly begged that Momotaro would give him a cake. 'Either you give me a cake,' said he, 'or I will kill you!'

When, however, the dog heard that the famous Momotaro stood before him, his tail dropped between his legs and he bowed with his head to the ground, requesting that he might follow 'Son of a Peach', and render to him all the service that lay in his power.

Momotaro readily accepted the offer, and after throwing the dog half a cake they proceeded on their way.

They had not gone far when they encountered a monkey, who also begged to be admitted to Momotaro's service. This was granted, but it was some time before the dog and the monkey ceased snapping at each other and became good friends.

Proceeding upon their journey, they came across a pheasant. Now the innate jealousy of the dog was again awakened, and he ran forward and tried to kill the bright-plumed creature. Momotaro separated the combatants, and in the end the pheasant was also admitted to the little band, walking decorously in the rear.

At length Momotaro and his followers reached the shore of the North-Eastern Sea. Here our hero discovered a boat, and after a good deal of timidity on the part of the dog, monkey, and pheasant, they all got aboard, and soon the little vessel was spinning away over the blue sea.

After many days upon the ocean they sighted an island. Momotaro bade the bird fly off, a winged herald to announce his coming, and bid the devils surrender.

The pheasant flew over the sea and alighted on the roof of a great castle and shouted his stirring message, adding that the devils, as a sign of submission, should break their horns.

The devils only laughed and shook their horns and shaggy red hair. Then they brought forth iron bars and hurled them furiously at the bird. The pheasant cleverly evaded the missiles, and flew at the heads of many devils.

In the meantime Momotaro had landed with his two companions. He had no sooner done so than he saw two beautiful damsels weeping by a stream, as they wrung out blood-soaked garments.

'Oh!' said they pitifully, 'we are daughters of *daimyōs*, and are now the captives of the Demon King of this dreadful island. Soon he will kill us, and alas! there is no one to come to our aid.' Having made these remarks the women wept anew.

'Ladies,' said Momotaro, 'I have come for the purpose of slaying your wicked enemies. Show me a way into yonder castle.'

So Momotaro, the dog, and the monkey entered through a small door in the castle. Once inside this fortification they fought tenaciously. Many of the devils were so frightened that they fell off the parapets and were dashed to pieces, while others were speedily killed by Momotaro and his companions. All were destroyed except the Demon King himself, and he wisely resolved to surrender, and begged that his life might be spared.

'No,' said Momotaro fiercely. 'I will not spare your wicked life. You have tortured many innocent people and robbed the country for many years.'

Having said these words he gave the Demon King into the monkey's keeping, and then proceeded through all the rooms of the castle, and set free the numerous prisoners he found there. He also gathered together much treasure.

The return journey was a very joyous affair indeed. The dog and the pheasant carried the treasure between them, while Momotaro led the Demon King.

Momotaro restored the two daughters or *daimyōs* to their homes, and many others who had been made captives in the island. The whole country rejoiced in his victory, but no one more than Momotaro's foster-parents, who ended their days in peace and plenty, thanks to the great treasure of the devils which Momotaro bestowed upon them.

My Lord Bag of Rice

ONE DAY THE GREAT HIDESATO came to a bridge that spanned the beautiful Lake Biwa. He was about to cross it when he noticed a great serpent-dragon fast asleep obstructing his progress. Hidesato, without a moment's hesitation, climbed over the monster and proceeded on his way.

He had not gone far when he heard someone calling to him. He looked back and saw that in the place of the dragon a man stood bowing to him with much ceremony. He was a strange-looking fellow with a dragon-shaped crown resting upon his red hair.

'I am the Dragon King of Lake Biwa,' explained the red-haired man. 'A moment ago I took the form of a horrible monster in the hope of finding a mortal who would not be afraid of me. You, my lord, showed no fear, and I rejoice exceedingly. A great centipede comes down from yonder mountain, enters my palace, and destroys my children and grandchildren. One by one they have become food for this dread creature, and I fear soon that unless something can be done to slay this centipede I myself shall become a victim. I have waited long for a brave mortal. All men who have hitherto seen me in my dragon-shape have run away. You are a brave man, and I beg that you will kill my bitter enemy.'

Hidesato, who always welcomed an adventure, the more so when it was a perilous one, readily consented to see what he could do for the Dragon King.

When Hidesato reached the Dragon King's palace he found it to be a very magnificent building indeed, scarcely less beautiful than the Sea King's palace itself. He was feasted with crystallised lotus leaves and flowers, and ate the delicacies spread before him with choice ebony chopsticks. While he feasted ten little goldfish danced, and just behind the goldfish ten carp made sweet music on the *koto* and *samisen*. Hidesato was just thinking how excellently he had been entertained, and how particularly good was the wine, when they all heard an awful noise like a dozen thunderclaps roaring together.

Hidesato and the Dragon King hastily rose and ran to the balcony. They saw that Mount Mikami was scarcely recognisable, for it was covered from top to bottom with the great coils of the centipede. In its head glowed two balls of fire, and its hundred feet were like a long winding chain of lanterns.

Hidesato fitted an arrow to his bowstring and pulled it back with all his might. The arrow sped forth into the night and struck the centipede in the middle of the head, but glanced off immediately without inflicting any wound. Again Hidesato sent an arrow whirling into the air, and again it struck the monster and fell harmlessly to the ground. Hidesato had only one arrow left. Suddenly remembering the magical effect of human saliva, he put the remaining arrow-head into his mouth for a moment, and then hastily adjusted it to his bow and took careful aim.

The last arrow struck its mark and pierced the centipede's brain. The creature stopped moving; the light in its eyes and legs darkened and then went out, and Lake Biwa, with its palace beneath, was shrouded in awful darkness. Thunder rolled, lightning flashed, and it seemed for the moment that the Dragon King's palace would topple to the ground.

The next day, however, all sign of storm had vanished. The sky was clear. The sun shone brightly. In the sparkling blue lake lay the body of the great centipede.

The Dragon King and those about him were overjoyed when they knew that their dread enemy had been destroyed. Hidesato was again feasted, even more royally than before. When he finally departed he did so with a retinue of fishes suddenly converted into men. The Dragon King bestowed upon our hero five precious gifts – two bells, a bag of rice, a roll of silk, and a cooking-pot.

The Dragon King accompanied Hidesato as far as the bridge, and then he reluctantly allowed the hero and the procession of servants carrying the presents to proceed on their way.

When Hidesato reached his home the Dragon King's servants put down the presents and suddenly disappeared.

The presents were no ordinary gifts. The rice-bag was inexhaustible, there was no end to the roll of silk, and the cooking-pot would cook without fire of any kind. Only the bells were without magical properties, and these were presented to a temple in the vicinity. Hidesato grew rich, and his fame spread far and wide. People now no longer called him Hidesato, but Tawara Toda, or 'My Lord Bag of Rice'.

Kintaro, the Golden Boy

SAKATA KURANDO was an officer of the Emperor's bodyguard, and though he was a brave man, well versed in the art of war, he had a gentle disposition, and during his military career chanced to love a beautiful lady named Yaegiri. Kurando eventually fell into disgrace, and was forced to leave the Court and to become a travelling tobacco merchant. Yaegiri, who was much distressed by her lover's flight, succeeded in escaping from her home, and wandered up and down the country in the hope of meeting Kurando. At length she found him, but the unfortunate man, who, no doubt, felt deeply his disgrace and his humble mode of living, put an end to his humiliation by taking his miserable life.

Animal Companions

When Yaegiri had buried her lover she went to the Ashigara Mountain, where she gave birth to a child, called Kintaro, or the Golden Boy. Now Kintaro was remarkable for his extreme strength. When only a few years old his mother gave him an axe, with which he felled trees as quickly and easily as an experienced woodcutter. Ashigara Mountain was a lonely and desolate spot, and as there were no children with whom Kintaro could play, he made companions of the bear, deer, hare, and monkey, and in a very short time was able to speak their strange language.

One day, when Kintaro was sitting on the mountain, with his favourites about him, he sought to amuse himself by getting his companions to join in a friendly wrestling match. A kindly old bear was delighted with the proposal, and at once set to work to dig up the earth and arrange it in the form of a small dais. When this had been made a hare and a monkey wrestled together, while a deer stood by to give encouragement and to see that the sport was conducted fairly. Both animals proved themselves to be equally strong, and Kintaro tactfully rewarded them with tempting rice-cakes.

After spending a pleasant afternoon in this way, Kintaro proceeded to return home, followed by his devoted friends. At length they came to a river, and the animals were wondering how they should cross such a wide stretch of water, when Kintaro put his strong arms round a tree which was growing on the bank, and pulled it across the river so that it formed a bridge. Now it happened that the famous hero, Yorimitsu, and his retainers witnessed this extraordinary feat of strength, and said to Watanabe Tsuna: 'This child is truly remarkable. Go and find out where he lives and all about him.'

A Famous Warrior

So Watanabe Tsuna followed Kintaro and entered the house where he lived with his mother. 'My master,' said he, 'Lord Yorimitsu, bids me find out who your wonderful son is.' When Yaegiri had narrated the story of her life and informed her visitor that her little one was the son of Sakata Kurando, the retainer departed and told Yorimitsu all he had heard.

Yorimitsu was so pleased with what Watanabe Tsuna told him that he went himself to Yaegiri, and said: 'If you will give me your child I will make him my retainer.' The woman gladly consented, and the Golden Boy went away with the great hero, who named him Sakata Kintoki. He eventually became a famous warrior, and the stories of his wonderful deeds are recited to this day. Children regard him as their favourite hero, and little boys, who would fain emulate the strength and bravery of Sakata Kintoki, carry his portrait in their bosoms.

The Wonderful Adventures of Funakoshi Jiuyemon

IN THE OLDEN TIME, in the island of Shikoku there lived one Funakoshi Jiuyemon, a brave Samurai and accomplished man, who was in great favour with the prince, his master. One day, at a drinking-bout, a quarrel sprung up between him and a brother-officer, which resulted in a duel upon the spot, in which Jiuyemon killed his adversary. When Jiuyemon awoke to a sense of what he had done, he was struck with remorse, and he thought to disembowel himself; but, receiving a private summons from his lord, he went to the castle, and the prince said to him:

'So it seems that you have been getting drunk and quarrelling, and that you have killed one of your friends; and now I suppose you will have determined to perform *hara-kiri*. It is a great pity, and in the face of the laws I can do nothing for you openly. Still, if you will escape and fly from this part of the country for a while, in two years' time the affair will have blown over, and I will allow you to return.'

And with these words the prince presented him with a fine sword, made by Sukesada, and a hundred ounces of silver, and, having bade him farewell, entered his private apartments; and Jiuyemon, prostrating himself, wept tears of gratitude; then, taking the sword and the money, he went home and prepared to fly from the province, and secretly took leave of his relations, each of whom made him some parting present. These gifts, together with his own money, and what he had received from the prince, made up a sum of two hundred and fifty ounces of silver, with which and his Sukesada sword he escaped under cover of darkness, and went to a sea-port called Marugame, in the province of Sanuki, where he proposed to wait for an opportunity of setting sail for Osaka. As ill luck would have it, the wind being contrary, he had to remain three days idle; but at last the wind changed; so he went down to the beach, thinking that he should certainly find a junk about to sail; and as he was looking about him, a sailor came up, and said:

'If your honour is minded to take a trip to Osaka, my ship is bound thither, and I should be glad to take you with me as passenger.'

'That's exactly what I wanted. I will gladly take a passage,' replied Jiuyemon, who was delighted at the chance.

'Well, then, we must set sail at once, so please come on board without delay.'

So Jiuyemon went with him and embarked; and as they left the harbour and struck into the open sea, the moon was just rising above the eastern hills, illumining the dark night like a noonday sun; and Jiuyemon, taking his place in the bows of the ship, stood wrapt in contemplation of the beauty of the scene.

Now it happened that the captain of the ship, whose name was Akagoshi Kuroyemon, was a fierce pirate who, attracted by Jiuyemon's well-to-do appearance, had determined to decoy him on board, that he might murder and rob him; and while Jiuyemon was looking at the moon, the pirate and his companions were collected in the stern of the ship, taking counsel together in whispers as to how they might slay him. He, on the other hand, having for some time past fancied their conduct somewhat strange, bethought him that it was not prudent to lay aside his sword, so he went towards the place where he had been sitting, and had left his weapon lying, to fetch it, when he was stopped by three of the pirates, who blocked up the gangway, saying:

'Stop, Sir Samurai! Unluckily for you, this ship in which you have taken a passage belongs to the pirate Akagoshi Kuroyemon. Come, sir! whatever money you may chance to have about you is our prize.'

When Jiuyemon heard this he was greatly startled at first, but soon recovered himself, and being an expert wrestler, kicked over two of the pirates, and made for his sword; but in the meanwhile Shichirohei, the younger brother of the pirate captain, had drawn the sword, and brought it towards him, saying:

'If you want your sword, here it is!' and with that he cut at him; but Jiuyemon avoided the blow, and closing with the ruffian, got back his sword. Ten of the pirates then attacked him with spear and sword; but he, putting his back against the bows of the ship, showed such good fight that he killed three of his assailants, and the others stood off, not daring to approach him. Then the pirate captain, Akagoshi Kuroyemon, who had been watching the fighting from the stern, seeing that his men stood no chance against Jiuyemon's dexterity, and that he was only losing them to no purpose, thought to shoot him with a matchlock. Even Jiuyemon, brave as he was, lost heart when he saw the captain's gun pointed at him, and tried to jump into the sea; but one of the pirates made a dash at him with a boat-hook, and caught him by the sleeve; then Jiuyemon, in despair, took the fine Sukesada sword which he had received from his prince, and throwing it at his captor, pierced him through the breast so that he fell dead, and himself plunging into the sea swam for his life. The pirate captain shot at him and missed him, and the rest of the crew made every endeavour to seize him with their boat-hooks, that they might avenge the death of their mates; but it was all in vain, and Jiuyemon, having shaken off his clothes that he might swim the better, made good his escape. So the pirates threw the bodies of their dead comrades into the sea, and the captain was partly consoled for their loss by the possession of the Sukesada sword with which one of them had been transfixed.

As soon as Jiuyemon jumped over the ship's side, being a good swimmer, he took a long dive, which carried him well out of danger, and struck out vigorously; and although he was tired and distressed by his exertions, he braced himself up to greater energy, and faced the waves boldly. At last, in the far distance, to his great joy, he spied a light, for which he made, and found that it was a ship carrying lanterns marked with the badge of the governor of Osaka; so he hailed her, saying:

'I have fallen into great trouble among pirates: pray rescue me.'

'Who and what are you?' shouted an officer, some forty years of age.

'My name is Funakoshi Jiuyemon, and I have unwittingly fallen in with pirates this night. I have escaped so far: I pray you save me, lest I die.'

'Hold on to this, and come up,' replied the other, holding out the butt end of a spear to him, which he caught hold of and clambered up the ship's side. When the officer saw before him a handsome gentleman, naked all but his loincloth, and with his hair all in disorder, he called to his servants to bring some of his own clothes, and, having dressed him in them, said:

'What clan do you belong to, sir?'

'Sir, I am a Ronin, and was on my way to Osaka; but the sailors of the ship on which I had embarked were pirates;' and so he told the whole story of the fight and of his escape.

'Well done, sir!' replied the other, astonished at his prowess. 'My name is Kajiki Tozayemon, at your service. I am an officer attached to the governor of Osaka. Pray, have you any friends in that city?'

'No, sir, I have no friends there; but as in two years I shall be able to return to my own country, and re-enter my lord's service, I thought during that time to engage in trade and live as a common wardsman.'

'Indeed, that's a poor prospect! However, if you will allow me, I will do all that is in my power to assist you. Pray excuse the liberty I am taking in making such a proposal.'

Jiuyemon warmly thanked Kajiki Tozayemon for his kindness; and so they reached Osaka without further adventures.

Jiuyemon, who had secreted in his girdle the two hundred and fifty ounces which he had brought with him from home, bought a small house, and started in trade as a vendor of perfumes, tooth-powder, combs, and other toilet articles; and Kajiki Tozayemon, who treated him with great kindness, and rendered him many services, prompted him, as he was a single man, to take to himself a wife. Acting upon this advice, he married a singing-girl, called O Hiyaku.

Now this O Hiyaku, although at first she seemed very affectionately disposed towards Jiuyemon, had been, during the time that she was a singer, a woman of bad and profligate character; and at this time there was in Osaka a certain wrestler, named Takasegawa Kurobei, a very handsome man, with whom O Hiyaku fell desperately in love; so that at last, being by nature a passionate woman, she became unfaithful to Jiuyemon. The latter, little suspecting that anything was amiss, was in the habit of spending his evenings at the house of his patron Kajiki Tozayemon, whose son, a youth of eighteen, named Tonoshin, conceived a great friendship for Jiuyemon, and used constantly to invite him to play a game at checkers; and it was on these occasions that O Hiyaku, profiting by her husband's absence, used to arrange her meetings with the wrestler Takasegawa.

One evening, when Jiuyemon, as was his wont, had gone out to play at checkers with Kajiki Tonoshin, O Hiyaku took advantage of the occasion to go and fetch the wrestler, and invite him to a little feast; and as they were enjoying themselves over their wine, O Hiyaku said to him:

'Ah! Master Takasegawa, how wonderfully chance favours us! and how pleasant these stolen interviews are! How much nicer still it would be if we could only be married. But, as long as Jiuyemon is in the way, it is impossible; and that is my one cause of distress.'

'It's no use being in such a hurry. If you only have patience, we shall be able to marry, sure enough. What you have got to look out for now is, that Jiuyemon does not find out what we are about. I suppose there is no chance of his coming home tonight, is there?'

'Oh dear, no! You need not be afraid. He is gone to Kajiki's house to play checkers; so he is sure to spend the night there.'

And so the guilty couple went on gossiping, with their minds at ease, until at last they dropped off asleep.

In the meanwhile Jiuyemon, in the middle of his game at checkers, was seized with a sudden pain in his stomach, and said to Kajiki Tonoshin, 'Young sir, I feel an unaccountable pain in my stomach. I think I had better go home, before it gets worse.'

'That is a bad job. Wait a little, and I will give you some physic; but, at any rate, you had better spend the night here.'

'Many thanks for your kindness,' replied Jiuyemon; 'but I had rather go home.'

So he took his leave, and went off to his own house, bearing the pain as best he might. When he arrived in front of his own door, he tried to open it; but the lock was fastened, and he could not get in, so he rapped violently at the shutters to try and awaken his wife. When O Hiyaku heard the noise, she woke with a start, and roused the wrestler, saying to him in a whisper:

'Get up! get up! Jiuyemon has come back. You must hide as fast as possible.'

'Oh dear! oh dear!' said the wrestler, in a great fright; 'here's a pretty mess! Where on earth shall I hide myself?' and he stumbled about in every direction looking for a hiding-place, but found none.

Jiuyemon, seeing that his wife did not come to open the door, got impatient at last, and forced it open by unfixing the sliding shutter and, entering the house, found himself face to face with his wife and her lover, who were both in such confusion that they did not know what to do. Jiuyemon, however, took no notice of them, but lit his pipe and sat smoking and watching them in silence. At last the wrestler, Takasegawa, broke the silence by saying:

'I thought, sir, that I should be sure to have the pleasure of finding you at home this evening, so I came out to call upon you. When I got here, the Lady O Hiyaku was so kind as to offer me some wine; and I drank a little more than was good for me, so that it got into my head, and I fell asleep. I must really apologize for having taken such a liberty in your absence; but, indeed, although appearances are against us, there has been nothing wrong.'

'Certainly,' said O Hiyaku, coming to her lover's support, 'Master Takasegawa is not at all to blame. It was I who invited him to drink wine; so I hope you will excuse him.'

Jiuyemon sat pondering the matter over in his mind for a moment, and then said to the wrestler, 'You say that you are innocent; but, of course, that is a lie. It's no use trying to conceal your fault. However, next year I shall, in all probability, return to my own country, and then you may take O Hiyaku and do what you will with her: far be it from me to care what becomes of a woman with such a stinking heart.'

When the wrestler and O Hiyaku heard Jiuyemon say this quite quietly, they could not speak, but held their peace for very shame.

'Here, you Takasegawa,' pursued he; 'you may stop here tonight, if you like it, and go home tomorrow.'

'Thank you, sir,' replied the wrestler, 'I am much obliged to you; but the fact is, that I have some pressing business in another part of the town, so, with your permission, I will take my leave;' and so he went out, covered with confusion.

As for the faithless wife, O Hiyaku, she was in great agitation, expecting to be severely reprimanded at least; but Jiuyemon took no notice of her, and showed no anger; only from that day forth, although she remained in his house as his wife, he separated himself from her entirely.

Matters went on in this way for some time, until at last, one fine day, O Hiyaku, looking out of doors, saw the wrestler Takasegawa passing in the street, so she called out to him:

'Dear me, Master Takasegawa, can that be you! What a long time it is since we have met! Pray come in, and have a chat.'

'Thank you, I am much obliged to you; but as I do not like the sort of scene we had the other day, I think I had rather not accept your invitation.'

'Pray do not talk in such a cowardly manner. Next year, when Jiuyemon goes back to his own country, he is sure to give me this house, and then you and I can marry and live as happily as possible.'

'I don't like being in too great a hurry to accept fair offers.'

'Nonsense! There's no need for showing such delicacy about accepting what is given you.'

And as she spoke, she caught the wrestler by the hand and led him into the house. After they had talked together for some time, she said:

'Listen to me, Master Takasegawa. I have been thinking over all this for some time, and I see no help for it but to kill Jiuyemon and make an end of him.'

'What do you want to do that for?'

'As long as he is alive, we cannot be married. What I propose is that you should buy some poison, and I will put it secretly into his food. When he is dead, we can be happy to our hearts' content.'

At first Takasegawa was startled and bewildered by the audacity of their scheme; but forgetting the gratitude which he owed to Jiuyemon for sparing his life on the previous occasion, he replied:

'Well, I think it can be managed. I have a friend who is a physician, so I will get him to compound some poison for me, and will send it to you. You must look out for a moment when your husband is not on his guard, and get him to take it.'

Having agreed upon this, Takasegawa went away, and, having employed a physician to make up the poison, sent it to O Hiyaku in a letter, suggesting that the poison should be mixed up with a sort of macaroni, of which Jiuyemon was very fond. Having read the letter, she put it carefully away in a drawer of her cupboard, and waited until Jiuyemon should express a wish to eat some macaroni.

One day, towards the time of the New Year, when O Hiyaku had gone out to a party with a few of her friends, it happened that Jiuyemon, being alone in the house, was in want of some little thing, and, failing to find it anywhere, at last bethought himself to look for it in O Hiyaku's cupboard; and as he was searching amongst the odds and ends which it contained, he came upon the fatal letter. When he read the scheme for putting poison in his macaroni, he was taken aback, and said to himself, 'When I caught those two beasts in their wickedness I spared them, because their blood would have defiled my sword; and now they are not even grateful for my mercy. Their crime is beyond all power of language to express, and I will kill them together.'

So he put back the letter in its place, and waited for his wife to come home. So soon as she made her appearance he said:

'You have come home early, O Hiyaku. I feel very dull and lonely this evening; let us have a little wine.'

And as he spoke without any semblance of anger, it never entered O Hiyaku's mind that he had seen the letter; so she went about her household duties with a quiet mind.

The following evening, as Jiuyemon was sitting in his shop casting up his accounts, with his counting-board in his hand, Takasegawa passed by, and Jiuyemon called out to him, saying:

'Well met, Takasegawa! I was just thinking of drinking a cup of wine tonight; but I have no one to keep me company, and it is dull work drinking alone. Pray come in, and drink a bout with me.'

'Thank you, sir, I shall have much pleasure,' replied the wrestler, who little expected what the other was aiming at; and so he went in, and they began to drink and feast.

'It's very cold tonight,' said Jiuyemon, after a while; 'suppose we warm up a little macaroni, and eat it nice and hot. Perhaps, however, you do not like it?'

'Indeed, I am very fond of it, on the contrary.'

'That is well. O Hiyaku, please go and buy a little for us.'

'Directly,' replied his wife, who hurried off to buy the paste, delighted at the opportunity for carrying out her murderous design upon her husband. As soon she had prepared it, she poured it into bowls and set it before the two men; but into her husband's bowl only she put poison. Jiuyemon, who well knew what she had done, did not eat the mess at once, but remained talking about this, that, and the other; and the wrestler, out of politeness, was obliged to wait also. All of a sudden, Jiuyemon cried out:

'Dear me! whilst we have been gossiping, the macaroni has been getting cold. Let us put it all together and warm it up again. As no one has put his lips to his bowl yet, it will all be clean; so none need be wasted.' And with these words he took the macaroni that was in the three bowls, and, pouring it altogether into an iron pot, boiled it up again. This time Jiuyemon served out the food himself, and, setting it before his wife and the wrestler, said:

'There! make haste and eat it up before it gets cold.'

Jiuyemon, of course, did not eat any of the mess; and the would-be murderers, knowing that sufficient poison had been originally put into Jiuyemon's bowl to kill them all three, and that now the macaroni, having been well mixed up, would all be poisoned, were quite taken aback, and did not know what to do.

'Come! make haste, or it will be quite cold. You said you liked it, so I sent to buy it on purpose. O Hiyaku! come and make a hearty meal. I will eat some presently.'

At this the pair looked very foolish, and knew not what to answer; at last the wrestler got up and said:

'I do not feel quite well. I must beg to take my leave; and, if you will allow me, I will come and accept your hospitality tomorrow instead.'

'Dear me! I am sorry to hear you are not well. However, O Hiyaku, there will be all the more macaroni for you.'

As for O Hiyaku, she put a bold face upon the matter, and replied that she had supped already, and had no appetite for any more.

Then Jiuyemon, looking at them both with a scornful smile, said:

'It seems that you, neither of you, care to eat this macaroni; however, as you, Takasegawa, are unwell, I will give you some excellent medicine;' and going to the cupboard, he drew out the letter, and laid it before the wrestler. When O Hiyaku and the wrestler saw that their wicked schemes had been brought to light, they were struck dumb with shame.

Takasegawa, seeing that denial was useless, drew his dirk and cut at Jiuyemon; but he, being nimble and quick, dived under the wrestler's arm, and seizing his right hand from behind, tightened his grasp upon it until it became numbed, and the dirk fell to the ground; for, powerful man as the wrestler was, he was no match for Jiuyemon, who held him in so fast a grip that he could not move. Then Jiuyemon took the dirk which had fallen to the ground, and said:

'Oh! I thought that you, being a wrestler, would at least be a strong man, and that there would be some pleasure in fighting you; but I see that you are but a poor feckless creature, after all. It would have defiled my sword to have killed such an ungrateful hound with it; but luckily here is your own dirk, and I will slay you with that.'

Takasegawa struggled to escape, but in vain; and O Hiyaku, seizing a large kitchen knife, attacked Jiuyemon; but he, furious, kicked her in the loins so violently that she fell powerless, then brandishing the dirk, he cleft the wrestler from the shoulder down to the nipple of his breast, and the big man fell in his agony. O Hiyaku, seeing this, tried to fly; but Jiuyemon, seizing her by the hair of the head, stabbed her in the bosom, and, placing her by her lover's side, gave her the death-blow.

On the following day, he sent in a report of what he had done to the governor of Osaka, and buried the corpses; and from that time forth he remained a single man, and pursued his trade as a seller of perfumery and such-like wares; and his leisure hours he continued to spend as before, at the house of his patron, Kajiki Tozayemon.

One day, when Jiuyemon went to call upon Kajiki Tozayemon, he was told by the servant-maid, who met him at the door, that her master was out, but that her young master, Tonoshin, was at home; so, saying that he would go in and pay his respects to the young gentleman, he entered the house; and as he suddenly pushed open the sliding-door of the room in which Tonoshin was sitting, the latter gave a great start, and his face turned pale and ghastly.

'How now, young sir!' said Jiuyemon, laughing at him, 'surely you are not such a coward as to be afraid because the sliding-doors are opened? That is not the way in which a brave Samurai should behave.'

'Really I am quite ashamed of myself,' replied the other, blushing at the reproof; 'but the fact is that I had some reason for being startled. Listen to me, Sir Jiuyemon, and I will tell you all about it. Today, when I went to the academy to study, there were a great number of my fellow-students gathered together, and one of them said that a ruinous old shrine, about two miles and a half to the east of this place, was the nightly resort of all sorts of hobgoblins, who have been playing pranks and bewitching the people for some time past; and he proposed that we should all draw lots, and that the one upon whom the lot fell should go tonight and exorcise those evil beings; and further that, as a proof of his having gone, he should write his name upon a pillar in the shrine. All the rest agreed that this would be very good sport; so I, not liking to appear a coward, consented to take my chance with the rest; and, as ill luck would have it, the lot fell upon me. I was thinking over this as you came in, and so it was that when you suddenly opened the door, I could not help giving a start.'

'If you only think for a moment,' said Jiuyemon, 'you will see that there is nothing to fear. How can beasts and hobgoblins exercise any power over men? However, do not let the matter trouble you. I will go in your place tonight, and see if I cannot get the better of these goblins, if any there be, having done which, I will write your name upon the pillar, so that everybody may think that you have been there.'

'Oh! thank you: that will indeed be a service. You can dress yourself up in my clothes, and nobody will be the wiser. I shall be truly grateful to you.'

So Jiuyemon having gladly undertaken the job, as soon as the night set in made his preparations, and went to the place indicated – an uncanny-looking, tumble-down, lonely old shrine, all overgrown with moss and rank vegetation. However, Jiuyemon, who was afraid of nothing, cared little for the appearance of the place, and having made himself as comfortable as he could in so dreary a spot, sat down on the floor, lit his pipe, and kept a sharp look-out for the goblins. He had not been waiting long before he saw a movement among the bushes; and presently he was surrounded by a host of elfish-looking creatures, of all shapes and kinds, who came and made hideous faces at him. Jiuyemon quietly knocked the ashes out of his pipe, and then, jumping up, kicked over first one and then another of the elves, until several of them lay sprawling in the grass; and the rest made off, greatly astonished at this unexpected reception. When Jiuyemon took his lantern and examined the fallen goblins attentively, he saw that they were all Tonoshin's fellow-students, who had painted their faces, and made themselves hideous, to frighten their companion, whom they knew to be a coward: all they got for their pains, however, was a good kicking from Jiuyemon, who left them groaning over their sore bones, and went home chuckling to himself at the result of the adventure.

The fame of this exploit soon became noised about Osaka, so that all men praised Jiuyemon's courage; and shortly after this he was elected chief of the Otokodate, or friendly society of the wardsmen, and busied himself no longer with his trade, but lived on the contributions of his numerous apprentices.

Now Kajiki Tonoshin was in love with a singing girl named Kashiku, upon whom he was in the habit of spending a great deal of money. She, however, cared nothing for him, for she had a sweetheart named Hichirobei, whom she used to contrive to meet secretly, although, in order to support her parents, she was forced to become the mistress of Tonoshin. One evening, when the latter was on guard at the office of his chief, the Governor of Osaka, Kashiku sent word privately to Hichirobei, summoning him to go to her house, as the coast would be clear.

While the two were making merry over a little feast, Tonoshin, who had persuaded a friend to take his duty for him on the plea of urgent business, knocked at the door, and Kashiku, in a great fright, hid her lover in a long clothes-box, and went to let in Tonoshin, who, on entering the room and seeing the litter of the supper lying about, looked more closely, and perceived a man's sandals, on which, by the light of a candle, he saw the figure seven. Tonoshin had heard some ugly reports of Kashiku's proceedings with this man Hichirobei, and when he saw this proof before his eyes he grew very angry; but he suppressed his feelings, and, pointing to the wine-cups and bowls, said:

'Whom have you been feasting with tonight?'

'Oh!' replied Kashiku, who, notwithstanding her distress, was obliged to invent an answer, 'I felt so dull all alone here, that I asked an old woman from next door to come in and drink a cup of wine with me, and have a chat.'

All this while Tonoshin was looking for the hidden lover; but, as he could not see him, he made up his mind that Kashiku must have let him out by the back door; so he secreted one of the sandals in his sleeve as evidence, and, without seeming to suspect anything, said:

'Well, I shall be very busy this evening, so I must go home.'

'Oh! won't you stay a little while? It is very dull here, when I am all alone without you. Pray stop and keep me company.'

But Tonoshin made no reply, and went home. Then Kashiku saw that one of the sandals was missing, and felt certain that he must have carried it off as proof; so she went in great trouble to open the lid of the box, and let out Hichirobei. When the two lovers talked over the matter, they agreed that, as they both were really in love, let Tonoshin kill them if he would, they would gladly die together: they would enjoy the present; let the future take care of itself.

The following morning Kashiku sent a messenger to Tonoshin to implore his pardon; and he, being infatuated by the girl's charms, forgave her, and sent a present of thirty ounces of silver to her lover, Hichirobei, on the condition that he was never to see her again; but, in spite of this, Kashiku and Hichirobei still continued their secret meetings.

It happened that Hichirobei, who was a gambler by profession, had an elder brother called Chobei, who kept a wine-shop in the Ajikawa Street, at Osaka; so Tonoshin thought that he could not do better than depute Jiuyemon to go and seek out this man Chobei, and urge him to persuade his younger brother to give up his relations with Kashiku; acting upon this resolution, he went to call upon Jiuyemon, and said to him:

'Sir Jiuyemon, I have a favour to ask of you in connection with that girl Kashiku, whom you know all about. You are aware that I paid thirty ounces of silver to her lover Hichirobei to induce him to give up going to her house; but, in spite of this, I cannot help suspecting that they still meet one another. It seems that this Hichirobei has an elder brother – one Chobei; now, if you would go to this man and tell him to reprove his brother for his conduct, you would be doing me a great service. You have so often stood my friend, that I venture to pray you to oblige me in this matter, although I feel that I am putting you to great inconvenience.'

Jiuyemon, out of gratitude for the kindness which he had received at the hands of Kajiki Tozayemon, was always willing to serve Tonoshin; so he went at once to find out Chobei, and said to him:

'My name, sir, is Jiuyemon, at your service; and I have come to beg your assistance in a matter of some delicacy.'

'What can I do to oblige you, sir?' replied Chobei, who felt bound to be more than usually civil, as his visitor was the chief of the Otokodate.

'It is a small matter, sir,' said Jiuyemon. 'Your younger brother Hichirobei is intimate with a woman named Kashiku, whom he meets in secret. Now, this Kashiku is the mistress of the son of a gentleman to whom I am under great obligation: he bought her of her parents for a large sum of money, and, besides this, he paid your brother thirty ounces of silver some time since, on condition of his separating himself from the girl; in spite of this, it appears that your brother continues to see her, and I have come to beg that you will remonstrate with your brother on his conduct, and make him give her up.'

'That I certainly will. Pray do not be uneasy; I will soon find means to put a stop to my brother's bad behaviour.'

And so they went on talking of one thing and another, until Jiuyemon, whose eyes had been wandering about the room, spied out a very long dirk lying on a cupboard, and all at once it occurred to him that this was the very sword which had been a parting gift to him from his lord: the hilt, the mountings, and the tip of the scabbard were all the same, only the blade had been shortened and made into a long dirk. Then he looked more attentively at Chobei's features, and saw that he was no other than Akagoshi Kuroyemon, the pirate chief. Two years had passed by, but he could not forget that face.

Jiuyemon would have liked to have arrested him at once; but thinking that it would be a pity to give so vile a robber a chance of escape, he constrained himself, and, taking his leave, went straightway and reported the matter to the Governor of Osaka. When the officers of justice heard of the prey that awaited them, they made their preparations forthwith. Three men of the secret police went to Chobei's wine-shop, and, having called for wine, pretended to get up a drunken brawl; and as Chobei went up to them and tried to pacify them, one of the policemen seized hold of him, and another tried to pinion him. It at once flashed across Chobei's mind that his old misdeeds had come to light at last, so with a desperate effort he shook off the two policemen and knocked them down, and, rushing into the inner room, seized the famous Sukesada sword and sprang upstairs. The three policemen, never thinking that he could escape, mounted the stairs close after him; but Chobei with a terrible cut cleft the front man's head in sunder, and the other two fell back appalled at their comrade's fate. Then Chobei climbed on to the roof, and, looking out, perceived that the house was surrounded on all sides by armed men. Seeing this, he made up his mind that his last moment was come, but, at any rate, he determined to sell his life dearly, and to die fighting; so he stood up bravely, when one of the officers, coming up from the roof of a neighbouring house, attacked him with a spear; and at the same time several other soldiers clambered up. Chobei, seeing that he was overmatched, jumped down, and before the soldiers below had recovered from their surprise he had dashed through their ranks, laying about him right and left, and cutting down three men. At top speed he fled, with his pursuers close behind him; and, seeing the broad river ahead of him, jumped into a small boat that lay moored there, of which the boatmen, frightened at the sight of his bloody sword, left him in undisputed possession. Chobei pushed off, and sculled vigorously into the middle of the river; and the officers – there being no other boat near – were for a moment baffled. One of them, however, rushing down the river bank, hid himself on a bridge, armed with. a spear, and lay in wait for Chobei to pass in his boat; but when the little boat came up, he missed his aim, and only scratched Chobei's elbow; and he, seizing the spear, dragged down his adversary into the river, and killed him as he was struggling in the water; then, sculling for his life, he gradually drew near to the sea. The other officers in the mean time had secured ten boats, and, having come up with Chobei, surrounded him; but he, having formerly been a pirate, was far better skilled in the management of a boat than his pursuers, and had no great difficulty in eluding them; so at last he pushed out to sea, to the great annoyance of the officers, who followed him closely.

Then Jiuyemon, who had come up, said to one of the officers on the shore:

'Have you caught him yet?'

'No; the fellow is so brave and so cunning that our men can do nothing with him.'

'He's a determined ruffian, certainly. However, as the fellow has got my sword, I mean to get it back by fair means or foul: will you allow me to undertake the job of seizing him?'

'Well, you may try; and you will have officers to assist you, if you are in peril.'

Jiuyemon, having received this permission, stripped off his clothes and jumped into the sea, carrying with him a policeman's mace, to the great astonishment of all the bystanders. When he got near Chobei's boat, he dived and came up alongside, without the pirate perceiving him until he had clambered into the boat. Chobei had the good Sukesada sword, and Jiuyemon was armed with nothing but a mace; but Chobei, on the other hand, was exhausted with his previous exertions, and was taken by surprise at a moment when he was thinking of nothing but how he should scull away from the pursuing boats; so it was not long before Jiuyemon mastered and secured him.

For this feat, besides recovering his Sukesada sword, Jiuyemon received many rewards and great praise from the Governor of Osaka. But the pirate Chobei was cast into prison.

Hichirobei, when he heard of his brother's capture, was away from home; but seeing that he too would be sought for, he determined to escape to Edo at once, and travelled along the Tokaido, the great highroad, as far as Kuana. But the secret police had got wind of his movements, and one of them was at his heels disguised as a beggar, and waiting for an opportunity to seize him.

Hichirobei in the meanwhile was congratulating himself on his escape; and, little suspecting that he would be in danger so far away from Osaka, he went to a house of pleasure, intending to divert himself at his ease. The policeman, seeing this, went to the master of the house and said:

'The guest who has just come in is a notorious thief, and I am on his track, waiting to arrest him. Do you watch for the moment when he falls asleep, and let me know. Should he escape, the blame will fall upon you.'

The master of the house, who was greatly taken aback, consented of course; so he told the woman of the house to hide Hichirobei's dirk, and as soon as the latter, wearied with his journey, had fallen asleep, he reported it to the policeman, who went upstairs, and having bound Hichirobei as he lay wrapped up in his quilt, led him back to Osaka to be imprisoned with his brother.

When Kashiku became aware of her lover's arrest, she felt certain that it was the handiwork of Jiuyemon; so she determined to kill him, were it only that she might die with Hichirobci. So hiding a kitchen knife in the bosom of her dress, she went at midnight to Jiuyemon's house, and looked all round to see if there were no hole or cranny by which she might slip in unobserved; but every door was carefully closed, so she was obliged to knock at the door and feign an excuse.

'Let me in! let me in! I am a servant-maid in the house of Kajiki Tozayemon, and am charged with a letter on most pressing business to Sir Jiuyemon.'

Hearing this, one of Jiuyemon's servants, thinking her tale was true, rose and opened the door; and Kashiku, stabbing him in the face, ran past him into the house. Inside she met another apprentice, who had got up, aroused by the noise; him too she stabbed in the belly, but as he fell he cried out to Jiuyemon, saying:

'Father, father! take care! Some murderous villain has broken into the house.'

And Kashiku, desperate, stopped his further utterance by cutting his throat. Jiuyemon, hearing his apprentice cry out, jumped up, and, lighting his night-lamp, looked about him in the half-gloom, and saw Kashiku with the bloody knife, hunting for him that she might kill him. Springing upon her before she saw him, he clutched her right hand, and, having secured her, bound her with cords so that she could not move. As soon as he had recovered from his surprise, he looked about him, and searched the house, when, to his horror, he found one of his apprentices dead, and the other lying bleeding from a frightful gash across the face. With the first dawn of day, he reported the affair to the proper authorities, and gave Kashiku in custody. So, after due examination, the two pirate brothers and the girl Kashiku were executed, and their heads were exposed together.

Now the fame of all the valiant deeds of Jiuyemon having reached his own country, his lord ordered that he should be pardoned for his former offence, and return to his allegiance; so, after thanking Kajiki Tozayemon for the manifold favours which he had received at his hands, he went home, and became a Samurai as before.

Heroes & Heroines in Literature & Poetry

Introduction

THE LITERATURE AND POETRY of a culture can be seen as being inherently heroic. Like the mythic hero or heroine, they represent that culture at its best. Like him or her, they perform an exemplary function, revealing the highest beauties of a people's language and modelling their values in the most moving and impressive way. It is no great surprise, then, to find that many ancient civilizations first found a poetic voice in high-flown heroic 'epics', recording their mythic origins in stirring poems of love and war. India's *Ramayana* and *Mahabharata*; East Africa's *Swahili Hadithi yar Liongon*; the Celtic stories of Cúchulainn; the Scandinavian Sagas; the stories of Britain's King Arthur and of China's Tchi-Niu … These great works draw on the deepest mythic memories of the cultures that brought them forth. But they also advertise these people's pretensions to a greater polish and sophistication – their claim to be truly 'civilized', in short.

Tales of Ramayana

THE RAMAYANA WAS AN EPIC POEM of about 50,000 lines, which was originally composed by the hermit Valmiki, probably in the third century BC. Many versions of this great work exist across India where Rama, the seventh incarnation of Vishnu, and hero of the poem, was worshipped. The Ramayana was originally divided into seven books, each of which celebrated a part of Rama's life. Rama was the greatest human hero of Hindu mythology, the son of a king and the avatar of Vishnu. He was the model of every good man, for he was brave, chivalrous, well versed and virtuous. He had but one wife and his name has become synonymous with loyalty and fidelity in many parts of the Indian nation.

It is believed that this epic poem is cleansing – even a reading of the Ramayana will remove the sins of the reader, for the text itself is regarded as charismatic. Many events befell Rama in his earthly form, and he left behind two sons. The following tales represent some of the most fascinating and profound occurrences in the life of Rama, whose name, even today, is in many parts of the Hindu community, the word for 'God'.

The Birth of Rama

Once, long, long ago, in the great city of Ayodhya there lived a king. Ayodhya was a prosperous city, one where its citizens were happy, pure of heart and well educated in the teachings of both man and god. Its king was also a good man and happy in almost every respect, for he had many wise counsellors and sages in his family and he had been blessed with a lovely daughter, Santa. This king was called Dasharatha, and he married his sweet daughter to the great sage Rishyasringa, who became a member of his inner circle, advising him on all matters with great wisdom and foresight. Two fine priests – Vashishtha and Vamadeva – were also part of his family, and they were known to all as the most saintly of men.

But Dasharatha had one hole in his glittering life; he longed for a son to carry on his line, a son who would one day be king. For many years he made offerings to the great powers, but to no avail, until such time as he made the most supreme sacrifice, that of a horse. His three wives were overjoyed by the prospect of having a son and when, after one year, the horse returned from the sacrifice, Rishyasringa and Vashishtha prepared the ceremony. With the greatest of respect and joy Rishyasringa was able to announce to Dasharatha that he would father four sons, and they would carry his name into the future.

When any sacrifice is made by man, all of the deities come together to take their portion of what has been offered, and so it was on this occasion that they had assembled to take from the sacrificial horse. There was, however, a dissenter among their ranks, one who was greedy and oppressive, and who caused in his colleagues such dissension that they came forward to Brahma with a request that he be destroyed. The evil rakshasa was called Ravana, and at an early age he had been granted immunity from death by yakshas, rakshasas or gods. His immunity had led him to become selfish and arrogant, and he took great pleasure in flaunting his exemption from the normal fates. Brahma spoke wisely to the gathered deities.

'Ravana is indeed evil,' he said quietly, 'and he had great foresight in requesting immunity from death by his equals. But,' and here Brahma paused. 'But,' he went on, 'he was not wise enough to seek immunity from death by humans – and it is in this way that he must be slain.'

The deities were relieved to find that Ravana was not invincible, and as they celebrated amongst themselves, they were quietened by a profound presence who entered their midst. It was the great God Vishnu himself, and he appeared in flowing yellow robes, his eyes sparkling. He carried with him mace, and discus and conch, and he appeared on the back of Garuda, the divine bird attendant of Narayana. The deities fell at his feet, and they begged him to be born as Dasharatha's four sons in order to destroy the deceitful Ravana.

And so it was that Vishnu threw himself into Dasharatha's fire and taking the form of a sacred tiger, spoke to the anxious father-to-be, pronouncing himself the ambassador of God himself. He presented Dasharatha with spiritual food, which he was to share with his wives – two portions to Sumitra, one to Kaikeyi, and one to Kaushalya. And soon, four strong, healthy babies were born to Dasharatha's wives and they were named by Vashishtha, the divine priest. They were Rama, born to Kaushalya, Bharata, born to Kaikeyi, and Lakshman and Satrughna born to Sumitra.

Rama and Vishvamitra

Dasharatha's four sons grew into robust and healthy young men. They were brave and above all good, and they were revered for their looks and good sense. The greatness of Vishnu was spread amongst them, and each glowed with great worth. The young men travelled in pairs – Satrughna devoting himself to his brother Bharata, and Lakshman dedicating himself to Rama. Rama was very much the favoured son, favourite of both Dasharatha and the people. He was a noble youth, well-versed in arts, sciences and physical applications alike; his spirituality was evident in all he did. By the age of sixteen, Rama was more accomplished than any man on earth, inspiring greatness in all who came into contact with him.

There lived, at this time, a rishi by the name of Vishvamitra who had become a brahma-rishi, an excellent status which had been accorded to him by the gods themselves. He lived in Siddhashrama, but his life there was far from easy. He was a religious man, and took enormous strength from his daily prayers and sacrifices. Each day his sacrificial fires and prayers were interrupted by two wily and evil rakshasas, Maricha and Suvahu, who received their orders from Ravana himself. Knowing that Rama was the incarnation of Vishnu, Vishvamitra approached Dasharatha and begged him to send Rama to rid him of these evil spirits.

Now Dasharatha was against the idea of sending his favourite son to what would surely be a dangerous and perhaps fatal mission, but he knew as well that a great brahma-rishi must be respected. And so it was that Rama and Lakshman travelled to Vishvamitra for ten days, in order to stand by the sacrificial fire. The young men were dressed in the finest of clothes, glittering with jewels and fine cloths. They were adorned with carefully wrought arms, and they glowed with pride and valour. All who witnessed their passing was touched by the glory, and a ray of light entered each of their lives.

They arrived at Siddhashrama in a cloud of radiance, and as the sacrifice began, Rama wounded Maricha and Suvahu, until they fled in dismay. The other evil spirits were banished, and the little hermitage was once again in peace, cleansed of the evil of Ravana.

Rama and the Bow of Janaka

Rama was greeted with great acclaim after he rid Vishvamitra's hermitage of the evil spirits, and his taste of heroism whetted in him a great appetite for further adventure. He begged Vishvamitra to present him with further tasks, and he was rewarded by the hallowed priest's plans to visit Janaka, the Raja of Mithila.

Janaka was owner of a splendid bow, one which no man was able to string. He had come by this bow through his ancestor, Devarata, who had received it personally from the gods, who had themselves been presented the bow by Shiva. The bow was now worshipped by all who had seen it, for gods, rakshasas and even the finest warriors had been unable to bend its mighty back.

Janaka was planning a marvellous sacrifice, and it was for Mithila that the three men would depart, in order to take part in the festivities, and to see the great bow in person. As they travelled along the Ganges, they were followed by all the birds and animals who inhabited Siddhashrama, and by the monkey protectors who had been presented to the two brothers upon their birth. They arrived in Mithila in a burst of splendid colour and radiance, and Janaka knew at once that the company he was about to keep was godly in every way. He bowed deeply to the men, and set them carefully among the other men of nobility.

The following day, Janaka brought the men to the bow, and explained to them its great significance.

He said to Rama, 'I have a daughter, Sita, who is not the product of man, or of animal, but who burst from a furrow of the earth itself as I ploughed and hallowed my field. She is a woman of supreme beauty and godliness, and she will be presented to any man or god who can bend the bow.'

Rama and his brother bent their heads respectfully, and Rama nodded towards the bow. A chariot pulled by four thousand men moved the bow forward, and he quietly reached towards it. The case sprung open at his touch, and as he strung it, it snapped into two pieces with a bolt of fire. There was a crack so loud that all the men in the room, bar Rama, Vishvamitra, Janaka and Lakshman, fell to the ground, clutching their ears and writhing. And there was silence – a quiet brought on by fear and reverence. The spectators struggled to their knees and bowed to the great Rama, and a jubilant Janaka shouted his blessing and ordered the wedding preparations to begin. Messengers were sent at once to the household of Dasharatha, and upon his arrival, the festivities began.

Sita was presented to Rama, and Urmila, the second daughter of Janaka was promised to Lakshman. Mandavya and Srutakirti, who were daughters of Kushadhwaja, were presented to Bharata and Satrughna. All around the world erupted in a fusion of light and colour – fragrant blossoms were cast down from the heavens upon the radiant brothers and their brides, and a symphony of angelic music wove its way around them. There was happiness like none ever known, and the four young men cast down their heads with deep gratitude. They returned home, in a shower of glory, to Ayodhya, where they would serve their proud and honoured father, Dasharatha.

Kaikeyi and the Heir Apparent

After many years of happiness at Ayodhya, Dasharatha decided that the time had come to appoint an heir apparent. Rama was still the most favoured of the brothers, a fine man of sterling integrity and wisdom.

He was known across the land for his unbending sense of justice, and he was friend to any man who was good. His brothers had no envy for their honourable brother for he was so kind and serene that he invited their good intentions and they wished him nothing but good fortune.

Rama was the obvious choice for heir, and Dasharatha took steps to prepare for his ascendance. He drew together all of his counsellors and kings, and he advised them of his plans. He explained how his years had been kind and bounteous, but that they weighed down on him now, and he felt the need to rest. He proposed that his son Rama become heir apparent.

The uproar astonished the elderly king. There was happiness and celebration at his proposal, and at once the air grew clear and the skies shone with celestial light. Bemused, he turned to the esteemed parliament of men and he said, 'Why, why do you wish him to be your ruler?'

'By reason of his many virtues, for indeed he towers among men as Sakra among the gods. He speaks the truth and he is a mighty and even bowman. He is ever busied with the welfare of the people, and not given to detraction where he finds one blemish among many virtues. He is skilled in music and his eyes are fair to look upon. Neither his pleasure nor his anger is in vain; he is easily approached, and self-controlled, and goes not forth to war or the protection of a city or province without victorious return. He is beloved of all. Indeed, the Earth desires him for her lord.' And once again the cheers rose and the preparations began.

The finest victuals were ordered – honey and butter, rices and milk and curds. There were golds, silvers and gems of great gleaming weight, and elephants and bulls and tigers ordered. Fine cloths and skins were draped around the palace, and everyone hummed with incessant, bustling excitement. And above it all was Rama, serene and calm, as cool as the winter waters of the Ganges, as pure of heart as the autumn moon. And just before the time when he would stand forward in his father's shoes, he was brought before the great Dasharatha, who greeted his kneeling form with warmth and lifted him up upon the seat of kings. He said to him then:

'Though you are virtuous by nature, I would advise you out of love and for your good: Practise yet greater gentleness and restraint of sense; avoid all lust and anger; maintain your arsenal and treasury; personally and by means of others make yourself well acquainted with the affairs of state; administer justice freely to all, that the people may rejoice. Gird yourself, my son, and undertake your task.'

Rama, for all his wisdom, found great solace in his father's words, and as the town around him buzzed with the activity of thousands of men preparing for the holy fast, he sat calmly, in worship and in gratitude.

Now throughout this time, all of Dasharatha's household celebrated the choice of Rama for heir apparent – his mother, Kaushalya, and his wife, Sita, were honoured, and his aunts, too, revelled in their relation to this fine young man. There was no room for envy in their hearts, until, that is, the deceitful old nurse, Manthara, took it upon herself to stir up the seeds of discontent. And this she did by the subtle but constant pressures she applied to her mistress, Kaikeyi, the mother of Bharata.

Kaikeyi was by nature a fair woman, easy natured and gentle. It took many months of persuasion before a hole was pierced in her goodness, and the beginnings of evil allowed to enter. It was a misfortune for Rama to become king, said Manthara, for Bharata would be cast out and Kaikeyi would be the subordinate of Kaushalya. Kaikeyi dismissed such nonsense and carried on with her daily work. Several days later, Manthara was back. Bharata would be sent away, she said. Did that not worry his mother? But Kaikeyi was calm. She said, 'Why grieve at Rama's fortune? He is well fitted to be king; and if the kingdom be his, it will also be Bharata's for Rama ever regards his brothers as himself.'

Manthara did not give up. She twisted her sword a little deeper and was rewarded by hitting at Kaikeyi's pride. 'Don't you know, Kaikeyi,' she said, 'that Rama's mother will seek revenge upon you. Yours will be a sorry lot when Rama rules the earth.'

Kaikeyi's rage burst from within her and she stalked around her chambers.

'Why he will have to be deported at once,' she said furiously. 'But how can I do it? How can I install Bharata as heir?'

The treacherous Manthara was again at her side, needling the pain and fury that she had inspired in her gentle mistress.

'You have two unused gifts from Dasharatha,' she reminded her. 'Have you forgotten that fateful day when you found him near dead on the battlefield? What did he promise you then, my mistress?' she asked her. 'Why he has made you his favourite of wives and he has done everything in his power to keep you happy. This is what you must do.' And the evil witch leaned forward and whispered in Kaikeyi's ear. Her eyes widened, and their glitter dimmed. She bowed her head and she left the room.

Kaikeyi cast off her jewels and fine clothes, and pulled down her hair. She dressed herself in sacks and she laid down on the floor of the anger chamber where she cried with such vigour that Dasharatha could not fail to hear her sobs. Finding her there, stripped of her finery, he laid beside her and spoke gently to his favourite wife.

'What has happened. What is it?' he whispered. 'If you are ill, there are many doctors who can cure what ails you. If someone has wronged you, we can right that wrong. Indeed, whatever you want, my dear Kaikeyi, I will ensure you have. Your desire is mine. You know that I can refuse you nothing.'

Kaikeyi sat up and brushed away her tears. 'You know,' she said, 'that you promised me that day long ago, when I carried you from the battlefield and administered your wounds, when I saved you from the jaws of death, you know, dear husband, that you promised me two gifts, two boons. You told me then that I could have my desire and until this day I have asked you for nothing.'

Dasharatha roared with approval. 'Of course, dear wife,' he said. 'Whatever you wish, it shall be yours. This I swear on Rama himself.'

'I wish,' she said softly, 'I wish, as Heaven and Earth and Day and Night are my witness, I wish that Bharata become heir and that Rama is cast out, clad only in deer-skins, to lead the life of a hermit in the forests of Dandaka, and that he remain there for fourteen years.'

Kaikeyi knew that in fourteen years her own son, who was good and true, could bind himself to the affections of the people and that Rama, upon his return, could not shift him from a well-regarded throne. Her plan was about to unfold and she shivered with anticipation. As expected, her husband let out a mighty roar and sank down to his knees once again. He begged Kaikeyi to change her mind, and he pleaded with her to allow his son to stay with him, but she refused to relent.

And so it was that Rama was summoned to the weeping Dasharatha, and as he travelled, the crowds rose to greet him, feeling their lives changed in some small way by the benefit of his smile, his wave, his celestial presence. And bolstered by the adoration, and glowing with the supreme eloquence of his righteousness, he entered his father's chamber with unwitting happiness and calm. His father's distress wiped the smile from his lips, and the clouds filled the autumn sky.

'What is it father,' he asked, sensing deep grief and misfortune. But his father could only mutter, 'Rama, Rama, I have wronged you.'

Rama turned to Kaikeyi, 'Mother, mother,' he asked, 'what ill has overcome my father?'

And Kaikeyi uttered with pride and something approaching glee, 'Nothing, Rama, but your imminent downfall. He cannot frame the words that will cause you distress and unhappiness, but you must do as he asks. You must help him to fulfil his promise to me. You see, Rama, long ago he promised me two gifts. If you swear to me now that you will do as he wishes, I will tell you all.'

Rama spluttered with indignation. 'Of course, dear Mother. Anything for my father. I would walk in fire. I would drink poison, or blood, for him. Tell me now, so that I may more quickly set about easing his poor soul.'

Kaikeyi related to him the story of her gifts from Dasharatha, and told him of her father's decision that he should be sent away to dwell as a hermit in Dandaka forest for fourteen years. Bharata, she said, would be installed as heir at once.

Rama smiled warmly and with such sincerity that Kaikeyi was stung with shame. 'Of course,' he said serenely, 'I am only sad for my father, who is suffering so. Send at once for Bharata while I go to the forest. Allow me some time to comfort my mother, and Sita, and I shall do as you wish.'

He saluted Kaikeyi, and he left at once. His mother was grieved by her son's fate, but she lifted her head high and she swore to him that she would follow him. 'My darling,' she said, 'I shall follow you to the forest even as a cow follows her young. I cannot bear to wait here for your return and I will come with you.'

Lakshman was greatly angered by the decision, and he vowed to fight for his brother who had been so wronged. But Rama calmed them both, and he spoke wisely and confidently.

'Gentle brother, I must obey the order of my father. I will never suffer degradation if I honour the words of my father.' Rama paused and turned to Kaushalya. 'Mother,' he said, taking her hands, 'Kaikeyi has ensnared the king, but if you leave him while I am gone he will surely die. You must remain and serve him. Spend your time in prayer, honouring the gods and the Brahmans and your virtue will be preserved.'

Sita greeted his news with dignity. 'I too will go forth into the forest with my husband,' she said. 'A wife shares in her husband's fate and I shall go before you, treading upon thorns and prickly grass, and I shall be happy there as in my own father's house, thinking only of your service.'

And Rama granted Sita her desire, and he said to her, 'Oh, my fair wife, since you do not fear the forest, you shall follow me and share my righteousness. Make haste, for we go at once.'

Rama's Exile

Lakshman could not bear to remain in his father's home without Rama and he too decided to leave with Rama and Sita for the forest, shunning the wealth and entrapments of his lifestyle to take a part of Rama's righteousness. There was hysteria in the household as the three prepared to leave, and a noble Brahman named Sumantra threw himself on the mercy of Kaikeyi to give in, begging her to allow Rama to remain. But Kaikeyi's will had turned her heart to stone and she refused all requests for clemency. Dasharatha sat dully, numbed by grief and shame at his wife's ill will. He motioned to send all his own wealth, and that of his city, with Rama into the forest, but Kaikeyi stood firm and insisted that Dasharatha stick to his vows and send Rama into the forest as a beggar.

As their new clothes of bark were set out for them, Sita collapsed and wept – fearing for her future and loathe to give up the easiness of her life, to which she had been both born and bred. The loyal subjects of Dasharatha begged him to allow Rama's wife to take the throne in his stead – there is no one, they said, who did not love Rama, and they would honour his wife as deeply as they honoured him. Yet again, Kaikeyi resisted all suggestions.

But then Dasharatha stood tall and he spoke firmly, drawing strength from his conviction. Sita shall not go without her jewels, and her robes, he commanded. So Sita's worldly goods were returned to her, and she shone like the sun in a summer sky, flanked by the bark-clad brothers whose goodness caused them to shine with even greater glory than Sita in her finery. They climbed up onto their chariot and set off for the forest, the citizens of Ayodhya falling in front of the carriage with despair.

And then Dasharatha turned to his wife Kaikeyi, and with all of his kingly disdain he cursed her, and cast her from his bed and his home.

'Take me to Kaushalya,' he said majestically. 'Take me swiftly for it is only there that I will find peace.'

At the same time, Lakshman, Sita and Rama had made their way from the city and had reached the shores of the blessed Ganges, a river as clear as the breath of the god, and inhabited by gods and angels alike. They were greeted there by Guha, the king of Nishadha, who fed their horses and made them comfortable for the night. Rama and his brother requested a paste of grain and water and they formed their hair into the customary locks of the forest hermits. The following night they slept by a great tree on the far bank of the Ganges, and the two brothers spoke quietly to one another, pledging to protect and care for the other, and for Sita. Rama expressed his great grief at leaving his father, and his concern for Ayodhya. He begged Lakshman to return in order to care for Kaushalya, but Lakshman gently rebuked him.

'Oh Rama,' he said softly, 'I can no more live without you than a fish can taken out of water – without you I do not wish to see my father, nor Sumitra, nor Heaven itself.' The two men slept silently, comforted by their love and devotion for one another. There was only one way to get through the years ahead, and that was as a united twosome.

The following day they reached the hermitage of Bharadwaja, where the great rishi told them of a wonderful place on the mountain of Chitrakuta, a place which teemed with trees, and peacocks and elephants, where there were rivers and caves and springs and many fruits and roots on which to feed. It was a place befitting their stature, he said, and they would be safe there. And so the following morning they set off, crossing the Jamna by raft and arriving at Shyama. There they prayed and set about building a house of wood, next to the hermitage of Valmiki.

A deer was slain by Lakshman, and a ritual sacrifice was offered to the divinities. And then they settled in together and allowed the happiness of their new life to enter their souls, banishing their grief for what they had left behind.

Bharata is King

Dasharatha was a broken man, and it was not long before his grief stripped him of his life. He died in the arms of Kaushalya, bewildered by his fate and recalling an incident which had occurred once in the forest, when as a youth he had accidentally slain a hermit with an errant arrow. Dasharatha had been spared punishment by a kind rishi, but he had been warned then that he would one day meet his death grieving for his son. That memory now clung to his mind, suffocating it until he gave in to his untimely death.

Ayodhya was in mourning for the loss of their finest son Rama, and the death of their king was a blow they could scarcely fathom. There was no rain and the earth dried up; an arid curse lay over the land and the dead Dasharatha's people could not even find the energy to go about their daily toil without the wisdom and leadership of the great and wise king. An envoy was half-heartedly sent for Bharata, with a message that he must return at once, but the people cared little about his arrival, and he was not told about the fate of his father and his brother Rama.

On the seventh day, Bharata, son of Kaikeyi, arrived at Ayodhya at sunrise, the first rays of morning failing to light the dark silence that the city had become. He entered his father's palace, and finding no one awake, entered the bed chamber, which he too found empty. And then Kaikeyi appeared, glowing with vanity and pride at her new position.

'Your father is gone,' she said crisply, caring little about the man who had once been her great love. Her son had taken her place in her affections, and she lusted now for the power that he was in the position to accord her.

Bharata wept silently for his father, and then, lifting a weary head, asked quietly, 'Where is Rama, I am happy for him. Was he present to perform the death-bed rites? Where is he, mother? I am his servant. I take refuge at his feet. Please inform him that I am here. I wish to know my father's last words.'

'Blessed are they that see Rama and the strong-armed Lakshman returning here with Sita,' said Kaikeyi. 'That is what he said.'

Bharata looked at her for a moment and paused. 'Where, may I ask, are Lakshman, Rama and Sita,' he asked then, his face losing colour.

'Rama has taken Sita and Lakshman and they have been exiled to Dandaka forest,' she said nobly, and then spilling over with the excitement of her conquest, she poured out the whole story to her son, explaining the wishes granted her by Dasharatha and the wonderful honours which would now be his.

'You are a murderer,' cried Bharata and leapt to his feet, casting his mother to one side. 'I loved Rama. I loved my father. It is for their sake alone that I call you mother, that I do not renounce you now. I do not want the kingdom. I want Rama – and I intend to bring him back from the forest! At once!'

Taking only the days necessary to prepare the funeral rites and to mourn his dead father, Bharata prepared to set out to find his brother. His tears were shared for his father and for his dear brother and he resolved to find him as soon as he could. He refused the throne which was offered to him by the ministers and preparing his chariots, he rode quickly towards the forest, following in the footsteps of Rama and the others. He reached him quickly, and was shocked and dismayed to find that Rama had adorned himself in the dress of a hermit – shaggy locks framed his pale face, and he wore the skin of a black deer upon his shoulders. But that pale face was serene, and he gently wiped away his brother's tears.

'Bharata,' he said, 'I cannot return. I have been commanded by both my father and my mother to live in the forest for fourteen years. That I must do. You must rule, as our father would have wished.'

Bharata thought for a moment. 'If it was our father's will for me to have the kingdom in your place, then I have the right to bestow it upon you.'

Rama smiled kindly then, and shook his head. 'The kingdom is yours, Bharata. Rule it wisely. For these fourteen years I shall live here as a hermit.'

Bharata took his brother's sandals and it was agreed that in fourteen years he would be joined by Rama, and that the sandals would be restored to him then – with the government and kingship of Ayodhya herself.

And Rama, Sita and Lakshman waved their farewells to Bharata and his men, and then they turned to leave themselves, no longer content in a house that had been trampled by feet of the outside world. They drew themselves deeper into Dandaka, where the cool darkness of the forest beckoned.

The Golden Deer

For ten years Rama, Sita and Lakshman wandered through the forests of Dandaka, resting and living for spells with hermits and other men of wisdom along their path. They befriended a vulture, Jatayu, who claimed to have been a friend of Dasharatha, and he pledged to guard Sita, and to offer Rama and Lakshman his help. They settled finally at Panchavati, by the river Godaveri, where lush blossoms hung over the rippling waters and the air was filled with the verdant scent of greenery. Sita, Rama and Lakshman lived happily there, in the green, fecund woodland, and lived virtually as gods, and undisturbed, until one day they were set upon by an evil rakshasi, sister of Ravana called Surpanakha. There ensued a terrible battle when this ugly sister sought to seduce Rama and Lakshman chased her away, cutting off her ears and nose in the process.

Surpanakha fled deep into the forest, angered and bleeding and she stumbled upon her brother Khara who flew into such a rage at his sister's plight that he set out for Rama's clearing, taking fourteen thousand rakshasas with him – each of which was great, courageous and more horrible in appearance that any rakshasa before him.

Rama had been warned of their coming by Jatayu and was prepared, sending Lakshman and Sita to a secret cave and fighting the rakshasas alone, slaying each of the fourteen thousand evil spirits until at last he stood face to face with Khara. Their battle was fierce and bloody, but Rama stood his ground. At last Khara was consumed by a fiery arrow. And there was silence.

Now far from this scene Ravana was brought news of his sister's maiming and his brother's death.

He was filled with such a rage that he plotted to destroy Rama by secreting away Sita. Ravana sought the advice of his most horrible accomplice, Maricha, who counselled him. Ravana was insistent that he could slay Rama single-handedly, and he ignored Maricha's advice to avoid meddling with Rama who could, if angered, quite easily destroy Ravana's city of Lanka.

Ravana's plan was put into action and the unwilling Maricha took on the form of a golden deer, with horn-like jewels and ears like two rich blue lotus flowers.

He entered the forest clearing, where he flitted between the trees, golden hide glinting. As expected, Sita looked up and cried out with delight. She called to Rama and to Lakshman and she begged them to catch the deer for her pleasure. Rama, too, suspecting nothing, was enchanted by the deer's beauty, and set out to catch her. He began to give chase.

Lakshman stayed behind, suspicious about the extraordinary beauty of the deer, where he kept watch over Sita. There was silence until, from the darkness of the woods, came the cry, 'Sita, Lakshman.'

The words were spoken in Rama's own voice, but they came from the body of the golden deer who had been hit by Rama's arrow. As the deer died he took on the shape of Maricha once again and in a last attempt to lure Lakshman from the forest clearing, he called out as Rama himself. And then he was dead.

Rama moved swiftly, realizing the ruse, but the cry had worked its magic. Lakshman was sent out into the forest by Sita, who feared for Rama's safety, and as that brave one made his way back to Panchavati, Sita was left alone.

Rama and Sita

Alone in the clearing of Panchavati, Sita paced restlessly, concern for her husband and his brother growing ever greater as the moments passed. And then she was startled by a movement in the trees. Into the clearing came a wandering yogi, and Sita smiled her welcome. She would not be alone after all.

She offered the yogi food and water, and told him her identity. She kindly asked for information in return and was startled when he called himself Ravana, and asked her to renounce Rama and become his wife. Ravana gazed at the lovely Sita and a deep jealousy and anger filled his soul. He determined to have her and he cared little now for his revenge of Rama.

Now Sita was enraged by the slight afforded her husband, the great Rama, by this insolent Ravana and she lashed out at him:

'I am the servant of Rama alone, lion among men, immovable as any mountain, as vast as the great ocean, radiant as Indra. Would you draw the teeth from a lion's mouth? Or swim in the sea with a heavy stone about your neck? You are as likely to seek the sun or moon as you are me, for Rama is little like you – he is as different as is the lion from the jackal, the elephant from the cat, the ocean from the tiny stream and gold from silver.' She stopped, fear causing her to tremble.

Ravana roared into the empty clearing, and taking his own shape once again, grabbed the lovely Sita by the hair and made to rise into the air with her. His cry woke the great vulture Jatayu, who had been sleeping in a nearby tree. He rose in outrage and warned the evil spirit of the wrath of Rama, who would certainly let no spirit live who had harmed his most prized possession. But Ravana sprang upon the poor great bird and after a heroic battle, cut away his wings, so that he fell down near death.

Ravana swept Sita into his carriage and rose into the sky. As she left the clearing, Sita cried out to the flowers, and the forest, begging them to pass on her fate to Rama and Lakshman upon their return. And then she cast down her veil and her jewels as a token for her husband.

Ravana returned her to his palace and begged her to become his wife. Her face crumpled in bitter pain and she refused to speak. And as he persisted, she turned to him then and prophesied his certain death at the hands of Rama. And she spoke no more.

Rama returned from the chase of the golden deer with an overwhelming sense of trepidation, and as he met with his brother, far from the clearing, his fears were confirmed. Rama and Lakshman raced towards the hermitage, but Sita had gone. There they found the weapons which had cut down the brave Jatayu, and the dying bird, who raised himself just enough to recount the events of the previous hours. And then, released of his burden, the soul of the great Jatayu rose above the clearing, leaving his body to sag to the ground below.

And so it was that Rama set out with Lakshman to search for Sita, travelling across the country but hearing little news and having no idea where Ravana kept his palace. He met with Sugriva, a king who had been robbed of his wife and his kingdom by his cruel brother Vali, and with the help of Hanuman, chief of the monkeys they continued their search.

Sugriva and Rama formed an alliance and it was agreed that Sugriva would be restored to his throne with the help of Rama. In return Sugriva would put at his disposal the monkey host, to find the poor Sita, already four months lost.

Rama's signet ring was put in Hanuman's possession, to show to Sita as a sign when he found her, but the monkey chief returned with his host, ashamed and saddened that they had been unable to find the beautiful princess. But then, as hope began to fade, there was news. On the coasts of the sea, where the monkeys sat deep in dejection, was a cave in which an old and very wise vulture made his home. He was Sampati, and he was brother to Jatayu. When he heard of his brother's fate he offered to the host his gift of foresight. Ravana, he announced, was with Sita in Lanka.

Hanuman was chosen for the task of retrieving Sita, and he swelled with pride at the prospect of his task. He sprang easily across the thousands of leagues, and across the sea – carelessly knocking down any foe who stood in his path. And so it was that he arrived on the walls of Lanka, and made his way towards the palace. The moon sat high in the sky, and the occupants of the golden city went about their nightly activities.

Making himself invisible, he entered the private apartments of Ravana, who lay sleeping with his many wives around him. But there was no sign of Sita. Hanuman roamed the city, increasingly anxious for the safety of Rama's wife, but she was not to be found. A deep desolation overtook him and he realized the enormity of his task. If he was unable to find the beautiful Sita then Lakshman and Rama would surely die of grief. And Bharata and Satrughna would die too. And the shame that would be brought on Sugriva, and the monkey host – it was too great to contemplate. Hanuman gritted his teeth, and in monkey fashion swung over the palace walls and into the wood.

The wood was cool and shining with gold and gems. In its midst was a marble palace, guarded by the ugliest of rakshasis. In the palace lay the form of a woman, scantily clad in rags and thinner than any living woman.

Hanuman watched as Ravana raised himself and approached the woman, who must surely be Sita. And he watched as the woman scorned him, and ignored his advances. The glitter in her eye betrayed her identity and Hanuman leapt up and down with glee. As Ravana left, the movement of the monkey caught Sita's eye and she looked at him with distrust. Probably Ravana in disguise, she thought tiredly, used to his tricks. But Hanuman whispered to her, and spoke reams of prayers for Rama, extolling his virtues. Sita was bemused and intrigued. She leant forward to hear more. Hanuman leapt down and spoke to Sita of Rama, presenting her with his ring as a token of his continual concern for his dear wife. Sita knew then that Hanuman was friend, not foe, and she poured out stories of Rama, begging Hanuman to return at once to Rama in order that she could be rescued.

Hanuman took with him a jewel from her hair, and departed. His high spirits caused him to frolic on the way, and he could not resist destroying a few of the trees around the palace. His activities drew attention, and he fought at the rakshasas who leapt up to meet him. He wounded or slayed all who approached him until at last he was caught by the enraged Ravana, who promised him instant death.

What could be worse for a monkey, he pronounced, than having his tail set fire? And so it was ordered that Hanuman's tail should be set alight, in order that he should burn to certain death. Now Sita still had powers of her own, and she prayed then, in Rama's name, that the fire should not burn Hanuman, but rage on at the end of his tail, leaving him unscathed. And so it was that Hanuman was able to leap away across Lanka, touching his tail here and there, in order to burn most of that glittering city to the ground. And then, dousing his tail in the wide, curving ocean, he flew across the sea to Rama.

Rama greeted Hanuman which caused the monkey to squirm with delight. He recounted all that had happened in the forest of Lanka, and he told what he had done with his burning tail. The monkey host leapt and cheered for Hanuman for he had brought them great glory with his bravery, and his craftiness.

Sugriva issued orders that all the monkey host should march to the south, in order to lay siege to Lanka. They reached the shores of the sea at Mahendra, and there they made camp. Rama joined them, and the plan to release Sita was formed.

Rama's Bridge

Vibhishana was brother to Ravana, and on the day that Rama set his camp on the shores of the sea, he was pacing around the palace at Lanka. He spoke angrily to his brother, pointing out that if a monkey could lay waste to half the city, what chance did they have against Rama and his monkey host? There could be nothing but death for all.

'From the day that Sita came,' said Vibhishana, 'there have been evil omens – the fire is ever obscured by smoke, serpents are found in kitchens, the milk of kine runs dry, wild beasts howl about the palace. Do restore Sita, lest we all suffer for your sin.'

But Ravana dismissed his brother and said that Sita would be his. Vibhishana begged his brother to see reason, but Ravana had become blind in his obsession with Sita and he would not allow anything to stand in his path. Vibhishana rose then, and heading over the sea with his four advisers, he said to Ravana, 'The fey refuse advice, as a man on the brink of death refuses medicine.'

And so it was that Vibhishana flew across the sea to Rama's camp and announced himself as an ally to the great Rama. A deal was struck.

The ocean was a formidable obstacle to the rescue of Sita, and Rama laid himself flat on the ground, begging the turbulent waters to open for him, in order that they could cross. After many days, if Rama had received no response, he would dry up the sea, and lay Varuna's home bare. Mighty storms erupted and across the world people trembled with fear. At last the ocean himself rose up and spoke to Rama, his head a mass of jewels pinning the great rivers Ganges and Sindhu to its peak. He spoke gently, his power simmering beneath a gentle exterior.

'Great Rama,' he said, 'you know that every element has its own qualities. Mine is this – to be fathomless and hard to cross. Neither for love nor fear can I stay the waters from their endless movement. But you can pass over me by way of a bridge, and I will suffer it and hold it firm.'

And so Rama was calmed, and plans were made to build a bridge. With the permission of the ocean, Rama dried up the waters of the north, causing the sea there to become a desert. Then he sent a shaft which caused that dry earth to bloom with woods and vines and flowers. The ocean presented to Rama and his men a fine monkey named Nala, Vishvakarma's son, and the monkey set in force a plan to build a bridge like none other. The host of monkeys began to follow his orders, and bit by bit, timber and rocks were thrust on to the sea until a mighty bridge was formed across its girth. And the monkey host and Rama passed over, in order that the siege of Lanka would begin.

The siege of Lanka was a story which took many years to resolve, and it involved the near deaths of Rama and each of his men. Garuda himself came down to heal their wounds, and the men fought on until, finally, Ravana was slain by Rama – with the Brahma weapon given to him by Agastya. Only this weapon had the force to take the life of the evil spirit, and the wind lay on the wings of this weapon, the sun and fire in its head, and in its mass the weight of Meru and Mandara. Rama held a mighty bow and the arrow was sent forth, where it met its mark on the breast of Ravana. The lord of the rakshasas was slain, and all of the gods poured bouquets of blossoms, rainbows of happiness upon Rama and his men. Rama's greatest achievement – the reason for Vishnu ever having taken human form – had been accomplished. Rama ordered Sita to be brought to him at once.

Rama knew that Sita would not be accepted by his people, for she had lived in another man's house and they had no reason to believe that she was not stained by his touch. Rama greeted her coldly, and told her that he had no choice but to renounce her, as he must renounce everything that had been in contact with the greatest of evils. Sita, begged and pleaded – insisting upon her dedication to her glorious husband, and her continual and undying devotion.

'Oh king,' wept Sita, throwing herself at Rama's feet, 'why did you not renounce me when Hanuman came? I could have given up my life at that time, and you need not have laboured to find me, nor laid a burden on your friends. You are angry – like a common man you are seeing nothing in me but womanhood. I am the daughter of Janaka, Rama, and I am also daughter of the earth. I was born of earth and you do not know my true self.'

She turned then to Lakshman, and she said bravely, 'Build me a funeral pyre, for there is my only refuge. I will not live with an undeserved brand.'

And the fire was prepared.

The gods threw themselves upon the mercy of Rama, praying that he should relent. And an elderly Brahma came forward and spoke words that fell on the ears of the gods and all around them like jewels: 'Sita is Lakshmi and you are Vishnu and Krishna. No stain has touched Sita, and although she was tempted in every way, she did not even consider Ravana in her innermost heart. She is spotless.' The fire roared up in approval, and added, 'Take her back.'

And so Sita was returned to Rama's side, where he pledged his undying love for her. He explained then that this test had been for her own safety – that their followers would now respect her once again for she had been proved pure. Together they set out for Ayodhya, and home.

It had been fourteen long years since Rama had left Ayodhya, but the memory of him and his goodness had remained etched in the hearts of every citizen. When they arrived through the gates of the city, they were greeted with uproarious cheers, and celebrations like none other were begun across the land. Bharata bowed to Sita and threw himself at Rama's feet. The kingdom was restored to Rama, and Bharata cried:

'Let the world behold you today, installed, like the radiant sun at midday. No one but you can bear the heavy burden of our empire. Sleep and rise to the sound of music and the tinkle of women's anklets. May you rule the people as long as the sun endures, and as far as the earth extends.'

'So it shall be,' said Rama.

Rama reigned happily in Ayodhya for ten thousand years, and then the day came when Sita conceived a child. Delighted by her news, he begged her to allow him to honour her with any wish, and she expressed a wish to visit the hermitages by the Ganges. Her wish was instantly granted and preparations were made for her travel. Lakshman was to accompany her, but before he left, he took counsel with his brother, the great Rama.

'I am concerned,' said Rama, 'that we know the feelings of our ministers and our people. We must call a conference to ensure that all is well in the kingdom.'

And so a conference was duly called and all of the counsellors and friends of Rama pledged their love for him, and their devotion. There was, however, one unhappiness which stained the otherwise perfect fabric of his rule.

'The people murmur that you have taken back Sita, although she was touched by Ravana and dwelt for many years in Lanka. For all that, they say, you still acknowledge her. That is the talk.' Rama's finest officer uttered these words and as he heard them, Rama's heart was chilled through and through. He sent for Lakshman and pronounced Sita's sorry fate.

'I am crushed by these slanders,' said Rama, 'for Sita was pronounced unstained by gods and fire and wind. But the censure of the people has pierced and this ill-fame can only bring me great disgrace. Take Sita tomorrow and leave her there, brother, and remove yourself now before I can change my mind.'

And so Sita and Lakshman travelled to the Ganges, armed with gifts for the hermits. When they arrived, Lakshman explained Rama's wish. Sita fell into a deep faint from which it took many minutes to recover. When she did, she spoke of her desolation, and her fear at being able to survive in the forest. She could not live there, she feared, and yet she would do so because her master had decreed it. She was faithful. She was unstained. She was prepared to prove it.

The Sons of Rama

The world about Rama was changing, and he was advised by the gods and by his counsellors that the age of Kali had begun. He continued to undertake acts of great kindness and goodness and his fine name sat comfortably on the tongues of subjects across the kingdom. But Rama was lonely. He longed for his great love Sita, and he longed for the day when she would be declared cleansed of all unrighteousness.

And that day came at last, when Rama prepared a horse sacrifice, and invited the hermit Valmiki to the ceremony. He was accompanied by two young boys, Kusha and Lava, and Rama was overjoyed to discover that these were the sons born of Sita, and that she was well and still living with the hermit Valmiki.

His two sons were born in his likeness, with voices as pure as a bird's. They were humble and kind, and when he offered them money for their performance to the people of the kingdom, they refused, saying that they had no need of money in the forest.

Sita was sent for, and Valmiki returned to his hermitage to fetch her. Sita followed Valmiki into a waiting assembly, where the hermit made a pronouncement: 'Oh Rama, Sita is pure and she did follow the path of righteousness but you renounced her because of the censure of your people. Do you now permit her to give testimony of her purity? These twin children are your sons, Rama, and I swear before you that if any sin can be found in Sita I will forgo the fruit of all austerities I have practised for many thousand years.'

And so Sita said quietly, 'I have never loved nor thought of anyone but Rama, even in my innermost heart. This is true. May the goddess of the earth be my protection. I pray now for Vasundhara to receive me.'

And the earth then thrust under the lovely Sita a throne so beautiful that each in the assembly gasped with pleasure. But the earth curled that throne around Sita and drew her back again into itself, home once again and part of the beginning and end of all things.

Rama screamed with despair and fought against the anger that threatened to engulf him Rama carried on ruling then, for some time, but his heart was no longer in his country. Lakshman travelled to a hermitage and was eventually returned to Indra as part of Vishnu. Bharata no longer wished the kingdom, although Rama begged him to take it back, and eventually it was decreed that Kusha and Lava should rule the kingdom as two cities. But Ayodhya, as it once was, was no longer a kingdom to be ruled, for when Rama left he was followed by all of his people.

Rama joined together with his brothers then, and with the blessing and prayers of the gods and the entire population of his kingdom, he returned to Heaven as Vishnu, in his own form, with his brothers. All of the gods knelt down before him and they rejoiced.

And Brahma appointed places in the heavens for all who had come after Rama, and the animals were given their godly form. Each reached his heavenly state, and in Heaven, all was once again at peace.

On earth it was decreed that the Ramayana should be told far and wide. And to this day, it is.

The Saga of Mahabharata

THE MAHABHARATA is one of the most magnificent epic poems of all time, and the longest in any language. The name *Mahabharata* probably applies to the Bharatas, who were descendants of King Bharata, the brother of Rama. The poem is unique in Indian literature, for it is driven mainly by the interplay of real people, rather than gods and demons, and it uses a plethora of very lively, dramatic and exciting personalities to present its message. Many believe that the entire philosophy of India is implicit in its romance, and its message is acted out in the great war waged between two ancient families – the Pandavas and the Kauravas.

Our narrative begins with the romantic stories centred around the names of the legendary ancestors of the Kauravas and the Pandavas. The sympathies of the Brahmanic compilers are with the latter, who are symbolized as 'a vast tree formed of religion and virtue', while their opponents are 'a great tree formed of passion'. The father of the great King Bharata was Dushyanta of the lunar race, the descendant of Atri, the Deva-rishi, and of Soma, the moon; his mother was beautiful Shakuntala, the hermit maiden, and daughter of a nymph from the celestial regions.

The poem was finally edited by Krishna Dvaipayana, or Vyasa the Compiler, but since this character is, too, mythical, it is doubtful that his contribution is authentic. There have been many interpretations and many hands turning the text and indeed the pages of the *Mahabharata* over the centuries – and they have served not to clutter but to make clear the extraordinary vividness of the characterization, and the reasons why this has become the Indian national saga.

Dushyanta and Shakuntala

One day King Dushyanta, that tiger among men, left his stately palace to go hunting with a great host and many horses and elephants. He entered a deep jungle and there killed numerous wild animals; his arrows wounded tigers at a distance; he felled those that came near with his great sword. Lions fled from before him, wild elephants stampeded in terror, deer sought to escape hastily, and birds rose in the air uttering cries of distress.

The king, attended by a single follower, pursued a deer across a desert plain, and entered a beautiful forest which delighted his heart, for it was deep and shady, and was cooled by soft winds; sweet-throated birds sang in the branches, and all round about there were blossoming trees and blushing flowers; he heard the soft notes of the kokila, and beheld many a green bower carpeted with grass and canopied by many-coloured creepers.

Dushyanta, abandoning the chase, wandered on until he came to a delightful and secluded hermitage, where he saw the sacred fire of that austere and high-souled Brahman, the saintly Kanva. It was a scene of peace and beauty. Blossoms from the trees covered the ground; tall were the trunks, and the branches were far-sweeping. A silvery stream went past, breaking on the banks in milk-white foam; it was the sacred River Malini, studded with green islands, loved by water fowl, and abounding with fish.

Then the king was taken with desire to visit the holy sage, Kanva, he who is without darkness. So he relieved himself of his royal insignia and entered the sacred grove alone. Bees were humming; birds trilled their many melodies; he heard the low chanting voices of Brahmans among the trees – those holy men who can take captive all human hearts....

When he reached the home of Kanva, he found that it was empty, and called out: 'Who is here?' and the forest echoed his voice.

Then a beautiful black-eyed virgin came towards him, clad in a robe of bark. She reverenced the king and said: 'What do you seek? I am your servant.'

Dushyanta replied to the maiden of faultless form and gentle voice: 'I have come to honour the wise and blessed Kanva. Tell me, fair and amiable one, where he has gone?'

The maiden answered: 'My illustrious father is gathering herbs, but if you will wait he will return before long.'

Dushyanta was entranced by the beauty and sweet smiles of the gentle girl, and his heart was moved towards her. So he spoke, saying: 'Who are you, fairest one? Where do you come from and why do you wander alone in the woods? Beautiful maiden, you have taken captive my heart.'

The bright-eyed one answered: 'I am the daughter of the holy and high-souled Kanva, the ever-wise and ever-constant.'

'But,' said the king, 'Kanva is chaste and austere and has always been celibate. He cannot have broken his rigid vow. How could it be that you were born the daughter of such a one?'

Then the maiden, who was named Shakuntala, because of the birds (shakunta) who had nursed her, revealed to the king the secret of her birth. Her real father was Vishwamitra, the holy sage who had been a Kshatriya and was made a Brahman in reward for his austerities. It came to pass that Indra became alarmed at his growing power, and he feared that the mighty sage of blazing energy would, by reason of his penances, cast down even him, the king of the gods, from his heavenly seat. So Indra commanded Menaka, the beautiful Apsara, to disturb the holy meditations of the sage, for he had already achieved such power that he created a second world and many stars. The nymph called on the wind god and on the god of love, and they went with her towards Vishwamitra.

Menaka danced before the brooding sage; then the wind god snatched away her moon-white garments, and the love god shot his arrows at Vishwamitra, whereupon that saintly man was stricken with love for the nymph of peerless beauty, and he wooed her and won her as his bride. So was he diverted from his austerities. In time Menaka became the mother of a girl babe, whom she cast away on the river bank.

Now the forest was full of lions and tigers, but vultures gathered round the infant and protected her from harm. Then Kanva found and took pity on the child; he said: 'She will be mine own daughter.'

Shakuntala said: 'I was that child who was abandoned by the nymph, and now you know how Kanva came to be my father.'

The king said: 'Blessed are your words, princess. You are of royal birth. Be my bride, beautiful maid, and you will have garlands of gold and golden earrings and white pearls and rich robes; my kingdom also will be yours, timid one.'

Then Shakuntala promised to be the king's bride, on condition that he would choose her son as the heir to his throne.

'As you desire, so let it be,' said Dushyanta. And the fair one became his bride.

When Dushyanta went away he promised Shakuntala that he would send a mighty host to escort her to his palace.

When Kanva returned, the maiden did not leave her hiding place to greet him; but he searched out and found her, and he read her heart. 'You have not broken the law,' he said.

'Dushyanta, my husband, is noble and true, and a son will be born to me who will achieve great renown.'

Shakuntala's Appeal

In time fair Shakuntala became the mother of a handsome boy, and the wheel mark was on his hands. He grew to be strong and brave, and when just six years old he sported with young lions, for he was suckled by a lioness; he rode on the backs of lions and tigers and wild boars in the midst of the forest. He was called All-tamer, because he tamed everything.

Now when Kanva perceived that the boy was of unequalled prowess, he spoke to Shakuntala and said: 'The time has come when he must be anointed as heir to the throne.' So he ordered his disciples to escort mother and son to the city of Gajasahvaya, where Dushyanta had his royal palace.

So it came that Shakuntala once again stood before the king, and she said to him: 'I have brought to your son, Dushyanta. Fulfil the promise you made, and let him be anointed as your heir.'

Dushyanta had no pleasure in her words, and answered: 'I have no memory of you. Who are you and where did you come from, wicked hermit woman? I never took you for my wife, nor care I whether you are to linger here or to depart speedily.'

Stunned by his cold answer, the sorrowing Shakuntala stood there like a log.... Soon her eyes became red as copper and her lips trembled; she cast burning glances at the monarch. For a time she was silent; then she exclaimed: 'King without shame, well do you know who I am. Why will you deny knowledge of me as if you were but an inferior person? Your heart is a witness against you. Be not a robber of your own affections.... The gods behold everything: nothing is hidden from them; they will not bless one who degrades himself by speaking falsely regarding himself. Spurn not the mother of your son; spurn not your faithful wife. A true wife bears a son; she is the first of friends and the source of salvation; she enables her husband to perform religious acts, her sweet speeches bring him joy; she is a solace and a comforter in sickness and in sorrow; she is a companion in this world and the next. If a husband dies, a wife follows soon afterwards; if she is gone before, she waits for her husband in heaven. She is the mother of the son who performs the funeral rite to secure everlasting bliss for his father, rescuing him from the hell called Put. Therefore a man should reverence the mother of his son, and look upon his son as if he saw his own self in a mirror, rejoicing as if he had found heaven.... Why, king, do you spurn your own child? Even the ants will protect their eggs; strangers far from home take the children of others on their knees to be made happy, but you have no compassion for this child, although he is your son, your own image.... What sin did I commit in my former state that I should have been deserted by my parents and now by you!... If I must go, take your son to your bosom.'

Dushyanta said: 'It has been well said that all women are liars. Who will believe you? I know nothing regarding you or your son.... Go away wicked woman, for you are without shame.'

Shakuntala replied, speaking boldly and without fear: 'King, you can perceive the shortcomings of others, although they may be as small as mustard seeds; you are blind to your own sins, although they may be big as Vilwa fruit. As the swine loves dirt even in a flower garden, so do the wicked perceive evil in all that the good relate. Honest men refrain from speaking ill of others: the wicked rejoice in scandal. Truth is the chief of all virtues. Truth is God himself. Do not break your vow of truth: let truth be ever a part of you. But if you would rather be false, I must go, for such a one as you should be avoided.... Yet know now, Dushyanta, that when you are gone, my son will be king of this world, which is surrounded by the four seas and adorned by the monarch of mountains.'

Shakuntala then turned from the king, but a voice out of heaven spoke softly down the wind, saying: 'Shakuntala has uttered what is true. Therefore, Dushyanta, cherish your son, and by command of the gods, let his name be Bharata ('the cherished').'

When the king heard these words, he spoke to his counsellors and said: 'The celestial messenger has spoken.... Had I welcomed this my son by pledge of Shakuntala alone, men would suspect the truth of her words and doubt his royal birth.'

Then Dushyanta embraced his son and kissed him, and he honoured Shakuntala as his chief rani; he said to her, soothingly: 'I have concealed our union from all men; and for the sake of your own good name I hesitated to acknowledge you. Forgive my harsh words, as I forgive yours. You spoke passionately because you love me, great-eyed and fair one, whom I love also.'

The son of Shakuntala was then anointed as heir to the throne, and he was named Bharata.

When Dushyanta died, Bharata became king. Great was his fame, as befitted a descendant of Chandra. He was a mighty warrior, and none could withstand him in battle; he made great conquests, and extended his kingdom all over Hindustan, which was called Bharatavarsha.

King Bharata was the father of King Hastin, who built the great city of Hastinapur; King Hastin the father of King Kuru, and King Kuru the father of King Shantanu.

King Shantanu and the Goddess Bride

It is said of the King Shantanu that he was pious and just and all-powerful, as was proper for the great grandson of King Bharata. His first wife was the goddess Ganga of the Ganges river. She was divinely beautiful. Before she assumed human form for a time, the eight Vasus (the attendants of Indra) came to her. It happened that when the Brahman Vasishtha was engaged in his holy meditations the Vasus flew between him and the sun, whereupon the angered sage cursed them, saying: 'Be born among men!' They could not escape this fate, so great was the Rishi's power over celestial beings. So they hastened to Ganga, and she consented to become their human mother, promising that she would cast them one by one into the Ganges soon after birth, so that they might return to their celestial state. For this service Ganga made each of the Vasus promise to confer an eighth part of his power on her son, who, according to her wishes, should remain among men for many years, but would never marry or have any offspring.

Soon a day came when King Shantanu walked beside the Ganges. Suddenly a maiden of surpassing beauty appeared before him. She was Ganga in human form. Her celestial garments had the splendour of lotus blooms; she was adorned with rare ornaments, and her teeth were as radiant as pearls. The king was silenced by her charms, and gazed at her.... In time he perceived that the maiden looked at him with love-lorn eyes, as if she sought to look at him forever, and he spoke to her, saying: 'Fair one, are you one of the Danavas, or are you of the race of Gandharvas, or are you of the Apsaras; are you one of the Yakshas or Nagas, or are you of human kind? Be my bride.'

The goddess answered that she would marry the king, but said she must leave him at once if he spoke harshly to her at any time, or attempted to stop her doing as she willed. Shantanu consented to her terms, and Ganga became his bride.

In time the goddess gave birth to a son, but soon afterwards she cast him into the Ganges, saying: 'This for your welfare.'

The king was stricken with horror, but he spoke not a word to his beautiful bride in case she should leave him.

So were seven babies, one after another, destroyed by their mother in this way. When the eighth was born, the goddess sought to drown him, too; but the king's pent-up wrath finally broke, and he reprimanded his heartless wife. Thus his marriage vow was broken, and Ganga was given power to leave him. But before she went she revealed to the king who she was, and also why she had cast the Vasus, her children, into the Ganges. Then she suddenly vanished from before his eyes, taking the last baby with her.

The Story of Satyavati

One day the fair goddess briefly returned to Shantanu. She brought with her a fair and noble son, who was endowed with the virtues of the Vasus. Then she departed never to come again. The heart of king Shantanu was moved towards the child, who became a handsome and powerful youth, and was named Satanava.

When Shantanu had grown old, he sought to marry a young and beautiful bride whom he loved. For one day as he walked beside the Jumna river he was attracted by a sweet and alluring perfume, which drew him through the trees until he beheld a maiden of celestial beauty with luminous black eyes. The king spoke to her and said: 'Who are you, and whose daughter, timid one? What are you doing here?'

The maiden blessed Shantanu and said: 'I am the daughter of a fisherman, and I ferry passengers across the river in my boat.'

Now, the name of this fair maiden was Satyavati. Like Shakuntala, she was of miraculous origin, and had been adopted by her reputed father. It happened that a fish once carried away in its stomach two unborn babies, a girl and a boy, whose father was a great king. This fish was caught by a fisherman, who opened it and found the children. He sent the boy to the king and kept the girl, who was reared as his own daughter. She grew to be beautiful, but a fishy odour ever clung to her.

One day, as she ferried pilgrims across the Jumna, the high and pious Brahman Parashara entered her boat. He was moved by the maiden's great beauty. He desired that she should become the mother of his son, and promised that ever afterwards an alluring perfume would emanate from her body. He then caused a cloud to fall on the boat, and it vanished from sight.

When the fisher girl became the mother of a son, he grew suddenly before her eyes, and in a brief space was a man. His name was Vyasa; he wished his mother farewell, and rushed to the depths of a forest to spend his days in holy meditation. Before he left he said to Satyavati: 'If ever you have need of me, think of me, and I will come to your aid.'

When this wonder had been accomplished, Satyavati became a virgin again through the power of the great sage Parashara, and a delicious odour lingered about her ever afterwards.

On this maiden King Shantanu gazed with love. Then he sought the fisherman, and said he desired the maiden to be his bride. But the man refused to give his daughter to the king in marriage until he promised that her son should be chosen as heir to the throne. Shantanu could not consent to disinherit Satanava, son of Ganga, and went away with a heavy heart.

Greatly the king sorrowed in his heart because of his love for the dark-eyed maiden, and eventually Satanava was told of his secret love. So the noble son of Ganga went to search for the beautiful daughter of the fisherman, and he found her. After he told the fisherman of his mission, the fisherman said to him: 'If Satyavati bears sons, they will not inherit the kingdom, for the king already has a son, and he will succeed him.'

So Satanava made a vow renouncing his claim to the throne, and said: 'If you will give your daughter to my father to be his queen, I, who am his heir, will never accept the throne, nor marry a wife, or be the father of children. If, then, Satyavati will become the mother of a son, he will surely be chosen as king.' After he said this, the gods and Apsaras (the mist fairies) caused flowers to fall out of heaven on to the prince's head, and a voice came down the wind, saying: 'This one is Bhishma.'

From that day on, the son of Ganga was called Bhishma, which signifies the 'Terrible', for the vow that he had taken was terrible indeed.

Then Satyavati was given in marriage to the king, and she bore him two sons, who were named Chitrangada and Vichitra-virya.

In time Shantanu sank under the burden of his years, and his soul departed from his body. Bhishma was left to care of the queen-mother, Satyavati, and the two princes.

When the days of mourning went past, Bhishma renounced the throne in accordance with his vow, and Chitrangada was proclaimed king. This youth was a haughty ruler, and his reign was brief. He waged war against the Gandharai of the hills for three years, and was slain in battle by their king. Then Bhishma placed Vichitra-virya on the throne, and, as he was but a boy, Bhishma ruled as regent for some years.

Marriage by Capture

Many years later the time came for the young king to marry, and Bhishma set out to find wives for him. It so happened that the King of Kasi (Benares) had three fair daughters whose swayamvara was being proclaimed. When Bhishma was told of this he immediately climbed aboard his chariot and drove from Hastinapur to Kasi to discover if the girls were worthy of the monarch of Bharatavarsha. He found that they had great beauty, which pleased him.

The great city was thronged with kings who had gathered from far and near to woo the maidens, but Bhishma would not wait until the day of the swayamvara. He immediately seized the king's fair daughters and placed them in his chariot. Then he challenged the assembled kings and sons of kings in a voice like thunder, saying: 'The sages have decreed that a king may give his daughter with many gifts to one he has invited when she has chosen him. Others may barter their daughters, and some may give them in exchange for gold. But maidens may also be taken captive. They may be married by consent, or forced to consent, or be obtained by sanction of their fathers. Some are given wives as reward for performing sacrifices, a form approved by the sages. Kings ever favour the swayamvara, and obtain wives according to its rules. But learned men have declared that the wife who is to be most highly esteemed is she who is taken captive after battle with the royal guests who attend a swayamvara. Hear and know, then, mighty kings, I will carry off these fair daughters of the king of Kasi, and I challenge all who are here to overcome me or else be overcome themselves by me in battle.'

The royal guests who were there accepted the challenge, and Bhishma fought against them with great fury. Bows were bent and ten thousand arrows were discharged against him, but he broke their flight with innumerable darts from his own mighty bow. Strong and brave was he indeed; there was no one who could overcome him; he fought and conquered all, until not one king was left to contend against him.

So Bhishma, the terrible son of the ocean-going Ganga, took the three fair daughters of the King of Kasi captive; and he drove away with them in his chariot towards Hastinapur.

When he reached the royal palace he presented the maidens to Queen Satyavati, who was very pleased. In return she gave many costly gifts to Bhishma. She decided that the captives should become the wives of her son, King Vichitra-virya.

Before the wedding ceremony was held, the eldest maiden, whose name was Amba, pleaded with the queen to be set free, saying: 'I have been betrothed already by my father to the King of Sanva. Oh, send me to him now, for I cannot marry a second time.'

Her prayer was granted, and Bhishma sent her with an escort to the King of Sanva. Then the fair Amba told him how she had been taken captive; but the king exclaimed, with anger: 'You have already dwelt in the house of a strange man, and I cannot take you for my wife.'

The maiden wept bitterly, and she knelt before the monarch and said: 'No man has wronged me, mighty king. Bhishma has taken a terrible vow of celibacy which he cannot break. If you will not have me for your wife, I pray you to take me as your concubine, so that I may live safely in your palace.'

But the king spurned the beautiful maiden, and his servants drove her from the palace and out of the city. So was she compelled to seek refuge in the lonely forest, and there she practised great austerities in order to secure power to slay Bhishma, who had wronged her. In the end she threw herself on a pyre, so that she might attain her desire in the next life.

Her two sisters, Amvika and Amvalika, became the wives of Vitchitra-virya, who loved them well; but his days were brief, and he wasted away with sickness until eventually he died. No children were born to the king, and his two widows mourned for him.

The heart of Queen Satyavati was stricken with grief because her two sons were dead, and there was no heir left to the throne of King Bharata.

Origin of Dhritarashtra, Pandu, and Vidura

Now it was the custom in those days that a kinsman should become the father of children to succeed the dead king. So Queen Satyavati spoke to Bhishma, saying: 'Take the widows of my son and raise up sons who will be as sons of the king.'

But Bhishma said: 'That I cannot do, as have I not vowed never to be the father of any children.'

In her despair Satyavati then thought of her son Vyasa, and he immediately appeared before her and consented to do what she wished.

Now Vyasa was a mighty sage, but, because of his austerities in his lonely jungle dwelling, he had grown gaunt and ugly so that women shrank from him; he was fearsome to look at.

Amvika closed her eyes with horror when she saw the sage, and she had a son who was born blind: he was named Dhritarashtra. Amvalika turned pale with fear: she had a son who was named Pandu, 'the pale one'.

Satyavati wished that Vyasa should be the father of a son who had no defect; but Amvika sent her handmaiden to him, and she bore a son who was called Vidura. As it happened, Dharma, god of justice, was put under the spell of a Rishi at this time, to be born among men, and he chose Vidura to be his human incarnation.

The three children were reared by Bhishma, who was regent over the kingdom, but nevertheless subject to Queen Satyavati. He taught them the laws and trained them as warriors. When the time came to select a king, Dhritarashtra was passed over because that he was blind, and Vidura because of his humble birth, and Pandu, 'the pale one', was set upon the throne.

The Birth of Karna

King Pandu became a mighty monarch, and was renowned as a warrior and a just ruler of his kingdom. He married two wives: Pritha, who was chief rani, and Madri, whom he loved best.

Now Pritha was of celestial origin, for her mother was a nymph; her father was a holy Brahman, and her brother, Vasudeva, was the father of Krishna. As a baby she had been adopted by the King of Shurasena, whose kingdom was among the Vindhya mountains. She was of pious heart, and ever showed reverence towards holy men. Once the great Rishi Durvasas came to the palace, and she ministered to him faithfully by serving food at any hour he desired, and by kindling the sacred fire in the sacrificial chamber. After his stay of a full year, Durvasas, in reward for her services, imparted to Pritha a powerful charm, by virtue of which she could compel the love of a celestial being. One day she had a vision of Surya, god of the sun; she muttered the charm, and received him when he came near in the attire of a king, wearing the celestial earrings. In secret she became in time the mother of his son, Karna, who was equipped at birth with celestial earrings and an invulnerable coat of mail, which had power to grow as the wearer increased in stature. The child had the eyes of a lion and the shoulders of a bull.

In her maidenly shame Pritha resolved to conceal her newborn babe. So she wrapped him in soft sheets and, laying his head on a pillow, placed him in a wicker basket which she had smeared over with wax. Then, weeping bitterly, she set the basket afloat on the river, saying: 'My babe, be you protected by all who are on land, and in the water, and in the sky, and in the celestial regions! May all who see you love you! May Varuna, god of the waters, shield you from harm. May your father, the sun, give you warmth!… I shall know you in days to come, wherever you may be, by your coat of golden mail.... She who will find you and adopt you will be surely blessed.... Oh my son, she who will cherish you will behold you in youthful prime like to a maned lion in Himalayan forests.'

The basket drifted down the River Aswa until it was no longer seen by that lotus-eyed damsel, and after some time it reached the Jumna; the Jumna gave it to the Ganges, and by that great and holy river it was carried to the country of Anga.... The child, lying in soft slumber, was kept alive because of the virtues possessed by the celestial armour and the earrings.

Now there was a woman of Anga whose name was Radha, and she had peerless beauty. Her husband was Shatananda, the charioteer. Both husband and wife had long wished for a son of their own. One day, however, their wish was granted. It happened that Radha went down to the river bank, and she saw the basket drifting on the waves. She brought it ashore; and when it was uncovered, she gazed with wonder at a sleeping babe who was as fair as the morning sun. Her heart was immediately filled with happiness, and she cried out: 'The gods have heard me at last, and they have sent me a son.' So she adopted the babe and cherished him. And the years went past, and Karna grew up and became a powerful youth and a mighty bowman.

King Pandu's Doom

Pritha, who was beautiful to behold, chose King Pandu at her swayamvara. Trembling with love, she placed the flower garland on his shoulders.

Madri came from the country of Madra, and was black-eyed and dusky-complexioned. She had been purchased by Bhishma for the king with gold, jewels, elephants and horses, as was the marriage custom among her people.

The glories of King Bharata's reign were revived by Pandu, who achieved great conquests and extended his territory. He loved well to go hunting, and eventually he retired to the Himalaya mountains with his two wives to hunt deer. There, as fate had decreed, he met with dire misfortune. One day he shot arrows at two deer; but as he discovered to his sorrow, they were a holy Brahman and his wife in animal form. The sage was mortally wounded, and before he died he assumed his human form. He cursed Pandu, and foretold that he would die in the arms of one of his wives.

The king was stricken with fear; he immediately took vows of celibacy, and gave all his possessions to Brahmans; then he went away to live in a solitary place with his two wives.

Some have told that Pandu never had children of his own, and that the gods were the fathers of his wives' great sons. Pritha was mother of Yudhishthira, son of Dharma, god of justice, and of Bhima, son of Vayu, the wind god, and also of Arjuna, son of mighty Indra, monarch of heaven. Madri received from Pritha the charm which Durvasas had given her, and she became the mother of Nakula and Sahadeva. These five princes were known as the Pandava brothers.

King Pandu was followed by his doom. One day he met with Madri, his favourite wife; they wandered together in a forest, and when he clasped her in his arms he immediately fell dead as the Brahman had foretold.

His sons, the Pandava brothers, built his funeral pyre, so that his soul might pass to heaven. Both Pritha and Madri wished to be burned with him, and they debated together which of them should follow her lord to the region of the dead.

Pritha said: 'I must go with my lord. I was his first wife and chief rani. Madri, yield me his body and raise our children together. Let me achieve what must be achieved.'

Madri said: 'I should be the chosen one. I was King Pandu's favourite wife, and he died because he loved me. If I survived you I would not be able to raise our children as you can. Do not refuse your sanction to this which is dear to my heart.'

So they could not agree; but the Brahmans, who heard them, said that Madri must be burned with King Pandu, having been his favourite wife. And so it came to pass that Madri laid herself on the pyre, and she passed in flames with her beloved lord, that bull among men.

The Rival Princes

Meanwhile King Pandu's blind brother, Dhritarashtra, had ascended the throne to reign over the kingdom of Bharatavarsha, with Bhishma as his regent, until the elder of the young princes should come of age.

Dhritarashtra had married Gandharai, daughter of the King of Gandhara. When she was betrothed she went to the king with eyes blindfolded, and ever afterwards she so appeared in his presence. She became the mother of a hundred sons, the eldest of whom was Duryodhana. These were the princes who were named the Kauravas.

The widowed Pritha returned to Hastinapur with her three sons and the two sons of Madri also. When she told Dhritarashtra that Pandu, his brother, had died, he wept and mourned. The blind king gave his protection to the five princes who were Pandu's heirs.

So the Pandavas and Kauravas were raised together in the royal palace at Hastinapur. Favour was not shown to one cousin more than another. The young princes were trained to throw the stone and to cast the noose, and they engaged lustily in wrestling bouts and practised boxing. As they grew up they shared work with the king's men; they marked the young calves, and every three years they counted and branded the cattle. Yet, despite all that could be done, the two families lived at enmity. Of all the young men Bhima, of the Pandavas, was the most powerful, and Duryodhana, the leader of the Kauravas, was jealous of him. Bhima was always the victor in sports and contests. The Kauravas could not endure his triumphs, and they plotted among themselves to accomplish his death.

It happened that the young men had gone to live in a royal palace on the banks of the Ganges. One day as they feasted together, Duryodhana put poison in Bhima's food. Shortly afterwards he fainted and seemed to be dead. Then Duryodhana bound him hand and foot and cast him into the Ganges; his body was swallowed by the waters.

But it was not fated that Bhima should perish. As his body sank down, the fierce snakes, which are called Nagas, attacked him; but their poison counteracted the poison he had already swallowed, so that he regained consciousness. Then, bursting his bonds, he scattered the reptiles before him, and they fled in terror.

Bhima found that he had sunk down to the city of serpents in the underworld. Vasuki, king of the Nagas, having heard of his prowess, hastened towards the young warrior, whom he greatly desired to behold.

Bhima was welcomed by Aryaka, the great grandfather of Pritha, who was a dweller in the underworld. He was loved by Vasuki, who, for Aryaka's sake, offered great gifts to the fearless Bhima. But Aryaka chose rather that the boy should be given a draught of strength which contained the virtues of a thousand Nagas. This great favour was granted by the king of serpents, and Bhima was permitted to drain the bowl eight times. He immediately fell into a deep sleep, which lasted for eight days. Then he awoke, and he returned again to his mother, who was mourning for him all the while. So it happened that Bhima triumphed over Duryodhana, forever afterwards he possessed the strength of a mighty giant. He told his brothers all that had happened to him, but they counselled him not to reveal his secret to the Kauravas, his cousins.

The Princes Learn to Shoot

Bhishma was royal grandfather to the houses of Pandava and Kauravas, and he was eager for the princes of these royal houses to have a teacher who could train them in the dignified and royal use of arms. He had put out a search for such a teacher when it happened that the boys themselves were playing ball in the forests outside Hastinapura, when their ball rolled away from them and fell into a well. Although they struggled, and used all of their inventiveness, all efforts to reach it failed, and the ball was lost to them.

The boys sat glumly by the well, gazing with frustration at its walls when suddenly there was a movement from the corner of their eyes. There, thin and dark, sat a Brahman who seemed to be resting after his daily worship.

The boys eagerly surrounded him and begged him to recover their ball.

The Brahman smiled at their boyish jinks and teased them, for what offspring of a royal house could not shoot well enough to retrieve a ball? He promised to do so himself, for the price of a dinner. And then the Brahman threw his ring into the well and promised to bring that up too – using only a few blades of grass.

The boys surrounded the Brahman, intrigued. 'Why that's magic,' said one of the boys. 'We could make you rich for life if you could do as you say.'

The Brahman was true to his word and selecting a piece of grass he threw it as if it were a sword, deep into the heart of the well and there it pierced the ball straight through. He immediately threw another blade, which pierced the first, and then another, which pierced the second, until soon he had a chain of grass with which to draw up the ball.

The boys had by now lost interest in their ball, but their fascination with the Brahman was growing by the moment.

'The ring,' they chorused. 'Show us how you can get the ring.'

And so it was that Drona, which was the name of that Brahman, took up his bow, which had been lying by his side, and choosing an arrow, and then carefully fitting it to the bow, he shot it into the well. Within seconds it had returned, bearing with it the ring. He handed it to the boys who whooped and hollered with glee.

They surrounded Drona again, begging him to allow them to help him, to offer him some gift. Drona grew silent and then with great effort he spoke, carefully choosing his words.

'There is something you can do,' he said quietly. 'You can tell Bhishma your guardian that Drona is here.'

The boys trooped home again and recounted their adventure to Bhishma. Their guardian was at once struck by the good fortune of this visit for he did indeed know of Drona and he would, it seemed, be the perfect teacher for these unruly boys. Bhishma had known Drona as the son of the great sage Gharadwaja, whose ashrama in the mountains had been a centre of higher learning. Many illustrious students had attended as scholars, and most of these had befriended Drona who had been, even then, gifted with divine weapons and the knowledge of how to use them.

Drona had fallen upon hard times when he had pledged his allegiance to Drupada, now king of the Panchalas. Drupada and Drona had been fast friends as scholars, but as regent, Drupada scorned their ancient friendship and set the poor Brahman in the position of a beggar. Hurt by his friend's actions, Drona had left to pursue his studies, and his first task was to find the best pupils to which he could apply his knowledge.

Bhishma did not ask what purpose Drona had for these good pupils, and it was with warmth and genuine delight that he welcomed Drona to his household.

'String your bow, Drona,' he said, 'and you may make the princes of my house accomplished in the use of arms. What we have is yours. Our house is at your disposal.'

The first morning of instruction found Drona lying the boys flat on their backs. He asked them then to promise that when they became skilled in the use of arms they would carry out for him a purpose that he had borne in mind. Ever eager, Arjuna, the third of the Pandavas, jumped up and promised that whatever that purpose might be, he was prepared to accomplish it. Drona drew Arjuna to him and the two men embraced. From that time there would be a special closeness between teacher and student.

The princes came from all the neighbouring kingdoms to learn of Drona and all the Kauravas and the Pandavas and the sons of the great nobles were his pupils. There was, among them, a shy and wild-looking boy called Karna who was by reputation the son of a royal charioteer. Arjuna and Karna became rivals, each seeking to outdo the other with his skill and accuracy.

At this time, Arjuna was becoming well versed in the vocabulary of arms. One night while eating, the lantern blew out and he realized that he could still continue to eat in the darkness. It set his mind on to the thought that it would certainly be possible to shoot in darkness, for it surely was habit as much as putting food to one's mouth. Drona applauded Arjuna's crafty mind and declared him to have no equal.

Another of those who travelled to Drona to become a pupil was a low-caste prince known as Ekalavya. Drona refused to take him on because of his caste, and Ekalavya retired to the forest where he made an image of Drona from the earth, which he worshipped and revered as the man himself. He practised often in the forest and soon became so fine a shot that his activities were drawn to the attention of Drona and his pupils.

Drona sought him out and when Ekalavya saw him coming, he fell to the ground. 'Please, Drona,' he cried, 'I am your pupil, struggling here in the woods to learn the skills of military science.'

Drona looked down on the boy. 'If you are,' he said, 'give me my fee.'

Ekalavya leapt to his feet. 'Master, just name your fee and you shall have it. There is nothing I would not do for you.' His face was broken by a wide smile.

'If you mean it,' said Drona coolly, 'cut off your thumb.'

Ekalavya allowed no reaction to cross his proud face and he did as his master bid at once. He laid the thumb of his left hand at the feet of Drona and held up his head.

Drona turned with Arjuna and left, and as Ekalavya bent to collect his bow he realized that he could no longer hold it. His lightness of touch was gone.

And so it was by these means, and others like them that Drona ensured the supremacy of the royal princes, who had, now, no rivals in the use of arms. Each had a speciality and they were all capable of fighting with resourcefulness, strength and perseverance.

The Princes' Trial

Drona's pupils had now come to the end of their education, and Drona applied to Dhritarashtra the king to hold a tournament in which they could exhibit their skill. Preparations began at once for the great event, and a hall was built for the queens and their ladies.

When the day arrived, the king took his place, surrounded by his ministers and minions, and by Bhishma and the early tutors of the princes. And then Gandharai, the mother of Duryodhana, and Pritha, the mother of the Pandavas, entered the area, beautifully dressed and bejewelled as befitted their stature. Last came Drona, who entered the lists dressed in white, as pure as the heart of Vishnu. Beside him walked his son, Ashvathaman, who held himself with great pride and authority.

In came the princes to a procession, led by Yudhishthira, and there began the most incredible display of expertise seen by any one of the noble spectators of that tournament. Arrow after arrow flew, never missing its mark. Horses pulled chariots and there was much vaulting and careering, but never did the princes lose control or exhibit anything other than the greatest of skill and precision. The princes fought together, and exhibited alone. Their mastery left none in any doubt that he was witnessing the finest example of marksmanship in the land. And then entered Arjuna, and Pritha gave a sigh of delight. Her son was even superior to his splendid cousins and he shot arrows that became water, and then fire, and then mountains, and then an arrow that made them all disappear. He fought with sword, and mace, and then pole and on the breast of his chariot. He met every mark with perfect precision. Here was a champion, and the audience hardly dared expel breath at this show of proficiency.

But the respectful silence that had fallen over the crowd was disturbed by a rustling in the corner. And then a great noise was heard in the direction of the gate. Into the centre of the ring came none other than Karna, grown to manhood and splendid in his arms. Far from the prying eyes of her neighbours, Pritha swooned and shivered with fear. Karna was none other than the son she had given up long ago, the son of the sun itself. He shone as brightly as any summer ray, his good looks matched by his eagerness to fight. He was tall and strong, and his presence caused the crowd to gasp with admiration.

Karna walked towards Arjuna and spoke quietly. 'Oh prince,' he said, 'I have a wish that we should engage in single combat.'

Arjuna could hardly hold back the spittle that multiplied on his tongue. He spluttered and then whispered angrily to Karna, 'The day will come when I will kill you.'

'That is yes, then?' shouted Karna. 'Today I will strike off your head before our master himself.'

The two men stood facing one another, antipathy growing between them like the strongest of armour. They moved into position for single combat, but just as they did so there was a cry from the master of ceremonies. Quietly he made his way across the field and drew the warriors to one side. Until Karna could show noble lineage, he was not by law able to fight with the sons of kings. Princes could not fight with men of inferior birth.

Karna's fury was tangible, but just as he turned to the master he was rewarded by a cry from Duryodhana, who was eager to see Arjuna defeated. 'I'll install him as king of Anga!' he shouted. 'And Arjuna can fight him on the morrow.'

Priests appeared at once, and a throne was brought for Karna, who beamed when he saw his old father Shatananda, the ancient charioteer.

He embraced his son, pride at his position as king causing him to weep with joy. There was some sniggering amongst the crowd, for how could a king have such a lowly father? But before anyone could speak, Duryodhana leapt forward once again, having pledged eternal support and friendship to Karna.

'We do not know the lineage of all heroes,' he shouted to the crowd. 'Who asks for the source of a river?' And to the cheers of the gathering, he wrapped his arms around Karna's shoulders and helped his aged father to a seat.

The princes and Karna left together. Pritha stared quietly at her sons – princes and now a king. She said nothing and watched them leave, undefeated and grand in every sense. Pritha looked then to the sun…and smiled.

Drona's War

The Pandavas and Kauravas had become accomplished warriors, and now it was time for their teacher, Drona to claim his reward. He said to his pupils, 'Go fight Drupada, King of the Panchalas; wound him in battle and bring him to me.'

The cousins were jealous of each other and could not agree to wage war together. So the Kauravas, led by Duryodhana, were first to attack Drupada; they rode in their chariots and invaded the hostile capital. The warriors of Panchala arose to fight; their shouting was like the roaring of lions, and their arrows were showered as thickly as rain dropping from the clouds. The Kauravas were defeated, and they left in disorder, uttering cries of despair.

The Pandavas then rushed against the enemies of Drona. Arjuna swept forward in his chariot, and he destroyed horses and cars and warriors. Bhima struck down elephants big as mountains, and many horses and charioteers also, and he covered the ground with rivers of blood.

Drupada endeavoured to turn the tide of battle; surrounded by his mightiest men, he opposed Arjuna. But the strong Pandava overcame him, and after fierce fighting, Arjuna seized Drupada. The remnant of the Panchalas forces then broke and fled, and the Pandavas began to lay waste the capital. Arjuna, however, cried to Bhima: 'Remember that Drupada is the kinsman of the Kauravas; therefore cease slaying his warriors.'

Drupada was led before Drona, who said: 'At last I have conquered your kingdom, and your life is in my hands. Is it your desire now to revive our friendship?' Drona smiled and continued: 'Brahmans are full of forgiveness; therefore have no fear for your life. I have not forgotten that we were children together. So once again I ask for your friendship, and I grant you half of the kingdom; the other half will be mine, and if it pleases you we will be friends.'

'You are indeed noble and great. I thank you, and desire to be your friend.' Drupada replied.

So Drona took possession of half of the kingdom. Drupada went to rule the southern Panchalas; he was convinced that he could not defeat Drona, and he resolved to discover means whereby he might obtain a son who could overcome his Brahman enemy.

Thereafter the Pandavas waged war against neighbouring kings, and they extended the territory over which the blind king held sway.

First Exile of the Pandavas

The Kauravas were rendered more jealous than ever by the successes achieved by the Pandavas, and also because the people favoured them. Duryodhana wanted to become heir to the throne, but the elder prince of the conquering Pandavas could not be set aside. In the end Yudhishthira was chosen by the blind king, and he became Yuva-rajah, 'Little Rajah', supplanting Bhishma, who had been regent during the minority. Yudhishthira, accordingly, ruled over the kingdom, and he was honoured and loved by the people; for although he was not a mighty warrior like Arjuna, or powerful like Bhima, he had great wisdom, and he was ever just and merciful, and a lover of truth.

Duryodhana remonstrated with his blind father, and he spoke to him, saying: 'Why, my father, have you so favoured the Pandavas and forgotten your own sons? You were Pandu's elder brother, and should have reigned before him. Now the children of your younger brother are to succeed you. The kingdom is your own by right of birth, and your sons are your heirs. Why, then, have you lowered us in the eyes of your subjects?'

Dhritarashtra replied: 'Duryodhana, my son, you know that Pandu, my brother, was the mightiest ruler in the world. Could I, who am blind, have set him aside? His sons have great wisdom and worth, and are loved by the people. How, then, could I pass them over? Yudhishthira has greater accomplishments for governing than you possess, my son. How could I turn against him and banish him from my council?'

Duryodhana said: 'I do not acknowledge Yudhishthira's superiority as a ruler of men. And this I know full well, I could combat against any number of Yudhishthiras on the battlefield.... If, my father, you will set me aside and deny me my right to a share of government in the kingdom, I will take my own life and end my sorrow.'

To this Dhritarashtra responded: 'Be patient, my son. If you wish, I will divide the kingdom between you and Yudhishthira, so that no jealousy may exist between you both.'

Duryodhana was pleased to hear these words, and he said: 'I agree and will accept your offer. Let the Pandavas take their own land and rule over it, and I and my brothers will remain at Hastinapur with you. If the Kauravas and Pandavas continue to live here together, there will be conflicts and bloodshed.'

Dhritarashtra replied: 'Neither Bhishma, the head of our family, nor Vidura, my brother, nor Drona, your teacher, will consent to the Pandavas being sent away.'

To which Duryodhana said: 'Do not consult them; they are beneath you. Command the Pandavas to go to the city of Varanavartha and live there; when they have gone no one will speak to you regarding this matter.'

Dhritarashtra listened to his son and followed his counsel. He commanded Yudhishthira to go with his brothers to the city of Varanavartha, rich in jewels and gold, to live there until he recalled them. So the Pandava brothers said farewell to Dhritarashtra and left Hastinapur, taking with them their mother, the widowed queen Pritha, and went towards the city of Varanavartha. The people of Hastinapur mourned for them.

Before they departed, Vidura spoke to them in secret, telling them to be aware of the perils of fire. He repeated a verse to Yudhishthira and said: 'Put your trust in the man who will recite these words to you; he will be your deliverer.'

Now Duryodhana had plotted with Shakuni, the brother of Queen Gandharai, to destroy his kinsmen. Then their ally, Kanika the Brahman, said in secret to Dhritarashtra: 'When your enemy is in your power, destroy him by whatever means is at your disposal, in secret or openly. Show him no mercy, nor give him your protection. If your son, or brother, or kinsman, or your father even, should become your enemy, do not hesitate to slay if it gives you prosperity. Let him be overcome either by spells, or by curses, or by deception, or by payment of money. Do not forget your enemy.'

The maharajah lent a willing ear thereafter to the counsel of his son, whom he secretly favoured most.

Before the Pandavas had left Hastinapur, Duryodhana sent his secret agent, Purochana, to build a roomy new dwelling for them in Varanavartha. This was accomplished quickly, and it became known as the 'house of lac'. It was built of combustible material: hemp and resin were packed in the walls and between the floors, and it was plastered over with mortar mixed with pitch and clarified butter.

Purochana welcomed the Pandavas when they arrived at their new home. But Yudhishthira smelt the mortar, and he closely examined the whole house before saying to Bhima: 'The enemy has built this house for us. It is full of hemp and straw, resin and bamboo, and the mortar is mixed with pitch and clarified butter.'

In due time a stranger visited the Pandavas, and he repeated the secret verse which Vidura had told to Yudhishthira. He said: 'I will construct for you a secret passage underground which will lead to a place of safety should you have to escape from this house when the doors are locked and it is set on fire.' So the man set to work in secret, and before long the underground passage was ready. Then Bhima resolved to deal with Purochana in the very manner that he had undertaken to deal with the princes.

One evening Pritha gave a feast in the new dwelling to all the poor people in Varanavartha. When the guests had left, a poor Bhil woman and her five sons remained behind. They had drunken heavily and were unable to rise up. They slept on the floor.

Meanwhile, a great windstorm had arisen, and the night was dark. So Bhima decided that the time had come to accomplish his mission. He went outside and secured the doors of Purochana's house, which stood beside that of the Pandavas; then he set it on fire. Soon the flames spread towards the new mansion and it burned fiercely and quickly. Pritha and her sons fled through the underground passage and took refuge in the jungle. In the morning the people discovered the blackened remains of Purochana's body and the bodies of his servants among the embers of his house. In the ruins of the Pandavas' mansion they found that a woman and five men had perished, and they lamented, believing that Pritha and her sons were dead. There was great sorrow in Hastinapur when the news reached there. Bhishma and Vidura wept, and blind Dhritarashtra was moved to tears also. But Duryodhana secretly rejoiced, believing that his enemies had all been destroyed.

Bhima and the Fair Demon

The Pandavas, having escaped through the subterranean passage, travelled southwards and entered the forest, which was full of reptiles and wild animals and with ferocious man-eating Asuras and gigantic Rakshasas. Weary and sore, they were overcome with tiredness and fear. So the mighty Bhima lifted up all the others and hastened on through the darkness: he took his mother on his back, and Madri's sons on his shoulders, and Yudhishthira and Arjuna under his arms.

He went swifter than the wind, breaking down trees by his breast and furrowing the ground that he stamped on. After some time the Pandavas found a place to rest in safety; and they all lay down to sleep under a great and beautiful Banyan tree, except mighty Bhima who kept watch over them.

Now in the forest there lived a ferocious Rakshasa named Hidimva. He was terrible to behold; his eyes were red, and he was red-haired and red-bearded; his mouth was large, with long, sharp-pointed teeth, which gleamed in darkness; his ears were shaped like arrows; his neck was as broad as a tree, his belly was large, and his legs were long.

The monster was exceedingly hungry on that fateful night. Scenting human flesh in the forest, he yawned and scratched his grizzly beard, and spoke to his sister, saying: 'I smell excellent food, and my mouth waters; tonight I will devour warm flesh and drink hot, frothy blood. Hurry now and bring the sleeping men to me; we will eat them together, and afterwards dance merrily in the wood.'

So the Rakshasa woman went towards the place where the Pandavas slept. When she saw Bhima, the long-armed one, clad in royal garments and wearing his jewels, she immediately fell in love with him, and said to herself: 'This man with the shoulders of a lion and eyes like lotus blooms is worthy to be my husband. I will not slay him for my evil brother.'

She transformed herself into a beautiful woman; her face became as fair as the full moon; on her head was a garland of flowers, her hair hung in ringlets; and she wore rich ornaments of gold with many gems.

Timidly she approached Bhima and said: 'Oh bull among men, who are you and where did you come from? Who are these fair ones sleeping there? Know that this forest is the abode of the wicked chief of the Rakshasas. He is my brother, and he has sent me here to kill you all for food, but I want to save you. Be my husband. I will take you to a secret place among the mountains, for I can speed through the air at will.'

Bhima said: 'I cannot leave my mother and my brothers to become food for a Rakshasa.'

The woman said: 'Let me help you. Awaken your mother and your brothers and I will rescue you all from my fierce brother.'

To which Bhima replied: 'I will not wake them, because I do not fear a Rakshasa. You can go as it pleases you, and I care not if you send your brother to me.'

Meantime the Rakshasa chief had grown impatient. He came down from his tree and went after his sister, with gaping mouth and head thrown back.

The Rakshasa woman said to Bhima: 'He comes here in anger. Wake up your family, and I will carry you all through the air to escape him.'

'Look at my arms,' said Bhima. 'They are as strong as the trunks of elephants; my legs are like iron maces, and my chest is powerful and broad. I will slay this man-eater, your brother.'

The Rakshasa chief heard Bhima's boast, and he fumed with rage when he saw his sister in her beautiful human form. He said to her: 'I will slay you and those whom you would help against me.' Then he rushed at her, but Bhima cried: 'You will not kill a woman while I am near. I challenge you to single combat now. Tonight your sister will see you slain by me as an elephant is slain by a lion.'

The Rakshasa replied: 'Boast not until you are the victor. I will kill you first of all, then your friends, and last of all my treacherous sister.'

Having said this, he rushed towards Bhima, who nimbly seized the monster's outstretched arms and, wrestling violently, cast him on the ground. Then as a lion drags off his prey, Bhima dragged the struggling Rakshasa into the depths of the forest, so that his yells should not wake his sleeping family. There they fought together like furious bull elephants, tearing down branches and overthrowing trees.

Eventually the clamour woke the Pandavas, and they gazed with wonder at the beautiful woman who kept watch in Bhima's place.

Pritha said to her: 'Oh celestial being, who are you? If you are the goddess of woods or an Apsara, tell me why you linger here?'

The fair demon said: 'I am the sister of the chief of the Rakshasas, and I was sent here to slay you all; but when I saw your mighty son the love god wounded me, and I chose him for my husband. Then my brother followed angrily, and your son is fighting with him. They are filling the forest with their shouting.'

All the brothers rushed to Bhima's aid, and they saw the two wrestlers struggling in a cloud of dust, and they appeared like two high cliffs shrouded in mist.

Arjuna cried out: 'Bhima, I am here to help you. Let me slay the monster.'

Bhima answered: 'Fear not, but look on. The Rakshasa will not escape from my hands.'

'Do not keep him alive too long,' Said Arjuna. 'We must act quickly. The dawn is near, and Rakshasas become stronger at daybreak; they exercise their powers of deception during the two twilights. Do not play with him, therefore, but kill him quickly.'

At these words Bhima became as strong as Vayu, his father, when he is angered. Raising the Rakshasa aloft, he whirled him round and round, crying: 'In vain have you gorged on unholy food. I will rid the forest of you. No longer will you devour human beings.'

Then, dashing the monster to the ground, Bhima seized him by the hair and by the waist, laid him over a knee, and broke his back. The Rakshasa was slain.

Day was breaking, and Pritha and her sons immediately turned away to leave the forest. The Rakshasa woman followed them, and Bhima cried to her: 'Be gone! Or I will send you after your brother.'

Yudhishthira then spoke to Bhima, saying: 'It is unseemly to slay a woman. Besides, she is the sister of that Rakshasa, and even although she became angry, what harm can she do us?'

Kneeling at Pritha's feet, the demon wailed: 'Oh illustrious and blessed lady, you know the sufferings women endure when the love god wounds them. Have pity on me now, and command your son to take me for his bride. If he continues to scorn me, I will kill myself. Let me be your slave, and I will carry you all wherever you desire and protect you from perils.'

Pritha heard her with compassion, and persuaded Bhima to take her for his bride. So the two were married by Yudhishthira; then the Rakshasa took Bhima on her back and sped through the air to a lonely place among the mountains which is sacred to the gods. They lived together beside silvery streams and lakes sparkling with lotus blooms; they wandered through woods of blossoming trees where birds sang sweetly, and by celestial sea-beaches covered with pearls and nuggets of gold. The demon bride had assumed celestial beauty, and often played sweet music. She made Bhima happy.

In time the woman became the mother of a mighty son; his eyes were fiercely bright, his ears were like arrows, and his mouth was large; he had copper-brown lips and long, sharp teeth. He grew to be a youth an hour after he was born. His mother named him Ghatotkacha.

Bhima then returned to his mother and his brothers with his demon bride and her son. They lived together for a time in the forest; then the Rakshasa bade all the Pandavas farewell and left with Ghatotkacha, who promised to come to the Pandavas' aid whenever they called on him.

The King of the Asuras

One day thereafter Vyasa appeared before the Pandavas and told them to go to the city of Ekachakra and to live there for a time in the house of a Brahman. Then he vanished from sight, promising to come again.

So the Pandavas went to Ekachakra and lived with a Brahman who had a wife and a daughter and an infant son. Disguised as holy men, the brothers begged for food. Every evening they brought home what they had obtained, and Pritha divided it into two portions; one half she gave to wolf-bellied Bhima, and the rest she kept for his brothers and herself.

Now the city of Ekachakra was protected against every enemy by a forest-dwelling Rakshasa named Vaka, who was king of the Asuras. Each day the people had to supply him with food, which consisted of a cartload of rice, two bullocks, and the man who carried the meal to him.

One morning a great wailing broke out in the Brahman's house because the holy man had been chosen to supply the demon's feast. He was too poor to purchase a slave, so he said he would deliver himself to Vaka. 'Although I reach Heaven,' he cried, 'I will have no joy, because my family will perish when I am gone.' His wife and his daughter pleaded to take his place, and the three wept together. Then the little boy plucked a long spear of grass, and with glowing eyes he spoke sweetly and said: 'Do not weep, Father; do not weep, Mother; do not weep, Sister. With this spear I will slay the demon who devours human beings.'

Pritha was deeply moved by the grief of the Brahman family, and she said: 'Sorrow not. I will send my son Bhima to slay the Asura king.'

The Brahman answered her, saying: 'That cannot be. Your sons are Brahmans and are under my protection. If I go, I will be obeying the king; if I send your son, I will be guilty of his death. The gods hate the man who causes a guest to be slain, or permits a Brahman to perish.'

To this Pritha said: 'Bhima is strong and mighty. A demon cannot do him any harm. He will kill this bloodthirsty Rakshasa and return again safely. But, Brahman, you must not reveal to anyone who has performed this mighty deed, so that the people do not trouble my son and try to obtain the secret of his power.'

So Bhima collected the rice and drove the bullocks towards the forest. When he got near to the appointed place, he began to eat the food himself, and called the Rakshasa's name over and over again. Vaka heard and came through the trees towards him. Red were his eyes, and his hair and his beard were red also; his ears were pointed like arrows; he had a mouth like a cave, and his forehead was puckered in three lines. He was terrible to look at; his body was huge, indeed.

The Rakshasa saw Bhima eating his meal, and approached angrily, biting his lower lip. 'Fool,' he cried, 'would you devour my food before my very eyes?'

Bhima smiled, and continued eating with his face averted. The demon struck him, but the hero only glanced round as if someone had touched his shoulder, and he went on eating as before.

Raging furiously, the Rakshasa tore up a tree, and Bhima rose leisurely and waited until it was flung at him. When that was done, he caught the trunk and hurled it back. Many trees were uprooted and flung by one at the other. Then Vaka attacked, but the Pandava overthrew him and dragged him round and round until the demon gasped with fatigue. The earth shook; trees were splintered into pieces. Then Bhima began to strike the monster with his iron fists, and he broke Vaka's back across his knee. Terrible were the loud screams of the Rakshasa while Bhima was bending him double. He died howling.

All the other Asuras were terror-stricken, and, bellowing horribly, they rushed towards Bhima and bowed before him. Bhima made them take vows never to eat human flesh again or to oppress the people of the city. They promised to do so, and he allowed them to depart.

Afterwards Pritha's son dragged the monster's body to the main gate of Ekachakra. He entered the city secretly and hurried to the Brahman's house, and he told Yudhishthira all that had taken place.

When the people of the city discovered that the Asura king was dead, they rejoiced, and hurried towards the house of the Brahman. But the holy man was evasive, saying that his deliverer was a certain high-souled Brahman who had offered to supply food to the demon. The people established a festival in honour of Brahmans.

Drupada's Children

The Pandavas remained in the city of Ekachakra. One day they were visited by a saintly man who told them the story of the miraculous births of Drupada's son and daughter from sacrificial fire.

When Drupada had lost half of his kingdom, he made pilgrimages to holy places. He promised great rewards to superior Brahmans, so that he might have offspring, ever desiring revenge against Drona. He offered the austere Upayája a million cows if he would procure a son for him, and that sage sent him to his brother Yája. Now Yája was reluctant to help the king; but eventually he consented to perform the sacrificial rite, and prevailed upon Upayája to help him.

So the rite was performed, and when the vital moment came, the Brahmans called for the queen to partake in it. But Drupada's wife was not prepared, and she asked them all to wait a little while. But the Brahmans could not delay the consummation of the sacrificial rite. Before the queen came, a son sprang from the flames: he was clad in full armour, and carried a sword and bow, and a crown gleamed brightly on his head. A voice out of the heavens said: 'This prince has come to destroy Drona and to increase the fame of the Panchalas'.

Next a daughter rose from the ashes on the altar. She was exceedingly beautiful, with long curling locks and lotus eyes. A sweet odour clung to her body. A voice out of heaven said: 'This dusky girl will become the chief of all women. Many Kshatriyas must die because of her, and the Kauravas will suffer from her. She will accomplish the decrees of the gods.'

The son was named Dhrishtadyumna and the daughter Draupadi.

The Bride of the Pandavas

Having heard the story of the birth of Draupadi, Pritha made up her mind to go to Panchala. Before they went away, the saintly man said that Draupadi had been destined to become a Pandava queen.

The princes were silent when their guest had gone and Pritha mourned for her sons who had been cast out. She smiled brightly at them and said, 'Perhaps it is time to depart from Ekachakra – I for one am glad to renew our wanderings.'

The spirits of the princes were lifted at once, and the following day they set off, thanking their gentle host for all his many kindnesses. Pritha and her sons wandered from the banks of the Ganges and went northwards on the road to Kampilya, the capital of Drupada. They soon fell in with a great number of people all going the same way. Yudhishthira spoke to a troop of Brahmans, and he asked them where they were going. They answered saying that Drupada of Panchala was observing a great festival, and that all the princes of the land were heading to the swayamvara of his daughter, the beautiful Draupadi.

So the Pandavas went towards Panchala with the troop of Brahmans. When they reached the city they took up home in the humble dwelling of a potter, still disguised as Brahmans, and they went out and begged food from the people. In their hearts the brothers secretly wished to win the fair bride whose fame had spread.

Alone in his castle, Drupada perused the swayamvara that he was about to hold and he wondered aloud at the choice of suitors. He had held for many years a secret wish that Arjuna should wed Draupadi, a wish that he had kept close to his breast over the last years. Arjuna's mastery of the bow at the tournament was fresh in his memory as he formed the instrument that would be required to shoot an arrow through a ring suspended at great height. It would not be easy to win his princess. In fact, thought Drupada, there was likely only one man who could do it.

The day of the swayamvara dawned bright and clear and the crowds poured in from adjoining kingdoms and lands. Duryodhana came with his dear friend Karna, and the Pandavas arrived in disguise, taking the form of Brahmans once again.

As the festivities began, the lovely Draupadi entered the arena, her stunning robes and jewellery matched only by her shimmering beauty. She held in her hands a wreath and she stood quietly while her twin brother Dhrishtadyumna stepped forward, his booming voice carrying across the crowds, 'Today you are assembled here for one purpose. He who can use this bow' – he gestured down and then up – 'to shoot five arrows through that ring, having birth, good looks and breeding, shall take today my sister for his bride.'

A cheer went up among the crowd and the first name on the list was called forward. Many men reached for that sturdy bow, but none was able even to string it. Karna, sensing the embarrassment of his peers, stood and moved toward the weapon, his head held high, his good looks glowing in the morning sunlight. But as Draupadi caught sight of Karna, her lips curled and she called out with great disdain, 'I will not be married to the son of a charioteer.'

Karna managed a smile and shrugging his shoulders, returned to the crowd. There appeared, then, a movement from its masses, and the gathering parted to let through the strong but bedraggled form of a Brahman. Some of the Brahmans in the crowd cheered aloud as a symbol of sovereignty. Others shook their heads at what was bound to be a disgrace for Brahmans altogether.

Arjuna walked forward in his Brahman disguise and he lifted the bow with ease. Stopping to say a quiet prayer he walked slowly round the weapon until as quick as a flash he drew it up and sent five arrows flying straight through the ring. The cheering was uproarious. Brahman's across the crowd waved their scarves and flowers were sent flying from each direction. The other Pandavas kept down their heads, fearing that Arjuna's victory would draw attention to them all.

So far no one had noticed that the Brahman was none other than Arjuna, and Draupadi brought forward a white robe and garland of marriage, which she placed eagerly about his neck.

'I take you as my lord,' she said happily.

Suddenly a roar went up from the crowds, and coming towards them were the other suitors, angered that a Brahman should steal what they thought was rightfully theirs. A great fight broke out and Arjuna and his brother Bhima stood firmly against the masses, proving themselves once again to be excellent fighters. Bhima tore out a tree by its roots and used it to fend off the crowds, a trick he had learned at the hand of Drona. The crowd gasped once again in delight. It was not often that they were treated to such a display.

In the royal gallery, a prince by the name of Krishna stood up.

'Look,' he shouted, pointing out Arjuna and Bhima to his brother, 'I would swear as my name is Krishna that those are the Pandavas.' He watched silently and said no more, waiting for his moment.

On the field the fighting continued until, finally, after much bloodshed, Arjuna was able to extract himself with his brothers and his new bride and return to the home of the potter. As they entered they addressed their mother, saying: 'We have won a great gift today.'

Pritha replied: 'Then share the gift between you, as brothers should.'

Yudhishthira was shocked to hear his mother's words, and said: 'What have you said, mother? The gift is the Princess Draupadi whom Arjuna won at the swayamvara.'

'Alas! What have I said?' said Pritha, 'But the fatal words have been spoken; you must work out how they can be obeyed without wronging one another.'

Each one of the Pandavas secretly yearned to have Draupadi for his bride, but the brothers agreed it should be Drupada's decision as to which of them his daughter should be given. Meanwhile Pritha greeted the princess warmly and welcomed her to the family, allowing her the honour of serving the food for them on that first night.

Back at the palace, King Drupada felt troubled after his daughter had been led away to the potter's house, so he sent his valiant son to watch her. To his joy Dhrishtadyumna discovered that the Brahmans were really the Pandava brothers. He returned to the king and related all that had happened. In the morning, Drupada sent two chariots to the potter's house with a messenger bidding the Pandavas to come to the palace for the nuptial feast.

The Pandava guests were made welcome, and the king and his son and all his counsellors sat down to feast with them. And after revealing to the king that they were in fact the Pandava princes, King Drupada glowed with joy and satisfaction. He asked the brothers to remain at the palace, and entertained them for many days.

After some time, the king spoke with Yudhishthira, saying: 'You are the elder brother. Is it your desire that Arjuna be given Draupadi for his bride.'

Yudhishthira replied: 'I would like to speak with Vyasa, the great Rishi, regarding this matter.'

So Vyasa was brought before the king, who spoke to him regarding Draupadi. The Rishi said: 'The gods have already declared that she will become the wife of all the five Pandava brothers.' Then Vyasa told that Draupadi was the reincarnation of a pious woman who once prayed to the god Shiva for a husband: five times she prayed, and the god rewarded her with the promise of five husbands in her next existence. Vyasa also revealed that the Pandava brothers were five incarnations of Indra, and therefore were but as one.

Drupada gave consent for his daughter to become the bride of all the brothers, so on five successive days she was led round the holy fire by each of the five Pandava princes. He gave many great gifts to his sons-in-law – much gold and many jewels, numerous horses and chariots and elephants, and also a hundred female servants clad in many-coloured robes.

But, when Duryodhana learned that the Pandava brothers were still alive, and had formed a powerful alliance with Drupada, he was furious. A great council was held, at which it was agreed that the Pandava princes should be invited to return to Hastinapur so that the kingdom might be divided between them and the sons of Dhritarashtra. Vidura was sent to Panchala to speak with Drupada and his sons-in-law regarding this matter.

Return to Hastinapur

And so the Pandava brothers returned to Hastinapur with Vidura. They took with them their mother, Queen Pritha, and their wife, Draupadi, and the people welcomed them home. There was much rejoicing and many banquets.

Dhritarashtra spoke at length to Yudhishthira and his brothers and said: 'I will now divide the kingdom between you and my sons. Your share will be the southwestern country of Khandava-prastha.' So the Pandava princes bade farewell to all their kinsmen and to wise Drona, and they went towards their own country.

On the banks of the Jumna they built a strong fort, and in time they made a great clearance in the forest. When they had gathered together the people who were subject to them, they erected a great and wonderful city called Indra-prastha. High walls, which resembled the Mandara mountains, were built round about, and these were surrounded by a deep moat as wide as the sea.

In time the fame of King Yudhishthira went far and wide. He ruled with wisdom and with power, and he had great piety. Forest robbers were pursued constantly and put to death, and wrongdoers were always brought to justice.

The brothers lived happily together. In accordance with the advice of a Rishi, they made a pact that when one of them was sitting beside Draupadi, none of the others should enter, and that if one of them should be guilty of intrusion, he must go into exile for twelve years.

As it chanced, Yudhishthira was sitting with Draupadi one day when a Brahman, whose cattle had been carried off, rushed to Arjuna and asked him to pursue the band of robbers. The weapons of the prince were in the king's palace, and to obtain them Arjuna entered the room in which Yudhishthira and Draupadi sat, therefore breaking the pact. He hurried after the robbers and recovered the stolen cattle, which he brought back to the Brahman.

On his return to the palace, Arjuna said to his brother that he must go into exile for twelve years to make amends for his offence. Yudhishthira, however, prevailed upon him not to go. But Arjuna replied that he had pledged his oath to fulfil the terms of the pact. 'I cannot waver from truth,' he said; 'truth is my weapon.' So after he said goodbye to Pritha and Draupadi and his four brothers, he left the city of Indra-prastha. A band of Brahmans went with him.

Arjuna's Exile

Arjuna wandered through the jungle, and he visited many holy places. One day he went to Hurdwar, where the Ganges flows on the plain, and he bathed in the holy waters. There he met Ulúpí, the beautiful daughter of Vasuka, king of the Nagas. She fell in love with him, and she led him to her father's palace, where he stayed for a time. She also gave him the power to render himself invisible in water. A child was born to them, and he was named Iravat.

Afterwards Arjuna went southwards until he came to the Mahendra mountain. He was received there by Parasu Rama, the Brahman hero, who gave him gifts of powerful weapons, and taught him the secret of using them.

So he wandered from holy place to holy place until he reached Manipur. Now the king of that place had a beautiful daughter whose name was Chitrángadá. Arjuna loved her, and sought her for his bride. The king said: 'I have no other child, and if I give her to you, her son must remain here to become my heir, for the god Shiva has decreed that the kings of this realm can have each but one child.' Arjuna married the maiden, and he lived in Manipur for three years. A son was born, and he was named Chitrangada. Afterwards Arjuna set out on his wanderings once more.

Travelling westward, he passed through many strange lands, eventually reaching the city of Prabhása on the southern sea, the capital of his kinsman Krishna, king of the Yádhavas.

Krishna welcomed Arjuna, and took the Pandava hero to live in his palace. Then he gave a great feast on the holy mountain of Raivataka, which lasted for two days. Arjuna looked with love at Krishna's fair sister, Subhadra, a girl of sweet smiles, and desired her for a bride.

Now it was the wish of Krishna'a brother, Balarama, that Subhadra should be given to Duryodhana, whom she would have chosen had a swayamvara been held. So Krishna advised Arjuna to carry her away by force, in accordance with the advice of the sages, who had said: 'Men applaud the princes who win brides by abducting them.'

When the feast was over, Arjuna drove his chariot from the holy mountain towards Dwaraka until he came close to Subhadra. Nimbly he leapt down and took her by the hand and lifted her into his chariot; then he drove quickly towards the city of Indra-prastha.

Balarama was furious and wanted to pursue Arjuna. He spoke to Krishna, saying: 'You are calm, and I can see that Arjuna has done this with your knowledge. You should not have given our sister to him without my consent. But let the deed be on his own head. I will pursue him and kill him and his brothers, one and all.'

Krishna replied: 'Arjuna is our kinsman and of noble birth, and is a worthy husband for Subhadra. If you pursue him and bring back our sister, no one else will marry her now because that she has been in the house of another. It is better if we send messengers after Arjuna and ask him to return here, so that the marriage may be held according to our rites.'

Balarama said: 'So be it, seeing that you are obviously pleased with this matter.'

And so it came to pass that messengers followed Arjuna and asked him to return with Subhadra to Dwaraka. A great feast was held, and they were married. Arjuna lived there for many months, until the time of his exile came to an end.

The Triumph of the Pandavas

When Arjuna returned to Indra-prastha with Subhadra, he was received with great rejoicing by his brothers, and Subhadra was welcomed by Draupadi. The two women grew to love one another, and were both very dear to Pritha. In time, Draupadi became the mother of five sons to her five husbands. Subhadra had one son only, whose name was Abhimanyu, and in the years that followed was an illustrious warrior.

As time went on, the Pandavas grew more and more powerful. They waged great wars, until many kings owed them allegiance; and eventually Yudhishthira decided that the time had come to hold his great Rajasúya sacrifice to celebrate the supremacy of his power over all.

Krishna came to Indra-prastha at this time and said: 'There is now just one king who must be overcome before the Imperial sacrifice can be performed: his name is Jarasandha, monarch of Magadha. He has already conquered a great number of kings, slaughtering our dear kinsmen.'

This king was of great valour and matchless strength. His body was invulnerable against weapons; not even the gods could wound him. He was also of miraculous birth – he was born of two mothers who had eaten a charmed mango which fell into the lap of his father. Also he had not come to life after birth until he was united by a Rakshasa woman, named Jara, the goddess of the household. So the child was called Jarasandha, meaning 'united by Jara'.

Krishna said to Yudhishthira: 'This monarch of Magadha cannot be defeated in battle even by gods or by demons. But he may be overcome in a conflict, fighting with bare arms. Now I am 'Policy', Bhima is 'Strength', and Arjuna is 'Protector'. Together we will surely accomplish the death of Jarasandha.'

So Yudhishthira agreed to let Krishna help them. Krishna, Arjuna, and Bhima disguised themselves as Brahmans and went towards the city of Mathura, Jarasandha's capital. When they arrived there they boldly entered the palace of the mighty king. They stood before him decked with flowers, and the king greeted them warmly.

Arjuna and Bhima were silent, but Krishna spoke to Jarasandha, saying: 'These two men are observing vows, and will not open their mouths until midnight; after then they will speak.'

The king provided for his guests in the sacrificial chamber, and after midnight he visited them. Discovering that they were warriors, he asked them: 'Tell me honestly who you are, and why you have come here.'

Krishna said: 'We are decked with flowers to achieve prosperity, and we have entered the home of our enemy to fulfil the vows of Kshatriyas.'

Jarasandha responded: 'I have never done you an injury. Why, therefore, do you regard me as your enemy?'

Then Krishna revealed himself, and said: 'You have slaughtered our kinsmen because you imagine there lives no man who is as powerful as you. For your sins you are doomed to go to Yama's kingdom to be tortured. But you can go instead to the Heaven of Indra by dying the death of a Kshatriya in battle with your peers. Now, we challenge you to combat. Set free the kings who are in your dungeons, or die at our hands!'

The king refused to set his captives free. Instead he agreed to meet one of them in battle, eventually choosing Bhima. It was agreed that they should fight without weapons, and the two got ready for the fray. Jarasandha fought so fiercely that the combat lasted for thirteen days. In the end the king was slain – his back broken over Bhima's knee.

Krishna went boldly into the palace and set free all the kings who were in captivity. And one by one they took vows to attend the Imperial sacrifice. Then Krishna met with Sahadeva, son of Jarasandha, and installed him as King of Magadha.

When Yudhishthira learned that Jarasandha had been slain, he sent his four brothers with great armies to collect tribute from every king in the world. Some welcomed them; others had to be conquered in battle. But when they had sworn allegiance to Yudhishthira, they joined the Pandava force and assisted in achieving further victories. A whole year went past before the brothers returned to Indra-prastha.

Krishna came from Dwaraka to help Yudhishthira at the ceremony, and he brought with him much wealth and a mighty army.

Stately pavilions were erected for the kings who came to attend the great sacrifice: their turrets were high, and they were swan-white and flecked with radiant gold. Silver and gold adorned the walls of the rooms, which were richly perfumed and carpeted and furnished to befit the royal guests.

The kings came to Indra-prastha in all their splendour and greeted mighty Yudhishthira. Those who were friends brought gifts, and those who had been subdued in battle brought tribute. White-haired and blind old Dhritarashtra came, and with him were Kripa and Bhishma and Vidura. Proud Duryodhana and his brothers also came, professing friendship, and Karna came with bow and spear and mace. Drona and his son, and their enemies Drupada and his son, were there also, and Balarama, Krishna's brother, and their father Vasudeva. And among many others were jealous Sishupala, King of Chedi, and his son, and both wore bright golden armour. Many Brahmans also assembled at Indra-prastha, and Krishna honoured them and washed their feet.

Now there were deep and smouldering jealousies among the assembled kings, and when the time came to honour him who was regarded as the greatest among them by presenting the Arghya, their passions were set ablaze. First Bhishma spoke and said that the honour should be given to Krishna, who was the noblest and greatest among them all. 'Krishna,' he said, 'is the origin of all things; the universe came into being for him alone. He is the incarnation of the Creator, the everlasting one, who is beyond man's comprehension.'

When the Arghya was given to Krishna, Sishupala, the King of Chedi, was angered and said: 'It does not become you, Yudhishthira, to honour an uncrowned chieftain. Gathered around you are ruling kings of the highest fame. If the honour is due to age, then Vasudeva can claim it before his son; if it is due to the foremost king, then Drupada should be honoured; if it is due to wisdom, Drona is the most worthy; if it is due to holiness, Vyasa is the greatest. Drona's son has more knowledge than Krishna, Duryodhana is peerless among younger men, Kripa is the worthiest priest, and Karna the greatest archer. For what reason should homage be paid to Krishna, who is neither the holiest priest, the wisest teacher, the greatest warrior, nor the foremost chieftain? To the shame of this assembly does it honour the murderer of his own king, this cowherd of low birth.' Sishupala hated Krishna because he had kidnapped the beautiful Rukmini, who had been betrothed to him, the mighty King of Chedi.

Krishna then spoke, his voice clam but his eyes bright. To the kings he said: 'The evil-tongued Sishupala is descended from a daughter of our race, and in my heart, I have never sought to work ill against a kinsman. But once, when I went eastward, he sacked my sea-swept Dwaraka and laid low its temple; once he broke faith with a king and cast him into prison; once he seized the consort of a king by force; and once he disguised himself as the husband of a chaste princess and deceived her. I have suffered because of his sins, but have sought vengeance because he was of our own race. He has even come after my consort Rukmini, and is worthy of death.'

As he spoke, the faces of many kings grew red with shame and anger, but Sishupala laughed aloud and said: 'I seek no mercy from Krishna, nor do I fear him.'

Then Krishna thought of his discus, and immediately it was in his hand. In anger he shouted: 'Hear me, lords of earth! I have promised the mother of Sishupala to pardon a hundred sins committed by her son. And I have fulfilled my vow. But now the number is more than full, and I will slay him before your eyes.' Krishna flung the discus, and it struck Sishupala on the neck, so that his head was severed from his body. Then the assembled kings saw a great wonder, for the passion-cleansed soul of Sishupala flowed from his body, beautiful as the sun in heaven, and went towards Krishna. Its eyes were like lotus blooms, and its form like a flame; and it adored Krishna and entered into his body.

The kings all looked on, silent and amazed, while thunder bellowed out of heaven, and lightning flashed, and rain poured down in torrents. Some grew angry, and laid hands on their weapons to avenge the death of Sishupala; others rejoiced that he had been slain; the Brahmans chanted the praises of Krishna.

Yudhishthira commanded his brothers to perform the funeral rites, so the body of Sishupala was burned and then his son was proclaimed King of Chedi.

Afterwards the great sacrifice was performed in peace. Krishna, who had maintained the supremacy of Yudhishthira by slaying a dangerous and jealous rival, looked on benignly.

Holy water was sprinkled by the Brahmans, and all the monarchs bowed and honoured Yudhishthira, saying: 'You have extended the fame of your mighty father, Pandu, and you have become even greater than he was. With this sacrifice you have graced your high station and fulfilled all our hopes. Now, emperor over all, permit us to return to our own homes, and bestow your blessing upon us.' So one by one they left, and the four Pandavas accompanied the greatest of them to the confines of their kingdoms. Krishna was the last to bid farewell.

Yudhishthira said to him: 'To you I owe all things. Because you were here, I was able to perform the great sacrifice.'

Krishna replied: 'Monarch of all! Rule over your people with a father's wisdom and care. Be to them like rain which nourishes the parched fields; be a shade in hot sunshine; be a cloudless heaven bending over all. Be ever free from pride and passion; ever rule with power and justice and holiness.' Then he was gone, and Yudhishthira turned homeward with tear-dimmed eyes.

Meanwhile, Duryodhana had witnessed the triumph of the Pandavas, and his heart burned with jealous rage. He envied the splendour of the palaces at Indra-prastha; he envied the glory achieved by Yudhishthira. He well knew that he could not overcome the Pandavas in open conflict, so he plotted with his brothers to accomplish their fall by artifice and by wrong.

The Great Gambling Match

Shakuni, Prince of Gandhara, and brother of Dhritarashtra's queen, was renowned for his skill as a gambler. He always enjoyed good fortune because he played with loaded dice. Duryodhana plotted with him, determined to conquer the Pandavas, and Shakuni said: 'Yudhishthira loves the dice, although he does not know how to play. Ask him to throw dice with me, because there is no gambler who is my equal. I will put him to shame. I will win his kingdom from him.'

Duryodhana was pleased at this proposal, and he went to his blind father and asked him to invite the Pandavas to Hastinapur for a friendly gambling match, despite the warnings of the royal counsellors. 'If the gods are merciful, my sons will cause no dispute,' said Dhritarashtra, 'No evil can happen so long as I am near, and Bhishma and Drona are near also. Therefore, let the Pandavas be invited here as my son wishes.'

So Vidura, who feared trouble, was sent to Indra-prastha to say: 'The maharajah is about to hold a great festival at Hastinapur, and he wishes that Yudhishthira and his brothers, their mother Pritha and their joint wife Draupadi, should be present. A great gambling match will be played.'

These words saddened Yudhishthira, who well knew that dice-throwing was often the cause of bitter disputes. Besides, he was unwilling to play Prince Shakuni, that desperate and terrible gambler.... But he could not refuse Dhritarashtra's invitation, or, like a true Kshatriya, disdain a challenge either to fight or to play with his peers.

So it came to pass that the Pandava brothers, with Pritha and Draupadi, travelled to Hastinapur in all their splendour. Dhritarashtra welcomed them in the presence of Bhishma, Drona, Duryodhana and Karna; then they were received by Queen Gandharai, and the wives of the Kaurava princes. All the daughters-in-law of the blind maharajah became sad because they were jealous of Draupadi's beauty.

The Pandava lords and ladies went to the dwelling which had been prepared for them, and there they were visited in turn by the lords and ladies of Hastinapur.

The following day, Yudhishthira and his brothers went together to the gambling match, which was held in a gorgeous pavilion, roofed with arching crystal and decorated with gold and lapis lazuli: it had a hundred doors and a thousand great columns, and it was richly carpeted. All the princes and great chieftains and warriors of the kingdom were gathered there. And Prince Shakuni of Gandharai was there also with his false dice.

Once the great company were seated, Shakuni invited Yudhishthira to play. Yudhishthira said: 'I will play if my opponent will promise to throw fairly, without trickery and deceit. Deceitful gambling is sinful, and unworthy a Kshatriya; there is no prowess in it. Wise men do not applaud a player who wins by foul means.'

To this Shakuni replied: 'A skilled gambler always plays to beat his opponent. Such is the practise in all contests; a man plays or fights to achieve victory.... But if you are in dread of me, Yudhishthira, and afraid that you will lose, perhaps it better if you did not play at all.'

'Having been challenged, I cannot withdraw,' said Yudhishthira. 'I do not fear to fight or to play with any man.... But first tell me who is to lay stakes equally with me.'

Then Duryodhana spoke, saying: 'I will supply jewels and gold and any stakes of equal value to what you can set down. It is for me that Shakuni, my uncle, is to throw the dice.'

Yudhishthira replied: 'This is a strange challenge. One man is to throw the dice and another is to lay the stakes. Such is contrary to all practice. If, however, you are determined to play in this fashion, let the game begin.'

The king of Indra-prastha knew then that the match would not be played fairly. But nevertheless he sat down to throw dice with Shakuni. At the first throw Yudhishthira lost; indeed, he lost at every throw on that fateful day. He gambled away all his money and all his jewels, his jewelled chariot with golden bells, and all his cattle; still he played on, and he lost his thousand war elephants, his slaves and beautiful slave girls, and the remainder of his goods; and next, he staked and lost the whole kingdom of the Pandavas, except for the lands which he had gifted to the Brahmans. Still he did not quit, despite the advice offered him by the chieftains who were there. One by one he staked and lost his brothers; he even staked himself and lost.

Shakuni then said to Yudhishthira: 'You have done wrong in staking your own self, for now you have become a slave; but if you will stake Draupadi now and win, all that you have lost will be restored to you.'

Yudhishthira replied: 'So be it. I will stake Draupadi.'

At these words the whole company was stricken with horror. Vidura fainted, and the faces of Bhishma and Drona grew pale; many groaned; but Duryodhana and his brothers openly rejoiced. So Shakuni threw the dice, and Yudhishthira lost this the last throw. Draupadi had been won by Duryodhana.

Then all the onlookers gazed at one another, silent and wide-eyed. Karna and Duhsasana and other young princes laughed aloud. Duryodhana rose proudly and spoke to Vidura, saying: 'Now go to Draupadi and ask her to come here to sweep the chambers with the other helpers.'

Vidura angrily replied: 'Your words are wicked, Duryodhana. You cannot command a lady of royal birth to become a household slave. Besides, she is not your slave, because Yudhishthira staked his own freedom before he staked Draupadi. You can win nothing from a slave who had no power to stake the princess.'

Duryodhana cursed Vidura, and asked one of his servants to bring Draupadi to him. But Vidura continued: 'Today Duryodhana is deprived of his reason. Dishonesty is one of the doors to hell. By practising dishonesty Duryodhana will accomplish the ruin of the Kauravas.'

The beautiful Draupadi was sitting peacefully outside the palace on the banks of the Ganges when suddenly, as a jackal stealthily enters the den of a lion, the servant sent by Duryodhana arrived and stood before her. He said to her: 'Oh Queen, the mighty son of Pandu has played and lost; he has lost all, even his reason, and he has staked you, and you have been won by Duryodhana. And now Duryodhana sends me to say that you are to become his slave, and must obey him like the other female slaves. So come with me.'

Draupadi was astonished by words, and in her anguish, she cried: 'Have I heard you right? Has my husband, the king, staked and lost me in his madness? Did he stake and loose anything else besides?'

The man replied: 'Yudhishthira has lost all his riches and his kingdom; he staked his brothers and lost them one by one; he staked himself and lost; and then he staked you and lost also. Therefore, come with me.'

To this Draupadi angrily replied: 'If my lord staked himself and became a slave, he could not wager me, because a slave owns neither his own life nor the life of another. Say this to my husband, and to Duryodhana say: 'Draupadi has not been won'.'

The man returned to the assembly and repeated the words which Draupadi had said, but Yudhishthira bowed his head and was silent.

Duryodhana was angered by the defiant answer of the proud queen, and he said to his brother Duhsasana: 'The sons of Pandu are our slaves, and your heart is without fear for them. Go to the palace and ask the princess, my humble servant, to come here quickly.'

Red-eyed and proud Duhsasana hurried to the palace. He entered the inner chambers and stood before Draupadi, who was dressed in a single robe, while her hair hung loosely.

The evil-hearted Kaurava said: 'Oh princess of Panchala with fair lotus eyes, you have been staked and lost fairly at the game of hazard. Hurry, therefore, and stand before your lord Duryodhana, for you are now his bright-eyed slave.'

Draupadi trembled with fear. She covered her eyes with her hands before the hated Duhsasana; her cheeks turned pale and her heart sickened. Then suddenly she leapt up and tried to escape to an inner room.

But the evil-hearted prince seized her by the hair. He no longer feared the sons of Pandu, and the beautiful princess quivered and shook. Crouching on her knees, she cried angrily, tears streaming from her lotus eyes: 'Be gone! Oh shameless prince. Can a modest woman appear before strangers in loose attire?'

The stern and cruel Duhsasana replied: 'Even you were naked now, you must follow me. Have you not become a slave, fairly staked and fairly won? From now on you will serve among the other slaves.'

Trembling and faint, Draupadi was dragged through the streets by Duhsasana. When she stood before the elders and the chieftains in the pavilion she cried: 'Forgive me for coming here in this unseemly plight....' Bhishma, Drona and the other elders who were there hung their heads in shame.

To Duhsasana Draupadi said angrily: 'Stop your wickedness! Defile me no longer with unclean hands.' Weeping, she cried: 'Hear and help me, elders. You have wives and children of your own. Will you permit this wrong to be continued. Answer me now.'

But no man said a word.

Draupadi wept and said: 'Why this silence?... Will no man among you protect a sinless woman?... Lost is the fame of the Kauravas, the ancient glory of Bharata, and the prowess of the Kshatriyas!... Why will the sons of Pandu not protect their outraged queen?... And has Bhishma lost his virtue and Drona his power?... Will Yudhishthira no longer defend one who is wronged?... Why are you all silent while this deed of shame is done before you?'

Draupadi glanced round the sons of Pandu one by one, and their hearts thirsted for vengeance. Bhishma's face was dark, Drona clenched his teeth, and Vidura, white and angry, gazed at Duhsasana with amazement while he tore off Draupadi's veil and addressed her with foul words. When she looked towards the Kaurava brothers, Duhsasana said: 'Ha! On whom dare you to look now, slave?'

Shakuni and Kama laughed to hear Draupadi called a slave, and they cried out: 'Well said, well said!'

Duhsasana tried to strip the princess naked before the assembly; but Draupadi, in her distress, prayed aloud to Krishna, invoking him as the creator of all and the soul of the universe, and begged him to help her. Krishna heard her, and multiplied her garments so that Duhsasana was unable to accomplish his wicked purpose.

Karna spoke to Draupadi and said: 'It is not your fault, princess, that you have fallen so low. A woman's fate is controlled by her husband; Yudhishthira has gambled you away. You were his, and must accept your fate. From now on, you will be the slave of the Kaurava princes. You must obey them and please them with your beauty.... You should now seek for yourself a husband who will love you too well to stake you at dice and suffer you to be put to shame.... Be assured that no one will blame a humble servant, as you now are, who looks lovingly at great and noble warriors. Remember that Yudhishthira is no longer your husband; he has become a slave, and a slave can have no wife.... Ah, sweet Princess of Panchala, those whom you chose at your swayamvara have gambled and lost you; they have lost their kingdom and also their power.'

At these words Bhima's chest heaved with anger and shame. Red-eyed he scowled at Karna; he seemed to be the image of flaming Wrath. To Yudhishthira he spoke grimly, saying: 'If you had not staked our freedom and our queen, elder brother, this son of a charioteer would not have taunted us in this manner.' Yudhishthira bowed his head in shame, not saying a word.

Arjuna reprimanded Bhima for his bitter words, but Pritha's mighty son, the slayer of Asuras, said: 'If I am not permitted to punish the tormentor of Draupadi, bring me a fire so that I may thrust my hands into it.'

A deep uproar rose from the assembly, and the elders applauded the wronged lady and censured Duhsasana.

Bhima clenched his hands and, with quivering lips, cried out: 'Hear my terrible words, Oh Kshatriyas.... May I never reach Heaven if I do not seize Duhsasana in battle and, tearing open his breast, drink his very life blood!...' He continued: 'If Yudhishthira will allow me, I will slay the wretched sons of Dhritarashtra without weapons, as a lion slays small animals.'

Bhishma, Vidura and Drona begged Bhima to refrain, whilst Duryodhana gloried in his hour of triumph. He taunted Yudhishthira saying: 'You are the spokesman for your brothers, and they owe you obedience. Speak and say, have you lost your kingdom and your brothers and your own self? Have you even lost the beautiful Draupadi? And has she, your wedded wife, become our humble servant?'

Yudhishthira heard him with downcast eyes, but his lips did not move.... Then Karna laughed; but Bhishma, pious and old, wept in silence.

Then Duryodhana looked at Draupadi, and, baring his knee, invited her to sit on it. Bhima gnashed his teeth – unable to restrain his pent-up anger. With eyes flashing like lightning, and in a voice like thunder he cried out: 'Hear my vow! May I never reach Heaven or meet my ancestors if, for these sinful deeds, I do not break Duryodhana in battle, and drink the blood of Duhsasana!'

Meanwhile, Dhritarashtra was sitting in his palace, knowing nothing of what was happening. The Brahmans were peacefully chanting their evening mantras, when a jackal howled in the sacrificial chamber. Asses brayed in response, and ravens answered their cries from all sides. Dhritarashtra shook with terror when he heard these dreadful omens, and when Vidura had told him all that had taken place, he said: 'The sinful Duryodhana has brought shame upon the head of King Drupada's sweet daughter, and so has courted death and destruction. May the prayers of a sorrowful old man remove the wrath of Heaven which these dark omens have revealed.'

The blind maharajah was led to Draupadi, and in front of all the elders and princes he spoke to her, kindly and gently, saying: 'Noble queen and virtuous daughter, wife of Yudhishthira, and purest of all women, you are very dear to my heart. My sons have wronged you today. Please forgive them now, and let the wrath of Heaven be averted. Whatever you ask of me will be yours.'

Draupadi replied: 'Oh mighty maharajah, you are merciful. I ask you to set free my lord and husband Yudhishthira. Having been a prince, it is not seemly that he should be called a slave.'

'Your wish is granted,' said Dhritarashtra. 'Ask a second favour and blessing, fair one. You deserve more than one.'

So Draupadi said: 'Let Arjuna and Bhima and their younger brothers also be set free and allowed to leave now with their horses and their chariots and their weapons.'

Dhritarashtra replied: 'So be it, princess. Ask yet another favour and blessing and it will be granted.' But to this Draupadi said: 'I seek no other favour: I am a Kshatriya by birth, and do not crave for gifts without end. You have freed my husbands from slavery: they will regain their fortunes by their own mighty deeds.'

Then the Pandava brothers departed from Hastinapur with Pritha and Draupadi, and returned to the city of Indra-prastha.

The Kauravas were furious. Duryodhana approached his royal father and said: 'You have permitted the Pandava princes to go in anger; now they will get ready to wage war against us to regain their kingdom and their wealth; when they return they will kill us all. Allow us, therefore, to throw dice with them once again. We will stake our liberty, and will agree that the side which loses shall go into exile for twelve years, and into hiding for a year thereafter. By this arrangement a bloody war may be averted.'

Dhritarashtra granted his son's wish and recalled the Pandavas. So it came to pass that Yudhishthira sat down once again to play with Shakuni, and once again Shakuni brought out the loaded dice. Before long the game ended, and Yudhishthira had lost.

Duhsasana danced with joy and cried out: 'Now the empire of Duryodhana is established.'

But Bhima replied: 'Do not be too happy, Duhsasana. Hear and remember my words: May I never reach Heaven until I drink your blood!'

The Pandava princes then cast off their royal garments and dressed themselves in deerskins like humble beggars. Yudhishthira said farewell to Dhritarashtra and Bhishma and Kripa and Vidura, one by one, and he even said farewell to the Kaurava brothers. Vidura said to him: 'Your mother, the royal Pritha, is too old to wander with you through forest and jungle. Let her remain here until the years of your exile have passed away.' Yudhishthira agreed and asked for his blessing. Vidura blessed each one of the Pandava princes, saying: 'Be saintly in exile, subdue your passions, learn truth in your sorrow, and return in happiness. May these eyes be blessed by seeing you in Hastinapur once again.'

Pritha wept over Draupadi and blessed her. But before the Princess of Panchala left the city she made a vow, saying: 'From this day on my hair will fall over my forehead until Bhima has slain Duhsasana; then Bhima shall tie up my tresses while his hands are still wet with Duhsasana's blood.'

The Pandava princes wandered towards the deep forest, and Draupadi followed them.

The Pandavas' Sorrow

Yudhishthira lamented his fate to the Brahmans as he wandered towards the forest. 'Our kingdom is lost to us,' he said, 'and our fortune; everything is lost; we go in sorrow, and must live on fruits and roots and the produce of the chase. In the woods are many perils – reptiles and hungry wild animals seeking their prey.'

A Brahman advised him to call upon the sun god, so Yudhishthira prayed: 'Oh sun, you are the eye of the universe, the soul of all things that are; you are the creator; you are Indra, you are

Vishnu, you are Brahma, you are Prajapati, lord of creatures, father of gods and man; you are fire, you are mind; you are lord of all, the eternal Brahma.' Then Surya appeared and gave Yudhishthira a copper pot, which was ever to be filled with food for the brothers.

For twelve long years the Pandavas lived in the woods with their wife Draupadi, and Dhaumya, the Brahman. Whatever food they obtained, they set apart a portion for the holy men and ate the rest. They visited holy shrines; they bathed in sacred waters; they performed their devotions. Often they talked with Brahmans and sages, who instructed them in religious works and blessed them, and also promised them that their lost kingdom would be restored in time.

They wandered in sunshine and in shade; they lived in pleasant places, amidst abundant fruits and surrounded by flowers. They also suffered from tempests and heavy rains, when their path would be torn by streams, and Draupadi would faint, and all the brothers would be weary and in despair. Then the mighty Bhima would carry them all on his back and under his arms.

The gods appeared before the brothers during their exile. Dharma, god of wisdom and holiness, asked his son, Yudhishthira many questions which he answered well. Hanuman, son of Vayu, the wind god, came to Bhima. One day the strong Pandava, who was also Vayu's son, was hurrying on his way and went swift as the wind; the earth shook under him and trees fell down, and at one touch of his foot he killed tigers and lions and even great elephants that sought to block his path. Hanuman shrank to the size of an ape, but his tail spread out in such great proportions across Bhima's path, that he was compelled to stop and stand still. He spoke to Bhima and told the tale of Rama and Sita. Suddenly he grew as tall as a mountain and transported his brother, the Pandava, to the garden of Kuvera, King of Yakshas, lord of treasure, who lived on Mount Kailasa in the Himalayas. There Bhima found sweet-scented flowers which gave youth to those who had grown old and turned grief into joy; these he gave to Draupadi.

Krishna came to visit the Pandavas in the forest, and Draupadi said to him: 'The evil-hearted Duryodhana dared to claim me for his slave. Shame on the Pandavas who looked on in silence when I was humiliated. Is it not the duty of a husband to protect his wife?... These husbands of mine, who have the prowess of lions, saw me afflicted, but did not lift a hand to save me.' Draupadi wept bitter tears from her exquisite coppery eyes, but Krishna comforted her by saying: 'You will yet live to see the wives of those men who persecuted you grieving over their fallen husbands as they lie soaked in their blood.... I will help the Pandavas, and you will once again be a queen over kings.'

Krishna said to Yudhishthira: 'Had I been at Dwaraka when you were called upon to visit Hastinapur, this unfair match would not have taken place, as I would have warned Dhritarashtra. But I was waging a war against demons.... What can I do, now that this disaster is done?... It is not easy to confine the waters after the dam has burst.'

After Krishna returned to his kingdom, Draupadi continued to lament her fate. She said to Yudhishthira: 'The sinful, evil-hearted Duryodhana has a heart of steel.... Oh king, I lie on the ground, remembering my soft luxurious bed. I, who sit on a grass mat, cannot forget my chairs of ivory. I have seen you in the court of kings; now you are a beggar. I have gazed at you in your silken robes, who are now dressed in rags.... What peace can my heart know now, remembering the things that have been? My heart is full of grief.... Does your anger not rise up, seeing your brothers in distress and me in sorrow? How can you forgive your cruel enemy? Are you devoid of anger, Yudhishthira?... A Kshatriya who does not act at the right moment – who forgives the enemy he should strike down, is the most despised of all men. The hour has now come for you to seek vengeance; the present is not a time for forgiveness.'

But the wise Yudhishthira replied: 'Anger is sinful; it is the cause of destruction. He who is angry cannot distinguish between right and wrong. An angry man may commit his own soul to hell. Wise men control their wrath in order to achieve prosperity both in this world and in the next. A weak man cannot control his wrath; but men of wisdom and insight seek to subdue their passions, knowing that he who is angry cannot see things in their true perspective. Only ignorant people regard anger as equivalent to energy.... Because fools commit folly, should I who seek wisdom do likewise?... If wrongs were not righted except by chastisement, the whole world would quickly be destroyed, because anger is destruction; it makes men kill one another. It is right to be forgiving; a man should forgive every wrong. He who is forgiving shall attain to eternal bliss; he who is foolish and cannot forgive is destroyed both in this world and in the next. Forgiveness is the greatest virtue; it is sacrifice; it is tradition; it is inspiration. Forgiveness, beautiful one, is holiness; it is truth; it is Brahma. The wise man who learns how to forgive attains to Brahma (the highest god). Draupadi, remember the verses of the sage:

Let not thy wrath possess thee,
But worship peace with joy;
Who yieldeth to temptation
That great god will destroy.

He who is self-controlled will attain to sovereignty, and the qualities of self-control are forgiveness and gentleness. Let me attain with self-control to everlasting goodness!'

To this Draupadi replied: 'I bow down before the Creator and Ordainer of life and the three worlds, because my mind, it seems, has been dimmed. Men are influenced by deeds, as deeds produce consequences; by works they are set free.... Man can never gain prosperity by forgiveness and gentleness; your virtue has not shielded you; you are following a shadow.... Men should not obey their own wills, but the will of the god who has ordained all things.... Like a doll is moved by strings, so are living creatures moved by the lord of all; he plays with them like a child with a toy.... Those who have done wrong are now happy, and I am full of grief and distress. Can I praise your god who allows such inequality? What reward does your god receive when he allows Duryodhana to prosper – he who is full of evil; he who destroys virtue and religion? If a sin does not rebound on the sinner, then a man's might is the greatest force and not your god, and I sorrow for those who are devoid of might.'

Shocked, Yudhishthira said: 'Your words are the words of an unbeliever! I do not act merely for the sake of reward. I give because it is right to give, and I sacrifice because it is my duty to do so. I follow in the paths of those who have lived wise and holy lives, because of that my heart turns toward goodness. I am no trader in goodness, ever looking for the rewards. The man who doubts virtue will be born among the brutes; he will never achieve everlasting bliss. Do not doubt the ancient religion of your people! God will reward; he is the giver of fruits for deeds; virtue and vice bear fruits.... The wise are content with little in this world; the fools are not content although they receive a lot, because they will have no joy in the future.... The gods are shrouded in mystery; who can pierce the cloud which covers the doings of the gods? Although you cannot see the fruits of goodness, do not doubt your religion or the gods. Let your scepticism give room to faith. Do not slander the great god, but endeavour to learn how to know him. Do not turn away from the Supreme One who gives eternal life, Draupadi.'

Draupadi said: 'I do not slander my god, the lord of all, for in my sorrow I simply rave.... But yet I believe that a man should act. Without acts no one can live. He who believes in chance and destiny and is inactive, lives a life of weakness and helplessness which cannot last long. Success comes to he who acts, and success depends on time and circumstance. So a wise Brahman once taught me.'

Bhima then spoke, charging Yudhishthira with weakness, and pleading with him to seize the sovereignty from Duryodhana: 'You are like froth,' he cried. 'You are unripe fruit! Oh king, strike down your enemies! Battle is the highest virtue for a Kshatriya.'

But Yudhishthira calmly replied: 'My heart burns because of our sufferings. But I have given my pledge to remain in exile, and it cannot be violated, Bhima. Virtue is greater than life and prosperity in this world; it is the way to celestial bliss.'

Then they were all silent, and they pondered over these things.

Arjuna's Celestial Gifts

Now the Pandavas needed celestial weapons, because these were owned by Drona, Bhishma and Karna. In time, therefore, the holy sage Vyasa appeared before Arjuna and told him to go to Mount Kailasa, the high seat of the gracious god Shiva, and to perform penances there with deep devotion in order to obtain gifts of arms. So Arjuna went on his way, and when he reached the mountain of Shiva he went through great austerities: he raised his arms in the air and, leaning on nothing, stood on his tiptoes; for food he ate withered leaves at first, then he fed on air alone.

The Rishis pleaded with Shiva, fearing disaster from the penances of Arjuna. Then the god assumed the form of a hunter and went towards Indra's warrior son, whom he challenged to single combat. First they fought with weapons; then they wrestled one another fiercely. In the end Arjuna fell to the ground. When that brave Pandava regained consciousness he made a clay image of Shiva, threw himself down in worship, and made an offering of flowers. Soon afterwards he saw his opponent wearing the garland he had given, and he knew that he had wrestled with Shiva himself. Arjuna fell down before him, and the god gave him a celestial weapon named Pasupata. Then a great storm broke out, and the earth shook, and the spirit of the weapon stood beside Arjuna, ready to obey his will.

Next appeared Indra, king of gods, Varuna, god of waters, Yama, king of the dead, and Kuvera, lord of treasures, and they stood on the mountain summit in all their glory; to Arjuna they gave gifts of other celestial weapons.

Afterwards Indra transported his son to his own bright city, the celestial Swarga, where the flowers always bloom and sweet music is forever wafted on fragrant winds. There he saw sea-born Apsaras, the heavenly brides of gods and heroes, and music-loving Gandharvas, who sang songs and danced merrily in their joy. Urvasi, a beautiful Apsara with bright eyes and silken hair, looked with love at Arjuna; but she sought in vain to subdue him, at which she scornfully said: 'Kama, god of love, has wounded me with his arrows, yet you scorn me. For this, Arjuna, you will live for a season as a dancer and musician, ignored by women.' Arjuna was troubled by this, but Indra told him that this curse would work in his favour. So Arjuna remained in Indra's fair city for five years. He achieved great skill in music, in dance and song. He was also trained to wield the celestial weapons which the gods had given to him.

Now the demons and giants who are named the Daityas and Danavas were the ancient enemies of Indra. They hailed from the lowest division of the underworld beneath the ocean floor, in a place called Patala. And a day came when Arjuna waged war with them. He rode away in Indra's great car, which sailed through the air like a bird, driven by Matali. When he reached the shore of the sea, the waves rose against him like great mountains, and the waters were divided; he saw demon fish and giant tortoises, and vessels laden down with rubies. But he did not pause, as he was without fear. Arjuna was eager for battle, and he blew a mighty blast on his war shell: the Daityas and Danavas heard him and quaked with terror. Then the demons beat their drums and blew their trumpets, and amid the dreadful racket the wallowing sea monsters rose up and leapt over the waves against Indra's great son. But Arjuna chanted mantras; he shot clouds of bright arrows; he fought with his bright celestial weapons, and the furies were thwarted and beaten back. They then sent fire against him and water, and they flung huge rocks; but he fought on until in the end he triumphed, killing all that stood against him.

Afterwards the valiant hero quickly rode towards the city of demons and giants which is named Hiranyapura. The women came out to lure him, calling aloud. He heard them but did not pause. All these evil giant women fled in confusion, terrified by the noise of Indra's celestial car and the driving of Matali, and their earrings and necklaces fell from their bodies like boulders tumbling and thundering down mountain slopes.

When Arjuna entered the city of Hiranyapura he gazed with wonder at the mighty chariots with ten thousand horses, which were stately and proud. And he wrecked the dwellings of the Daityas and Danavas.

Indra praised his warrior son for his valour in overcoming the demons and giants of the ocean, and he gave him a chain of gold, a bright crown, and the war shell which gave a mighty, thunderous blast.

Second Exile of the Pandavas

During the years that Arjuna lived in Indra's celestial city, Yudhishthira and his three younger brothers, with Draupadi and the priest Dhaumya, stayed for a time in the forest of Kamyaka. Great sages visited them there, one teaching Yudhishthira the skill of throwing dice. Others led the wanderers to sacred waters, in which they were cleansed of their sins, and they achieved great virtues. And the sages told them many tales of men and women who suffered and made self-sacrifices, undergoing long exiles and performing penances so as to learn great wisdom and win favour from the gods.

Thereafter the exiles went northward towards the Himalayas, and eventually in the distance they saw the home of Kuvera, lord of treasure and King of Yakshas. They gazed at palaces of crystal and gold; the high walls were studded with jewels, and the gleaming ramparts and turrets were adorned by dazzling streamers. They saw beautiful gardens of bright flowers, and soft winds came towards them laden with perfume; wonderful were the trees, and they were vocal with the songs of birds.

Kuvera came and spoke words of wisdom to Yudhishthira, counselling him to be patient and long-suffering, and to wait for the right time and place to display his Kshatriya prowess.

The exiles wandered on, and one day they saw the bright car of Indra, and they worshipped Matali, the charioteer. Then Indra arrived with his hosts of Apsaras and Gandharvas, and when they had adored him, the god promised Yudhishthira that he would once again reign in splendour over all men.

Arjuna appeared, and the Pandavas family rejoiced. They all returned together to Kamyaka. There they were visited by Markandeya, the mighty sage, whose life endures through all the world's ages, and he spoke of the mysteries and all that had taken place from the beginning, and revealed to them full knowledge of the Deluge.

Now while the Pandavas were enduring great suffering in the forest, Karna spoke to Duryodhana and prevailed upon him to spy on their misery. So Dhritarashtra's son left, as was the custom every three years, to inspect the cattle and brand the calves. And with him went Karna and many princes and courtiers, and also a thousand ladies of the royal household. However, when they all drew near to the forest, they found that the Gandharvas and Apsaras, who had descended to make merry there, would not permit the royal train to advance. Duryodhana sent messages to the

Gandharva king, commanding him to leave; but the celestial spirits did not fear him, and instead came forward to fight. A great war was waged, and the Kauravas were defeated. Karna fled, whilst Duryodhana and many of his courtiers and all the royal ladies were taken prisoners.

It happened that some of Duryodhana's followers who managed to flee soon reached the place where the Pandavas were, and told them how their kinsmen had been overcome. So Arjuna, Bhima and the two younger brothers went to the Gandharvas and fought with them until they were compelled to release the royal prisoners. The proud Duryodhana was humbled by his enemies' actions.

Yudhishthira gave a feast to the Kauravas, and he called Duryodhana his 'brother'. Duryodhana pretended to be pleased, although in his heart he was mortified. After this the sullen and angry Duryodhana resolved to end his life. His friends protested with him, but he said: 'I have nothing to live for now. I do not desire friendship, or wealth, or power, or enjoyment. Do not delay my purpose, but leave me now. I will eat no more food, and I will wait here until I die. Return, therefore, to Hastinapur and respect and obey those who are greater than me.' Then he purified himself with water, and sat down to wait for the end, dressed in rags and absorbed in silent meditation.

But the Daityas and Danavas did not want their favourite king to end his life in case their power should be weakened, so they sent a strange goddess to the forest, who carried him away in the night. Then the demons promised to help him in the coming struggle against the Pandavas. Duryodhana was comforted by this, and abandoned his vow to die in solitude. So he quickly returned to Hastinapur and resumed his position.

Soon afterwards, when the princes and the elders sat in council with the maharajah, wise old Bhishma praised the Pandava princes for their valour and generosity, and advised Duryodhana to offer them his friendship, so that the kinsmen might ever afterwards live together in peace. Duryodhana did not answer. Instead, smiling bitterly, he rose up and walked out of the council chamber. This made Bhishma angry, and he too left and went to his own house.

Then Duryodhana sought to rival the glory of Yudhishthira by holding an Imperial sacrifice. Duhsasana, with evil heart, sent messengers to Yudhishthira, inviting him to attend with his brothers; but Yudhishthira said: 'Although this great sacrifice will reflect honour on all the descendants of King Bharata, and therefore on me and my brothers, I cannot be present because our years of exile have not yet come to an end.'

He spoke calmly and with dignity, but Bhima was enraged and exclaimed: 'Messengers of Duryodhana, tell your master that when our years of exile are over, Yudhishthira will offer up a mighty sacrifice with weapons and burn the whole family of Dhritarashtra.'

Duryodhana received these messages in silence. And when the sacrifice was held, Karna took a vow and said Duryodhana: 'I will neither eat venison nor wash my feet until I have slain Arjuna.'

Spies rushed to the Pandavas and related all that had taken place at the sacrifice, and also the words which Karna had spoken. When Yudhishthira heard of Karna's terrible vow, it caused him great sorrow, because he knew that a day must come when Arjuna and Karna would meet in deadly conflict.

One day Surya, god of the sun, warned Karna that Indra had resolved to strip him of his celestial armour and earrings. 'But,' said Surya, 'you can demand in exchange a heavenly weapon which has the power to slay gods and demons and mortal men.'

So it came that Indra stood before Karna, disguised as a Brahman, and asked for his armour and earrings. Having vowed to give the Brahmans whatever they might ask of him, Karna took off his armour and earrings and gave them to the king of the gods. In exchange he demanded an infallible weapon. Indra granted his request, but smiled and went on his way, knowing that the triumph of the Pandavas was now assured.

One day soon after this Jayadratha, King of Sindhu, passed through the wood when the Pandavas had gone hunting. He watched Draupadi with eyes of love, and, despite her warnings, carried her away in his chariot.

When the Pandavas returned and were told what had taken place, they set out in pursuit of the king of Sindhu, who left his chariot and hid when they came near. Bhima turned to Yudhishthira and said: 'Return now with Draupadi and our brothers. Although the king should seek refuge in the underworld, he will not escape my vengeance.'

Yudhishthira replied: 'Remember, Bhima, that although Jayadratha has committed a grievous sin, he is our kinsman. He is married to the sister of Duryodhana.'

To this Draupadi exclaimed: 'He is worthy of death. He is the worst of kings and the vilest of men! Have the sages not said that he who carries off the wife of another in times of peace must certainly be put to death?'

When Bhima found Jayadratha, he threw him down and cut off his hair except five locks; then the strong warrior promised to spare the king's life if he would swear allegiance to Yudhishthira and declare himself his slave. So the King of Sindhu had to bow down to Yudhishthira like a humble servant. He then left in shame and returned to his own country.

The Voice of the Waters

When the twelfth year of exile was near to an end, the Pandava brothers thought it was time to leave the forest. But before they went a strange and awful adventure threatened them with disaster. One day a stag appeared and carried away the twigs with which a Brahman was accustomed to use to kindle his holy fire. The Brahman begged Yudhishthira to pursue the animal, and the Pandavas endeavoured in vain to kill it or recover the sacred twigs. Weary with the chase, they eventually sat down to rest. They were all thirsty, and one of them climbed a tree to look for signs of water. When it was discovered that a pond was nearby, Yudhishthira sent Nakula towards it. The young man approached the water, and as he bend down he heard a voice which said: 'Answer what I shall ask of you before you drink or draw water.'

But Nakula's thirst was greater than his fear, so he drank the waters; then he fell dead. Sahadeva followed him, wondering what had delayed his brother. He too gazed greedily at the pool, and he too heard the voice, but did not listen and drank; and he also fell dead.

Arjuna was next to go towards the water. The voice spoke to him, and he answered with anger: 'Who are you that would hinder me so? Reveal yourself, and my arrows will speak to you!' Then he drew his bow, and his arrows flew thick and fast like raindrops. But his bravery was for nothing, because when he drank he also fell dead like the others. Bhima followed him, and stooped and drank, unheeding the voice, and he was stricken down just like Arjuna, Nakula and Sahadeva before him.

Eventually wise Yudhishthira approached the pond. He saw his brothers lying dead, and grieved over them. Then, as he neared the water, the voice spoke once again, and he answered it, saying: 'Who are you?'

The voice said: 'I am a Yaksha. I warned your brothers not to drink this water until they had answered what I should ask them, but they disregarded my warning and I laid them in death. If you will answer my questions you can, however, drink here and not be afraid.'

Yudhishthira replied: 'Speak and I will answer you.'

The voice said: 'Who makes the sun rise? Who keeps him company? Who makes the sun go down? In whom is the sun established?'

Yudhishthira responded: 'Brahma makes the sun rise; the gods accompany him; Dharma makes the sun set; in truth is the sun established.'

The voice then said: 'What sleeps with open eyes? What does not move after birth? What is that which has no heart? What is that which swells of itself?'

Yudhishthira answered: 'A fish sleeps with open eyes; an egg does not move after birth; a stone has no heart; a river swells of itself.'

The Voice went on: 'What makes The Way? What is called Water? What is called Food? What is called Poison?'

Yudhishthira retorted: 'They that are devout make The Way; space is called Water; the cow is Food; a request is Poison.'

The voice said: 'Who is spoken of as the unconquered enemy of man? What is spoken of as the enemy's disease? Who is regarded as holy? Who is regarded as unholy?'

Yudhishthira replied: 'Man's unconquered enemy is anger, and his disease is greed; he who seeks the good of all is holy; he who is selfishly cold is unholy.'

The voice said: 'Who are worthy of eternal torment?'

Yudhishthira responded: 'He who says to the Brahman whom he has asked to his house, I have nothing to give; he who declares the Vedas to be false; he who is rich and yet gives nothing to the poor.'

The voice addressed many such questions to wise Yudhishthira, and he answered each one patiently and with knowledge. Then the Yaksha revealed himself in the form of Dharma, god of wisdom and justice. He was the celestial father of Yudhishthira. To his son he granted two favours; and Yudhishthira requested that his brothers should be restored to life, and that they should all have the power to remain unrecognized by anyone in the three worlds for the space of a year.

An End to the Exile

Before the Pandavas left the forest, Yudhishthira invoked the goddess Durga, giver of favours, saying: 'Oh slayer of the Buffalo Asura, you are worshipped by the gods, for you are the protector of the three worlds. Chief of all deities, bless us. Grant us victory, and help us in our distress.' The goddess heard Yudhishthira, and confirmed the promise of Dharma that the Pandava brothers and Draupadi would remain unrecognized during the last year of their exile.

Then the wanderers concealed their weapons in a tree, and went together towards the city of Virata so that they might hide themselves. According to the terms of their banishment, they would have to spend a further twelve years in the jungle if the Kauravas discovered their whereabouts.

The Pandavas found favour in the eyes of the king. Yudhishthira became his instructor in the art of playing with dice, because he was accustomed to lose heavily. Bhima was made chief cook. Arjuna taught dancing and music to the ladies of the harem. Nakula was given care of horses, and Sahadeva of cattle. The queen was drawn towards Draupadi, who offered to become a servant on condition that she should not have to wash the feet of anyone, or eat food left over after meals; and on these terms she was engaged. The queen feared that Draupadi's great beauty would attract lovers and cause strife; but the forlorn woman said that she was protected by five Gandharvas, and was without fear.

Bhima soon won renown for his matchless strength. At a great festival he overcame a wrestler from a far country who was named Jimúta, and he received many gifts. The king took great pride in him, and often took him to the apartments of the women, where he wrestled with caged tigers and lions and bears, slaying each one at will with a single blow. Indeed, all the brothers were well loved by the monarch because of their loyal services.

It happened that the queen's brother, Kichaka, a mighty warrior and commander of the royal army, was smitten with the beautiful Draupadi, and in time he sought to carry her away. But one night Bhima waited for him when he came stealthily towards Draupadi, and after a long struggle the strong Pandava killed him. Then Bhima broke all this prince's bones and rolled up his body into a ball of flesh.

Kichaka's kinsmen were horrified when they discovered what had happened, and they said: 'No man has done this awful deed; the Gandharvas have taken vengeance.' In their anger they seized Draupadi, intent on burning her on the pyre with the body of Kichaka; but Bhima disguised himself and went to her rescue. He scattered her tormentors in flight, killing many with a great tree which he had uprooted.

The king was terror-stricken, and spoke to the queen, who in turn asked Draupadi to leave Virata. But the wife of the Pandavas begged to remain in the royal service; and she said that her Gandharva protectors would serve the king in his greatest hour of peril, which, she foretold, was already near to him. So the queen supported her, and Draupadi stayed there.

Soon afterwards the King of Trigartis, hearing that mighty Kichaka was dead, plotted with the Kauravas at Indra-prastha to attack the city of Virata in order to capture the kingdom. Duryodhana agreed to help him, so the King of Trigartis invaded the kingdom from the north, while the Kauravas marched against Virata from the south.

And so it came to pass that on the last day of the thirteenth year of the Pandavas' exile, the first raid took place from the north, and many cattle were carried off. Yudhishthira and Bhima, with Nakula and Sahadeva, offered to help when they heard that the King of Virata had been captured by his enemies. The Pandavas went off to rescue the monarch. They soon defeated the raiders and rescued their prisoner; they also seized the King of Trigartis, and forced him to submit to his rival before he was allowed to return to his own city.

Meanwhile the Kauravas had advanced from the south. Uttar, son of the King of Virata, went against them, with Arjuna as his charioteer. When the young man, however, saw his enemies, he wanted to flee, but his driver forced him to remain in the chariot.

Arjuna recovered his own weapons from the tree in which they were hidden. Then, fully armed, he rode against the Kauravas, who said: 'If this is Arjuna, he and his brothers must go into exile for another twelve years.'

Bhishma responded: 'The thirteenth year of concealment is now ended.' The Kauravas, however, persisted that Arjuna had appeared before the full time was spent.

Indra's great son advanced boldly. Suddenly he blew his celestial war shell, and all the Kauravas were stricken with fear. They fainted and lay on the field like they were sleeping. Arjuna refrained from killing them, instead he commanded Uttar to take possession of their royal attire. Then the great archer of the Pandavas returned to the city with the king's son.

Now when the monarch discovered how Arjuna had served him by warding off the attack of the Kauravas, he offered the brave Pandava his daughter, Uttara, for a bride; but Arjuna said: 'Let her be given to my son.'

It was then that the Pandava brothers revealed to the King of Virata who they were. All those who had assembled in the palace rejoiced and honoured them.

Many great kings came to the marriage of Abhimamju, son of Arjuna and Subhadra. Krishna came with his brother Balarama, and the King Drupada came with his son Dhrishtadyumna.

Now the King of Virata resolved to help Yudhishthira claim back his kingdom from the Kauravas, who continued to protest that their kinsmen had been discovered before the complete term of exile had ended.

Shakuni, the cunning gambler, and the vengeful Karna supported the proud and evil-hearted Duryodhana in refusing to make peace with the Pandava brothers, despite the warnings of the sages who sat around the Maharajah Dhritarashtra.

Duryodhana's Defiance

Before the wedding guests departed from Virata, the elders and princes and chieftains assembled in the council chamber. Drupada was there with his son, and Krishna with his brother Balarama and Satyaki his kinsman, and all the Pandava brothers were there also, and many others both valiant and powerful. As bright and numerous as the stars were the gems that glittered on the robes of the mighty warriors.

For a time they spoke kindly greetings one to another, and joked and made merry. Krishna sat pondering in silence, and after some time he rose and said: 'Oh kings and princes, may your fame endure forever! You well know that Yudhishthira was deprived of his kingdom by the evil trickster Shakuni. He has endured twelve years of exile, and has served, like his brothers, as a humble servant for a further year in the palace of the King of Virata. After all his suffering Yudhishthira desires peace; his heart is without anger, although he has endured great shame. The heart of Duryodhana, however, still burns with hate and jealous anger; still, as in his youth, he desires to work evil by deceit against the Pandava brothers. Now we must consider what Yudhishthira should do. Should he call many chieftains to his aid and wage war to punish his ancient enemies? Or should he send friendly messengers to Duryodhana, asking him to restore the kingdom which he still continues to possess?'

Balarama then spoke and said: 'Kings, you have heard the words of my brother, who loves Yudhishthira. It is true, indeed, that the Kauravas have wronged the Pandavas. Yet I would counsel peace, so that this matter may be arranged between kinsmen. Yudhishthira has brought his sufferings upon his own head. He was unwise to play with cunning Shakuni, and also to continue playing, despite the warnings of the elders and his friends. He has suffered for his mistake. Now let a messenger be sent to Duryodhana, asking him to restore the throne to Yudhishthira. I do not advise war. What has been gambled away cannot be restored in battle.'

Next stood Satyaki, the kinsman of Krishna. He said: 'Oh Balarama, you have spoken like to a woman! You remind me that weaklings are sometimes born to warriors, like barren saplings sprung from sturdy trees. Timid words come from timid hearts. Proud monarchs do not listen to such weak counsel. Can you justify Duryodhana and blame the pious-hearted and gracious Yudhishthira? If it had happened that Yudhishthira while playing with his brothers had been visited by Duryodhana, who, having thrown the dice, had won, then the contest would have been fair in the eyes of all men. But Duryodhana plotted to ruin his kinsman, and invited him to Hastinapur to play with the evil-hearted Shakuni, who threw loaded dice. But that is ended. Yudhishthira has fulfilled his obligation; his exile is past, and he is entitled to his kingdom. Why, therefore, should he beg for that which is his? A Kshatriya begs of no man; what is refused him he seizes in battle at all times.... Duryodhana still clings to Yudhishthira's kingdom, despite the wise counsel of Bhishma and Drona. Remember Balarama, it is not sinful to kill one's enemies, but it is shameful to beg from them. I now declare my advice to be that we should give the Kauravas an opportunity to restore the throne of Yudhishthira; if they hesitate to do so, then let the Pandavas secure justice on the battlefield.'

Then Drupada, King of Panchala, rose to his feet and said: 'Monarchs, I fear that Satyaki has spoken truly. The Kauravas are a stubborn people. I think it is useless to ask Duryodhana, whose heart is consumed with greed. It is useless to plead with Dhritarashtra, who is like clay in the hands of his proud son. Bhishma and Drona have already counselled in vain. Karna thirsts for war, and Duryodhana plots with him and also with false and cunning Shakuni. I think it would be wrong to follow the advice of Balarama. Duryodhana will never give up what he now possesses, nor does he desire peace. If we should send to him an ambassador who will speak mild words, he will think that we are weak, and become more boastful and arrogant than before. My advice is that we should gather together a great army without delay: the kings will side with him who askes first. Meanwhile let us offer peace and friendship to Duryodhana: my family priest will carry our message. If Duryodhana is willing to give up the kingdom of Yudhishthira, there will be peace; if he scorns our friendship, he will find us ready for war.'

Krishna again addressed the assembly and said: 'Drupada has spoken wisely. The Pandavas would do well to accept his counsel. If Duryodhana will agree to restore the kingdom to Yudhishthira, there will be no strife or bloodshed.... You all know that the Pandavas and Kauravas are my kinsmen; know also that they are equally dear to me.... I will now be gone. When you send out messengers of war, let them enter my kingdom last of all.'

After Krishna had returned home, he was visited by Duryodhana and Arjuna, both parties wanting his help in the war. He spoke to the rival kinsmen and said: 'I stand before you as in the balance; I have put myself on one side, and all my army is on the other. Choose now between you whether you want me or my forces. I will not fight, but will give my advice in battle.'

Duryodhana asked for the army, but Arjuna preferred to have Krishna alone. Krishna promised to be Arjuna's charioteer.

Duryodhana also tried to persuade Balarama to help him, but Krishna's brother said: 'I have no heart for this war. You know that you have wronged Yudhishthira, and that you should act justly in this matter. Do your duty, and your renown will be great.' Angered by Balamara's words, Duryodhana returned home.

In time Drupada's priest appeared in the city of Hastinapur, and the elders and princes sat with Dhritarashtra to hear his message. The Brahman said: 'So speaks the Pandavas – 'Pandu and Dhritarashtra were brothers: why, therefore, should Dhritarashtra's sons possess the whole kingdom, while the sons of Pandu are denied inheritance? Duryodhana has worked evil against his kinsman. He invited them to a gambling match to play with loaded dice, and they lost their possessions and had to go into exile like beggars. Now they have fulfilled the conditions, and are prepared to forget the past if their kingdom is restored to them. If their rightful claim is rejected, then Arjuna will scatter the Kauravas in battle.'

Bhishma said: 'What you have said is well justified, but it is wrong to boast regarding Arjuna. It would be wise of you not to speak of him in such a manner again.'

Karna angrily added: 'If the Pandavas have suffered, they are themselves to blame. It is fitting that they should plead for peace, because they are without followers. If they can prove their right to possessions, Duryodhana will give them; but he will not be forced by vain threats, or because the Kings of Panchala and Virata support them. Brahman, tell the Pandavas that they have failed to fulfil their obligations, because Arjuna was seen by us before the thirteenth year of banishment was completed. Let them return to the jungle for another term, and then come here and submit to Duryodhana and beg for his favours.'

To this Bhishma replied: 'You did not boast in this manner, Karna, when Arjuna opposed you at the Virata cattle raid. Remember that Arjuna is still powerful. If war comes, he will trample you into the dust.'

Dhritarashtra scolded Karna for his hasty speech, and said to Bhishma: 'He is young and unaccustomed to debate; do not be angry with him.'

Then the blind old king sent his minister and charioteer, Sanjaya, to the Pandavas to say: 'If you desire to have peace, come to me and I will do justice. Except wicked Duryodhana and hasty Karna all who are here are willing to make peace.'

When Sanjaya reached the Pandavas, he was astonished to see that they had assembled a mighty army. He greeted the brothers and delivered his message.

Yudhishthira said: 'We honour Dhritarashtra, but fear that he has listened to the counsel of his son Duryodhana, who wishes to have us in his power. The maharajah offers us protection, but not the fulfilment of our claims.'

Krishna added: 'The Pandavas have assembled a mighty army, and cannot reward these soldiers unless they receive their kingdom. It is not too late to make peace. Sanjaya, deliver this message to the Kauravas: 'If you seek peace, you will have peace; if you desire war, then let there be war.'

Before Sanjaya left, Yudhishthira spoke to him once more, saying: 'Tell Duryodhana that we will accept that portion of the kingdom which we ourselves have conquered and settled: he can keep the rest. My desire is for peace.'

Many days went past, and the Pandavas waited in vain for an answer to their message. Then Yudhishthira spoke to Krishna, saying: 'We have offered to make peace by accepting just a portion of our kingdom, yet the Kauravas remain silent.'

Krishna replied: 'I will go to Hastinapur and address the maharajah and his counsellors on your behalf.'

Yudhishthira responded: 'May you secure peace between kinsmen.'

Then Draupadi entered and, addressing Krishna, she said: 'Yudhishthira is too generous towards the Kauravas in offering to give up part of his kingdom to them. He pleads with them too much, as well, to grant him that which does not belongs to them. If the Kauravas wage war, my father and many other kings will assist the Pandavas.... Oh, can it be forgotten how Duhsasana dragged me by the hair to the Gambling Pavilion, and how I was put to shame before the elders and the princes?...'

She wept bitterly, and Krishna pitied her. 'Why do you despair?' he asked with gentle voice. 'The time is drawing near when all the Kauravas will be laid low, and their wives will shed tears more bitter than yours that fall now, fair one.'

Messengers who arrived at Hastinapur announced the coming of Krishna. Wise Vidura counselled that he should be welcomed in state, so Duryodhana proclaimed a public holiday, and all the people rejoiced, and decorated the streets with streamers and flowers.

Vidura was very pleased, and he said to Duryodhana: 'You have done well. But these preparations are in vain if you are unwilling to do justice to the Pandavas.'

Duryodhana was irate, and said: 'I will give nothing except what they can win in battle. If the success of the Pandavas depends on Krishna, then let us seize Krishna and put him in prison.'

Dhritarashtra was horror-stricken, and cried out: 'You cannot so treat an ambassador, and especially an ambassador like Krishna.'

Bhishma rose up and said: 'Oh maharajah, your son desires to work evil and bring ruin and shame on us all. I thinks disaster is now not far off.' He then departed to his own house, and Vidura did likewise.

All the Kauravas went forward to meet the royal ambassador except Duryodhana, who scarcely looked at Krishna when he arrived at the palace. Krishna went to the house of Vidura, and there he saw Pritha, who wept and said: 'How are my sons, whom I have not seen for fourteen years? How is Draupadi? I have heard about their sufferings in desolate places. Who can understand my own misery, as every day is full of weariness and grief to me?'

Krishna comforted her and said: 'Your sons have many allies, and before long they will triumphantly return to their own land.'

Afterwards Krishna went to the house of Duryodhana, who sat haughtily in the feasting chamber. Eventually Dhritarashtra's son spoke to his kinsman, who ate nothing. He said: 'Why are you unfriendly towards me?'

Krishna replied: 'I cannot be your friend until you act justly towards your kinsmen, the Pandavas.'

When Krishna went again to the house of Vidura, the aged counsellor said to him: 'It would have been better if you had not come here. Duryodhana will take no man's advice. When he speaks he expects all men to agree with him.'

Krishna said: 'It is my desire to prevent bloodshed. I came to Hastinapur to save the Kauravas from destruction, and I will warn them in the council chamber tomorrow. If they will listen to me, all will be well; if they scorn my advice, then let their blood be on their own heads.'

When the princes and the elders sat with Dhritarashtra in the council chamber, Narada and other great Rishis appeared in the heavens and were invited to come down and share in the deliberations. After a few moments Krishna stood, and in a voice like thunder said: 'I have come here not to seek war, but to utter words of peace and love. Maharajah, do not let your heart be stained with sin. Your sons have wronged their kinsmen, and a danger threatens all: it approaches now like an angry comet, and I can see kinsmen slaying kinsmen, and many noble lords laid in the dust. All of you here gathered together are already in the clutch of death. Dhritarashtra, man of peace, stretch forward your hand and avert the dreadful calamity which is about to fall on your house. Grant the Pandavas their rightful claim, and your reign will close in unsurpassed glory and in blessed peace.... What if all the Pandavas were killed in battle! Would their fall bring you joy? Are they not your own brother's children?... But you know that the Pandavas are as ready for war as they are eager for peace; and if war comes, it will be polluted with the blood of your sons. Oh gracious maharajah, let the last years of your life be peaceful and pleasant, so that you may indeed be blessed.'

Dhritarashtra wept and said: 'I would gladly do as you have counselled so wisely, Krishna, but Duryodhana, my vicious son, will not listen to me or obey, nor will he listen to his mother, nor to Vidura, nor to Bhishma.'

Next Bhishma spoke, and he addressed Duryodhana, saying: 'All would be well if you would follow the advice of Krishna. You are evil-hearted and a wrongdoer; you are the curse of our family; you take pleasure in disobeying your royal father and in scorning the advice of Krishna and Vidura. Soon your father will be stripped of his kingdom because of your actions; your pride will bring death to your kinsmen. Hear and follow my advice; do not bring eternal sorrow to your aged parents.'

Duryodhana heard these words in anger, but was silent.

Then Drona addressed him, and said: 'I join with Bhishma and Krishna in appealing to you. Those who advise you to make peace are your friends; those who counsel war are your enemies. Do not be too certain of victory; do not tempt the hand of vengeance; leave the night-black road of evil and seek out the road of light and well-doing, Duryodhana.'

Next Vidura stood up. He spoke with slow, gentle voice, and said: 'You have heard words of wisdom, Duryodhana.... I am deeply saddened. My grief is not for you, but for your old mother and father, who will fall into the hands of your enemies; my grief is for kinsmen and friends who must die in battle, and for those who will afterwards be driven away as beggars, friendless and without a home. The few survivors of war will curse the day of your birth.'

Again Bhishma spoke. He praised the courage of the Pandavas, and said: 'It is not too late to avoid calamity. The field of battle is still unstained by the blood of thousands; your army has not yet met the arrows of death. Before it is too late, make your peace with your kinsmen, the Pandavas, so that all men may rejoice. Banish evil from your heart forever; rule the whole world with the heirs of Pandu.'

The Rishis, too counselled peace like the elders. And all the while Dhritarashtra still wept.

When Duryodhana finally spoke, his eyes burned bright and his brows hung darkly. He said: 'Krishna counsels me to be just, yet he hates me and loves the Pandavas. Bishma scowls on me, and Vidura and Drona look coldly on; my father weeps for my sins. Yet what have I done that you all should turn my father's affection from me? If Yudhishthira loved gambling and staked and lost his throne and freedom, am I to blame? If he played a second time after being set free, and became an exile, why should he now call me a robber? Dull is the star of the Pandavas' destiny: their friends are few, and their army is feeble. Shall we, who do not fear Indra even, be threatened by the weak sons of Pandu? No warrior lives who can overcome us. A Kshatriya fears no enemy; he may fall in battle, but he will never give in. So the sages have spoken…. Hear me, my kinsmen! My father gifted Indra-prastha to the Pandavas in a moment of weakness. Never, so long as I and my brother live, will they possess it again. Never again will the kingdom of Maharajah Dhritarashtra be severed in two. It has been united, and so it will remain forever. My words are firm and plain. So tell the Pandavas, Krishna, that they ask in vain for territory. No town or village will they possess again with my consent. I swear by the gods that I will never humble myself in front of the Pandavas.'

Krishna responded: 'How can you speak in such a manner, Duryodhana? How can you pretend that you never wronged your kinsmen? Be mindful of your evil thoughts and deeds.'

Duhsasana whispered to his elder brother: 'I fear, if you do not make peace with the Pandavas, the elders will seize you and send you as a prisoner to Yudhishthira. They desire to make you and me and Karna kneel before the Pandavas.'

Duryodhana was furious. He rose and left the council chamber. Duhsasana, Karna and Shakuni followed him.

Krishna then turned to Dhritarashtra and said: 'You should arrest these four rebellious princes and act freely and justly towards the Pandavas.'

The weak old maharajah was stricken with grief, and he sent Vidura for his elder son. Shakuni, Karna and Duhsasana waited outside for Duryodhana, and they plotted to seize Krishna so that the power of the Pandavas might be weakened. But to Krishna came knowledge of their thoughts, and he informed the elders.

Once again the maharajah summoned Duryodhana before him, and Krishna said: 'Ah! You of little understanding, is it your desire to take me captive? Know now that I am not alone here; all the gods and holy beings are with me.'

Having uttered these words, Krishna suddenly revealed himself in divine splendour. His body was transformed into a tongue of flame; gods and divine beings appeared around him; fire flowed out from his mouth and eyes and ears; sparks broke from his skin, which became as radiant as the sun…. All the kings closed their eyes; they trembled when an earthquake shook the palace. But Duryodhana remained defiant.

Krishna, having resumed his human form, then said farewell to the maharajah, who lamented the doings of Duryodhana. The divine one spoke and said: 'Dhritarashtra, you I forgive freely; but a father is often cursed by the people because of the wicked doings of his own son.'

Before Krishna left the city he met Karna and spoke to him, saying: 'Come with me, and the Pandavas will regard you as their elder brother, and you will become the king.'

Karna responded: 'Although Duryodhana is the future king, he rules according to my counsel…. I know, without doubt, that a great battle is coming which will cover the earth with blood. Terrible are the omens. Calamity awaits the Kauravas…. Yet I cannot desert those who have given me their friendship. Besides, if I went with you now, men would regard me as Arjuna's inferior. Arjuna and I must meet in battle, and fate will decide who is greater. I know I shall fall in this war, but I must fight for my friends.... Oh mighty one, may we meet again on earth. If not, may we meet in heaven.'

Then Krishna and Karna embraced one another, and each went his own way.

Vidura spoke to Pritha, mother of the Pandavas, and said: 'My desire is always for peace, but although I cry myself hoarse, Duryodhana will not listen to my words. Dhritarashtra is old, yet he does not work for peace; he is intoxicated with pride for his sons. When Krishna returns to the Pandavas, war will certainly break out; the sin of the Kauravas will cause much bloodshed. I cannot sleep, thinking of approaching disaster.'

Pritha sighed and wept. 'To hell with wealth!' she said, 'That it should cause kinsmen to slaughter one another. War should be waged between enemies, not friends. If the Pandavas do not fight, they will suffer poverty; if they go to war and win, the destruction of kinsmen will not bring triumph. My heart is full of sorrow. And it is Karna who supports Duryodhana in his foolishness; he has again become powerful.'

Pritha regretted the mistakes of her girlhood which caused Karna to be, and she went out to look for him. She found her son bathing in sacred waters, and she said to him: 'You are my own son, and your father is Surya. I hid you at birth, and Radha, who found you, is not your mother. It is not right that you should plot in ignorance with Duryodhana against your own brothers. Let the Kauravas see the friendship of you and Arjuna. If you two were side by side you would conquer the world. My eldest son, you should be with your brothers now. Be no longer known as one of lowly birth.'

A voice spoke from the sun, saying: 'What Pritha has said is truth. Oh tiger among men, great good will be accomplished if you will obey her command.'

Karna remained steadfast, because his heart was full of honour. He said to Pritha, his mother: 'It is too late to command my obedience now. Why did you abandon me at birth? If I am a Kshatriya, I have been deprived of my rank. No enemy could have done me a greater injury than you have done. You have never been a mother to me, nor do your sons know I am their brother. How can I now desert the Kauravas, who trust me to wage this war. I am their boat on which to cross a stormy sea.... I will speak without deceit to you. For the sake of Duryodhana I will fight your sons. I cannot forget his kindness; I cannot forget my own honour. Your command cannot be obeyed by me. Yet your solicitation to me will not be fruitless. I have the power to kill Yudhishthira, and Bhima, and Nakula, and Sahadeva, but I promise they shall not fall by my hand. I will fight with Arjuna alone. If I slay Arjuna, I will achieve great fame; if I am slain by him, I will be covered with glory.'

Pritha responded: 'You have pledged the lives of four of your brothers. You must remembered this in the perils of battle. I bless you.'

Karna said: 'So be it,' and then they parted, the mother going one way and the son another.

After this the Pandavas and Kauravas gathered together their mighty armies and marched to the field of battle.

The Epic Battle of Eighteen Days

Soon after Krishna had returned from Hastinapur, Duryodhana sent a challenge to the Pandavas. His messenger spoke, saying: 'You have vowed to wage war against us. The time has come for you to fulfil your vow. Your kingdom was seized by me, your wife Draupadi was put to shame, and you were all made exiles. Why have you not yet sought to be avenged in battle? Where is drowsy Bhima, who boasted that he would drink the blood of Duhsasana? Duhsasana is weary with waiting for him. Where is arrogant Arjuna, who has Drona to meet? When mountains are blown about like dust, and men hold back the wind with their hands, Arjuna will take captive the mighty Drona.... Of what account was the mace of Bhima and the bow of Arjuna on the day when your kingdom was taken from you, and you were banished like vagabonds?... Krishna's help will be of no use when you meet us in battle.'

Krishna answered the messenger, saying: 'Vainly do you boast of prowess, but before long your fate will be made known to you. I will consume your army like fire consumes withered grass. You will not escape me, because I will drive Arjuna's chariot. And let Duhsasana know that the Bhima's vow will be fulfilled before long.'

Arjuna then added: 'Tell Duryodhana, it is unseemly for warriors to boast like women.... It is well that Duhsasana comes to battle.'

When the messenger repeated these words to Duryodhana, Karna said: 'Stop this chatter! Let the drums of war be sounded.'

So at dawn on the following day the armies of the Kauravas and the Pandavas were assembled for battle on the wide plain of Kuru-Kshetra. Bhishma had been chosen to lead Duryodhana's army, and Karna, who had quarrelled with him, vowed not to fight so long as the older warrior remained alive. 'Should he fall, however,' Karna said, 'I will attack Arjuna.'

The army of the Pandavas was commanded by Dhrishtadyumna, son of Drupada, and brother of Draupadi. Among the young heroes were Arjuna's two sons, the noble Abhimanyu, whose mother was Krishna's beautiful sister Subhadra, and brave Iravat, whose mother was Ulupi, the serpent nymph, daughter of the king of the Nagas. Bhima's Rakshasa son, the terrible Ghatotkacha, who had the power to change his shape and create illusions, had also rushed to assist his kinsmen. Krishna drove the chariot of Arjuna, who carried his celestial bow, named Gandiva, the gift of the god Agni; and his standard was the image of Hanuman, the chief ape god, who was the son of Vayu, the wind god. But the army of Duryodhana was much larger than the army of Yudhishthira.

Drona led the right wing of the Kaurava forces, which was strengthened by Shakuni, the gambler, and his Gandharai lancers. The left wing was led by Duhsasana, who was followed by Kamboja cavalry and fierce Sakas and Yavanas mounted on fast horses. The peoples of the north were there and the peoples of the south, and also of the east. Blind old Dhritarashtra was in the rear, and with him was Sanjaya, his charioteer, who told him all that took place, having been gifted with divine vision by Vyasa.

Yet before the conflict began, Yudhishthira walked unarmed towards the Kauravas, at which his kinsmen laughed, thinking he was terror-stricken. But Pandu's noble son first spoke to Bhishma and asked permission to fight against him. Bhishma gave consent. Then he addressed Drona in similar terms, and Drona also gave consent. And before he returned to his place, Yudhishthira called out to the Kaurava army: 'Whoever desires to help our cause, let him follow me.' When he had said this, Yuyutsu, the half-brother of Duryodhana, called out: 'If you will elevate me, I will serve you well.' Yudhishthira replied: 'Be my brother.' Then Yuyutsu followed Yudhishthira with all his men, and no man tried to hold him back.

As the armies were getting ready for battle, Arjuna urged Krishna to drive his chariot to the open space on which the struggle would take place. Indra's mighty son surveyed the hosts, and when he saw his kinsmen, young and old, and his friends and all the elders and princes on either side ready to attack one another, his heart was touched, and he trembled with pity and sorrow. He spoke to Krishna, saying: 'I do not seek victory, or kingdom, or any joy on earth. Those for whose sake we might wish for power are gathered against us in battle. What joy can come to us if we commit the crime of slaying our own kinsmen?' Then he dropped his celestial bow and sat down on the bench of his chariot with a heart full of grief.

Krishna admonished Arjuna, saying: 'You are a Kshatriya, and it is your duty to fight, no matter what may happen to you or to others. He who has wisdom does not sorrow for the living or for the dead. As one casts off old clothing and puts on new, so the soul casts off this body and enters the new body. Nothing exists that is not of the soul.'

After long instruction, Krishna revealed himself to Arjuna in his celestial splendour and power and said: 'Let your heart and your understanding be fixed in me, and you shall dwell in me from now on. I will deliver you from all your sins.... I am the same to all creatures; there is none hateful to me – none dear. Those who worship me are in me and I am in them. Those who hate me are consigned to evil births: they are deluded birth after birth.'

Arjuna listened to Krishna's counsel, and prepared for the fray. The war shell bellowed loudly, and the drums of battle were sounded. The Kauravas got ready to attack with horsemen, footmen, charioteers, and elephants of war. The Pandavas were gathered to meet them. And the air was filled with the shouting of men, the roaring of elephants, the blasts of trumpets, and the beating of drums: the rattling of chariots was like thunder rolling in heaven. The gods and Gandharvas assembled in the clouds and saw the hosts which had gathered for mutual slaughter.

As both armies waited for sunrise, a tempest rose up and the dawn was darkened by dust clouds, so that men could scarcely see one another. Evil were the omens. Blood dropped like rain out of heaven, while jackals howled impatiently, and kites and vultures screamed hungrily for human flesh. The earth shook, peals of thunder were heard, although there were no clouds, and angry lightning broke the horrid gloom; flaming thunderbolts struck the rising sun and broke in fragments....

The undaunted warriors never faltered, despite these signs and warnings. Shouting defiance, they mingled in conflict, eager for victory, and strongly armed. Swords were wielded and ponderous maces, javelins were hurled, and numerous darts too; countless arrows whistled in flight.

When the wind fell and the air cleared, the battle rose in fury. Bhishma achieved mighty deeds. Duryodhana led his men against Bhima's, and they fought with courage. Yudhishthira fought with Salya, King of Madra; Dhrishtadyumna, son of Drupada, went against Drona, who had once captured half of the Panchala kingdom with the help of the Pandavas. Drupada was opposed to Jayadratha, the King of Sindhu, who had attempted to carry off Draupadi, and was compelled to acknowledge himself as the slave of Yudhishthira. Many single combats were fought with uncertain result.

All day the armies battled with growing enthusiasm. As evening was coming on, Abhimanyu, son of Arjuna, perceived that the advantage lay with the Kauravas, mainly because of Bhishma's prowess. So he hurried towards that mighty warrior, and cut down the flag of his chariot. Bhishma said he had never seen such a youthful hero who could perform greater deeds. Then he advanced to attack the Pandava army. Victoriously he went, cutting a blood-red path through the stricken legions; no one could resist him for long. The heart of Arjuna was filled with shame, and he rode against Bhishma, whose advance was stopped. The two heroes fought desperately until dusk. Then Bhishma withdrew; but Arjuna followed him, and pierced the heart of the Kaurava host, achieving great slaughter. The truce was sounded, and the first day's battle came to an end.

Yudhishthira was despondent because the fortunes of war seemed to be against him; in the darkness he went to Krishna, who told him to lift his spirits, and Yudhishthira was comforted.

On the morning of the second day Bhishma once again attacked the Pandava forces, shattering their ranks; but Arjuna drove him back. Seeing this, Duryodhana lamented to Bhishma that he had quarrelled with Karna. The old warrior answered: 'I am a Kshatriya and must fight even against my beloved kinsman.' Then he rode against Arjuna once more, and the two warriors fought fiercely and wounded one another.

Drupada's son waged a long battle with Drona, and Bhima performed mighty deeds. He leapt on the back of an elephant and killed the son of the King of Maghadha; and with a single blow of his mace he killed the king and his elephant, too.

Towards evening a furious battle was being fought by Abhimanyu, son of Arjuna, and Lakshmana, son of Duryodhana. The young Pandava was about to achieve victory, when Duryodhana came to his son's aid with many kings. Shouts were raised: 'Abhimanyu is in peril; he will be overcome by force of numbers!' Arjuna heard these words, and rode to the rescue. Then the Kauravas cried out in terror: 'Arjuna! Arjuna!' and scattered in flight. That evening Bhishma spoke to Drona and said: 'I think the gods are against us.'

On the third day the army of the Pandavas advanced in crescent formation and drove back the Kaurava army. Many were slain, and rivers of blood stained the earth; horses writhed in agony, and the air was filled with the shrieking and moaning of wounded men. Terrible were the omens, for headless men rose up and fought against one another; then the people feared that all who fought in that dreadful battle would be slain.

When he saw the fallen standard, and the heaps of murdered elephants, horses and men, Duryodhana said to Bhishma: 'You should give your place to Karna. I think you are swayed by Arjuna and the Pandavas.'

Bhishma replied: 'Your struggle is in vain, foolish Duryodhana. No one can wipe away the stain of your sins; cunning is of no avail against a righteous cause. You shall perish because of your mistakes.... I have no fear of battle, and I will lead the Kauravas until I triumph or fall.'

Then angry Bhishma urged his charioteer to attack the enemy; and he drove back all who opposed him, even Arjuna. The fighting became general, nor did it end until night obscured the plain.

Bhima was the hero of the fourth day of battle. He swept against the Kauravas like a whirlwind; darts were thrown and arrows shot at the strong Pandava but all were in vain. He wounded both Duryodhana and Salya, King of Sindhu. Then fourteen of Duryodhana's brothers rushed to attack him. Like the lion who licks his lips when he sees his prey coming close, Bhima awaited them. Brief and terrible was the conflict, and before six princes fled in terror, eight were slaughtered by the mighty Pandava.

Another day dawned, and Arjuna and Bhima advanced in triumph until they were met and held back by Drona. Once again the sons of Duryodhana and Arjuna sought out one another. Their blows were swift and mighty, and for a time all men watched them in wonder. Eventually Lakshmana was grievously wounded, and was carried from the field by his kinsmen. Abhimanyu returned in triumph to Yudhishthira. On that same day the ten great sons of Satyaki, Krishna's kinsman were killed.

Another day dawned, and it was a day of peril for Bhima. Confident of victory, he pressed too far into the midst of the Kaurava forces, and was surrounded by overwhelming numbers. Drupada saw this threat and rushed to help him, but neither could retreat. Then Arjuna's fearless son, the slayer of Lakshmana, with twelve brave chieftains shattered the Kaurava hosts and rescued Bhima and Drupada from the surging warriors who thirsted for their blood.

The seventh day was the day of Bhishma. No one could withstand him in his battle fury. The Pandavas cowered before him, nor could Bhima or Arjuna drive him back. Before night fell, the standard of Yudhishthira was cut down, and the Kauravas rejoiced, believing that they would achieve a great victory.

On the day that followed, however, the tide of battle turned. As Bhishma advanced, his charioteer was slain, and the horses took flight in terror. Then confusion fell on the Kaurava army. For a time the Pandavas made resistless advance amidst mighty slaughter. Then the six Gandharai princes advanced to beat back the forces of Yudhishthira. Riding on milk-white horses, they swept like sea birds across the ocean. They had vowed to kill Iravat, son of Arjuna and the Naga princess. The gallant youth did not fear them and fought triumphantly, stirred with the joy of battle; he killed five of the princes, but the sixth, the eldest prince, struck down Arjuna's son, taking his life. When Arjuna was told that his son had fallen he was stricken with grief. Then with tear-dimmed eyes he raced towards his enemies, thirsting for vengeance; he broke through the Kaurava ranks, and Bhima, who followed him, killed more of Duryodhana's brothers.

Bhima's terrible son, the Rakshasa Ghatotkacha, also sought vengeance after Iravat fell. Roaring like the sea, he assumed an awesome shape, and advanced with flaming spears like the Destroyer at the end of Time, followed by other Rakshasas. Warriors fled from his path, until Duryodhana went against him with many elephants; but Ghatotkacha scattered the elephant host. Duryodhana fought like a lion and killed four Rakshasas, whereupon Bhima's son, raging furiously, his eyes red as fire, charged at Duryodhana; but that mighty Kaurava shot arrows like angry snakes, and he wounded his enemy. An elephant was brought in front of Duryodhana's chariot for protection. Ghatotkacha cut down the great animal with a flaming dart. Next Bhishma pressed forward with a division to shield Dhritarashtra's son, and the Rakshasa fought fiercely; he wounded Kripa, and with an arrow severed the string of Bhishma's bow. Then the Panchalas rushed to help Bhima's son, and the Kauravas were scattered in flight.

Duryodhana was stricken with sorrow, and went to the snow-white tent of Bhishma that night and said: 'Forgive my harsh words, mighty chieftain. The Pandavas are brave in battle, but they are unable to resist you. If, however, you love them too much to overcome them, let Karna take your place, so that he may lead the army against our enemies.'

Bhishma replied: 'Duryodhana, your struggle is of no avail. The just cause must win; they who fight for the right are doubly armed. Besides, Krishna is with the Pandavas: he drives Arjuna's chariot, and not even the gods could strike them down. You are confronted by utter ruin! I will fight as I have fought until the end, which is not far off.'

The next day Bhishma was like a fire which burns up a dry and withering forest. In his chariot he advanced triumphantly, wreaking havoc and carnage as he went.

Yudhishthira was in despair, and when night fell he spoke to Krishna, who said: 'Bhishma has vowed that he will not kill one who had been born a woman, knowing that the righteous would defame him if he murdered a female. Therefore let Sikhandin be sent against him with Arjuna.'

Arjuna responded: 'No! I cannot fight behind another, or achieve the fall of Bhishma by foul means. I loved him as a child; I sat on his knee and called him 'Father'. I would rather perish than slay the saintly hero.'

Krishna replied: 'It is fated that Bhishma will fall tomorrow, a victim of wrong. As he has fought against those whom he loves, so must you, Arjuna, fight against him. He has shown you how Kshatriyas must always wage war, whether their enemies are hated or loved.'

And so on the tenth day of battle, Arjuna left for battle with Sikhandin, who had been born a woman and made a male by a Yaksha.

Once again Duryodhana tried to persuade Bhishma to give his place to Karna, and Bhishma answered him in anger: 'Today will I overcome the Pandavas or perish on the battlefield.'

Then the ancient hero advanced and challenged Arjuna. A terrible conflict ensued, lasting for many hours; all the warriors on either side stopped fighting and watched. In time Sikhandin rushed forward like a foaming wave, and when Bhishma saw him his arms fell, because he could not fight against one who had been born a woman. Then the arrows of Arjuna pierced Bhishma's body, and the old hero fell from his chariot and lay dying.... The sun went down, and darkness swept over the plain.

There was misery on the blood-drenched plain that night. Arjuna wept like a son weeps for a father, and he carried water to Bhishma. Yudhishthira cursed the day the war began. Duryodhana and his brothers also came to the dying chieftain. Friends and enemies grieved together over the fallen hero.

Bhishma spoke to Duryodhana, saying: 'Hear the counsel of your dying kinsman; his voice speaks as from the dead. If your heart of stone can be moved, you will bring this slaughter of kinsmen by kinsmen to an end now. Restore to Yudhishthira his kingdom and make your peace with him, and let Pandavas and Kauravas be friends and comrades together.'

But he spoke in vain, as his words stirred Duryodhana's heart to hate the Pandavas with a deeper hatred than before.

Karna came to the battlefield, and Bhishma said to him: 'We have been proud rivals; always jealous of one another, and ever in conflict. My voice fails, yet I must tell you that Arjuna is not greater than you are on the battlefield. Nor is he of higher birth, because you are the son of Pritha and the sun god Surya. As Arjuna is your own brother, it would be good for you to bring this trouble to an end.'

But again Bhishma spoke in vain. Karna hated his brother and thirsted for his life.

A guard was set around Bhishma, who lay supported by a pillow of arrows, waiting for the hour of his death. But he was not to die until after the great war was over.

The Kauravas held a war council, and they chose Drona to be their leader. The battle standard of the Brahman was a water jar and a golden altar on a deerskin. He vowed to Duryodhana that he would take Yudhishthira prisoner.

On the first day of Drona's command, and the eleventh day of the great war, Abhimanyu was leading in the fight. He dragged a chieftain by the hair out of his chariot, and would have taken him prisoner, but Jayadratha, the king who had endeavoured to abduct Draupadi, intervened, and broke his sword on the young man's shield. Jayadratha fled, and Salya, King of Madra, attacked Arjuna's noble son. But Bhima dashed forward and engaged him in fierce combat. Both were mighty wielders of the mace; they were like two tigers, like two great elephants; they were like eagles tearing one another with blood-red claws. The sound of their blows was like the echoing thunder, and each stood as firm as a cliff which is struck in vain by fiery lightning.... After a long time both staggered and fell, but Bhima immediately sprang up to strike the final blow. Before he could accomplish his fierce desire, however, Salya was rescued by his followers and carried to safety.... Afterwards the battle raged with more fury than ever, until night fell and all the living and the dead were hidden from sight.

Drona sought to fulfil his vow on the second day of his command, and he prompted Susarman, the king who had invaded Virata when the Pandavas were servants there, to send a challenge to Arjuna for single combat. Susarman selected a place away from the main battlefield. Arjuna fought for many hours, until at last he put the boastful king and his followers to flight; then he taunted them for their cowardice. Meanwhile Drona had attacked Yudhishthira, who, when confronted by certain death, leapt on the back of a horse and escaped from the battlefield. But it was no shame for a Kshatriya to flee a Brahman.

Duryodhana went against Bhima: he was wounded after a brief combat, and retreated from the field. Many warriors then pressed against Bhima, but Arjuna had returned after fighting Susarman, and drove furiously against the Kauravas; he swept over the blood-red plain in triumph. Karna watched his rival with jealous rage and entered the fray. The fire burned in his eyes, and he attacked Arjuna, resolved to conquer or die. The fight raged for hours, and when night fell the two great warriors reluctantly withdrew from the field.

The next day Drona arranged his army like a spider's web, and once again Susarman challenged Arjuna, in order to draw him away from the battle-front. It was the day of Abhimanyu's triumph and the day of his death. Yudhishthira sent Arjuna's son to break the web of enemies, and he rode his chariot against elephants and horses with conquering fury. Duryodhana attacked the youthful hero with a band of warriors, but fell wounded by Abhimanyu, who also killed the warriors. Salya next dashed against Arjuna's son, but before long he was carried from the field grievously wounded. Then Duhsasana came forward, frowning and fierce.

Abhimanyu cried out: 'Evil prince, who plotted with Shakuni to win the kingdom of Yudhishthira and put Draupadi to shame, I welcome you, as I have waited a long time for you. Now you will receive proper punishment for your sins.'

As he spoke, the fearless youth flung a dart, and Duhsasana fell stunned and bleeding, but was rescued from death by his followers.

Lakshmana, son of Duryodhana, rode proudly against Arjuna's son, and fought bravely and well; but he was cut down, and died on the battlefield.

Then the evil Jayadratha, who had vowed to be Yudhishthira's slave in the forest, stealthily advanced with six warriors to fight the lordly youth. The seven men surged forwards, and Abhimanyu stood alone. His charioteer was killed and his chariot was shattered; he leapt to the ground and fought on, slaying one by one.... Noticing his peril, the Pandavas tried to rescue Arjuna's son; but Jayadratha held them back, and Karna helped him. Eventually Abhimanyu was wounded on the forehead, blood streamed into his eyes and blinded him, and he stumbled. Before he could recover, the son of Duhsasana leapt forward and dashed out his brains with a mace. So died the gallant youth, pure as he was at birth. He died like a forest lion surrounded by hunters; he sank like the red sun at evening; he perished like a tempest whose strength is spent; Abhimanyu was lost.

So that day's battle ended, and Abhimanyu slumbered in the soft starlight, lifeless and cold.

When Arjuna was told that his son was gone, the mighty warrior lay on the ground and silently wept. After some time he leapt up and cried: 'May the curse of a father and the vengeance of a warrior smite the murderers of my boy!... May I never reach heaven if I do not slay Jayadratha tomorrow....' A spy hurried to the Kauravas' camp and told of Arjuna's vow.. Jayadratha trembled with fear.

Early the next morning Arjuna said to Krishna: 'Drive swiftly, as this will be a day of great slaughter.' He wanted to find Jayadratha; with him went Bhima and Satyaki. Many warriors engaged them in battle, as the Kauravas hoped that the sun should go down before Arjuna could fulfil his terrible vow.

Mounted on an elephant, Duhsasana opposed Arjuna; but he took flight when the rattling chariot drew near. Drona blocked the way; but Arjuna refused combat, saying: 'You are like a father to me.... Let me find my son's killer....' He passed on. Then Duryodhana came up and engaged him. Karna fought with Bhima, and Bhurisrava attacked Satyaki. Long waged the bitter conflicts, and after a while Krishna saw that his kinsman was about to be slain. He called to Arjuna, who cast a celestial weapon at Bhurisrava, which cut off both his arms; then Satyaki killed him. Afterwards many warriors confronted Arjuna, and many fell. But the day wore on and evening drew near, and he could not find Jayadratha. Eventually Arjuna urged Krishna to drive furiously onward, and not to stop not until he found his son's killer. The chariot sped like a whirlwind, until at last Arjuna saw the evil-hearted Jayadratha; he was guarded by Karna and five great warriors, and at that time the sun had begun to set.

Karna leapt forward and engaged Arjuna; but Krishna used his divine power to cause a dark cloud to obscure the sun. Everyone believed that night had fallen. Karna immediately withdrew;

but Arjuna drove on, and as the sun shot out its last ray of dazzling light, he pounced on Jayadratha like a falcon swoops down on its prey. The struggle was brief, and before daylight faded completely, Arjuna overthrew the slayer of his son and cut off his head. Bhima uttered a roar of triumph when he saw Jayadratha's head held high, and the Kauravas despaired because their wicked plan had been thwarted.

Night fell, but the fighting was renewed. In the darkness and confusion men killed their kinsmen, fathers cut down their sons, and brothers fought against brothers. Yudhishthira sent men with torches to light up the blood-red plain, and the battle was waged for many hours. Swords were splintered and spears were lost, and warriors threw great boulders and chariot wheels against one another. All men were maddened with the thirst for blood, and the night was filled with horrors.

At last Arjuna called for a truce, and it was agreed that the warriors should sleep on the battlefield. So all lay down, the charioteer in his chariot, the rider on his horse, and the driver of the elephant on his elephant's back....

Duryodhana scolded Drona for not slaying the Pandavas in their sleep.... 'Let Karna,' he said, 'lead the army to victory.'

But Drona replied: 'You are reaping the red harvest of your sins.... But know now that tomorrow either Arjuna will fall or I will be slain by him.'

When the bright moon rose in the heavens the conflict was renewed. Many fell on that awful night. Ghatotkacha, the Rakshasa son of Bhima, was leading the fray, and he slaughtered numerous Kaurava warriors. At last Karna went against him, and then the air was filled with blazing arrows. Each struck the other with powerful weapons, and for a time the conflict hung in the balance. Ghatotkacha created illusions, but Karna kept his senses in that great fight, even after his horses had been slain; he leapt to the ground, then flung a celestial dart, the gift of Indra, and Ghatotkacha, uttering terrible cries, fell down and breathed his last breath. The Kauravas shouted with gladness, and the Pandavas wept.

Before the night was ended, Drona killed his ancient enemy Drupada, King of Southern Panchala, and he also cut down the King of Virata.

Before dawn broke, Dhrishtadyumna, son of Drupada, went out in search of Drona, the slayer of his beloved father. But Bhima said to him: 'You are too young to strike down as great a warrior as Drona. I will fight with him until he is wearied, then you can approach and be avenged.'

Bhima struggled with the sage, his teacher, for many hours; then Dhrishtadyumna engaged him, but neither could prevail over Drupada's killer. Eventually the Pandava warriors falsely shouted: 'Aswatthaman, son of Drona, is slain.' When Drona heard this he fainted in his chariot, and vengeful Dhrishtadyumna rushed forward and cut off his head. Then the son of Drupada threw the head of Drona towards Duryodhana, saying: 'Here is the head of your mighty warrior; I will cut off the heads of each Kaurava prince!'

The fall of Drona was like the sinking of heaven's sun; it was like the drying up of the ocean; the Kauravas fled in fear.

When Aswatthaman returned that evening and found that his father had been slain he was grief-stricken. Night fell while he wept, and he vowed to kill Dhrishtadyumna and all his family.

Karna was next chosen to be the leader of the Kaurava army, and Duryodhana praised him and said: 'You alone can stem the tide of our disasters. Arjuna has been spared by Bhishma and by Drona because they loved him. But the arm of Karna is strengthened by hatred of the proud Pandava archer.'

When morning broke over the plain, the first battle of Karna began, and it continued all day long. Countless warriors were slain; blood ran in streams, and the dead and mangled bodies of men and elephants and horses were strewn in confusion. The air was darkened with arrows and darts, and it rang with the shouts of the fighters and the moans of the wounded, the bellowing of trumpets, and the clamour of drums.

At last evening came and the carnage ended.... Duryodhana summoned his war council and said: 'This is the sixteenth day of the war, and many of our strongest heroes have fallen. Bhishma and Drona are gone, and many of my brothers are now dead.'

Karna then said: 'Tomorrow will be the great day of the war. I have vowed to kill Arjuna or fall by his hand.'

Duryodhana was cheered by Karna's words, and all the Kauravas were once again hopeful of victory.

In the morning Karna rode out in his chariot. He chose Salya, King of Madra, as his driver whose skill was so great that even Krishna was not his superior.

Arjuna was again engaged in combat with Susarman when Karna attacked the Pandava army. So the son of Surya went against Yudhishthira and cast him on the ground, saying: 'If you were Arjuna I would kill you.'

Bhima then attacked Karna, and they fought fiercely for a time, until Arjuna, having overcome Susarman, returned to fight with Karna.

Duhsasana, who put Draupadi to shame, came up to help Karna, and Bhima attacked him. Bhima had always hoped to meet this evil-hearted son of the blind maharajah, so that he might fulfil his vow. He swung his mace and struck so mighty a blow that the advancing chariot was shattered. Duhsasana fell heavily on the ground and broke his back. Then Bhima seized him and, whirling his body up in the air, cried out: 'Oh Kauravas, come those who dare and rescue Karna's helper.'

No one dared to approach, and Bhima cast down Duhsasana's body, cut off his head, and drank his blood as he had vowed to do. Many Kaurava warriors fled, and they cried out: 'This is not a man, because he drinks human blood!'

All men watched the deadly combat which was waged between the mighty heroes Arjuna and Karna. They began by shooting arrows one at another, while Krishna and Salya skilfully guided the chariots. Arjuna's arrows fell on Karna like summer rain; Karna's arrows were like stinging snakes, and they drank blood. Eventually Arjuna's celestial bow Gandiva was struck and the bowstring severed.... Arjuna said: 'Pause, Karna. According to the rules of battle, you cannot attack a disabled enemy.' But Karna did not listen. He showered countless arrows, until his proud rival was grievously wounded.

When Arjuna had restrung his bow, he rose up like a stricken and angry tiger held at bay, and cast a screen of arrows against his enemy. But Karna did not fear him, nor could Arjuna take him down. The fight hung in the balance.... Then suddenly a wheel of Karna's chariot sank in the soft ground, and Salya could not get the horses to advance.

Karna cried out: 'Pause now, Arjuna, do not wage unequal war. It is not manly to attack a helpless enemy.'

Arjuna paused; but Krishna spoke quickly, saying: 'Oh Karna, you speak the truth; but was it manly to shoot arrows at Arjuna whilst he was restringing his bow? Was it manly to scoff at Draupadi when she was put to shame before elders and princes in the gambling hall? Was it manly of you and six warriors to surround Abhimanyu in order to murder him without compassion?'

When Arjuna heard his son's name, his heart burned with consuming fury. He drew his bow and shot a crescent-bladed arrow at Karna, whose head was immediately struck off. So fell in that dreadful battle a brother by a brother's hand.

The Kauravas fled in terror when Karna was killed, and Kripa said to Duryodhana: 'Now that our greatest warriors are dead, it would be wise to ask for peace.'

Duryodhana replied: 'After the wrongs I have done the Pandavas, how can I ask or expect mercy at their hands? Let the war go on till the end comes.'

Salya was then chosen as the new leader of the Kaurava army, which had greatly shrunken in numbers, and on the morning of the eighteenth day of the war the battle was waged with fury. But the Pandavas were irresistible, and when Duryodhana saw that they were sweeping all before them, he secretly fled, carrying his mace. He had the power to hide under water for as long as he wished, thanks to a mighty charm which had been given to him by the demons; so he plunged into a lake and lay hidden below the waters.

Salya was slain by Yudhishthira, and he fell like a thunder-splintered rock. Sahadeva overthrew Shakuni, the gambler, who had played against Yudhishthira with loaded dice, and Bhima cut down all Duryodhana's brothers who had survived until that last fateful day. Of all the Kaurava heroes the only ones left alive were Aswa-thaman, son of Drona, Kripa, Kritavarman and the hidden Duryodhana.

Finally Bhima discovered where Duryodhana was hidden. Yudhishthira went to the lakeside and urged him to come out and fight.

Duryodhana cried: 'Take my kingdom now and have pleasure in it. Go and leave me, as I must retire to the jungle and engage in meditation.'

Yudhishthira replied: 'I cannot accept anything from you except what is won in battle.'

So Duryodhana said: 'If you promise to fight one by one, I will come out of the water and kill you all.'

Yudhishthira said: 'Come out, and the battle will be fought as you wish. Now you have spoken like a true Kshatriya.'

Still Duryodhana hung back, and Bhima shouted: 'If you do not come out of the lake at once, I will plunge in and drag you to the shore.'

Then Duryodhana came forward, and the Pandavas laughed at the sight of him, as he was covered with mud, and water streamed down from his clothing.

Duryodhana responded: 'Soon your high spirits will be turned to grief.'

Now, all during the time of the Pandava exile, Duryodhana had practised with the mace, so that he became the equal of Bhima. But he had no one to support him there. The other survivors remained in hiding. Then Balarama appeared, and he caused the fight to be waged in the middle of the blood-red plain; he was Duryodhana's supporter.

The warriors fought like two fierce bulls, and hit one another with heavy blows, until their faces were reddened with blood. Once Duryodhana almost achieved victory; he struck Bhima on the head so hard that everyone thought the Pandava hero had received his death blow. Bhima staggered but recovered himself, and soon afterwards he struck Duryodhana a foul blow to the knee, which smashed the bone so that he fell to the ground. He danced around Duryodhana for a while then, kicking his enemy's head, cried out: 'Draupadi is avenged.' The vow of Bhima was at last fulfilled.

Yudhishthira was angry; he struck Bhima on the face and said: 'You will cause all men to speak ill of us.'

Then Arjuna led Bhima away, and Yudhishthira knelt beside Duryodhana and said: 'You are still our ruler, and if you order me to kill Bhima, your command will be obeyed. You are now very close to death, and I despair for the Kaurava wives and children, who will curse us because you have been laid low.'

Balarama added: 'Bhima has broken the laws of combat, because he struck Duryodhana below the waist.'

But Krishna responded, saying: 'My brother, did Duryodhana not wrong the Pandavas with foul play at dice? And did Bhima not, when he saw Draupadi put to shame, vow to break the knee of Duryodhana?'

Balarama replied: 'So you approve of this?... Can I forget that Bhima kicked the head of our wounded kinsman?'

Krishna held off the vengeful hand of Balarama, and persuaded him to take vows not to fight against the Pandavas.

When night fell, the dying Duryodhana was visited on the battlefield by Aswatthaman, son of Drona, and Kripa and Kritavarman. He gave Aswatthaman permission to attack the Pandavas while they slept.... Then Drona's son went out in the darkness to satisfy his hunger for vengeance because his father had been slain.... The pale stars looked down on the dead and the dying as Aswatthaman crossed the battlefield and went stealthily towards the tents of his enemies with Kripa and Kritavarman.

At the gate of the Pandava camp an awful figure rose up against the conspirators. Aswatthaman was not afraid, and he fought with his adversary until he realised that he was the god Shiva, the Blue-throated Destroyer. Then Drona's son drew back, and he kindled a fire to worship the all-powerful deity. Then, having nothing else to sacrifice, he cast his own body on the flames. By this supremely religious act Shiva was appeased; he accepted Drona's son and entered his body, saying: 'Until now, for the sake of Krishna, I have protected the sons of Draupadi, but now their hour of doom has come.'

Then Aswatthaman rushed into the camp and slaughtered with the cruel arm of vengeance. He rudely awakened Dhrishtadyumna, who cried out: 'Coward! Would you attack a naked man?'

Aswatthaman did not answer his father's killer, but took his life with a single blow.... Through the camp he went, striking down everyone he met, and shrieks and moans rose up on every side.

Draupadi was awakened by the noise, and her five young sons sprang up to protect her. Aswatthaman murdered each one without pity.... Then he lit a great fire to discover those who had concealed themselves, and he completed his ghastly work of slaughter. Meanwhile Kripa and Kritavarman, with weapons in their hands, kept watch at the gate, and cut down everyone who tried to escape.

Meanwhile, on that night of horror, the Pandava princes slept safely in the camp of the Kauravas, so that they all escaped the sword of Drona's son.

When his job was done, the bloodthirsty Aswatthaman cut off the heads of Draupadi's five sons and carried them to Duryodhana, who rejoiced, believing that they were the heads of Yudhishthira and his brothers. But when he saw that the avenger of night had killed the children of Draupadi instead, he cried out: 'What horror have you committed? You have murdered innocent children, who, had they lived, would have perpetuated our name and our fame. My heart burns with anger against the fathers and not their harmless sons.'

Duryodhana groaned heavily: his heart was oppressed with grief, and, bowing his head down, he died in despair.

Aswatthaman, Kripa and Kritavarman quickly fled, fearing the wrath of the Pandavas.

The Aftermath of War

When the Pandava brothers were told that their camp had been raided in darkness by the bloodthirsty Aswatthaman, Yudhishthira exclaimed: 'After all our suffering, now the greatest sorrow of all has fallen. Draupadi mourns the death of her brother and her five sons, and I fear she will die of grief!'

Draupadi came to her husbands and, weeping bitterly, said: 'For thirteen cruel years you have endured shame and exile so that your children might prosper. But now that they are all slain, can you desire to have power and kingdom?'

Krishna said: 'Oh daughter of a king, is your grief as great as is Pritha's and Gandharai's, and as great as those who mourn the loss or their husbands on the battlefield? You have less cause than others to wail now.'

Draupadi was somewhat soothed, but she turned to Bhima and said: 'If you will not bring to me the head of Aswatthaman, I will never look at your face again.'

Yudhishthira replied: 'Aswatthaman is a Brahman, and Vishnu, the greatest of the gods, will punish him if he has done wrong. If we kill him now, Draupadi, your sons and your brother and your father would not be restored to you.'

Draupadi said. 'So be it. But Aswatthaman has a great jewel which gleams in darkness. Let it be taken from him, because it is as dear to him as his life.'

Then Arjuna went in pursuit of Aswatthaman and found him, and returned with the jewel.

Blind old Dhritarashtra then came to the battlefield, mourning the death of his hundred sons. And with the weeping maharajah were Queen Gandharai and the wives of the Kaurava princes, who cried and sobbed. Wives wept for their husbands, their children wailed beside them, and mothers moaned for their sons. The anguish of tender-hearted women was bitter, and the air was filled with wailing on that blood-red plain of Kuru-kshetra.

When Queen Gandharai saw the Pandavas she cried out: 'The smell of Duryodhana is on you all.'

Dhritarashtra plotted in his weak mind to crush Bhima, the slayer of Duryodhana. When he embraced Yudhishthira he said: 'Where is Bhima?' and they placed in front of him an image of the strong Pandava. Dhritarashtra put forward his arms, and he crushed the image in his embrace and fell back fainting. Then he wailed: 'Bhima was as a son to me. Although I have killed him, the dead cannot return.'

The maharajah was pleased when he was told that Bhima still lived; and he embraced his son's slayer tenderly and with forgiveness, saying: 'I have no children now except the sons of Pandu, my brother.'

Pritha was delighted to see her five sons, and she embraced them one by one. Then she went towards Draupadi, who fainted in her arms. They wept together for the dead.

The bodies of the dead kings and princes were collected together. Each was wrapped in perfumed linen and laid on a funeral pyre and burned. The first pyre which was kindled was that of Duryodhana. The Pandavas mourned for their kinsmen. Then they bathed in the holy Ganges, and took up water and sprinkled it in the name of each dead hero. Yudhishthira poured out the oblation for Karna, his brother, and he gave great gifts to his widows and his children. Afterwards all the remaining bodies were burned on the battlefield.

Yudhishthira was proclaimed king in the city of Hastinapur, and he wore the great jewel in his crown. A great sacrifice was offered up, and Dhaumya, the family priest of the Pandavas, poured the Homa offering to the gods on the sacred fire. Yudhishthira and Draupadi were anointed with holy water.

The Atonement

In the days that followed, Yudhishthira mourned over the carnage of the great war; he could not be comforted. Eventually Vyasa, the sage, appeared and advised that he should perform the horse sacrifice to atone for his sins.

So a search was made for a moon-white horse with a yellow tail and one black ear, and when it was found a plate of gold, inscribed with the name of Yudhishthira, was tied to its forehead. The horse was then let loose, and was allowed to wander wherever it wished. A great army, led by Arjuna, followed the horse.

Now it was the custom in those days that when the sacred horse entered a kingdom, that kingdom was proclaimed to be subject to the king who performed the ceremony. And if any ruler detained the horse, he was compelled to fight with the army that followed the wandering animal. Should he be overcome in battle, the opposing king immediately joined forces with those of the conqueror, and followed the horse from kingdom to kingdom. For a whole year the animal was allowed to wander.

The horse was let loose on the night of full moon.

Arjuna met with many adventures. He fought against a king and the son of a king, who had a thousand wives in the country of Malwa, and defeated them. But Agni, who had married a daughter of the king, came to rescue his family. He fought against Arjuna with fire, but Arjuna shot celestial arrows which produced water. Then the god made peace, and the king who had detained the horse went away with Arjuna. After that the horse came to a rock which was the wife of a Rishi who had been transformed because of her wickedness. 'So will you stay,' her husband had said, 'until Yudhishthira performs the Aswa-medha ceremony.' The horse was unable to leave the rock. Then Arjuna touched the rock, which immediately became a woman, and the horse was set free.

In time the horse entered the land of Amazons, and the queen detained it, and came out with her women warriors to fight against Arjuna, who, however, made peace with them and went on his way. Next the holy animal reached a strange country where men, women, horses, cows and goats grew on mighty trees like fruit, and came to maturity and died each day. The king fought against Arjuna, but was defeated. Then all the army fled to the islands of the sea, for they were Daityas, and Arjuna plundered their homes and took their treasure.

Once the horse entered a pond, and was cursed by the goddess Parvati, and it became a mare; it entered another pond and became a lion, owing to a Brahman's spell.

In the kingdom of Manipura the horse was seized, and soldiers armed with fire weapons were ready to fight against the Pandavas and their allies. But when the king, whose name was Babhru-váhana, discovered that the horse bore the name of Yudhishthira, he said: 'Arjuna is my father;' and he went forward and bowed, and put his head under the foot of the Pandava hero. But Arjuna spurned him, saying: 'If I were your father, you would have no fear of me.'

Then the king challenged Arjuna to battle, and was victorious on that day. He took all the great men prisoners, and he severed Arjuna's head from his body with a crescent-bladed arrow. The king's mother, Chitrangada, was stricken with grief, as was Ulupi, the daughter of Vasuka, the king of serpents, who had borne a son to Arjuna. But Ulupi remembered that her father possessed a magic jewel which had power to restore a dead man to life, and she sent the king of Manipura to get it from the underworld. But the Nagas refused to give up the jewel, so Arjuna's mighty son fought against them with arrows which were transformed into peacocks; and the peacocks devoured the serpents. Then the Naga king delivered up the magic jewel, and the king returned with it. He touched the body of Arjuna with the jewel, and the hero came back to life, and all his wounds were healed. When he left Manipura city the king, his son, accompanied him.

So from kingdom to kingdom the horse wandered while the army followed, until a year had gone by. Then it returned to Hastinapur.

In the meantime, Yudhishthira had lived a life of purity and self-restraint. Each night he lay on the ground, and always slept within the city. Beside him lay Draupadi, and a naked sword was always between them.

When the horse came back the people rejoiced: they came to welcome the army with gifts of fine clothing, jewels and flowers. Money was scattered in the streets, and the poor were made happy. Yudhishthira embraced Arjuna, kissed him and wept tears of joy. He welcomed Arjuna's son, Babhru-váhana, King of Manipura, and also the other kings who had followed the sacred horse.

Twelve days after Arjuna's return, and on the day when the full moon marked the close of the winter season, the people assembled in great crowds from far and near to share Yudhishthira's generous hospitality and witness the Aswa-medha ceremony, which was held on a green and level portion of consecrated ground. Stately pavilions, glittering with jewels and gold, had been erected for the royal guests, and there were humbler places for the Brahmans. Maharajah Dhritarashtra and King Yudhishthira sat on gold thrones, and the other kings had thrones of sandalwood and gold. The royal ladies were brought together in their appointed places. Wise Vyasa was there, and he directed the ceremony. And Krishna, the holy one, was there too.

When all the guests were assembled, Yudhishthira and Draupadi bathed together in the sacred waters of the Ganges. Then a portion of ground was measured out, and Yudhishthira ploughed it with a golden plough. Draupadi followed him, and sowed the seeds of every kind in the kingdom, while all the women and the Brahmans chanted holy mantras. Then a golden altar was built with four broad layers of golden bricks, and stakes of sacred wood from the forest and from Himalaya, and it was canopied and winged with gold-brocaded silk.

Then eight pits were dug for Homa of milk and butter to be made ready for the sacrificial fire. Then portions of every kind of vegetable and curative herb which grew in the kingdom were wrapped and placed in the Homa pits.

On the ground there were numerous sacrificial stakes, to which countless animals were tied – bulls, buffaloes and horses, wild beasts from the forests and mountains and caves, birds of every kind, fishes from rivers and lakes, and even insects.

The priests offered up animals in sacrifice to each celestial power, and the feasting was watched by sacred beings. The Gandharvas sang, and the Apsaras, whom the Gandharvas wooed, danced like sunbeams on the grass. Messengers of the gods were also gathered there, and Vyasa and his disciples chanted mantras to celestial music. The people lifted up their voices at the sound of the rain drum and the blast of the rain trumpet. The glory of Yudhishthira's fame was bright.

When all the kings, royal ladies and sages took their places to be blessed by the horse sacrifice, Yudhishthira sat on his throne, and in his hand he held the horn of a stag.

Vyasa sent many kings and their wives to draw water from the holy Ganges. Many musicians went with them beating drums and blowing trumpets and playing sweet instruments, and girls danced in front. And all the kings and their wives were given splendid clothing by Yudhishthira, and also jewelled necklaces. The Brahmans were given gold and jewels, as well as elephants, horses and cattle.

Yudhishthira then sat naked in his throne, and each one who had drawn holy water poured some over his head; pouring what remained over the head of the sacred white horse.

Nákula held the horse's head, and said: 'The horse speaks.'

Those who were near him asked in loud voices: 'What does the horse say?'

Nákula replied: 'So speaks the horse – 'In other such ceremonies the horse that is sacrificed goes to Swarga, but I shall rise far above Swarga, because Krishna is here'.'

Then Dhaumya, having washed the horse, gave Bhima a sword to strike off the head at a single blow. But before this was done, Dhaumya pressed an ear of the holy animal, and milk flowed out. Then he said to Bhima: 'The horse is pure; the gods will certainly accept the sacrifice. Strike now, strong one.'

Bhima raised the sword and severed the head, which immediately ascended to heaven and vanished from view. The assembled crowd was filled with joy and wonder.

Krishna, along with other kings and sages, then cut open the horse's body, from which a bright light shone out. They found that the animal was pure, and Krishna said to Yudhishthira: 'This, your sacrifice, is acceptable to Vishnu.'

Draupadi was made Queen of the Sacrifice, and mantras were chanted, and she was adored and given rich offerings, because of her virtue and her wisdom.

The body of the slain horse was divided, and the flesh gave off the smell of camphor. Priests lifted portions in their ladles and placed these on the sacrificial fire, and they made Soma. And King Yudhishthira and all his brothers stood in the sin-cleansing smoke and breathed its fragrance.

As he laid a piece of flesh on the altar fire, Dhaumya cried out: 'Oh Indra, accept this flesh which has turned to camphor.'

When he had uttered these words, Indra, accompanied by many gods, appeared in front of the people, who bowed with fear and secret joy. Indra took portions of the flesh from Vyasa and gave these to each of the gods. Then he vanished from sight with all his companions.

Vyasa blessed Yudhishthira, and Krishna embraced him and said: 'Your fame will last forever.'

Yudhishthira responded by saying: 'I owe all these blessings to you.'

After that Krishna and the kings poured holy water over the heads of Yudhishthira and Draupadi.

All the fragments of the herbs which had been provided for Homa were then ground into powder. And Yudhishthira gave balls of the powder to everyone present, so that they might eat of the sacred herbs and share in the blessings of the Aswa-medha. He ate his own portion last of all. The fragments of the offerings that remained were burnt on the altar.

Then Pritha and all the maidens who were with her enjoyed themselves, while the musicians played sweet music.

Yudhishthira distributed more gifts. To Vyasa he assigned an estate. And to the Brahmans who officiated he gave many animals, pearls and slaves. To the kings he gave war elephants, horses and money, and to the kings' wives gifts of clothing, jewels and gold.

Finally, he wept as he said farewell to Krishna, his friend in peace and in war, who climbed aboard his chariot bound for sea-washed Dwaraka.

A Night of Wonder

There was prosperity in the kingdom under Yudhishthira's wise and just government; but blind old Dhritarashtra never ceased to mourn the death of Duryodhana, his first-born, and eventually he retired to live in a humble dwelling in the jungle. With him went Queen Gandharai, and Pritha, the mother of the Pandavas, and Vidura, and others who were of great age.

Years went past, and a day came when Yudhishthira and his brothers and their wife Draupadi travelled to the home of their elders. They found them all there except for Vidura, who had gone to a sacred place on the banks of the Ganges to undergo penance and wait for the coming of Yama, god of the dead. Then all the relatives, young and old, went off to find Vidura; but when they found him he was wasted with hunger and old age, nor could he speak to them. They waited beside him until he died, and then they mourned together. This new sorrow awakened their grief, and they spoke of all those who had fallen in the great war. Fathers and mothers mourned for their sons, and wives for their husbands….

While they wept and moaned together, the great sage Vyasa came and said: 'I will soothe all your sorrows…. Let each one bathe at sunset in the holy waters of the Ganges, and when night falls your lost ones will return to you once again.'

Then they all sat waiting on the river bank until evening arrived. The day passed slowly; it seemed to be as long as a year.

Eventually the sun went down, and they chanted mantras and went into the Ganges. Vyasa bathed beside the old Maharajah Dhritarashtra and Yudhishthira…. Then all came out and stood on the bank.

Suddenly the waters began to heave and foam, and Vyasa muttered holy words and called out the names of the dead one by one…. Soon all the heroes who had been slain appeared one by one. They came in chariots, on horseback and on the backs of elephants. They all uttered triumphant cries; drums were sounded and trumpets were blown; and it seemed as if the armies of the Pandavas and Kauravas were once again assembled for battle. They swept over the river like a mighty tempest.

Many of the onlookers trembled with fear, until they saw Bhishma and Drona, clad in armour, standing overhead in their chariots in splendour and pride; then came Arjuna's son, the noble Abhimanyu, and Bhima's Asura son. Soon Gandharai saw Duryodhana and all his brothers, while Pritha looked with glad eyes at Karna, and Draupadi welcomed her brother Dhrishtadyumna and her five children who had all been killed by vengeful Aswatthaman. All the warriors who had fallen in battle returned again on that night of wonder.

With the army came minstrels who sang of the deeds of the heroes, and beautiful girls who danced in front of them. All strife had ended between kinsmen and rivals; in death there was peace and sweet companionship.

The ghostly warriors crossed the Ganges and were welcomed by those who waited on the bank around Vyasa. It was a night of supreme and heart-stirring happiness.

Fathers and mothers found their sons, widows clung to their husbands, sisters embraced their brothers, and all wept tears of joy. The elders who were living conversed with those who were dead; the burdens of grief and despair fell from all hearts after years of mourning; the past was suddenly forgotten in the rapture of seeing those who had died.

The night passed swiftly as if it had last for an hour. Then when dawn began to break, the dead men returned to their chariots and their horses and their elephants and said their farewells….

Vyasa spoke to the widows and said that those of them who desired to be with their husbands could go with them. Then the Kaurava princesses and other high-born ladies, who never ceased to mourn for their own, kissed the feet of the Maharajah Dhritarashtra and Queen Gandharai and plunged into the Ganges with the departing army…. Vyasa chanted mantras, and all the drowned widows were transported to heaven with their husbands.

The Ascent to Heaven

The Pandavas returned to Hastinapur, and after two years had gone past they received more tragic news. One day Narada, the sage, arrived and told Yudhishthira that a great fire had swept through the jungle, and that Dhritarashtra, Gandharai and Pritha, and all who were with them, had perished.

Soon afterwards the Pandavas began to see terrible omens, and realised that another great tragedy was coming, but no man could tell what it was or when it would take place.

Before long it became known that the city of Dwaraka was doomed to be destroyed. A horror in human shape was seen in the night; it was yellow and black, its head was bald and its limbs misshapen, and men said it was Yama, god of the dead.... Visions of headless men fighting in battle were seen at sunset.... The moon was eclipsed, a tempest ravaged the land, and a plague of rats afflicted the city.

Krishna forbade all the people, on pain of death, to drink wine, and commanded them to perform devotions on the seashore....

Then the night was haunted by a black woman with yellow teeth who grinned horribly at house doors. All the inhabitants of the city were stricken with terror.... Evil spirits also came and robbed the jewels of the women and the weapons of the men.... Eventually the chakra of Krishna went up to heaven, and his chariot and horses followed it.... The end of the Yádavas was not far off, and the day came when Apsaras called out of heaven: 'Depart from here,' and all the people heard them.

When the people gathered on the seashore they held a feast, and being allowed to drink wine for one day, they drank heavily and began to argue. After some time Satyaki killed Kritavarman, who had gone to the Pandava camp with Drona's son on the night of slaughter. Then Kritavarman's friends killed Satyaki and one of Krishna's sons. Krishna put the rebels to death, but he could not stop the tumult and the fighting which ensued; fathers murdered their sons, and sons their fathers, and kinsmen fought fiercely against kinsmen.

Then Krishna and Balarama left the city, and both died in the jungle. From Balarama's mouth emerged a mighty snake, as he was the incarnation of the world serpent.... Krishna was mistaken for a gazelle by a hunter, who shot an arrow which pierced his foot at the only spot where he could be mortally wounded. He then departed to his heaven, which is called Goloka.

Before Krishna had left Dwaraka he sent messengers to Arjuna, who came quickly to find the women wailing for the dead. Then Vasudeva, father of Krishna, died, and Arjuna laid the body of the old man on the pyre, and he was burned with four of his widows, who no longer wanted to live. The bodies of Krishna and Balarama were also cremated.

Arjuna then set off towards Indra-prastha with a remnant of the people; and when they had left Dwaraka, the sea rose up and swallowed the whole city, with those who had refused to leave.

A deep gloom fell on the Pandavas after this, and Vyasa, the sage, appeared before them, and revealed that their time had come to leave this world.

Then Yudhishthira divided the kingdom in half. He made Parikshit, son of Abhimanyu, one King of Hastinapur; and Yuyutsu, the half-brother of Duryodhana, who had joined the Pandava army on the first day of the great war, was made the second King of Hastinapur. He counselled them to live at peace one with another.

Afterwards the Pandavas cast off their royal attire and their jewels and put on the clothing of hermits, and the bright-eyed and faithful Draupadi did likewise. Yudhishthira left first of all, and his brothers walked behind him one by one, and Draupadi went last of all, followed by a hound. They all walked towards the rising sun on the long path which leads to Mount Meru, through forests and over streams and across the burning plains, never to return again.

One by one they fell by the wayside, all except Yudhishthira. Draupadi was the first to sink down, and Bhima cried: 'Why has she fallen who has never done wrong?'

Yudhishthira replied: 'Her heart was bound up in Arjuna, and she has her reward.'

Sahadeva was next to fall, and then Nakula. After some time Yudhishthira heard the voice of Bhima crying in distress: 'No! Now the noble Arjuna has fallen. What sin has he committed?'

Yudhishthira explained: 'He boasted confidently that he could destroy all his enemies in one day, and because he failed in his vow he has fallen.'

The two surviving brothers walked on in silence; but the time came when mighty Bhima sank down. He cried: 'Yudhishthira, tell me why I have fallen now.'

Yudhishthira said: 'Because of your cursing and gluttony and your pride.'

Yudhishthira walked on, calm and unmoved, followed by his faithful hound. When he came close to sacred Mount Meru, the world-spine, Indra, king of the gods, came out to welcome him, saying: 'Ascend, resolute prince.'

Yudhishthira replied: 'Oh king of the gods, let my brothers who have fallen by the wayside come with me. I cannot enter heaven without them. Let the fair and gentle princess come too; Draupadi has been a faithful wife, and is worthy of bliss. Hear my prayer, Indra, and have mercy.'

Indra said to him: 'Your brothers and Draupadi have gone before you.'

Then Yudhishthira pleaded that his faithful hound should also enter heaven; but Indra said: 'Heaven is no place for those who are followed by hounds. Do you not know that demons rob religious ordinances of their virtues when dogs are nearby?'

To this Yudhishthira replied: 'No evil can come from the noble. I cannot have joy if I desert this faithful friend.'

Indra said: 'You left behind your brothers and Draupadi. Why, therefore, can you not abandon your hound?'

Yudhishthira answered: 'I have no power to bring back to life those who have fallen by the wayside: there can be no abandonment of the dead.'

As he spoke, the hound was transformed into Dharma, god of justice. He stood by the king's side and said: 'Yudhishthira, you are indeed my son. You would not abandon me, your hound, because I was faithful to you. Your equal cannot be found in heaven.'

Then Yudhishthira was transported to the city of eternal bliss, and there he found Duryodhana sat on a throne. All the Kauravas were in heaven too, but the king could not find his brothers or Draupadi.

Indra said: 'Yudhishthira, here you will live in eternal bliss. Forget all earthly ties and attain to perfection; your brothers have fallen short, therefore they sank by the wayside.'

Yudhishthira said: 'I cannot stay here with the Kauravas who have done me wrong. Where my brothers are, is where I should be with our wife Draupadi.'

Then a celestial being led Yudhishthira to the home of his brothers and the Princess of Panchala. He entered the forest of the nether regions, where the leaves were like sharp weapons and the path was covered with knives. Darkness hung heavily, and the way was sodden with blood and strewn with foul and mutilated corpses. Shapes of horror flitted round about like shadows; fierce birds of prey feasted on human flesh. The damned were burning in everlasting fires, and the air reeked with foul odours. A boiling river went past, and Yudhishthira saw the place of torture with thorns, and the desert of fiery sand: he gazed mutely at each horror that was unfolded before his eyes.

Gladly would Yudhishthira have turned back, but in the darkness he heard the voices of his brothers and Draupadi calling him to stay a little while to comfort them while they suffered torment.

Yudhishthira said to the celestial being: 'Leave me here; I must stay to relieve the sufferings of my brothers and Draupadi.' As he spoke the gods appeared, and the scene of horror vanished from before his eyes, for it was an illusion conjured up to test his constancy.

Then Yudhishthira was led to the heavenly Ganges, and having bathed in its sacred waters, he cast off his mortal body and became a celestial.

Then, rejoicing, he entered Swarga, the celestial city of Indra, and was welcomed by Krishna in all his divine glory, and by his brothers and by Draupadi, and all whom he had loved on earth.

Indra spoke and said: 'This is the beautiful and immortal one, who sprang from the altar to be your wife, and these bright beings are her five children. Here is Dhritarashtra, who is now the king of the Gandharvas; there is Karna, son of Surya, the peerless archer who was slain by Arjuna. Here comes towards you Abhimanyu, son of Arjuna; he is now the star-bright companion of the lord of night.... Here are Pandu, your father and Pritha, your mother, now united in heaven. See too, Yudhishthira, the wise Bhishma, whose place is with the Vasus round my throne: Drona sits with Dharma, god of wisdom. Here are all the peerless warriors who fell in battle and have won heaven by their courage and their constancy. So may all mortals rise to eternal bliss, casting off their mortal bodies and entering by the shining door of the celestial city, by doing good deeds, by uttering gentle words, and by enduring all suffering with patience. The holy life is prepared for all the sons of men.'

So ends the story of the Great War of the Bharatas.

Legends of Indra & Yama

THE ANCIENT EURASIAN 'HAMMER GOD', bearing the tribal name of Indra, was accompanied to India by the earliest invading bands of Aryans. He was the Thunderer who brought rain to quicken dried-up pasture lands; he was the god of fertility; he was 'the friend of man'; he was the artisan of the Universe which he shaped with his hammer, the dragon slayer, the giant killer, the slaughterer of enemies, the god of war. But although his name may belong to the early Iranian period, the Vedic King of the Gods assumed a distinctly Indian character after localization in the land of the 'Five Rivers'; he ultimately stepped from his chariot, drawn by the steeds of the Aryan horse tamers, and mounted an elephant.

Yama, King of the Dead, was the first man, he explored the hidden regions and discovered the road which became known as 'the path of the fathers'. In the Vedic 'land of the fathers', the shining Paradise, the two kings Varuna and Yama sit beneath a tree. Yama gathers his people to him like a shepherd gathers his flock. To the faithful he gives a drink of Soma; unbelievers were destroyed or committed to a hell called Put. In post-Vedic times he presided over a complicated system of Hells; he was Danda-dhara, 'the wielder of the rod or mace'. He carried out the decrees of the gods, taking possession of souls at their appointed time.

The Vedic character of Yama survives in Epic narrative and the two touching and beautiful stories, preserved in the *Mahabharata*, are probably very ancient Aryan folk tales which were cherished by the people and retold by the poets, who attached to them later religious beliefs and practices.

The final tale in this section tells of the beauties of Indra, Yama and Varuna's heaven.

Tales of Indra, King of the Gods

Indra's combats are reflections of the natural phenomena of India. When the hot Indian summer draws to a close, the whole land is parched and thirsty for rain; rivers are low and many hill streams have dried up; man and beast are weary and wait release from the breathless atmosphere; they are even threatened by famine. Then dense masses of cloud gather in the sky; the tempest bellows, lightnings flash and thunder peals loudly; rain descends in a deluge; once again torrents pour down from the hills and rivers become swollen. Indra has waged his battle with the Drought Demons, broken down their fortress walls, and released the imprisoned cow-clouds which give nourishment to his human friends; the withered pastures become green with generous and rapid growth, and the rice harvest follows.

According to Vedic myth, Indra achieved his first great victory immediately after birth. Vritra, 'the encompasser', the Demon of Drought, was holding the cloud-cattle captive in his mountain fortress. Mankind begged for help from the gods, the shining ones, the world guardians.

Who will take pity? Who will bring refreshment?
Who will come nigh to help us in distress?
Counsels the thoughts within our hearts are counselling,
Wishes are wished and soar towards the highest –
O none but them, the shining ones, are merciful,
My longing wings itself towards the Eternals.

Indra heroically rose up to do battle for the sacrificers. Impulsively he seized the nectar of the gods, called Soma, and he drank that intoxicating juice. Then he snatched up his thunderstone which had been fashioned by the divine artisan Twashtri. His favourite horses, named the Bold and the Brown, were yoked in his golden chariot by his attendants and followers, the youthful Maruts.

Now, at the very beginning, Indra, the golden child, became the king of the three worlds. It was he who gave the air of life; he also gave strength. All the shining gods revered him and obeyed his commands. 'His shadow is immortality; his shadow is death.'

The Maruts, the sons of red Rudra, were the spirits of tempest and thunder. Their chariots were pulled by two spotted deer and one swift-footed, never-wearying red deer as leader. They were loyal and courageous youths; on their heads were golden helmets and they had golden breastplates, and wore bright skins on their shoulders; their ankles and arms were decked with golden bracelets. The Maruts were always strongly armed with bows and arrows and axes, and especially with gleaming spears. All beings feared those 'cloud shakers' when they charged forward with their lightning spears which 'shattered cattle like the thunderstone'; they were known to cleave cloud-rocks and drench the earth with quickening showers.

When Indra set off to attack the Drought Demon, the Maruts followed him, shouting with loud voices. They dashed towards the imprisoned cows of the clouds and chased them up into the air.

The dragon Vritra roared when Indra came near; at which heaven shook and the gods retreated. Mother Earth, the goddess Prithivi, was troubled regarding her golden son. But Indra advanced boldly with the roaring Maruts; he was inspired by the hymns of the priests; he had drank the Soma; he was strengthened by the sacrifices offered on earth's altars; and he wielded the thunderstone.

The Drought Demon deemed itself invulnerable, but Indra cast his weapon and soon discovered the vulnerable parts of its writhing body. He killed the monster and, as it lay face down in front of him, the torrents burst and carried it away to the sea of eternal darkness. Then Indra rejoiced and cried out:

I have slain Vritra, O ye hastening Maruts;
I have grown mighty through my own great vigour;
I am the hurler of the bolt of Thunder –
For man flow freely now the gleaming waters.

On earth the worshippers of the god were happy and the Rishi hymned his praises.

A post-Vedic version of the encounter between Indra and Vritra is found in the *Mahabharata*. Although it is coloured by the change which, in the process of time, passed over the religious beliefs of the Aryans, it retains some features of the original myth.

The story goes that in the first Age of the Universe a host of Danavas, or giants and demons, were so strongly armed that they were invincible in battle. They selected the dragon Vritra as their leader, and waged war against the gods, whom they scattered in all directions.

Realizing that they could not regain their power until they accomplished the death of Vritra, the celestials appeared before the Supreme Being, Brahma, the incarnation of the Soul of the Universe. Brahma instructed them to obtain the bones of a Rishi named Dadhicha, from which to construct a demon-slaying weapon. So the gods visited the Rishi and bowed down before him, and begged the request according to Brahma's advice.

Dadhicha agreed to renounce his body for the benefit of the gods. So the Rishi gave up his life, and from his bones Twashtri, the artisan god, shaped Indra's great weapon, which is called Vajra.

Twashtri spoke to Indra and said: 'Oh chief of the celestials, with this, the best of weapons, reduce that fierce enemy of the gods to ashes! And, having slain him, happily rule the entire domain of heaven with those who follow you.'

Then Indra led the gods against the mighty army. They found that Vritra was surrounded by dreaded Danavas, who resembled mountain peaks. A terrible battle was waged, but once again the gods were put to flight. Then Indra saw Vritra growing bolder, and he became dejected. But the Supreme Being protected him and the gods endowed him with their strength, so that he became mightier than before. Vritra was enraged, and roared loudly and fiercely, so that the heavens shook and the earth trembled with fear. Deeply agitated, Indra flung his divine weapon, which killed the leader of the Danavas. But Indra, thinking the demon was still alive, fled from the field in terror to seek shelter in a lake. The celestials, however, saw that Vritra had been slain, and they rejoiced and shouted the praises of Indra. Then, rallying once more, the gods attacked the panic-stricken Danavas, who turned and fled to the depths of ocean. There in the fathomless darkness they assembled together, and began to plot how they would accomplish the destruction of the three worlds.

Eventually the conspirators resolved to destroy all the Rishis who were possessed of knowledge and ascetic virtue, because the world was supported by them. So they made the ocean their home, raising waves high as hills for their protection, and they began to come out from their fortress to attack the mighty saints.

The Call of Yama, King of the Dead

Once upon a time Menaka, the beautiful Apsara (celestial fairy) left her newborn baby, the daughter of the King of Gandharvas (celestial elves) beside a hermitage. A Rishi, named Sthulakesha, found the child and raised her. She was called Pramadarva, and grew to be the most beautiful and most devout of all young women. Ruru, the great grandson of Bhrigu, looked at her with eyes of love, and at the request of his father, Pramati, the virgin was betrothed to the young Brahman.

Pramadarva was spending time with her friends a few days before the morning of the nuptials. As her time had come, she trod on a serpent, and the death-compelling reptile bit her. She then fell down and died, becoming more beautiful in death than she had been in life.

Brahmans assembled around the body of Pramadarva and sorrowed. Ruru crept away alone and went to a solitary place in the forest where he wept and cried out: 'The fair one, whom I love more dearly than ever, lies dead on the bare ground. If I have performed penances and attained to great ascetic merit, let the power which I have achieved restore my beloved to life again.'

Suddenly an emissary from the celestial regions appeared in front of Ruru, who said: 'Your prayer is of no use, Ruru. One whose days have been numbered can never get back her own life again. Therefore you should not abandon your heart to grief. But the gods have decreed a means whereby you can receive back your beloved.'

Ruru pleaded with him, and said: 'Tell me how I can comply with the will of the celestials, so that I may be delivered from my grief.'

The messenger replied: 'If you will give up half of your own life to Pramadvara, she will rise up again.'

Ruru happily consented, saying: 'I will give up half of my own life so that my beloved may be restored to me.'

Then the king of the Gandharvas and the celestial messenger stood before Dharma-rajah (Yama) and said: 'If it be your will, Oh Mighty One, let Pramadarva rise up endowed with a part of Ruru's life.'

The King of the Dead responded: 'So be it.'

After Dharma-rajah had spoken, the serpent-bitten young woman rose from the ground, and Ruru, whose life was curtailed for her sake, obtained the sweetest wife on earth. The happy pair spent their days deeply devoted to each other, awaiting the call of Yama at the appointed time.

Yama and Savitri

There was once a princess in the country of Madra, and her name was Savitri. She was the gift of the goddess Gayatri, wife of Brahma, the self-created, who had heard the prayers and received the offerings of Aswapati, the childless king of Madra, when he practised austere penances so that he might have children of his own. The young woman grew to be beautiful; her eyes had burning splendour, and were as fair as lotus leaves; she had exceeding sweetness and grace.

It came to pass that Savitri looked with eyes of love at a youth named Satyavan 'the Truthful'. Although Satyavan lived in a hermitage, he was of royal birth. His father was a virtuous king, named Dyumatsena, who became blind, and was then deprived of his kingdom by an old enemy living nearby. The dethroned monarch retired to the forest with his faithful wife and his only son, who in time grew up to be a handsome youth.

When Savitri confessed her love to her father, the great sage Narada, who sat beside him, spoke and said: 'The princess has done wrong in choosing this royal youth Satyavan for her husband. He is attractive and courageous, he is truthful and magnanimous and forgiving, he is modest and patient and without malice; he possesses every virtue. But he has one defect, and no other. He is to have a short life; it has been decreed that within a year from this day he must die; within a year Yama, god of the dead, will come for him.'

The king turned to his daughter: 'Savitri, you have heard the words of Narada. Therefore go and choose another lord for yourself, for the days of Satyavan are numbered.'

The beautiful young woman said to her father the king: 'The die is cast; it can fall only once; only once can a daughter be given away by her father; only once can a woman say, 'I am yours'. I have chosen my lord. Let his life be brief or be long, I must marry Satyavan.'

Narada said: 'Oh king, the heart of your daughter will not waver; she will not be turned away from the path she has chosen. Therefore I approve of the marriage of Savitri and Satyavan.'

The king replied: 'As you advise, so I must do, Narada, because you are my teacher. I cannot disobey.'

Then Narada said: 'Peace be with Savitri! I must go now. My blessing to all of you!'

Aswapati went to visit Dyumatsena in the forest, and his daughter went with him. Dyumatsena asked his visitors: 'Why have you come here?'

Aswapati replied: 'Royal sage, this is my beautiful daughter Savitri. Take her for your daughter-in-law.'

Dyumatsena responded by saying: 'I have lost my kingdom, and live here in the woods with my wife and my son. We live as ascetics and perform great penances. How will your daughter endure the hardships of a forest life?'

Aswapati answered: 'My daughter well knows that joy and sorrow come and go and that nowhere is bliss assured. Therefore accept her from me.'

Dyumatsena consented that his son should marry Savitri. Satyavan was happy because he was given a wife who had every accomplishment. Savitri also rejoiced because she obtained a husband after her own heart, and she took off her royal garments and ornaments and dressed herself in bark and red cloth.

So Savitri became a hermit woman. She honoured Satyavan's father and mother, and she gave joy to her husband with her sweet speeches, her skill at work, her subdued and even temper, and especially her love. She lived the life of the ascetics and practised every austerity. But she never forgot the dreadful prophecy of Narada the sage; his sad words were always present in her secret heart, and she counted the days as they went past.

Soon the time came when Satyavan must cast off his mortal body. When he had just four days to live, Savitri took the Tritatra vow of three nights of sleepless penance and fast.

Dyumatsena warned her of how hard this would be, but Savitri was determined not to break her vow. So Savitri began to fast. She grew pale and became wasted by her rigid penance. Three days passed, and then, believing that her husband would die the following day, Savitri spent a night of bitter anguish through all the dark and lonely hours.

As the sun rose on the fateful morning, she said to herself, 'Today is the day.' Her face was bloodless but brave; she prayed in silence and made offerings at the morning fire; then she stood before her father-in-law and her mother-in-law in reverent silence with joined hands, concentrating her senses. All the hermits of the forest blessed her and said: 'May you never suffer widowhood.'

Dyumatsena spoke to Savitri then, saying: 'Now that your vow has been completed you may eat the morning meal.'

But Savitri replied: 'I will eat when the sun goes down.'

Hearing her words Satyavan stood up, and taking his axe on his shoulder, turned towards the distant jungle to find fruits and herbs for his wife, whom he loved. He was strong and self-possessed.

Savitri spoke to him sweetly and said: 'You must not go alone, my husband. It is my heart's desire to go with you. I cannot endure to be parted from you today.'

Satyavan replied: 'It is not for you to enter the dark jungle; the way is long and difficult, and you are weak on account of your severe penance. How can you walk so far on foot?'

Savitri laid her head on his chest and said: 'I have not been made weary by my fast. Indeed I am now stronger than before. I will not feel tired when you are by my side. I have resolved to go with you: therefore do not seek to stand in the wat of my wish – the wish and the longing of a faithful wife to be with her lord.'

Satyavan replied: 'If it is your desire to accompany me I will allow it. But you must ask permission of my parents so that they do not find fault with me for taking you through the trackless jungle.'

Then Savitri spoke to the blind sage and her husband's mother and said: 'Satyavan is going towards the deep jungle to find fruits and herbs for me, and also fuel for the sacrificial fires. It is my heart's wish to go too, for today I cannot endure to be parted from him.'

Dyumatsena said: 'Since you have come to live with us in our hermitage you have not asked anything of us. So have your wish in this matter, but do not delay your husband in his duties.'

Having received permission to leave the hermitage, Savitri turned towards the jungle with Satyavan, her beloved lord. Smiles covered her face, but her heart was torn with secret sadness.

Peacocks fluttered in the green woodland through which they walked together, and the sun shone in all its splendour in the blue heaven.

In a sweet voice Satyavan said: 'How beautiful are the bright streams and the blossoming trees!'

The heart of Savitri was divided into two parts: with one she talked with her husband while she watched his face and followed his moods; with the other she awaited the dreaded coming of Yama, but she never uttered her fears. Birds sang sweetly in the forest, but sweeter to Savitri was the voice of her beloved. It was very dear to her to walk on in silence, listening to his words.

Satyavan gathered fruits and stored them in his basket. Then he began to cut down the branches of trees. The sun was hot and he perspired. Suddenly he felt weary and he said: 'My head aches; my senses are confused and my limbs have grown weak. A sickness has seized me. My body seems to be pierced by a hundred darts. I would gladly lie down and rest, my beloved; I would gladly sleep even now.'

Speechless and terror-stricken, the gentle Savitri wound her arms about her husband's body; she sat on the ground and she pillowed his head on her lap. Remembering the words of Narada, she knew that the dreaded hour had come; the very moment of death was at hand. Gently she held her husband's head with caressing hands; she kissed his panting lips; her heart was beating fast and loud. The forest grew dark and lonesome.

Suddenly an awful shape emerged from the shadows. He was of great stature; his clothing was blood-red; on his head he wore a gleaming crown; he had red eyes and was fearsome to look at; he carried a noose.... The shape was Yama, God of Death. He stood in silence, and gazed at the sleeping Satyavan.

Savitri looked up, and when she saw that a celestial had come near, her heart trembled with misery and with fear. She laid her husband's head on the green grass and stood up quickly: then she spoke, saying, 'Who are you, divine one, and what is your mission to me?'

Yama replied: 'You do love your husband; you are endued also with ascetic merit. I will therefore speak with you. I am the Monarch of Death. The days of this man, your husband, are now spent, and I have come to bind him and take him away.'

Savitri responded by saying: 'Wise sages have told me that your messengers carry mortals away. Why, then, mighty King, have you come here yourself?'

Yama replied: 'This prince is of spotless heart; his virtues are without number; he is, indeed, an ocean of accomplishments. It would not be fitting to send messengers for him, so I have come here myself.'

The face of Satyavan had grown ashen. Yama cast his noose and tore out from the prince's body the soul-form, which was no larger than a man's thumb; it was tightly bound and subdued.

So Satyavan lost his life; he stopped breathing; his body became unsightly; it was robbed of its lustre and deprived of its power to move.

Yama fettered the soul with tightness, and turned abruptly towards the south; silently and speedily he went on his way. Savitri followed him. Her heart was drowned in grief. She could not desert her beloved lord. She followed Yama, the Monarch of Death.

Yama said to her: 'Turn back, Savitri. Do not follow me. Perform the funeral rites of your lord. Your allegiance to Satyavan has now come to an end: you are free from all wifely duties. Dare not to proceed further on this path.'

But Savitri answered: 'I must follow my husband whether he is carried or whether he goes of his own will. I have undergone great penance. I have observed my vow, and I cannot be turned back…. I have already walked with you seven paces, and the sages have declared that one who walks seven paces with another becomes a companion. I must converse with you, I must speak and you must listen…. I have attained the perfect life on earth by performing my vows and by reason of my devotion to my lord. It is not right that you should part me from my husband now, and prevent me from attaining bliss by saying that my allegiance to him has ended and another mode of life is opened to me.'

Yama responded: 'Turn back now…. Your words are wise and pleasing; therefore, before you go, you can ask a favour of me and I will grant it. Except the soul of Satyavan, I will give you whatever you desire.'

Savitri said: 'Because my husband's father became blind, he was deprived of his kingdom. Restore his eyesight, mighty One.'

Yama agreed and said: 'The wish is granted. I will restore the vision of your father-in-law…. But you have now grown faint on this difficult journey. Turn back, therefore, and your weariness will pass away.'

Savitri responded: 'How can I be weary when I am with my husband? The fate of my husband will be my fate also; I will follow him even to the place where you carry him…. Hear me, mighty One, whose friendship I cherish! It is a blessed thing to see a celestial; still more blessed is it to converse with one; the friendship of a god must bear great fruit.'

Yama replied: 'Your wisdom delights my heart. Therefore you can ask of me a second favour, except the life of your husband, and it will be granted to you.'

So Savitri said: 'May my wise and saintly father-in-law regain the kingdom he has lost. May he once again become the protector of his people.'

Yama replied: 'The wish is granted. The king will return to his people and be their wise protector…. Turn back now, princess; your desire is fulfilled.'

To this Savitri said: 'All people must obey your decrees; you take away life in accordance with divine ordinances and not of your own will. Therefore you are called Yama – he that rules by decrees. Hear my words, divine One. It is the duty of celestials to love all creatures and to award them according to their merit. The wicked are without holiness and devotion, but the saintly protect all creatures and show mercy even to their enemies.'

Yama responded by saying: 'Your wise words are like water to a thirsty soul. Therefore ask of me a third favour, except your husband's life, and it will be granted to you.'

Savitri said: 'My father, King Aswapati, has no son. Grant that a hundred sons may be born to him.'

Yama replied: 'A hundred sons will be born to your royal father. Your wish is granted…. Now turn back, princess; you cannot come any further. Long is the path you have already travelled.'

But Savitri would not give up. She said: 'I have followed my husband and the way has not seemed long. Indeed, my heart desires to go on much further. Hear my words, Yama, as you proceed on your journey. You are great and wise and powerful; you deal equally with all human creatures; you are the lord of justice…. One cannot trust oneself as one can trust a celestial; therefore, one seeks to win the friendship of a celestial. It is proper that one who seeks the friendship of a celestial should make answer to his words.'

Yama responded: 'No mortal has ever spoken to me as you have spoken. Indeed your words are pleasing, princess. I will grant you a fourth wish, except your husband's life, before you go.'

Savitri said: 'May a century of sons be born to my husband and me so that our race may endure. Grant me this, the fourth favour, Mighty One.'

Then Yama said: 'I grant to you a century of sons, princess; they will be wise and powerful and your race will endure.... Be without weariness now, and turn back; you have come too far already.'

Savitri replied: 'Those who are pious must practise eternal morality, Yama. The pious uphold the universe. The pious hold communion with the pious only, and are never weary; the pious do good to others without ever expecting any reward. A good deed done to the righteous is never thrown away; such an act does not entail loss of dignity nor is any interest impaired. Indeed, the doing of good is the chief office of the righteous, and the righteous therefore are the true protectors of all.'

To this Yama said: 'The more you speak, the more I respect you, princess. You, who are so deeply devoted to your husband, you can now ask of me some incomparable favour.'

So Savitri said: 'Mighty One, bestower of favours, you have already promised what cannot be fulfilled unless my husband is restored to me; you have promised me a century of sons. Therefore, I ask you, Yama, to give me back Satyavan, my beloved, my lord. Without him, I am like one who is dead; without him, I have no desire for happiness; without him I have no longing even for Heaven; I will have no desire to prosper if my lord is snatched away; I cannot live without Satyavan. You have promised me sons, Yama, yet you take away my husband from my arms. Hear me and grant this favour: Let Satyavan be restored to life so that your decree may be fulfilled.'

Eventually Yama replied: 'So be it. With cheerful heart I now unbind your husband. He is free.... Disease cannot afflict him again and he will prosper. Together you will both have a long life; you will live for four hundred years; you will have a century of sons and they will be kings, and their sons will be kings too.'

Yama, the lord of death, then departed. And Savitri returned to the forest where her husband's body lay cold and pale; she sat on the ground and pillowed his head on her lap. Then Satyavan was given back his life.... He looked at Savitri with eyes of love; he was like one who had returned from a long journey in a strange land. He said: 'My sleep was long; why did you not wake me, my beloved?... Where is that dark One who dragged me away?'

Savitri replied: 'Yama has come and gone, and you have slept long, resting your head on my lap, and are now refreshed, blessed one. If you can rise up, let us now leave because the night is already dark....'

Satyavan rose up refreshed and strong. He looked round about and saw that he was in the middle of the forest.

Then he said: 'Oh fair one, I came here to gather fruit for you, and while I cut down branches from the trees a pain afflicted me. I grew faint, I sank to the ground, I laid my head on your lap and fell into a deep sleep even whilst you embraced me. Then it seemed to me that I was enveloped in darkness, and that I saw someone.... Was this a vision or a reality?'

Savitri responded: 'The darkness deepens.... I will tell you everything tomorrow.... Now let us find our parents. The beasts of the night are coming; I hear their awesome voices; they tread the forest in glee; the howl of the jackal makes my heart afraid.'

Satyavan said: 'Darkness has covered the forest with fear; we cannot find the path by which to return home.'

So Savitri said: 'I will gather sticks and make a fire and we will wait here until daylight comes.'

Satyavan replied: 'My sickness has gone and I would gladly see my parents again. I have never before spent a night away from the hermitage. My mother and father are old, and I am their crutch. They will be afflicted with sorrow because we have not returned.'

Satyavan lifted up his arms and wept, but Savitri dried his tears and said: 'I have performed penances, I have given away in charity, I have offered up sacrifices, I have never uttered a falsehood. May your parents be protected by virtue of the power which I have obtained, and may you, my husband, be protected too.'

Satyavan replied: 'Beautiful one, let us now return to the hermitage.'

Savitri raised up her despairing husband. Then she placed his left arm on her left shoulder and wound her right arm around his body, and they walked on together.... After some time the moon came out and shone on their path.

Meanwhile Dyumatsena, the father of Satyavan, had regained his sight, and he went with his wife to search for his lost son, but had to return to the hermitage in despair. The sages comforted the weeping parents and said: 'Savitri has practised great austerities, and there can be no doubt that Satyavan is still alive.'

Finally Satyavan and Savitri reached the hermitage, and their own hearts and the hearts of their parents were freed from sorrow.

Then Savitri told of all that had taken place, and the sages said: 'Oh chaste and illustrious lady, you have rescued the race of Dyumatsena, the foremost of kings, from the ocean of darkness.'

The following morning messengers came to Dyumatsena and told him that the king who had deprived him of his kingdom was now dead, having fallen by the hand of his chief minister. All the people clamoured for their legitimate ruler. 'Chariots are waiting for you, king. Therefore return to your kingdom,' said the messengers.

So the king was restored to his kingdom, in accordance with the favour Savitri had obtained from Yama. And in time sons were born to her father. The gentle Savitri, because of her great devotion, had raised the family of her husband and her own father from misery to high fortune. She was the rescuer of all; the bringer of happiness and prosperity.... He who hears the story of Savitri will never endure misery again.

Tales of Heaven

In that fair domain it is neither too hot nor too cold. Life there is devoid of sorrow; age does not bring frailties, and no one is ever hungry or thirsty; it is without wretchedness, or fatigue, or evil feelings. Everything, whether celestial or human, that the heart seeks after is found there. Sweet are the juicy fruits, delicious the fragrance of flowers and tree blossoms, and waters are there, both cold and hot, to give refreshment and comfort. Nymphs dance and sing to the piping of celestial elves, and merry laughter always blends with the strains of alluring music.

The Assembly House of Yama, which was made by Twashtri, has splendour equal to the sun; it shines like burnished gold. There the servants of the Lord of Justice measure out the allotted days of mortals. Great rishis and ancestors wait on Yama, King of the Pitris (fathers), and adore him. Sanctified by holiness, their shining bodies are dressed in swan-white garments, and decked with many-coloured bracelets and golden earrings. Sweet sounds, alluring perfumes, and brilliant flower garlands make that building eternally pleasant and supremely blessed. Hundreds of thousands of saintly beings worship the illustrious King of the Pitris.

The heaven of Indra was constructed by the great artisan-god himself. Like a chariot it can be moved anywhere at will. The Assembly House has many rooms and seats, and is adorned by celestial trees. Indra sits there with his beautiful queen, wearing his crown, with gleaming bracelets on his upper arms; he is decked with flowers, and dressed in white garments. He is waited on by brilliant Maruts, and all the gods and the rishis and saints, whose sins have been washed off their pure souls, which are as resplendent as fire. There is no sorrow, or fear, or suffering in Indra's home, which is inhabited by the spirits of wind and thunder, fire and water, plants and clouds, and planets and stars, and also the spirits of Prosperity, Religion, Joy, Faith, and Intelligence. Fairies and elves (Apsaras and Gandharvas) dance and sing to sweet music; feats of skill are performed by celestial battle heroes; auspicious rites are also practised. Divine messengers come and go in celestial chariots, looking as bright as Soma himself.

The heaven of Varuna was built by Vishwakarman (Twashtri) within the sea. Its walls and arches are pure white, and they are surrounded by celestial trees, made of sparkling jewels, which always blossom and always bear fruit. In the many-coloured bowers beautiful and variegated birds sing delightful melodies. In the Assembly House, which is also pure white, there are many rooms and many seats. Varuna, richly decked with jewels and golden ornaments and flowers, is throned there with his queen. Adityas wait on the lord of the waters, as also do hooded snakes (Nagas) with human heads and arms, and Daityas and Danavas (giants and demons) who have taken vows and have been rewarded with immortality. All the holy spirits of rivers and oceans are there, and the holy spirits of lakes and springs and pools, and the personified forms of the points of the heavens, the ends of the earth, and the great mountains. Music and dances provide entertainment, while sacred hymns are sung in praise of Varuna.

The 'Hadithi yar Liongo'

THIS POEM ('The Story of Liongo') relates how certain Galla people (now 'Oromo', native to Ethiopia), coming to Pate to trade, heard of Liongo (hero, warrior and poet of the Swahili people) from the sultan, who dwelt so much on his prowess that their curiosity was aroused, and they expressed a wish to see him. So he sent a letter to Liongo at Shaka, desiring him to come. Liongo replied with respect and courtesy that he would come, and he set out on the following day, fully armed and carrying three tr umpets. The journey from Shaka to Pate was reckoned at four days, but Liongo arrived the day after he had started. At the city gate he blew such a blast that the trumpet was split, and the Galla asked, 'What is it? Who has raised such a cry?' He answered, 'It is Liongo who has come!'

Liongo sounded his second trumpet, and burst it; he then took the third, and the townsfolk all ran together, the Galla among them, to see what this portended. He then sent a messenger to say, 'Our lord Liongo asks leave to enter.' The gate was thrown open, and he was invited in, all the Galla being struck with astonishment and terror at the sight of him. 'This is a lord of war,' they said; 'he can put a hundred armies to flight.'

He sat down, at the same time laying on the ground the wallet which he had been carrying. After resting awhile he took out from it a mortar and pestle, a millstone, cooking pots of no common size, and the three stones used for supporting them over the fire. The Galla stood by, gaping with amazement, and when at last they found speech they said to the sultan, 'We want him for a prince, to marry one of our daughters, that a son of his may bring glory to our tribe.'

The sultan undertook to open the matter to Liongo, who agreed, on certain conditions (what these were we are not told), and the wedding was celebrated with great rejoicing at the Galla kraals. In due course a son was born, who, as he grew up, bade fair to resemble his father in strength and beauty.

It would seem as if Liongo had been living for some time at Pate (for he did not take up his abode permanently with the Galla) – no doubt as a result of the quarrel with his brother. But now someone – whether an emissary of Mringwari's or some of the Galla whom he had offended – stirred up trouble; enmity arose against him, and, finding that the sultan had determined on his death, he left Pate for the mainland. There he took refuge with the forest folk, the Wasanye and Wadahalo. These soon received a message from Pate, offering them a hundred reals (silver dollars) if they would bring in Liongo's head. They were not proof against the temptation, and, unable to face him in fight, planned a treacherous scheme for his destruction. They approached him one day with a suggestion for a kikoa, since a regular feast – in their roving forest life – is not to be done. They were to dine off makoma (the fruit of the Hyphaene palm), each man taking his turn at climbing a tree and gathering for the party, the intention being to shoot Liongo when they had him at a disadvantage. However, when it came to his turn, having chosen the tallest palm, he defeated them by shooting down the nuts, one by one, where he stood. This, by the by, is the only instance recorded of his marksmanship, though his skill with the bow is one of his titles to fame.

Liongo Escapes from Captivity

The Wasanye now gave up in despair, and sent word to the sultan that Liongo was not to be overcome either by force or guile. He, unwilling to trust them any further, left them and went to Shaka, where he met his mother and his son. His Galla wife seems to have remained with her people, and we hear nothing from this authority of any other wives he may have had. Here, at last, he was captured by his brother's men, seized while asleep – one account says: 'first having been given wine to drink' (it was probably drugged). He was then secured in the prison in the usual way, his feet chained together with a post between them, and fetters on his hands. He was guarded day and night by warriors. There was much debating as to what should be done with him. There was a general desire to get rid of him, but some of Mringwari's councillors were of opinion that he was too dangerous to be dealt with directly: it would be better to give him the command of the army and let him perish, like Uriah, in the forefront of the battle, Mringwari thought this would be too great a risk, and there could be none in killing him, fettered as he was.

Meanwhile Liongo's mother sent her slave girl Saada every day to the prison with food for her son, which the guards invariably seized, only tossing him the scraps.

Mringwari, when at last he had come to a decision, sent a slave lad to the captive, to tell him that he must die in three days' time, but if he had a last wish it should be granted, 'that you may take your leave of the world.' Liongo sent word that he wished to have a gungu dance performed where he could see and hear it, and this was granted.

He then fell to composing a song, which is known and sung to this day:

O thou handmaid Saada, list my words today!
Haste thee to my mother, tell her what I say.
Bid her bake for me a cake of chaff and bran, I pray,
And hide therein an iron file to cut my bonds away,
File to free my fettered feet, swiftly as I may;
Forth I'll glide like serpent's child, silently to slay.

When Saada came again he sang this over to her several times, till she knew it by heart-the guards either did not understand the words or were too much occupied with the dinner of which they had robbed him to pay any attention to his music. Saada went home and repeated the song to her mistress, who lost no time, but went out at once and bought some files. Next morning she prepared a better meal than usual, and also baked such a loaf as her son asked for, into which she inserted the files, wrapped in a rag.

When Saada arrived at the prison the guards took the food as usual, and, after a glance at the bran loaf, threw it contemptuously to Liongo, who appeared to take it with a look of sullen resignation to his fate.

When the dance was arranged he called the chief performers together and taught them a new song – perhaps one of the 'Gungu Dance Songs' which have been handed down under his name. There was an unusually full orchestra: horns, trumpets, cymbals (matoazi), gongs (tasa), and the complete set of drums, while Liongo himself led the singing. When the band was playing its loudest he began filing at his fetters, the sound being quite inaudible amid the din; when the performers paused he stopped filing and lifted up his voice again. So he gradually cut through his foot shackles and his handcuffs, and, rising up in his might, like Samson, burst the door, seized two of the guards, knocked their heads together, and threw them down dead. The musicians dropped their instruments and fled, the crowd scattered like a flock of sheep, and Liongo took to the woods, after going outside the town to take leave of his mother, none daring to stay him.

Liongo Undone by Treachery at Last

Here he led an outlaw's life, raiding towns and plundering travellers, and Mringwari was at his wits' end to compass his destruction. At last Liongo's son – or, as some say, his sister's son – was gained over and induced to ferret out the secret of Liongo's charmed life, since it had been discovered by this time that neither spear nor arrow could wound him. The lad sought out his father, and greeted him with a great show of affection; but Liongo was not deceived. He made no difficulty, however, about revealing the secret – perhaps he felt that his time had come and that it was useless to fight against destiny. When his son said to him, after some hesitation, 'My father, it is the desire of my heart – since I fear danger for you – that I might know for certain what it is that can kill you,' Liongo replied, 'I think, since you ask me this, that you are seeking to kill me.' The son, of course, protested: 'I swear by the Bountiful One I am not one to do this thing! Father, if you die, to whom shall I go? I shall be utterly destitute.'

Liongo answered, 'My son, I know how you have been instructed and how you will be deceived in your turn. Those who are making use of you now will laugh you to scorn, and you will bitterly regret your doings! Yet, though it be so, I will tell you! That which can slay me is a copper nail driven into the navel. From any other weapon than this I can take no hurt.' The son waited two days, and on the third made an excuse to hasten back to Pate, saying that he was anxious about his mother's health. Mringwari, on receiving the information, at once sent for a craftsman and ordered him to make a copper spike of the kind required. The youth was feasted and made much of for the space of ten days, and then dispatched on his errand, with the promise that a marriage should be arranged for him when he returned successful. On arriving at Shaka he was kindly welcomed by his father (who perhaps thought that, after all, he had been wrong in his suspicions), and remained with him for a month without carrying out his design – either from lack of opportunity or, as one would fain hope, visited by some compunction. As time went on Mringwari grew impatient and wrote, reproaching him in covert terms for the delay. 'We, here, have everything ready' – i.e., for the promised wedding festivities, which were to be of the utmost magnificence. It chanced that on the day when this letter arrived Liongo, wearied out with hunting, slept more soundly than usual during the midday heat. The son, seizing his opportunity, screwed his courage to the sticking place, crept up, and stabbed him in the one vulnerable spot.

Liongo started up in the death pang and, seizing his bow and arrows, walked out of the house and out of the town. When he had reached a spot halfway between the city gate and the well at which the folk were wont to draw water his strength failed him: he sank on one knee, fitted an arrow to the string, drew it to the head, and so died, with his face towards the well.

The townsfolk could see him kneeling there, and did not know that he was dead. Then for three days neither man nor woman durst venture near the well. They used the water stored for ablutions in the tank outside the mosque; when that was exhausted there was great distress in the town. The elders of the people went to Liongo's mother and asked her to intercede with her son. 'If she goes to him he will be sorry for her.' She consented, and went out, accompanied by the principal men, chanting verses (perhaps some of his own poems) with the purpose of soothing him. Gazing at him from a distance, she addressed him with piteous entreaties, but when they came nearer and saw that he was dead she would not believe it. 'He cannot be killed; he is angry, and therefore he does not speak; he is brooding over his wrongs in his own mind and refuses to hear me!' So she wailed; but when he fell over they knew that he was dead indeed.

They came near and looked at the body, and drew out the copper needle which had killed him, and carried him into the town, and waked and buried him. And there he lies to this day, near Kipini by the sea.

The Traitor's Doom

The news reached Pate, and Mringwari, privately rejoicing at the removal of his enemy, sent for Mani Liongo, the son (who meanwhile had been sumptuously entertained in the palace), and told him what had happened, professing to be much surprised when he showed no signs of sorrow. When the son replied that, on the contrary, he was very glad Mringwari turned on him. 'You are an utterly faithless one! Depart out of my house and from the town; take off the clothes I have given you and wear your own, you enemy of God!' Driven from Pate, he betook himself to his Galla kinsmen, but there he was received coldly, and even his mother cast him off. So, overcome with remorse and grief, he fell into a wasting sickness and died unlamented.

The Transformation of Arachne into a Spider

IN BOOK VI of Roman poet Ovid's epic narrative poem *Metamorphoses*, we meet Arachne – that rare example of an ancient heroine who is neither goddess, princess nor other-worldy nymph. Her downfall is simply to be supremely skilled at her art – and vocally proud of it...

Pallas, attending to the Muse's song,
Approv'd the just resentment of their wrong;
And thus reflects: While tamely I commend
Those who their injur'd deities defend,
My own divinity affronted stands,
And calls aloud for justice at my hands;
Then takes the hint, asham'd to lag behind,
And on Arachne' bends her vengeful mind;
One at the loom so excellently skill'd,
That to the Goddess she refus'd to yield.
Low was her birth, and small her native town,
She from her art alone obtain'd renown.
Idmon, her father, made it his employ,
To give the spungy fleece a purple dye:
Of vulgar strain her mother, lately dead,
With her own rank had been content to wed;
Yet she their daughter, tho' her time was spent
In a small hamlet, and of mean descent,
Thro' the great towns of Lydia gain'd a name,
And fill'd the neighb'ring countries with her fame.
Oft, to admire the niceness of her skill,
The Nymphs would quit their fountain, shade, or hill:
Thither, from green Tymolus, they repair,
And leave the vineyards, their peculiar care;
Thither, from fam'd Pactolus' golden stream,
Drawn by her art, the curious Naiads came.
Nor would the work, when finish'd, please so much,
As, while she wrought, to view each graceful touch;
Whether the shapeless wool in balls she wound,
Or with quick motion turn'd the spindle round,
Or with her pencil drew the neat design,
Pallas her mistress shone in every line.
This the proud maid with scornful air denies,
And ev'n the Goddess at her work defies;
Disowns her heav'nly mistress ev'ry hour,
Nor asks her aid, nor deprecates her pow'r.
Let us, she cries, but to a tryal come,
And, if she conquers, let her fix my doom.
The Goddess then a beldame's form put on,
With silver hairs her hoary temples shone;
Prop'd by a staff, she hobbles in her walk,
And tott'ring thus begins her old wives' talk.
Young maid attend, nor stubbornly despise
The admonitions of the old, and wise;
For age, tho' scorn'd, a ripe experience bears,
That golden fruit, unknown to blooming years:
Still may remotest fame your labours crown,

And mortals your superior genius own;
But to the Goddess yield, and humbly meek
A pardon for your bold presumption seek;
The Goddess will forgive. At this the maid,
With passion fir'd, her gliding shuttle stay'd;
And, darting vengeance with an angry look,
To Pallas in disguise thus fiercely spoke.
Thou doating thing, whose idle babling tongue
But too well shews the plague of living long;
Hence, and reprove, with this your sage advice,
Your giddy daughter, or your aukward neice;
Know, I despise your counsel, and am still
A woman, ever wedded to my will;
And, if your skilful Goddess better knows,
Let her accept the tryal I propose.
She does, impatient Pallas strait replies,
And, cloath'd with heavenly light, sprung from her odd disguise.
The Nymphs, and virgins of the plain adore
The awful Goddess, and confess her pow'r;
The maid alone stood unappall'd; yet show'd
A transient blush, that for a moment glow'd,
Then disappear'd; as purple streaks adorn
The opening beauties of the rosy morn;
Till Phoebus rising prevalently bright,
Allays the tincture with his silver light.
Yet she persists, and obstinately great,
In hopes of conquest hurries on her fate.
The Goddess now the challenge waves no more,
Nor, kindly good, advises as before.
Strait to their posts appointed both repair,
And fix their threaded looms with equal care:
Around the solid beam the web is ty'd,
While hollow canes the parting warp divide;
Thro' which with nimble flight the shuttles play,
And for the woof prepare a ready way;
The woof and warp unite, press'd by the toothy slay.
Thus both, their mantles button'd to their breast,
Their skilful fingers ply with willing haste,
And work with pleasure; while they chear the eye
With glowing purple of the Tyrian dye:
Or, justly intermixing shades with light,
Their colourings insensibly unite.
As when a show'r transpierc'd with sunny rays,
Its mighty arch along the heav'n displays;
From whence a thousand diff'rent colours rise,
Whose fine transition cheats the clearest eyes;
So like the intermingled shading seems,

And only differs in the last extreams.
Then threads of gold both artfully dispose,
And, as each part in just proportion rose,
Some antique fable in their work disclose.
Pallas in figures wrought the heav'nly Pow'rs,
And Mars's hill among th' Athenian tow'rs.
On lofty thrones twice six celestials sate,
Jove in the midst, and held their warm debate;
The subject weighty, and well-known to fame,
From whom the city shou'd receive its name.
Each God by proper features was exprest,
Jove with majestick mein excell'd the rest.
His three-fork'd mace the dewy sea-God shook,
And, looking sternly, smote the ragged rock;
When from the stone leapt forth a spritely steed,
And Neptune claims the city for the deed.
Herself she blazons, with a glitt'ring spear,
And crested helm that veil'd her braided hair,
With shield, and scaly breast-plate, implements of war.
Struck with her pointed launce, the teeming Earth
Seem'd to produce a new surprizing birth;
When, from the glebe, the pledge of conquest sprung,
A tree pale-green with fairest olives hung.
And then, to let her giddy rival learn
What just rewards such boldness was to earn,
Four tryals at each corner had their part,
Design'd in miniature, and touch'd with art.
Haemus in one, and Rodope of Thrace
Transform'd to mountains, fill'd the foremost place;
Who claim'd the titles of the Gods above,
And vainly us'd the epithets of Jove.
Another shew'd, where the Pigmaean dame,
Profaning Juno's venerable name,
Turn'd to an airy crane, descends from far,
And with her Pigmy subjects wages war.
In a third part, the rage of Heav'n's great queen,
Display'd on proud Antigone, was seen:
Who with presumptuous boldness dar'd to vye,
For beauty with the empress of the sky.
Ah! what avails her ancient princely race,
Her sire a king, and Troy her native place:
Now, to a noisy stork transform'd, she flies,
And with her whiten'd pinions cleaves the skies.
And in the last remaining part was drawn
Poor Cinyras that seem'd to weep in stone;
Clasping the temple steps, he sadly mourn'd
His lovely daughters, now to marble turn'd.

With her own tree the finish'd piece is crown'd,
And wreaths of peaceful olive all the work surround.
Arachne drew the fam'd intrigues of Jove,
Chang'd to a bull to gratify his love;
How thro' the briny tide all foaming hoar,
Lovely Europa on his back he bore.
The sea seem'd waving, and the trembling maid
Shrunk up her tender feet, as if afraid;
And, looking back on the forsaken strand,
To her companions wafts her distant hand.
Next she design'd Asteria's fabled rape,
When Jove assum'd a soaring eagle's shape:
And shew'd how Leda lay supinely press'd,
Whilst the soft snowy swan sate hov'ring o'er her breast,
How in a satyr's form the God beguil'd,
When fair Antiope with twins he fill'd.
Then, like Amphytrion, but a real Jove,
In fair Alcmena's arms he cool'd his love.
In fluid gold to Danae's heart he came,
Aegina felt him in a lambent flame.
He took Mnemosyne in shepherd's make,
And for Deois was a speckled snake.
She made thee, Neptune, like a wanton steer,
Pacing the meads for love of Arne dear;
Next like a stream, thy burning flame to slake,
And like a ram, for fair Bisaltis' sake.
Then Ceres in a steed your vigour try'd,
Nor cou'd the mare the yellow Goddess hide.
Next, to a fowl transform'd, you won by force
The snake-hair'd mother of the winged horse;
And, in a dolphin's fishy form, subdu'd
Melantho sweet beneath the oozy flood.
All these the maid with lively features drew,
And open'd proper landskips to the view.
There Phoebus, roving like a country swain,
Attunes his jolly pipe along the plain;
For lovely Isse's sake in shepherd's weeds,
O'er pastures green his bleating flock he feeds,
There Bacchus, imag'd like the clust'ring grape,
Melting bedrops Erigone's fair lap;
And there old Saturn, stung with youthful heat,
Form'd like a stallion, rushes to the feat.
Fresh flow'rs, which twists of ivy intertwine,
Mingling a running foliage, close the neat design.
This the bright Goddess passionately mov'd,
With envy saw, yet inwardly approv'd.
The scene of heav'nly guilt with haste she tore,

Nor longer the affront with patience bore;
A boxen shuttle in her hand she took,
And more than once Arachne's forehead struck.
Th' unhappy maid, impatient of the wrong,
Down from a beam her injur'd person hung;
When Pallas, pitying her wretched state,
At once prevented, and pronounc'd her fate:
Live; but depend, vile wretch, the Goddess cry'd,
Doom'd in suspence for ever to be ty'd;
That all your race, to utmost date of time,
May feel the vengeance, and detest the crime.
Then, going off, she sprinkled her with juice,
Which leaves of baneful aconite produce.
Touch'd with the pois'nous drug, her flowing hair
Fell to the ground, and left her temples bare;
Her usual features vanish'd from their place,
Her body lessen'd all, but most her face.
Her slender fingers, hanging on each side
With many joynts, the use of legs supply'd:
A spider's bag the rest, from which she gives
A thread, and still by constant weaving lives.

The Story of Tereus, Procne and Philomela

ALSO IN BOOK VI of Ovid's *Metamorphoses*, we hear the bloody and grotesque tale of Tereus, Procne and Philomela. Philomela's heroism lies in her use of art as a means to escape her confinement. We join the story after the death of Thebes' founder Amphion and his family:

To Thebes the neighb'ring princes all repair,
And with condolance the misfortune share.
Each bord'ring state in solemn form address'd,
And each betimes a friendly grief express'd.
Argos, with Sparta's, and Mycenae's towns,
And Calydon, yet free from fierce Diana's frowns.
Corinth for finest brass well fam'd of old,
Orthomenos for men of courage bold:
Cleonae lying in the lowly dale,
And rich Messene with its fertile vale:
Pylos, for Nestor's City after fam'd,

And Troezen, not as yet from Pittheus nam'd.
And those fair cities, which are hem'd around
By double seas within the Isthmian ground;
And those, which farther from the sea-coast stand,
Lodg'd in the bosom of the spacious land.
Who can believe it? Athens was the last:
Tho' for politeness fam'd for ages past.
For a strait siege, which then their walls enclos'd,
Such acts of kind humanity oppos'd:
And thick with ships, from foreign nations bound,
Sea-ward their city lay invested round.
These, with auxiliar forces led from far,
Tereus of Thrace, brave, and inur'd to war,
Had quite defeated, and obtain'd a name,
The warrior's due, among the sons of Fame.
This, with his wealth, and pow'r, and ancient line,
From Mars deriv'd, Pandions's thoughts incline
His daughter Procne with the prince to joyn.
Nor Hymen, nor the Graces here preside,
Nor Juno to befriend the blooming bride;
But Fiends with fun'ral brands the process led,
And Furies waited at the Genial bed:
And all night long the scrieching owl aloof,
With baleful notes, sate brooding o'er the roof.
With such ill Omens was the match begun,
That made them parents of a hopeful son.
Now Thrace congratulates their seeming joy,
And they, in thankful rites, their minds employ.
If the fair queen's espousals pleas'd before,
Itys, the new-born prince, now pleases more;
And each bright day, the birth, and bridal feast,
Were kept with hallow'd pomp above the rest.
So far true happiness may lye conceal'd,
When, by false lights, we fancy 'tis reveal'd!
Now, since their nuptials, had the golden sun
Five courses round his ample zodiac run;
When gentle Procne thus her lord address'd,
And spoke the secret wishes of her breast:
If I, she said, have ever favour found,
Let my petition with success be crown'd:
Let me at Athens my dear sister see,
Or let her come to Thrace, and visit me.
And, lest my father should her absence mourn,
Promise that she shall make a quick return.
With thanks I'd own the obligation due
Only, o Tereus, to the Gods, and you.
Now, ply'd with oar, and sail at his command,

The nimble gallies reach'd th' Athenian land,
And anchor'd in the fam'd Piraean bay,
While Tereus to the palace takes his way;
The king salutes, and ceremonies past,
Begins the fatal embassy at last;
The occasion of his voyage he declares,
And, with his own, his wife's request prefers:
Asks leave that, only for a little space,
Their lovely sister might embark for Thrace.
Thus while he spoke, appear'd the royal maid,
Bright Philomela, splendidly array'd;
But most attractive in her charming face,
And comely person, turn'd with ev'ry grace:
Like those fair Nymphs, that are describ'd to rove
Across the glades, and op'nings of the grove;
Only that these are dress'd for silvan sports,
And less become the finery of courts.
Tereus beheld the virgin, and admir'd,
And with the coals of burning lust was fir'd:
Like crackling stubble, or the summer hay,
When forked lightnings o'er the meadows play.
Such charms in any breast might kindle love,
But him the heats of inbred lewdness move;
To which, tho' Thrace is naturally prone,
Yet his is still superior, and his own.
Strait her attendants he designs to buy,
And with large bribes her governess would try:
Herself with ample gifts resolves to bend,
And his whole kingdom in th' attempt expend:
Or, snatch'd away by force of arms, to bear,
And justify the rape with open war.
The boundless passion boils within his breast,
And his projecting soul admits no rest.
And now, impatient of the least delay,
By pleading Procne's cause, he speeds his way:
The eloquence of love his tongue inspires,
And, in his wife's, he speaks his own desires;
Hence all his importunities arise,
And tears unmanly trickle from his eyes.
Ye Gods! what thick involving darkness blinds
The stupid faculties of mortal minds!
Tereus the credit of good-nature gains
From these his crimes; so well the villain feigns.
And, unsuspecting of his base designs,
In the request fair Philomela joyns;
Her snowy arms her aged sire embrace,
And clasp his neck with an endearing grace:

Only to see her sister she entreats,
A seeming blessing, which a curse compleats.
Tereus surveys her with a luscious eye,
And in his mind forestalls the blissful joy:
Her circling arms a scene of lust inspire,
And ev'ry kiss foments the raging fire.
Fondly he wishes for the father's place,
To feel, and to return the warm embrace;
Since not the nearest ties of filial blood
Would damp his flame, and force him to be good.
At length, for both their sakes, the king agrees;
And Philomela, on her bended knees,
Thanks him for what her fancy calls success,
When cruel fate intends her nothing less.
Now Phoebus, hastning to ambrosial rest,
His fiery steeds drove sloping down the west:
The sculptur'd gold with sparkling wines was fill'd,
And, with rich meats, each chearful table smil'd.
Plenty, and mirth the royal banquet close,
Then all retire to sleep, and sweet repose.
But the lewd monarch, tho' withdrawn apart,
Still feels love's poison rankling in his heart:
Her face divine is stamp'd within his breast,
Fancy imagines, and improves the rest:
And thus, kept waking by intense desire,
He nourishes his own prevailing fire.
Next day the good old king for Tereus sends,
And to his charge the virgin recommends;
His hand with tears th' indulgent father press'd,
Then spoke, and thus with tenderness address'd.
Since the kind instances of pious love,
Do all pretence of obstacle remove;
Since Procne's, and her own, with your request,
O'er-rule the fears of a paternal breast;
With you, dear son, my daughter I entrust,
And by the Gods adjure you to be just;
By truth, and ev'ry consanguineal tye,
To watch, and guard her with a father's eye.
And, since the least delay will tedious prove,
In keeping from my sight the child I love,
With speed return her, kindly to asswage
The tedious troubles of my lingring age.
And you, my Philomel, let it suffice,
To know your sister's banish'd from my eyes;
If any sense of duty sways your mind,
Let me from you the shortest absence find.
He wept; then kiss'd his child; and while he speaks,

The tears fall gently down his aged cheeks.
Next, as a pledge of fealty, he demands,
And, with a solemn charge, conjoyns their hands;
Then to his daughter, and his grandson sends,
And by their mouth a blessing recommends;
While, in a voice with dire forebodings broke,
Sobbing, and faint, the last farewel was spoke.
Now Philomela, scarce receiv'd on board,
And in the royal gilded bark secur'd,
Beheld the dashes of the bending oar,
The ruffled sea, and the receding shore;
When strait (his joy impatient of disguise)
We've gain'd our point, the rough Barbarian cries;
Now I possess the dear, the blissful hour,
And ev'ry wish subjected to my pow'r.
Transports of lust his vicious thoughts employ,
And he forbears, with pain, th' expected joy.
His gloting eyes incessantly survey'd
The virgin beauties of the lovely maid:
As when the bold rapacious bird of Jove,
With crooked talons stooping from above,
Has snatcht, and carry'd to his lofty nest
A captive hare, with cruel gripes opprest;
Secure, with fix'd, and unrelenting eyes,
He sits, and views the helpless, trembling prize.
Their vessels now had made th' intended land,
And all with joy descend upon the strand;
When the false tyrant seiz'd the princely maid,
And to a lodge in distant woods convey'd;
Pale, sinking, and distress'd with jealous fears,
And asking for her sister all in tears.
The letcher, for enjoyment fully bent,
No longer now conceal'd his base intent;
But with rude haste the bloomy girl deflow'r'd,
Tender, defenceless, and with ease o'erpower'd.
Her piercing accents to her sire complain,
And to her absent sister, but in vain:
In vain she importunes, with doleful cries,
Each unattentive godhead of the skies.
She pants and trembles, like the bleating prey,
From some close-hunted wolf just snatch'd away;
That still, with fearful horror, looks around,
And on its flank regards the bleeding wound.
Or, as the tim'rous dove, the danger o'er,
Beholds her shining plumes besmear'd with gore,
And, tho' deliver'd from the faulcon's claw,
Yet shivers, and retains a secret awe.

But when her mind a calm reflection shar'd,
And all her scatter'd spirits were repair'd:
Torn, and disorder'd while her tresses hung,
Her livid hands, like one that mourn'd, she wrung;
Then thus, with grief o'erwhelm'd her languid eyes,
Savage, inhumane, cruel wretch! she cries;
Whom not a parent's strict commands could move,
Tho' charg'd, and utter'd with the tears of love;
Nor virgin innocence, nor all that's due
To the strong contract of the nuptial vow:
Virtue, by this, in wild confusion's laid,
And I compell'd to wrong my sister's bed;
Whilst you, regardless of your marriage oath,
With stains of incest have defil'd us both.
Tho' I deserv'd some punishment to find,
This was, ye Gods! too cruel, and unkind.
Yet, villain, to compleat your horrid guilt,
Stab here, and let my tainted blood be spilt.
Oh happy! had it come, before I knew
The curs'd embrace of vile perfidious you;
Then my pale ghost, pure from incestuous love,
Had wander'd spotless thro' th' Elysian grove.
But, if the Gods above have pow'r to know,
And judge those actions that are done below;
Unless the dreaded thunders of the sky,
Like me, subdu'd, and violated lye;
Still my revenge shall take its proper time,
And suit the baseness of your hellish crime.
My self, abandon'd, and devoid of shame,
Thro' the wide world your actions will proclaim;
Or tho' I'm prison'd in this lonely den,
Obscur'd, and bury'd from the sight of men,
My mournful voice the pitying rocks shall move,
And my complainings eccho thro' the grove.
Hear me, o Heav'n! and, if a God be there,
Let him regard me, and accept my pray'r.
Struck with these words, the tyrant's guilty breast
With fear, and anger, was, by turns, possest;
Now, with remorse his conscience deeply stung,
He drew the faulchion that beside her hung,
And first her tender arms behind her bound,
Then drag'd her by the hair along the ground.
The princess willingly her throat reclin'd,
And view'd the steel with a contented mind;
But soon her tongue the girding pinchers strain,
With anguish, soon she feels the piercing pain:
Oh father! father! would fain have spoke,

But the sharp torture her intention broke;
In vain she tries, for now the blade has cut
Her tongue sheer off, close to the trembling root.
The mangled part still quiver'd on the ground,
Murmuring with a faint imperfect sound:
And, as a serpent writhes his wounded train,
Uneasy, panting, and possess'd with pain;
The piece, while life remain'd, still trembled fast,
And to its mistress pointed to the last.
Yet, after this so damn'd, and black a deed,
Fame (which I scarce can credit) has agreed,
That on her rifled charms, still void of shame,
He frequently indulg'd his lustful flame,
At last he ventures to his Procne's sight,
Loaded with guilt, and cloy'd with long delight;
There, with feign'd grief, and false, dissembled sighs,
Begins a formal narrative of lies;
Her sister's death he artfully declares,
Then weeps, and raises credit from his tears.
Her vest, with flow'rs of gold embroider'd o'er,
With grief distress'd, the mournful matron tore,
And a beseeming suit of gloomy sable wore.
With cost, an honorary tomb she rais'd,
And thus th' imaginary ghost appeas'd.
Deluded queen! the fate of her you love,
Nor grief, nor pity, but revenge should move.
Thro' the twelve signs had pass'd the circling sun,
And round the compass of the Zodiac run;
What must unhappy Philomela do,
For ever subject to her keeper's view?
Huge walls of massy stone the lodge surround,
From her own mouth no way of speaking's found.
But all our wants by wit may be supply'd,
And art makes up, what fortune has deny'd:
With skill exact a Phrygian web she strung,
Fix'd to a loom that in her chamber hung,
Where in-wrought letters, upon white display'd,
In purple notes, her wretched case betray'd:
The piece, when finish'd, secretly she gave
Into the charge of one poor menial slave;
And then, with gestures, made him understand,
It must be safe convey'd to Procne's hand.
The slave, with speed, the queen's apartment sought,
And render'd up his charge, unknowing what he brought.
But when the cyphers, figur'd in each fold,
Her sister's melancholy story told
(Strange that she could!) with silence, she survey'd

The tragick piece, and without weeping read:
In such tumultuous haste her passions sprung,
They choak'd her voice, and quite disarm'd her tongue.
No room for female tears; the Furies rise,
Darting vindictive glances from her eyes;
And, stung with rage, she bounds from place to place,
While stern revenge sits low'ring in her face.
Now the triennial celebration came,
Observ'd to Bacchus by each Thracian dame;
When, in the privacies of night retir'd,
They act his rites, with sacred rapture fir'd:
By night, the tinkling cymbals ring around,
While the shrill notes from Rhodope resound;
By night, the queen, disguis'd, forsakes the court,
To mingle in the festival resort.
Leaves of the curling vine her temples shade,
And, with a circling wreath, adorn her head:
Adown her back the stag's rough spoils appear,
Light on her shoulder leans a cornel spear.
Thus, in the fury of the God conceal'd,
Procne her own mad headstrong passion veil'd;
Now, with her gang, to the thick wood she flies,
And with religious yellings fills the skies;
The fatal lodge, as 'twere by chance, she seeks,
And, thro' the bolted doors, an entrance breaks;
From thence, her sister snatching by the hand,
Mask'd like the ranting Bacchanalian band,
Within the limits of the court she drew,
Shading, with ivy green, her outward hue.
But Philomela, conscious of the place,
Felt new reviving pangs of her disgrace;
A shiv'ring cold prevail'd in ev'ry part,
And the chill'd blood ran trembling to her heart.
Soon as the queen a fit retirement found,
Stript of the garlands that her temples crown'd,
She strait unveil'd her blushing sister's face,
And fondly clasp'd her with a close embrace:
But, in confusion lost, th' unhappy maid,
With shame dejected, hung her drooping head,
As guilty of a crime that stain'd her sister's bed.
That speech, that should her injur'd virtue clear,
And make her spotless innocence appear,
Is now no more; only her hands, and eyes
Appeal, in signals, to the conscious skies.
In Procne's breast the rising passions boil,
And burst in anger with a mad recoil;
Her sister's ill-tim'd grief, with scorn, she blames,

Then, in these furious words her rage proclaims.
Tears, unavailing, but defer our time,
The stabbing sword must expiate the crime;
Or worse, if wit, on bloody vengeance bent,
A weapon more tormenting can invent.
O sister! I've prepar'd my stubborn heart,
To act some hellish, and unheard-of part;
Either the palace to surround with fire,
And see the villain in the flames expire;
Or, with a knife, dig out his cursed eyes,
Or, his false tongue with racking engines seize;
Or, cut away the part that injur'd you,
And, thro' a thousand wounds, his guilty soul pursue.
Tortures enough my passion has design'd,
But the variety distracts my mind.
A-while, thus wav'ring, stood the furious dame,
When Itys fondling to his mother came;
From him the cruel fatal hint she took,
She view'd him with a stern remorseless look:
Ah! but too like thy wicked sire, she said,
Forming the direful purpose in her head.
At this a sullen grief her voice suppress't,
While silent passions struggle in her breast.
Now, at her lap arriv'd, the flatt'ring boy
Salutes his parent with a smiling joy:
About her neck his little arms are thrown,
And he accosts her in a pratling tone.
Then her tempestuous anger was allay'd,
And in its full career her vengeance stay'd;
While tender thoughts, in spite of passion, rise,
And melting tears disarm her threat'ning eyes.
But when she found the mother's easy heart,
Too fondly swerving from th' intended part;
Her injur'd sister's face again she view'd:
And, as by turns surveying both she stood,
While this fond boy (she said) can thus express
The moving accents of his fond address;
Why stands my sister of her tongue bereft,
Forlorn, and sad, in speechless silence left?
O Procne, see the fortune of your house!
Such is your fate, when match'd to such a spouse!
Conjugal duty, if observ'd to him,
Would change from virtue, and become a crime;
For all respect to Tereus must debase
The noble blood of great Pandion's race.
Strait at these words, with big resentment fill'd,
Furious her look, she flew, and seiz'd her child;

Like a fell tigress of the savage kind,
That drags the tender suckling of the hind
Thro' India's gloomy groves, where Ganges laves
The shady scene, and rouls his streamy waves.
Now to a close apartment they were come,
Far off retir'd within the spacious dome;
When Procne, on revengeful mischief bent,
Home to his heart a piercing ponyard sent.
Itys, with rueful cries, but all too late,
Holds out his hands, and deprecates his fate;
Still at his mother's neck he fondly aims,
And strives to melt her with endearing names;
Yet still the cruel mother perseveres,
Nor with concern his bitter anguish hears.
This might suffice; but Philomela too
Across his throat a shining curtlass drew.
Then both, with knives, dissect each quiv'ring part,
And carve the butcher'd limbs with cruel art;
Which, whelm'd in boiling cauldrons o'er the fire,
Or turn'd on spits, in steamy smoak aspire:
While the long entries, with their slipp'ry floor,
Run down in purple streams of clotted gore.
Ask'd by his wife to this inhuman feast,
Tereus unknowingly is made a guest:
Whilst she her plot the better to disguise,
Styles it some unknown mystick sacrifice;
And such the nature of the hallow'd rite,
The wife her husband only could invite,
The slaves must all withdraw, and be debarr'd the sight.
Tereus, upon a throne of antique state,
Loftily rais'd, before the banquet sate;
And glutton like, luxuriously pleas'd,
With his own flesh his hungry maw appeas'd.
Nay, such a blindness o'er his senses falls,
That he for Itys to the table calls.
When Procne, now impatient to disclose
The joy that from her full revenge arose,
Cries out, in transports of a cruel mind,
Within your self your Itys you may find.
Still, at this puzzling answer, with surprise,
Around the room he sends his curious eyes;
And, as he still inquir'd, and call'd aloud,
Fierce Philomela, all besmear'd with blood,
Her hands with murder stain'd, her spreading hair
Hanging dishevel'd with a ghastly air,
Stept forth, and flung full in the tyrant's face
The head of Itys, goary as it was:

Nor ever so much to use her tongue,
And with a just reproach to vindicate her wrong.
The Thracian monarch from the table flings,
While with his cries the vaulted parlour rings;
His imprecations eccho down to Hell,
And rouze the snaky Furies from their Stygian cell.
One while he labours to disgorge his breast,
And free his stomach from the cursed feast;
Then, weeping o'er his lamentable doom,
He styles himself his son's sepulchral tomb.
Now, with drawn sabre, and impetuous speed,
In close pursuit he drives Pandion's breed;
Whose nimble feet spring with so swift a force
Across the fields, they seem to wing their course.
And now, on real wings themselves they raise,
And steer their airy flight by diff'rent ways;
One to the woodland's shady covert hies,
Around the smoaky roof the other flies;
Whose feathers yet the marks of murder stain,
Where stampt upon her breast, the crimson spots remain.
Tereus, through grief, and haste to be reveng'd,
Shares the like fate, and to a bird is chang'd:
Fix'd on his head, the crested plumes appear,
Long is his beak, and sharpen'd like a spear;
Thus arm'd, his looks his inward mind display,
And, to a lapwing turn'd, he fans his way.
Exceeding trouble, for his children's fate,
Shorten'd Pandion's days, and chang'd his date;
Down to the shades below, with sorrow spent,
An earlier, unexpected ghost he went.

Stories of Cúchulainn of the Red Guard

THE ULSTER CYCLE, also known as the Red Branch Cycle, is compiled of tales of Ulster's traditional heroes, chief among whom is Cúchulainn (pronounced 'Koo khul-in'), arguably the most important war-champion in ancient Irish literature. An account of his birth dating from the ninth century is retold here, although a great many variations exist.

From the age of six, Cúchulainn displays his supernatural ancestry and astounding strength. While still a child, he slays the terrifying hound of Culann. As a mere youth he is sent to train with the Knights of the Red Guard under Scathach and he alone is entrusted with the diabolical weapon known as the Gae Bolg. Later, he single-handedly defends Ulster against Queen Medb (pronounced 'Maev') while the rest of the province sleeps under the charm of Macha. His most notable exploits spanning his hectic warrior's life up until his early death are recounted here.

Cúchulainn is said to have fallen at the battle of Muirthemne, *c.* 12 BC. He was finally overcome by his old enemy Lugaid, aided by the monstrous daughters of Calatin. As death approaches, Cúchulainn insists that he be allowed to bind himself upright to a pillar-stone. With his dying breath, he gives a loud, victorious laugh and when Lugaid attempts to behead his corpse, the enemy's right hand is severed as the sword of Cúchulainn falls heavily upon it. The hero's death is avenged by Conall the Victorious, but with the defeat of Cúchulainn, the end is sealed to the valiant reign of the Red Guard Knights in ancient Irish legend.

The Birth of Cúchulainn

King Conchobar mac Nessa was ruler of Ulster at the time when Cúchulainn, the mightiest hero of the Red Guard, came to be born. It happened that one day, the King's sister Dechtire, whom he cherished above all others, disappeared from the palace without warning, taking fifty of her maidens and her most valuable possessions with her. Although Conchobar summoned every known person in the court before him for questioning, no explanation could be discovered for his sister's departure. For three long years, the King's messengers scoured the country in search of Dechtire, but not one among them ever brought him news of her whereabouts.

At last, one summer's morning, a strange flock of birds descended on the palace gardens of Emain Macha and began to gorge themselves on every fruit tree and vegetable patch in sight. Greatly disturbed by the greed and destruction he witnessed, the King immediately gathered together a party of his hunters, and they set off in pursuit of the birds, armed with powerful slings and the sharpest of arrows. Fergus mac Roig, Conchobar's chief huntsman and guide, was among the group, as were his trusted warriors Amergin and Bricriu. As the day wore on, they found themselves being lured a great distance southward by the birds, across Sliab Fuait, towards the Plain of Gossa, and with every step taken they grew more angry and frustrated that not one arrow had yet managed to ruffle a single feather.

Nightfall had overtaken them before they had even noticed the light begin to fade, and the King, realizing that they would never make it safely back to the palace, gave the order for Fergus and some of the others to go out in search of a place of lodging for the party. Before long, Fergus came upon a small hut whose firelight was extremely inviting, and he approached and knocked politely on the door. He received a warm and hearty welcome from the old married couple within, and they at once offered him food and a comfortable bed for the evening. But Fergus would not accept their kind hospitality, knowing that his companions were still abroad without shelter.

'Then they are all invited to join us,' said the old woman, and as she bustled about, preparing food and wine for her visitors, Fergus went off to deliver his good news to Conchobar and the rest of the group.

Bricriu had also set off in search of accommodation, and as he had walked to the opposite side of the woodlands, he was certain that he heard the gentle sound of harp music. Instinctively drawn towards the sweet melody, he followed the winding path through the trees until he came upon a regal mansion standing proudly on the banks of the river Boyne. He timidly approached the noble structure, but there was no need for him to knock, since the door was already ajar and a young maiden, dressed in a flowing gown of shimmering gold, stood in the entrance hall ready to greet him. She was accompanied by a young man of great stature and splendid appearance who smiled warmly at Bricriu and extended his hand in friendship:

'You are indeed welcome,' said the handsome warrior, 'we have been waiting patiently for your visit to our home this day.'

'Come inside, Bricriu,' said the beautiful maiden, 'why is it that you linger out of doors?'

'Can it be that you do not recognize the woman who appears before you?' asked the warrior.

'Her great beauty stirs a memory from the past,' replied Bricriu, 'but I cannot recall anything more at present.'

'You see before you Dechtire, sister of Conchobar mac Nessa,' said the warrior, 'and the fifty maidens you have been seeking these three years are also in this house. They have today visited Emain Macha in the form of birds in order to lure you here.'

'Then I must go at once to the King and inform him of what I have discovered,' answered Bricriu, 'for he will be overjoyed to know that Dechtire has been found and will be eager for her to accompany him back to the palace where there will be great feasting and celebration.'

He hurried back through the woods to rejoin the King and his companions. And when Conchobar heard the news of Bricriu's discovery, he could scarcely contain his delight and was immediately anxious to be reunited with his sister. A messenger was sent forth to invite Dechtire and the warrior to share in their evening meal, and a place was hurriedly prepared for the couple at the table inside the welcoming little hut. But Dechtire was already suffering the first pangs of childbirth by the time Conchobar's messenger arrived with his invitation. She excused herself by saying that she was tired and agreed instead to meet up with her brother at dawn on the following morning.

When the first rays of sunshine had brightened the heavens, Conchobar arose from his bed and began to prepare himself for Dechtire's arrival. He had passed a very peaceful night and went in search of Fergus and the others in the happiest of moods. Approaching the place where his men were sleeping, he became convinced that he had heard the stifled cries of an infant. Again, as he drew nearer, the sound was repeated. He stooped down and began to examine a small, strange bundle lying on the ground next to Bricriu. As he unwrapped it, the bundle began to wriggle in his arms and a tiny pink hand revealed itself from beneath the cloth covering.

Dechtire did not appear before her brother that morning, or on any morning to follow. But she had left the King a great gift – a newborn male child fathered by the noble warrior, Lugh of the Long Arm, a child destined to achieve great things for Ulster. Conchobar took the infant back to the palace with him and gave him to his sister Finnchoem to look after. Finnchoem reared the child alongside her own son Conall and grew to love him as if he had been born of her own womb. He was given the name of Setanta, a name he kept until the age of six, and the druid Morann made the following prophecy over him:

'His praise will be sung by the most valorous knights,
And he will win the love of all
His deeds will be known throughout the land
For he will answer Ulster's call.'

How Setanta Won the Name of Cúchulainn

Within the court of Emain Macha, there existed an élite group of boy athletes whose outstanding talents filled the King with an overwhelming sense of pride and joy. It had become a regular part of Conchobar's daily routine to watch these boys at their various games and exercises, for nothing brought him greater pleasure than to witness their development into some of the finest sportsmen in Erin. He had named the group the Boy-Corps, and the sons of the most powerful chieftains and princes of the land were among its members, having proven their skill and dexterity in a wide and highly challenging range of sporting events.

Before Setanta had grown to the age of six, he had already expressed his desire before the King to be enrolled in the Boy-Corps. At first, Conchobar refused to treat the request seriously, since his nephew was a great deal younger than any other member, but the boy persisted, and the King at last agreed to allow him to try his hand. It was decided that he should join in a game of hurling one morning, and when he had dressed himself in the martial uniform of the Boy-Corps, he was presented with a brass hurley almost his own height off the ground.

A team of twelve boys was assembled to play against him and they sneered mockingly at the young lad before them, imagining they would have little difficulty keeping the ball out of his reach. But as soon as the game started up, Setanta dived in among the boys and took hold of the ball, striking it with his hurley and driving it a powerful distance to the other end of the field where it sailed effortlessly through the goal-posts. And after this first onslaught, he made it impossible for his opponents to retrieve the ball from him, so that within a matter of minutes he had scored fifty goals against the twelve of them. The whole corps looked on in utter amazement and the King, who had been eagerly following the game, was flushed with excitement. His nephew's show of prowess was truly astonishing and he began to reproach himself for having originally set out to humour the boy.

'Have Setanta brought before me,' he said to his steward, 'for such an impressive display of heroic strength and impertinent courage deserves a very special reward.'

Now on that particular day, Conchobar had been invited to attend a great feast at the house of Culann, the most esteemed craftsman and smith in the kingdom. A thought had suddenly entered Conchobar's head that it would be a very fitting reward for Setanta to share in such a banquet, for no small boy had ever before accompanied the King and the Knights of the Red Guard on such a prestigious outing. It was indeed a great honour and one Setanta readily acknowledged. He desperately wanted to accept the invitation, but only one thing held him back. He could not suppress the desire of a true sportsman to conclude the game he had begun and pleaded with the King to allow him to do so:

'I have so thoroughly enjoyed the first half of my game with the Boy-Corps,' he told the King, 'that I am loathe to cut it short. I promise to follow when the game is over if you will allow me this great liberty.'

And seeing the excitement and keenness shining in the boy's eyes, Conchobar was more than happy to agree to this request. He instructed Setanta to follow on before nightfall and gave him directions to the house of Culann. Then he set off for the banquet, eager to relate the morning's stirring events to the rest of Culann's house guests.

It was early evening by the time the royal party arrived at the dwelling place of Culann. A hundred blazing torches guided them towards the walls of the fort and a carpet of fresh green rushes formed a mile-long path leading to the stately entrance. The great hall was already lavishly prepared for the banquet and the sumptuous aroma of fifty suckling pigs turning on the spit filled every room of the house. Culann himself came forward to greet each one of his guests and he bowed respectfully before the King and led him to his place of honour at the centre of the largest table. Once his royal guest had taken his seat, the order was given for the wine to be poured and the laughter and music followed soon afterwards. And when it was almost time for the food to be served, Culann glanced around him one last time to make certain that all his visitors had arrived.

'I think we need wait no longer,' he said to the King. 'My guests are all present and it will now be safe to untie the hound who keeps watch over my home each night. There is not a hound in Erin who could equal mine for fierceness and strength, and even if a hundred men should attempt to do battle with him, every last one would be torn to pieces in his powerful jaws.'

'Release him then, and let him guard this place,' said Conchobar, quite forgetting that his young nephew had not yet joined the party. 'My men are all present and our appetites have been whetted by our long journey here. Let us delay no longer and begin the feasting at once.'

And after the gong had been sounded, a procession of elegantly-clad attendants entered the room carrying gilded trays of roasted viands and freshly harvested fruit and vegetables, which they set down on the table before the King and the hungry warriors of the Red Guard.

It was just at this moment that the young Setanta came to the green of Culann's fort carrying with him the hurley and the ball that had brought him victory against the Boy-Corps. As the boy drew nearer to the entrance of the fort, the hound's ears pricked up warily and it began to growl and bark in such a way as to be heard throughout the entire countryside. The whole company within the great hall heard the animal snarling ferociously and raced outdoors to discover what exactly it was that had disturbed the creature. They saw before them a young boy, who showed little sign of fear as he stood facing the fierce dog with gaping jaws. The child was without any obvious weapon of defence against the animal, but as it charged at him, he thrust his playing ball forcefully down its throat causing it to choke for breath. Then he seized the hound by the hind legs and dashed its head against a rock until blood spewed from its mouth and the life had gone out of it.

Those who witnessed this extraordinary confrontation hoisted the lad triumphantly into the air and bore him on their shoulders to where Conchobar and Culann stood waiting. The King, although more than gratified by the boy's demonstration of courage, was also much relieved to know that Setanta was safe. Turning to his host, he began to express his joy, but it was immediately apparent that Culann could share none of Conchobar's happiness. He walked instead towards the body of his dead hound and fell into a mournful silence as he stroked the lifeless form, remembering the loyal and obedient animal who had given its life to protect its master's property. Seeing Culann bent over the body of his faithful dog, Setanta came forward without hesitation and spoke the following words of comfort to him:

'If in all of Erin there is a hound to replace the one you have lost, I will find it, nurture it and place it in your service when it is fit for action. But, in the meantime, I myself will perform the duty of that hound and will guard your land and your possessions with the utmost pride.'

There was not one among the gathering who remained unmoved by this gesture of contrition and friendship. Culann, for his part, was overcome with gratitude and appreciation and declared that Setanta should bear the name of Cúchulainn, 'Culann's Hound', in remembrance of his first great act of valour. And so, at the age of six, the boy Setanta was named Cúchulainn, a name by which he was known and feared until the end of his days.

The Tragedy of Cúchulainn and Connla

As soon as Cúchulainn had reached the appropriate age to begin his formal training as a Knight of the Red Guard, it was decided at the court of Conchobar mac Nessa that he should depart for the Land of Shadows, where Scathach, the wisest, strongest, most celebrated woman-warrior, had prepared the path of his instruction in the feats of war. The stronghold of Scathach lay in a mysterious land overseas, beyond the bounds of the Plain of Ill-luck. It could only be reached by crossing the Perilous Glen, a journey very few had survived, for the Glen teemed with the fiercest of goblins lying in wait to devour hopeful young pilgrims. But even if a youth managed to come through the Perilous Glen unharmed, he had then to cross the Bridge of Leaps, underneath which the sea boiled and hissed furiously. This bridge was the highest and narrowest ever built and it spanned the steepest gorge in the western world. Only a handful of people had ever crossed it, but those who did were privileged to become the highest-ranking scholars of Scathach and the very finest of Erin's warriors.

Within a week of leaving the court of Emain Macha, Cúchulainn had arrived at the Plain of Ill-luck and although he had already suffered many trials along the way, he knew in his heart that the worst still lay ahead. As he gazed out over the vast stretch of barren land he was obliged to traverse, he grew despondent, for he could see that one half was covered in a porous clay which would certainly cause his feet to stick fast, while the other was overgrown with long, coarse, straw-coloured grass, whose pointed blades were designed to slash a man's limbs to pieces. And as he stood crestfallen, attempting to decide which of the two routes would prove less hazardous, he noticed a young man approaching on horseback from the east. The very appearance of the rider lifted Cúchulainn's spirits, but when he observed that the youth's countenance shone as splendidly as the golden orb of the sun (though he does not reveal himself, this is, of course, Cúchulainn's father, Lugh of the Long Arm), he immediately felt hopeful and reassured once more. The two began to converse together and Cúchulainn enquired of the young man which track he considered the best to follow across the Plain of Ill-luck. The youth pondered the question awhile and then, reaching beneath his mantel, he handed Cúchulainn a leather pouch containing a small golden wheel.

'Roll this before you as you cross the quagmire,' he told Cúchulainn, 'and it will scorch a path in the earth which you may follow safely to the stronghold of Scathach.'

Cúchulainn gratefully received the gift and bid farewell to the youth. And after he had set the wheel in motion, it led him safely, just as the young rider had promised, across the Plain of Ill-luck and through the Perilous Glen until he reached the outskirts of the Land of Shadows.

It was not long before he happened upon a small camp in the heart of the woodlands where the scholars of Scathach, the sons of the noblest princes and warriors of Erin, were busy at their training. He recognized at once his friend Ferdia, son of the Firbolg, Daman, and the two men embraced each other warmly. After Cúchulainn had told Ferdia all of the latest news from Ulster, he began to question his friend about the great woman-warrior who was set to educate him in arms.

'She dwells on the island beyond the Bridge of Leaps,' Ferdia told him, 'which no man, not even myself, has ever managed to cross. It is said that when we have achieved a certain level of valour, Scathach herself will teach us to cross the bridge, and she will also teach us to thrust the Gae Bolg, a weapon reserved for only the bravest of champions.'

'Then I must prove to her that I am already valorous,' replied Cúchulainn, 'by crossing that bridge without any assistance from her.'

'You are unlikely to succeed,' warned Ferdia, 'for if a man steps on one end of the bridge, the middle rises up and flings him into the waters below where the mouths of sea-monsters lie open, ready to swallow him whole.'

But these words of caution merely fired Cúchulainn's ambition to succeed in his quest. Retiring to a quiet place, he sat down to recover his strength from his long journey and waited anxiously for evening to fall.

The scholars of Scathach had all gathered to watch Cúchulainn attempt to cross the Bridge of Leaps and they began to jeer him loudly when after the third attempt he had failed to reach the far side. The mocking chorus that greeted his failure greatly infuriated the young warrior but prompted him at the same time to put all his strength and ability into one final, desperate leap. And at the fourth leap, which came to be known as 'the hero's salmon-leap', Cúchulainn landed on the ground of the island at the far side of the bridge. Lifting himself off the ground, he strode triumphantly to the fortress of Scathach and beat loudly on the entrance door with the shaft of his spear. Scathach appeared before him, wonder-struck that a boy so young and fresh of face had demonstrated such courage and vigour. She agreed at once to accept him as her pupil, promising to teach him all the feats of war if he would pledge himself to remain under her tuition and guidance for a period not less than a full year and a day.

During the time that Cúchulainn dwelt with Scathach, he grew to become her favourite pupil, for he acquired each new skill with the greatest of ease and approached every additional challenge set him with the utmost enthusiasm. Scathach had never before deemed any of her students good enough to be trained in the use of the Gae Bolg, but she now considered Cúchulainn a champion worthy of this special honour and presented him one morning with the terrible weapon. Then she instructed him on how to use it and explained that it should be hurled with the foot, and upon entering the enemy it would fill every inch of his body with deadly barbs, killing him almost instantly.

It was while Cúchulainn remained under Scathach's supervision that the Land of Shadows came under attack from the fiercest of tribal warriors, led by the Princess Aífe. After several weeks of bloody battle, during which no solution to the conflict could be reached, it was agreed that Scathach and Aífe should face each other in single combat. On hearing this news, Cúchulainn expressed the gravest concern and was adamant that he would accompany Scathach to the place where the contest was due to take place. Yet Scathach feared that something untoward might befall her young protégé, and she placed a sleeping-potion in Cúchulainn's drink with the power to prevent him waking until she was safely reached her meeting place with Aífe. But the potion, which would have lasted twenty-four hours in any other man, held Cúchulainn in a slumber for less than one hour and when he awoke he seized his weapon and went forth to join the war against Aífe.

And not only did he slay three of Aífe's finest warriors in the blink of an eyelid, he insisted on trading places with Scathach and facing the tribal-leader by himself. But before going into battle against her, he asked Scathach what it was that Aífe prized above all other things.

'What she most loves are her two horses, her chariot, and her charioteer,' she informed Cúchulainn. So he set off to meet Aífe, forearmed with this knowledge.

The two opponents met on the Path of Feats and entered into a vicious combat there. They had only clashed swords three or four times however, before Aífe delivered Cúchulainn a mighty blow, shattering his powerful sword to the hilt and leaving him defenceless. Seeing the damage to his weapon, Cúchulainn at once cried out:

'What a terrible fate that charioteer beyond has met with. Look, his chariot and his two beautiful horses have fallen down the glen.'

And as Aífe glanced around, Cúchulainn managed to seize her by the waist, squeezing firmly with his hands until she could hardly breathe and had dropped her sword at his feet. Then he carried her over his shoulder back to the camp of Scathach and flung her on the ground where he placed his knife at her throat.

'Do not take my life from me, Cúchulainn,' Aífe begged, 'and I will agree to whatever you demand.'

It was soon settled between Scathach and Cúchulainn that Aífe should agree to a lasting peace and, as proof of her commitment, they pronounced that she should bind herself over to remain a full year as Cúchulainn's hostage in the Land of Shadows. And after nine months, Aífe gave birth to a son whom she named Connla, for she and Cúchulainn had grown to become the best of friends and the closest of lovers with the passing of time.

Now sadly, the day arrived for Cúchulainn to depart the Land of Shadows, and knowing that Aífe would not accompany him, he spoke the following wish for his son's future:

'I give you this golden ring for our child,' he told Aífe. 'And when he has grown so that the ring fits his finger, send him away from here to seek out his father in Erin.

'Counsel him on my behalf to keep his identity secret,' he added, 'so that he may stand proud on his own merit and never refuse a combat, or turn out of his way for any man.'

Then after he had uttered these words, Cúchulainn took his leave of Aífe and made his way back to his own land and his people.

Seven years had passed, during which time Cúchulainn had chosen Emer, daughter of Forgall, one of the finest maidens in Ulster, to become his wife, and the two lived a very happy life together. He rarely thought of Aífe and the son he had left behind in the Land of Shadows, for he had also risen to become captain of the House of the Red Branch of Conchobar mac Nessa and was by far the busiest and most respected warrior in the kingdom.

It was at this time, however, that Connla, son of Cúchulainn, set out on his journey to be reunited with his father in Erin, approaching her shores on the precise day that all the great warriors and noble lords of Ulster were assembled for an annual ceremony on the Strand of Footprints. They were very much surprised to see a little boat of bronze appear on the crest of the waves, and in it a small boy clutching a pair of gilded oars, steering his way steadily towards them. The boy seemed not to notice them and every so often he stopped rowing and bent down to pick up a stone from the heap he had collected at the bottom of the boat. Then, putting one of these stones into a sling, he launched a splendid shot at the sea-birds above, bringing the creatures down, stunned, but unharmed, one after another, in a manner far too quick for the naked eye to perceive. The whole party looked on in amazement as the lad performed these wonderful feats, but the King soon grew uncomfortable at the spectacle he witnessed and called Condere, son of Eochaid, to him:

'This boy's arrival here does not bode well for us,' said the King. 'For if grown-up men of his kind were to follow in his wake, they would grind us all to dust. Let someone go to meet him and inform him that he is not welcome on Erin's soil.'

And as the boy came to moor his boat, Condere approached him and delivered Conchobar's message.

'Go and tell your King,' said the boy, 'that even if everyone among you here had the strength of a hundred men, and you all came forward to challenge me, you would not be able to persuade me to turn back from this place.'

Hearing these words, the King grew even more concerned and he called Conall the Victorious to him:

'This lad mocks us,' Conchobar told him, 'and it is now time for a show of force against him.'

So Conall was sent against the boy, but as he approached the lad put a stone in his sling and sent it whizzing with a noise like thunder through the air. It struck Conall on the forehead, knocking him backwards to the ground and before he could even think about rising to his feet, the boy had bound his arms and legs with the strap from his shield. And in this manner, the youth made a mockery of the host of Ulster, challenging man after man to confront him, and succeeding on every occasion to defeat his opponents with little or no effort.

At last, when King Conchobar could suffer this humiliation no longer, he sent a messenger to Dundalk to the house of Cúchulainn requesting that he come and do battle against the young boy whom Conall the Victorious could not even manage to overcome. And hearing that her husband was prepared to meet this challenge, Emer, his wife, went and pleaded with him not to go forward to the Strand of Footprints:

'Do not go against the boy,' she begged Cúchulainn, 'since the great courage he possesses has convinced me that he is Connla, son of Aífe. Hear my voice, Cúchulainn, and do not go forward to murder your only child.'

'Even if he were my son,' replied Cúchulainn, 'I would slay him for the honour of Ulster.'

And he ordered his chariot to be yoked without further delay and set off in the direction of the strand.

Soon afterwards, he came upon the young boy sitting in his boat polishing stones and calmly awaiting his next opponent. Cúchulainn strode towards him, demanding to know his name and lineage. But the boy would not reveal his identity or the slightest detail of the land of his birth. Then Cúchulainn lost patience with him and they began to exchange blows. With one daring stroke, the boy cut off a lock of Cúchulainn's hair, and as he watched it fall to the ground, the older warrior became greatly enraged.

'Enough of this child's play,' he shouted and, dragging the boy from the boat, he began to wrestle with him in the water. But the boy's strength was astonishing and he managed twice to push Cúchulainn's head beneath the waves, almost causing him to drown. And it was on the third occasion that this occurred, when Cúchulainn gasped helplessly for air, that he remembered the Gae Bolg which Scathach had entrusted him with, and he flung it at the boy through the water. At once, the boy loosened his powerful hold and reached agonizingly towards his stomach, where the blood flowed freely from the vast gaping wound the weapon had made there.

'That is a weapon Scathach has not yet taught me to use,' said the boy. 'Carry me now from the water, for I am gravely injured.'

And as Cúchulainn bore the boy in his arms towards the shore he noticed a golden ring on his middle finger.

'It is true then,' he murmured sadly to himself, and set the boy down on the ground before the King and the men of Ulster.

'You see here before you my son,' Cúchulainn announced solemnly, 'the child I have mortally wounded for the good of Ulster.'

'Alas, it is so,' spoke Connla in a feeble voice, 'and I wish with all my heart that I could remain with you to the end of five years. For in that time, I would grow among you and conquer the world before you on every side, so that soon you would rule as far as Rome. But since this cannot be, let me now take my leave of the most famous among you before I die.'

So, one after another, the most courageous knights of the Red Guard were brought before Connla and he placed his arms around the neck of each of them and embraced them affectionately. Then Cúchulainn came forward and his son kissed his father tenderly before drawing his last breath. And as he closed his eyes, a great lament was raised among them and they dug a grave for the boy and set a splendid pillar-stone at its head. Connla, son of Aífe, was the only son Cúchulainn ever had and he lived to regret for the rest of his days that he had destroyed so precious a gift.

The Combat of Ferdia and Cúchulainn

Beyond the borders of Ulster in the province of Connacht, there ruled a spirited and domineering queen named Medb, daughter of Eochaid Fedlech, whose husband, King Ailill, was the meekest and gentlest of creatures. Medb's nature was such that whatever she desired she took for her own, and whatever law displeased her, she refused to obey, so that her husband gave her whatever she demanded and nothing was ever too great a task for him to complete on her behalf. Medb was also the strongest and mightiest of warriors and she had gathered together a powerful army, convinced that one day she would conquer the whole land of Erin.

One evening as Medb and her husband lay together, they began to count up and compare their numerous possessions, for it was one of Medb's favourite entertainments to ridicule Ailill by proving that she had acquired far more treasures and wealth than he had over the years. Weapons, rings and jewellery were counted out, as well as chariots, horses, mansions and plots of land, but each of them was found to possess precisely the same amount as the other. So they began to count the herds of cattle and sheep that roamed the pastures beyond the walls of the castle and it was then that Ailill remembered the Bull of Finnbennach and began to tease his wife about the animal, reminding her of how the bull had deserted her herd in favour of his because it refused to remain in the hands of a woman. As soon as Medb heard these words, all of her property lost its value for her, and she grew adamant that she would soon find a bull to equal the Bull of Finnbennach even if she had to scour the entire countryside for it and bring it back to Connacht by force.

Mac Roth, the King's steward, was summoned to appear before Medb and when she questioned him on the whereabouts of such a bull, he was able to tell her without any hesitation exactly where the best specimen in the country might be found:

'It belongs to Daire mac Fiachna in the province of Ulster,' he told the Queen. 'It is known as the Brown Bull of Cooley and is regarded as the finest beast in the whole of Erin.'

'Then you must go to the son of Fiachna and ask him for the loan of the bull for a year,' replied Medb, 'informing him that at the end of this time, the beast will be safely returned to him, together with fifty of the finest heifers my kingdom has to offer. And if Daire chooses to bring the bull here himself, he may add to his reward a measure of land equalling the size of his present domain in Ulster and a splendid war chariot worthy of the bravest of Connacht's warriors.'

On the following morning, a group of nine foot-messengers led by mac Roth set off in the direction of Ulster, carrying with them a number of gifts from Queen Medb to the owner of the bull, including an oak chest loaded with gold and silver ornaments and several decorated bronze flagons filled with the finest mead in the land. The mere sight of such a treasure-laden party approaching the fort of Daire mac Fiachna raised the spirits of all who set eyes on them and a very warm welcome was lavished on the men. Then Daire himself came forward to greet the party and enquired of them the purpose of their journey to his home. Mac Roth began to tell him of the squabble between Medb and Ailill and of how the Queen had decided that she must quickly find a bull to match the impressive Bull of Finnbennach. Flattered that his own beast had achieved such fame in Connacht, Daire was immediately disposed to help Queen Medb as best he could, but when he heard of the generous reward he would receive in return for the loan of his property, he was well pleased with himself and gave the order at once for the Bull of Cooley to be prepared for its journey to Connacht the next day.

The evening was spent feasting and drinking and a happy atmosphere prevailed for a time as the men of the two provinces exchanged friendly conversation. But as the wine flowed, the tongues of Queen Medb's messengers began to loosen and in the company of their hosts they began to brag of their army's great strength:

'It is just as well for Daire,' boasted one of Medb's envoys, 'that he has surrendered the beast willingly to us. For if he had refused to do so, the Queen's mighty army would have marched on Ulster and taken the bull from him without any trouble at all.'

When Daire's men heard these offensive remarks, they went straightaway to their master's quarters and demanded that he avenge such a dreadful insult. Mac Roth was immediately summoned to appear before Daire who angrily informed him of the conversation that had been overheard.

'Go back to your Queen,' said Daire, 'and tell her that she shall never take from me by foul means what she cannot win by fair. Let Medb and Ailill invade Ulster if they dare, for we are well equipped to meet the challenge.'

Before the break of day, Medb's messengers had set off for Connacht to deliver the unhappy tidings to their Queen. But when Medb saw that they had not returned with the Brown Bull of Cooley, she did not fly into the rage they had expected. Instead, she spoke calmly to mac Roth:

'I have foreseen this result,' she told him. 'Your dispute with the son of Fiachna is of little consequence, for I have always known that if the Brown Bull of Cooley was not given willingly, he would be taken by force. That time is now arrived, and taken he shall be!'

So began the Queen of Connacht's great war on Ulster, one of the bloodiest wars the country had ever before endured. From every corner of Erin came the allies of Medb and Ailill, including Fraech, son of Fidach, and Calatin, accompanied by his twenty-seven sons. Warriors of great renown from the provinces of Leinster and Munster swelled the numbers of Medb's armed legions, and they were joined by many heroic Ulstermen, among them Fergus mac Roy and Cormac, son of Conchobar, who had defected from their own army, unhappy with their King's leadership.

Not a day or a night passed without a fierce and fiery combat between the armies of Connacht and Ulster. Rivers and streams ran crimson with blood and the bodies of the slain littered the emerald hills and plains. Medb was not slow to display her true worth as a warrior in her own right and Fergus, her chief scout, proved himself a most loyal and courageous comrade in arms. Yet there was none among Medb's great army who could emulate the feats of one particular Ulster warrior, a youthful figure who seemed utterly invincible and who drove himself against them time and time again, bursting with renewed vitality and strength on each occasion.

Cúchulainn, leader of Ulster's Red Guard, was well known to both Fergus and Cormac, but he had grown stronger and more powerful than they had ever imagined possible during their brief time of exile. And as they observed his powers of command and his exceptional skill on the battlefield, they became increasingly alarmed and went before the Queen to warn her that she was faced with no ordinary opponent. Medb grew worried at this news and took counsel with the most prominent figures of her army. After some deliberation, it was decided that her most valiant warrior should be sent to do battle against Cúchulainn. The son of Daman, known as Ferdia, was nominated for this task, for he had been trained alongside Cúchulainn under the great woman-warrior Scathach in the Land of Shadows and had risen to become Connacht's champion warrior, a man feared and respected by all who encountered him.

Nothing had ever yet challenged the deep bond of friendship formed between Ferdia and Cúchulainn during their time together in the Land of Shadows. The love and respect the two men felt for each other had remained constant over the years, and whenever they found occasion to be together, it was not unusual for people to mistake them for brothers. When Ferdia discovered what Medb demanded of him, he was greatly disturbed, and though he was loathe to oppose the wishes of his sovereign, he immediately refused the Queen's request and dismissed her messengers. Then Medb sent her druids and men of poetry to Ferdia's tent, instructing them to recite the most savage and mocking verses in the loudest of voices for everybody to hear.

It was for the sake of his own honour that Ferdia agreed to meet with Medb and Ailill without any further delay. The King and Queen were more than delighted to receive him and Medb wasted no time reeling off the numerous rewards Ferdia could hope to receive if he would only obey her simple wish. But Ferdia showed no interest in the riches that were intended for him, so that Medb grew more and more angry and frustrated. She had little or nothing to lose by playing her one last card and with a tone of false resignation she addressed Ferdia once more:

'It must be true what Cúchulainn has said of you,' said Medb slyly. 'He said that you feared death by his hands and that you would be wise not to go against him. Perhaps it is just as well that the two of you do not meet.'

On hearing this, Ferdia could scarcely contain his anger:

'It was unjust of Cúchulainn to say such a thing,' he roared. 'He well knows that it is not cowardice, but love, that prevents me facing him. So it is settled then. Tomorrow I will go forth to his camp and raise my weapon against him.'

But even as he spoke these words, a mood of gloom and despair descended upon Ferdia and he walked out into the black night, his head bowed in sadness. His closest companions and servants were also overcome with grief to discover what it was that Ferdia was compelled to do, for each was troubled by the knowledge that one of the two great champion warriors of Erin would fail to return home alive.

Word had soon reached Cúchulainn that Medb had chosen his dearest friend to face him in combat and, as he watched Ferdia's war chariot approach, he was forced to acknowledge in his own mind that he would much rather fall by his friend's weapon than slay Ferdia with his own. Yet, at the same time, he could not fully understand why his fosterbrother had so easily given into the wishes of Queen Medb. The betrayal he felt could not be ignored and he prepared himself to greet Ferdia with a degree of caution and reserve. As Ferdia stood down from his chariot, Cúchulainn did not rush forward to embrace him as he would have done in the past, but remained at a distance, waiting for his friend to make the first gesture of friendship.

'I wish that we could have met again in more favourable circumstances,' said Ferdia. 'With all my heart I long to embrace you, old friend.'

'I once would have trusted such words,' answered Cúchulainn, 'but I no longer place any trust in what you say when I know that you have abandoned our friendship for the sake of a treacherous queen and the rewards she no doubt promised you.'

'I see that treason has overcome our love,' replied Ferdia sadly, 'but it is just as well that you think this way. It is best not to remember our friendship, but to meet each other as true enemies of war.'

And so they began to choose the weapons they would use against each other and it was agreed that they would begin the day's fighting with small javelins. They hurled these at each other, backwards and forwards through the air with great energy and speed, but by the close of day, not one spear had pierced the shield of either champion. As nightfall approached, they called a truce, and agreed to resume combat with different weapons at dawn on the following morning.

On the second day, Cúchulainn and Ferdia took up the fight once more, remaining seated in their chariots as they cast heavy, broad-bladed spears at each other across the ford from noon until sundown. But on this day, they both suffered many wounds that stained their flesh red with blood. When they had grown weary of the battle, they again agreed to stop fighting until morning and, placing their weapons in the hands of their servants, they moved towards each other and kissed and embraced warmly in remembrance of their friendship. Their horses shared the same paddock that evening and their charioteers gathered round the same fire. Healing herbs were laid on their wounds and they both rested until daybreak.

As the third day of combat was about to commence and the two men stood opposite each other once more, Cúchulainn was suddenly struck by the change which seemed to have occurred overnight in his friend. Ferdia's brow was now deeply furrowed and his eyes reflected a deep, dark sadness. He no longer held himself upright and he lurched forward wearily to meet his opponent. Filled with pity and sorrow, Cúchulainn pleaded with Ferdia to abandon the fighting, but his friend merely shook his head, insisting that he must fulfil his contract with Queen Medb and King Ailill. They proceeded to choose their weapons and armed themselves with full-length shields and hard-smiting swords. Then they began to strike each other savagely and viciously until they had each carved great wedges of flesh from the other's shoulder-blades and thighs. Still the combat could not be resolved and they decided to part once more for the evening, their bodies torn to shreds and their friendship shattered irreparably. And on this occasion, no kiss was exchanged between them, no curing herbs were exchanged, and their horses and charioteers slept in separate quarters.

As the sun was about to rise on the fourth morning, Ferdia arose and walked out alone to the ford of combat. He wore the jaded, sorrowful expression of a man who senses death close at hand and he began to arm himself with particular care and attention. He knew instinctively that the decisive day of the battle had arrived and that one of them would certainly fall before the evening had drawn to a close. Next to his skin he wore a tunic of silk, speckled with gold and over this he placed a thick leather smock. He then laid a huge, flat stone, which he had carried all the way from Africa, across his torso and covered it with a solid iron apron. On his head he placed a crested war-helmet, adorned with crystals and rubies. He carried in his left hand a massive shield with fifty bosses of bronze and in his right, he clutched his mighty battle-sword. And when at last he was satisfied that he had protected himself against injury as best he could, he remained by the ford, performing many impressive feats with his sword while he awaited the arrival of Cúchulainn.

It was decided between the two warriors on this fourth day that they should use whatever weapons they had to hand and once they had gathered these together the fighting began in earnest. So wild was their rage on that morning, so bitter and violent the clashing of their swords, even the goblins and demons of the air fled in fear. Every creature of the forest shrieked in terror and ran for cover, while the waters themselves changed course, recoiling from the horror and ruthlessness of the combat. And as the afternoon came and went, the wounds inflicted were now deeper and more savage. Each man, although staggering with exhaustion, sought to outdo the other and remained watchful of just such an opportunity. Then, at last, in a moment of acute weariness, Cúchulainn lowered his heavy shield and as soon as he had done so, Ferdia thrust at him with his blade, driving it cleanly through his breast, causing the blood to flow freely down the battle-warrior's tunic. Again, Ferdia struck with his sword and this time it entered Cúchulainn's stomach so that he curled over in agony and began writhing on the earth. And knowing that he must save himself before it was too late, Cúchulainn reached for the Gae Bolg, a weapon he was resolved to use only as a last resort. Taking careful aim, he let fly the instrument with his right foot so that it passed through Ferdia's protective iron apron, through to the flat stone which it broke in three pieces and into the body of his friend filling every joint and every limb with its deadly barbs.

Cúchulainn hastened towards where his friend lay and pulled him gently to his bosom.

'Death is almost upon me,' sighed Ferdia, 'and it is a sad day for us that our friendship should come to such an end. Do not forget the love we once had, Cúchulainn.'

And as Ferdia perished in his arms, Cúchulainn wept piteously, clasping his friend's cold hand lovingly in his own. Then he lifted the body from the damp earth and carried it northwards across the ford to a place where they would not be disturbed by the approaching armies of Ulster. Daylight faded and as Cúchulainn lay down next to Ferdia he fell into a death-like swoon from which he could not be roused for a full seven days.

Tales of Finn Mac Cumaill and the Fianna

THE CENTRAL CHARACTER of the Fenian, or Ossianic Cycle, of Irish mythology, is Finn mac Cumaill (pronounced 'Finn mac Cool'), thought to be a real historical person who lived in Ireland some time in the third century ad. A myriad of stories now exists detailing the adventures of this distinguished warrior who rose to leadership of the Fianna and whose stronghold was situated on the Hill of Allen near Co. Kildare. The tales in this cycle generally take place in the Midlands of Ireland and describe a much later epoch when life was less turbulent and the climate of war had been replaced by a more harmonious and romantic atmosphere. The men of the Fianna were not merely military soldiers therefore, but highly accomplished hunter-fighters, often trained in the wilderness, and forced to submit to a number of rigourous tests before they were accepted into the Fianna. Alongside warrior attributes, members of the Fianna were also expected to know by heart the full poet's repertoire, numbering twelve books, and to possess the gift of poetic composition. Oisín (pronounced 'Usheen'), son of Finn mac Cumaill, is traditionally regarded as the greatest poet of all ancient Irish tales.

The parentage of Finn and the cause of the feud between himself and the Clan of Morna are recounted in this chapter, followed by the story of The Pursuit of Diarmuid and Gráinne which is considered to be one of the most striking and inventive tales of the cycle. The visit of Oisín to Tír na nÓg is a much later addition to the Fenian tales, and only made a first appearance in literary form in the mid-eighteenth century.

Finn also appears in mythology from the Isle of Man and Scotland where he is known as Finn MacCool, and Fingal, depending on the part of the country, and there are many variations of the spelling of his surname. His son Ossian, from the Irish Oisín of the Fenian Cycle, has a different number of brothers in different legends, as well as variations in the spelling of his name. The feats of the great Féinn, of the wise warrior Fionn, and his sons, Osgar and Ossian, form the basis of some of the most dazzling Scottish legends.

The Coming of Finn mac Cumaill

Many hundreds of years after the death of Cúchulainn and the Knights of the Red Guard, the Fianna of Erin reached the height of their fame under the leadership of Finn mac Cumaill. The great warriors of the Fianna were every bit as courageous as their forerunners and each was carefully chosen for his strength and fearlessness on the battlefield. They were also powerful hunters who loved the outdoor life, and many among them possessed the gift of poetry which led to the writing of beautiful tributes to the land of their birth, with its breathtaking mountain valleys and swift-flowing, silver streams. These noble Fenian fighters were above all champion protectors of Erin and during their reign no foreign invader ever dared to set foot on her illustrious shores.

Cumall, son of Trenmor of Clan Brascna, was the father of Finn mac Cumaill and he served as one of the bravest leaders of the Fianna until the day he was slain by his rival, Goll mac Morna, at the battle of Cnucha. Following his death, the Clan of Morna took control of the Fianna and the relatives and friends of Cumall were forced into hiding in the dense forests of the midlands where they built for themselves makeshift homes and yearned for the day when their household would again be restored to power. The Clan of Morna stole from the dead leader the Treasure Bag of the Fianna, filled with strange magical instruments from the Eastern World that had the power to heal all wounds and illnesses. It was placed in the charge of Lia, a chieftain of Connacht, for it was he who had dealt Cumall the first significant wound in the battle of Cnucha.

After the defeat of her husband, Muirne, wife of Cumall, hurriedly abandoned her home and fled to the west to the woodlands of Kerry, accompanied by two of her most trusted handmaidens. For she was carrying the child of the deceased warrior and wished to bring it safely into the world, out of the reach of the bloodthirsty sons of Morna. Within the month, Muirne had given birth to a son and she gave him the name of Demna. And as she gazed upon the infant's face, she was struck by its likeness to the face of Cumall, not yet cold in his grave. Tears of sorrow and anguish flooded down her cheeks and she grasped the child fiercely to her bosom, making a solemn promise to protect him from all harm and evil until he should grow to manhood.

But it was not long before Goll mac Morna received news of the birth of Cumall's heir and he rode forth in great haste through the forests of Erin towards Kerry, intent on destroying the infant. That evening, as she lay sleeping, Muirne had a disturbing vision of a war chariot with wheels of fire approaching her home and she arose at once and summoned her handmaidens to her.

'The sons of Morna have knowledge of our whereabouts,' she told them, 'and the child is unsafe while he remains here with me. Take him under cover of darkness to a safe retreat and do not rest until you are certain you have discovered the remotest dwelling in Erin where he may grow to adulthood unharmed and untroubled.'

The two handmaidens took the tiny bundle from Muirne's arms and set off in the piercingly cold night air towards the protection of the woods. They journeyed for fourteen days by secret paths until they reached the mountains of Slieve Bloom and here, under the shelter of the sprawling oak trees, they finally came to rest, satisfied at last that they had found a true place of sanctuary.

In the fullness of time, the boy Demna grew fair and strong and the two women who cared for him taught him how to hunt and how to spear fish and they marvelled at the speed and zealousness with which he learned to do these things. Before he had reached the age of ten, he could outrun the fastest wild deer of the forests and was so accomplished in the use of his various weapons that he could bring down a hawk with a single shot from his sling, or pin down a charging wild boar with one simple thrust of his spear. It was obvious too that he had the makings of a fine poet, for he was at one with nature and grew to love her fruits, whether listening for hours to the sound of a running brook, or gazing in awe and wonder at the delicate petals of mountain snowdrops. And his nursemaids were overjoyed with their charge and knew that Muirne would be proud of the son they had reared on her behalf, though she may never again lay eyes on the child.

One day, when Demna was in his fourteenth year and had grown more adventurous in spirit, he went out alone and journeyed deep into the mountains until he had reached the place known as Mag Life on the shores of the Liffey. Here, he came upon a chieftain's stronghold and, as he peered beyond the walls of the castle, he observed a group of young boys his own age engaged in a game of hurling. He boldly approached them and expressed his desire to join them in their sport, so they presented him with a hurley and invited him to play along. Though he was outnumbered by the rest of them and was unfamiliar with the rules of the game, Demna quickly proved that he could play as well as any of them and managed, on every occasion, to take the ball from the best players in the field. He was invited to join the group for another game on the following day and, this time, they put one half of their number against him. But again, he had little difficulty beating them off. On the third day, the group decided to test his ability even further and all twelve of them went against him. Demna was triumphant once more and his athletic skill was much admired and applauded. After this, the boys went before their chieftain and told him the story of the youth who had bravely defeated them. The chieftain asked for the young man to be brought before him and when he laid eyes on Demna's beautiful golden hair and saw the milky whiteness of his skin, he pronounced that he should be given the name of Finn, meaning 'fair one', and it was by this name that he was always known thereafter.

At the end of three months, there was not a living person in the land who had not heard rumours of the daring feats of Finn, the golden-haired youth. And it was not long before Goll mac Morna had dispatched his horsemen throughout the countryside to track down the son of Cumall, ordering them to bring him back dead or alive. Finn's two foster-mothers grew anxious that he would be found and they called Finn back home to them and advised him to leave his home in the mountains of Slieve Bloom:

'The champion warriors of the sons of Morna will arrive soon,' they told him, 'and they have been instructed to kill you if they find you here. It was Goll, son of Morna, who murdered your father Cumall. Go from us now, Finn, and keep your identity secret until you are strong enough to protect yourself, for the sons of Morna know that you are the rightful leader of the Fianna and they will stop at nothing until you are dead.'

And so Finn gathered together his belongings and set off in the direction of Loch Lein in the west where he lived for a time in the outdoors, safe from the attention of everyone. At length, however, he began to yearn for the company of other warriors and could not suppress his desire to volunteer himself in military service to the King of Bantry. Even though he did not make himself known to any of his companions, it was not long before their suspicions were aroused, for there was not a soldier more intrepid, nor a hunter more accomplished in the whole of the kingdom. The King himself was curious to learn more about the young warrior and invited him to visit the palace. The two men sat down to a game of chess and the King was greatly surprised to witness the ease with which the youth managed to defeat him. They decided to play on, and Finn won seven games, one after another. Then the King gave up the contest and began to question his opponent warily:

'Who are you,' he asked, 'and who are your people?'

'I am the son of a peasant of the Luagni of Tara,' replied Finn.

'I do not believe this to be the truth,' said the King, 'I am convinced that you are the son that Muirne bore to Cumall. You need not fear me if this is so and I advise you, as proof, to depart here without delay, since I do not wish you to be slain by the sons of Morna while under my poor protection.'

Then Finn realized that he had little choice but to continue his wanderings over the lonely plains of Erin. And it was always the case that whenever he came into contact with other people, his beauty and noble bearing betrayed him, so that the eyes of all were fixed upon him, and the news of his presence promptly spread throughout the region.

He journeyed onwards into Connacht, restricting himself to those areas of the wilderness where he felt certain he would not encounter another living soul. But as he was on his way one morning, he heard the unmistakable sound of a woman wailing and soon came upon her in a clearing of the woods, kneeling over the body of a dead youth.

'I have good cause to mourn in such a fashion,' said the woman looking up at Finn, 'for my only son has been struck down without mercy by the tall warrior who has just passed by here.'

'And what was your son's name who suffered this cruel, unwarranted fate?' enquired Finn.

'Glonda was his name,' replied the woman, 'and I ask you, under bond as a warrior, to avenge his death, since I know of no other who can help me.'

Without hesitating a moment longer, Finn set off in pursuit of the warrior, following the tracks through the woods until he came to the dwelling place of Lia Luachair on the outskirts of Connacht. Taking up the old woman's challenge, he drew his sword and began attacking Lia, striking him down with little effort. It was then that Finn noticed a strange bag on the floor at the older man's feet, and as he looked inside, the treasures of Cumall and the Fianna were revealed to him, and he was overcome with pride that he had unwittingly slain the man who had dealt his father the first wound at Cnucha.

It was at this time that Finn grew weary of his solitary life and began to gather around him all the young warriors of the country who had come to admire his courage and determination. And one of the first tasks he set himself was to go in search of his uncle Crimall and the rest of the Clan Brascna who were still in hiding from the sons of Morna. Accompanied by his followers, he crossed the River Shannon and marched into Connacht where he found his uncle and a number of the old Fianna lying low in the heart of the forest. Crimall stepped forwards and lovingly embraced his nephew, for it was apparent at once that the young stranger before him was the son of Cumall. Then Finn presented the old man with the Bag of Treasures and told him the story from beginning to end of how he had come upon it and slain its custodian. And as he spoke, Crimall laid out the treasures on the ground before them and all who gazed upon them grew fresh of face and strong in body and the burden of age and sorrow was instantly lifted from their brows.

'Our time of deliverance is close at hand,' shouted Crimall joyfully, 'for it has been foretold that he who recovers the Treasure Bag of the Fianna from the hands of the enemy is the one who will lead the Clan of Brascna to victory once more. Go now Finn,' he added, 'and seek out the ancient bard known as Finnegas, since he is the one destined to prepare you for the day when you will rise to your rightful position as head of the Fianna.'

Hearing these words, Finn bade the company farewell and set off alone towards the shores of the River Boyne in the east, eager to meet with the wise old druid who had schooled his father in the ways of poetry and story-telling, whose masterful instruction was deemed essential for any man aspiring to leadership of the Fianna.

For seven long years, Finnegas had lived on the banks of the Boyne, seeking to catch the Salmon of Fec. The salmon, which swam in a deep pool overhung by hazel boughs, was famous throughout the land, for it was prophesied that the first person to eat of its flesh would enjoy all the wisdom of the world. And it happened one day that while Finn was sitting by the river with Finnegas at his side, the salmon swam boldly towards them, almost daring them to cast their rods into the water. Finnegas lost no time in doing so and was astounded when the fish got caught on his hook, struggling only very weakly to release itself. He hauled the salmon onto the shore and watched its silver body wriggle in the sand until all life had gone out of it. When it finally lay still, he gave the salmon over to Finn and ordered him to build a fire on which to cook it.

'But do not eat even the smallest morsel,' Finnegas told him, 'for it is my reward alone, having waited patiently for seven years.'

Finn placed a spit over the fire and began turning it as requested until the fish was cooked through. He then placed it on a plate and took it to Finnegas.

'And have you eaten any of the salmon?' asked the poet.

'No,' answered Finn, 'but I burned my thumb while cooking it and put it in my mouth to relieve the pain.'

'Then you are indeed Finn mac Cumaill,' said Finnegas, 'and I bear you no ill-will for having tasted the salmon, for in you the prophecy is come true.'

Then Finnegas gave Finn the rest of the salmon to eat and it brought him instant knowledge of all he desired to know. And that evening he composed the finest of verses, proving that he possessed a talent equal to the most gifted poets in Erin:

May-day! delightful day!
Bright colours play the vale along.
Now wakes at morning's slender ray
Wild and gay the Blackbird's song.

Now comes the bird of dusty hue,
The loud cuckoo, the summer-lover;
Branchy trees are thick with leaves;
The bitter, evil time is over.

Loaded bees with puny power
Goodly flower-harvest win;
Cattle roam with muddy flanks;
Busy ants go out and in.

Through the wild harp of the wood
Making music roars the gale–
Now it settles without motion,
On the ocean sleeps the sail.
Men grow mighty in the May,
Proud and gay the maidens grow;
Fair is every wooded height;
Fair and bright the plain below.

A bright shaft has smit the streams,
With gold gleams the water-flag;
Leaps the fish and on the hills
Ardour thrills the leaping stag.

Loudly carols the lark on high,
Small and shy his tireless lay,
Singing in wildest, merriest mood,
Delicate-hued, delightful May.
T.W. Rolleston, May-Day

The Rise of Finn to Leadership of the Fianna

After Finn had eaten of the Salmon of Fec which gave him all the gifts of wisdom, he had only to put his thumb in his mouth and whatever he wished to discover was immediately revealed to him. He knew beyond all doubt that he had been brought into the world to take the place of Cumall as head of the Fianna, and was confident at last that he had learned from Finnegas all that he would ever need to know. Turning his back on the valley of the Boyne, he set off to join Crimall and his followers in the forests of Connacht once more in order to plan in earnest for his future. He had by now become the most courageous of warriors, yet this quality was tempered by a remarkable generosity and gentleness of spirit that no man throughout the length and breath of the country could ever hope to rival. Finn was loved and admired by every last one of his comrades and they devoted their lives to him, never once slackening in their efforts to prove themselves worthy of his noble patronage.

It was decided among this loyal group that the time had come for Finn to assert his claim to the leadership of the Fianna and they went and pledged him their support and friendship in this bravest of quests. For it was well known that the Clan of Morna, who continued to rule the Fenian warriors, would not surrender their position without a bitter struggle. Finn now believed himself ready for such a confrontation and the day was chosen when he and his army would march to the Hill of Tara and plead their case before Conn Céadchathach, the High King of Erin.

As it was now the month of November and the Great Assembly of Tara was once more in progress, a period of festivity and good-will, when every man was under oath to lay aside his weapon. Chieftains, noblemen, kings and warriors all journeyed to Tara for the splendid event and old feuds were forgotten as the wine and mead flowed freely and the merry-making and dancing lasted well into the small hours. It was not long before Finn and his band of followers had arrived at Tara and they proceeded at once to the main banqueting hall where they were welcomed by the King's attendants and seated among the other Fenian warriors. As soon as he had walked into the hall, however, all eyes had been turned towards Finn, and a flurry of hushed enquiries circulated around the room as to the identity of the golden-haired youth. The King too, was quick to acknowledge that a stranger had entered his court, and he picked up a goblet of wine and instructed one of his servants to present it to the young warrior. At this gesture of friendship, Finn felt reassured in approaching the King, and he walked forward to the royal table and introduced himself to one and all.

'I am Finn, son of Cumall,' he declared, 'and I have come to take service with you, High King of Erin, just as my father did before me as head of the Fianna.'

And when he heard these words, Goll mac Morna, who sat at the King's right hand, grew pale in anger, and shuddered to hear the King respond favourably to the young warrior:

'I would be honoured to have you serve in my ranks,' replied Conn Céadchathach. 'If you are the son of Cumall, son of Trenmor, then you are also a friend of mine.'

After this, Finn bound himself in loyalty to the King, and his own band of men followed his example, and each was presented with a sword of the Fianna which they accepted with great pride and humility.

Everybody in the kingdom had either heard of Aillen the goblin or seen the creature with their own eyes. Every year during the Great Assembly, Conn Céadchathach increased the number of men guarding the royal city, but still the goblin managed to pass undetected through the outer gates, moving swiftly towards the palace and setting it alight with its flaming breath. Not even the bravest of warriors could prevent Aillen from reeking havoc on Tara, for he carried with him a magic harp and all who heard its fairy music were gently lulled to sleep. The King lived in hope however, that one day the goblin would be defeated and he adamantly refused to be held to ransom by the creature, insisting that the annual festivities take place as normal. A handsome reward awaited that warrior who could capture or destroy Aillen, but none had yet succeeded in doing so. It was at this time that Goll mac Morna conceived of his wicked plan to belittle his young rival before the King, for he could see that Conn Céadchathach secretly entertained the hope that Finn would rescue Tara from further destruction. He called the young warrior to him and told him of the one true way to win the King's favour, being careful not to mention the enchanting harp or the difficulty of the task that lay ahead:

'Go and bind yourself before the King to rid this city of the terrible goblin who every year burns it to the ground,' said Goll. 'You alone possess the courage to do this Finn, and you may name your price if you are successful.'

So Finn went before the King and swore that he would not rest in peace until he had slain Aillen the goblin.

'And what would you have as your reward?' asked the King.

'If I manage to rid you of the goblin,' Finn replied, 'I should like to take up my rightful position as captain of the Fianna. Will you agree, under oath, to such a reward?'

'If this is what you desire,' answered the King, 'then I bind myself to deliver such a prize.'

Satisfied with these words, Finn took up his weapon and ventured out into the darkness to begin his lonely vigil over the palace.

As night fell and the November mists began to thicken round the hill of Tara, Finn waited anxiously for the goblin to appear. After some time, he saw an older warrior enter the courtyard and make his way towards him. He noticed that the warrior held in his hand a long, pointed spear, protected by a case of the soft, shining leather.

'I am Fiacha,' said the warrior gently, 'and I was proud to serve under your father, Cumall, when he was leader of the Fianna. The spear I carry is the spear of enchantment which Cumall placed in my charge upon his death.

'Take this weapon,' he added, 'and as soon as you hear the fairy music, lay its blade against your forehead and you will not fall under the melody's spell.'

Finn thanked the warrior for his gift and turned it over to inspect it, admiring its shining handle of Arabian gold and the sharp steel body of the blade that glinted challengingly in the moonlight. Then he began to roam the ramparts once more, straining his ear to catch the first notes of the magic harp. He gazed out over the wide, frosty plains of Meath but still there was no sign of the evil goblin. He had almost given up hope that Aillen would appear and had sat down wearily on the hard, frozen earth, when he caught sight of a shadowy, phantom-like figure in the distance, floating eerily over the plain towards the royal palace. At first the strange music that wafted through the air was scarcely audible, but as the goblin drew nearer, the sweet sound of the harp strings filled the air like a potent fragrance, intoxicating the senses and inducing a warm, drowsy feeling. Finn was immediately enraptured by the sound and his eyelids slowly began to droop as the music weaved its magic spell over him. But something within him struggled against the opiate of the melody and his fingers searched for the spear of enchantment. Releasing the weapon from its leather shroud, he lay the cold steel blade against his forehead and drew a long, deep breath as he allowed its rejuvenating strength to flow through his tired limbs.

As soon as Aillen had reached the crest of the Hill of Tara he began to spit blazing fire-balls through the palace gates, unaware that Finn had escaped the enchantment of the harp. Now Aillen had never before come face to face with an alert and animate mortal, and the sudden appearance of the young warrior quenching the flames with the cloak off his back prompted a shriek of terror and alarm. Turning swiftly around in the direction he had come from, Aillen fled for his safety, hoping to reach the fairy mound at Sliabh Fuaid before Finn could overtake him. But the young warrior was far too fleet of foot and before the goblin had managed to glide through the entrance of the mound, Finn had cast his spear, striking down the goblin with a single fatal blow through the chest. Then Finn bent over the corpse and removed Aillen's head and carried it back to the palace so that all were made aware that he had put an end to the reign of destruction.

When the sun had risen on the following morning, the King was overjoyed to discover that his kingdom remained untouched by the goblin's flame. He knew at once that Finn must have fulfilled his promise and was eager to express his gratitude. He called together all the men of the

Fianna and sent his messenger to Finn's chamber requesting him to appear before him. Then the King stood Finn at his right hand and addressed his audience slowly and solemnly with the following words:

'Men of Erin,' said the King, 'I have pledged my word to this young warrior that if he should ever destroy the goblin Aillen, he would be granted leadership of the Fianna. I urge you to embrace him as your new leader and to honour him with your loyalty and service. If any among you cannot agree to do this, let him now resign his membership of the Fianna.'

And turning to face Goll mac Morna, the King asked him:

'Do you swear service to Finn mac Cumaill, or is it your decision to quit the Fianna?'

'The young warrior has risen nobly to his position,' replied Goll, 'and I now bow to his superiority and accept him as my captain.'

Then Goll mac Morna swore allegiance to Finn and each warrior came forward after him and did the same in his turn. And from this day onwards it was deemed the highest honour to serve under Finn mac Cumaill, for only the best and bravest of Erin's warriors were privileged to stand alongside the most glorious leader the Fianna had ever known.

The Pursuit of Diarmuid and Gráinne

Following the death of his wife Maignes, Finn mac Cumaill had spent an unhappy year alone as a widower. The loss of his wife had come as a severe blow to the hero of the Fianna and even though he was surrounded by loved ones, including his beloved son Oisín and his grandson Oscar, who watched over and comforted him, he could not rid himself of thoughts of Maignes and was increasingly overwhelmed by deep feelings of loneliness and despair.

One morning, seeing his father in such a pitiful state of grief, Oisín called upon his most trusted friend, Diorruing O'Baoiscne, and together they agreed that something must be done to rescue Finn from his prolonged melancholy. It was Diorruing who suggested that perhaps the time had come for Finn to take a new wife and the two young men began to consider who best would fill this role. And as they pondered this question, Oisín suddenly remembered that the High King of Erin, Cormac mac Art, was said to possess one of the most beautiful daughters in the land. Her name was Gráinne, and although several suitors had sought her hand, it was known that she had not consented to marry any of them and was still in search of a husband.

Oisín and Diorruing went before Finn and expressed their concern that he had not yet recovered his good spirits. Finn listened attentively, and he could not deny that every word they spoke was the truth. But he had tried, he told them, to put aside all memory of his wife, and his attempts so far had been utterly futile.

'Will you let us help you then?' Oisín asked his father. 'For we feel certain that you would be better off with a strong woman by your side. The maiden you seek is named Gráinne, daughter of Cormac mac Art, and if you will allow it, we will journey to Tara on your behalf and request her hand in marriage.'

After they had persuaded Finn that he had little to lose by agreeing to such a venture, both Oisín and Doirruing set off for the royal residence at Tara. So impressive was their stature as warriors of the Fianna, that as soon as they arrived, they were respectfully escorted through the palace gates and permitted an immediate audience with the King. And when Cormac mac Art heard that Finn mac Cumaill desired to take his daughter for a wife, he was more than pleased at the prospect, yet at the same time, he felt it his duty to inform Oisín of thc outcome of Gráinne's previous courtships:

'My daughter is a wilful and passionate woman,' the King told Oisín. 'She has refused the hand of some of the finest princes and battle-champions Erin has ever known. Let her be brought before us so that she may give you her own decision on the matter, for I would rather not incur your displeasure by saying yes, only to have her go against me.'

So Gráinne was brought before them and the question was put to her whether or not she would have Finn mac Cumaill for a husband. And it was without the slightest show of interest or enthusiasm that Gráinne made the following reply:

'If you consider this man a fitting son-in-law for you, father, then why shouldn't he be a suitable husband for me?'

But Oisín and Doirruing were satisfied with this answer and taking their leave of the King after having promised to visit as soon as possible in the company of Finn mac Cumaill, they hastened back to the Hill of Allen to deliver the good news.

Within a week, the royal household of Tara was busy preparing itself to welcome the leader of the Fianna and the captains of the seven battalions of his great army. An elaborate banquet was prepared in their honour and King Cormac mac Art received his visitors with great pride and excitement. Then he led the way to the vast dining hall and they all sat down to enjoy a merry evening of feasting and drinking. Seated at Cormac's left hand was his wife, Eitche, and next to her sat Gráinne, resplendent in a robe of emerald silk which perfectly enhanced her breathtaking beauty. Finn mac Cumaill took pride of place at the King's right hand and beside him were seated the most prominent warriors of the Fianna according to his rank and patrimony.

After a time, Gráinne struck up a conversation with her father's druid Daire who sat close by, demanding to know of him the cause of the great celebrations taking place.

'If you are not aware of the reason,' said the druid, 'then it will indeed be hard for me to explain it to you.'

But Gráinne continued to pester Daire with the same question until eventually he was forced to give her a more direct answer:

'That warrior next to your father is none other than Finn mac Cumaill,' said the druid, 'and he has come here tonight to ask you to be his wife.'

And so, for the first time, Gráinne scrutinized the figure she had so flippantly agreed to marry, and having studied his face at some length she fell silent for a time. Then she addressed the druid once more:

'It comes as a great surprise to me,' said Gráinne, 'that it is not for his own son Oisín, or even his grandson Oscar, that Finn seeks me as a wife, since it would be far more appropriate if I married one of these two than marry this man who must be three times my own age.'

'Do not say such things,' answered Daire worriedly, 'for if Finn were to hear you, he would certainly now refuse you and none among the Fianna would ever dare to look at you afterwards.'

But Gráinne merely laughed to hear these words and her eye began to wander in the direction of the young Fenian warriors at the banqueting table. As she surveyed each of them in turn, she questioned the druid as to their identity, desiring to know what exceptional qualities they each had to recommend them. And when her eyes came to rest upon one particularly handsome warrior with dusky-black hair, her interest was very keenly aroused.

'That is Diarmuid, son of Dubne,' the druid informed her, 'who is reputed to be the best lover of women and of maidens in all the world.'

As she continued to sip her wine, Gráinne stared even more closely at the black-haired youth until eventually she called her attendant to her and whispered in her ear:

'Bring me the jewelled goblet from my chamber closet that holds enough wine for nine times nine men.' she told her. 'Have it filled to the brim with wine, then set it down before me.'

When her servant returned with the heavy goblet Gráinne added to it the contents of a small phial she had secretly hidden in a fold of her gown.

'Take the goblet to Finn first of all,' she urged her handmaiden, 'and bid him swallow a draught of wine in honour of our courtship. After he has done so, pass the goblet to all of the company at the high table, but be careful not to allow any of the youthful warriors of the Fianna to drink from it.'

The servant did as she was requested and it was not long before all who swallowed the wine from Gráinne's cup had fallen into a deep and peaceful slumber. Then Gráinne rose quietly from her place at the table and made her way towards where Diarmuid was seated.

'Will you receive my love, Diarmuid,' Gráinne asked him, 'and escape with me tonight to a place far away from here?'

'It is Finn mac Cumaill you are set to wed,' answered the young warrior, stunned at her suggestion. 'I would not do such a thing for any woman who is betrothed to the leader of the Fianna.'

'Then I place you under bonds as a warrior of the King,' said Gráinne, 'to take me out of Tara tonight and to save me from an unhappy union with an old man.'

'These are evil bonds indeed,' said Diarmuid, 'and I beg you to withdraw them, for I cannot understand what it is I have done to deserve such unwarranted punishment.'

'You have done nothing except allow me to fall in love with you,' replied Gráinne, 'ever since the day, many years ago, when you visited the palace and joined in a game of hurling on the green of Tara. I turned the light of my eyes on you that day, and I never gave my love to any other man from that time until now, nor will I ever, Diarmuid.'

Torn between his loyalty to Finn, and an allegiance to the sacred bonds Gráinne had placed him under, Diarmuid turned to his Fenian friends for counsel and advice. But all of them, including Oisín, Oscar, Diorruing and Cailte, advised that he had little choice but to go with Gráinne:

'You have not invited Gráinne's love,' Oisín told him, 'and you are not responsible for the bonds she has laid upon you. But he is a miserable wretch who does not honour his warrior's oath. You must follow Gráinne therefore, and accept this destiny, though your own death may come of it.'

Filled with despair and sorrow at these words, Diarmuid gathered up his weapons and then moving towards his comrades, he embraced each of them sadly, knowing that his days with the Fianna had now come to an end, to be replaced by days of tortured exile, when Finn mac Cumaill would ruthlessly pursue the couple from one end of Erin to the next.

As soon as the flight of Diarmuid and Gráinne had been brought to his attention, the leader of the Fianna was consumed with violent jealousy and rage and swore the bitterest revenge on the pair. At once, Finn mac Cumaill called for his horses to be saddled and a great host of his men set off on the trail of the couple, journeying for days along the most secluded tracks through the densest forests of Erin until they had crossed the river Shannon and arrived near to the place known as Doire Da Both. On the outskirts of this forest, the Fenian trackers discovered a makeshift camp dusted with the ashes of a small fire, which although now cold, left them in little doubt that they were moving very closely behind their prey.

On the following evening, after they had travelled a lengthy distance deeper into the forest, Finn and his men came upon a form of wooden enclosure built of saplings, stones and mud, containing seven narrow doors. Climbing to one of the tallest trees, Finn's chief scout peered inside the structure and saw there Diarmuid and a woman lying next to him on a blanket of deer-skin. The men of the Fianna were ordered to stand guard at each of the seven exits and then Finn himself approached the hut and shouted loudly for Diarmuid to come forward and surrender himself to them. Diarmuid awoke abruptly from his sleep and taking Gráinne by the hand thrust his head through the smallest of the doors. But his eyes betrayed not the slightest glimmer of fear to see Finn and his great warriors surrounding the hut. Instead, he clasped Gráinne closer to him and planted three kisses on her lips for all the men of the Fianna to observe. Finn mac Cumaill was seized by a fury on seeing this, and proclaimed at once that the removal of Diarmuid's head by whatever method his men were forced to employ would alone prove fitting reprisal for so brazen a show of disrespect.

Now Aengus Óg, the god of love, was the foster-father of Diarmuid, son of Dubne, the deity who had protected and watched over the couple since the night they had fled the palace of Tara. And witnessing their plight at the hands of the Fianna, Aengus now took it upon himself to come to their aid, drifting invisibly towards them on the breeze.

'Come and take shelter under my cloak,' he appealed to them, 'and we will pass unseen by Finn and his people to a place of refuge and safety.'

But Diarmuid insisted that he would remain behind to face his former comrades as a true warrior, and requested that Aengus take only Gráinne with him. So Aengus drew Gráinne under his mantel for protection and they both rose up into the air, gliding towards the woodlands of the south where they felt certain Diarmuid would survive to meet up with them later.

After he had bid Aengus and Gráinne farewell, Diarmuid stood upright, tall and proud, and prepared himself for the task of fighting his way through the formidable band of Fenian warriors. Taking up his weapon, he approached the first of the seven doors and demanded to know which of his former comrades stood behind it waiting to do combat with him:

'I wish you no harm, Diarmuid,' replied the gentle voice of Oisín. 'Let me guide you out through this door, and I promise I will not raise a finger to hurt you.'

And on each of the other doors upon which he knocked, apart from the very last, Diarmuid met with the same response, for it appeared that not one among his old friends of the Fianna was prepared to meet him with hostility. Finally, however, Diarmuid arrived at the seventh door and this time when he knocked, the response was anything but warm and friendly:

'It is I, Finn mac Cumaill,' came the thundering reply, 'a man who bears you no love, as you well know. And if you should come out through this gate I would take great pleasure in striking you down and cleaving asunder every last bone in your body.'

'I will not go out by any other door in that case,' answered Diarmuid, 'for I would not wish such raw anger to be unleashed on any of my friends gathered here whose desire it is to let me go free.'

And then, having driven the shafts of his mighty spears firmly into the earth, Diarmuid used them to spring high into the air, leaping over the walls of the wooden hut, clean over the heads of Finn and his men. So swift was this manoeuvre, so light his descent on the grass beyond the warrior group, that none could trace the path of his escape and they stood looking on in amazement, deliberating a long time whether or not it was some goblin of the air who had helped carry Diarmuid so effortlessly to freedom.

It was not long before Diarmuid had arrived at the clearing in the woods where Aengus and Gráinne waited anxiously to see him. Great was their relief to know that he had escaped the Fianna unharmed and they both listened in admiration as he related to them the tale of his daring escape. When the excitement of the reunion had abated however, Aengus Óg grew more serious and spoke earnestly to his foster-son and Gráinne:

'I must now depart from you,' he said to them, 'but I leave you with these words of advice. Do not slacken in caution while Finn mac Cumaill remains in pursuit of you. Never enter a cave with only one opening; and never take refuge on an island with only one harbour. Always eat your meals in a place different to where you have cooked them; never rest your head where you eat your meal, and wherever you sleep tonight, make sure you choose a fresh bed on the following night.'

For many months afterwards, Diarmuid and Gráinne followed the advice of Aengus Óg and lived precisely as he had counselled them. But the time came when they grew weary once more of shifting from place to place and they longed for even two nights together when they might sleep under the same familiar oak tree or heather bush. They had by now reached the forests of the west and had entered a bower guarded by the fierce giant Searbhán.

'Surely we may rest awhile here, Diarmuid,' said Gráinne. 'Is it not the most unlikely thing in the world that Finn and his men would find us out in such a lonely and shaded part of the woods?'

And seeing the look of exhaustion on Gráinne's face, Diarmuid agreed to go in search of Searbhán to beg permission to shelter in the forest. The giant also took pity on Gráinne and it was soon settled that the couple were free to roam the forests and hunt for their food for up to three days provided neither of them touched the quicken tree of Dubros growing in its centre or ate any of its sweet-smelling berries. For this particular tree belonged to the people of the Fairy mounds who did not wish that any mortal should eat of its fruit and share the gift of immortality. And so Diarmuid accepted responsibility for both himself and Gráinne and swore upon his sword that during their short stay the berries would remain the sacred property of the fairies.

As for Finn mac Cumaill and his loyal followers of the Fianna, they had not tired in their quest for revenge and were little more than half a day's journey away from the outskirts of Searbhán's forest. And it was while Finn awaited news from his scouts, sent forth to search for evidence of Diarmuid and Gráinne, that he observed a group of horsemen approaching the Fenian camp. He recognized these riders at once as the offspring of the sons of Morna who had murdered his father at the battle of Cnucha and with whom he still had a long-standing feud. But it soon became apparent that these young warriors had travelled a great distance to beg forgiveness for the sins of their fathers and to be reconciled to the Fianna.

Now when Finn's scouts returned to inform him that Diarmuid and Gráinne rested under the protection of Searbhán beneath the tree of Dubros, Finn made up his mind to test the commitment of the warriors of the Clan of Morna:

'If you truly seek forgiveness,' he told them, 'go forth into the woods and bring me one of two things, either the head of Diarmuid, son of Dubne, or a fistful of berries from the tree of Dubros.'

And when the offspring of Morna heard this request, they answered the leader of the Fianna innocently:

'We would be honoured to perform such a task. Point us in the direction of the woods and we shall soon return with one of these two prizes.'

When they were still quite a long way off however, Diarmuid spotted the warriors of Clan Morna approaching and he made ready his weapon for attack. And as they came closer he jumped to the earth from a tree above, blocking the path of their progress.

'Who are you,' Diarmuid asked them, 'and why have you come to the forest of Searbhán?'

'We are of the Clan of Morna,' they replied, 'and we have been sent here by Finn mac Cumaill to perform one of two tasks, either to recover the head of Diarmuid, son of Dubne, or to escape here with a fistful of berries from the tree of Dubros.'

'I am the man whose head you seek,' replied Diarmuid, 'and over there is the tree bearing the fruit you are required to remove. But it will be no easy task for you to accomplish either of these things. Choose now which of the two feats you would attempt to perform.'

'I would sooner fight for your head,' answered the eldest of the warriors, 'than go against the giant Searbhán.'

So the children of Morna began wrestling with Diarmuid who had little or no difficulty overcoming them and within minutes they had been bound hand and foot by him.

Then Gráinne, who had been watching the struggle with some amusement, came forward and began to question Diarmuid about the berries. And when she heard of their magic properties, and of how, in particular, they could make the old young and beautiful once more, she insisted that she must taste them before putting any other food in her mouth again. It was useless for Diarmuid to try and persuade her otherwise, and he began to sharpen his spear, resigned to the fact that he must soon confront the tree's ferocious guardian. Seeing that he was reluctant to break his bond of friendship with the giant, the children of Morna offered to go and get the berries for Gráinne. But although Diarmuid would not agree to this, he was nonetheless touched by their generosity and offered to loosen their bonds so that they might witness the combat.

And so Diarmuid, accompanied by the children of Morna, went forward and roused the giant from his sleep, demanding that he hand over some of the precious berries for Gráinne to eat. Furious at this request, the giant swung his mighty club over his shoulder and brought it down hard in Diarmuid's direction. But Diarmuid managed to leap aside, avoiding any injury, and then hurled himself at the giant forcing him to loosen his hold on the club so that it fell heavily to the ground. Seizing the weapon, Diarmuid delivered three strong blows to the giant's head, dashing his brains to pieces. And when he was certain that Searbhán was dead, he climbed the tree of Dubros and plucked the juiciest berries, handing one bunch to Gráinne and the other to the children of Morna.

'Take these berries to Finn,' he told the warriors, 'and do not pretend to him that you have seen me. Tell him instead that you have earned his forgiveness by slaying the giant with your own bare hands.'

The children of Morna were more than happy to do this, and they expressed their gratitude to Diarmuid that he had finally brought peace between the two clans. And having placed the berries carefully in their saddlebags, they made their way back towards Finn and the men of the Fianna.

As soon as he laid eyes on the berries, Finn mac Cumaill placed them under his nose and announced at once that it was Diarmuid, not the offspring of Morna, who had gathered them:

'For I can smell his skin on them,' roared Finn, 'and I will now go myself in search of him and remove his head with my own sword.'

And he tore through the forest as fast as his horse could carry him until he reached the tree of Dubros where he suspected Diarmuid and Gráinne must be hiding. Here he sat down and called for Oisín to bring his chess-board to him. The two began to play a long and complicated game, for they were each as skilled as the other, until eventually they reached a point where the victor of the game would be decided by Oisín's next move. And Diarmuid, who had been closely following the game from above, could not prevent himself from helping his friend. Impulsively, he threw a berry down from one of the branches where it landed on the board indicating to Oisín how the game should be won. At this, Finn rose rapidly to his feet and calling all the warriors of the Fianna together he ordered them to surround the tree. Then Garb of Sliab Cua announced that Diarmuid had slain his father and that nothing would make him happier than to avenge this death. So Finn agreed to this and Garb climbed the tree in pursuit of Diarmuid.

Again, however, Aengus Óg was watchful of his foster-son and rushed to his aid without the Fianna's knowledge. And as Diarmuid flung Garb backwards from the branches with one swift movement of his foot, Aengus put the form of his foster-son upon him so that his own warriors took off his head believing him to be Diarmuid, son of Dubne. After they had done this, Garb was again changed back into his own shape causing great distress to all who witnessed the transformation. And of the nine Fenian warriors Finn mac Cumaill ordered to ascend the tree in search of Diarmuid, the same fate befell each of them so that Finn fell into a heavy mood of anguish and grief. And when Diarmuid announced that he would descend the tree and slaughter every living person under Finn's protection, Finn at last could tolerate the killing no longer and begged for it to come to an end.

So Diarmuid and Aengus Óg appeared before Finn and it was agreed among the three of them that peace should be restored between Finn and Diarmuid. Then the leader of the Fianna and five of his captains went to the stronghold of the High King of Erin to secure a pardon for Diarmuid and Gráinne. Once this had been done, the couple were allowed to return to their native country of west Kerry where they built for themselves a fine home and lived in peace and harmony together for a great many years to follow.

Oisín in Tír na N-Óg (The Land of Youth)

Finn mac Cumaill, the mightiest warrior of the Fianna, had no equal among mortal men and his reputation as one of the fiercest fighters in Ireland spread with each glorious victory on the battlefield. His young son, Oisín, was a particular favourite with him, for the boy showed signs of remarkable courage at an early age and had clearly inherited his father's voracious thirst for adventure. Each time Finn gazed at his golden-haired son a memory of Blaí, the boy's mother, stirred within his breast, filling him with both joy and sorrow. Blaí was now lost to him, but the child she had borne him possessed her great beauty and gift of poetry. Oisín was a true warrior and the greatest of Fenian poets. Many women had fallen in love with him, but none had yet succeeded in winning his heart. The son of Finn mac Cumaill was happiest fighting alongside his father, or roaming the dense forests that chimed with birdsong in the company of his trusty hounds.

While hunting in the middle of the woods one summer's morning, just as the silver veil of mist was rising from the shores of Loch Lein, Oisín was struck by the most enchanting vision. A young maiden appeared before him, seated majestically on a milk-white steed. Oisín had never seen her kind before, but felt certain she must have come from the fairy world. Her luxuriant golden hair, adorned by an elaborate jewelled crown, cascaded over her shoulders and she was clothed in a mantle of the finest red silk. Her saddle was made of purple and gold and her horse's hooves were placed in four shoes of gold, studded with the most precious gems. She moved gracefully towards Oisín, who was immediately entranced by her radiance and perfection. The maiden's cheeks were as delicate as the satin petals of a rose; her eyes were as bright and pure as two drops of dew on a violet; her skin was as white and delicate as the first snows of winter.

'I am Niamh daughter of the great King who rules the Land of Youth,' she spoke softly. 'Your name is well known to me, brave Oisín, son of the noble Finn mac Cumaill. I have hastened here for love's sake, to woo you.'

Oisín stood bewitched before the maiden as she began to sing to him of Tír na N-Óg, the Land of Youth. Her music drifted lightly towards him like a perfumed summer breeze, and it was the sweetest sound the young warrior had ever heard.

'Delightful land of honey and wine
Beyond what seems to thee most fair –
Rich fruits abound the bright year round
And flowers are found of hues most rare.
Unfailing there the honey and wine

And draughts divine of mead there be,
No ache nor ailing night or day –
Death or decay thou ne'er shalt see!
A hundred swords of steel refined,
A hundred cloaks of kind full rare,
A hundred steeds of proudest breed,
A hundred hounds – thy meed when there!

The royal crown of the King of Youth
Shall shine in sooth on thy brow most fair,
All brilliant with gems of luster bright
Whose worth aright none might declare.

All things I've named thou shalt enjoy
And none shall cloy – to endless life –
Beauty and strength and power thou'lt see
And I'll e'er be thy own true wife!'
Michael Comyn, Niamh sings to Oisín

'Niamh of the Golden Hair,' Oisín spoke to her. 'I have never before met a maiden so pleasing to the eye and I long to visit the kingdom of which you sing. I would be honoured to take you as my bride and will depart this land of mortals without delay to be with you.' –

Before reaching up to grasp her hand, he looked around him only once, catching a final glimpse of his father's great palace and the beautiful woodlands he had now chosen to leave behind. Bidding a valiant farewell in his heart to the men of the Fianna, he mounted the powerful horse which carried them both away towards the cliffs of the west, and further on into the crashing waves.

For five days and five nights they rode, crossing the great plains of Erin and journeying on through various kingdoms of the Otherworld. The deep sea opened up to greet them and they passed underneath the bed of the ocean into a land of golden light. Regal citadels, surrounded by luscious green lawns and exotic, vibrantly coloured blooms, gleamed in the rays of sparkling sunshine. A youthful knight, clad in a magnificent raiment of purple and silver, suddenly appeared alongside them, riding a white mare. A fair young maiden sat next to him on the saddle holding a golden apple in the palm of her hand. Niamh again told Oisín of the beauty of Tír na N-Óg, a land even more beautiful than the splendid images now before them. They journeyed onwards, passing from this luminous world through a raging, violent tempest, moving as swiftly as the howling winds and driving rains would carry them across mountains, valleys and bottomless dark lakes until the bright orb of the sun emerged in all its splendour once more.

The kingdom now before them was far more breathtaking than Oisín had ever imagined possible. A silver-pebbled stream wound its way towards a gently undulating hill dotted with purple and yellow orchids which breathed a rich, opulent fragrance into the air. A magnificent castle stood on the hilltop, shaded by giant leafy trees laden with ripe golden pears. The sound of honey-bees buzzing from flower to flower united melodiously with the singing of birds, languidly pruning their feathers in the amber glow of early twilight. A large crowd moved forward to welcome the couple. Minstrels played soothing, magical airs and delicate blossoms were strewn at their feet creating a soft carpet for them to tread on. The happy pair were escorted to the palace where the King and Queen had prepared a large wedding banquet. The King warmly embraced his new son-in-law and ordered the seven days of feasting and celebrations to commence.

As each new day dawned in the Land of Youth it brought with it an abundance of joy for Oisín and Niamh. Time stood absolutely still in this perfect world and they had only to wish for something and it would instantly appear. Before long, the couple were blessed with three healthy children: two handsome sons, and a beautiful daughter. The son of Finn mac Cumaill had won the admiration and respect of every person in the kingdom and he enthralled each and every subject with tales of his Fenian friends and the splendid adventures they had survived together. Only one thing now threatened to destroy his happiness. At night, Oisín was tormented by dreams of Erin and of his people, the Fianna. These dreams became more and more powerful with the passing of time and he ached with the desire to visit his homeland once again. Such a dreadful anxiety could not be hidden from Niamh, for she knew what troubled her husband and could not bear to see him suffer this deep sadness and unrest.

'Go, Oisín,' she told him, 'though it breaks my heart, I will not hinder you. But you must promise me, in the name of our love for each other and for our children, that you will not dismount on Erin's soil, for time has autonomy in the land of Erin. Hear my warning that if you touch the earth, you will never again return to the Land of Youth.'

Having listened carefully to these words of caution, Oisín rode away, guided by his magical steed across the plains leading back to his beloved country. After five long days, he arrived in his native land and made his way to the home of his father. Cheered by memories of his youth and the joyous welcome home he knew he would soon receive, he rode to the far side of the forest and waited anxiously for the thick mist to clear so that the great house would be revealed in all its regal splendour. Yet when the drizzling clouds finally dispersed, Oisín was shocked to discover only a pile of crumbling stones where the stronghold of Finn mac Cumaill had once stood firm. Utterly distressed and bewildered, he turned his horse swiftly around and galloped away in search of any mortal creature who might bring him news of the Fianna.

After what seemed an eternity, he spotted on the horizon a strange band of men toiling and sweating in their efforts to lift a slab of granite from the ground. Oisín marvelled at their small frames and their lack of strength in lifting such a trifling load.

'I am searching for the dwelling place of Finn mac Cumaill and the Fianna,' he shouted to the men.

'We have often heard of Finn,' replied a stooped, wizened figure, the eldest of the group. 'But it has been many hundreds of years since the great battle of Gabra where he and the last of the Fianna lost their lives.'

'I can see you possess the blood of such mighty ancestors,' added another of the band. 'Can you lend us your strength to shift this stone?'

Niamh's words of counsel to Oisín had not been forgotten, but he was angered by these men of Erin who stood before him so weak and feeble. Filled with a great pride in his own strength and ability, he bent forward from his horse to assist in the lifting of the slab. But the angle at which he had leaned towards the men, added to the weight of the stone, caused the animal's saddle-girth to snap and Oisín could not save himself from falling to the ground. In an instant, his steed had disappeared into thin air, his royal garments had turned to grimy sackcloth and his youthful warrior's face had become creased and lined as the burden of three hundred years of mortal life fell on him. Withered and blind, he reached out with his bony arms, grasping in the dark for some form of comfort. A wretched, pitiful cry escaped his lips and he heard again Niamh's parting words to him. As he lay helpless on the cold, damp earth, he began to weep inconsolably for the wife and children to whom he could never now return in the Land of Eternal Youth.

The Legend of Tchi-Niu

IN THE QUAINT COMMENTARY accompanying the text of that holy book of Lao-tseu called Kan-ing-p'ien may be found a little story so old that the name of the one who first told it has been forgotten for a thousand years, yet so beautiful that it lives still in the memory of four hundred millions of people, like a prayer that, once learned, is forever remembered. The Chinese writer makes no mention of any city nor of any province, although even in the relation of the most ancient traditions such an omission is rare; we are only told that the name of the hero of the legend was Tong-yong, and that he lived in the years of the great dynasty of Han, some twenty centuries ago.

* * *

Tong-Yong's mother had died while he was yet an infant; and when he became a youth of nineteen years his father also passed away, leaving him utterly alone in the world, and without resources of any sort; for, being a very poor man, Tong's father had put himself to great straits to educate the lad, and had not been able to lay by even one copper coin of his earnings. And Tong lamented greatly to find himself so destitute that he could not honor the memory of that good father by having the customary rites of burial performed, and a carven tomb erected upon a propitious site. The poor only are friends of the poor; and among all those whom Tong knew; there was no one able to assist him in defraying the expenses of the funeral. In one way only could the youth obtain money – by selling himself as a slave to some rich cultivator; and this he at last decided to do. In vain his friends did their utmost to dissuade him; and to no purpose did they attempt to delay the accomplishment of his sacrifice by beguiling promises of future aid. Tong only replied that he would sell his freedom a hundred times, if it were possible, rather than suffer his father's memory to remain unhonored even for a brief season. And furthermore, confiding in his youth and strength, he determined to put a high price upon his servitude – a price which would enable him to build a handsome tomb, but which it would be well-nigh impossible for him ever to repay.

* * *

Accordingly he repaired to the broad public place where slaves and debtors were exposed for sale, and seated himself upon a bench of stone, having affixed to his shoulders a placard inscribed with the terms of his servitude and the list of his qualifications as a laborer. Many who read the characters upon the placard smiled disdainfully at the price asked, and passed on without a word; others lingered only to question him out of simple curiosity; some commended him with hollow praise; some openly mocked his unselfishness, and laughed at his childish piety. Thus many hours wearily passed, and Tong had almost despaired of finding a master, when there rode up a high official of the province – a grave and handsome man, lord of a thousand slaves, and owner of vast estates. Reining in his Tartar horse, the official halted to read the placard and to consider the value of the slave. He did not smile, or advise, or ask any questions; but having observed the price asked, and the fine strong limbs of the youth, purchased him without further ado, merely ordering his attendant to pay the sum and to see that the necessary papers were made out.

* * *

Thus Tong found himself enabled to fulfil the wish of his heart, and to have a monument built which, although of small size, was destined to delight the eyes of all who beheld it, being designed by cunning artists and executed by skilful sculptors. And while it was yet designed only, the pious rites were performed, the silver coin was placed in the mouth of the dead, the white lanterns were hung at the door, the holy prayers were recited, and paper shapes of all things the departed might need in the land of the Genii were consumed in consecrated fire. And after the geomancers and the necromancers had chosen a burial-spot which no unlucky star could shine upon, a place of rest which no demon or dragon might ever disturb, the beautiful chih was built. Then was the phantom money strewn along the way; the funeral procession departed from the dwelling of the dead, and with prayers and lamentation the mortal remains of Tong's good father were borne to the tomb.

Then Tong entered as a slave into the service of his purchaser, who allotted him a little hut to dwell in; and thither Tong carried with him those wooden tablets, bearing the ancestral names, before which filial piety must daily burn the incense of prayer, and perform the tender duties of family worship.

* * *

Thrice had spring perfumed the breast of the land with flowers, and thrice had been celebrated that festival of the dead which is called Siu-fan-ti, and thrice had Tong swept and garnished his father's tomb and presented his fivefold offering of fruits and meats. The period of mourning had passed, yet he had not ceased to mourn for his parent. The years revolved with their moons, bringing him no hour of joy, no day of happy rest; yet he never lamented his servitude, or failed to perform the rites of ancestral worship – until at last the fever of the rice-fields laid strong hold upon him, and he could not arise from his couch; and his fellow-laborers thought him destined to die. There was no one to wait upon him, no one to care for his needs, inasmuch as slaves and servants were wholly busied with the duties of the household or the labor of the fields – all departing to toil at sunrise and returning weary only after the sundown.

Now, while the sick youth slumbered the fitful slumber of exhaustion one sultry noon, he dreamed that a strange and beautiful woman stood by him, and bent above him and touched his forehead with the long, fine fingers of her shapely hand. And at her cool touch a weird sweet shock passed through him, and all his veins tingled as if thrilled by new life. Opening his eyes in wonder, he saw verily bending over him the charming being of whom he had dreamed, and he knew that her lithe hand really caressed his throbbing forehead. But the flame of the fever was gone, a delicious coolness now penetrated every fibre of his body, and the thrill of which he had dreamed still tingled in his blood like a great joy. Even at the same moment the eyes of the gentle visitor met his own, and he saw they were singularly beautiful, and shone like splendid black jewels under brows curved like the wings of the swallow. Yet their calm gaze seemed to pass through him as light through crystal; and a vague awe came upon him, so that the question which had risen to his lips found no utterance. Then she, still caressing him, smiled and said: 'I have come to restore thy strength and to be thy wife. Arise and worship with me.'

Her clear voice had tones melodious as a bird's song; but in her gaze there was an imperious power which Tong felt he dare not resist. Rising from his couch, he was astounded to find his strength wholly restored; but the cool, slender hand which held his own led him away so swiftly that he had little time for amazement. He would have given years of existence for courage to speak of his misery, to declare his utter inability to maintain a wife; but something irresistible in the long dark eyes of his companion forbade him to speak; and as though his inmost thought had been discerned by that wondrous gaze, she said to him, in the same clear voice, 'I will provide.' Then shame made him blush at the thought of his wretched aspect and tattered apparel; but he observed that she also was poorly attired, like a woman of the people – wearing no ornament of any sort, nor even shoes upon her feet. And before he had yet spoken to her, they came before the ancestral tablets; and there she knelt with him and prayed, and pledged him in a cup of wine – brought he knew not from whence – and together they worshipped Heaven and Earth. Thus she became his wife.

* * *

A mysterious marriage it seemed, for neither on that day nor at any future time could Tong venture to ask his wife the name of her family, or of the place whence she came, and he could not answer any of the curious questions which his fellow-laborers put to him concerning her; and she, moreover, never uttered a word about herself, except to say that her name was Tchi. But although Tong had such awe of her that while her eyes were upon him he was as one having no will of his own, he loved her unspeakably; and the thought of his serfdom ceased to weigh upon him from the hour of his marriage. As through magic the little dwelling had become transformed: its misery was masked with charming paper devices – with dainty decorations created out of nothing by that pretty jugglery of which woman only knows the secret.

Each morning at dawn the young husband found a well-prepared and ample repast awaiting him, and each evening also upon his return; but the wife all day sat at her loom, weaving silk after a fashion unlike anything which had ever been seen before in that province. For as she wove, the silk flowed from the loom like a slow current of glossy gold, bearing upon its undulations strange forms of violet and crimson and jewel-green: shapes of ghostly horsemen riding upon horses, and of phantom chariots dragon-drawn, and of standards of trailing cloud. In every dragon's beard glimmered the mystic pearl; in every rider's helmet sparkled the gem of rank. And each day Tchi would weave a great piece of such figured silk; and the fame of her weaving spread abroad. From far and near people thronged to see the marvellous work; and the silk-merchants of great cities heard of it, and they sent messengers to Tchi, asking her that she should weave for them and teach them her secret. Then she wove for them, as they desired, in return for the silver cubes which they brought her; but when they prayed her to teach them, she laughed and said, 'Assuredly I could never teach you, for no one among you has fingers like mine.' And indeed no man could discern her fingers when she wove, any more than he might behold the wings of a bee vibrating in swift flight.

* * *

The seasons passed, and Tong never knew want, so well did his beautiful wife fulfil her promise – 'I will provide'; and the cubes of bright silver brought by the silk-merchants were piled up higher and higher in the great carven chest which Tchi had bought for the storage of the household goods.

One morning, at last, when Tong, having finished his repast, was about to depart to the fields, Tchi unexpectedly bade him remain; and opening the great chest, she took out of it and gave him a document written in the official characters called li-shu. And Tong, looking at it, cried out and leaped in his joy, for it was the certificate of his manumission. Tchi had secretly purchased her husband's freedom with the price of her wondrous silks!

'Thou shalt labor no more for any master,' she said, 'but for thine own sake only. And I have also bought this dwelling, with all which is therein, and the tea-fields to the south, and the mulberry groves hard by, all of which are thine.'

Then Tong, beside himself for gratefulness, would have prostrated himself in worship before her, but that she would not suffer it.

* * *

Thus he was made free; and prosperity came to him with his freedom; and whatsoever he gave to the sacred earth was returned to him centupled; and his servants loved him and blessed the beautiful Tchi, so silent and yet so kindly to all about her. But the silk-loom soon remained untouched, for Tchi gave birth to a son, a boy so beautiful that Tong wept with delight when he looked upon him. And thereafter the wife devoted herself wholly to the care of the child.

Now it soon became manifest that the boy was not less wonderful than his wonderful mother. In the third month of his age he could speak; in the seventh month he could repeat by heart the proverbs of the sages, and recite the holy prayers; before the eleventh month he could use the writing-brush with skill, and copy in shapely characters the precepts of Lao-tseu. And the priests of the temples came to behold him and to converse with him, and they marvelled at the charm of the child and the wisdom of what he said; and they blessed Tong, saying: 'Surely this son of thine is a gift from the Master of Heaven, a sign that the immortals love thee. May thine eyes behold a hundred happy summers!'

* * *

It was in the Period of the Eleventh Moon: the flowers had passed away, the perfume of the summer had flown, the winds were growing chill, and in Tong's home the evening fires were lighted. Long the husband and wife sat in the mellow glow – he speaking much of his hopes and joys, and of his son that was to be so grand a man, and of many paternal projects; while she, speaking little, listened to his words, and often turned her wonderful eyes upon him with an answering smile. Never had she seemed so beautiful before; and Tong, watching her face, marked not how the night waned, nor how the fire sank low, nor how the wind sang in the leafless trees without.

All suddenly Tchi arose without speaking, and took his hand in hers and led him, gently as on that strange wedding-morning, to the cradle where their boy slumbered, faintly smiling in his dreams. And in that moment there came upon Tong the same strange fear that he knew when Tchi's eyes had first met his own – the vague fear that love and trust had calmed, but never wholly cast out, like unto the fear of the gods. And all unknowingly, like one yielding to the pressure of mighty invisible hands, he bowed himself low before her, kneeling as to a divinity. Now, when he lifted his eyes again to her face, he closed them forthwith in awe; for she towered before him taller than any mortal woman, and there was a glow about her as of sunbeams, and the light of her limbs shone through her garments. But her sweet voice came to him with all the tenderness of other hours, saying: 'Lo! my beloved, the moment has come in which I must forsake thee; for I was never of mortal born, and the Invisible may incarnate themselves for a time only. Yet I leave with thee the pledge of our love – this fair son, who shall ever be to thee as faithful and as fond as thou thyself hast been. Know, my beloved, that I was sent to thee even by the Master of Heaven, in reward of thy filial piety, and that I must now return to the glory of His house: I AM THE GODDESS XXHI-NIU.'

Even as she ceased to speak, the great glow faded; and Tong, re-opening his eyes, knew that she had passed away forever – mysteriously as pass the winds of heaven, irrevocably as the light of a flame blown out. Yet all the doors were barred, all the windows unopened. Still the child slept, smiling in his sleep. Outside, the darkness was breaking; the sky was brightening swiftly; the night was past. With splendid majesty the East threw open high gates of gold for the coming of the sun; and, illuminated by the glory of his coming, the vapors of morning wrought themselves into marvellous shapes of shifting color – into forms weirdly beautiful as the silken dreams woven in the loom of Tchi-Niu.

Tales of King Arthur, from Le Morte d'Arthur: Book I

Chapter V: How Arthur Was Chosen King, and of Wonders and Marvels of a Sword Taken out of a Stone by the Said Arthur

THEN STOOD THE REALM in great jeopardy long while, for every lord that was mighty of men made him strong, and many weened to have been king. Then Merlin went to the Archbishop of Canterbury, and counselled him for to send for all the lords of the realm, and all the gentlemen of arms, that they should to London come by Christmas, upon pain of cursing; and for this cause, that Jesus, that was born on that night, that he would of his great mercy show some miracle, as he was come to be king of mankind, for to show some miracle who should be rightwise king of this realm. So the Archbishop, by the advice of Merlin, sent for all the lords and gentlemen of arms that they should come by Christmas even unto London. And many of them made them clean of their life, that their prayer might be the more acceptable unto God. So in the greatest church of London, whether it were Paul's or not the French book maketh no mention, all the estates were long or day in the church for to pray. And when matins and the first mass was done, there was seen in the churchyard, against the high altar, a great stone four square, like unto a marble stone; and in midst thereof was like an anvil of steel a foot on high, and therein stuck a fair sword naked by the point, and letters there were written in gold about the sword that said thus:

Whoso pulleth out this sword of this stone and anvil,
is rightwise king born of all England.

Then the people marvelled, and told it to the Archbishop. I command, said the Archbishop, that ye keep you within your church and pray unto God still, that no man touch the sword till the high mass be all done. So when all masses were done all the lords went to behold the stone and the sword. And when they saw the scripture some assayed, such as would have been king. But none might stir the sword nor move it.

'He is not here,' said the Archbishop, 'that shall achieve the sword, but doubt not God will make him known. But this is my counsel,' said the Archbishop, 'that we let purvey ten knights, men of good fame, and they to keep this sword.'

So it was ordained, and then there was made a cry, that every man should assay that would, for to win the sword. And upon New Year's Day the barons let make a jousts and a tournament, that all knights that would joust or tourney there might play, and all this was ordained for to keep the lords together and the commons, for the Archbishop trusted that God would make him known that should win the sword.

So upon New Year's Day, when the service was done, the barons rode unto the field, some to joust and some to tourney, and so it happened that Sir Ector, that had great livelihood about London, rode unto the jousts, and with him rode Sir Kay his son, and young Arthur that was his nourished brother; and Sir Kay was made knight at All Hallowmass afore. So as they rode to the jousts-ward, Sir Kay lost his sword, for he had left it at his father's lodging, and so he prayed young Arthur for to ride for his sword.

'I will well,' said Arthur, and rode fast after the sword, and when he came home, the lady and all were out to see the jousting. Then was Arthur wroth, and said to himself, 'I will ride to the churchyard, and take the sword with me that sticketh in the stone, for my brother Sir Kay shall not be without a sword this day.' So when he came to the churchyard, Sir Arthur alighted and tied his horse to the stile, and so he went to the tent, and found no knights there, for they were at the jousting. And so he handled the sword by the handles, and lightly and fiercely pulled it out of the stone, and took his horse and rode his way until he came to his brother Sir Kay, and delivered him the sword. And as soon as Sir Kay saw the sword, he wist well it was the sword of the stone, and so he rode to his father Sir Ector, and said: Sir, lo here is the sword of the stone, wherefore I must be king of this land. When Sir Ector beheld the sword, he returned again and came to the church, and there they alighted all three, and went into the church. And anon he made Sir Kay swear upon a book how he came to that sword.

'Sir,' said Sir Kay, 'by my brother Arthur, for he brought it to me.'

'How gat ye this sword?' said Sir Ector to Arthur.

'Sir, I will tell you. When I came home for my brother's sword, I found nobody at home to deliver me his sword; and so I thought my brother Sir Kay should not be swordless, and so I came hither eagerly and pulled it out of the stone without any pain.'

'Found ye any knights about this sword?' said Sir Ector.

'Nay,' said Arthur.

'Now,' said Sir Ector to Arthur, 'I understand ye must be king of this land.'

'Wherefore I,' said Arthur, 'and for what cause?'

'Sir,' said Ector, 'for God will have it so; for there should never man have drawn out this sword, but he that shall be rightwise king of this land. Now let me see whether ye can put the sword there as it was, and pull it out again.'

'That is no mastery,' said Arthur, and so he put it in the stone; wherewithal Sir Ector assayed to pull out the sword and failed.

Chapter VI: How King Arthur Pulled Out the Sword Divers Times

'Now assay,' said Sir Ector unto Sir Kay. And anon he pulled at the sword with all his might; but it would not be. 'Now shall ye assay,' said Sir Ector to Arthur.

'I will well,' said Arthur, and pulled it out easily. And therewithal Sir Ector knelt down to the earth, and Sir Kay. 'Alas,' said Arthur, 'my own dear father and brother, why kneel ye to me?'

'Nay, nay, my lord Arthur, it is not so; I was never your father nor of your blood, but I wot well ye are of an higher blood than I weened ye were.' And then Sir Ector told him all, how he was betaken him for to nourish him, and by whose commandment, and by Merlin's deliverance.

Then Arthur made great dole when he understood that Sir Ector was not his father.

'Sir,' said Ector unto Arthur, 'will ye be my good and gracious lord when ye are king?'

'Else were I to blame,' said Arthur, 'for ye are the man in the world that I am most beholden to, and my good lady and mother your wife, that as well as her own hath fostered me and kept. And if ever it be God's will that I be king as ye say, ye shall desire of me what I may do, and I shall not fail you.'

'God forbid I should fail you Sir,' said Sir Ector, 'I will ask no more of you, but that ye will make my son, your foster brother, Sir Kay, seneschal of all your lands.'

'That shall be done,' said Arthur, 'and more, by the faith of my body, that never man shall have that office but he, while he and I live.'

Therewithal they went unto the Archbishop, and told him how the sword was achieved, and by whom; and on Twelfth-day all the barons came thither, and to assay to take the sword, who that would assay. But there afore them all, there might none take it out but Arthur; wherefore there were many lords wroth, and said it was great shame unto them all and the realm, to be overgoverned with a boy of no high blood born. And so they fell out at that time that it was put off till Candlemas and then all the barons should meet there again; but always the ten knights were ordained to watch the sword day and night, and so they set a pavilion over the stone and the sword, and five always watched. So at Candlemas many more great lords came thither for to have won the sword, but there might none prevail. And right as Arthur did at Christmas, he did at Candlemas, and pulled out the sword easily, whereof the barons were sore aggrieved and put it off in delay till the high feast of Easter. And as Arthur sped before, so did he at Easter; yet there were some of the great lords had indignation that Arthur should be king, and put it off in a delay till the feast of Pentecost.

Then the Archbishop of Canterbury by Merlin's providence let purvey then of the best knights that they might get, and such knights as Uther Pendragon loved best and most trusted in his days. And such knights were put about Arthur as Sir Baudwin of Britain, Sir Kay, Sir Ulfius, Sir Brastias. All these, with many other, were always about Arthur, day and night, till the feast of Pentecost.

Chapter VII: How King Arthur Was Crowned, and How He Made Officers

And at the feast of Pentecost all manner of men assayed to pull at the sword that would assay; but none might prevail but Arthur, and pulled it out afore all the lords and commons that were there, wherefore all the commons cried at once, 'We will have Arthur unto our king, we will put him no more in delay, for we all see that it is God's will that he shall be our king, and who that holdeth against it, we will slay him.'

And therewithal they kneeled at once, both rich and poor, and cried Arthur mercy because they had delayed him so long, and Arthur forgave them, and took the sword between both his hands, and offered it upon the altar where the Archbishop was, and so was he made knight of the best man that was there. And so anon was the coronation made. And there was he sworn unto his lords and the commons for to be a true king, to stand with true justice from thenceforth the days of this life. Also then he made all lords that held of the crown to come in, and to do service as they ought to do. And many complaints were made unto Sir Arthur of great wrongs that were done since the death of King Uther, of many lands that were bereaved lords, knights, ladies, and gentlemen. Wherefore King Arthur made the lands to be given again unto them that owned them.

When this was done, that the king had stablished all the countries about London, then he let make Sir Kay seneschal of England; and Sir Baudwin of Britain was made constable; and Sir Ulfius was made chamberlain; and Sir Brastias was made warden to wait upon the north from Trent forwards, for it was that time the most party the king's enemies. But within few years after Arthur won all the north, Scotland, and all that were under their obeissance. Also Wales, a part of it, held against Arthur, but he overcame them all, as he did the remnant, through the noble prowess of himself and his knights of the Round Table.

Chapter VIII: How King Arthur Held in Wales, at a Pentecost, a Great Feast, and What Kings and Lords Came to His Feast

Then the king removed into Wales, and let cry a great feast that it should be holden at Pentecost after the incoronation of him at the city of Carlion. Unto the feast came King Lot of Lothian and of Orkney, with five hundred knights with him. Also there came to the feast King Uriens of Gore with four hundred knights with him. Also there came to that feast King Nentres of Garlot, with seven hundred knights with him. Also there came to the feast the king of Scotland with six hundred knights with him, and he was but a young man. Also there came to the feast a king that was called the King with the Hundred Knights, but he and his men were passing well beseen at all points. Also there came the king of Carados with five hundred knights. And King Arthur was glad of their coming, for he weened that all the kings and knights had come for great love, and to have done him worship at his feast; wherefore the king made great joy, and sent the kings and knights great presents. But the kings would none receive, but rebuked the messengers shamefully, and said they had no joy to receive no gifts of a beardless boy that was come of low blood, and sent him word they would none of his gifts, but that they were come to give him gifts with hard swords betwixt the neck and the shoulders: and therefore they came thither, so they told to the messengers plainly, for it was great shame to all them to see such a boy to have a rule of so noble a realm as this land was. With this answer the messengers departed and told to King Arthur this answer. Wherefore, by the advice of his barons, he took him to a strong tower with five hundred good men with him. And all the kings aforesaid in a manner laid a siege to-fore him, but King Arthur was well victualed. And within fifteen days there came Merlin among them into the city of Carlion. Then all the kings were passing glad of Merlin, and asked him, 'For what cause is that boy Arthur made your king?'

'Sirs,' said Merlin, 'I shall tell you the cause, for he is King Uther Pendragon's son, born in wedlock, gotten on Igraine, the duke's wife of Tintagil.'

'Then is he a bastard,' they said all.

'Nay,' said Merlin, 'after the death of the duke, more than three hours, was Arthur begotten, and thirteen days after King Uther wedded Igraine; and therefore I prove him he is no bastard. And who saith nay, he shall be king and overcome all his enemies; and, or he die, he shall be long king of all England, and have under his obeissance Wales, Ireland, and Scotland, and more realms than I will now rehearse.'

Some of the kings had marvel of Merlin's words, and deemed well that it should be as he said; and some of them laughed him to scorn, as King Lot; and more other called him a witch. But then were they accorded with Merlin, that King Arthur should come out and speak with the kings, and to come safe and to go safe, such surance there was made. So Merlin went unto King Arthur, and told him how he had done, and bade him fear not, but come out boldly and speak with them, and spare them not, but answer them as their king and chieftain; for ye shall overcome them all, whether they will or nill.

Chapter IX: Of the First War that King Arthur Had, and How He Won the Field

Then King Arthur came out of his tower, and had under his gown a jesseraunt of double mail, and there went with him the Archbishop of Canterbury, and Sir Baudwin of Britain, and Sir

Kay, and Sir Brastias: these were the men of most worship that were with him. And when they were met there was no meekness, but stout words on both sides; but always King Arthur answered them, and said he would make them to bow an he lived. Wherefore they departed with wrath, and King Arthur bade keep them well, and they bade the king keep him well. So the king returned him to the tower again and armed him and all his knights. What will ye do? said Merlin to the kings; ye were better for to stint, for ye shall not here prevail though ye were ten times so many. Be we well advised to be afeared of a dream-reader? said King Lot. With that Merlin vanished away, and came to King Arthur, and bade him set on them fiercely; and in the meanwhile there were three hundred good men, of the best that were with the kings, that went straight unto King Arthur, and that comforted him greatly. Sir, said Merlin to Arthur, fight not with the sword that ye had by miracle, till that ye see ye go unto the worse, then draw it out and do your best. So forthwithal King Arthur set upon them in their lodging. And Sir Baudwin, Sir Kay, and Sir Brastias slew on the right hand and on the left hand that it was marvel; and always King Arthur on horseback laid on with a sword, and did marvellous deeds of arms, that many of the kings had great joy of his deeds and hardiness.

Then King Lot brake out on the back side, and the King with the Hundred Knights, and King Carados, and set on Arthur fiercely behind him. With that Sir Arthur turned with his knights, and smote behind and before, and ever Sir Arthur was in the foremost press till his horse was slain underneath him. And therewith King Lot smote down King Arthur. With that his four knights received him and set him on horseback. Then he drew his sword Excalibur, but it was so bright in his enemies' eyes, that it gave light like thirty torches. And therewith he put them a-back, and slew much people. And then the commons of Carlion arose with clubs and staves and slew many knights; but all the kings held them together with their knights that were left alive, and so fled and departed. And Merlin came unto Arthur, and counselled him to follow them no further.

Extracts from the Sigurd Saga

The Sword in the Branstock

THE STORY OF THE VOLSUNGS begins with Sigi, a son of Odin, a powerful man, and generally respected, until he killed a man from motives of jealousy, the latter having slain more game when they were out hunting together. In consequence of this crime, Sigi was driven from his own land and declared an outlaw. But it seems that he had not entirely forfeited Odin's favour, for the god now provided him with a well-equipped vessel, together with a number of brave followers, and promised that victory should ever attend him.

Thus aided by Odin, the raids of Sigi became a terror to his foes, and in the end he won the glorious empire of the Huns and for many years reigned as a powerful monarch. But in extreme old age his fortune changed, Odin forsook him, his wife's kindred fell upon him, and he was slain in a treacherous encounter.

His death was soon avenged, however, for Rerir, his son, returning from an expedition upon which he had been absent from the land at the time, put the murderers to death as his first act upon mounting the throne. The rule of Rerir was marked by every sign of prosperity, but his dearest wish, a son to succeed him, remained unfulfilled for many a year. Finally, however, Frigga decided to grant his constant prayer, and to vouchsafe the heir he longed for. She accordingly despatched her swift messenger Gna, or Liod, with a miraculous apple, which she dropped into his lap as he was sitting alone on the hillside. Glancing upward, Rerir recognised the emissary of the goddess, and joyfully hastened home to partake of the apple with his wife. The child who in due time was born under these favourable auspices was a handsome little lad. His parents called him Volsung, and while he was still a mere infant they both died, and the child became ruler of the land.

Years passed and Volsung's wealth and power ever increased. He was the boldest leader, and rallied many brave warriors around him. Full oft did they drink his mead underneath the Branstock, a mighty oak, which, rising in the middle of his hall, pierced the roof and overshadowed the whole house.

Ten stalwart sons were born to Volsung, and one daughter, Signy, came to brighten his home. So lovely was this maiden that when she reached marriageable age many suitors asked for her hand, among whom was Siggeir, King of the Goths, who finally obtained Volsung's consent, although Signy had never seen him.

When the wedding-day came, and the bride beheld her destined husband she shrank in dismay, for his puny form and lowering glances contrasted sadly with her brothers' sturdy frames and open faces. But it was too late to withdraw – the family honour was at stake – and Signy so successfully concealed her dislike that none save her twin brother Sigmund suspected with what reluctance she became Siggeir's wife.

While the wedding feast was in progress, and when the merry-making was at its height, the entrance to the hall was suddenly darkened by the tall form of a one-eyed man, closely enveloped in a mantle of cloudy blue. Without vouchsafing word or glance to any in the assembly, the stranger strode to the Branstock and thrust a glittering sword up to the hilt in its great bole. Then, turning slowly round, he faced the awe-struck and silent assembly, and declared that the weapon would be for the warrior who could pull it out of its oaken sheath, and that it would assure him victory in every battle. The words ended, he then passed out as he had entered, and disappeared, leaving a conviction in the minds of all that Odin, king of the gods, had been in their midst.

Volsung was the first to recover the power of speech, and, waiving his own right first to essay the feat, he invited Siggeir to make the first attempt to draw the divine weapon out of the tree-trunk. The bridegroom anxiously tugged and strained, but the sword remained firmly embedded in the oak and he resumed his seat, with an air of chagrin. Then Volsung tried, with the same result. The weapon was evidently not intended for either of them, and the young Volsung princes were next invited to try their strength.

The nine eldest sons were equally unsuccessful; but when Sigmund, the tenth and youngest, laid his firm young hand upon the hilt, the sword yielded easily to his touch, and he triumphantly drew it out as though it had merely been sheathed in its scabbard.

Nearly all present were gratified at the success of the young prince; but Siggeir's heart was filled with envy, and he coveted possession of the weapon. He offered to purchase it from his young brother-in-law, but Sigmund refused to part with it at any price, declaring that it was clear that the weapon had been intended for him to wear. This refusal so offended Siggeir that he secretly resolved to exterminate the proud Volsungs, and to secure the divine sword at the same time that he indulged his hatred towards his new kinsmen.

Concealing his chagrin, however, he turned to Volsung and cordially invited him to visit his court a month later, together with his sons and kinsmen. The invitation was immediately accepted, and although Signy, suspecting evil, secretly sought her father while her husband slept, and implored him to retract his promise and stay at home, he would not consent to withdraw his plighted word and so exhibit fear.

Siggeir's Treachery

A few weeks after the return of the bridal couple, therefore, Volsung's well-manned vessels arrived within sight of Siggeir's shores. Signy had been keeping anxious watch, and when she perceived them she hastened down to the beach to implore her kinsmen not to land, warning them that her husband had treacherously planned an ambush, whence they could not escape alive. But Volsung and his sons, whom no peril could daunt, calmly bade her return to her husband's palace, and donning their arms they boldly set foot ashore.

It befell as Signy had said, for on their way to the palace the brave little troop fell into Siggeir's ambush, and, although they fought with heroic courage, they were so borne down by the superior number of their foes that Volsung was slain and all his sons were made captive. The young men were led bound into the presence of the cowardly Siggeir, who had taken no part in the fight, and Sigmund was forced to relinquish his precious sword, after which he and his brothers were condemned to death.

Signy, hearing the cruel sentence, vainly interceded for her brothers: all she could obtain by her prayers and entreaties was that they should be chained to a fallen oak in the forest, to perish of hunger and thirst if the wild beasts should spare them. Then, lest she should visit and succour her brothers, Siggeir confined his wife in the palace, where she was closely guarded night and day.

Every morning early Siggeir himself sent a messenger into the forest to see whether the Volsungs were still living, and every morning the man returned saying a monster had come during the night and had devoured one of the princes, leaving nothing but his bones. At last, when none but Sigmund remained alive, Signy thought of a plan, and she prevailed on one of her servants to carry some honey into the forest and smear it over her brother's face and mouth.

When the wild beast came that night, attracted by the smell of the honey, it licked Sigmund's face, and even thrust its tongue into his mouth. Clinching his teeth upon it, Sigmund, weak and wounded as he was, held on to the animal, and in its frantic struggles his bonds gave way, and he succeeded in slaying the prowling beast who had devoured his brothers. Then he vanished into the forest, where he remained concealed until the king's messenger had come as usual, and until Signy, released from captivity, came speeding to the forest to weep over her kinsmen's remains.

Seeing her intense grief, and knowing that she had not participated in Siggeir's cruelty, Sigmund stole out of his place of concealment and comforted her as best he could. Together they then buried the whitening bones, and Sigmund registered a solemn oath to avenge his family's wrongs. This vow was fully approved by Signy, who, however, bade her brother bide a favourable time, promising to send him aid. Then the brother and sister sadly parted, she to return to her distasteful palace home, and he to a remote part of the forest, where he built a tiny hut and plied the craft of a smith.

Siggeir now took possession of the Volsung kingdom, and during the next few years he proudly watched the growth of his eldest son, whom Signy secretly sent to her brother when he was ten years of age, that Sigmund might train up the child to help him to obtain vengeance if he should prove worthy. Sigmund reluctantly accepted the charge; but as soon as he had tested the boy he found him deficient in physical courage, so he either sent him back to his mother, or, as some versions relate, slew him.

Some time after this Signy's second son was sent into the forest for the same purpose, but Sigmund found him equally lacking in courage. Evidently none but a pure-blooded Volsung would avail for the grim work of revenge, and Signy, realising this, resolved to commit a crime.

Her resolution taken, she summoned a beautiful young witch, and exchanging forms with her, she sought the depths of the dark forest and took shelter in Sigmund's hut. The Volsung did not penetrate his sister's disguise. He deemed her nought but the gypsy she seemed, and being soon won by her coquetry, he made her his wife. Three days later she disappeared from the hut, and, returning to the palace, she resumed her own form, and when she next gave birth to a son, she rejoiced to see in his bold glance and strong frame the promise of a true Volsung hero.

The Story of Sinfiotli

When Sinfiotli, as the child was called, was ten years of age, she herself made a preliminary test of his courage by sewing his garment to his skin, and then suddenly snatching it off, and as the brave boy did not so much as wince, but laughed aloud, she confidently sent him to the forest hut. Sigmund speedily prepared his usual test, and ere leaving the hut one day he bade Sinfiotli take meal from a certain sack, and knead it and bake some bread. On returning home, Sigmund asked whether his orders had been carried out. The lad replied by showing the bread, and when closely questioned he artlessly confessed that he had been obliged to knead into the loaf a great adder which was hidden in the meal. Pleased to see that the boy, for whom he felt a strange affection, had successfully stood the test which had daunted his brothers, Sigmund bade him refrain from eating of the loaf, for although he was proof against the bite of a reptile, he could not, like his mentor, taste poison unharmed.

Sigmund now began patiently to teach Sinfiotli all that a warrior of the North should know, and the two soon became inseparable companions. One day while ranging the forest together they came to a hut, where they found two men sound asleep. Near by hung two wolf-skins, which suggested immediately that the strangers were werewolves, whom a cruel spell prevented from bearing their natural form save for a short space at a time. Prompted by curiosity, Sigmund and Sinfiotli donned the wolf-skins, and they were soon, in the guise of wolves, rushing through the forest, slaying and devouring all that came in their way.

Such were their wolfish passions that soon they attacked each other, and after a fierce struggle Sinfiotli, the younger and weaker, fell dead. This catastrophe brought Sigmund to his senses, and he hung over his murdered companion in despair.

While thus engaged he saw two weasels come out of the forest and attack each other fiercely until one lay dead. The victor then sprang into the thicket, to return with a leaf, which it laid upon its companion's breast. Then was seen a marvellous thing, for at the touch of the magic herb the dead beast came back to life. A moment later a raven flying overhead dropped a similar leaf at Sigmund's feet, and he, understanding that the gods wished to help him, laid it upon Sinfiotli, who was at once restored to life.

In dire fear lest they might work each other further mischief, Sigmund and Sinfiotli now crept home and patiently waited until the time of their release should come. To their great relief the skins dropped off on the ninth night, and they hastily flung them into the fire, where they were entirely consumed, and the spell was broken for ever.

Sigmund now confided the story of his wrongs to Sinfiotli, who swore that, although Siggeir was his father (for neither he nor Sigmund knew the secret of his birth), he would aid him in his revenge. At nightfall, therefore, he accompanied Sigmund to the king's hall, and they entered unseen, concealing themselves in the cellar, behind the huge vats of beer. Here they were discovered by Signy's two youngest children, who, while playing with golden rings, which rolled into the cellar, came suddenly upon the men in ambush.

They loudly proclaimed their discovery to their father and his guests, but, before Siggeir and his men could take up arms, Signy took both children, and dragging them into the cellar bade her brother slay the little traitors. This Sigmund utterly refused to do, but Sinfiotli struck off their heads ere he turned to fight against the assailants, who were now closing in upon them.

In spite of all efforts Sigmund and his brave young companion soon fell into the hands of the Goths, whereupon Siggeir sentenced them to be buried alive in the same mound, with a stone partition between them so that they could neither see nor touch each other. The prisoners were accordingly confined in their living grave, and their foes were about to place the last stones on the roof, when Signy drew near, bearing a bundle of straw, which she was allowed to throw at Sinfiotli's feet, for the Goths fancied that it contained only a few provisions which would prolong his agony without helping him to escape.

When all was still, Sinfiotli undid the sheaf, and great was his joy when he found instead of bread the sword which Odin had given to Sigmund. Knowing that nothing could dull or break the keen edge of this fine weapon, Sinfiotli thrust it through the stone partition, and, aided by Sigmund, he succeeded in cutting an opening, and in the end both effected their escape through the roof.

As soon as they were free, Sigmund and Sinfiotli returned to the king's hall, and piling combustible materials around it, they set fire to the mass. Then stationing themselves on either side of the entrance, they prevented all but the women from passing through. They loudly adjured Signy to escape ere it was too late, but she did not desire to live, and so coming to the entrance for a last embrace she found opportunity to whisper the secret of Sinfiotli's birth, after which she sprang back into the flames and perished with the rest.

The long-planned vengeance for the slaughter of the Volsungs having thus been carried out, Sigmund, feeling that nothing now detained him in the land of the Goths, set sail with Sinfiotli and returned to Hunaland, where he was warmly welcomed to the seat of power under the shade of his ancestral tree, the mighty Branstock. When his authority was fully established, Sigmund married Borghild, a beautiful princess, who bore him two sons, Hamond and Helgi. The latter was visited by the Norns as he lay in his cradle, and they promised him sumptuous entertainment in Valhalla when his earthly career should be ended.

Northern kings generally entrusted their sons' upbringing to a stranger, for they thought that so they would be treated with less indulgence than at home. Accordingly Helgi was fostered by Hagal, and under his care the young prince became so fearless that at the age of fifteen he ventured alone into the hall of Hunding, with whose race his family was at feud. Passing through the hall unmolested and unrecognised, he left an insolent message, which so angered Hunding that he immediately set out in pursuit of the bold young prince, whom he followed to the dwelling of Hagal. Helgi would then have been secured but that meanwhile he had disguised himself as a servant-maid, and was busy grinding corn as if this were his wonted occupation. The invaders marvelled somewhat at the maid's tall stature and brawny arms, nevertheless they departed without suspecting that they had been so near the hero whom they sought.

Having thus cleverly escaped, Helgi joined Sinfiotli, and collecting an army, the two young men marched boldly against the Hundings, with whom they fought a great battle, over which the Valkyrs hovered, waiting to convey the slain to Valhalla. Gudrun, one of the battle-maidens, was so struck by the courage which Helgi displayed, that she openly sought him and promised to be his wife. Only one of the Hunding race, Dag, remained alive, and he was allowed to go free after promising not to endeavour to avenge his kinsmen's death. This promise was not kept, however, and Dag, having obtained possession of Odin's spear Gungnir, treacherously slew Helgi with it. Gudrun, who in the meantime had fulfilled her promise to become his wife, wept many tears at his death, and laid a solemn curse upon his murderer; then, hearing from one of her maids that her slain husband kept calling for her from the depths of the tomb, she fearlessly entered the mound at night and tenderly inquired why he called and why his wounds continued to bleed after death. Helgi answered that he could not rest happy because of her grief, and declared that for every tear she shed a drop of his blood must flow.

To appease the spirit of her beloved husband, Gudrun from that time ceased to weep, but they did not long remain separated; for soon after the spirit of Helgi had ridden over Bifrost and entered Valhalla, to become leader of the Einheriar, he was joined by Gudrun who, as a Valkyr once more, resumed her loving tendance of him. When at Odin's command she left his side for scenes of human strife, it was to seek new recruits for the army which her lord was to lead into battle when Ragnarok, the twilight of the gods, should come.

Sinfiotli, Sigmund's eldest son, also met an early death; for, having slain in a quarrel the brother of Borghild, she determined to poison him. Twice Sinfiotli detected the attempt and told his father that there was poison in his cup. Twice Sigmund, whom no venom could injure, drained the bowl; and when Borghild made a third attempt, he bade Sinfiotli let the wine flow through his beard. Mistaking the meaning of his father's words, Sinfiotli forthwith drained the cup, and fell lifeless to the ground, for the poison was of the most deadly kind.

Speechless with grief, Sigmund tenderly raised his son's body in his arms, and strode out of the hall and down to the shore, where he deposited his precious burden in a skiff which an old one-eyed boatman brought at his call. He would fain have stepped aboard also, but ere he could do so the boatman pushed off and the frail craft was soon lost to sight. The bereaved father then slowly wended his way home, taking comfort from the thought that Odin himself had come to claim the young hero and had rowed away with him 'out into the west.'

The Birth of Sigurd

Sigmund deposed Borghild as his wife and queen in punishment for this crime, and when he was very old he sued for the hand of Hiordis, a fair young princess, daughter of Eglimi, King of the Islands. This young maiden had many suitors, among others King Lygni of Hunding's race, but so great was Sigmund's fame that she gladly accepted him and became his wife. Lygni, the discarded suitor, was so angry at this decision, that he immediately collected a great army and marched against his successful rival, who, though overpowered by superior numbers, fought with the courage of despair.

From the depths of a thicket which commanded the field of battle, Hiordis and her maid anxiously watched the progress of the strife. They saw Sigmund pile the dead around him, for none could stand against him, until at last a tall, one-eyed warrior suddenly appeared, and the press of battle gave way before the terror of his presence.

Without a moment's pause the new champion aimed a fierce blow at Sigmund, which the old hero parried with his sword. The shock shattered the matchless blade, and although the strange assailant vanished as he had come, Sigmund was left defenceless and was soon wounded unto death by his foes.

As the battle was now won, and the Volsung family all slain, Lygni hastened from the battlefield to take possession of the kingdom and force the fair Hiordis to become his wife. As soon as he had gone, however, the beautiful young queen crept from her hiding-place in the thicket, and sought the spot where Sigmund lay all but dead. She caught the stricken hero to her breast in a last passionate embrace, and then listened tearfully while he bade her gather the fragments of his sword and carefully treasure them for their son whom he foretold was soon to be born, and who was destined to avenge his father's death and to be far greater than he.

While Hiordis was mourning over Sigmund's lifeless body, her handmaiden suddenly warned her of the approach of a band of vikings. Retreating into the thicket once more, the two women exchanged garments, after which Hiordis bade the maid walk first and personate the queen, and they went thus to meet the viking Elf (Helfrat or Helferich). Elf received the women graciously, and their story of the battle so excited his admiration for Sigmund that he caused the remains of the slain hero to be reverentially removed to a suitable spot, where they were interred with all due ceremony. He then offered the queen and her maid a safe asylum in his hall, and they gladly accompanied him over the seas.

As he had doubted their relative positions from the first, Elf took the first opportunity after arriving in his kingdom to ask a seemingly idle question in order to ascertain the truth. He asked the pretended queen how she knew the hour had come for rising when the winter days were short and there was no light to announce the coming of morn, and she replied that, as she was in the habit of drinking milk ere she fed the cows, she always awoke thirsty. When the same question was put to the real Hiordis, she answered, with as little reflection, that she knew it was morning because at that hour the golden ring which her father had given her grew cold on her hand.

The suspicions of Elf having thus been confirmed, he offered marriage to the pretended handmaiden, Hiordis, promising to cherish her infant son, a promise which he nobly kept. When the child was born Elf himself sprinkled him with water – a ceremony which our pagan ancestors scrupulously observed – and bestowed upon him the name of Sigurd. As he grew up he was treated as the king's own son, and his education was entrusted to Regin, the wisest of men, who knew all things, his own fate not even excepted, for it had been revealed to him that he would fall by the hand of a youth.

Under this tutor Sigurd grew daily in wisdom until few could surpass him. He mastered the smith's craft, and the art of carving all manner of runes; he learned languages, music, and eloquence; and, last but not least, he became a doughty warrior whom none could subdue. When he had reached manhood Regin prompted him to ask the king for a war-horse, a request which was immediately granted, and Gripir, the stud-keeper, was bidden to allow him to choose from the royal stables the steed which he most fancied.

On his way to the meadow where the horses were at pasture, Sigurd met a one-eyed stranger, clad in grey and blue, who accosted the young man and bade him drive the horses into the river and select the one which could breast the tide with least difficulty.

Sigurd received the advice gladly, and upon reaching the meadow he drove the horses into the stream which flowed on one side. One of the number, after crossing, raced round the opposite meadow; and, plunging again into the river, returned to his former pasture without showing any signs of fatigue. Sigurd therefore did not hesitate to select this horse, and he gave him the name of Grane or Greyfell. The steed was a descendant of Odin's eight-footed horse Sleipnir, and besides being unusually strong and indefatigable, was as fearless as his master.

One winter day while Regin and his pupil were sitting by the fire, the old man struck his harp, and, after the manner of the Northern scalds, sang or recited in the following tale, the story of his life.

The Treasure of the Dwarf King

Hreidmar, king of the dwarf folk, was the father of three sons. Fafnir, the eldest, was gifted with a fearless soul and a powerful arm; Otter, the second, with snare and net, and the power of changing his form at will; and Regin, the youngest, with all wisdom and deftness of hand. To please the avaricious Hreidmar, this youngest son fashioned for him a house lined with glittering gold and flashing gems, and this was guarded by Fafnir, whose fierce glances and Aegis helmet none dared encounter.

Now it came to pass that Odin, Hoenir, and Loki once came in human guise, upon one of their wonted expeditions to test the hearts of men, unto the land where Hreidmar dwelt.

As the gods came near to Hreidmar's dwelling, Loki perceived an otter basking in the sun. This was none other than the dwarf king's second son, Otter, who now succumbed to Loki's usual love of destruction. Killing the unfortunate creature he flung its lifeless body over his shoulders, thinking it would furnish a good dish when meal time came.

Loki then hastened after his companions, and entering Hreidmar's house with them, he flung his burden down upon the floor. The moment the dwarf king's glance fell upon the seeming otter, he flew into a towering rage, and ere they could offer effective resistance the gods found themselves lying bound, and they heard Hreidmar declare that never should they recover their liberty until they could satisfy his thirst for gold by giving him of that precious substance enough to cover the skin of the otter inside and out.

As the otter-skin developed the property of stretching itself to a fabulous size, no ordinary treasure could suffice to cover it, and the plight of the gods, therefore, was a very bad one. The case, however, became a little more hopeful when Hreidmar consented to liberate one of their number. The emissary selected was Loki, who lost no time in setting off to the waterfall where the dwarf Andvari dwelt, in order that he might secure the treasure there amassed.

In spite of diligent search, however, Loki could not find the dwarf, until, perceiving a salmon sporting in the foaming waters, it occurred to him that the dwarf might have assumed this shape. Borrowing Ran's net he soon caught the fish, and learned, as he had suspected, that it was Andvari. Finding that there was nothing else for it, the dwarf now reluctantly brought forth his mighty treasure and surrendered it all, including the Helmet of Dread and a hauberk of gold, reserving only a ring which was gifted with miraculous powers, and which, like a magnet, attracted the precious ore. But the greedy Loki, catching sight of it, wrenched it from off the dwarf's finger and departed laughing, while his victim hurled angry curses after him, declaring that the ring would ever prove its possessor's bane and would cause the death of many.

On arriving at Hreidmar's house, Loki found the mighty treasure none too great, for the skin became larger with every object placed upon it, and he was forced to throw in the ring Andvaranaut (Andvari's loom), which he had intended to retain, in order to secure the release of himself and his companions. Andvari's curse of the gold soon began to operate. Fafnir and Regin both coveted a share, while Hriedmar gloated over his treasure night and day, and would not part with an item of it. Fafnir the invincible, seeing at last that he could not otherwise gratify his lust, slew his father, and seized the whole of the treasure, then, when Regin came to claim a share he drove him scornfully away and bade him earn his own living.

Thus exiled, Regin took refuge among men, to whom he taught the arts of sowing and reaping. He showed them how to work metals, sail the seas, tame horses, yoke beasts of burden, build houses, spin, weave, and sew – in short, all the industries of civilised life, which had hitherto been unknown. Years elapsed, and Regin patiently bided his time, hoping that some day he would find a hero strong enough to avenge his wrongs upon Fafnir, whom years of gloating over his treasure had changed into a horrible dragon, the terror of Gnîtaheid (Glittering Heath), where he had taken up his abode.

His story finished, Regin turned suddenly to the attentive Sigurd, saying he knew that the young man could slay the dragon if he wished, and inquiring whether he were ready to aid him to avenge his wrongs.

Sigurd immediately assented, on the condition, however, that the curse should be assumed by Regin, who, also, in order to fitly equip the young man for the coming fight, should forge him a sword, which no blow could break. Twice Regin fashioned a marvellous weapon, but twice Sigurd broke it to pieces on the anvil. Then Sigurd bethought him of the broken fragments of Sigmund's weapon which were treasured by his mother, and going to Hiordis he begged these from her; and either he or Regin forged from them a blade so strong that it divided the great anvil in two without being dinted, and whose temper was such that it neatly severed some wool floating gently upon the stream.

The Fight with the Dragon

Sigurd now went upon a farewell visit to Gripir, who, knowing the future, foretold every event in his coming career; after which he took leave of his mother, and accompanied by Regin set sail for the land of his fathers, vowing to slay the dragon when he had fulfilled his first duty, which was to avenge the death of Sigmund.

On his way to the land of the Volsungs a most marvellous sight was seen, for there came a man walking on the waters. Sigurd straightway took him on board his dragon ship, and the stranger, who gave his name as Feng or Fiollnir, promised favourable winds. Also he taught Sigurd how to distinguish auspicious omens. In reality the old man was Odin or Hnikar, the wave-stiller, but Sigurd did not suspect his identity.

Sigurd was entirely successful in his descent upon Lygni, whom he slew, together with many of his followers. He then departed from his reconquered kingdom and returned with Regin to slay Fafnir. Together they rode through the mountains, which ever rose higher and higher before them, until they came to a great tract of desert which Regin said was the haunt of Fafnir. Sigurd now rode on alone until he met a one-eyed stranger, who bade him dig trenches in the middle of the track along which the dragon daily dragged his slimy length to the river to quench his thirst, and to lie in wait in one of these until the monster passed over him, when he could thrust his sword straight into its heart.

Sigurd gratefully followed this counsel, and was rewarded with complete success, for as the monster's loathsome folds rolled overhead, he thrust his sword upward into its left breast, and as he sprang out of the trench the dragon lay gasping in the throes of death.

Regin had prudently remained at a distance until all danger was past, but seeing that his foe was slain, he now came up. He was fearful lest the young hero should claim a reward, so he began to accuse him of having murdered his kin, but, with feigned magnanimity, he declared that instead of requiring life for life, in accordance with the custom of the North, he would consider it sufficient atonement if Sigurd would cut out the monster's heart and roast it for him on a spit.

Sigurd was aware that a true warrior never refused satisfaction of some kind to the kindred of the slain, so he agreed to the seemingly small proposal, and immediately prepared to act as cook, while Regin dozed until the meat was ready. After an interval Sigurd touched the roast to ascertain whether it were tender, but burning his fingers severely, he instinctively thrust them into his mouth to allay the smart. No sooner had Fafnir's blood thus touched his lips than he discovered, to his utter surprise, that he could understand the songs of the birds, many of which were already gathering round the carrion. Listening attentively, he found that they were telling how Regin meditated mischief against him, and how he ought to slay the old man and take the gold, which was his by right of conquest, after which he ought to partake of the heart and blood of the dragon. As this coincided with his own wishes, he slew the evil old man with a thrust of his sword and proceeded to eat and drink as the birds had suggested, reserving a small portion of Fafnir's heart for future consumption. He then wandered off in search of the mighty hoard, and, after donning the Helmet of Dread, the hauberk of gold, and the ring Andvaranaut, and loading Greyfell with as much gold as he could carry, he sprang to the saddle and sat listening eagerly to the birds' songs to know what his future course should be.

The Sleeping Warrior Maiden

Soon he heard of a warrior maiden fast asleep on a mountain and surrounded by a glittering barrier of flames, through which only the bravest of men could pass to arouse her.

This adventure was the very thing for Sigurd, and he set off at once. The way lay through trackless regions, and the journey was long and cheerless, but at length he came to the Hindarfiall in Frankland, a tall mountain whose cloud-wreathed summit seemed circled by fiery flames.

Sigurd rode up the mountain side, and the light grew more and more vivid as he proceeded, until when he had neared the summit a barrier of lurid flames stood before him. The fire burned with a roar which would have daunted the heart of any other, but Sigurd remembered the words of the birds, and without a moment's hesitation he plunged bravely into its very midst.

The threatening flames having now died away, Sigurd pursued his journey over a broad tract of white ashes, directing his course to a great castle, with shield-hung walls. The great gates stood wide open, and Sigurd rode through them unchallenged by warders or men at arms. Proceeding cautiously, for he feared some snare, he at last came to the centre of the courtyard, where he saw a recumbent form cased in armour. Sigurd dismounted from his steed and eagerly removed the helmet, when he started with surprise to behold, instead of a warrior, the face of a most beautiful maiden.

All his efforts to awaken the sleeper were vain, however, until he had removed her armour, and she lay before him in pure-white linen garments, her long hair falling in golden waves around her. Then as the last fastening of her armour gave way, she opened wide her beautiful eyes, which met the rising sun, and first greeting with rapture the glorious spectacle, she turned to her deliverer, and the young hero and the maiden loved each other at first sight.

The maiden now proceeded to tell Sigurd her story. Her name was Brunhild, and according to some authorities she was the daughter of an earthly king whom Odin had raised to the rank of a Valkyr. She had served him faithfully for a long while, but once had ventured to set her own wishes above his, giving to a younger and therefore more attractive opponent the victory which Odin had commanded for another.

In punishment for this act of disobedience, she had been deprived of her office and banished to earth, where Allfather decreed she should wed like any other member of her sex. This sentence filled Brunhild's heart with dismay, for she greatly feared lest it might be her fate to mate with a coward, whom she would despise. To quiet these apprehensions, Odin took her to Hindarfiall or Hindfell, and touching her with the Thorn of Sleep, that she might await in unchanged youth and beauty the coming of her destined husband, he surrounded her with a barrier of flame which none but a hero would venture through.

From the top of Hindarfiall, Brunhild now pointed out to Sigurd her former home, at Lymdale or Hunaland, telling him he would find her there whenever he chose to come and claim her as his wife; and then, while they stood on the lonely mountain top together, Sigurd placed the ring Andvaranaut upon her finger, in token of betrothal, swearing to love her alone as long as life endured.

According to some authorities, the lovers parted after thus plighting their troth; but others say that Sigurd soon sought out and wedded Brunhild, with whom he lived for a while in perfect happiness until forced to leave her and his infant daughter Aslaug. This child, left orphaned at three years of age, was fostered by Brunhild's father, who, driven away from home, concealed her in a cunningly fashioned harp, until reaching a distant land he was murdered by a peasant couple for the sake of the gold they supposed it to contain. Their surprise and disappointment were great indeed when, on breaking the instrument open, they found a beautiful little girl, whom they deemed mute, as she would not speak a word. Time passed, and the child, whom they had trained as a drudge, grew to be a beautiful maiden, and she won the affection of a passing viking, Ragnar Lodbrog, King of the Danes, to whom she told her tale. The viking sailed away to other lands to fulfil the purposes of his voyage, but when a year had passed, during which time he won much glory, he came back and carried away Aslaug as his bride.

In continuation of the story of Sigurd and Brunhild, however, we are told that the young man went to seek adventures in the great world, where he had vowed, as a true hero, to right the wrong and defend the fatherless and oppressed.

The Niblungs

In the course of his wanderings, Sigurd came to the land of the Niblungs, the land of continual mist, where Giuki and Grimhild were king and queen. The latter was specially to be feared, as she was well versed in magic lore, and could weave spells and concoct marvellous potions which had power to steep the drinker in temporary forgetfulness and compel him to yield to her will.

The king and queen had three sons, Gunnar, Hogni, and Guttorm, who were brave young men, and one daughter, Gudrun, the gentlest as well as the most beautiful of maidens. All welcomed Sigurd most warmly, and Giuki invited him to tarry awhile. The invitation was very agreeable after his long wanderings, and Sigurd was glad to stay and share the pleasures and occupations of the Niblungs. He accompanied them to war, and so distinguished himself by his valour, that he won the admiration of Grimhild and she resolved to secure him as her daughter's husband. One day, therefore, she brewed one of her magic potions, and when he had partaken of it at the hand of Gudrun, he utterly forgot Brunhild and his plighted troth, and all his love was diverted unto the queen's daughter.

Although there was not wanting a vague fear that he had forgotten some event in the past which should rule his conduct, Sigurd asked for and obtained Gudrun's hand, and their wedding was celebrated amid the rejoicings of the people, who loved the young hero very dearly. Sigurd gave his bride some of Fafnir's heart to eat, and the moment she had tasted it her nature was changed, and she began to grow cold and silent to all except him. To further cement his alliance with the two eldest Giukings (as the sons of Giuki were called) Sigurd entered the 'doom ring' with them, and the three young men cut a sod which was placed upon a shield, beneath which they stood while they bared and slightly cut their right arms, allowing their blood to mingle in the fresh earth. Then, when they had sworn eternal friendship, the sod was replaced.

But although Sigurd loved his wife and felt a true fraternal affection for her brothers, he could not lose his haunting sense of oppression, and was seldom seen to smile as radiantly as of old. Giuki had now died, and his eldest son, Gunnar, ruled in his stead. As the young king was unwedded, Grimhild, his mother, besought him to take a wife, suggesting that none seemed more worthy to become Queen of the Niblungs than Brunhild, who, it was reported, sat in a golden hall surrounded by flames, whence she had declared she would issue only to marry the warrior who would dare brave the fire for her sake.

Gunnar immediately prepared to seek this maiden, and strengthened by one of his mother's magic potions, and encouraged by Sigurd, who accompanied him, he felt confident of success. But when on reaching the summit of the mountain he would have ridden into the fire, his steed drew back affrighted and he could not induce him to advance a step. Seeing that his companion's steed did not show signs of fear, he asked him of Sigurd; but although Greyfell allowed Gunnar to mount, he would not stir because his master was not on his back.

Now as Sigurd carried the Helmet of Dread, and Grimhild had given Gunnar a magic potion in case it should be needed, it was possible for the companions to exchange their forms and features, and seeing that Gunnar could not penetrate the flaming wall Sigurd proposed to assume the appearance of Gunnar and woo the bride for him. The king was greatly disappointed, but as no alternative offered he dismounted, and the necessary exchange was soon effected. Then Sigurd mounted Greyfell in the semblance of his companion, and this time the steed showed not the least hesitation, but leaped into the flames at the first touch on his bridle, and soon brought his rider to the castle, where, in the great hall, sat Brunhild. Neither recognised the other: Sigurd because of the magic spell cast over him by Grimhild; Brunhild because of the altered appearance of her lover.

The maiden shrank in disappointment from the dark-haired intruder, for she had deemed it impossible for any but Sigurd to ride through the flaming circle. But she advanced reluctantly to meet her visitor, and when he declared that he had come to woo her, she permitted him to take a husband's place at her side, for she was bound by solemn injunction to accept as her spouse him who should thus seek her through the flames.

Three days did Sigurd remain with Brunhild, and his bright sword lay bared between him and his bride. This singular behaviour aroused the curiosity of the maiden, wherefore Sigurd told her that the gods had bidden him celebrate his wedding thus.

When the fourth morning dawned, Sigurd drew the ring Andvaranaut from Brunhild's hand, and, replacing it by another, he received her solemn promise that in ten days' time she would appear at the Niblung court to take up her duties as queen and faithful wife.

The promise given, Sigurd again passed out of the palace, through the ashes, and joined Gunnar, with whom, after he had reported the success of his venture, he hastened to exchange forms once more. The warriors then turned their steeds homeward, and only to Gudrun did Sigurd reveal the secret of her brother's wooing, and he gave her the fatal ring, little suspecting the many woes which it was destined to occasion.

True to her promise, Brunhild appeared ten days later, and solemnly blessing the house she was about to enter, she greeted Gunnar kindly, and allowed him to conduct her to the great hall, where sat Sigurd beside Gudrun. The Volsung looked up at that moment and as he encountered Brunhild's reproachful eyes Grimhild's spell was broken and the past came back in a flood of bitter recollection. It was too late, however: both were in honour bound, he to Gudrun and she to Gunnar, whom she passively followed to the high seat, to sit beside him as the scalds entertained the royal couple with the ancient lays of their land.

The days passed, and Brunhild remained apparently indifferent, but her heart was hot with anger, and often did she steal out of her husband's palace to the forest, where she could give vent to her grief in solitude.

Meanwhile, Gunnar perceived the cold indifference of his wife to his protestations of affection, and began to have jealous suspicions, wondering whether Sigurd had honestly told the true story of the wooing, and fearing lest he had taken advantage of his position to win Brunhild's love. Sigurd alone continued the even tenor of his way, striving against none but tyrants and oppressors, and cheering all by his kindly words and smile.

On a day the queens went down together to the Rhine to bathe, and as they were entering the water Gudrun claimed precedence by right of her husband's courage. Brunhild refused to yield what she deemed her right, and a quarrel ensued, in the course of which Gudrun accused her sister-in-law of not having kept her faith, producing the ring Andvaranaut in support of her charge. The sight of the fatal ring in the hand of her rival crushed Brunhild, and she fled homeward, and lay in speechless grief day after day, until all thought she must die. In vain did Gunnar and the members of the royal family seek her in turn and implore her to speak; she would not utter a word until Sigurd came and inquired the cause of her unutterable grief. Then, like a long-pent-up stream, her love and anger burst forth, and she overwhelmed the hero with reproaches, until his heart so swelled with grief for her sorrow that the tight bands of his strong armour gave way.

Words had no power to mend that woeful situation, and Brunhild refused to heed when Sigurd offered to repudiate Gudrun, saying, as she dismissed him, that she would not be faithless to Gunnar. The thought that two living men had called her wife was unendurable to her pride, and the next time her husband sought her presence she implored him to put Sigurd to death, thus increasing his jealousy and suspicion.

He refused to deal violently with Sigurd, however, because of their oath of good fellowship, and so she turned to Hogni for aid. He, too, did not wish to violate his oath, but he induced Guttorm, by means of much persuasion and one of Grimhild's potions, to undertake the dastardly deed.

The Death of Sigurd

Accordingly, in the dead of night, Guttorm stole into Sigurd's chamber, weapon in hand; but as he bent over the bed he saw Sigurd's bright eyes fixed upon him, and fled precipitately. Later on he returned and the scene was repeated; but towards morning, stealing in for the third time, he found the hero asleep, and traitorously drove his spear through his back.

Although wounded unto death, Sigurd raised himself in bed, and seizing his renowned sword which hung beside him, he flung it with all his remaining strength at the flying murderer, cutting him in two as he reached the door. Then, with a last whispered farewell to the terrified Gudrun, Sigurd sank back and breathed his last.

Sigurd's infant son was slain at the same time, and poor Gudrun mourned over her dead in silent, tearless grief; while Brunhild laughed aloud, thereby incurring the wrath of Gunnar, who repented, too late, that he had not taken measures to avert the dastardly crime.

The grief of the Niblungs found expression in the public funeral celebration which was shortly held. A mighty pyre was erected, to which were brought precious hangings, fresh flowers, and glittering arms, as was the custom for the burial of a prince; and as these sad preparations took shape, Gudrun was the object of tender solicitude from the women, who, fearing lest her heart would break, tried to open the flood-gate of her tears by recounting the bitterest sorrows they had known, one telling of how she too had lost all she held dear. But these attempts to make her weep were utterly vain, until at length they laid her husband's head in her lap, bidding her kiss him as if he were still alive; then her tears began to flow in torrents.

The reaction soon set in for Brunhild also; her resentment was all forgotten when she saw the body of Sigurd laid on the pyre, arrayed as if for battle in burnished armour, with the Helmet of Dread at his head, and accompanied by his steed, which was to be burned with him, together with several of his faithful servants who would not survive his loss. She withdrew to her apartment, and after distributing her possessions among her handmaidens, she donned her richest array, and stabbed herself as she lay stretched upon her bed.

The Story of Frithiof the Bold

Part One

Chapter 1: Of King Beli and Thorstein Vikingson and Their Children

Thus beginneth the tale, telling how that King Beli ruled over Sogn-land; three children had he, whereof Helgi was his first son, and Halfdan his second, but Ingibjorg his daughter. Ingibjorg was fair of face and wise of mind, and she was ever accounted the foremost of the king's children.

Now a certain strand went west of the firth, and a great stead was thereon, which was called Balder's Meads; a Place of Peace was there, and a great temple, and round about it a great garth of pales: many gods were there, but amidst them all was Balder held of most account. So jealous were the heathen men of this stead, that they would have no hurt done therein to man nor beast, nor might any man have dealings with a woman there.

Sowstrand was the name of that stead whereas the king dwelt; but on the other side the firth was an abode named Foreness, where dwelt a man called Thorstein, the son of Viking; and his stead was over against the king's dwelling.

Thorstein had a son by his wife called Frithiof: he was the tallest and strongest of men, and more furnished of all prowess than any other man, even from his youth up. Frithiof the Bold was he called, and so well beloved was he, that all prayed for good things for him.

Now the king's children were but young when their mother died; but a goodman of Sogn, named Hilding, prayed to have the king's daughter to foster: so there was she reared well and needfully: and she was called Ingibjorg the Fair. Frithiof also was fostered of goodman Hilding, wherefore was he foster-brother to the king's daughter, and they two were peerless among children.

Now King Beli's chattels began to ebb fast away from his hands, for he was grown old.

Thorstein had rule over the third part of the realm, and in him lay the king's greatest strength.

Every third year Thorstein feasted the king at exceeding great cost, and the king feasted Thorstein the two years between.

Helgi, Beli's son, from his youth up turned much to blood-offering: neither were those brethren well-beloved.

Thorstein had a ship called Ellidi, which pulled fifteen oars on either board; it ran up high stem and stern, and was strong-built like an ocean-going ship, and its bulwarks were clamped with iron.

So strong was Frithiof that he pulled the two bow oars of Ellidi; but either oar was thirteen ells long, and two men pulled every oar otherwhere.

Frithiof was deemed peerless amid the young men of that time, and the king's sons envied him, whereas he was more praised than they.

Now King Beli fell sick; and when the sickness lay heavy on him he called his sons to him and said to them: 'This sickness will bring me to mine end, therefore will I bid you this, that ye hold fast to those old friends that I have had; for meseems in all things ye fall short of that father and son, Thorstein and Frithiof, yea, both in good counsel and in hardihood. A mound ye shall raise over me.'

So with that Beli died.

Thereafter Thorstein fell sick; so he spake to Frithiof: 'Kinsman,' says he, 'I will crave this of thee, that thou bow thy will before the king's sons, for their dignity's sake; yet doth my heart speak goodly things to me concerning thy fortune. Now would I be laid in my mound over against King Beli's mound, down by the sea on this side the firth, whereas it may be easiest for us to cry out each to each of tidings drawing nigh.'

A little after this Thorstein departed, and was laid in mound even as he had bidden; but Frithiof took the land and chattels after him. Biorn and Asmund were Frithiof s foster-brethren; they were big and strong men both.

Chapter 2: Frithiof Wooeth Ingibjorg of Those Brethren

So Frithiof became the most famed of men, and the bravest in all things that may try a man.

Biorn, his foster-brother, he held in most account of all, but Asmund served the twain of them.

The ship Ellidi, he gat, the best of good things, of his father's heritage, and another possession therewith – a gold ring; no dearer was in Norway.

So bounteous a man was Frithiof withal, that it was the talk of most, that he was a man of no less honour than those brethren, but it were for the name of king; and for this cause they held Frithiof in hate and enmity, and it was a heavy thing to them that he was called greater than they: furthermore they thought they could see that Ingibjorg, their sister, and Frithiof were of one mind together.

It befell hereon that the kings had to go to a feast to Frithiof s house at Foreness; and there it happened according to wont that he gave to all men beyond that they were worthy of. Now Ingibjorg was there, and she and Frithiof talked long together; and the king's daughter said to him:

'A goodly gold ring hast thou.'

'Yea, in good sooth,' said he.

Thereafter went those brethren to their own home, and greater grew their enmity of Frithiof.

A little after grew Frithiof heavy of mood, and Biorn, his foster-brother, asked him why he fared so.

He said he had it in his mind to woo Ingibjorg. 'For though I be named by a lesser name than those brethren, yet am I not fashioned lesser.'

'Even so let us do then,' quoth Biorn. So Frithiof fared with certain men unto those brethren; and the kings were sitting on their father's mound when Frithiof greeted them well, and then set forth his wooing, and prayed for their sister Ingibjorg, the daughter of Beli.

The kings said: 'Not overwise is this thine asking, whereas thou wouldst have us give her to one who lacketh dignity; wherefore we gainsay thee this utterly.'

Said Frithiof: 'Then is mine errand soon sped; but in return never will I give help to you henceforward, nay, though ye need it ever so much.'

They said they heeded it nought: so Frithiof went home, and was joyous once more.

Chapter 3: Of King Ring and Those Brethren

There was a king named Ring, who ruled over Ringrealm, which also was in Norway: a mighty folk-king he was, and a great man, but come by now unto his latter days.

Now he spake to his men: 'Lo, I have heard that the sons of King Beli have brought to nought their friendship with Frithiof, who is the noblest of men; wherefore will I send men to these kings, and bid them choose whether they will submit them to me and pay me tribute, or else that I bring war on them: and all things then shall lie ready to my hand to take, for they have neither might nor wisdom to withstand me; yet great fame were it to my old age to overcome them.'

After that fared the messengers of King Ring, and found those brethren, Helgi and Halfdan, in Sogn, and spake to them thus: 'King Ring sends bidding to you to send him tribute, or else will he war against your realm.'

They answered and said that they would not learn in the days of their youth what they would be loth to know in their old age, even how to serve King Ring with shame. 'Nay, now shall we draw together all the folk that we may.'

Even so they did; but now, when they beheld their force that it was but little, they sent Hilding their fosterer to Frithiof to bid him come help them against King Ring. Now Frithiof sat at the knave-play when Hilding came thither, who spake thus: 'Our kings send thee greeting, Frithiof, and would have thy help in battle against King Ring, who cometh against their realm with violence and wrong.'

Frithiof answered him nought, but said to Biorn, with whom he was playing: 'A bare place in thy board, foster-brother, and nowise mayst thou amend it; nay, for my part I shall beset thy red piece there, and wot whether it be safe.'

Then Hilding spake again:

'King Helgi bade me say thus much, Frithiof, that thou shouldst go on this journey with them, or else look for ill at their hands when they at the last come back.'

'A double game, foster-brother,' said Biorn; 'and two ways to meet thy play.'

Frithiof said: 'Thy play is to fall first on the knave, yet the double game is sure to be.'

No other outcome of his errand had Hilding: he went back speedily to the kings, and told them Frithiof's answer.

They asked Hilding what he made out of those words. He said:

'Whereas he spake of the bare place he will have been thinking of the lack in this journey of yours; but when he said he would beset the red piece, that will mean Ingibjorg, your sister; so give ye all the heed ye may to her. But whereas I threatened him with ill from you, Biorn deemed the game a double one; but Frithiof said that the knave must be set on first, speaking thereby of King Ring.'

So then the brethren arrayed them for departing; but, ere they went, they let bring Ingibioig and eight women with her to Balder's Meads, saying that Frithiof would not be so mad rash as to go see her thither, since there was none who durst make riot there.

Then fared those brethren south to Jadar, and met King Ring in Sogn-Sound.

Now, herewith was King Ring most of all wroth that the brothers had said that they accounted it a shame to fight with a man so old that he might not get a-horseback unholpen.

Chapter 4: Frithiof Goes to Balder's Meads

Straightway whenas the kings were gone away Frithiof took his raiment of state and set the goodly gold ring on his arm; then went the foster-brethren down to the sea and launched Ellidi. Then said Biorn: 'Whither away, foster-brother?'

'To Balder's Meads,' said Frithiof, 'to be glad with Ingibjorg.'

Biorn said: 'A thing unmeet to do, to make the gods wroth with us.'

'Well, it shall be risked this time,' said Frithiof; 'and withal, more to me is Ingibjorg's grace than Balder's grame.'

Therewith they rowed over the firth, and went up to Balder's Meads and to Ingibjorg's bower, and there she sat with eight maidens, and the new comers were eight also.

But when they came there, lo, all the place was hung with cloth of pall and precious webs.

Then Ingibjorg arose and said:

'Why art thou so overbold, Frithiof, that thou art come here without the leave of my brethren to make the gods angry with thee?'

Frithiof says: 'Howsoever that may be, I hold thy love of more account than the gods' hate.'

Ingibjorg answered: 'Welcome art thou here, thou and thy men!'

Then she made place for him to sit beside her, and drank to him in the best of wine; and thus they sat and were merry together.

Then beheld Ingibjorg the goodly ring on his arm, and asked him if that precious thing were his own.

Frithiof said Yea, and she praised the ring much. Then Frithiof said:

'I will give thee the ring if thou wilt promise to give it to no one, but to send it to me when thou no longer shalt have will to keep it: and hereon shall we plight troth each to other.'

So with this troth-plighting they exchanged rings.

Frithiof was oft at Balder's Meads a-night time, and every day between whiles would he go thither to be glad with Ingibjorg.

Chapter 5: Those Brethren Come Home Again

Now tells the tale of those brethren, that they met King Ring, and he had more folk than they: then went men betwixt them, and sought to make peace, so that no battle should be: thereto King Ring assented on such terms that the brethren should submit them to him, and give him in marriage Ingibjorg their sister, with the third part of all their possessions.

The kings said Yea thereto, for they saw that they had to do with overwhelming might: so the peace was fast bound by oaths, and the wedding was to be at Sogn whenas King Ring should go see his betrothed.

So those brethren fare home with their folk, right ill content with things. But Frithiof, when he deemed that the brethren might be looked for home again, spake to the king's daughter:

'Sweetly and well have ye done to us, neither has goodman Balder been wroth with us; but now as soon as ye wot of the kings' coming home, spread the sheets of your beds abroad on the Hall of the Goddesses, for that is the highest of all the garth, and we may see it from our stead.'

The king's daughter said: 'Thou dost not after the like of any other: but certes, we welcome dear friends whenas ye come to us.'

So Frithiof went home; and the next morning he went out early, and when he came in then he spake and sang:

'Now must I tell
To our good men
That over and done
Are our fair journeys;
No more a-shipboard
Shall we be going,
For there are the sheets
Spread out a-bleaching.'

Then they went out, and saw that the Hall of the Goddesses was all thatched with white linen. Biorn spake and said: 'Now are the kings come home, and but a little while have we to sit in peace, and good were it, meseems, to gather folk together.'

So did they, and men came flocking thither.

Now the brethren soon heard of the ways of Frithiof and Ingibjorg, and of the gathering of men. So King Helgi spake:

'A wondrous thing how Balder will bear what shame soever Frithiof and she will lay on him! Now will I send men to him, and wot what atonement he will offer us, or else will I drive him from the land, for our strength seemeth to me not enough that we should fight with him as now.'

So Hilding, their fosterer, bare the king's errand to Frithiof and his friends, and spake in such wise: 'This atonement the kings will have of thee, Frithiof, that thou go gather the tribute of the Orkneys, which has not been paid since Beli died, for they need money, whereas they are giving Ingibjorg their sister in marriage, and much of wealth with her.'

Frithiof said: 'This thing only somewhat urges us to peace, the good will of our kin departed; but no trustiness will those brethren show herein. But this condition I make, that our lands be in good peace while we are away.' So this was promised and all bound by oaths.

Then Frithiof arrays him for departing, and is captain of men brave and of good help, eighteen in company.

Now his men asked him if he would not go to King Helgi and make peace with him, and pray himself free from Balder's wrath.

But he answered: 'Hereby I swear that I will never pray Helgi for peace.'

Then he went aboard Ellidi, and they sailed out along the Sognnrth.

But when Frithiof was gone from home, King Halfdan spake to Helgi his brother: 'Better lordship and more had we if Frithiof had payment for his masterful deed: now therefore let us burn his stead, and bring on him and his men such a storm on the sea as shall make an end of them.'

Helgi said it was a thing meet to be done.

So then they burned up clean all the stead at Foreness and robbed it of all goods; and after that sent for two witch-wives, Heidi and Hamglom, and gave them money to raise against Frithiof and his men so mighty a storm that they should all be lost at sea. So they sped the witch-song, and went up on the witch-mount with spells and sorcery.

Chapter 6: Frithiof Sails for the Orkneys

So when Frithiof and his men were come out of the Sognfirth there fell on them great wind and storm, and an exceeding heavy sea: but the ship drave on swiftly, for sharp built she was, and the best to breast the sea. So now Frithiof sang:

'Oft let I swim from Sogn
My tarred ship sooty-sided,
When maids sat o'er the mead-horn
Amidst of Balder's Meadows;
Now while the storm is wailing
Farewell I bid you maidens,
Still shall ye love us, sweet ones,
Though Ellidi the sea fill.'

Said Biorn: 'Thou mightest well find other work to do than singing songs over the maids of Balder's Meadows.'

'Of such work shall I not speedily run dry, though,' said Frithiof. Then they bore up north to the sounds nigh those isles that are called Solundir, and therewith was the gale at its hardest.

Then sang Frithiof:

'Now is the sea a-swelling,
And sweepeth the rack onward;
Spells of old days cast o'er us
Make ocean all unquiet;
No more shall we be striving
Mid storm with wash of billows,
But Solundir shall shelter
Our ship with ice-beat rock-walls.'

So they lay to under the lee of the isles hight Solundir, and were minded to abide there; but straightway thereon the wind fell: then they turned away from under the lee of the islands, and now their voyage seemed hopeful to them, because the wind was fair awhile: but soon it began to freshen again.

Then sang Frithiof:

'In days foredone
From Foreness strand
I rowed to meet
Maid Ingibjorg;
But now I sail
Through chilly storm
And wide away
My long-worm driveth.'

And now when they were come far out into the main, once more the sea waxed wondrous troubled, and a storm arose with so great drift of snow, that none might see the stem from the stern; and they shipped seas, so that they must be ever a-baling.

So Frithiof sang:

'The salt waves see we nought
As seaward drive we ever
Before the witch-wrought weather,
We well-famed kings'-defenders:
Here are we all a-standing,
With all Solundir hull-down,
Eighteen brave lads a-baling
Black Ellidi to bring home.'

Said Biorn: 'Needs must he who fareth far fall in with diverse hap.'

'Yea, certes, foster-brother,' said Frithiof. And he sang withal:

'Helgi it is that helpeth
The white-head billows' waxing;
Cold time unlike the kissing
In the close of Balder's Meadow!
So is the hate of Helgi
To that heart's love she giveth.
O would that here I held her,
Gift high above all giving!'

'Maybe,' said Biorn, 'she is looking higher than thou now art: what matter when all is said?'

'Well,' says Frithiof, 'now is the time to show ourselves to be men of avail, though blither tide it was at Balder's Meadows.'

So they turned to in manly wise, for there were the bravest of men come together in the best ship of the Northlands. But Frithiof sang a stave:

'So come in the West-sea,
Nought see I the billows,
The sea-water seemeth
As sweeping of wild-fire.
Topple the rollers,
Toss the hills swan-white,
Ellidi wallows
O'er steep of the wave-hills.'

Then they shipped a huge sea, so that all stood a-baling. But Frithiof sang:

'With love-moved mouth the maiden
Mepledgeth though I founder.
Ah! bright sheets lay a-bleaching,
East there on brents the swan loves.'

Biorn said: 'Art thou of mind belike that the maids of Sogn will weep many tears over thee?'

Said Frithiof: 'Surely that was in my mind.'

Therewith so great a sea broke over the bows, that the water came in like the in-falling of a river; but it availed them much that the ship was so good, and the crew aboard her so hardy.

Now sang Biorn:

'No widow, methinks,
To thee or me drinks;
No ring-bearer fair
Biddeth draw near;
Salt are our eyne
Soaked in the brine;
Strong our arms are no more,
And our eyelids smart sore.'

Quoth Asmund: 'Small harm though your arms be tried somewhat, for no pity we had from you when we rubbed our eyes whenas ye must needs rise early a-mornings to go to Balder's Meadows.'

'Well,' said Frithiof, 'why singest thou not, Asmund?'

'Not I,' said Asmund; yet sang a ditty straightway:

'Sharp work about the sail was
When o'er the ship seas tumbled,
And there was I a-working
Within-board 'gainst eight balers;
Better it was to bower,
Bringing the women breakfast,
Than here to be 'mid billows
Black Ellidi a-baling.'

'Thou accountest thy help of no less worth than it is?' said Frithiof, laughing therewith; 'but sure it showeth the thrall's blood in thee that thou wouldst fain be awaiting at table.'

Now it blew harder and harder yet, so that to those who were aboard liker to huge peaks and mountains than to waves seemed the sea-breakers that crashed on all sides against the ship.

Then Frithiof sang:

'On bolster I sat.
In Balder's Mead erst,
And all songs that I could
To the king's daughter sang;
Now on Ran's bed belike
Must I soon be a-lying,
And another shall be
By Ingibjorg's side.'

Biorn said: 'Great fear lieth ahead of us, foster-brother, and now dread hath crept into thy words, which is ill with such a good man as thou.'

Says Frithiof: 'Neither fear nor fainting is it, though I sing now of those our merry journeys; yet perchance more hath been said of them than need was: but most men would think death surer than life, if they were so bested as we be.'

'Yet shall I answer thee somewhat,' said Biorn, and sang:

'Yet one gain have I gotten
Thou gatst not 'mid thy fortune,
For meet play did I make me
With Ingibjorgs eight maidens;
Red rings we laid together
Aright in Balder's Meadow,
When far off was the warder
Of the wide land of Halfdan.'

'Well,' said he, 'we must be content with things as they are, foster-brother.'

Therewith so great a sea smote them, that the bulwark was broken and both the sheets, and four men were washed overboard and all lost.

Then sang Frithiof:

'Both sheets are bursten
Amid the great billows,
Four swains are sunk
In the fathomless sea?'

'Now, meseems,' said Frithiof, 'it may well be that some of us will go to the house of Ran, nor shall we deem us well sped if we come not thither in glorious array; wherefore it seems good to me that each man of us here should have somewhat of gold on him.'

Then he smote asunder the ring, Ingibjorg's gift, and shared it between all his men, and sang a stave withal:

'The red ring here I hew me
Once owned of Halfdan's father,
The wealthy lord of erewhile,
Or the sea waves undo us,
So on the guests shall gold be,
If we have need of guesting;
Meet so for mighty men-folk
Amid Ran's hall to hold them.'

'Not all so sure is it that we come there,' said Biorn; 'and yet it may well be so.'

Now Frithiof and his folk found that the ship had great way on her, and they knew not what lay ahead, for all was mirk on either board, so that none might see the stem or stern from amidships; and therewith was there great drift of spray amid the furious wind, and frost, and snow, and deadly cold.

Now Frithiof went up to the masthead, and when he came down he said to his fellows: 'A sight exceeding wondrous have I seen, for a great whale went in a ring about the ship, and I misdoubt me that we come nigh to some land, and that he is keeping the shore against us; for certes King Helgi has dealt with us in no friendly wise, neither will this his messenger be friendly. Moreover I saw two women on the back of the whale, and they it is who will have brought this great storm on us with the worst of spells and witchcraft; but now we shall try which may prevail, my fortune or their devilry, so steer ye at your straightest, and I will smite these evil things with beams.'

Therewith he sang a stave:

'See I troll women
Twain on the billows,
Een they whom Helgi
Hither hath sent.
Ellidi now
Or ever her way stop
Shall smile the backs
Of these asunder.'

So tells the tale that this wonder went with the good ship Ellidi, that she knew the speech of man.

But Biorn said: 'Now may we see the treason of those brethren against us.' Therewith he took the tiller, but Frithiof caught up a forked beam, and ran into the prow, and sang a stave:

'Ellidi, hail!
Leap high o'er the billows!
Break of the troll wives
Brow or teeth now!
Break cheek or jaw
Of the cursed woman,
One foot or twain
Of the ogress filthy.'

Therewith he drave his fork at one of the skin-changers, and the beak of Ellidi smote the other on the back, and the backs of both were broken; but the whale took the deep, and gat him gone, and they never saw him after.

Then the wind fell, but the ship lay waterlogged; so Frithiof called out to his men, and bade bale out the ship, but Biorn said:

'No need to work now, verily!'

'Be thou not afeard, foster-brother,' said Frithiof, 'ever was it the wont of good men of old time to be helpful while they might, whatsoever should come after.' And therewith he sang a stave:

'No need, fairfellows,
To fear the death-day;
Rather be glad,
Good men of mine:
For if dreams wot aught
All nights they say
I yet shall have
My Ingibjorg.'

Then they baled out the ship; and they were now come nigh unto land; but there was yet a flaw of wind in their teeth. So then did Frithiof take the two bow oars again, and rowed full mightily. Therewith the weather brightened, and they saw that they were come out to Effia Sound, and so there they made land.

The crew were exceeding weary; but so stout a man was Frithiof that he bore eight men a-land over the foreshore, but Biorn bore two, and Asmund one. Then sang Frithiof:

'Fast bare I up
To the fire-lit house
My men all dazed
With the drift of the storm;
And the sail moreover
To the sand I carried;
With the might of the sea
Is there no more to do.'

Chapter 7: Frithiof at the Orkneys

Now Earl Angantyr was at Effia whenas Frithiof and his folk came a-land there. But his way it was, when he was sitting at the drink, that one of his men should sit at the watch-window, looking weatherward from the drinking hall, and keep watch there. From a great horn drank he ever: and still as one was emptied another was filled for him. And he who held the watch when Frithiof came a-land was called Hallward; and now he saw where Frithiof and his men went, and sang a stave:

'Men see I a-baling
Amid the storm's might;
Six bale on Ellidi
Seven are a-rowing;
Like is he in the stem,
Straining hard at the oars,
To Frithiof the bold,
The brisk in the battle.'

So when he had drunk out the horn, he cast it in through the window, and spake to the woman who gave him drink:

'Take up from the floor,
O fair-going woman,
The horn cast adown
Drunk out to the end!
I behold men at sea
Who, storm-beaten, shall need
Help at our hands
Ere the haven they make.'

Now the Earl heard what Hallward sang; so he asked for tidings, and Hallward said: 'Men are come a-land here, much forewearied, yet brave lads belike: but one of them is so hardy that he beareth the others. ashore.'

Then said the Earl, 'Go ye, and meet them, and welcome them in seemly wise; if this be Frithiof, the son of Hersir Thorstein, my friend, he is a man famed far and wide for all prowess.'

Then there took up the word a man named Atli, a great viking, and he spake: 'Now shall that be proven which is told of, that Frithiof hath sworn never to be first in the craving of peace.'

There were ten men in company with him, all evil and outrageous, who often wrought berserksgang.

So when they met Frithiof they took to their weapons.

But Atli said:

'Good to turn hither, Frithiof! Clutching ernes should claw; and we no less, Frithiof! Yea, and now may'st thou hold to thy word, and not crave first for peace.'

So Frithiof turned to meet them, and sang a stave:

'Nay, nay, in nought
Now shall ye cow us.
Blenching hearts
Isle-abiders!
Alone with you ten
The fight will I try,
Rather than pray
For peace at your hands.'

Then came Hallward thereto, and spake: 'The Earl wills that ye all be made welcome here: neither shall any set on you.'

Frithiof said he would take that with a good heart; howsoever he was ready for either peace or war.

So thereon they went to the Earl, and he made Frithiof and all his men right welcome, and they abode with him, in great honour holden, through the wintertide; and oft would the Earl ask of their voyage: so Biorn sang:

'There baled we, wight fellows,
Washed over and over
On both boards
By billows;
For ten days we baled there,
And eight thereunto.'

The Earl said: 'Well nigh did the king undo you; it is ill seen of such-like kings as are meet for nought but to overcome men by wizardry. But now I wot,' says Angantyr, 'of thine errand hither, Frithiof, that thou art sent after the scat: whereto I give thee a speedy answer, that never shall King Helgi get scat of me, but to thee will I give money, even as much as thou wilt; and thou mayest call it scat if thou hast a mind to, or whatso else thou wilt.'

So Frithiof said that he would take the money.

Chapter 8: King Ring Weddeth Ingibjorg

Now shall it be told of what came to pass in Norway the while Frithiof was away: for those brethren let burn up all the stead at Foreness. Moreover, while the weird sisters were at their spells they tumbled down from off their high witch-mount, and brake both their backs.

That autumn came King Ring north to Sogn to his wedding, and there at a noble feast drank his bridal with Ingibjorg.

'Whence came that goodly ring which thou hast on thine arm?' said King Ring to Ingibjorg.

She said her father had owned it, but he answered and said:

'Nay, for Frithiof s gift it is: so take it off thine arm straightway; for no gold shalt thou lack whenas thou comest to Elfhome.'

So she gave the ring to King Helgi's wife, and bade her give it to Frithiof when he came back.

Then King Ring wended home with his wife, and loved her with exceeding great love.

Chapter 9: Frithiof Brings the Tribute to the Kings

The spring after these things Frithiof departed from the Orkneys and Earl Angantyr in all good liking; and Hallward went with Frithiof.

But when they came to Norway they heard tell of the burning of Frithiof's stead.

So when he was gotten to Foreness, Frithiof said: 'Black is my house waxen now; no friends have been at work here.' And he sang withal:

'Frank and free,
With my father dead,
In Foreness old
We drank aforetime.
Now my abode
Behold I burned;
For many ill deeds
The kings must I pay.'

Then he sought rede of his men what was to be done; but they bade him look to it: then he said that the scat must first be paid out of hand. So they rowed over the Firth to Sowstrand; and there they heard that the kings were gone to Balder's Meads to sacrifice to the gods; so Frithiof and Biorn went up thither, and bade Hallward and Asmund break up meanwhile all ships, both great and small, that were anigh; and they did so. Then went Frithiof and his fellow to the door at Balder's Meads, and Frithiof would go in. Biorn bade him fare warily, since he must needs go in alone; but Frithiof charged him to abide without, and keep watch; and he sang a stave:

'All alone go I
Unto the stead;
No folk I need
For the finding of kings;
But cast ye the fire
O'er the kings' dwellingly

If I come not again
In the cool of the even.'

'Ah,' said Biorn, 'a goodly singing!'

Then went Frithiof in, and saw but few folk in the Hall of the Goddesses; there were the kings at their blood-offering, sitting a-drinking; a fire was there on the floor, and the wives of the kings sat thereby, a-warming the gods, while others anointed them, and wiped them with napkins.

So Frithiof went up to King Helgi and said: 'Have here thy scat!'

And therewith he heaved up the purse wherein was the silver, and drave it on to the face of the king; whereby were two of his teeth knocked out, and he fell down stunned in his high seat; but Halfdan got hold of him, so that he fell not into the fire.

Then sang Frithiof:
'Have here thy scat,
High lord of the warriors!
Heed that and thy teeth,
Lest all tumble about thee!
Lo the silver abideth
At the bight of this bag here,
That Biorn and I
Betwixt us have borne thee.'

Now there were but few folk in the chamber, because the drinking was in another place; so Frithiof went out straightway along the floor, and beheld therewith that goodly ring of his on the arm of Helgi's wife as she warmed Balder at the fire; so he took hold of the ring, but it was fast to her arm, and he dragged her by it over the pavement toward the door, and Balder fell from her into the fire; then Halfdan's wife caught hastily at Balder, whereby the god that she was warming fell likewise into the fire, and the fire caught both the gods, for they had been anointed, and ran up thence into the roof, so that the house was all ablaze: but Frithiof got the ring to him ere he came out. So then Biorn asked him what had come of his going in there; but Frithiof held up the ring and sang a stave:

'The heavy purse smote Helgi
Hard 'midst his scoundrel's visage:
Lowly bowed Halfdan's brother,
Fell bundling 'mid the high seat;
There Balder fell a-burning.
But first my bright ring gat I.
Fast from the roaring fire
I dragged the bent crone forward.'

Men say that Frithiof cast a firebrand up on to the roof, so that the hall was all ablaze, and therewith sang a stave:

'Down stride we toward the sea-strand,
And strong deeds set a-going,

For now the blue flame bickers
Amidst of Balder's Meadow.'

And therewith they went down to the sea.

Chapter 10: Frithiof Made an Outlaw

But as soon as King Helgi had come to himself he bade follow after Frithiof speedily, and slay them all, him and his fellows: 'A man of forfeit life, who spareth no Place of Peace!'

So they blew the gathering for the kings' men, and when they came out to the hall they saw that it was afire; so King Halfdan went thereto with some of the folk, but King Helgi followed after Frithiof and his men, who were by then gotten a-shipboard and were lying on their oars.

Now King Helgi and his men find that all the ships are scuttled, and they have to turn back to shore, and have lost some men: then waxed King Helgi so wroth that he grew mad, and he bent his bow, and laid an arrow on the string, and drew at Frithiof so mightily that the bow brake asunder in the midst.

But when Frithiof saw that, then he gat him to the two bow oars of Ellidi, and laid so hard on them that they both brake, and with that he sang a stave:

'Young Ingibjorg
Kissed I aforetime,
Kissed Beli's daughter
In Balder's Meadow.
So shall the oars
Of Ellidi
Break both together
As Helgi's bow breaks.'

Then the land-wind ran down the firth and they hoisted sail and sailed; but Frithiof bade them look to it that they might have no long abiding there. And so withal they sailed out of the Sognfirth, and Frithiof sang:

'Sail we away from Sogn,
E'en as we sailed aforetime,
When flared the fire all over
The house that was my father's.
Now is the bale a-burning
Amidst of Balder's Meadow:
But wend I as a wild-wolf,
Well wot I they have sworn it.'

'What shall we turn to now, foster-brother?' said Biorn.

'I may not abide here in Norway,' said Frithiof: 'I will learn the ways of warriors, and sail a-warring.'

So they searched the isles and out-skerries the summer long, and gathered thereby riches and renown; but in autumn-tide they made for the Orkneys, and Angantyr gave them good welcome, and they abode there through the winter-tide.

But when Frithiof was gone from Norway the kings held a Thing, whereat was Frithiof made an outlaw throughout their realm: they took his lands to them, moreover, and King Halfdan took up his abode at Foreness, and built up again all Balder's Meadow, though it was long ere the fire was slaked there. This misliked King Helgi most, that the gods were all burned up, and great was the cost or ever Balder's Meadow was built anew fully equal to its first estate.

So King Helgi abode still at Sowstrand.

Part Two

Chapter 11: Frithiof Fareth to See King Ring and Ingibjorg

Frithiof waxed ever in riches and renown whithersoever he went: evil men he slew, and grimly strong-thieves, but husbandmen and chapmen he let abide in peace; and now was he called anew Frithiof the Bold; he had gotten to him by now a great company well arrayed, and was become exceeding wealthy of chattels.

But when Frithiof had been three winters a-warring he sailed west, and made the Wick; then he said that he would go a-land: 'But ye shall fare a-warring without me this winter; for I begin to weary of warfare, and would fain go to the Uplands, and get speech of King Ring: but hither shall ye come to meet me in the summer, and I will be here the first day of summer.'

Biorn said: 'This counsel is naught wise, though thou must needs rule; rather would I that we fare north to Sogn, and slay both those kings, Helgi and Halfdan.'

'It is all naught,' said Frithiof; 'I must needs go see King Ring and Ingibjorg.'

Says Biorn: 'Loth am I hereto that thou shouldst risk thyself alone in his hands; for this Ring is a wise man and of great kin, though he be somewhat old.'

But Frithiof said he would have his own way: 'And thou, Biorn, shalt be captain of our company meanwhile.'

So they did as he bade, and Frithiof fared to the Uplands in the autumn, for he desired sore to look upon the love of King Ring and Ingibjorg. But or ever he came there he did on him, over his clothes, a great cloak all shaggy; two staves he had in his hand, and a mask over his face, and he made as if he were exceeding old.

So he met certain herdsmen, and, going heavily, he asked them: 'Whence are ye?'

They answered and said: 'We are of Streitaland, whereas the king dwelleth.'

Quoth the carle: 'Is King Ring a mighty king, then?'

They answered: 'Thou lookest to us old enough to have cunning to know what manner of man is King Ring in all wise.'

The carle said that he had heeded salt-boiling more than the ways of kings; and therewith he goes up to the king's house.

So when the day was well worn he came into the hall, blinking about as a dotard, and took an outward place, pulling his hood over him to hide his visage.

Then spake King Ring to Ingibjorg: 'There is come into the hall a man far bigger than other men.'

The queen answered: 'That is no such great tidings here.'

But the king spake to a serving-man who stood before the board, and said: 'Go thou, and ask yon cowled man who he is, whence he cometh, and of what kin he is.'

So the lad ran down the hall to the new-comer and said: 'What art thou called, thou man? Where wert thou last night? Of what kin art thou?'

Said the cowled man: 'Quick come thy questions, good fellow! but hast thou skill to understand if I shall tell thee hereof?'

'Yea, certes,' said the lad.

'Well,' said the cowl-bearer, 'Thief is my name, with Wolf was I last night, and in Grief-ham was I reared.'

Then ran the lad back to the king, and told him the answer of the new-comer.

'Well told, lad,' said the king; 'but for that land of Grief-ham, I know it well: it may well be that the man is of no light heart, and yet a wise man shall he be, and of great worth I account him.'

Said the queen: 'A marvellous fashion of thine, that thou must needs talk so freely with every carle that cometh hither! Yea, what is the worth of him, then?'

'That wottest thou no clearer than I,' said the king; 'but I see that he thinketh more than he talketh, and is peering all about him.'

Therewith the king sent a man after him, and so the cowl-bearer went up before the king, going somewhat bent, and greeted him in a low voice. Then said the king: 'What art thou called, thou big man?'

And the cowl-bearer answered and sang:

'Peace-thief they called me
On the prow with the Vikings;
But War-thief whenas
I set widows a-weeping;
Spear-thief when I
Sent forth the barbed shafts;
Battle-thief when I
Burst forth on the king;
Hel-thief when I
Tossed up the small babies:
Isle-thief when I
In the outer isles harried;
Slaws-thief when I
Sat aloft over men:
Yet since have I drifted
With salt-boiling carls,
Needy of help
'Ere hither I came.'

Said the king: 'Thou hast gotten thy name of Thief from many a matter, then; but where wert thou last night, and what is thy home?'

The cowl-bearer said: 'In Grief-ham I grew up; but heart drave me hither, and home have I nowhere.'

The king said: 'Maybe indeed that thou hast been nourished in Grief-ham a certain while; yet also maybe that thou wert born in a place of peace. But in the wild-wood must thou have lain last night, for no goodman dwelleth anigh named Wolf; but whereas thou sayest thou hast no home, so is it, that thou belike deemest thy home nought, because of thy heart that drave thee hither.'

Then spake Ingibjorg: 'Go, Thief, get thee to some other harbour, or in to the guest-hall.'

'Nay,' said the king, 'I am old enow to know how to marshal guests; so do off thy cowl, new-comer, and sit down on my other hand.'

'Yea, old, and over old,' said the queen, 'when thou settest staff-carles by thy side.'

'Nay, lord, it beseemeth not,' said Thief; 'better it were as the queen sayeth. I have been more used to boiling salt than sitting beside lords.'

'Do thou my will,' said the king, 'for I will rule this time.'

So Thief cast his cowl from him, and was clad thereunder in a dark blue kirtle; on his arm, moreover, was the goodly gold ring, and a thick silver belt was round about him, with a great purse on it, and therein silver pennies glittering; a sword was girt to his side, and he had a great fur hood on his head, for his eyes were bleared, and his face all wrinkled.

'Ah! now we fare better, say I,' quoth the king; 'but do thou, queen, give him a goodly mantle, well shapen for him.'

'Thou shalt rule, my lord,' said the queen; 'but in small account do I hold this Thief of thine.'

So then he gat a good mantle over him, and sat down in the high-seat beside the king.

The queen waxed red as blood when she saw the goodly ring, yet would she give him never a word; but the king was exceeding blithe with him and said: 'A goodly ring hast thou on thine arm there; thou must have boiled salt long enough to get it.'

Says he, 'That is all the heritage of my father.'

'Ah!' says the king, 'maybe thou hast more than that; well, few salt-boiling carles are thy peers, I deem, unless eld is deep in mine eyes now.'

So Thief was there through the winter amid good entertainment, and well accounted of by all men; he was bounteous of his wealth, and joyous with all men: the queen held but little converse with him; but the king and he were ever blithe together.

Chapter 12: Frithiof Saves the King and Queen on the Ice

The tale tells that on a time King Ring and the queen, and a great company, would go to a feast. So the king spake to Thief: 'Wilt thou fare with us, or abide at home?'

He said he had liefer go; and the king said: 'Then am I the more content.'

So they went on their ways, and had to cross a certain frozen water. Then said Thief: 'I deem this ice untrustworthy; meseemeth ye fare unwarily.'

Quoth the king: 'It is often shown how heedful in thine heart thou wilt be to us.'

So a little after the ice broke in beneath them, and Thief ran thereto, and dragged the wain to him, with all that was therein; and the king and the queen both sat in the same: so Thief drew it all up on to the ice, with the horses that were yoked to the wain.

Then spake King Ring: 'Right well drawn, Thief! Frithiof the Bold himself would have drawn no stronger had he been here; doughty followers are such as thou!'

So they came to the feast, and there is nought to tell thereof, and the king went back again with seemly gifts.

Chapter 13: The King Sleeps Before Frithiof

Now weareth away the mid-winter, and when spring cometh, the weather groweth fair, the wood bloometh, the grass groweth, and ships may glide betwixt land and land. So on a day the king says to his folk: 'I will that ye come with us for our disport out into the woods, that we may look upon the fairness of the earth.'

So did they, and went flock-meal with the king into the woods; but so it befell, that the king and Frithiof were gotten alone together afar from other men, and the king said he was heavy, and would fain sleep. Then said Thief: 'Get thee home, then, lord, for it better beseemeth men of high estate to lie at home than abroad.'

'Nay,' said the king, 'so will I not do.' And he laid him down therewith, and slept fast, snoring loud.

Thief sat close by him, and presently drew his sword from his sheath and cast it far away from him.

A little while after the king woke up, and said: 'Was it not so, Frithiof, that a many things came into thy mind e'en now? But well hast thou dealt with them, and great honour shalt thou have of me. Lo, now, I knew thee straightway that first evening thou earnest into our hall: now nowise speedily shalt thou depart from us; and somewhat great abideth thee.'

Said Frithiof: 'Lord king, thou hast done to me well, and in friendly wise; but yet must I get me gone soon, because my company cometh speedily to meet me, as I have given them charge to do.'

So then they rode home from the wood, and the king's folk came flocking to him, and home they fared to the hall and drank joyously; and it was made known to all folk that Frithiof the Bold had been abiding there through the winter-tide.

Chapter 14: King Ring's Gift to Frithiof

Early of a morning-tide one smote on the door of that hall, wherein slept the king and queen, and many others: then the king asked who it was that called at the hall door; and so he who was without said: 'Here am I, Frithiof; and I am arrayed for my departure.'

Then was the door opened, and Frithiof came in, and sang a stave:

'Have great thanks for the guesting
Thou gavest with all bounty;
Dight fully for wayfaring
Is the feeder of the eagle;
But, Ingidiorg, I mind thee
While yet on earth we tarry;
Live gloriously! I give thee
This gift for many kisses.'

And therewith he cast the goodly ring towards Ingibjorg, and bade her take it.

The king smiled at this stave of his, and said: 'Yea, forsooth, she hath more thanks for thy winter quarters than I; yet hath she not been more friendly to thee than I.'

Then sent the king his serving-folk to fetch victuals and drink, and saith that they must eat and drink before Frithiof departed. 'So arise, queen, and be joyful!' But she said she was loth to fall a-feasting so early.

'Nay, we will eat all together,' said King Ring; and they did so.

But when they had drank a while King Ring spake: 'I would that thou abide here, Frithiof; for my sons are but children and I am old, and unmeet for the warding of my realm, if any should bring war against it.' Frithiof said: 'Speedily must I be gone, lord.' And he sang:

'Oh, live, King Ring,
Both long and hale!
The highest king
Neath heaven's skirt!

Ward well, O king,
Thy wife and land,
For Ingibjorg now
Never more shall I meet.'
Then quoth King Ring:

'Fare not away,
O Frithiof, thus,
With downcast heart,
O dearest of chieftains!
For now will I give thee
For all thy good gifts,
Far better things
Than thou wottest thyself.'

And again he sang:

'To Frithiof the famous
My fair wife I give,
And all things therewith
That are unto me.'

Then Frithiof took up the word and sang:

'Nay, how from thine hands
These gifts may I have,
But if thou hast fared
By the last way of fate.'

The king said: 'I would not give thee this, but that I deem it will soon be so, for I sicken now. But of all men I would that thou shouldst have the joy of this; for thou art the crown of all Norway. The name of king will I give thee also; and all this, because Ingibjorg's brethren would begrudge thee any honour; and would be slower in getting thee a wife than I am.'

Said Frithiof: 'Have all thanks, lord, for thy goodwill beyond that I looked for! But I will have no higher dignity than to be called earl.'

Then King Ring gave Frithiof rule over all his realm in due wise, and the name of earl therewith; and Frithiof was to rule it until such time as the sons of King Ring were of age to rule their own realm. So King Ring lay sick a little while, and then died; and great mourning was made for him; then was there a mound cast over him, and much wealth laid therein, according to his bidding.

Thereafter Frithiof made a noble feast, whereunto his folk came; and thereat was drunken at one and the same time the heritage feast after King Ring, and the bridal of Frithiof and Ingibjorg.

After these things Frithiof abode in his realm, and was deemed therein a most noble man; he and Ingibjorg had many children.

Chapter 15: Frithiof King in Sogn

Now those kings of Sogn, the brethren of Ingibjorg, heard these tidings, how that Frithiof had gotten a king's rule in Ringrealm, and had wedded Ingibjorg their sister. Then says Helgi to

Halfdan, his brother, that unheard of it was, and a deed over-bold, that a mere hersir's son should have her to wife: and so thereat they gather together a mighty army, and go their ways therewith to Ringrealm, with the mind to slay Frithiof, and lay all his realm under them.

But when Frithiof was ware of this, he gathered folk, and spake to the queen moreover: 'New war is come upon our realm; and now, in whatso wise the dealings go, fain am I that thy ways to me grow no colder.'

She said: 'In such wise have matters gone that I must needs let thee be the highest.'

Now was Biorn come from the east to help Frithiof; so they fared to the fight, and it befell, as ever erst, that Frithiof was the foremost in the peril: King Helgi and he came to handy-blows, and there he slew King Helgi.

Then bade Frithiof raise up the Shield of Peace, and the battle was stayed; and therewith he cried to King Halfdan: 'Two choices are in thine hands now, either that thou give up all to my will, or else gettest thou thy bane like thy brother; for now may men see that mine is the better part.'

So Halfdan chose to lay himself and his realm under Frithiof's sway; and so now Frithiof became ruler over Sogn-folk, and Halfdan was to be Hersir in Sogn and pay Frithiof tribute, while Frithiof ruled Ringrealm. So Frithiof had the name of King of Sogn-folk from the time that he gave up Ringrealm to the sons of King Ring, and thereafter he won Hordaland also. He and Ingibjorg had two sons, called Gunnthiof and Hunthiof, men of might, both of them.

And so here endeth the story of Frithiof the Bold.

Legends of the Gods, Demigods & Culture Heroes

Introduction

CATHOLIC CLAIMS of miraculous cures or apparitions; the Pentecostalist Protestant belief that the faithful can safely handle snakes … these days such direct interventions by God in human life are widely derided. Even among Christians, the prevailing view is that the presiding deity does not become involved in the daily ins and outs of his (or her) creation. But in earlier, pre-Christian traditions the divine and mortal realms interpenetrated: gods and goddesses were forever interfering in the lives of humans. There were, moreover, demigods: heroes who straddled the two realms. Often because they had been born out of liaisons between gods and human women: Krishna's relationship with Radha, for example, or Zeus' with Alcmene (which was to produce Heracles). Some stories show us gods intervening to bring the skills of civilization and culture to humankind – like the Mesoamerican deities Quetzalcoatl or Viracocha.

The Mexican Legend of Quetzalcoatl

IT IS HIGHLY PROBABLE that Quetzalcoatl was a deity of the pre-Nahua people of Mexico. He was regarded by the Aztec race as a god of somewhat alien character, and had but a limited following in Mexico, the city of Huitzilopochtli. In Cholula, however, and others of the older towns his worship flourished exceedingly. He was regarded as 'The Father of the Toltecs', and, legend says, was the seventh and youngest son of the Toltec Abraham, Iztacmixcohuatl. Quetzalcoatl (whose name means 'Feathered Serpent' or 'Feathered Staff') became, at a relatively early period, ruler of Tollan, and by his enlightened sway and his encouragement of the liberal arts did much to further the advancement of his people. His reign had lasted for a period sufficient to permit of his placing the cultivated arts upon a satisfactory basis when the country was visited by the cunning magicians Tezcatlipoca and Coyotlinaual, god of the Amantecas. Disentangled from its terms of myth, this statement may be taken to imply that bands of invading Nahua first began to appear within the Toltec territories. Tezcatlipoca, descending from the sky in the shape of a spider by way of a fine web, proffered him a draught of *pulque*, which so intoxicated him that the curse of lust descended upon him, and he forgot his chastity with Quetzalpetlatl. The doom pronounced upon him was the hard one of banishment, and he was compelled to forsake Anahuac. His exile wrought peculiar changes upon the face of the country. He secreted his treasures of gold and silver, burned his palaces, transformed the cacao-trees into mezquites, and banished all the birds from the neighbourhood of Tollan. The magicians, nonplussed at these unexpected happenings, begged him to return, but he refused on the ground that the sun required his presence. He proceeded to Tabasco, the fabled land of Tlapallan, and, embarking upon a raft made of serpents, floated away to the east. A slightly different version of this myth has already been given. Other accounts state that the king cast himself upon a funeral pyre and was consumed, and that the ashes arising from the conflagration flew upward, and were changed into birds of brilliant plumage. His heart also soared into the sky, and became the morning star. The Mexicans averred that Quetzalcoatl died when the star became visible, and thus they bestowed upon him the title 'Lord of the Dawn'. They further said that when he died he was invisible for four days, and that for eight days he wandered in the underworld, after which time the morning star appeared, when he achieved resurrection, and ascended his throne as a god.

It is the contention of some authorities that the myth of Quetzalcoatl points to his status as god of the sun. That luminary, they say, begins his diurnal journey in the east, whence Quetzalcoatl returned as to his native home. It will be recalled that Montezuma and his subjects imagined that Cortés was no other than Quetzalcoatl, returned to his dominions, as an old prophecy declared he would do. But that he stood for the sun itself is highly improbable, as will be shown. First of all, however, it will be well to pay some attention to other theories concerning his origin.

Perhaps the most important of these is that which regards Quetzalcoatl as a god of the air. He is connected, say some, with the cardinal points, and wears the insignia of the cross, which symbolizes them. Dr Seler says of him: 'He has a protruding, trumpet-like mouth, for the wind-god blows.... His figure suggests whirls and circles. Hence his temples were built in circular form.... The head of the wind-god stands for the second of the twenty day signs, which was called Ehecatl (Wind).' The same authority, however, in his essay on Mexican chronology, gives to Quetzalcoatl a dual nature, 'the dual nature which seems to belong to the wind-god Quetzalcoatl, who now appears simply a wind-god, and again seems to show the true characters of the old god of fire and light.'

Dr Brinton perceived in Quetzalcoatl a similar dual nature. 'He is both lord of the eastern light and of the winds,' he writes (*Myths of the New World*, page 214). 'Like all the dawn heroes, he too was represented as of white complexion, clothed in long, white robes, and, as many of the Aztec gods, with a full and flowing beard.... He had been overcome by Tezcatlipoca, the wind or spirit of night, who had descended from heaven by a spider's web, and presented his rival with a draught supposed to confer immortality, but in fact producing an intolerable longing for home. For the wind and the light both depart when the gloaming draws near, or when the clouds spread their dark and shadowy webs along the mountains, and pour the vivifying rain upon the fields.'

The theory which derives Quetzalcoatl from a 'culture-hero' who once actually existed is scarcely reconcilable with probability. It is more than likely that, as in the case of other mythical paladins, the legend of a mighty hero arose from the somewhat weakened idea of a great deity. Some of the early Spanish missionaries professed to see in Quetzalcoatl the Apostle St Thomas, who had journeyed to America to effect its conversion!

The Man of the Sun

A more probable explanation of the origin of Quetzalcoatl and a more likely elucidation of his nature is that which would regard him as the Man of the Sun, who has quitted his abode for a season for the purpose of inculcating in mankind those arts which represent the first steps in civilization, who fulfils his mission, and who, at a late period, is displaced by the deities of an invading race. Quetzalcoatl was represented as a traveller with staff in hand, and this is proof of his solar character, as is the statement that under his rule the fruits of the earth flourished more abundantly than at any subsequent period. The abundance of gold said to have been accumulated in his reign assists the theory, the precious metal being invariably associated with the sun by most barbarous peoples. In the native *pinturas* it is noticeable that the solar disc and semi-disc are almost invariably found in connection with the feathered serpent as the symbolical attributes of Quetzalcoatl. The Hopi Indians of Mexico at the present day symbolize the sun as a serpent, tail in mouth, and the ancient Mexicans introduced the solar disc in connection with small images of Quetzalcoatl, which they attached to the head-dress. In still other examples Quetzalcoatl is pictured as if emerging or stepping from the luminary, which is represented as his dwelling-place.

Several tribes tributary to the Aztecs were in the habit of imploring Quetzalcoatl in prayer to return and free them from the intolerable bondage of the conqueror. Notable among them were the Totonacs, who passionately believed that the sun, their father, would send a god who would free them from the Aztec yoke. On the coming of the Spaniards the European conquerors were hailed as the servants of Quetzalcoatl, thus in the eyes of the natives fulfilling the tradition that he would return.

Various Forms of Quetzalcoatl

Various conceptions of Quetzalcoatl are noticeable in the mythology of the territories which extended from the north of Mexico to the marshes of Nicaragua. In Guatemala the Kiches recognized him as Gucumatz, and in Yucatan proper he was worshipped as Kukulcan, both of which names are but literal translations of his Mexican title of 'Feathered Serpent' into Kiche and Mayan. That the three deities are one and the same there can be no shadow of doubt. Several authorities have seen in Kukulcan a 'serpent-and-rain god'. He can only be such in so far as he is a solar god also. The cult of the feathered snake in Yucatan was unquestionably a branch of sun-worship. In tropical latitudes the sun draws the clouds round him at noon. The rain falls from the clouds accompanied by thunder and lightning – the symbols of the divine serpent. Therefore the manifestations of the heavenly serpent were directly associated with the sun, and no statement that Kukulcan is a mere serpent-and-water god satisfactorily elucidates his characteristics.

Quetzalcoatl's Northern Origin

It is by no means improbable that Quetzalcoatl was of northern origin, and that on his adoption by southern peoples and tribes dwelling in tropical countries his characteristics were gradually and unconsciously altered in order to meet the exigencies of his environment. The mythology of the Indians of British Columbia, whence in all likelihood the Nahua originally came, is possessed of a central figure bearing a strong resemblance to Quetzalcoatl. Thus the Thlingit tribe worship Yetl; the Quaquiutl Indians, Kanikilak; the Salish people of the coast, Kumsnöotl, Quäaqua, or Släalekam. It is noticeable that these divine beings are worshipped as the Man of the Sun, and totally apart from the luminary himself, as was Quetzalcoatl in Mexico. The Quaquiutl believe that before his settlement among them for the purpose of inculcating in the tribe the arts of life, the sun descended as a bird, and assumed a human shape. Kanikilak is his son, who, as his emissary, spreads the arts of civilization over the world. So the Mexicans believed that Quetzalcoatl descended first of all in the form of a bird, and was ensnared in the fowler's net of the Toltec hero Hueymatzin.

The titles bestowed upon Quetzalcoatl by the Nahua show that in his solar significance he was god of the vault of the heavens, as well as merely son of the sun. He was alluded to as Ehecatl (The Air), Yolcuat (The Rattlesnake), Tohil (The Rumbler), Nanihehecatl (Lord of the Four Winds), Tlauizcalpantecutli (Lord of the Light of the Dawn). The whole heavenly vault was his, together with all its phenomena. This would seem to be in direct opposition to the theory that Tezcatlipoca was the supreme god of the Mexicans. But it must be borne in mind that Tezcatlipoca was the god of a later age, and of a fresh body of Nahua immigrants, and as such inimical to Quetzalcoatl, who was probably in a similar state of opposition to Itzamna, a Maya deity of Yucatan.

The Worship of Quetzalcoatl

The worship of Quetzalcoatl was in some degree antipathetic to that of the other Mexican deities, and his priests were a separate caste. Although human sacrifice was by no means so prevalent among his devotees, it is a mistake to aver, as some authorities have done, that it did not exist in connection with his worship. A more acceptable sacrifice to Quetzalcoatl appears to have been the blood of the celebrant or worshipper, shed by himself. When we come to consider the mythology of the Zapotecs, a people whose customs and beliefs appear to have formed a species of link between the Mexican and Mayan civilizations, we shall find that their high-priests occasionally enacted the legend of Quetzalcoatl in their own persons, and that their worship, which appears to have been based upon that of Quetzalcoatl, had as one of its most pronounced characteristics the shedding of blood. The celebrant or devotee drew blood from the vessels lying under the tongue or behind the ear by drawing across those tender parts a cord made from the thorn-covered fibres of the agave. The blood was smeared over the mouths of the idols. In this practice we can perceive an act analogous to the sacrificial substitution of the part for the whole, as obtaining in early Palestine and many other countries – a certain sign that tribal or racial opinion has contracted a disgust for human sacrifice, and has sought to evade the anger of the gods by yielding to them a portion of the blood of each worshipper, instead of sacrificing the life of one for the general weal.

Viracocha

THE AYMARA-QUICHUA RACE worshipped Viracocha as a great culture hero. They did not offer him sacrifices or tribute, as they thought that he, being creator and possessor of all things, needed nothing from men, so they only gave him worship. After him they idolized the sun. They believed, indeed, that Viracocha had made both sun and moon, after emerging from Lake Titicaca, and that then he made the earth and peopled it. On his travels westward from the lake he was sometimes assailed by men, but he revenged himself by sending terrible storms upon them and destroying their property, so they humbled themselves and acknowledged him as their lord. He forgave them and taught them everything, obtaining from them the name of Pachayachachic. In the end he disappeared in the western ocean. He either created or there were born with him four beings who, according to mythical beliefs, civilized Peru. To them he assigned the four quarters of the earth, and they are thus known as the four winds, north, south, east, and west. One legend avers they came from the cave Pacari, the Lodging of the Dawn.

Thonapa

SOME MYTHS tell of a divine personage called Thonapa, who appears to have been a hero-god or civilizing agent like Quetzalcoatl. He seems to have devoted his life to preaching to the people in the various villages, beginning in the provinces of Colla-suya. When he came to Yamquisupa he was treated so badly that he would not remain there. He slept in the open air, clad only in a long shirt and a mantle, and carried a book. He cursed the village. It was soon immersed in water, and is now a lake.

There was an idol in the form of a woman to which the people offered sacrifice at the top of a high hill, Cachapucara. This idol Thonapa detested, so he burnt it, and also destroyed the hill. On another occasion Thonapa cursed a large assembly of people who were holding a great banquet to celebrate a wedding, because they refused to listen to his preaching. They were all changed into stones, which are visible to this day.

Wandering through Peru, Thonapa came to the mountain of Caravaya, and after raising a very large cross he put it on his shoulders and took it to the hill Carapucu, where he preached so fervently that he shed tears. A chief's daughter got some of the water on her head, and the Indians, imagining that he was washing his head (a ritual offence), took him prisoner near the Lake of Carapucu. Very early the next morning a beautiful youth appeared to Thonapa, and told him not to fear, for he was sent from the divine guardian who watched over him. He released Thonapa, who escaped, though he was well guarded. He went down into the lake, his mantle keeping him above the water as a boat would have done.

After Thonapa had escaped from the barbarians he remained on the rock of Titicaca, afterwards going to the town of Tiya-manacu, where again he cursed the people and turned them into stones. They were too bent upon amusement to listen to his preaching. He then followed the river Chacamarca till it reached the sea, and, like Quetzalcoatl, disappeared. This is good evidence that he was a solar deity, or 'man of the sun', who, his civilizing labours completed, betook himself to the house of his father.

Anansi Obtains the Sky-God's Stories

KWAKU ANANSI had one great wish. He longed to be the owner of all the stories known in the world, but these were kept by the Sky-God, Nyame [The Ashanti refer to God as 'Nyame'. The Dagomba call him 'Wuni', while the Krachi refer to him as 'Wulbari'.], in a safe hiding-place high above the clouds.

One day, Anansi decided to pay the Sky-God a visit to see if he could persuade Nyame to sell him the stories.

'I am flattered you have come so far, little creature,' the Sky-God told Anansi, 'but many rich and powerful men have preceded you and none has been able to purchase what they came here for. I am willing to part with my stories, but the price is very high. What makes you think that you can succeed where they have all failed?'

'I feel sure I will be able to buy them,' answered Anansi bravely, 'if you will only tell me what the price is.'

'You are very determined, I see,' replied Nyame, 'but I must warn you that the price is no ordinary one. Listen carefully now to what I demand of you.

'First of all, you must capture Onini, the wise old python, and present him to me. When you have done this, you must go in search of the Mmoboro, the largest nest of hornets in the forest, and bring them here also. Finally, look for Osebo, the fastest of all leopards and set a suitable trap for him. Bring him to me either dead or alive.

'When you have delivered me these three things, all the stories of the world will be handed over to you.'

'I shall bring you everything you ask for,' Anansi declared firmly, and he hastened towards his home where he began making plans for the tasks ahead.

That afternoon, he sat down with his wife, Aso, and told her all about his visit to the Sky-God.

'How will I go about trapping the great python, Onini?' he asked her.

His wife, who was a very clever woman, instructed her husband to make a special trip to the centre of the woods:

'Go and cut yourself a long bamboo pole,' she ordered him, 'and gather some strong creeper-vines as well. As soon as you have done this, return here to me and I will tell you what to do with these things.'

Anansi gathered these objects as his wife had commanded and after they had spent some hours consulting further, he set off enthusiastically towards the house of Onini.

As he approached closer, he suddenly began arguing with himself in a loud and angry voice:

'My wife is a stupid woman,' he pronounced, 'she says it is longer and stronger. I say it is shorter and weaker. She has no respect. I have a great deal. She is stupid. I am right.'

'What's all this about?' asked the python, suddenly appearing at the door of his hut. 'Why are you having this angry conversation with yourself?'

'Oh! Please ignore me,' answered the spider. 'It's just that my wife has put me in such a bad mood. For she says this bamboo pole is longer and stronger than you are, and I say she is a liar.'

'There is no need for the two of you to argue so bitterly on my account,' replied the python, 'bring that pole over here and we will soon find out who is right.'

So Anansi laid the bamboo pole on the earth and the python stretched himself out alongside it.

'I'm still not certain about this,' said Anansi after a few moments. 'When you stretch at one end, you appear to shrink at the other end. Perhaps if I tied you to the pole I would have a clearer idea of your size.'

'Very well,' answered the python, 'just so long as we can sort this out properly.'

Anansi then took the creeper-vine and wrapped it round and round the length of the python's body until the great creature was unable to move.

'Onini,' said Anansi, 'it appears my wife was right. You are shorter and weaker than this pole and more foolish into the bargain. Now you are my prisoner and I must take you to the Sky-God, as I have promised.'

The great python lowered his head in defeat as Anansi tugged on the pole, dragging him along towards the home of Nyame.

'You have done well, spider,' said the god, 'but remember, there are two more, equally difficult quests ahead. You have much to accomplish yet, and it would not be wise to delay here any longer.'

So Anansi returned home once more and sat down to discuss the next task with his wife.

'There are still hornets to catch,' he told her, 'and I cannot think of a way to capture an entire swarm all at once.'

'Look for a gourd,' his wife suggested, 'and after you have filled it with water, go out in search of the hornets.'

Anansi found a suitable gourd and filled it to the brim. Fortunately, he knew exactly the tree where the hornets had built their nest. But before he approached too close, he poured some of the water from the gourd over himself so that his clothes were dripping wet. Then, he began sprinkling the nest with the remaining water while shouting out to the hornets:

'Why do you remain in such a flimsy shelter Mmoboro, when the great rains have already begun? You will soon be swept away, you foolish people. Here, take cover in this dry gourd of mine and it will protect you from the storms.'

The hornets thanked the spider for this most timely warning and disappeared one by one into the gourd. As soon as the last of them had entered, Anansi plugged the mouth of the vessel with some grass and chuckled to himself:

'Fools! I have outwitted you as well. Now you can join Onini, the python. I'm certain Nyame will be very pleased to see you.'

Anansi was delighted with himself. It had not escaped his notice that even the Sky-God appeared rather astonished by his success and it filled him with great excitement to think that very soon he would own all the stories of the world.

Only Osebo, the leopard, stood between the spider and his great wish, but Anansi was confident that with the help of his wife he could easily ensnare the creature as he had done all the others.

'You must go and look for the leopard's tracks,' his wife told him, 'and then dig a hole where you know he is certain to walk.'

Anansi went away and dug a very deep pit in the earth, covering it with branches and leaves so that it was well-hidden from the naked eye. Night-time closed in around him and soon afterwards, Osebo came prowling as usual and fell right into the deep hole, snarling furiously as he hit the bottom.

At dawn on the following morning, Anansi approached the giant pit and called to the leopard:

'What has happened here? Have you been drinking, leopard? How on earth will you manage to escape from this great hole?'

'I have fallen into a silly man-trap,' said the leopard impatiently. 'Help me out at once. I am almost starving to death in this wretched place.'

'And if I help you out, how can I be sure you won't eat me?' asked Anansi. 'You say you are very hungry, after all.'

'I wouldn't do a thing like that,' Osebo reassured him. 'I beg you, just this once, to trust me. Nothing bad will happen to you, I promise.'

Anansi hurried away from the opening of the pit and soon returned with a long, thick rope. Glancing around him, he spotted a tall green tree and bent it towards the ground, securing it with a length of the rope so that the top branches hung over the pit. Then he tied another piece of rope to these branches, dropping the loose end into the pit for the leopard to tie to his tail.

'As soon as you have tied a large knot, let me know and I will haul you up,' shouted Anansi.

Osebo obeyed the spider's every word, and as soon as he gave the signal that he was ready, Anansi cut the rope pinning the tree to the ground. It sprung upright at once, pulling the leopard out of the hole in one swift motion. Osebo hung upside down, wriggling and twisting helplessly, trying with every ounce of his strength to loosen his tail from the rope. But Anansi was not about to take any chances and he plunged his knife deep into the leopard's chest, killing him instantly. Then he lifted the leopard's body from the earth and carried it all the way to the Sky-God.

Nyame now called together all the elders of the skies, among them the Adonten, the Oyoko, the Kontire and Akwam chiefs, and informed them of the great exploits of Anansi, the spider:

'Many great warriors and chiefs have tried before,' the Sky-God told the congregation, 'but none has been able to pay the price I have asked of them. Kwaku Anansi has brought me Onini the python, the Mmoboro nest and the body of the mighty Osebo. The time has come to repay him as he deserves. He has won the right to tell my stories. From today, they will no longer be called stories of the Sky-God, but stories of Anansi, the spider.'

And so, with Nyame's blessing, Anansi became the treasurer of all the stories that have ever been told. And even now, whenever a man wishes to tell a story for the entertainment of his people, he must acknowledge first of all that the tale is a great gift, given to him by Anansi, the spider.

The Legend of Ra and Isis

THE EGYPTIAN LEGEND opens with a list of the titles of Ra, the 'self-created god', creator of heaven, earth, breath of life, fire, gods, men, beasts, cattle, reptiles, feathered fowl, and fish, the King of gods and men, to whom cycles of 120 years are as years, whose manifold names are unknown even by the gods.

The text continues: Isis had the form of a woman, and knew words of power, but she was disgusted with men, and she yearned for the companionship of the gods and the spirits, and she meditated and asked herself whether, supposing she had the knowledge of the Name of Ra, it was not possible to make herself as great as Ra was in heaven and on the earth? Meanwhile Ra appeared in heaven each day upon his throne, but he had become old, and he dribbled at the mouth, and his spittle fell on the ground. One day Isis took some of the spittle and kneaded up dust in it, and made this paste into the form of a serpent with a forked tongue, so that if it struck anyone the person struck would find it impossible to escape death. This figure she placed on the path on which Ra walked as he came into heaven after his daily survey of the Two Lands (i.e. Egypt). Soon after this Ra rose up, and attended by his gods he came into heaven, but as he went along the serpent drove its fangs into him. As soon as he was bitten Ra felt the living fire leaving his body, and he cried out so loudly that his voice reached the uttermost parts of heaven. The gods rushed to him in great alarm, saying, 'What is the matter?' At first Ra was speechless, and found himself unable to answer, for his jaws shook, his lips trembled, and the poison continued to run through every part of his body. When he was able to regain a little strength, he told the gods that some deadly creature had bitten him, something the like of which he had never seen, something which his hand had never made. He said, 'Never before have I felt such pain; there is no pain worse than this.' Ra then went on to describe his greatness and power, and told the listening gods that his father and mother had hidden his name in his body so that no one might be able to master him by means of any spell or word of power. In spite of this something had struck him, and he knew not what it was. 'Is it fire?' he asked. 'Is it water? My heart is full of burning fire, my limbs are shivering, shooting pains are in all my members.' All the gods round about him uttered cries of lamentation, and at this moment Isis appeared. Going to Ra she said, 'What is this, Oh divine father? What is this? Has a serpent bitten you? Has something made by you lifted up its head against you? Verily my words of power shall overthrow it; I will make it depart in the sight of your light.' Ra then repeated to Isis the story of the incident, adding, 'I am colder than water, I am hotter than fire. All my members sweat. My body quakes. My eye is unsteady. I cannot look on the sky, and my face is bedewed with water as in the time of the Inundation' (i.e. in the period of summer). Then Isis said, 'Father, tell me your name, for he who can utter his own name lives.'

Ra replied, 'I am the maker of heaven and earth. I knit together the mountains and whatsoever lives on them. I made the waters. I made Mehturit (an ancient Cow-goddess of heaven) to come into being. I made Kamutef (a form of Amen-Ra). I made heaven, and the two hidden gods of the horizon, and put souls into the gods. I open my eyes, and there is light; I shut my eyes, and there is darkness. I speak the word[s], and the waters of the Nile appear. I am he whom the gods know not. I make the hours. I create the days. I open the year. I make the river [Nile]. I create the living fire whereby works in the foundries and workshops are carried out. I am Khepera in the morning, Ra at noon, and Temu in the evening.' Meanwhile the poison of the serpent was coursing through the veins of Ra, and the enumeration of his works afforded the god no relief from it. Then Isis said to Ra, 'Among all the things which you have named to me you have not named your name. Tell me your name, and the poison shall come forth from you.' Ra still hesitated, but the poison was burning in his blood, and the heat thereof was stronger than that of a fierce fire. At length he said, 'Isis shall search me through, and my name shall come forth from my body and pass into hers.' Then Ra hid himself from the gods, and for a season his throne in the Boat of Millions of Years was empty. When the time came for the heart of the god to pass into Isis, the goddess said to Horus, her son, 'The great god shall bind himself by an oath to give us his two eyes (i.e. the sun and the moon).' When the great god had yielded up his name Isis pronounced the following spell: 'Flow poison, come out of Ra. Eye of Horus, come out of the god, and sparkle as you come through his mouth. I am the worker. I make the poison fall on the ground. The poison is conquered. Truly the name of the great god has been taken from him. Ra lives! The poison dies! If the poison live Ra shall die.' These were the words which Isis spoke, Isis the great lady, the Queen of the gods, who knew Ra by his own name.

In late times magicians used to write the above legend on papyrus above figures of Temu and Heru-Hekenu, who gave Ra his secret name, and over figures of Isis and Horus, and sell the rolls as charms against snake bites.

The Legend of Horus of Behutet

THE GREAT HISTOROCAL FACT underlying this legend is the conquest of Egypt by some very early king who invaded Egypt from the south, and who succeeded in conquering every part of it, even the northern part of the Delta. The events described are supposed to have taken place whilst Ra was still reigning on the earth.

The legend states that in the three hundred and sixty-third year of the reign of Ra-Harmakhis, the ever living, His Majesty was in Ta-sti (i.e. the Land of the Bow, or Nubia) with his soldiers; the enemy had reviled him, and for this reason the land is called 'Uauatet' to this day. From Nubia Ra sailed down the river to Apollinopolis (Edfu), and Heru-Behutet, or Horus of Edfu, was with him. On arriving there Horus told Ra that the enemy were plotting against him, and Ra told him to go out and slay them. Horus took the form of a great winged disk, which flew up into the air and pursued the enemy, and it attacked them with such terrific force that they could neither see nor hear, and they fell upon each other, and slew each other, and in a moment not a single foe was left alive. Then Horus returned to the Boat of Ra-Harmakhis, in the form of the winged disk which shone with many colours, and said, 'Advance, Oh Ra, and look upon your enemies who are lying under you in this land.' Ra set out on the journey, taking with him the goddess Ashtoreth, and he saw his enemies lying on the ground, each of them being fettered. After looking upon his slaughtered foes Ra said to the gods who were with him, 'Behold, let us sail in our boat on the water, for our hearts are glad because our enemies have been overthrown on the earth.'

So the Boat of Ra moved onwards towards the north, and the enemies of the god who were on the banks took the form of crocodiles and hippopotami, and tried to frighten the god, for as his boat came near them they opened their jaws wide, intending to swallow it up together with the gods who were in it. Among the crew were the Followers of Horus of Edfu, who were skilled workers in metal, and each of these had in his hands an iron spear and a chain. These 'Blacksmiths' threw out their chains into the river and allowed the crocodiles and hippopotami to entangle their legs in them, and then they dragged the beasts towards the bows of the Boat, and driving their spears into their bodies, slew them there. After the slaughter the bodies of six hundred and fifty-one crocodiles were brought and laid out before the town of Edfu. When Thoth saw these he said, 'Let your hearts rejoice, Oh gods of heaven, Let your hearts rejoice, Oh gods who dwell on the earth. The Young Horus comes in peace. On his way he has made manifest deeds of valour, according to the Book of slaying the Hippopotamus.' And from that day they made figures of Horus in metal.

Then Horus of Edfu took the form of the winged disk, and set himself on the prow of the Boat of Ra. He took with him Nekhebet, goddess of the South, and Uatchet, goddess of the North, in the form of serpents, so that they might make all the enemies of the Sun-god to quake in the South and in the

North. His foes who had fled to the north doubled back towards the south, for they were in deadly fear of the god. Horus pursued and overtook them, and he and his blacksmiths had in their hands spears and chains, and they slew large numbers of them to the south-east of the town of Thebes in Upper Egypt. Many succeeded in escaping towards the north once more, but after pursuing them for a whole day Horus overtook them, and made a great slaughter among them. Meanwhile the other foes of the god, who had heard of the defeats of their allies, fled into Lower Egypt, and took refuge among the swamps of the Delta. Horus set out after them, and came up with them, and spent four days in the water slaying his foes, who tried to escape in the forms of crocodiles and hippopotami. He captured one hundred and forty-two of the enemy and a male hippopotamus, and took them to the fore part of the Boat of Ra. There he hacked them in pieces, and gave their inward parts to his followers, and their mutilated bodies to the gods and goddesses who were in the Boat of Ra and on the river banks in the town of Heben.

Then the remnant of the enemy turned their faces towards the Lake of the North, and they attempted to sail to the Mediterranean in boats; but the terror of Horus filled their hearts, and they left their boats and fled to the district of Mertet-Ament, where they joined themselves to the worshippers of Set, the god of evil, who dwelt in the Western Delta. Horus pursued them in his boat for one day and one night without seeing them, and he arrived at the town of Per-Rehui. At length he discovered the position of the enemy, and he and his followers fell upon them, and slew a large number of them; he captured three hundred and eighty-one of them alive, and these he took to the Boat of Ra, then, having slain them, he gave their carcasses to his followers or bodyguard, who presumably devoured them. The custom of eating the bodies of enemies is very old in Egypt, and survives in some parts of Africa to this day.

Then Set, the great antagonist of Horus, came out and cursed him for the slaughter of his people, using most shameful words of abuse. Horus stood up and fought a duel with Set, the 'Stinking Face,' as the text calls him, and Horus succeeded in throwing him to the ground and spearing him. Horus smashed his mouth with a blow of his mace, and having fettered him with his chain, he brought him into the presence of Ra, who ordered that he was to be handed over to Isis and her son Horus, that they might work their will on him. Here we must note that the ancient editor of the legend has confounded Horus the ancient Sun-god with Horus, son of Isis, son of Osiris. Then Horus, the son of Isis, cut off the heads of Set and his followers in the presence of Ra, and dragged Set by his feet round about throughout the district with his spear driven through his head and back, according to the order of Ra. The form which Horus of Edfu had at that time was that of a man of great strength, with the face and back of a hawk; on his head he wore the Double Crown, with feathers and serpents attached, and in his hands he held a metal spear and a metal chain. And Horus, the son of Isis, took upon himself a similar form, and the two Horuses slew all the enemies on the bank of the river to the west of the town of Per-Rehui. This slaughter took place on the seventh day of the first month of the season Pert (about the middle of November), which was ever afterwards called the 'Day of the Festival of Sailing'.

Now, although Set in the form of a man had been slain, he reappeared in the form of a great hissing serpent, and took up his abode in a hole in the ground without being noticed by Horus. Ra, however, saw him, and gave orders that Horus, the son of Isis, in the form of a hawk-headed staff, should set himself at the mouth of the hole, so that the monster might never reappear among men. This Horus did, and Isis his mother lived there with him. Once again it became known to Ra that a remnant of the followers of Set had escaped, and that under the direction of the Smait fiends, and of Set, who had reappeared, they were hiding in the swamps of the Eastern Delta. Horus of Edfu, the winged disk, pursued them, speared them, and finally slew them in the presence of Ra. For the moment, there were no more enemies of Ra to be found in the district on land, although Horus passed six days and six nights in looking for them; but it seems that several of the followers of Set in the forms of water reptiles were lying on the ground under water, and that Horus saw them there. At this time Horus had strict guard kept over the tomb of Osiris in Anrutef (a district of Herakleopolis), because he learned that the Smait fiends wanted to come and wreck both it and the body of the god. Isis, too, never ceased to recite spells and incantations in order to keep away her husband's foes from his body. Meanwhile the 'blacksmiths' of Horus, who were in charge of the 'middle regions' of Egypt, found a body of the enemy, and attacked them fiercely, slew many of them, and took one hundred and six of them prisoners. The 'blacksmiths' of the west also took one hundred and six prisoners, and both groups of prisoners were slain before Ra. In return for their services Ra bestowed dwelling-places upon the 'blacksmiths', and allowed them to have temples with images of their gods in them, and arranged for offerings and libations to be made to them by properly appointed priests of various classes.

Shortly after these events Ra discovered that a number of his enemies were still at large, and that they had sailed in boats to the swamps that lay round about the town of Tchal, or Tchar, better known as Zoan or Tanis. Once more Horus unmoored the Boat of Ra, and set out against them; some took refuge in the waters, and others landed and escaped to the hilly land on the east. For some reason, which is not quite apparent, Horus took the form of a mighty lion with a man's face, and he wore on his head the triple crown. His claws were like flints, and he pursued the enemy on the hills, and chased them hither and thither, and captured one hundred and forty-two of them. He tore out their tongues, and ripped their bodies into strips with his claws, and gave them over to his allies in the mountains, who, no doubt, ate them. This was the last fight in the north of Egypt, and Ra proposed that they should sail up the river and return to the south. They had traversed all Egypt, and sailed over the lakes in the Delta, and down the arms of the Nile to the Mediterranean, and as no more of the enemy were to be seen the prow of the boat of Ra was turned southwards. Thoth recited the spells that produced fair weather, and said the words of power that prevented storms from rising, and in due course the Boat reached Nubia. When it arrived, Horus found in the country of Uauatet men who were conspiring against him and cursing him, just as they had at one time blasphemed Ra. Horus, taking the form of the winged disk, and accompanied by the two serpent-goddesses, Nekhebet and Uatchet, attacked the rebels, but there was no fierce fighting this time, for the hearts of the enemy melted through fear of him. His foes cast themselves before him on the ground in submission, they offered no resistance, and they died straightway. Horus then returned to the town of Behutet (Edfu), and the gods acclaimed him, and praised his prowess. Ra was so pleased with him that he ordered Thoth to have a winged disk, with a serpent on each side of it, placed in every temple in Egypt in which he (i.e. Ra) was worshipped, so that it might act as a protector of the building, and drive away any and every fiend and devil that might wish to attack it. This is the reason why we find the winged disk, with a serpent on each side of it, above the doors of temples and religious buildings throughout the length and breadth of Egypt.

The Legend of Khnemu and the Seven Years' Famine

THE SUBJECT OF THIS LEGEND is a terrible famine, which lasted for seven years, in the reign of King Tcheser, and which recalls the seven years' famine that took place in Egypt when Joseph was there. This famine was believed to have been caused by the king's neglect to worship properly the god Khnemu, who was supposed to control the springs of the Nile, which were asserted by the sages to be situated between two great rocks on the Island of Elephantine.

The legend sets forth that the Viceroy of Nubia, in the reign of Tcheser, was a nobleman called Meter, who was also the overseer of all the temple properties in the South. His residence was in Abu, or Elephantine, and in the eighteenth year of his reign the king sent him a despatch in which it was written thus: 'This is to inform you that misery has laid hold upon me as I sit upon the great throne, and I grieve for those who dwell in the Great House. My heart is grievously afflicted by reason of a very great calamity, which is due to the fact that the waters of the Nile have not risen to their proper height for seven years. Grain is exceedingly scarce, there are no garden herbs and vegetables to be had at all, and everything which men use for food has come to an end. Every man robs his neighbour. The people wish to walk about, but are unable to move. The baby wails, the young man shuffles along on his feet through weakness. The hearts of the old men are broken down with despair, their legs give way under them, they sink down exhausted on the ground, and they lay their hands on their bellies [in pain]. The officials are powerless and have no counsel to give, and when the public granaries, which ought to contain supplies, are opened, there comes forth from them nothing but wind. Everything is in a state of ruin. I go back in my mind to the time when I had an adviser, to the time of the gods, to the Ibis-god [Thoth], and to the chief Kher-heb priest Imhetep (Imouthis), the son of Ptah of his South Wall (a part of Memphis). [Tell me, I pray you], Where is the birthplace of the Nile? What god or what goddess presides over it? What kind of form has the god? For it is he that makes my revenue, and who fills the granaries with grain. I wish to go to [consult] the Chief of Het-Sekhmet (i.e. Hermopolis, the town of Thoth), whose beneficence strengthens all men in their works. I wish to go into the House of Life (i.e. the library of the temple), and to take the rolls of the books in my own hands, so that I may examine them [and find out these things].'

Having read the royal despatch the Viceroy Meter set out to go to the king, and when he came to him he proceeded to instruct the king in the matters about which he had asked questions. The text makes the king say: '[Meter] gave me information about the rise of the Nile, and he told me all that men had written concerning it; and he made clear to me all the difficult passages [in the books], which my ancestors had consulted haveily, and which had never before been explained to any king since the time when Ra [reigned]. And he said to me: There is a town in the river wherefrom the Nile makes his appearance. 'Abu' was its name in the beginning: it is the City of the Beginning, it is the Name of the City of the Beginning. It reaches to Uauatet, which is the first land [on the south]. There is a long flight of steps there (a nilometer?), on which Ra rests when he determines to prolong life to mankind. It is called 'Netchemtchem ankh'. Here are the 'Two Qerti' (the two caverns which contained the springs of the Nile), which are the two breasts wherefrom every good thing comes. Here is the bed of the Nile, here the Nile-god renews his youth, and here he sends out the flood on the land. Here his waters rise to a height of twenty-eight cubits; at Hermopolis (in the Delta) their height is seven cubits. Here the Nile-god smites the ground with his sandals, and here he draws the bolts and throws open the two doors through which the water pours forth. In this town the Nile-god dwells in the form of Shu, and he keeps the account of the products of all Egypt, in order to give to each his due. Here are kept the cord for measuring land and the register of the estates. Here the god lives in a wooden house with a door made of reeds, and branches of trees form the roof; its entrance is to the south-east. Round about it are mountains of stone to which quarrymen come with their tools when they want stone to build temples to the gods, shrines for sacred animals, and pyramids for kings, or to make statues. Here they offer sacrifices of all kinds in the sanctuary, and here their sweet-smelling gifts are presented before the face of the god Khnemu. In the quarries on the river bank is granite, which is called the 'stone of Abu'. The names of its gods are: Sept (Sothis, the dog-star), Anqet, Hep (the Nile-god), Shu, Keb, Nut, Osiris, Horus, Isis, and Nephthys. Here are found precious stones (a list is given), gold, silver, copper, iron, lapis-lazuli, emerald, crystal, ruby, etc., alabaster, mother-of-emerald, and seeds of plants that are used in making incense. These were the things which I learned from Meter [the Viceroy].'

Having informed the king concerning the rise of the Nile and the other matters mentioned in his despatch, Meter made arrangements for the king to visit the temple of Khnemu in person. This he did, and the legend gives us the king's own description of his visit. He says: I entered the temple, and the keepers of the rolls untied them and showed them to me. I was purified by the sprinkling of holy water, and I passed through the places that were prohibited to ordinary folk, and a great offering of cakes, ale, geese, oxen, etc., was offered up on my behalf to the gods and goddesses of Abu. Then I found the god [Khnemu] standing in front of me, and I propitiated him with the offerings that I made to him, and I made prayer and supplication before him. Then he opened his eyes (the king was standing before a statue with movable eyes), and his heart inclined to me, and in a majestic manner he said to me: 'I am Khnemu who fashioned you. My two hands grasped you and knitted together your body; I made your members sound, and I gave you your heart. Yet the stones have been lying under the ground for ages, and no man has worked them in order to build a god-house, to repair the [sacred] buildings which are in ruins, or to make shrines for the gods of the South and North, or to do what he ought to do for his lord, even though I am the Lord [the Creator]. I am Nu, the self-created, the Great God, who came into being in the beginning. [I am] Hep [the Nile-god] who rises at will to give health to him that works for me. I am the Governor and Guide of all men, in all their periods, the Most Great, the Father of the gods, Shu, the Great One, the Chief of the earth. The two halves of heaven are my abode. The Nile is poured out in a stream by me, and it goes round about the tilled lands, and its embrace produces life forevery one that breathes, according to the extent of its embrace.... I will make the Nile rise for you, and in no year shall it fail, and it shall spread its water out and cover every land satisfactorily. Plants, herbs, and trees shall bend beneath [the weight of] their produce. The goddess Rennet (the Harvest goddess) shall be at the head of everything, and every product shall increase a hundred thousandfold, according to the cubit of the year. The people shall be filled, verily to their hearts' desire, yea, everyone. Want shall cease, and the emptiness of the granaries shall come to an end. The Land of Mera (i.e. Egypt) shall be one cultivated land, the districts shall be yellow with crops of grain, and the grain shall be good. The fertility of the land shall be according to the desire [of the husbandman], and it shall be greater than it has ever been before.' At the sound of the word 'crops' the king awoke, and the courage that then filled his heart was as great as his former despair had been.

Having left the chamber of the god the king made a decree by which he endowed the temple of Khnemu with lands and gifts, and he drew up a code of laws under which every farmer was compelled to pay certain dues to it. Every fisherman and hunter had to pay a tithe. Of the calves cast one tenth were to be sent to the temple to be offered up as the daily offering. Gold, ivory, ebony, spices, precious stones, and woods were tithed, whether their owners were Egyptians or not, but no local tribe was to levy duty on these things on their road to Abu. Every artisan also was to pay tithe, with the exception of those who were employed in the foundry attached to the temple, and whose occupation consisted in making the images of the gods. The king further ordered that a copy of this decree, the original of which was cut in wood, should be engraved on a stele to be set up in the sanctuary, with figures of Khnemu and his companion gods cut above it. The man who spat upon the stele [if discovered] was to be 'admonished with a rope'.

Perseus and the Gorgon

THERE ONCE WAS A TROUBLED KING who learned, through an Oracle, that he would reach his death through the hand of his own grandson. This king was Acrisius, king of Argos, and he had only one child, the fair Danae. Acrisius shut her away in a cave, in order to keep her unwedded, and there she grew older, and more beautiful, as time passed. No man could reach her, although many tried, and eventually word of her beauty reached the gods, and finally the king of the Gods himself, Zeus.

He entered her prison in a cascade of light, and planted in her womb the seed of the gods, and from this the infant Perseus was spawned. Acrisius heard the infant's cries, and unable to kill him outright, he released Danae from her prison, and with her child she was placed on a raft, and sent out on the stormy seas to meet their death.

Now Poseidon knew of Zeus's child, and calmed the seas, lifting the mother and child carefully to the island of Seriphos, where they washed onto safe shores. They were discovered there by a kind fisherman, who brought them to his home. It was in this humble and peaceful abode that Perseus grew up, a boy of effortless intelligence, cunning and nobility. He was a sportsman beyond compare, and a hero among his playmates. He was visited in his dreams by Athene, the goddess of war, who filled his head with lusty ambition and inspired him to seek danger and excitement.

The fisherman became a father figure to Perseus, but another schemed to take his place. The fisherman's brother Polydectes, chief of the island, was besotted by the beautiful Danae, and longed to have her for his wife. He showered her with priceless jewels, succulent morsels of food, rich fabrics and furs, but her heart belonged to Perseus, and she refused his attentions. Embittered, he resolved to dispose of the youth, and set Perseus a task at which he could not help but fail, and from which no mortal man could ever return.

The task was to slay the creature Medusa, one of the three Gorgon sisters. Medusa was the only mortal of the Gorgons, with a face so hideous, so repulsive, that any man who laid eyes on her would be turned to stone before he could attack. Her hair was a nest of vipers, which writhed around that flawed and fatal face. Perseus was enthralled by the idea of performing an act of such bravery and that night, as he slept, he summoned again the goddess Athene, who provided him with the tools by which the task could be shouldered.

Athene came to him, a glorious figure of war, and with her she brought Hermes, her brother, who offered the young man powerful charms with which he could make his way. Perseus was provided with Hermes own crooked sword, sturdy enough to cut through even the strongest armour, and Perseus's feet were fitted with winged sandals, by which he could make his escape. From Hades he received a helmet which had the power to make its wearer invisible. Athene offered her mirrored shield, which would allow Perseus to strike Medusa without seeing her horrible face. Finally, he was given a skin bag, to carry the Gorgon's head from the site.

Perseus set out the next morning, his first assignment to find the half-sisters of the Gorgons, in the icy wilderness of the northern steppes of Graiae. They alone could provide him with the whereabouts of Medusa. With the aid of his winged sandals, Perseus flew north, till he came to the frosted mists of the mountains. There the earth was so cold, a fabulous crack was rent across her surface. The land was barren, icy, empty, and although he felt no fear, Perseus had to struggle to carry on, his breath frozen on his lips. There, on the edge of the Hyperborean sea were the Gray Sisters, witches from another era who had come there to end their days, wreaking a wretched existence from the snow-capped mountains, toothless and haggard with age. They had but one eye between them, and one tooth, without which they would surely have died.

Perseus chose his moment carefully, and lunged into their midst, grasping their single eye, and stepping out of reach.

'I require your assistance,' he said firmly. 'I must know the way to the Gorgons. If you cannot help me I shall take your tooth as well, and you shall starve in this wilderness.'

The Gray Sisters swayed and muttered, lolling upon the snow and fumbling across its icy surface towards the awe-inspiring voice.

A cry rose up when they realized that he had their eye, and they threatened and cursed Perseus, their howls echoing in the blackness of the wasteland. Finally, they succumbed, the fear of blindness in that empty place enlivening their tongues, loosening their resolve. Perseus graciously returned their eye, and on a breath of Arctic air, he rose and headed southwards, out of sight of the sisters, who struggled to see their tormentor.

Back through the mists he flew, where the sea sent spirals of spray that lashed at his heels and tried to drag him down. On he went, and the snows melted away into a sea so blue he seemed enveloped in it. The sky grew bright, the grass of the fields green and inviting, and as he flew he grew hotter, his eyes heavy with exhaustion, his perfect skin dripping with effort. The other end of the world rose up, a land and a sea where no human dared enter, a land of burning heat, of fiery hatred and fear, where none lived but the Gorgons themselves, surrounded by the hapless stone statues of man and beast who had dared to look upon them.

He came across the sisters as they slept in the midday sun. Medusa lay between her sisters, who protectively laid their arms across her mass. Her body was scaled and repellent, her limbs clawed and gnarled. Perseus dared look no further, but from the corner of his eye he saw the coiling vipers, and the serpent's tongue which even in sleep darted from her razor-sharp lips. Her fearsome eyes were shut. He was safe.

With one decisive movement he plunged himself and his sword towards this creature, Athene's shield held high. And Medusa's answering howl pierced the air, ripping the breath from his lungs, and dragging him down towards her. He struggled to maintain his composure, shivering and drawn to look at the source of this violent cry. He fell on her, shaking his head to clear it, fighting the temptation to give in. And then the courage that was deep inside him, born within him, the gift of his father Zeus, redeemed him. He lifted his head, and with shield held high, thrust his sword in one wild swoop that lopped off the head of Medusa.

He packed it hastily in his bag, and leapt up, away from the arms of the Sisters Gorgon who had woken abruptly, and now hissed and struck out at him. The Gorgons were not human, and could not, like Medusa, be slain by humans. They rose on wings, like murderous vultures, yowling and gnashing their teeth, screaming of revenge.

But Perseus had disappeared. His helmet took him from their side, enshrouded him with a curtain that protected him from their eyes. He was safe.

For days on end he flew with his booty, across the desert, where the dripping blood of Medusa hit the sand and bred evil vipers and venomous snakes, ever to populate the sunburnt earth. The Gorgons flew behind him, a whirlwind of hatred and revenge, but Perseus soared above them, until he was safe, at the edge of his world.

He came to rest at the home of Atlas, the giant, who held up with great pillars the weight of the sky. He begged for a place to lay his weary head, for sustenance and water. But the giant refused him. Tired and angry, Perseus thrust his hand into his bag and drew out the monstrous head. To this day, Atlas stands, a stone giant holding up the skies, his head frosted with snow, his face frozen with horror.

And Perseus flew on, although it was several months and many more challenges before he was able to present his trophy. But his travels are another story, involving passion, bravery and an ultimate battle. He would meet Polydectes once again, would defend his hostage mother, and face his long-lost grandfather. He would make his own mark at Olympus, and become, eventually, a bright star, a divine beacon which would guide courageous wanderers, as he had once been.

Theseus

WHEN YET BUT A VERY YOUNG MAN, Aegeus, King of Athens, journeyed off to Troezene, where he fell in love with and married a pretty young princess by the name of Aethra. For some reason, which mythologists do not make known, the king was forced to return alone to Athens; but ere he departed he concealed his sword and sandals beneath a stone, bidding his wife remember, that, as soon as the strength of their son Theseus permitted, he must raise the rock, appropriate sword and sandals, and come and join him in Athens, where he should be introduced to the people as his son and heir. These instructions given, Aegeus bade a fond farewell to his wife and infant son, and returned home.

As the years passed by, they brought strength, beauty, and wisdom to Theseus, whose fame began to be published abroad. At last Aethra deemed him strong enough to raise the rock beneath which his father's trusty weapon lay; and, conducting him to the spot where it was, she told him the whole story, and bade him try his strength.

Theseus immediately obeyed. With a mighty effort he raised the rock, and, to his great satisfaction, found the sword and sandals in a perfect state of preservation. Sword in hand, he then set out for Athens, – a long and dangerous journey. He proceeded slowly and cautiously, for he knew that many dangers lurked along his pathway, and that ere he reached his father's city he would have to encounter both giants and monsters, who would strive to bar his way.

He was not at all mistaken in his previsions; for Troezene was scarcely lost to sight ere he came across the giant Periphetes, son of Vulcan, who stood in the road and attacked with a huge club, whose blows were generally fatal, all who strove to pass. Adroitly evading the giant's first onslaught, Theseus plunged his sword deep into his huge side ere he could renew the attack, and brought him lifeless to the ground.

Theseus then disarmed his fallen foe, and, retaining the club for future use, continued his journey in peace, until he came to the Isthmus of Corinth, where two adventures awaited him. The first was with a cruel giant named Sinis, nicknamed The Pine-bender, whose usual practice was to bend some huge pine until its top touched the ground, and call to any unsuspecting passer-by to seize it and lend him a helping hand for a moment. Then, as soon as the innocent stranger had complied with his request, he would suddenly let go the pine, which, freed from his gigantic grasp, sprang back to its upright position, and hurled the unfortunate traveler way up in the air, to be dashed to pieces against the rocky mountain side.

Theseus, who had already heard of the giant's stratagem, skillfully eluded the danger, and finally caused Sinis to perish by the same cruel death which he had dealt out to so many others.

In one place the Isthmus of Corinth was exceedingly narrow, and the only practicable pathway led along a rocky ledge, guarded by a robber named Sciron, who forced all who tried to pass him to wash his feet. While the traveler was thus engaged, and knelt in the narrow pathway to do his bidding, he would suddenly raise his foot, kick him over the side, and hurl him down into the sea below, where a huge tortoise was ever waiting with gaping jaws to devour the victims.

Instead of yielding to Sciron's exactions, Theseus drew his sword, and by his determined bearing so terrified the robber, that he offered him a free passage. This offer, however, did not satisfy Theseus, who said he would sheathe his sword only on condition that Sciron performed for him the menial office he had imposed upon so many others. Sciron dared not refuse, and obeyed in fear and trembling; but he was doomed never to molest any one again, for Theseus kicked him over the precipice, into the breakers, where the tortoise feasted upon his remains with as keen a relish as upon former victims.

After disposing of another world-renowned robber, Cercyon (The Wrestler), Theseus encountered Procrustes (The Stretcher), a cruel giant, who, under pretext of entertainment, deluded travelers into entering his home, where he had two beds of very different dimensions, – one unusually short, the other unusually long. If the unfortunate traveler were a short man, he was put to bed in the long bedstead, and his limbs were pulled out of joint to make him fit it; but if, on the contrary, he were tall, he was assigned the short bed, and the superfluous length of limb was lopped off under the selfsame pretext. Taking Procrustes quite unawares, Theseus gave him a faint idea of the sufferings he had inflicted upon others by making him try each bed in turn, and then, to avoid his continuing these evil practices, put an end to his wretched existence.

Theseus successfully accomplished a few more exploits of a similar character, and finally reached Athens, where he found that his fame had preceded him.

The first tidings that there reached his ear were that Aegeus had just married Medea, the enchantress; but, although these tidings were very unwelcome, he hastened on to his father's court, to make himself known, and receive the welcome promised so many years before. Medea, seated by Aegeus' side, no sooner saw the young stranger draw near, than she knew him, and foresaw that he had come to demand his rights. To prevent his making known claims which might interfere with the prospects of her future offspring, she hastily mixed a deadly poison in a cup, which she filled with fragrant wine, and bade Aegeus offer it to the stranger.

The monarch was about to execute her apparently hospitable purpose, when his eye suddenly rested upon the sword at Theseus' side, which he immediately recognized. One swift glance into the youth's open face convinced him that Aethra's son stood before him, and he eagerly stretched out his arms to clasp him to his heart. This sudden movement upset the goblet, and the poisonous contents, falling upon a dog lying at the king's feet, caused his almost instantaneous death. Seeing her crime discovered and Theseus recognized, Medea quickly mounted her magic dragon car, and fled to Media, whence she never returned.

One day, some time after his arrival at Athens, Theseus heard a sound of weeping and great lamentation throughout all the city, and in reply to his wondering inquiries was told, that ever since an unfortunate war between the Cretans and Athenians, the latter, who had been vanquished, were obliged to pay a yearly tribute of seven youths and as many maidens, destined to serve as food for the Minotaur. Further questions evolved the fact that the Minotaur was a hideous monster, the property of Minos, King of Crete, who kept it in an intricate labyrinth, constructed for that express purpose by Daedalus, the far-famed architect. This labyrinth was so very intricate, that those who entered could not find their way out.

These varied details kindled Theseus' love of adventure, and still further strengthened him in his sudden resolve to join the mournful convoy, try his strength against the awful Minotaur, and, if possible, save his country from further similar exactions.

Even his father's tears and entreaties were powerless to move him from his purpose, and, the hour having come, he embarked upon the black-sailed vessel which was to bear the yearly tribute to Crete, promising to change the black sails for snowy white ones if he were fortunate enough to return victorious.

Favourable winds soon wafted the galley to distant Crete, and as they sailed along the coast, searching for the port, they were challenged by the brazen giant Talus, who walked daily thrice around the whole island, killing, by contact with his red-hot body, all who had no business to land on that coast. Knowing, however, that the black-sailed galley brought a fresh supply of youths and maidens for the terrible Minotaur, Talus let it pass unharmed; and the victims were brought into the presence of Minos, who personally inspected each new freight-load, to make sure he was not being cheated by the Athenians.

At the monarch's side stood his fair daughter Ariadne, whose tender heart was filled with compassion when she beheld the frail maidens and gallant youths about to perish by such a loathsome death. Theseus, by right of his birth, claimed the precedence, and proffered a request to be the first victim, – a request which the king granted with a sardonic smile, ere he returned unmoved to his interrupted feast.

Unnoticed by all, Ariadne slipped out of the palace, and, under cover of the darkness, entered the prison where Theseus was confined. There she tremblingly offered him a ball of twine and a sharp sword, bidding him tie one end of the twine to the entrance of the labyrinth, and keep the other in his hand as a clew to find the way out again should the sword enable him to kill the dreaded Minotaur. In token of gratitude for this timely assistance, Theseus solemnly promised Ariadne to take her with him to Athens as his bride, were he only successful in his undertaking.

At dawn the next day Theseus was conducted to the entrance of the labyrinth, and there left to await the tender mercies of the Minotaur. Like all heroes, he preferred to meet any danger rather than remain inactive: so, mindful of Ariadne's instructions, he fastened his twine to the entrance, and then boldly penetrated into the intricate ways of the labyrinth, where many whitening bones plainly revealed the fate of all who had preceded him.

He had not gone very far before he encountered the Minotaur, – a creature more hideous than fancy can paint, – and he was obliged to use all his skill and ingenuity to avoid falling a prey to the monster's appetite, and all his strength to lay him low at last. The Minotaur slain, Theseus hastily retraced his footsteps.

Arrived at the place where his ship rode at anchor, he found his companions and Ariadne awaiting him, and, springing on board, bade the sailors weigh anchor as quickly as possible. They were almost out of reach of the Cretan shores, when Talus came into view, and, perceiving that his master's prisoners were about to escape, leaned forward to catch the vessel by its rigging. Theseus, seeing this, sprang forward, and dealt the giant such a blow, that he lost his balance and fell into the deep sea, where he was drowned, and where thermal springs still bear witness to the heat of his brazen body.

The returning vessel, favoured by wind and tide, made but one port, Naxos; and here youths and maidens landed to view the beautiful island. Ariadne strayed apart, and threw herself down upon the ground to rest, where, before she was aware of it, sleep overtook her. Now, although very brave, Theseus was not very constant. He had already grown weary of Ariadne's love; and, when he saw her thus asleep, he basely summoned his companions, embarked with them, and set sail, leaving her alone upon the island, where Bacchus soon came to console her for the loss of her faithless lover.

Theseus, having committed a deed heinous in the eyes of gods and men, was doomed to suffer just punishment. In his preoccupation he entirely forgot his promise to change the black sails for white; and Aegeus, from Attica's rocky shore, seeing the sable sails when the vessel was yet far from land, immediately concluded that his son was dead, and in his grief cast himself into the sea since known as the Aegean, where he perished.

Theseus, on entering the city, heard of his father's death; and when he realized that it had been caused by his carelessness, he was overwhelmed with grief and remorse. All the cares of royalty and the wise measures he introduced for the happiness of his people could not divert his mind from this terrible catastrophe: so he finally resolved to resign his authority and set out again in search of adventures, which might help him forget his woes. He therefore made an excursion into the land of the Amazons, where Hercules had preceded him, and whence he brought back Hippolyte, whom he married. Theseus was now very happy indeed, and soon all his hopes were crowned by the birth of a son, whom he called Hippolytus. Shortly after this joyful event, the Amazons invaded his country under pretext of rescuing their kidnapped queen, and in the battle which ensued Hippolyte was accidentally wounded by an arrow, and breathed her last in Theseus' arms.

Theseus next set out with an Athenian army to fight Pirithous, king of the Lapithae, who had dared to declare war; but when the armies were face to face, the two chiefs, seized with a sudden liking for each other, simultaneously cast down their weapons, and, falling on each other's necks, embraced, and swore an eternal friendship.

To show his devotion to this newly won friend, Theseus consented to accompany him to the court of Adrastus, King of Argos, and witness his marriage to Hippodamia, daughter of the king. Many guests were, of course, present to witness the marriage ceremony, among others Hercules and a number of the Centaurs. The latter, struck with admiration for the bride's unusual beauty, made an attempt to kidnap her, which was frustrated by the Lapithae, seconded by Theseus and Hercules. The terrible struggle which ensued between the conflicting parties has ever been a favourite subject in art, and is popularly known as the 'Battle between the Centaurs and Lapithae.'

The hotly contested bride did not, however, enjoy a very long life, and Pirithous soon found himself, like Theseus, a disconsolate widower. To avoid similar bereavement in future, they both resolved to secure goddesses, who, being immortal, would share their thrones forever. Aided by Pirithous, Theseus carried off Helen, the daughter of Zeus, and, as she was still but a child, entrusted her to the care of his mother, Aethra, until she attained a suitable age for matrimony. Then, in return for Pirithous' kind offices, he accompanied him to Hades, where they intended to carry off Proserpina.

While they were thus engaged, Helen's twin brothers, Castor and Pollux, came to Athens, delivered her from captivity, and carried her home in triumph. As for Theseus and Pirithous, their treacherous intention was soon discovered by Hades, who set the first on an enchanted rock, from which he could not descend unassisted, and bound the second to the constantly revolving wheel of his father, Ixion.

When Hercules was in Hades in search of Cerberus, he delivered Theseus from his unpleasant position, and thus enabled him to return to his own home, where he now expected to spend the remainder of his life in peace.

Although somewhat aged by this time, Theseus was still anxious to marry, and looked about him for a wife to cheer his loneliness. Suddenly he remembered that Ariadne's younger sister, Phaedra, must be a charming young princess, and sent an embassy to obtain her hand in marriage. The embassy proved successful, and Phaedra came to Athens; but, young and extremely beautiful, she was not at all delighted with her aged husband, and, instead of falling in love with him, bestowed all her affections upon his son, Hippolytus, a virtuous youth, who utterly refused to listen to her proposals to elope. In her anger at finding her advances scorned, Phaedra went to Theseus and accused Hippolytus of attempting to kidnap her. Theseus, greatly incensed at what he deemed his son's shameful actions, implored Poseidon to punish the youth, who was even then riding in his chariot close by the shore. In answer to this prayer, a great wave suddenly arose, dashed over the chariot, and drowned the young charioteer, whose lifeless corpse was finally flung ashore at Phaedra's feet. When the unfortunate queen saw the result of her false accusations, she confessed her crime, and, in her remorse and despair, hung herself.

As for Theseus, soured by these repeated misfortunes, he grew so stern and tyrannical, that he gradually alienated his people's affections, until at last they hated him, and banished him to the Island of Scyros, where, in obedience to a secret order, Lycomedes, the king, treacherously slew him by hurling him from the top of a steep cliff into the sea. As usual, when too late, the Athenians repented of their ingratitude, and in a fit of tardy remorse deified this hero, and built a magnificent temple on the Acropolis in veneration of him. This building, now used as a museum, contains many relics of Greek art. Theseus' bones were piously brought back, and inhumed in Athens, where he was long worshiped as a demigod.

Tales of Heracles

SON OF ZEUS, father of the Greek Gods, and Alcmene, a human, Heracles (also known by his Roman name Hercules) was born a mortal who could feel pain, but was possessed with immense strength, courage and intelligence; a man who bridged the gap between mortals and gods. As such, tales of his extraordinary life are legendary and his twelve labours rank as the most incredible of all. As penance for the murder of his children in a fit of insanity brought on by Hera – Zeus' queen who was jealous of Heracles – Heracles was forced to serve his cousin, the spiteful and cowardly King Eurystheus of Argos, for 12 years, performing any tasks that were asked of him, no matter how deadly and perilous. If Heracles could do this, his soul would be purified and he would earn immortality.

Young Heracles

At the time of his birth Alcmene was living at Thebes with her husband Amphitryon, and thus the infant Heracles was born in the palace of his stepfather.

Aware of the animosity with which Hera persecuted all those who rivalled her in the affections of Zeus, Alcmene, fearful lest this hatred should be visited on her innocent child, entrusted him, soon after his birth, to the care of a faithful servant, with instructions to expose him in a certain field, and there leave him, feeling assured that the divine offspring of Zeus would not long remain without the protection of the gods.

Soon after the child had been thus abandoned, Hera and Pallas-Athene happened to pass by the field, and were attracted by its cries. Athene pityingly took up the infant in her arms, and prevailed upon the queen of heaven to put it to her breast; but no sooner had she done so, than the child, causing her pain, she angrily threw him to the ground, and left the spot. Athene, moved with compassion, carried him to Alcmene, and entreated her kind offices on behalf of the poor little foundling. Alcmene at once recognized her child, and joyfully accepted the charge.

Soon afterwards Hera, to her extreme annoyance, discovered whom she had nursed, and became filled with jealous rage. She now sent two venomous snakes into the chamber of Alcmene, which crept, unperceived by the nurses, to the cradle of the sleeping child. He awoke with a cry, and grasping a snake in each hand, strangled them both. Alcmene and her attendants, whom the cry of the child had awakened, rushed to the cradle, where, to their astonishment and terror, they beheld the two reptiles dead in the hands of the infant Heracles. Amphitryon was also attracted to the chamber by the commotion, and when he beheld this astounding proof of supernatural strength, he declared that the child must have been sent to him as a special gift from Zeus. He accordingly consulted the famous seer Tiresias, who now informed him of the divine origin of his stepson, and prognosticated for him a great and distinguished future.

When Amphitryon heard the noble destiny which awaited the child entrusted to his care, he resolved to educate him in a manner worthy of his future career. At a suitable age he himself taught him how to guide a chariot; Eurytus, how to handle the bow; Autolycus, dexterity in wrestling and boxing; and Castor, the art of armed warfare; whilst Linus, the son of Apollo, instructed him in music and letters.

Heracles was an apt pupil; but undue harshness was intolerable to his high spirit, and old Linus, who was not the gentlest of teachers, one day corrected him with blows, whereupon the boy angrily took up his lyre, and, with one stroke of his powerful arm, killed his tutor on the spot.

Apprehensive lest the ungovernable temper of the youth might again involve him in similar acts of violence, Amphitryon sent him into the country, where he placed him under the charge of one of his most trusted herdsmen. Here, as he grew up to manhood, his extraordinary stature and strength became the wonder and admiration of all beholders. His aim, whether with spear, lance, or bow, was unerring, and at the age of eighteen he was considered to be the strongest as well as the most beautiful youth in all Greece.

Heracles felt that the time had now arrived when it became necessary to decide for himself how to make use of the extraordinary powers with which he had been endowed by the gods; and in order to meditate in solitude on this all-important subject, he repaired to a lonely and secluded spot in the heart of the forest.

Here two females of great beauty appeared to him. One was Vice, the other Virtue. The former was full of artificial wiles and fascinating arts, her face painted and her dress gaudy and attractive; whilst the latter was of noble bearing and modest mien, her robes of spotless purity.

Vice stepped forward and thus addressed him: 'If you will walk in my paths, and make me your friend, your life shall be one round of pleasure and enjoyment. You shall taste of every delight which can be procured on earth; the choicest viands, the most delicious wines, the most luxuriant of couches shall be ever at your disposal; and all this without any exertion on your part, either physical or mental.'

Virtue now spoke in her turn: 'If you will follow me and be my friend, I promise you the reward of a good conscience, and the love and respect of your fellowmen. I cannot undertake to smooth your path with roses, or to give you a life of idleness and pleasure; for you must know that the gods grant no good and desirable thing that is not earned by labour; and as you sow, so must you reap.'

Heracles listened patiently and attentively to both speakers, and then, after mature deliberation, decided to follow in the paths of virtue, and henceforth to honour the gods, and to devote his life to the service of his country.

Full of these noble resolves he sought once more his rural home, where he was informed that on Mount Cithaeron, at the foot of which the herds of Amphitryon were grazing, a ferocious lion had fixed his lair, and was committing such frightful ravages among the flocks and herds that he had become the scourge and terror of the whole neighbourhood. Heracles at once armed himself and ascended the mountain, where he soon caught sight of the lion, and rushing at him with his sword succeeded in killing him. The hide of the animal he wore ever afterwards over his shoulders, and the head served him as a helmet.

As he was returning from this, his first exploit, he met the heralds of Erginus, king of the Minyans, who were proceeding to Thebes to demand their annual tribute of 100 oxen. Indignant at this humiliation of his native city, Heracles mutilated the heralds, and sent them back, with ropes round their necks, to their royal master.

Erginus was so incensed at the ill-treatment of his messengers that he collected an army and appeared before the gates of Thebes, demanding the surrender of Heracles. Creon, who was at this time king of Thebes, fearing the consequences of a refusal, was about to yield, when the hero, with the assistance of Amphitryon and a band of brave youths, advanced against the Minyans.

Heracles took possession of a narrow defile through which the enemy were compelled to pass, and as they entered the pass the Thebans fell upon them, killed their king Erginus, and completely routed them. In this engagement Amphitryon, the kind friend and foster-father of Heracles, lost his life. The hero now advanced upon Orchomenus, the capital of the Minyans, where he burned the royal castle and sacked the town.

After this signal victory all Greece rang with the fame of the young hero, and Creon, in gratitude for his great services, bestowed upon him his daughter Megara in marriage. The Olympian gods testified their appreciation of his valour by sending him presents; Hermes gave him a sword, Phoebus-Apollo a bundle of arrows, Hephaestus a golden quiver, and Athene a coat of leather.

Heracles and Eurystheus

And now it will be necessary to retrace our steps. Just before the birth of Heracles, Zeus, in an assembly of the gods, exultingly declared that the child who should be born on that day to the house of Perseus should rule over all his race. When Hera heard her lord's boastful announcement she knew well that it was for the child of the hated Alcmene that this brilliant destiny was designed; and in order to rob the son of her rival of his rights, she called to her aid the goddess Eilithyia, who retarded the birth of Heracles, and caused his cousin Eurystheus (another grandson of Perseus) to precede him into the world. And thus, as the word of the mighty Zeus was irrevocable, Heracles became the subject and servant of his cousin Eurystheus.

When, after his splendid victory over Erginus, the fame of Heracles spread throughout Greece, Eurystheus (who had become king of Mycenae), jealous of the reputation of the young hero, asserted his rights, and commanded him to undertake for him various difficult tasks. But the proud spirit of the hero rebelled against this humiliation, and he was about to refuse compliance, when Zeus appeared to him and desired him not to rebel against the Fates. Heracles now repaired to Delphi in order to consult the oracle, and received the answer that after performing ten tasks for his cousin Eurystheus his servitude would be at an end.

Soon afterwards Heracles fell into a state of the deepest melancholy, and through the influence of his inveterate enemy, the goddess Hera, this despondency developed into raving madness, in which condition he killed his own children. When he at length regained his reason he was so horrified and grieved at what he had done, that he shut himself up in his chamber and avoided all intercourse with men. But in his loneliness and seclusion the conviction that work would be the best means of procuring oblivion of the past decided him to enter, without delay, upon the tasks appointed him by Eurystheus.

12 Tasks: The Nemean Lion

His first task was to bring to Eurystheus the skin of the much-dreaded Nemean lion, which ravaged the territory between Cleone and Nemea, and whose hide was invulnerable against any mortal weapon.

Heracles proceeded to the forest of Nemea, where, having discovered the lion's lair, he attempted to pierce him with his arrows; but finding these of no avail he felled him to the ground with his club, and before the animal had time to recover from the terrible blow, Heracles seized him by the neck and, with a mighty effort, succeeded in strangling him. He then made himself a coat of mail of the skin, and a new helmet of the head of the animal. Thus attired, he so alarmed Eurystheus by appearing suddenly before him, that the king concealed himself in his palace, and henceforth forbade Heracles to enter his presence, but commanded him to receive his behests, for the future, through his messenger Copreus.

12 Tasks: The Hydra

His second task was to slay the Hydra, a monster serpent (the offspring of Typhon and Echidna), bristling with nine heads, one of which was immortal. This monster infested the neighbourhood of Lerna, where she committed great depredations among the herds.

Heracles, accompanied by his nephew Iolaus, set out in a chariot for the marsh of Lerna, in the slimy waters of which he found her. He commenced the attack by assailing her with his fierce arrows, in order to force her to leave her lair, from which she at length emerged, and sought refuge in a wood on a neighbouring hill. Heracles now rushed forward and endeavoured to crush her heads by means of well-directed blows from his tremendous club; but no sooner was one head destroyed than it was immediately replaced by two others. He next seized the monster in his powerful grasp; but at this juncture a giant crab came to the assistance of the Hydra and commenced biting the feet of her assailant. Heracles destroyed this new adversary with his club, and now called upon his nephew to come to his aid. At his command Iolaus set fire to the neighbouring trees, and, with a burning branch, seared the necks of the monster as Heracles cut them off, thus effectually preventing the growth of more. Heracles next struck off the immortal head, which he buried by the road-side, and placed over it a heavy stone. Into the poisonous blood of the monster he then dipped his arrows, which ever afterwards rendered wounds inflicted by them incurable.

12 Tasks: The Horned Hind

The third labour of Heracles was to bring the horned hind Cerunitis alive to Mycenae. This animal, which was sacred to Artemis, had golden antlers and hoofs of brass.

Not wishing to wound the hind Heracles patiently pursued her through many countries for a whole year, and overtook her at last on the banks of the river Ladon; but even there he was compelled, in order to secure her, to wound her with one of his arrows, after which he lifted her on his shoulders and carried her through Arcadia. On his way he met Artemis with her brother Phoebus-Apollo, when the goddess angrily reproved him for wounding her favourite hind; but Heracles succeeded in appeasing her displeasure, whereupon she permitted him to take the animal alive to Mycenae.

12 Tasks: The Erymanthian Boar

The fourth task imposed upon Heracles by Eurystheus was to bring alive to Mycenae the Erymanthian boar, which had laid waste the region of Erymantia, and was the scourge of the surrounding neighbourhood.

On his way thither he craved food and shelter of a Centaur named Pholus, who received him with generous hospitality, setting before him a good and plentiful repast. When Heracles expressed his surprise that at such a well-furnished board wine should be wanting, his host explained that the wine cellar was the common property of all the Centaurs, and that it was against the rules for a cask to be broached, except all were present to partake of it. By dint of persuasion, however, Heracles prevailed on his kind host to make an exception in his favour; but the powerful, luscious odour of the good old wine soon spread over the mountains, and brought large numbers of Centaurs to the spot, all armed with huge rocks and fir-trees. Heracles drove them back with fire-brands, and then, following up his victory, pursued them with his arrows as far as Malea, where they took refuge in the cave of the kind old Centaur Chiron. Unfortunately, however, as Heracles was shooting at them with his poisoned darts, one of these pierced the knee of Chiron. When Heracles discovered that it was the friend of his early days that he had wounded, he was overcome with sorrow and regret. He at once extracted the arrow, and anointed the wound with a salve, the virtue of which had been taught him by Chiron himself. But all his efforts were unavailing. The wound, imbued with the deadly poison of the Hydra, was incurable, and so great was the agony of Chiron that, at the intercession of Heracles, death was sent him by the gods; for otherwise, being immortal, he would have been doomed to endless suffering.

Pholus, who had so kindly entertained Heracles, also perished by means of one of these arrows, which he had extracted from the body of a dead Centaur. While he was quietly examining it, astonished that so small and insignificant an object should be productive of such serious results, the arrow fell upon his foot and fatally wounded him. Full of grief at this untoward event, Heracles buried him with due honours, and then set out to chase the boar.

With loud shouts and terrible cries he first drove him out of the thickets into the deep snow-drifts which covered the summit of the mountain, and then, having at length wearied him with his incessant pursuit, he captured the exhausted animal, bound him with a rope, and brought him alive to Mycenae.

12 Tasks: The Augean Stables

After slaying the Erymanthian boar Eurystheus commanded Heracles to cleanse in one day the stables of Augeas.

Augeas was a king of Elis who was very rich in herds. Three thousand of his cattle he kept near the royal palace in an enclosure where the refuse had accumulated for many years. When Heracles presented himself before the king, and offered to cleanse his stables in one day, provided he should receive in return a tenth part of the herds, Augeas, thinking the feat impossible, accepted his offer in the presence of his son Phyleus.

Near the palace were the two rivers Peneus and Alpheus, the streams of which Heracles conducted into the stables by means of a trench which he dug for this purpose, and as the waters rushed through the shed, they swept away with them the whole mass of accumulated filth.

But when Augeas heard that this was one of the labours imposed by Eurystheus, he refused the promised guerdon. Heracles brought the matter before a court, and called Phyleus as a witness to the justice of his claim, whereupon Augeas, without waiting for the delivery of the verdict, angrily banished Heracles and his son from his dominions.

12 Tasks: The Stymphalian Birds

The sixth task was to chase away the Stymphalides, which were immense birds of prey who, as we have seen (in the legend of the Argonauts), shot from their wings feathers sharp as arrows. The home of these birds was on the shore of the lake Stymphalis, in Arcadia (after which they were called), where they caused great destruction among men and cattle.

On approaching the lake, Heracles observed great numbers of them; and, while hesitating how to commence the attack, he suddenly felt a hand on his shoulder. Looking round he beheld the majestic form of Pallas-Athene, who held in her hand a gigantic pair of brazen clappers made by Hephaestus, with which she presented him; whereupon he ascended to the summit of a neighbouring hill, and commenced to rattle them violently. The shrill noise of these instruments was so intolerable to the birds that they rose into the air in terror, upon which he aimed at them with his arrows, destroying them in great numbers, whilst such as escaped his darts flew away, never to return.

12 Tasks: The Cretan Bull

The seventh labour of Heracles was to capture the Cretan bull. Minos, king of Crete, having vowed to sacrifice to Poseidon any animal which should first appear out of the sea, the god caused a magnificent bull to emerge from the waves in order to test the sincerity of the Cretan king, who, in making this vow, had alleged that he possessed no animal, among his own herds, worthy the acceptance of the mighty sea-god. Charmed with the splendid animal sent by Poseidon, and eager to possess it, Minos placed it among his herds, and substituted as a sacrifice one of his own bulls. Hereupon Poseidon, in order to punish the cupidity of Minos, caused the animal to become mad, and commit such great havoc in the island as to endanger the safety of the inhabitants. When Heracles, therefore, arrived in Crete for the purpose of capturing the bull, Minos, far from opposing his design, gladly gave him permission to do so.

The hero not only succeeded in securing the animal, but tamed him so effectually that he rode on his back right across the sea as far as the Peloponnesus. He now delivered him up to Eurystheus, who at once set him at liberty, after which he became as ferocious and wild as before, roamed all over Greece into Arcadia, and was eventually killed by Theseus on the plains of Marathon.

12 Tasks: The Mares of Diomedes

The eighth labour of Heracles was to bring to Eurystheus the mares of Diomedes, a son of Ares, and king of the Bistonians, a warlike Thracian tribe. This king possessed a breed of wild horses of tremendous size and strength, whose food consisted of human flesh, and all strangers who had the misfortune to enter the country were made prisoners and flung before the horses, who devoured them.

When Heracles arrived he first captured the cruel Diomedes himself, and then threw him before his own mares, who, after devouring their master, became perfectly tame and tractable. They were then led by Heracles to the sea-shore, when the Bistonians, enraged at the loss of their king, rushed after the hero and attacked him. He now gave the animals in charge of his friend Abderus, and made such a furious onslaught on his assailants that they turned and fled.

But on his return from this encounter he found, to his great grief, that the mares had torn his friend in pieces and devoured him. After celebrating due funereal rites to the unfortunate Abderus, Heracles built a city in his honour, which he named after him. He then returned to Tiryns, where he delivered up the mares to Eurystheus, who set them loose on Mount Olympus, where they became the prey of wild beasts.

It was after the performance of this task that Heracles joined the Argonauts in their expedition to gain possession of the Golden Fleece, and was left behind at Chios, as already narrated. During his wanderings he undertook his ninth labour, which was to bring to Eurystheus the girdle of Hippolyte, queen of the Amazons.

12 Tasks: The Girdle of Hippolyte

The Amazons, who dwelt on the shores of the Black Sea, near the river Thermodon, were a nation of warlike women, renowned for their strength, courage, and great skill in horsemanship. Their queen, Hippolyte, had received from her father, Ares, a beautiful girdle, which she always wore as a sign of her royal power and authority, and it was this girdle which Heracles was required to place in the hands of Eurystheus, who designed it as a gift for his daughter Admete.

Foreseeing that this would be a task of no ordinary difficulty the hero called to his aid a select band of brave companions, with whom he embarked for the Amazonian town Themiscyra. Here they were met by queen Hippolyte, who was so impressed by the extraordinary stature and noble bearing of Heracles that, on learning his errand, she at once consented to present him with the coveted girdle. But Hera, his implacable enemy, assuming the form of an Amazon, spread the report in the town that a stranger was about to carry off their queen. The Amazons at once flew to arms and mounted their horses, whereupon a battle ensued, in which many of their bravest warriors were killed or wounded. Among the latter was their most skilful leader, Melanippe, whom Heracles afterwards restored to Hippolyte, receiving the girdle in exchange.

On his voyage home the hero stopped at Troy, where a new adventure awaited him.

During the time that Apollo and Poseidon were condemned by Zeus to a temporary servitude on earth, they built for king Laomedon the famous walls of Troy, afterwards so renowned in history; but when their work was completed the king treacherously refused to give them the reward due to them. The incensed deities now combined to punish the offender. Apollo sent a pestilence which decimated the people, and Poseidon a flood, which bore with it a marine monster, who swallowed in his huge jaws all that came within his reach.

In his distress Laomedon consulted an oracle, and was informed that only by the sacrifice of his own daughter Hesione could the anger of the gods be appeased. Yielding at length to the urgent appeals of his people he consented to make the sacrifice, and on the arrival of Heracles the maiden was already chained to a rock in readiness to be devoured by the monster.

When Laomedon beheld the renowned hero, whose marvellous feats of strength and courage had become the wonder and admiration of all mankind, he earnestly implored him to save his daughter from her impending fate, and to rid the country of the monster, holding out to him as a reward the horses which Zeus had presented to his grandfather Tros in compensation for robbing him of his son Ganymede.

Heracles unhesitatingly accepted the offer, and when the monster appeared, opening his terrible jaws to receive his prey, the hero, sword in hand, attacked and slew him. But the perfidious monarch once more broke faith, and Heracles, vowing future vengeance, departed for Mycenae, where he presented the girdle to Eurystheus.

12 Tasks: The Oxen of Geryon

The tenth labour of Heracles was the capture of the magnificent oxen belonging to the giant Geryon or Geryones, who dwelt on the island of Erythia in the bay of Gadria (Cadiz). This giant, who was the son of Chrysaor, had three bodies with three heads, six hands, and six feet. He possessed a herd of splendid cattle, which were famous for their size, beauty, and rich red colour. They were guarded by another giant named Eurytion, and a two-headed dog called Orthrus, the offspring of Typhon and Echidna.

In choosing for him a task so replete with danger, Eurystheus was in hopes that he might rid himself for ever of his hated cousin. But the indomitable courage of the hero rose with the prospect of this difficult and dangerous undertaking.

After a long and wearisome journey he at last arrived at the western coast of Africa, where, as a monument of his perilous expedition, he erected the famous 'Pillars of Hercules,' one of which he placed on each side of the Straits of Gibraltar. Here he found the intense heat so insufferable that he angrily raised his bow towards heaven, and threatened to shoot the sun-god. But Helios, far from being incensed at his audacity, was so struck with admiration at his daring that he lent to him the golden boat with which he accomplished his nocturnal transit from West to East, and thus Heracles crossed over safely to the island of Erythia.

No sooner had he landed than Eurytion, accompanied by his savage dog Orthrus, fiercely attacked him; but Heracles, with a superhuman effort, slew the dog and then his master. Hereupon he collected the herd, and was proceeding to the sea-shore when Geryones himself met him, and a desperate encounter took place, in which the giant perished.

Heracles then drove the cattle into the sea, and seizing one of the oxen by the horns, swam with them over to the opposite coast of Iberia (Spain). Then driving his magnificent prize before him through Gaul, Italy, Illyria, and Thrace, he at length arrived, after many perilous adventures and hair-breadth escapes, at Mycenae, where he delivered them up to Eurystheus, who sacrificed them to Hera.

Heracles had now executed his ten tasks, which had been accomplished in the space of eight years; but Eurystheus refused to include the slaying of the Hydra and the cleansing of the stables of Augeas among the number, alleging as a reason that the one had been performed by the assistance of Iolaus, and that the other had been executed for hire. He therefore insisted on Heracles substituting two more labours in their place.

12 Tasks: The Apples of the Hesperides

The eleventh task imposed by Eurystheus was to bring him the golden apples of the Hesperides, which grew on a tree presented by Gaea to Hera, on the occasion of her marriage with Zeus. This sacred tree was guarded by four maidens, daughters of Night, called the Hesperides, who were assisted in their task by a terrible hundred-headed dragon. This dragon never slept, and out of its hundred throats came a constant hissing sound, which effectually warned off all intruders. But what rendered the undertaking still more difficult was the complete ignorance of the hero as to the locality of the garden, and he was forced, in consequence, to make many fruitless journeys and to undergo many trials before he could find it.

He first travelled through Thessaly and arrived at the river Echedorus, where he met the giant Cycnus, the son of Ares and Pyrene, who challenged him to single combat. In this encounter Heracles completely vanquished his opponent, who was killed in the contest; but now a mightier adversary appeared on the scene, for the war-god himself came to avenge his son. A terrible struggle ensued, which had lasted some time, when Zeus interfered between the brothers, and put an end to the strife by hurling a thunderbolt between them. Heracles proceeded on his journey, and reached the banks of the river Eridanus, where dwelt the Nymphs, daughters of Zeus and Themis. On seeking advice from them as to his route, they directed him to the old sea-god Nereus, who alone knew the way to the Garden of the Hesperides. Heracles found him asleep, and seizing the opportunity, held him so firmly in his powerful grasp that he could not possibly escape, so that notwithstanding his various metamorphoses he was at last compelled to give the information required. The hero then crossed over to Libya, where he engaged in a wrestling-match with king Anteos, son of Poseidon and Gaea, which terminated fatally for his antagonist.

From thence he proceeded to Egypt, where reigned Busiris, another son of Poseidon, who (acting on the advice given by an oracle during a time of great scarcity) sacrificed all strangers to Zeus. When Heracles arrived he was seized and dragged to the altar; but the powerful demi-god burst asunder his bonds, and then slew Busiris and his son.

Resuming his journey he now wandered on through Arabia until he arrived at Mount Caucasus, where Prometheus groaned in unceasing agony. It was at this time that Heracles (as already related) shot the eagle which had so long tortured the noble and devoted friend of mankind. Full of gratitude for his deliverance, Prometheus instructed him how to find his way to that remote region in the far West where Atlas supported the heavens on his shoulders, near which lay the Garden of the Hesperides. He also warned Heracles not to attempt to secure the precious fruit himself, but to assume for a time the duties of Astlas, and to despatch him for the apples.

On arriving at his destination Heracles followed the advice of Prometheus. Atlas, who willingly entered into the arrangement, contrived to put the dragon to sleep, and then, having cunningly outwitted the Hesperides, carried off three of the golden apples, which he now brought to Heracles. But when the latter was prepared to relinquish his burden, Atlas, having once tasted the delights of freedom, declined to resume his post, and announced his intention of being himself the bearer of the apples to Eurystheus, leaving Heracles to fill his place. To this proposal the hero feigned assent, merely begging that Atlas would be kind enough to support the heavens for a few moments whilst he contrived a pad for his head. Atlas good-naturedly threw down the apples and once more resumed his load, upon which Heracles bade him adieu, and departed.

When Heracles conveyed the golden apples to Eurystheus the latter presented them to the hero, whereupon Heracles placed the sacred fruit on the altar of Pallas-Athene, who restored them to the garden of the Hesperides.

12 Tasks: Cerberus

The twelfth and last labour which Eurystheus imposed on Heracles was to bring up Cerberus from the lower world, believing that all his heroic powers would be unavailing in the Realm of Shades, and that in this, his last and most perilous undertaking, the hero must at length succumb and perish.

Cerberus was a monster dog with three heads, out of whose awful jaws dripped poison; the hair of his head and back was formed of venomous snakes, and his body terminated in the tail of a dragon.

After being initiated into the Eleusinian Mysteries, and obtaining from the priests certain information necessary for the accomplishment of his task, Heracles set out for Taenarum in Lacolia, where there was an opening which led to the under-world. Conducted by Hermes, he commenced his descent into the awful gulf, where myriads of shades soon began to appear, all of whom fled in terror at his approach, Meleager and Medusa alone excepted. About to strike the latter with his sword, Hermes interfered and stayed his hand, reminding him that she was but a shadow, and that consequently no weapon could avail against her.

Arrived before the gates of Hades he found Theseus and Pirithöus, who had been fixed to an enchanted rock by Aïdes for their presumption in endeavouring to carry off Persephone. When they saw Heracles they implored him to set them free. The hero succeeded in delivering Theseus, but when he endeavoured to liberate Pirithöus, the earth shook so violently beneath him that he was compelled to relinquish his task.

Proceeding further Heracles recognized Ascalaphus, who, as we have seen in the history of Demeter, had revealed the fact that Persephone had swallowed the seeds of a pomegranate offered to her by her husband, which bound her to Aïdes for ever. Ascalaphus was groaning beneath a huge rock which Demeter in her anger had hurled upon him, and which Heracles now removed, releasing the sufferer.

Before the gates of his palace stood Aïdes the mighty ruler of the lower world, and barred his entrance; but Heracles, aiming at him with one of his unerring darts, shot him in the shoulder, so that for the first time the god experienced the agony of mortal suffering. Heracles then demanded of him permission to take Cerberus to the upper-world, and to this Aïdes consented on condition that he should secure him unarmed. Protected by his breastplate and lion's skin Heracles went in search of the monster, whom he found at the mouth of the river Acheron. Undismayed by the hideous barking which proceeded from his three heads, he seized the throat with one hand and the legs with the other, and although the dragon which served him as a tail bit him severely, he did not relinquish his grasp. In this manner he conducted him to the upper-world, through an opening near Troezen in Argolia.

When Eurystheus beheld Cerberus he stood aghast, and despairing of ever getting rid of his hated rival, he returned the hell-hound to the hero, who restored him to Aïdes, and with this last task the subjection of Heracles to Eurystheus terminated.

Heracles' Freedom

Free at last Heracles now returned to Thebes; and it being impossible for him to live happily with Megara in consequence of his having murdered her children he, with her own consent, gave her in marriage to his nephew Iolaus. Heracles himself sought the hand of Iole, daughter of Eurytus, king of Oechalia, who had instructed him when a boy in the use of the bow. Hearing that this king had promised to give his daughter to him who could surpass himself and his three sons in shooting with the bow, Heracles lost no time in presenting himself as a competitor. He soon proved that he was no unworthy pupil of Eurytus, for he signally defeated all his opponents. But although the king treated him with marked respect and honour he refused, nevertheless, to give him the hand of his daughter, fearing for her a similar fate to that which had befallen Megara. Iphitus, the eldest son of Eurytus, alone espoused the cause of Heracles, and essayed to induce his father to give his consent to the marriage; but all to no purpose, and at length, stung to the quick at his rejection, the hero angrily took his departure.

Soon afterwards the oxen of the king were stolen by the notorious thief Autolycus, and Heracles was suspected by Eurytus of having committed the theft. But Iphitus loyally defended his absent friend, and proposed to seek out Heracles, and with his assistance to go in search of the missing cattle.

The hero warmly welcomed his staunch young friend, and entered cordially into his plan. They at once set out on their expedition; but their search proved altogether unsuccessful. When they approached the city of Tiryns they mounted a tower in hopes of discovering the missing herd in the surrounding country; but as they stood on the topmost summit of the building, Heracles became suddenly seized with one of his former attacks of madness, and mistaking his friend Iphitus for an enemy, hurled him down into the plain below, and he was killed on the spot.

Heracles now set forth on a weary pilgrimage, begging in vain that someone would purify him from the murder of Iphitus. It was during these wanderings that he arrived at the palace of his friend Admetus, whose beautiful and heroic wife (Alcestes) he restored to her husband after a terrible struggle with Death, as already related.

Soon after this event Heracles was struck with a fearful disease, and betook himself to the temple of Delphi, hoping to obtain from the oracle the means of relief. The priestess, however, refused him a response on the ground of his having murdered Iphitus, whereupon the angry hero seized upon the tripod, which he carried off, declaring that he would construct an oracle for himself. Apollo, who witnessed the sacrilege, came down to defend his sanctuary, and a violent struggle ensued. Zeus once more interfered, and, flashing his lightnings between his two favourite sons, ended the combat. The Pythia now vouchsafed an answer to the prayer of the hero, and commanded him, in expiation of his crime, to allow himself to be sold by Hermes for three years as a slave, the purchase-money to be given to Eurytus in compensation for the loss of his son.

Heracles bowed in submission to the divine will, and was conducted by Hermes to Omphale, queen of Lydia. The three talents which she paid for him were given to Eurytus, who, however, declined to accept the money, which was handed over to the children of Iphitus.

Heracles now regained his former vigour. He rid the territory of Omphale of the robbers which infested it and performed for her various other services requiring strength and courage. It was about this time that he took part in the Calydonian boar-hunt, details of which have already been given.

When Omphale learned that her slave was none other than the renowned Heracles himself she at once gave him his liberty, and offered him her hand and kingdom. In her palace Heracles abandoned himself to all the enervating luxuries of an oriental life, and so completely was the great hero enthralled by the fascination which his mistress exercised over him, that whilst she playfully donned his lion's skin and helmet, he, attired in female garments, sat at her feet spinning wool, and beguiling the time by the relation of his past adventures.

But when at length, his term of bondage having expired, he became master of his own actions, the manly and energetic spirit of the hero reasserted itself, and tearing himself away from the palace of the Maeonian queen, he determined to carry out the revenge he had so long meditated against the treacherous Laomedon and the faithless Augeas.

Gathering round him some of his old brave companions-in-arms, Heracles collected a fleet of vessels and set sail for Troy, where he landed, took the city by storm, and killed Laomedon, who thus met at length the retribution he had so richly deserved.

To Telamon, one of his bravest followers, he gave Hesione, the daughter of the king, in marriage. When Heracles gave her permission to release one of the prisoners of war she chose her own brother Podarces, whereupon she was informed that as he was already a prisoner of war she would be compelled to ransom him. On hearing this Hesione took off her golden diadem, which she joyfully handed to the hero. Owing to this circumstance Podarces henceforth bore the name of Priamus (or Priam), which signifies the 'ransomed one.'

Heracles now marched against Augeas to execute his vengeance on him also for his perfidious conduct. He stormed the city of Elis and put to death Augeas and his sons, sparing only his brave advocate and staunch defender Phyleus, on whom he bestowed the vacant throne of his father.

Heracles now proceeded to Calydon, where he wooed the beautiful Deianeira, daughter of Oeneus, king of Aetolia; but he encountered a formidable rival in Achelous, the river-god, and it was agreed that their claims should be decided by single combat. Trusting to his power of assuming various forms at will, Achelous felt confident of success; but this availed him nothing, for having at last transformed himself into a bull, his mighty adversary broke off one of his horns, and compelled him to acknowledge himself defeated.

After passing three happy years with Deianeira an unfortunate accident occurred, which for a time marred their felicity. Heracles was one day present at a banquet given by Oeneus, when, by a sudden swing of his hand, he had the misfortune to strike on the head a youth of noble birth, who, according to the custom of the ancients, was serving the guests at table, and so violent was the blow that it caused his death. The father of the unfortunate youth, who had witnessed the occurrence, saw that it was the result of accident, and therefore absolved the hero from blame. But Heracles resolved to act according to the law of the land, banished himself from the country, and bidding farewell to his father-in-law, set out for Trachin to visit his friend King Ceyx, taking with him his wife Deianeira, and his young son Hyllus.

In the course of their journey they arrived at the river Evenus, over which the Centaur Nessus was in the habit of carrying travellers for hire. Heracles, with his little son in his arms, forded the stream unaided, entrusting his wife to the care of the Centaur, who, charmed with the beauty of his fair burden, attempted to carry her off. But her cries were heard by her husband, who without hesitation shot Nessus through the heart with one of his poisoned arrows. Now the dying Centaur was thirsting for revenge. He called Deianeira to his side, and directed her to secure some of the blood which flowed from his wound, assuring her that if, when in danger of losing her husband's affection, she used it in the manner indicated by him, it would act as a charm, and prevent her from being supplanted by a rival. Heracles and Deianeira now pursued their journey, and after several adventures at length arrived at their destination.

Death of Heracles

The last expedition undertaken by the great hero was against Eurytus, king of Oechalia, to revenge himself upon this king and his sons for having refused to bestow upon him the hand of Iole, after having fairly won the maiden. Having collected a large army Heracles set out for Euboea in order to besiege Oechalia, its capital. Success crowned his arms. He stormed the citadel, slew the king and his three sons, reduced the town to ashes, and carried away captive the young and beautiful Iole.

Returning from his victorious expedition, Heracles halted at Cenoeus in order to offer a sacrifice to Zeus, and sent to Deianeira to Trachin for a sacrificial robe. Deianeira having been informed that the fair Iole was in the train of Heracles was fearful lest her youthful charms might supplant her in the affection of her husband, and calling to mind the advice of the dying Centaur, she determined to test the efficacy of the love-charm which he had given to her. Taking out the phial which she had carefully preserved, she imbued the robe with a portion of the liquid which it contained, and then sent it to Heracles.

The victorious hero clothed himself with the garment, and was about to perform the sacrifice, when the hot flames rising from the altar heated the poison with which it was imbued, and soon every fibre of his body was penetrated by the deadly venom. The unfortunate hero, suffering the most fearful tortures, endeavoured to tear off the robe, but it adhered so closely to the skin that all his efforts to remove it only increased his agonies.

In this pitiable condition he was conveyed to Trachin, where Deianeira, on beholding the terrible suffering of which she was the innocent cause, was overcome with grief and remorse, and hanged herself in despair. The dying hero called his son Hyllus to his side, and desired him to make Iole his wife, and then ordering his followers to erect a funeral pyre, he mounted it and implored the by-standers to set fire to it, and thus in mercy to terminate his insufferable torments. But no one had the courage to obey him, until at last his friend and companion Philoctetes, yielding to his piteous appeal, lighted the pile, and received in return the bow and arrows of the hero.

Soon flames on flames ascended, and amidst vivid flashes of lightning, accompanied by awful peals of thunder, Pallas-Athene descended in a cloud, and bore her favourite hero in a chariot to Olympus.

Heracles became admitted among the immortals; and Hera, in token of her reconciliation, bestowed upon him the hand of her beautiful daughter Hebe, the goddess of eternal youth.

The Heraclidae

After the apotheosis of Heracles, his children were so cruelly persecuted by Eurystheus, that they fled for protection to king Ceyx at Trachin, accompanied by the aged Iolaus, the nephew and life-long friend of their father, who constituted himself their guide and protector. But on Eurystheus demanding the surrender of the fugitives, the Heraclidae, knowing that the small force at the disposal of king Ceyx would be altogether inadequate to protect them against the powerful king of Argos, abandoned his territory, and sought refuge at Athens, where they were hospitably received by king Demophoon, the son of the great hero Theseus. He warmly espoused their cause, and determined to protect them at all costs against Eurystheus, who had despatched a numerous force in pursuit of them.

When the Athenians had made all necessary preparations to repel the invaders, an oracle announced that the sacrifice of a maiden of noble birth was necessary to ensure to them victory; whereupon Macaria, the beautiful daughter of Heracles and Deianira, magnanimously offered herself as a sacrifice, and, surrounded by the noblest matrons and maidens of Athens, voluntarily devoted herself to death.

While these events were transpiring in Athens, Hyllus, the eldest son of Heracles and Deianira, had advanced with a large army to the assistance of his brothers, and having sent a messenger to the king announcing his arrival, Demophoon, with his army, joined his forces.

In the thick of the battle which ensued, Iolaus, following a sudden impulse, borrowed the chariot of Hyllus, and earnestly entreated Zeus and Hebe to restore to him, for this one day only, the vigour and strength of his youth. His prayer was heard. A thick cloud descended from heaven and enveloped the chariot, and when it disappeared, Iolaus, in the full plenitude of manly vigour, stood revealed before the astonished gaze of the combatants. He then led on his valiant band of warriors, and soon the enemy was in headlong flight; and Eurystheus, who was taken prisoner, was put to death by the command of king Demophoon.

After gratefully acknowledging the timely aid of the Athenians, Hyllus, accompanied by the faithful Iolaus and his brothers, took leave of king Demophoon, and proceeded to invade the Peloponnesus, which they regarded as their lawful patrimony; for, according to the will of Zeus, it should have been the rightful possession of their father, the great hero Heracles, had not Hera maliciously defeated his plans by causing his cousin Eurystheus to precede him into the world.

For the space of twelve months the Heraclidae contrived to maintain themselves in the Peloponnesus; but at the expiration of that time a pestilence broke out, which spread over the entire peninsula, and compelled the Heraclidae to evacuate the country and return to Attica, where for a time they settled.

After the lapse of three years Hyllus resolved on making another effort to obtain his paternal inheritance. Before setting out on the expedition, however, he consulted the oracle of Delphi, and the response was, that he must wait for the third fruit before the enterprise would prove successful. Interpreting this ambiguous reply to signify the third summer, Hyllus controlled his impatience for three years, when, having collected a powerful army, he once more entered the Peloponnesus.

At the isthmus of Corinth he was opposed by Atreus, the son of Pelops, who at the death of Eurystheus had inherited the kingdom. In order to save bloodshed, Hyllus offered to decide his claims by single combat, the conditions being, that if he were victorious, he and his brothers should obtain undisputed possession of their rights; but if defeated, the Heraclidae were to desist for fifty years from attempting to press their claim.

The challenge was accepted by Echemon, king of Tegea, and Hyllus lost his life in the encounter, whereupon the sons of Heracles, in virtue of their agreement, abandoned the Peloponnesus and retired to Marathon.

Hyllus was succeeded by his son Cleodaeus, who, at the expiration of the appointed time, collected a large army and invaded the Peloponnesus; but he was not more successful than his father had been, and perished there with all his forces.

Twenty years later his son Aristomachus consulted an oracle, which promised him victory if he went by way of the defile. The Heraclidae once more set out, but were again defeated, and Aristomachus shared the fate of his father and grandfather, and fell on the field of battle.

When, at the expiration of thirty years, the sons of Aristomachus, Temenus, Cresphontes, and Aristodemus again consulted the oracle, the answer was still the same; but this time the following explanation accompanied the response: the third fruit signified the third generation, to which they themselves belonged, and not the third fruit of the earth; and by the defile was indicated, not the isthmus of Corinth, but the straits on the right of the isthmus.

Temenus lost no time in collecting an army and building ships of war; but just as all was ready and the fleet about to sail, Aristodemus, the youngest of the brothers, was struck by lightning. To add to their misfortunes, Hippolytes, a descendant of Heracles, who had joined in the expedition, killed a soothsayer whom he mistook for a spy, and the gods, in their displeasure, sent violent tempests, by means of which the entire fleet was destroyed, whilst famine and pestilence decimated the ranks of the army.

The oracle, on being again consulted, advised that Hippolytes, being the offender, should be banished from the country for ten years, and that the command of the troops should be delegated to a man having three eyes. A search was at once instituted by the Heraclidae for a man answering to this description, who was found at length in the person of Oxylus, a descendant of the Aetolian race of kings. In obedience to the command of the oracle, Hippolytes was banished, an army and fleet once more equipped, and Oxylus elected commander-in-chief.

And now success at length crowned the efforts of the long-suffering descendants of the great hero. They obtained possession of the Peloponnesus, which was divided among them by lot. Argos fell to Temenus, Lacedaemon to Aristodemus, and Messene to Cresphontes. In gratitude for the services of their able leader, Oxylus, the kingdom of Elis, was conferred upon him by the Heraclidae.

Legends of Krishna

KRISHNA WAS ORIGINALLY THE HERO of the *Mahabharata*, a destructive, evil and immoral warrior who was known for his cunning and martial skills.

Later, as Krishna became associated with Vishnu – his third human incarnation – his evil deeds were explained philosophically, and all manner of excuses was devised to explain his previous acts. The murders he had committed were to rid the earth of demons; his forays with women, and their subsequent search for him, have been explained in a metaphor of a worshipper seeking his god. Indeed, he came to represent the doctrine that devotion is a way to salvation.

Krishna was a popular god, and the late addition of the Bhagavadgita to the *Mahabharata* presents him, alongside work and knowledge, as the means by which believers can be saved. But it is his childhood pranks that have come to characterize Krishna, and it is some of these which follows.

Krishna's Birth

There once was a king of Mathura, named Ugrasena, who had a beautiful wife. Now his wife was barren, a fact which dismayed them both and caused her to hold her head down in shame. One day, when walking in the wood, she lost her companions and found herself in the company of a demon who assumed her husband's form. Knowing not the difference between this man and the man who was her husband, she allowed him to lie with her and the product of this liaison was a long-awaited son, who they named Kansa.

When Kansa was a child he was cruel and a source of great sorrow to his family and his country. He shunned the religious teachings of the day and taunted his father for his devotion to Rama, the god of his race. His father could only reply, 'Rama is my lord, and the dispeller of my grief. If I do not worship him, how shall I cross over the sea of the world?'

The ruthless Kansa laughed heartily at what he considered to be his father's foolishness and immediately usurped his place on the throne. Immediately a proclamation was issued throughout the kingdom, forbidding men to worship Rama and commanding them to pay their devotions to Siva instead.

This arrogance and tyranny went on for many years, and every man and woman throughout the kingdom prayed for relief from the rule of this truly evil man. Finally, the Earth, assuming the form of a cow, went to Indra and complained. And so it was that Brahma listened to the pleas of the Earth and led them to Siva, and then Vishnu. Vishnu had in the past taken on the incarnation of man and they reminded him of that now, begging him to do so in order to afford the destruction of the seemingly invincible Kansa. Each of the gods and goddesses cheered Vishnu in this mission and promised to leave their heavenly homes in order that they could accompany him on earth. Vishnu arranged that Lakshman, Bharata and Sutraghna would accompany him and that Sita, who would take the name of Rukmini, would be his wife.

One day Kansa was carrying the great Vasudeva and his wife Devaki through the sky when a voice set out the following prophecy:

'Kansa, fool that you are, the eighth child of the damsel you are now driving shall take away your life!' And so Kansa drew his sword and was about to take the life of Devaki when Vasudeva intervened, and said:

'Spare her life and I will deliver to you every child she brings forth.' Kansa laid down his sword, but he placed a guard with her who stayed by her side for her every living hour. And as child after child was given up to him and slain, he continued in his wretched mission.

But Devaki was a woman with a mind as quick as a tree squirrel, and although Kansa had been advised that the children he had destroyed were her own, this was not the case. The children that had been handed over to him were the children of Hiranyakasipu who had been lodged in the womb of Devaki in order that the cruel Kansa might be fooled. Vishnu said to the goddess Yoganindra, who brought the children from the nether regions:

'Go Yoganindra, go and by my command conduct successively six of their princes to be conceived by Devaki. When these shall have been put to death by Kansa, the seventh conception shall be formed of a portion of Sesha, who is part of me; and you shall transfer before the time of birth to Rohini, another wife of Vasudeva, who resides at Gokula. The report shall run that Devaki miscarries and I will myself become incarnate in her eighth conception; and you shall take a similar character as the embryo offspring of Yasoda, the wife of a herdsman called Nanda. In the night of the eighth of the dark half of the month Nabhas I shall be born, and you will be born on the ninth. Aided by my power, Vasudeva shall bear me to the bed of Yasoda, and you to the bed of Devaki. Kansa shall take you and hold you up to dash you against a stone, but you shall escape into the sky, where Indra shall meet and do homage to you through reverence of me.'

And so it was that when Devaki gave birth to her eighth son, Vasudeva took the child and hurried through the city. When he reached the River Yamuna, which he had to cross, the water rose only to his knees instead of seeking to drown him. And as he reached the house of Nanda, Yasoda had given birth to her child, which Vasudeva seized and, leaving Devaki's child in its place, returned to his wife's bed.

Soon after, the guard heard the cry of a newborn, and summoning himself from the depths of a good sleep, he called for Kansa, who immediately rushed into the home of Devaki and thrust the child against a stone. But as soon as this child touched the ground there was a cry as deep and angry as that of any rakshasa. It rose into the sky and grew into a huge figure with eight arms, each holding a great weapon. It laughed and said to Kansa, 'What use is it to you to have hurled me to the ground? He is born that shall kill you, the mighty one amongst the gods.'

Kansa collected his ministers and gathered them round. He insisted that every man who was generous in gifts and sacrifices and prayers to the gods must be put to death so that no god shall have subsistence. He said then, 'I know now that the tool of my fate is still living. Let therefore active search be made for whatever young children there may be upon earth, and let every boy in whom there are signs of unusual vigour be slain without remorse.'

Soon after this Vasudeva and Devaki were released from their confinement, and quickly sought out Nanda, who was still unaware of the change in their children. Vasudeva had brought with him another of his child, by Rohini, who was Balarama, and placed him under the care of Nanda to be brought up as his own child. By this means, as Rama and Lakshman were inseparable companions in previous incarnations, Krishna and Balarama were intimately connected.

Nanda and his family had not been settled long at Gokula before efforts were made to destroy the infant Krishna. A female fiend called Putana, whose breast caused instant death when sucked, had taken the child in her arms and offered him a drink. The infant Krishna seized it with such fervour and sucked with such violence that the horrible fiend roared with pain and met with an instant death.

The birth of Krishna had caused great happiness, despite the evil decrees of Kansa, and throughout the land trees blossomed, flowers bloomed and there was music in the souls of all who lived on earth.

The Young Krishna

The young Krishna was a very mischievous boy and his merry-making became legend throughout the land. One day, as a mere infant lying under the wagon of Nanda, he cried for his mother's breast, and impatient that she did not come to him at once, kicked the wagon over, to the great astonishment of all who witnessed this momentous occurrence.

When Krishna was but five months old, another fiend came in the form of a whirlwind to sweep him away, but at once he grew so heavy that his own surrogate mother could not hold him and had to lay him down. But when the storm became a cyclone, the infant allowed himself to be swept into the sky, and while all the people on the ground wept and bemoaned his sorry fate, he dashed the rakshasa down, killing him and ending the storm.

On another occasion, Krishna and Balarama played with the calves in the fields to such an extent that Yasoda became angry, and tied the errant Krishna to a heavy wooden mortar in which the corn from the farm was threshed. Krishna, trying to free himself, dragged it until it became wedged between two Arjuna trees and then, with a strong pull, uprooted the trees altogether. Again, the people of the surrounding farms were astonished because there had been no storm and yet the trees had fallen, and their roots were exposed. The land must be unlucky, they thought, and they moved away to Vrindavana.

Krishna's tricks were not only for the benefit of himself, for his companions were also defended by his fiery nature, trickery and quick thinking. One day, Brahma came and stole away the calves and the herd-boys, taking them to a cave among the mountains. Krishna quickly made another herd and another group of herd-boys in their likeness and placed them where he had found them. No one but Krishna knew their true identities and he waited impatiently for Brahma to come upon his trick. Now it was nearly a year later before Brahma remembered the herd and the children, and he found the boys and the calves asleep in the cave. But, when he went to Brindaban, he found the boys and the calves there too.

Brahma was puzzled, but he drew back in fear when Krishna, not content with his changelings, drew the herd-boys into the likeness of gods, with four arms and the shape of Brahma, Rudra and Indra. Krishna quickly returned the boys to their shape when he saw Brahma's fright, and Brahma restored them at once. When they awoke they knew nothing of the time that had passed, and Brahma was now in awe of the young Krishna, whose eager mind had caused such devilry.

There are many other tales related of Krishna's youth, for he liked nothing more than to stir a little trouble amongst the local gopis and cow-herds. There is a tale told of the day that Krishna stole the gopis' clothes. The girls had sought out a quiet place to bathe, and laying their clothes on the bank, they frolicked in the fresh water, their lotus eyes glowing with frivolity and the fervour of youth. They sang and played, and Krishna sat in the tree, watching his cows, but drawn to the happy songs of the gopis. Slipping down the bank, he snatched the clothes, and climbed up a kadamb tree which hugged the bank of the water hold.

When the gopis had completed their bath they returned to the banks to retrieve their clothes. They looked everywhere, raising their arms and brows in puzzlement at such a seemingly magical occurrence. Until one of the gopis looked up and saw Krishna sitting in the tree, gently laying out the clothes of each girl. He was wearing a crown and yellow robes and she called out, 'There he is, Krishna, who steals our hearts and our clothes.'

The girls squealed, as all girls across the ages would have done, and plunged into the water to hide themselves. They prayed silently for Krishna to return their clothes but he would not hand them over.

'You must come and fetch them,' he said smartly, grinning from ear to ear.

'We shall tell on you,' said the girls, 'we shall tell your father and ours, and all our friends and you will be punished. Our husbands will protect our honour.'

But Krishna only laughed and said to them then, 'If you are bathing for me, then cast away your shame and come and take your clothes.'

The girls said to each other, 'We must respect him, for he knows our minds and our bodies. There is no shame with Krishna.' And they strolled then from the water, their arms at their sides but their heads lowered in deference to Krishna. At Krishna's encouragement they joined hands and waited for their clothes, which were duly presented. And so the gopis returned home, wiser in some small way that was unknown to them, and more attracted to and confused by the mischievous Krishna than ever.

Krishna and Kaliya

One day, the cow-herds set out early, wandering through the woods and along the banks of the river until they came to a place called Kaliya. There they drank of the river waters, and allowed their cows to drink as well. Suddenly there was blackness and each of the cow-herds and cows laid down, the rich and instant poison of the naga or water snake called Kaliya entering their veins and causing them to die a painful death. Kaliya had come there from Ramanaka Dwipa, where he had once made his home. Garuda, who was the enemy of all serpents, had gone to live at Ramanaka Dwipa and Kaliya had fled immediately, taking refuge in the only place that Garuda was unable to visit, due to an ancient curse. Kaliya was an evil, frothing snake, and for miles around his shimmering form, the river bubbled with the heat of his poison.

Now on this day, Krishna set out to seek the company of the cow-herds and their cows, and he came upon their lifeless forms by the banks of the Jamna with some surprise. Krishna's powers were such that it took only a glance to restore the life to their bodies once more, and this he did at once. But Krishna was unhappy about his friends being plagued and he leapt into the water. Now the great Kaliya rose with all one hundred and ten hoods spluttering his poison, and the cowherds wept and wrung their hands at his certain death in that water. But Balarama was calm.

'Krishna will not die,' he said calmly. 'He cannot be slain.'

Now Kaliya had wrapped himself around the body of Krishna, and he tightened his grip with all of his force. But Krishna outwitted him, and making himself so large, he caused the serpent to set him free. Again, Kaliya squeezed his bulk around the youth, but once again Krishna cast him aside by growing in size.

Then, Krishna suddenly leapt onto Kaliya's heads, and taking on the weight of the entire universe, he danced on the serpent's heads until Kaliya began to splutter, and then die. But there was silence and weeping, and the serpent's many wives came forward and begged Krishna to set their husband free. They laid themselves at his feet, and pledged eternal worship.

'Please release him,' they asked, 'or slay us with him. Please, Krishna, know that a serpent is venomous through nature not through will. Please pardon him.'

And so it was that Krishna stepped from Kaliya's head and set the serpent free. Kaliya gasped his gratefulness, and prayed forgiveness for failing to recognize the great Krishna, the Lord, earlier. Krishna commanded Kaliya to return to Ramanaka Dwipa, but Kaliya lowered his head and explained that he could not return there for Garuda would make a meal of him at first sight. Krishna laughed, and pointed to the mark on Kaliya's head.

'Show him my mark, my friend,' he said to the serpent, 'for when Garuda sees that he will not touch you.'

From that day, the waters were cleared of poisons and the people rejoiced. Krishna was Lord.

Krishna and the Mountain

Krishna had long wished to annoy Indra – partly because he was mischievous by nature and partly because he envied the giver of rain for all the gifts he received from the people. And so it was on this day that Krishna spoke to the gopis who were preparing to worship Indra, and he urged them instead to worship the mountain that had supplied their cattle with food, and their cattle that yielded them with milk. And following the wise Krishna's advice, the gopis presented the mountain Govarddhana with curds and milk and flesh, the finest offerings they had.

The crafty Krishna at once transformed himself, appearing on the summit of the mountain saying 'I am the mountain.' There he ate greedily of the offerings while in his own form, as Krishna, he worshipped the mountains with the gopis. Little did they know that Krishna wished only to divert the worship of Indra to himself and that he could appear both as the mountain and in his own form at will.

Now Indra was not pleased that his offerings had all but dried up and pledging to punish the people, he sent down great floods and storms to destroy them and their cattle. An army of clouds swept across the skies and a rain like none had ever seen before was cast down.

'You told us to give up the worship of Indra,' chanted the gopis angrily. 'And now we will lose everything. You told us to worship the mountain and that we did. And so, great Krishna, bring that mountain to us now.'

And so it was that Krishna filled Govarddhana with all of the burning energy that filled his celestial body and he lifted it easily on the tip of one finger. Laying it over the people of Braj and their cows, he sheltered them from the rains and the floods until Indra gave up. Not even a drop of rain had fallen in Braj and Indra knew he had met the Primal Male.

The following day, as Balarama and Krishna laid lazily in the meadows, enjoying the sun and good fortune, Indra arrived and laid himself at Krishna's feet. Krishna was Lord.

Krishna and Radha

One day, as the cool breeze wafted lazily at the ripples on the river, Krishna and Balarama lay in the grasses under the trees, playing on the flute and joking amongst themselves. As was usually the case they were soon joined by the lovely gopis, who had fallen under the spell of Krishna and who longed for his company. They came towards the music and took up his hands to dance. Now there were too many of these gopis to dance with Krishna and to hold his hands, but as they danced he multiplied himself into as many forms as there were woman so that each woman believed she held the hand of the true Krishna.

It was on this same day that Krishna watched the gopis bathe in the Yamuna river after their dance. He loved them all, of course, but his particular favourite was Radha, the wife of Ayanagosha. Radha's sister-in-law told her brother of his wife's misconduct with Krishna, and Radha was afraid that she would be murdered as she slept. But when she spoke her fears to Krishna he calmed her, and reassured her easily that when her husband came, he would transform himself into Kali, and instead of finding Radha with her lover, Ayanagosha would find her worshipping a goddess instead.

Krishna took Radha into his embrace, and as he did so, her husband passed. Looking up, he noticed his wife bowing down with Krishna, who appeared at once as the goddess Kali.

The love affair with Radha went on for many years. They walked together in the flowering woods, and she spent many hours worshipping his feet. When Radha made love to Krishna, they made the world, and their love-making was passionate and playful. After their love-making Krishna combed her hair and plaited and pinned it, a servant to his mistress, a servant to his great love. He helped her with her sari. Theirs was a true, divine love – personifying all that is good in the union of man and woman.

There are many more stories of Krishna, who continued his tricks and his love-making, eventually taking on some 16,000 wives, but that is the story of the *Mahabharata* and other tales.

The Ten Suns of Dijun and Xihe

THE GOD OF THE EAST, Dijun, had married the Goddess of the Sun, Xihe, and they lived together on the far eastern side of the world just at the edge of the great Eastern Ocean. Shortly after their marriage, the Goddess gave birth to ten suns, each of them a fiery, energetic, golden globe, and she placed the children lovingly in the giant Fusang tree close to the sea where they could frolic and bathe whenever they became overheated.

Each morning before breakfast, the suns took it in turns to spring from the enormous tree into the ocean below in preparation for their mother's visit when one of them would be lifted into her chariot and driven across the sky to bring light and warmth to the world. Usually the two remained together all day until they had travelled as far as the western abyss known as the Yuyuan. Then, when her sun had grown weary and the light had begun to fade from his body, Xihe returned him to the Fusang tree where he slept the night peacefully with his nine brothers. On the following morning, the Goddess would collect another of her suns, sit him beside her in her chariot, and follow exactly the same route across the sky. In this way, the earth was evenly and regularly heated, crops grew tall and healthy, and the people rarely suffered from the cold.

But one night, the ten suns began to complain among themselves that they had not yet been allowed to spend an entire day playing together without at least one of them being absent. And realizing how unhappy this situation made them feel, they decided to rebel against their mother and to break free of the tedious routine she insisted they follow. So the next morning, before the Goddess had arrived, all ten of them leapt into the skies at once, dancing joyfully above the earth, intent on making the most of their forbidden freedom. They were more than pleased to see the great dazzling light they were able to generate as they shone together, and made a solemn vow that they would never again allow themselves to become separated during the daytime.

The ten suns had not once paused to consider the disastrous consequences of their rebellion on the world below. For with ten powerful beams directed at the earth, crops began to wilt, rivers began to dry up, food became scarce and people began to suffer burns and wretched hunger pangs. They prayed for rains to drive away the suns, but none appeared. They called upon the great sorceress Nu Chou to perform her acts of magic, but her spells had no effect. They hid beneath the great trees of the forests for shade, but these were stripped of leaves and offered little or no protection. And now great hungry beasts of prey and dreaded monsters emerged from the wilderness and began to devour the human beings they encountered, unable to satisfy their huge appetites any longer. The destruction spread to every corner of the earth and the people were utterly miserable and filled with despair. They turned to their Emperor for help, knowing he was at a loss to know what to do, but he was their only hope, and they prayed that he would soon be visited by the God of Wisdom.

Yi, the Archer, is Summoned

Tijun and Xihe were horrified to see the effect their unruly children were having upon the earth and pleaded with them to return to their home in the Fusang tree. But in spite of their entreaties, the ten suns continued on as before, adamant that they would not return to their former lifestyle. Emperor Yao now grew very impatient, and summoning Dijun to appear before him, he demanded that the God teach his suns to behave. Dijun heard the Emperor's plea but still he could not bring himself to raise a hand against the suns he loved so dearly. It was eventually settled between them, however, that one of Yao's officials in the heavens, known as Yi, should quickly descend to earth and do whatever he must to prevent any further catastrophe.

Yi was not a God of very impressive stature, but his fame as one of the most gifted archers in the heavens was widespread, for it was well known that he could shoot a sparrow down in full flight from a distance of fifty miles. Now Dijun went to meet with Yi to explain the problem his suns had created, and he handed the archer a new red bow and a quiver of white arrows and advised him what he must do.

'Try not to hurt my suns any more than you need to,' he told Yi, 'but take this bow and ensure that you bring them under control. See to it that the wicked beasts devouring mankind are also slain and that order and calm are restored once more to the earth.'

Yi readily accepted this challenge and, taking with him his wife Chang E, he departed the Heavenly Palace and made his descent to the world below. Emperor Yao was overjoyed to see the couple approach and immediately organized a tour of the land for them, where Yi witnessed for himself the devastation brought about by Dijun's children, as he came face to face with half-burnt, starving people roaming aimlessly over the scorched, cracked earth.

And witnessing all of this terrible suffering, Yi grew more and more furious with the suns of Dijun and it slipped his mind entirely that he had promised to treat them leniently. 'The time is now past for reasoning or persuasion,' Yi thought to himself, and he strode to the highest mountain, tightened the string of his powerful bow and took aim with the first of his arrows. The weapon shot up into the sky and travelled straight through the centre of one of the suns, causing it to erupt into a thousand sparks as it split open and spun out of control to the ground, transforming itself on impact into a strange three-legged raven.

Now there were only nine suns left in the sky and Yi fitted the next arrow to his bow. One after another the arrows flew through the air, expertly hitting their targets, until the earth slowly began to cool down. But when the Emperor saw that there were only two suns left in the sky and that Yi had already taken aim, he wisely remembered that at least one sun should survive to brighten the earth and so he crept up behind the archer and stole the last of the white arrows from his quiver.

Having fulfilled his undertaking to rid Emperor Yao of the nine suns, Yi turned his attention to the task of hunting down the various hideous monsters threatening the earth. Gathering a fresh supply of arrows, he made his way southwards to fight the man-eating monster of the marsh with six feet and a human head, known as Zao Chi. And with the help of his divine bow, he quickly overcame the creature, piercing his huge heart with an arrow of steel. Travelling northwards, he tackled a great many other ferocious beasts, including the nine-headed monster, Jiu Ying, wading into a deep, black pool and throttling the fiend with his own bare hands. After that, he moved onwards to the Quingqiu marshes of the east where he came upon the terrible vulture Dafeng, a gigantic bird of unnatural strength with a wing span so enormous that whenever the bird took to the air, a great typhoon blew up around it. And on this occasion, Yi knew that his single remaining arrow would only wound the bird, so he tied a long black cord to the shaft of the arrow before taking aim. Then as the creature flew past, Yi shot him in the chest and even though the vulture pulled strongly on the cord as it attempted to make towards a place of safety, Yi dragged it to the ground, plunging his knife repeatedly into its breast until all life had gone from it.

All over the earth, people looked upon Yi as a great hero, the God who had single-handedly rescued them from destruction. Numerous banquets and ceremonial feasts were held in his honour, all of them attended by the Emperor himself, who could not do enough to thank Yi for his assistance. Emperor Yao invited Yi to make his home on earth, promising to build him the a very fine palace overlooking Jade Mountain, but Yi was anxious to return to the heavens in triumph where he felt he rightly belonged and where, in any event, Dijun eagerly awaited an account of his exploits.

Tales of the Five Emperors

AFTER NU WA HAD peopled the earth, several of the heavenly gods began to take a greater interest in the world below them. The five most powerful of these gods descended to earth in due course and each was assigned various territories of the new world.

The Yellow Emperor (Huang Ti), the most important of the five sovereigns, is a part-mythical, part-historical figure who is reputed to have founded the Chinese nation around 4000 BC. During his 'historical' reign he is said to have developed a number of important astronomical instruments and mathematical theories, as well as introducing the first calendar to his people and a system for telling the time. He is always depicted as a figure who takes particular pride in humanity and one who consistently reveals a great love of nature and of peaceful existence.

Yet in order to achieve peace, the Yellow Emperor is forced, at one time or another, to battle against the other four gods. These include the Fiery or Red Emperor (Chih Ti), who is the Yellow Emperor's half-brother by the same mother, the White Emperor (Shao Hao), the Black Emperor (Zhuan Xu), and the Green Emperor (Tai Hou). The Yellow Emperor is victorious over all of these gods and he divides up the earth into four equal regions. The Red Emperor is placed in charge of the south, the White Emperor is in charge of the west, the Black Emperor rules the north, while the Green Emperor rules the east.

The Yellow Emperor's Earthly Kingdom

After he had grown for twenty-five months in his mother's womb, the infant God Huang Ti was safely delivered at last, bringing great joy to his celestial father, the God of Thunder. As soon as he appeared, Huang Ti had the gift of speech, and in each of his four faces the determination and energy of a born leader shone brightly for all to see. By the time the young God had grown to manhood, he alone among other deities had befriended every known spirit-bird, and a great many phoenixes travelled from afar simply to nest in his garden, or to perch themselves on the palace roof and terraces to serenade him with the sweetest of melodies.

When the five most powerful Gods decided to explore the earth, it was already in the minds of each that one among them should be assigned absolute and supreme control over the others. But the God of Fire, who was later known as the Red Emperor, was reluctant to share power with anyone, especially with his half-brother Huang Ti who seemed to be everyone else's natural choice. So when the time of the election came, the Red Emperor launched a vicious attack on the Yellow Emperor, instigating one of the fiercest battles the earth had ever witnessed. It was fought on the field of Banquan where the allies of Huang Ti, including wolves, leopards, bears and huge birds of prey, gathered together and rushed at the Red Emperor's troops until every last one of them lay slain.

Once this great battle was over and the Yellow Emperor had been acknowledged by all as supreme ruler, he set about building for himself a divine palace at the top of Mount Kunlun, which reached almost to the clouds. The magnificent royal residence, consisting of no less than five cities and twelve towers surrounded by solid walls of priceless jade, was flanked by nine fire-mountains which burnt day and night casting their warm red glow on the palace walls.

The front entrance faced eastwards and was guarded by the Kaiming, the loyal protector of the Gods, who had nine heads with human faces and the body of a giant panther. The exquisite gardens of the royal palace, where the Emperor's precious pearl trees and jade trees blossomed all year round, were protected by the three-headed God Li Zhu who sat underneath the branches never once allowing his three heads to sleep at the same time. This God was also guardian of the dan trees which bore five different exotic fruits once every five years, to be eaten exclusively by the Emperor himself.

From the largest garden, which was known as the Hanging Garden, a smooth path wound its way upwards to the heavens so that many of the most prestigious Gods and the rarest divine beasts chose to make the Emperor's wondrous kingdom their home, content that they had discovered earthly pleasures equal to their heavenly experience. And it was here, in this garden, that the supreme ruler particularly loved to sit each evening, taking time to admire his newly discovered world just as the setting sun bathed it in a gentle golden light. As he looked below him, he saw the reviving spring of Yaoshui flowing jubilantly into the crystal-clear waters of the Yaochi Lake. To the west he saw the great Emerald trees swaying delicately in the breeze, shedding a carpet of jewels on the earth beneath them. When he looked northwards his eyes were fixed upon the towering outline of Mount Zhupi where eagles and hawks soared merrily before their rest. The Yellow Emperor saw that all of this was good and knew that he would spend many happy years taking care of the earth.

The Fiery Emperor and the First Grain

The Fiery Emperor, who ruled as God of the south, had the head of an ox and the body of a human being. He was also known as the God of the Sun and although in the past he had led his people in a disastrous rebellion against the Yellow Emperor, he was still much loved by his subjects and they held him in the highest esteem. The Fiery Emperor taught mankind how to control and make constructive use of fire through the art of forging, purifying and welding metals so that eventually his subjects were able to use it for cooking, lighting and for making domestic tools and hunting weapons. In those early times, the forests were filled with venomous reptiles and savage wild animals and the Fiery Emperor ordered his people to set fire to the undergrowth to drive away these dangerous and harmful creatures. He was also the first to teach them how to plant grain, together with a whole variety of medicinal herbs that could cure any ailment which might trouble them.

It was said that when the Fiery Emperor first appeared on earth he very wisely observed that there was not enough fruit on the trees, or vegetables in the ground to satisfy the appetite of his people. Knowing that mankind was forced to eat the flesh of other living creatures, the Emperor became unhappy and quickly set about instructing his subjects in the use of the plough and other tools of the land until they learned how to cultivate the soil around them. And when he saw that the soil was ready, the Emperor called for his people to pray aloud for a new and abundant food to rise up before them out of the ground.

As the people raised their faces to the heavens, a red bird carrying nine seedlings in its beak suddenly appeared through the clouds. As it swooped to the ground it began to scatter grains on to the upturned soil. After it had done this, the Fiery Emperor commanded the sun to warm the earth and from the seeds emerged five young cereal plants which began to multiply rapidly until a vast area of land was covered with luscious vegetation.

The fruits of these plants were harvested at the close of day to fill eight hundred wicker baskets. Then the Fiery Emperor showed his people how to set up market stalls and explained to them how to keep time according to the sun in order that they might barter among themselves in the future for whatever food they lacked. But even after having provided all of this, the Fiery Emperor was still not satisfied with his work. And so, taking his divine whip, he began to lash a number of the plants, which caused them to be endowed with healing properties, and he set them aside to be used by mankind whenever disease struck. The people, overjoyed that they were so well cared for, decided that the Fiery Emperor should henceforth go by the name of the Divine Peasant and they built in his honour a giant cauldron for boiling herbs and carried it to the summit of the Shenfu Mountains where it stands to this day.

The Bird and the Sea

The Fiery Emperor had three daughters whom he loved and cared for very much, but it was his youngest daughter who had always occupied a special place in his heart. She was named Nu Wa, after the great Goddess who created mankind, and like her sisters she possessed a cheerful disposition and a powerful spirit of adventure.

One day Nu Wa went out in search of some amusement and seeing a little boat moored in the tiny harbour at a short distance from the palace gates, she went towards it, untied it and jumped aboard, allowing it to carry her out over the waves of the Eastern Sea. The young girl smiled happily to see the sun sparkle on the water and the graceful gulls circling overhead, but became so preoccupied in her joy that she failed to notice she had drifted out of sight, further and further towards the centre of the ocean. Suddenly, the wind picked up speed and the waves began to crash violently against the side of the boat. There was nothing Nu Wa could do to prevent herself being tossed overboard into the foaming spray and even though she struggled with every ounce of strength to save herself, she eventually lost the fight and was sadly drowned.

Just at that time, a small jingwei bird happened to approach the place where Nu Wa had fallen. And at that moment, her spirit, resentful of the fact that life had been cut short so unfairly, rose up in anger and entered the creature. Nu Wa now lived on in the form of a bird with a speckled head, white beak and red claws, and all day long she circled the skies angrily, vowing to take revenge on the sea which had deprived her of her life and left her father grieving for his beloved child.

It was not long before she conceived of a plan to fill up the sea with anything she could find, hoping that in time there would no longer be any room left for people to drown in it. So every day the little bird flew back and forth from the land out over the Eastern ocean until she grew weary with exhaustion. In her beak she carried pebbles, twigs, feathers and leaves which she dropped into the water below. But this was no easy task, and the sea laughed and jeered at the sight of the tiny bird labouring so strenuously:

'How do you imagine you will ever complete your work,' hissed the waves mockingly. 'Never in a million years will you be able to fill up the sea with twigs and stones, so why not amuse yourself somewhere else.'

But the little jingwei would not be deterred: 'If it takes me a hundred times a million years, I will not stop what I am doing. I will carry on filling you up until the end of the world, if necessary.'

And although the sea continued to laugh even more loudly over the years, the jingwei never ceased to drop into the ocean whatever she managed to collect. Later, after she had found herself a mate and they had produced children together, a flock of jingwei birds circled above the water, helping to fill up the sea. And they continue to do so to this day in China, where their persistent courage and strength have won the admiration and applause of each and every Chinese citizen.

Tai Hou, the Green Emperor

Even in the world of deities, the birth of the Green Emperor, God of the East, was judged quite an extraordinary affair. The story handed down among the other Gods was that the Emperor's mother, a beautiful young mortal named Hua Xu, lived originally in the ancient kingdom of Huaxushi, a place so remote and inaccessible, that many people had begun to question its very existence. Those who believed in this land, however, knew that its inhabitants possessed unique powers and gifts and often they were referred to as partial-Gods. They could move underwater as freely as they did above the earth, for example, and it was said that they could pass through fire without suffering any injury to the flesh. They walked through the air as easily as they walked on the ground and could see through the clouds as clearly as they could through glass.

One day the young girl Hua Xu was out walking across the northern plain of Leize, a name which means 'marshes of thunder', when she happened upon a gigantic footprint in the earth. She had never before encountered an imprint of its size and stooped to the ground to inspect it more closely. Imagining that a strange and wonderful being must have passed through the marshes, she grew very excited and found that she could not suppress the urge to compare the size of the footprint with her own. Slowly and carefully, Hua Xu placed her tiny foot in the enormous hollow and as she did so a strange vibration travelled up from the ground through the entire length of her body.

Shortly afterwards, the young girl found that she was pregnant and she was more than happy to be carrying a child, for there was no doubt in her mind that the Gods had intervened on that strange day to bring about her condition. After nine months Hua Xu gave birth to a son who bore the face of a man and the body of a snake. The elders of the people of Huanxushi advised that he should be named Tai Hou, a name fit for a supreme being they were convinced had been fathered by the God of Thunder.

Shao Hao, Son of the Morning Star

The Emperor of the West, Shao Hao, was also said to have come into being as the result of a strange and wonderful union. His mother, who was considered to be one of the most beautiful females in the firmament, worked as a weaver-girl in the Palace of Heaven. And it was always the case that after she had sat weaving the whole day, she preferred nothing better than to cruise through the Milky Way in a raft of silver that had been specially built for her use. On these occasions, she would pause for rest underneath the old mulberry tree which reached more than ten thousand feet into the skies. The branches of this tree were covered in huge clusters of shining berries, hidden from the naked eye by delicately spiced, scarlet-coloured leaves. It was a well-known fact that whoever ate the fruit of this tree would immediately receive the gift of immortality and many had journeyed to the centre of the Milky Way with this purpose in mind.

At that time, a very handsome young star-God named Morning Star, who was also known as Prince of the White Emperor, regularly took it upon himself to watch over these berries. Often he came and sat under the Mulberry Tree where he played his stringed instrument and sang the most enchanting songs. One evening, however, Morning Star was surprised to find his usual place occupied by a strange and beautiful maiden. Timidly, he approached her, but there was hardly any need for such caution, for as the maiden raised her head, their eyes met and the two fell in love almost instantly.

The maiden invited the young God aboard her raft and together they floated off into the night sky, along the silver river of the Milky Way down towards the earth and the waves of the sea. And as Morning Star played his magical music, the maiden carved a turtledove from a precious piece of white jade and set it on the top of the mast where it stood as a joint symbol of their mutual love and their deep desire to be guided by each other through the various storms of life. The lovers drifted together over the earth's ocean as their immortal music echoed through the air. And from this joyful union a son was born whom the happy couple named Shao Hao, and it was the child's great destiny to become White Emperor of the western realms and to rule wisely over his people.

Zhuan Xu, Emperor of the North

The Yellow Emperor and his wife once had a son called Chang Yi who turned out to be a very disappointing and disobedient child. One day, Chang Yi committed a crime so terrible, even his own father could not bring himself to discuss it, and immediately banished his son to a remote corner of the world where he hoped he would never again set eyes on him. After a time, Chang Yi had a son of his own, a very foolish-looking creature it was said, with a long, thin neck, round, beady eyes, and a pig's snout where his mouth should have been. By some form of miracle, Chang Yi's son also managed to find a mate and eventually married a strong and wholesome woman named Ah Nu. From this marriage, the Yellow Emperor's great grandson, Zhuan Xu, was produced, a God who managed to redeem the family name and who, after a careful trial period, was appointed ruler of the earth's northern territories.

Following the Yellow Emperor's great battle against Chiyou, he began to look around for a successor, for he had grown extremely weary of the rebellion and discontent he had experienced during his long reign. His great-grandson had proven himself a faithful servant and everyone now agreed that Zhuan Xu should be the next God to ascend the divine throne.

Chiyou had brought widespread destruction and suffering to the earth which led Zhuan Xu to believe that the alliance between mortals and immortals must be dissolved to prevent an even greater disaster in the future. And so he set about the task of separating the people from the Gods and turned his attention first of all to the giant ladder which ran between heaven and earth. For in those days, it was not unusual for people to ascend the ladder to consult with the Gods when they were in trouble, and the Gods, in turn, often made regular visits to the earth's surface. Chiyou had made such a visit when he secretly plotted with the Maio tribe in the south to put an end to the Yellow Emperor's sovereignty. The bloodshed which followed would never again be tolerated by Zhaun Xu and he enlisted the aid of two Gods in his destruction of the ladder.

With their help, the world became an orderly place once more. The God Chong was assigned control of the heavens and his task was to ensure that immortals no longer descended to earth. The God Li, together with his son Yi, were put in charge of the earth. Yi had the face of a human but his feet grew out of his head to form a fan-shaped bridge to the heavens behind which the sun and the stars set each evening. Zhaun Xu supervised the work of the other Gods and took it upon himself to re-introduce discipline to a race which had become untamed. It was said that he banished all cruel instruments of war and taught mankind respect for his own kind once again. He forbade women to stand in the path of men and severely punished a sister and brother who lived together as husband and wife.

By the time Zhuan Xu died, the world was a much more peaceful place and on the day he passed away it was said that the elements rose up in a great lament. Jagged lightning lit up the skies and thunder clouds collided furiously with each other. The north wind howled fiercely and the underground streams burst to the surface in torrents of grief. Legend has it that Zhuan Xu was swept away by the water and his upper-half transformed into a fish so that he might remain on the earth in another form, ever watchful of mankind's progress.

Chiyou Challenges the Yellow Emperor

Chiyou was a ferocious and ambitious God who had begun life as an aide and companion to the young deity, Huang Ti, in the days before he had risen to become Yellow Emperor on earth. During this time, the two had become firm friends and close confidants, but as soon as Huang Ti ascended the throne, this favourable relationship came to an abrupt end. For Chiyou could not bear to see his friend achieve the success he secretly longed for, and it became his obsession to find a way to reverse this situation and take the throne for himself.

Chiyou was the eldest of seventy-two brothers, all of them huge and powerful in stature. They each spoke the language of humans, but their bodies below the neckline were those of animals with cloven feet. Their heads were made of iron and their hideous copper faces contained four repulsive eyeballs protruding from mottled foreheads. These brothers ate all kinds of food, but they particularly liked to eat stones and chunks of metal, and their special skill was the manufacture of battle weapons, including sharp lances, spears, axes, shields and strong bows.

Now Chiyou had become convinced that he could easily overthrow the Yellow Emperor and so, gathering together his brothers and other minor Gods who were discontented with the Emperor's reign, he made an arrogant and boisterous descent to earth. First of all, however, he decided to establish a reputation for himself as a great warrior and immediately led a surprise attack on the ageing Fiery Emperor, knowing that he would seize power without a great deal of effort. The Fiery Emperor, who had witnessed his fair share of war, had no desire to lead his people into a climate of further suffering and torment, and soon fled from his home, leaving the way open for Chiyou to take control of the south. Shortly after this event, one of the largest barbarian tribes known as the Miao, who had been severely punished for their misdemeanours under the Fiery Emperor's authority, decided to take their revenge against the ruling monarchy and enthusiastically joined ranks of Chiyou and his brothers.

It was not long before the Yellow Emperor received word of the disturbances in the south, and hearing that it was his old friend who led the armies to rebellion, he at first tried to reason with him. But Chiyou refused to listen and insisted on war as the only path forward. The Yellow Emperor found that he had little choice but to lead his great army of Gods, ghosts, bears, leopards and tigers to the chosen battlefield of Zhuolu and here the terrible war began in earnest.

It was in Chiyou's nature to stop at nothing to secure victory against his opponent. Every subtle trick and sudden manoeuvre, no matter how underhanded, met with his approval and he had no hesitation in using his magic powers against the enemy. When he observed that his army had not made the progress he desired, he grew impatient and conjured up a thick fog which surrounded the Yellow Emperor and his men. The dense blanket of cloud swirled around them, completely obscuring their vision and they began to stab blindly with their weapons at the thin air. Then suddenly, the wild animals who made up a large part of the Emperor's forces started to panic and to flee in every direction straight into the arms of the enemy. The Yellow Emperor looked on desperately and, realizing that he was helpless to dispel the fog himself, he turned to his ministers and pleaded for help.

Fortunately, a little God named Feng Hou was among the Emperor's men, a deity renowned for his intelligence and inventiveness. And true to his reputation, Feng Hou began to puzzle a solution to the problem and within minutes he was able to offer a suggestion.

'I cannot banish from my mind an image of the Plough which appears in our skies at night-time and always points in the same direction,' he informed the Emperor. 'Now if only I could design something similar, we would be able to pinpoint our direction no matter which way we were forced to move through the mist.'

And so Feng Hou set to work at once, using his magic powers to assist him, and within a very short time he had constructed a device, rather like a compass, which continued to point southwards, regardless of its position. And with this incredible new instrument, the Yellow Emperor finally managed to make his way out of the fog, through to the clear skies once more.

But the battle was far from over, and the Emperor began to plan his revenge for the humiliation Chiyou had brought upon his men. At once, he summoned another of his Gods before him, a dragon-shaped deity named Ying Long, who possessed the ability to make rain at will, and commanded him to produce a great flood that would overwhelm the enemy. But Chiyou had already anticipated that the Yellow Emperor would not gladly suffer his defeat, and before the dragon had even begun to prepare himself for the task ahead, Chiyou had called upon the Master of Wind and the Master of Rain who together brought heavy rains and howling winds upon the Yellow Emperor's army, leaving them close to defeat once more.

As a last desperate measure, the Emperor introduced one of his own daughters into the battlefield. Ba was not a beautiful Goddess, but she had the power to generate tremendous heat in her body, enough heat to dry up the rain which now threatened to overcome her father's legions. So Ba stood among them and before long, the rains had evaporated from the earth and the sun began to shine brilliantly through the clouds. Its bright rays dazzled Chiyou's men which enabled Ying Long to charge forward unnoticed, and as he did so, hundreds of enemy bodies were crushed beneath his giant feet, lying scattered behind him on the plains.

And seeing this result, the Yellow Emperor managed to recover some of his dignity and pride, but his army lay exhausted and the morale of his men was very low. He was worried also that they would not be able to withstand another onslaught, for although Chiyou had retreated, the Emperor was certain he would soon return with reinforcements. He knew that he must quickly find something to lift the spirits of his men, and after much thought it suddenly came to him. What he needed most was to fill their ears with the sound of a victory drum, a drum which would resound with more power and volume than anyone had ever before imagined possible.

'With such a drum, I would bring fear to the enemy and hope to my own men,' the Emperor thought to himself. 'Two of my finest warriors must go out on my behalf and fetch a very special skin needed to produce this instrument.'

And having decided that the great beast from the Liubo Mountain possessed the only skin which would suffice, the Yellow Emperor dispatched two of his messengers to kill the strange creature. It resembled an ox without horns, he told them, and they would find it floating on the waves of the Eastern Sea. Sometimes the beast was known to open its mouth to spit out great tongues of lightning, and its roar, it was said, was worse than that of any wild cat of the forests.

But in spite of the creature's terrifying description, the Emperor's men found the courage to capture and skin it without coming to any great harm. After they had done so, they carried the hide back to the battlefield where it was stretched over an enormous bamboo frame to create an impressively large drum. At first, the Yellow Emperor was satisfied with the result, but when his men began to beat upon it with their hands, he decided that the sound was not loud enough to please him. So again, he sent two of his finest warriors on an expedition, and this time they went in search of the God of Thunder, Lei Shen. They found the God sleeping peacefully and crept up on him to remove both his thigh bones as the Emperor had commanded them to do. With these thigh bones a suitable pair of drumsticks was made and handed over to the principal drummer who stood awaiting his signal to beat on the giant instrument.

At last, the drum was struck nine times, releasing a noise louder than the fiercest thunder into the air. Chiyou's men stood paralysed with terror and fear as all around them the earth began to quake and the mountains to tremble. But this was the opportunity the Yellow Emperor's men had waited for and they rushed forward with furious energy, killing as many of Chiyou's brothers and the Miao warriors as they could lay their hands on. And when the battlefield was stained with blood and the casualties were too heavy for Chiyou to bear much longer, he called for his remaining men to withdraw from the fighting.

Refusing to surrender to the Yellow Emperor, the defeated leader fled to the north of the country to seek the help of a group of giants who took particular delight in warfare. These giants were from a tribe known as the Kua Fu and with their help Chiyou revived the strength of his army and prepared himself for the next attack.

The Yellow Emperor Returns to the Heavens

Chiyou had spent three days and three nights after his defeat at the battle of Zhuolu in the kingdom of the Kua Fu giants gathering rebel forces for his ongoing war against the Yellow Emperor. Both sides, it seemed, were now evenly matched once more and Chiyou relished the thought of a return to battle. But the Yellow Emperor saw that a renewal of conflict would only result in more loss of life and he was deeply disturbed and saddened by the prospect.

On the day before the second great battle was due to commence, the Emperor was sitting deep in thought in his favourite garden at the palace of Mount Kunlun when a strange Goddess suddenly appeared before him. She told him she was the Goddess of the Ninth Heaven and that she had been sent to help him in his plight.

'I fear for the lives of my men,' the Yellow Emperor told her, 'and I long for some new battle plan that will put an end to all this bloodshed.'

So the Goddess sat down on the soft grass and began to reveal to him a number of new strategies conceived by the highest, most powerful Gods of the heavens. And having reassured the Emperor that his trouble would soon be at an end, she presented him with a shining new sword furnished of red copper that had been mined in the sacred Kunwu Mountains.

'Treat this weapon with respect,' she told him as she disappeared back into the clouds, 'and its magic powers will never fail you.'

The next morning, the Emperor returned to the battlefield armed with his new strategies and the sacred weapon the Goddess had given him. And in battle after battle, he managed to overcome Chiyou's forces until at last they were all defeated and Chiyou himself was captured alive. The evil God was dragged in manacles and chains before the Yellow Emperor, but he showed no sign of remorse for the anguish he had caused and the destruction he had brought to the earth. The Yellow Emperor shook his head sadly, knowing that he now had little option but to order his prisoner's execution. The death sentence was duly announced, but Chiyou struggled so fiercely that the shackles around his ankles and wrists were stained crimson with blood.

When it was certain that he lay dead, Chiyou's manacles were cast into the wilderness where it is said they were transformed into a forest of maple trees whose leaves never failed to turn bright red each year, stained with the blood and anger of the fallen God.

And now that relative peace had been restored to the world once more, the Yellow Emperor spent his remaining time on earth re-building the environment around him. He taught the people how to construct houses for themselves where they could shelter from the rains; he brought them the gift of music and he also introduced them to the skill of writing. Mankind wanted to believe that the Yellow Emperor would always be with them on earth, but soon a divine dragon appeared in the skies, beckoning him back to the heavens. The time had arrived for the Yellow Emperor to answer this call and to acknowledge an end to the long reign of the Gods on earth. And so in the company of his fifty officials and all the other willing immortals whose stay had also run its course, he climbed on to the dragon's back and was carried up into the sky back to the heavens to take up his position again as crowned head of the celestial realms.

Hou-Ji, the Ice-Child

JIANG YUAN was one of four wives of Di Ku, God of the East. For many years the couple had tried to have a child together but they had not been successful and their marriage was not a very happy one as a result. One day, however, Jiang Yaun was walking along by the riverbank when she spotted a trail of large footprints in the earth. She was intrigued by them and began to follow where they led, placing her own tiny feet in the hollows of the ground. She was unaware that by doing this, she would conceive a child, and not long afterwards she gave birth to a son, an event which under normal circumstances would have brought her great joy.

But Jiang Yuan was filled with shame to see the tiny bundle wriggling in her arms, knowing that she had absolutely no knowledge of its father. And realizing that she would have great difficulty explaining the infant's birth to her husband, Jiang Yaun made up her mind to dispose of the child before she became a victim of scandalous gossip and derision. So she took the baby to a deserted country lane and left him to perish in the cold among the sheep and cattle. But then a strange thing happened. For instead of rejecting the baby and trampling him to death, the sheep and cattle treated him as one of their own, carrying him to a nearby barn where they nestled up close to him to keep him warm and suckled him with their own milk until he grew fit and strong.

Now Jiang Yuan had sent her scouts into the countryside to make sure that her unwanted child no longer lived. The news that he had survived and that he was being cared for by the animals of the pastures threw her into a fit of rage and she ordered her men to take the infant deep into the forests, to the most deserted spot they could find, where he was to be abandoned without any food or water. Jiang Yuan's messengers performed their duty exactly as they had been commanded, but again, fate intervened to save the child.

For one morning, a group of woodcutters who had travelled into the heart of the forest to find sturdier trees, spotted the child crawling through the undergrowth. Alarmed by his nakedness and grimy appearance, they immediately swept him up off the ground and carried him back to their village. Here, the woman Chingti, who was herself without child, took charge of the infant. She wrapped him in warm clothing and filled him with nourishing food until gradually he grew plump and healthy. His foster-mother doted on her son and it brought her great pleasure to see him thrive in her care.

But again, Jiang Yuan managed to track down the child and this time she was resolved to stop at nothing until she was certain of his destruction. And so, as a last resort, she carried him herself to a vast frozen river in the north where she stripped him naked and threw him on to the ice. For two years, the infant remained on the frozen waters, but from the very first day, he was protected from the piercing cold by a flock of birds who took it in turn to fly down with morsels of food and to shelter him under their feathered wings.

The people grew curious to know why the birds swooped on to the icy surface of the river every day when clearly there were no fish to be had. Eventually a group of them set off across the ice to investigate further and soon they came upon the young child, curled up against the warm breast of a motherly seagull. They were amazed at the sight and took it as a sign that the child they had discovered was no ordinary mortal, but a very precious gift from the Gods. They rescued the young boy and named him Hou-Ji and as they watched him grow among them, his outstanding talents began to manifest themselves one by one.

Hou-Ji became an excellent farmer in time, but he did not follow any conventional model. He was a born leader and from a very early age he had learned to distinguish between every type of cereal and edible grain. He made agricultural tools for the people, such as hoes and spades, and soon the land delivered up every variety of crop, including wheat, beans, rice and large, succulent wild melons. The people had a bountiful supply of food and when the Emperor himself heard of Hou-Ji's great work he appointed him a minister of the state so that his knowledge of agriculture would spread throughout the nation.

When Hou-Ji died he left behind a 'Five-Crop-Stone' which guaranteed the Chinese people a constant supply of food even in times of famine. He was buried on the Duguang Plain, a magnificent region of rolling hills and clear-flowing rivers where the land has always remained exceptionally fertile.

Kuan Ti, the God of War

A YOUNG MAN whose name was Yun-chang was born near Chieh Liang in Ho Tung (now the town of Chieh Chou in Shansi). The boy had a difficult nature and, having exasperated his parents, he was shut up in a room from which he escaped by breaking through the window. In one of the neighbouring houses he heard a young lady and an old man weeping. Running to the foot of the wall of the compound, he asked the reason for their grief. The old man replied that though his daughter was already engaged, the uncle of the local official, smitten by her beauty, wished to make her his concubine. His petitions to the official had only been rejected with curses.

Beside himself with rage, the youth seized a sword and went and killed both the official and his uncle. He escaped through the T'ung Kuan, the pass to Shensi. Having successfully avoided capture by the barrier officials, he knelt down at the side of a brook to wash his face. As he did so he discovered his appearance was completely transformed. His complexion had become reddish-grey and he was absolutely unrecognizable. He then presented himself with assurance before the officers, who asked him his name. 'My name is Kuan,' he replied. It was by that name that he was then known.

One day Kuan arrived at the town of Chu-chou, in Chihli. There he met Chang Fei, a butcher who had been selling his meat all morning. At noon the butcher lowered what remained of his meat into a well. He placed a stone weighing twenty-five pounds over the mouth of the well and said with a sneer: 'If anyone can lift that stone and take my meat, I will make him a present of it!' Kuan Yu, going up to the edge of the well, lifted the stone with the same ease as he would a tile, took the meat and made off. Chang Fei pursued him and eventually the two came to blows, but no one dared to separate them. Just then Liu Pei, a hawker of straw shoes arrived, and put a stop to the fight. The community of ideas which they found they possessed soon gave rise to a firm friendship between the three men.

Another account represents Liu Pei and Chang Fei as having entered a village inn to drink wine, when a man of gigantic stature pushing a wheelbarrow stopped at the door to rest. As he sat himself down he hailed the waiter, saying: 'Bring me some wine quickly, because I have to rush to the town to enlist in the army.'

Liu Pei looked at this man, nine feet in height, with a beard two feet long. His face was the colour of the fruit of the jujube tree and his lips were carmine. Eyebrows like sleeping silkworms shaded his phoenix eyes, which were a scarlet red. Terrible was his appearance.

'What is your name?' asked Liu Pei. 'My family name is Kuan, my own name is Yu, my surname Yun Chang,' he replied. 'I am from the Ho Tung country. For the last five or six years I have been wandering around the world as a fugitive to escape from my pursuers, because I killed a powerful man of my country who was oppressing the poor people. I hear that they are collecting a body of troops to crush the brigands, and I should like to join the expedition.'

Chang Fei (also named Chang I Te), is described as eight feet in height, with round shining eyes in a panther's head and a pointed chin bristling with a tiger's beard. His voice resembled the rumbling of thunder. His enthusiasm was like that of a fiery steed. He was a native of Cho Chun, where he owned some fertile farms. He was a butcher and wine merchant.

Liu Pei, surnamed Hsuan Te, (otherwise Hsien Chu), was the third member of the group.

The three men went to Chang Fei's farm. The following day they met in his peach orchard and sealed their friendship with an oath. Having bought a black ox and a white horse, with the various accessories to perform a sacrifice, they killed the victims, burnt the incense of friendship, and after twice prostrating themselves took this oath:

'We three, Liu Pei, Kuan Yu, and Chang Fei, already united by mutual friendship, although belonging to different clans, now bind ourselves by the union of our hearts and join our forces in order to help each other in times of danger. We wish to pay to the State our debt of loyal citizens and give peace to our black-haired compatriots. We do not inquire if we were born in the same year, the same month or on the same day, but we desire only that the same year, the same month and the same day may find us united in death. May Heaven our King and Earth our Queen see clearly our hearts! If any one of us violate justice or forget benefits, may Heaven and Man unite to punish him!'

The oath having been formally taken, Liu Pei was saluted as elder brother, Kuan Yu as the second and Chang Fei as the youngest. Their sacrifice to Heaven and earth over, they killed an ox and served a feast, to which they invited over three hundred of the soldiers from the district. They all drank copiously until they were intoxicated. Liu Pei enrolled the peasants; Chang Fei bought them horses and arms; and then they set out to make war on the Yellow Turbans (Huang Chin Tsei).

Kuan Yu proved himself worthy of the affection which Liu Pei showed him; brave and generous, he never turned aside from danger. His fidelity was shown especially on one occasion when, having been taken prisoner by Ts'ao Ts'ao, together with two of Liu Pei's wives and having been allotted a common sleeping apartment with his fellow captives, he preserved the ladies' reputation and his own trustworthiness by standing at the door of the room all night with a lighted lantern in his hand.

Kuan Yu remained faithful to his oath, even though tempted with a marquisate by the great Ts'ao Ts'ao, but he was eventually captured by Sun Ch'uan and put to death in ad 219. Long celebrated as the most renowned of China's military heroes, he was ennobled in ad 1120 as Faithful and Loyal Duke. Eight years later he was given the still more glorious title of Magnificent Prince and Pacificator. The Emperor Wen of the Yuan dynasty added the appellation Warrior Prince and Civilizer and, finally, the Emperor Wan Li of the Ming dynasty, in 1594, gave him the title of Faithful and Loyal Great Ti, Supporter of Heaven and Protector of the Kingdom. He therefore became a god, a ti, and has ever since received worship as Kuan Ti or Wu Ti, the God of War.

Temples erected in his honour are to be seen in all parts of the country. He is one of the most popular gods of China. During the last half-century of the Manchu Period his fame greatly increased. In 1856 he is said to have appeared in the heavens and successfully turned the tide of battle in favour of the Imperialists. His portrait hangs in every tent but his worship is not confined to the officials and the army. Many trades and professions have elected him as a patron saint. The sword of the public executioner used to be kept within the precincts of his temple and after an execution the presiding magistrate would stop there to worship for fear the ghost of the criminal might follow him home. He knew that the spirit would not dare to enter Kuan Ti's presence.

Legends of Thor

Thor's Visit to the Giants

Nowadays, since their journey to get the stolen hammer, Thor and Loki were good friends, for Loki seemed to have turned over a new leaf and to be a very decent sort of fellow; but really he was the same sly rascal at heart, only biding his time for mischief. However, in this tale he behaves well enough.

It was a long time since Thor had slain any giants, and he was growing restless for an adventure. 'Come, Loki,' he said one day, 'let us fare forth to Giant Land and see what news there is among the Big Folk.'

Loki laughed, saying, 'Let us go, Thor. I know I am safe with you;' which was a piece of flattery that happened to be true.

So they mounted the goat chariot as they had done so many times before and rumbled away out of Asgard. All day they rode; and when evening came they stopped at a little house on the edge of a forest, where lived a poor peasant with his wife, his son, and daughter.

'May we rest here for the night, friend?' asked Thor; and noting their poverty, he added, 'We bring our own supper, and ask but a bed to sleep in.' So the peasant was glad to have them stay. Then Thor, who knew what he was about, killed and cooked his two goats, and invited the family of peasants to sup with him and Loki; but when the meal was ended, he bade them carefully save all the bones and throw them into the goatskins which he had laid beside the hearth. Then Thor and Loki lay down to sleep.

In the morning, very early, before the rest were awake, Thor rose, and taking his hammer, Miolnir, went into the kitchen, where were the remains of his faithful goats. Now the magic hammer was skillful, not only to slay, but to restore, when Thor's hand wielded it. He touched with it the two heaps of skin and bones, and lo! up sprang the goats, alive and well, and as good as new. No, not quite as good as new. What was this? Thor roared with anger, for one of the goats was lame in one of his legs, and limped sorely. 'Some one has meddled with the bones!' he cried. 'Who has touched the bones that I bade be kept so carefully?'

Thialfi, the peasant's son, had broken one of the thigh-bones in order to get at the sweet marrow, and this Thor soon discovered by the lad's guilty face; then Thor was angry indeed. His knuckles grew white as he clenched the handle of Miolnir, ready to hurl it and destroy the whole unlucky house and family; but the peasant and the other three fell upon their knees, trembling with fear, and begged him to spare them. They offered him all that they owned, – they offered even to become his slaves, – if he would but spare their wretched lives.

They looked so miserable that Thor was sorry for them, and resolved at last to punish them only by taking away Thialfi, the son, and Roskva, the daughter, thenceforth to be his servants. And this was not so bad a bargain for Thor, for Thialfi was the swiftest of foot of any man in the whole world.

So he left the goats behind, and fared forth with his three attendants straight towards the east and Jotunheim. Thialfi carried Thor's wallet with their scanty store of food. They crossed the sea and came at last to a great forest, through which they tramped all day, until once more it was night; and now they must find a place in which all could sleep safely until morning. They wandered about here and there, looking for some sign of a dwelling, and at last they came to a big, queer-shaped house. Very queer indeed it was; for the door at one end was as broad as the house itself! They entered, and lay down to sleep; but at midnight Thor was wakened by a terrible noise. The ground shook under them like an earthquake, and the house trembled as if it would fall to pieces. Thor arose and called to his companions that there was danger about, and that they must be on guard. Groping in the dark, they found a long, narrow chamber on the right, where Loki and the two peasants hid trembling, while Thor guarded the doorway, hammer in hand. All night long the terrible noises continued, and Thor's attendants were frightened almost to death; but early in the morning Thor stole forth to find out what it all meant. And lo! close at hand in the forest lay an enormous giant, sound asleep and snoring loudly. Then Thor understood whence all their night's terror had proceeded, for the giant was so huge that his snoring shook even the trees of the forest, and made the mountains tremble. So much the better! Here at last was a giant for Thor to tackle. He buckled his belt of power more tightly to increase his strength, and laid hold of Miolnir to hurl it at the giant's forehead; but just at that moment the giant waked, rose slowly to his feet, and stood staring mildly at Thor. He did not seem a fierce giant, so Thor did not kill him at once. 'Who are you?' asked Thor sturdily.

'I am the giant Skrymir, little fellow,' answered the stranger, 'and well I know who you are, Thor of Asgard. But what have you been doing with my glove?'

Then the giant stooped and picked up – what do you think? – the queer house in which Thor and his three companions had spent the night! Loki and the two others had run out of their chamber in affright when they felt it lifted; and their chamber was the thumb of the giant's glove. That was a giant indeed, and Thor felt sure that they must be well upon their way to Giant Land.

When Skrymir learned where they were going, he asked if he might not wend with them, and Thor said that he was willing. Now Skrymir untied his wallet and sat down under a tree to eat his breakfast, while Thor and his party chose another place, not far away, for their picnic. When all had finished, the giant said, 'Let us put our provisions together in one bag, my friends, and I will carry it for you.' This seemed fair enough, for Thor had so little food left that he was not afraid to risk losing it; so he agreed, and Skrymir tied all the provisions in his bag and strode on before them with enormous strides, so fast that even Thialfi could scarcely keep up with him.

The day passed, and late in the evening Skrymir halted under a great oak-tree, saying, 'Let us rest here. I must have a nap, and you must have your dinner. Here is the wallet, – open it and help yourselves.' Then he lay down on the moss, and was soon snoring lustily.

Thor tried to open the wallet, in vain; he could not loosen a single knot of the huge thongs that fastened it. He strained and tugged, growing angrier and redder after every useless attempt. This was too much; the giant was making him appear absurd before his servants. He seized his hammer, and bracing his feet with all his might, struck Skrymir a blow on his head. Skrymir stirred lazily, yawned, opened one eye, and asked whether a leaf had fallen on his forehead, and whether his companions had dined yet. Thor bit his lip with vexation, but he answered that they were ready for bed; so he and his three followers retired to rest under another oak.

But Thor did not sleep that night. He lay thinking how he had been put to shame, and how Loki had snickered at the sight of Thor's vain struggles with the giant's wallet, and he resolved that it should not happen again. At about midnight, once more he heard the giant's snore resounding like thunder through the forest. Thor arose, clenching Miolnir tight, and stole over to the tree where Skrymir slept; then with all his might he hurled the hammer and struck the giant on the crown of his head, so hard that the hammer sank deep into his skull. At this the giant awoke with a start, exclaiming, 'What is that? Did an acorn fall on my head? What are you doing there, Thor?'

Thor stepped back quickly, answering that he had waked up, but that it was only midnight, so they might all sleep some hours longer. 'If I can only give him one more blow before morning,' he thought, 'he will never see daylight again.' So he lay watching until Skrymir had fallen asleep once more, which was near daybreak; then Thor arose as before, and going very softly to the giant's side, smote him on the temple so sore that the hammer sank into his skull up to the very handle. 'Surely, he is killed now,' thought Thor.

But Skrymir only raised himself on his elbow, stroked his chin, and said, 'There are birds above me in the tree. Methinks that just now a feather fell upon my head. What, Thor! are you awake? I am afraid you slept but poorly this night. Come, now, it is high time to rise and make ready for the day. You are not far from our giant city, – Utgard we call it. Aha! I have heard you whispering together. You think that I am big; but you will see fellows taller still when you come to Utgard. And now I have a piece of advice to give you. Do not pride yourselves overmuch upon your importance. The followers of Utgard's king think little of such manikins as you, and will not bear any nonsense, I assure you. Be advised; return homeward before it is too late. If you will go on, however, your way lies there to the eastward. Yonder is my path, over the mountains to the north.'

So saying, Skrymir hoisted his wallet upon his shoulders, and turning back upon the path that led into the forest, left them staring after him and hoping that they might never see his big bulk again.

Thor and his companions journeyed on until noon, when they saw in the distance a great city, on a lofty plain. As they came nearer, they found the buildings so high that the travelers had to bend back their necks in order to see the tops. 'This must be Utgard, the giant city,' said Thor. And Utgard indeed it was. At the entrance was a great barred gate, locked so that no one might enter. It was useless to try to force a passage in; even Thor's great strength could not move it on its hinges. But it was a giant gate, and the bars were made to keep out other giants, with no thought of folk so small as these who now were bent upon finding entrance by one way or another. It was not dignified, and noble Thor disliked the idea. Yet it was their only way; so one by one they squeezed and wriggled between the bars, until they stood in a row inside. In front of them was a wonderful great hall with the door wide open. Thor and the three entered, and found themselves in the midst of a company of giants, the very hugest of their kind. At the end of the hall sat the king upon an enormous throne. Thor, who had been in giant companies ere now, went straight up to the throne and greeted the king with civil words. But the giant merely glanced at him with a disagreeable smile, and said:

'It is wearying to ask travelers about their journey. Such little fellows as you four can scarcely have had any adventures worth mentioning. Stay, now! Do I guess aright? Is this manikin Thor of Asgard, or no? Ah, no! I have heard of Thor's might. You cannot really be he, unless you are taller than you seem, and stronger too. Let us see what feats you and your companions can perform to amuse us. No one is allowed here who cannot excel others in some way or another. What can you do best?'

At this word, Loki, who had entered last, spoke up readily: 'There is one thing that I can do, – I can eat faster than any man.' For Loki was famished with hunger, and thought he saw a way to win a good meal.

Then the king answered, 'Truly, that is a noble accomplishment of yours, if you can prove your words true. Let us make the test.' So he called forth from among his men Logi, – whose name means 'fire,' – and bade him match his powers with the stranger.

Now a trough full of meat was set upon the floor, with Loki at one end of it and the giant Logi at the other. Each began to gobble the meat as fast as he could, and it was not a pretty sight to see them. Midway in the trough they met, and at first it would seem as if neither had beaten the other. Loki had indeed done wondrous well in eating the meat from the bones so fast; but Logi, the giant, had in the same time eaten not only meat but bones also, and had swallowed his half of the trough into the bargain. Loki was vanquished at his own game, and retired looking much ashamed and disgusted.

The king then pointed at Thialfi, and asked what that young man could best do. Thialfi answered that of all men he was the swiftest runner, and that he was not afraid to race with any one whom the king might select.

'That is a goodly craft,' said the king, smiling; 'but you must be a swift runner indeed if you can win a race from my Hugi. Let us go to the racing-ground.'

They followed him out to the plain where Hugi, whose name means 'thought,' was ready to race with young Thialfi. In the first run Hugi came in so far ahead that when he reached the goal he turned about and went back to meet Thialfi. 'You must do better than that, Thialfi, if you hope to win,' said the king, laughing, 'though I must allow that no one ever before came here who could run so fast as you.'

They ran a second race; and this time when Hugi reached the goal there was a long bow-shot between him and Thialfi.

'You are truly a good runner,' exclaimed the king. 'I doubt not that no man can race like you; but you cannot win from my giant lad, I think. The last time shall show.' Then they ran for the third time, and Thialfi put forth all his strength, speeding like the wind; but all his skill was in vain. Hardly had he reached the middle of the course when he heard the shouts of the giants announcing that Hugi had won the goal. Thialfi, too, was beaten at his own game, and he withdrew, as Loki had done, shamefaced and sulky.

There remained now only Thor to redeem the honor of his party, for Roskva the maiden was useless here. Thor had watched the result of these trials with surprise and anger, though he knew it was no fault of Loki or of Thialfi that they had been worsted by the giants. And Thor was resolved to better even his own former great deeds. The king called to Thor, and asked him what he thought he could best do to prove himself as mighty as the stories told of him. Thor answered that he would undertake to drink more mead than any one of the king's men. At this proposal the king laughed aloud, as if it were a giant joke. He summoned his cup-bearer to fetch his horn of punishment, out of which the giants were wont to drink in turn. And when they returned to the hall, the great vessel was brought to the king.

'When any one empties this horn at one draught, we call him a famous drinker,' said the king. 'Some of my men empty it in two trials; but no one is so poor a manikin that he cannot empty it in three. Take the horn, Thor, and see what you can do with it.'

Now Thor was very thirsty, so he seized the horn eagerly. It did not seem to him so very large, for he had drunk from other mighty vessels ere now. But indeed, it was deep. He raised it to his lips and took a long pull, saying to himself, 'There! I have emptied it already, I know.' Yet when he set the horn down to see how well he had done, he found that he seemed scarcely to have drained a drop; the horn was brimming as before. The king chuckled.

'Well, you have drunk but little,' he said. 'I would never have believed that famous Thor would lower the horn so soon. But doubtless you will finish all at a second draught.'

Instead of answering, Thor raised the horn once more to his lips, resolved to do better than before. But for some reason the tip of the horn seemed hard to raise, and when he set the vessel down again his heart sank, for he feared that he had drunk even less than at his first trial. Yet he had really done better, for now it was easy to carry the horn without spilling. The king smiled grimly. 'How now, Thor!' he cried. 'You have left too much for your third trial. I fear you will never be able to empty the little horn in three draughts, as the least of my men can do. Ho, ho! You will not be thought so great a hero here as the folk deem you in Asgard, if you cannot play some other game more skillfully than you do this one.'

At this speech Thor grew very angry. He raised the horn to his mouth and drank lustily, as long as he was able. But when he looked into the horn, he found that some drops still remained. He had not been able to empty it in three draughts. Angrily he flung down the horn, and said that he would have no more of it.

'Ah, Master Thor,' taunted the king, 'it is now plain that you are not so mighty as we thought you. Are you inclined to try some other feats? For indeed, you are easily beaten at this one.'

'I will try whatever you like,' said Thor; 'but your horn is a wondrous one, and among the Aesir such a draught as mine would be called far from little. Come, now, – what game do you next propose, O King?'

The king thought a moment, then answered carelessly, 'There is a little game with which my youngsters amuse themselves, though it is so simple as to be almost childish. It is merely the exercise of lifting my cat from the ground. I should never have dared suggest such a feat as this to you, Thor of Asgard, had I not seen that great tasks are beyond your skill. It may be that you will find this hard enough.' So he spoke, smiling slyly, and at that moment there came stalking into the hall a monstrous gray cat, with eyes of yellow fire.

'Ho! Is this the creature I am to lift?' queried Thor. And when they said that it was, he seized the cat around its gray, huge body and tugged with all his might to lift it from the floor. Then the wretched cat, lengthening and lengthening, arched its back like the span of a bridge; and though Thor tugged and heaved his best, he could manage to lift but one of its huge feet off the floor. The other three remained as firmly planted as iron pillars.

'Oho, oho!' laughed the king, delighted at this sight. 'It is just as I thought it would be. Poor little Thor! My cat is too big for him.'

'Little I may seem in this land of monsters,' cried Thor wrathfully, 'but now let him who dares come hither and try a hug with me.'

'Nay, little Thor,' said the king, seeking to make him yet more angry, 'there is not one of my men who would wrestle with you. Why, they would call it child's play, my little fellow. But, for the joke of it, call in my old foster-mother, Elli. She has wrestled with and worsted many a man who seemed no weaker than you, O Thor. She shall try a fall with you.'

Now in came the old crone, Elli, whose very name meant 'age.' She was wrinkled and gray, and her back was bent nearly double with the weight of the years which she carried, but she chuckled when she saw Thor standing with bared arm in the middle of the floor. 'Come and be thrown, dearie,' she cried in her cracked voice, grinning horribly.

'I will not wrestle with a woman!' exclaimed Thor, eyeing her with pity and disgust, for she was an ugly creature to behold. But the old woman taunted him to his face and the giants clapped their hands, howling that he was 'afraid.' So there was no way but that Thor must grapple with the hag.

The game began. Thor rushed at the old woman and gripped her tightly in his iron arms, thinking that as soon as she screamed with the pain of his mighty hug, he would give over. But the crone seemed not to mind it at all. Indeed, the more he crushed her old ribs together the firmer and stronger she stood. Now in her turn the witch attempted to trip up Thor's heels, and it was wonderful to see her power and agility. Thor soon began to totter, great Thor, in the hands of a poor old woman! He struggled hard, he braced himself, he turned and twisted. It was no use; the old woman's arms were as strong as knotted oak. In a few moments Thor sank upon one knee, and that was a sign that he was beaten. The king signaled for them to stop. 'You need wrestle no more, Thor,' he said, with a curl to his lip, 'we see what sort of fellow you are. I thought that old Elli would have no difficulty in bringing to his knees him who could not lift my cat. But come, now, night is almost here. We will think no more of contests. You and your companions shall sup with us as welcome guests and bide here till the morrow.'

Now as soon as the king had pleased himself in proving how small and weak were these strangers who had come to the giant city, he became very gracious and kind. But you can fancy whether or no Thor and the others had a good appetite for the banquet where all the giants ate so merrily. You can fancy whether or no they were happy when they went to bed after the day of defeats, and you can guess what sweet dreams they had.

The next morning at daybreak the four guests arose and made ready to steal back to Asgard without attracting any more attention. For this adventure alone of all those in which Thor had taken part had been a disgraceful failure. Silently and with bowed heads they were slipping away from the hall when the king himself came to them and begged them to stay.

'You shall not leave Utgard without breakfast,' he said kindly, 'nor would I have you depart feeling unfriendly to me.'

Then he ordered a goodly breakfast for the travelers, with store of choicest dainties for them to eat and drink. When the four had broken fast, he escorted them to the city gate where they were to say farewell. But at the last moment he turned to Thor with a sly, strange smile and asked:

'Tell me now truly, brother Thor; what think you of your visit to the giant city? Do you feel as mighty a fellow as you did before you entered our gates, or are you satisfied that there are folk even sturdier than yourself?'

At this question Thor flushed scarlet, and the lightning flashed angrily in his eye. Briefly enough he answered that he must confess to small pride in his last adventure, for that his visit to the king had been full of shame to the hero of Asgard. 'My name will become a joke among your people,' quoth he. 'You will call me Thor the puny little fellow, which vexes me more than anything; for I have not been wont to blush at my name.'

Then the king looked at him frankly, pleased with the humble manner of Thor's speech. 'Nay,' he said slowly, 'hang not your head so shamedly, brave Thor. You have not done so ill as you think. Listen, I have somewhat to tell you, now that you are outside Utgard, – which, if I live, you shall never enter again. Indeed, you should not have entered at all had I guessed what noble strength was really yours, – strength which very nearly brought me and my whole city to destruction.'

To these words Thor and his companions listened with open-mouthed astonishment. What could the king mean, they wondered? The giant continued:

'By magic alone were you beaten, Thor. Of magic alone were my triumphs, – not real, but seeming to be so. Do you remember the giant Skrymir whom you found sleeping and snoring in the forest? That was I. I learned your errand and resolved to lower your pride. When you vainly strove to untie my wallet, you did not know that I had fastened it with invisible iron wire, in order that you might be baffled by the knots. Thrice you struck me with your hammer, – ah! what mighty blows were those! The least one would have killed me, had it fallen on my head as you deemed it did. In my hall is a rock with three square hollows in it, one of them deeper than the others. These are the dents of your wondrous hammer, my Thor. For, while you thought I slept, I slipped the rock under the hammer-strokes, and into this hard crust Miolnir bit. Ha, ha! It was a pretty jest.'

Now Thor's brow was growing black at this tale of the giant's trickery, but at the same time he held up his head and seemed less ashamed of his weakness, knowing now that it had been no weakness, but lack of guile. He listened frowningly for the rest of the tale. The king went on:

'When you came to my city, still it was magic that worsted your party at every turn. Loki was certainly the hungriest fellow I ever saw, and his deeds at the trencher were marvelous to behold. But the Logi who ate with him was Fire, and easily enough fire can consume your meat, bones, and wood itself. Thialfi, my boy, you are a runner swift as the wind. Never before saw I such a race as yours. But the Hugi who ran with you was Thought, my thought. And who can keep pace with the speed of winged thought? Next, Thor, it was your turn to show your might. Bravely indeed you strove. My heart is sick with envy of your strength and skill. But they availed you naught against my magic. When you drank from the long horn, thinking you had done so ill, in truth you had performed a miracle, – never thought I to behold the like. You guessed not that the end of the horn was out in the ocean, which no one might drain dry. Yet, mighty one, the draughts you swallowed have lowered the tide upon the shore. Henceforth at certain times the sea will ebb; and this is by great Thor's drinking. The cat also which you almost lifted, – it was no cat, but the great Midgard serpent himself who encircles the whole world. He had barely length enough for his head and tail to touch in a circle about the sea. But you raised him so high that he almost touched heaven. How terrified we were when we saw you heave one of his mighty feet from the ground! For who could tell what horror might happen had you raised him bodily. Ah, and your wrestling with old Elli! That was the most marvelous act of all. You had nearly overthrown Age itself; yet there has never lived one, nor will such ever be found, whom Elli, old age, will not cast to earth at last. So you were beaten, Thor, but by a mere trick. Ha, ha! How angry you looked, – I shall never forget! But now we must part, and I think you see that it will be best for both of us that we should not meet again. As I have done once, so can I always protect my city by magic spells. Yes, should you come again to visit us, even better prepared than now, yet you could never do us serious harm. Yet the wear and tear upon the nerves of both of us is something not lightly forgotten.'

He ceased, smiling pleasantly, but with a threatening look in his eye. Thor's wrath had been slowly rising during this tedious, grim speech, and he could control it no longer.

'Cheat and trickster!' he cried, 'your wiles shall avail you nothing now that I know your true self. You have put me to shame, now my hammer shall shame you beyond all reckoning!' and he raised Miolnir to smite the giant deathfully. But at that moment the king faded before his very eyes. And when he turned to look for the giant city that he might destroy it, – as he had so many giant dwellings, – there was in the place where it had been but a broad, fair plain, with no sign of any palace, wall, or gate. Utgard had vanished. The king had kept one trick of magic for the last.

Then Thor and his three companions wended their way back to Asgard. But they were slower than usual about answering questions concerning their last adventure, their wondrous visit to the giant city. Truth to tell, magic or no magic, Thor and Loki had showed but a poor figure that day. For the first time in all their meeting with Thor the giants had not come off any the worse for the encounter. Perhaps it was a lesson that he sorely needed. I am afraid that he was rather inclined to think well of himself. But then, he had reason, had he not?

The Quest of the Hammer

One morning Thor the Thunderer awoke with a yawn, and stretching out his knotted arm, felt for his precious hammer, which he kept always under his pillow of clouds. But he started up with a roar of rage, so that all the palace trembled. The hammer was gone!

Now this was a very serious matter, for Thor was the protector of Asgard, and Miolnir, the magic hammer which the dwarf had made, was his mighty weapon, of which the enemies of the Aesir stood so much in dread that they dared not venture near. But if they should learn that Miolnir was gone, who could tell what danger might not threaten the palaces of heaven?

Thor darted his flashing eye into every corner of Cloud Land in search of the hammer. He called his fair wife, Sif of the golden hair, to aid in the search, and his two lovely daughters, Thrude and Lora. They hunted and they hunted; they turned Thrudheim upside down, and set the clouds to rolling wonderfully, as they peeped and pried behind and around and under each billowy mass. But Miolnir was not to be found. Certainly, some one had stolen it.

Thor's yellow beard quivered with rage, and his hair bristled on end like the golden rays of a star, while all his household trembled.

'It is Loki again!' he cried. 'I am sure Loki is at the bottom of this mischief!' For since the time when Thor had captured Loki for the dwarf Brock and had given him over to have his bragging lips sewed up, Loki had looked at him with evil eyes; and Thor knew that the red rascal hated him most of all the gods.

But this time Thor was mistaken. It was not Loki who had stolen the hammer, – he was too great a coward for that. And though he meant, before the end, to be revenged upon Thor, he was waiting until a safe chance should come, when Thor himself might stumble into danger, and Loki need only to help the evil by a malicious word or two; and this chance came later, as you shall hear in another tale.

Meanwhile Loki was on his best behavior, trying to appear very kind and obliging; so when Thor came rumbling and roaring up to him, demanding, 'What have you done with my hammer, you thief?' Loki looked surprised, but did not lose his temper nor answer rudely.

'Have you indeed missed your hammer, brother Thor?' he said, mumbling, for his mouth was still sore where Brock had sewed the stitches. 'That is a pity; for if the giants hear of this, they will be coming to try their might against Asgard.'

'Hush!' muttered Thor, grasping him by the shoulder with his iron fingers. 'That is what I fear. But look you, Loki: I suspect your hand in the mischief. Come, confess.'

Then Loki protested that he had nothing to do with so wicked a deed. 'But,' he added wheedlingly, 'I think I can guess the thief; and because I love you, Thor, I will help you to find him.'

'Humph!' growled Thor. 'Much love you bear to me! However, you are a wise rascal, the nimblest wit of all the Aesir, and it is better to have you on my side than on the other, when giants are in the game. Tell me, then: who has robbed the Thunder-Lord of his bolt of power?'

Loki drew near and whispered in Thor's ear. 'Look, how the storms rage and the winds howl in the world below! Some one is wielding your thunder-hammer all unskillfully. Can you not guess the thief? Who but Thrym, the mighty giant who has ever been your enemy and your imitator, and whose fingers have long itched to grasp the short handle of mighty Miolnir, that the world may name him Thunder-Lord instead of you. But look! What a tempest! The world will bc shattered into fragments unless we soon get the hammer back.'

Then Thor roared with rage. 'I will seek this impudent Thrym!' he cried. 'I will crush him into bits, and teach him to meddle with the weapon of the Aesir!'

'Softly, softly,' said Loki, smiling maliciously. 'He is a shrewd giant, and a mighty. Even you, great Thor, cannot go to him and pluck the hammer from his hand as one would slip the rattle from a baby's pink fist. Nay, you must use craft, Thor; and it is I who will teach you, if you will be patient.'

Thor was a brave, blunt fellow, and he hated the ways of Loki, his lies and his deceit. He liked best the way of warriors, – the thundering charge, the flash of weapons, and the heavy blow; but without the hammer he could not fight the giants hand to hand. Loki's advice seemed wise, and he decided to leave the matter to the Red One.

Loki was now all eagerness, for he loved difficulties which would set his wit in play and bring other folk into danger. 'Look, now,' he said. 'We must go to Freyia and borrow her falcon dress. But you must ask; for she loves me so little that she would scarce listen to me.'

So first they made their way to Folkvang, the house of maidens, where Freyia dwelt, the loveliest of all in Asgard. She was fairer than fair, and sweeter than sweet, and the tears from her flower-eyes made the dew which blessed the earth-flowers night and morning. Of her Thor borrowed the magic dress of feathers in which Freyia was wont to clothe herself and flit like a great beautiful bird all about the world. She was willing enough to lend it to Thor when he told her that by its aid he hoped to win back the hammer which he had lost; for she well knew the danger threatening herself and all the Aesir until Miolnir should be found.

'Now will I fetch the hammer for you,' said Loki. So he put on the falcon plumage, and, spreading his brown wings, flapped away up, up, over the world, down, down, across the great ocean which lies beyond all things that men know. And he came to the dark country where there was no sunshine nor spring, but it was always dreary winter; where mountains were piled up like blocks of ice, and where great caverns yawned hungrily in blackness. And this was Jotunheim, the land of the Frost Giants.

And lo! when Loki came thereto he found Thrym the Giant King sitting outside his palace cave, playing with his dogs and horses. The dogs were as big as elephants, and the horses were as big as houses, but Thrym himself was as huge as a mountain; and Loki trembled, but he tried to seem brave.

'Good-day, Loki,' said Thrym, with the terrible voice of which he was so proud, for he fancied it was as loud as Thor's. 'How fares it, feathered one, with your little brothers, the Aesir, in Asgard halls? And how dare you venture alone in this guise to Giant Land?'

'It is an ill day in Asgard,' sighed Loki, keeping his eye warily upon the giant, 'and a stormy one in the world of men. I heard the winds howling and the storms rushing on the earth as I passed by. Some mighty one has stolen the hammer of our Thor. Is it you, Thrym, greatest of all giants, – greater than Thor himself?'

This the crafty one said to flatter Thrym, for Loki well knew the weakness of those who love to be thought greater than they are.

Then Thrym bridled and swelled with pride, and tried to put on the majesty and awe of noble Thor; but he only succeeded in becoming an ugly, puffy monster.

'Well, yes,' he admitted. 'I have the hammer that belonged to your little Thor; and now how much of a lord is he?'

'Alack!' sighed Loki again, 'weak enough he is without his magic weapon. But you, O Thrym, – surely your mightiness needs no such aid. Give me the hammer, that Asgard may no longer be shaken by Thor's grief for his precious toy.'

But Thrym was not so easily to be flattered into parting with his stolen treasure. He grinned a dreadful grin, several yards in width, which his teeth barred like jagged boulders across the entrance to a mountain cavern.

'Miolnir the hammer is mine,' he said, 'and I am Thunder-Lord, mightiest of the mighty. I have hidden it where Thor can never find it, twelve leagues below the sea-caves, where Queen Ran lives with her daughters, the white-capped Waves. But listen, Loki. Go tell the Aesir that I will give back Thor's hammer. I will give it back upon one condition, – that they send Freyia the beautiful to be my wife.'

'Freyia the beautiful!' Loki had to stifle a laugh. Fancy the Aesir giving their fairest flower to such an ugly fellow as this! But he only said politely, 'Ah, yes; you demand our Freyia in exchange for the little hammer? It is a costly price, great Thrym. But I will be your friend in Asgard. If I have my way, you shall soon see the fairest bride in all the world knocking at your door. Farewell!'

So Loki whizzed back to Asgard on his falcon wings; and as he went he chuckled to think of the evils which were likely to happen because of his words with Thrym. First he gave the message to Thor, – not sparing of Thrym's insolence, to make Thor angry; and then he went to Freyia with the word for her, – not sparing of Thrym's ugliness, to make her shudder. The spiteful fellow!

Now you can imagine the horror that was in Asgard as the Aesir listened to Loki's words. 'My hammer!' roared Thor. 'The villain confesses that he has stolen my hammer, and boasts that he is Thunder-Lord! Gr-r-r!'

'The ugly giant!' wailed Freyia. 'Must I be the bride of that hideous old monster, and live in his gloomy mountain prison all my life?'

'Yes; put on your bridal veil, sweet Freyia,' said Loki maliciously, 'and come with me to Jotunheim. Hang your famous starry necklace about your neck, and don your bravest robe; for in eight days there will be a wedding, and Thor's hammer is to pay.'

Then Freyia fell to weeping. 'I cannot go! I will not go!' she cried. 'I will not leave the home of gladness and Father Odin's table to dwell in the land of horrors! Thor's hammer is mighty, but mightier the love of the kind Aesir for their little Freyia! Good Odin, dear brother Frey, speak for me! You will not make me go?'

The Aesir looked at her and thought how lonely and bare would Asgard be without her loveliness; for she was fairer than fair, and sweeter than sweet.

'She shall not go!' shouted Frey, putting his arms about his sister's neck.

'No, she shall not go!' cried all the Aesir with one voice.

'But my hammer,' insisted Thor. 'I must have Miolnir back again.'

'And my word to Thrym,' said Loki, 'that must be made good.'

'You are too generous with your words,' said Father Odin sternly, for he knew his brother well. 'Your word is not a gem of great price, for you have made it cheap.'

Then spoke Heimdall, the sleepless watchman who sits on guard at the entrance to the rainbow bridge which leads to Asgard; and Heimdall was the wisest of the Aesir, for he could see into the future, and knew how things would come to pass. Through his golden teeth he spoke, for his teeth were all of gold.

'I have a plan,' he said. 'Let us dress Thor himself like a bride in Freyia's robes, and send him to Jotunheim to talk with Thrym and to win back his hammer.'

But at this word Thor grew very angry. 'What! dress me like a girl!' he roared. 'I should never hear the last of it! The Aesir will mock me, and call me 'maiden'! The giants, and even the puny dwarfs, will have a lasting jest upon me! I will not go! I will fight! I will die, if need be! But dressed as a woman I will not go!'

But Loki answered him with sharp words, for this was a scheme after his own heart. 'What, Thor!' he said. 'Would you lose your hammer and keep Asgard in danger for so small a whim? Look, now: if you go not, Thrym with his giants will come in a mighty army and drive us from Asgard; then he will indeed make Freyia his bride, and moreover he will have you for his slave under the power of his hammer. How like you this picture, brother of the thunder? Nay, Heimdall's plan is a good one, and I myself will help to carry it out.'

Still Thor hesitated; but Freyia came and laid her white hand on his arm, and looked up into his scowling face pleadingly.

'To save me, Thor,' she begged. And Thor said he would go.

Then there was great sport among the Aesir, while they dressed Thor like a beautiful maiden. Brunhilde and her sisters, the nine Valkyr, daughters of Odin, had the task in hand. How they laughed as they brushed and curled his yellow hair, and set upon it the wondrous headdress of silk and pearls! They let out seams, and they let down hems, and set on extra pieces, to make it larger, and so they hid his great limbs and knotted arms under Freyia's fairest robe of scarlet; but beneath it all he would wear his shirt of mail and his belt of power that gave him double strength. Freyia herself twisted about his neck her famous necklace of starry jewels, and Queen Frigga, his mother, hung at his girdle a jingling bunch of keys, such as was the custom for the bride to wear at Norse weddings. Last of all, that Thrym might not see Thor's fierce eyes and the yellow beard, that ill became a maiden, they threw over him a long veil of silver white which covered him to the feet. And there he stood, as stately and tall a bride as even a giant might wish to see; but on his hands he wore his iron gloves, and they ached for but one thing, – to grasp the handle of the stolen hammer.

'Ah, what a lovely maid it is!' chuckled Loki; 'and how glad will Thrym be to see this Freyia come! Bride Thor, I will go with you as your handmaiden, for I would fain see the fun.'

'Come, then,' said Thor sulkily, for he was ill pleased, and wore his maiden robes with no good grace. 'It is fitting that you go; for I like not these lies and maskings, and I may spoil the mummery without you at my elbow.'

There was loud laughter above the clouds when Thor, all veiled and dainty seeming, drove away from Asgard to his wedding, with maid Loki by his side. Thor cracked his whip and chirruped fiercely to his twin goats with golden hoofs, for he wanted to escape the sounds of mirth that echoed from the rainbow bridge, where all the Aesir stood watching. Loki, sitting with his hands meekly folded like a girl, chuckled as he glanced up at Thor's angry face; but he said nothing, for he knew it was not good to joke too far with Thor, even when Miolnir was hidden twelve leagues below the sea in Ran's kingdom.

So off they dashed to Jotunheim, where Thrym was waiting and longing for his beautiful bride. Thor's goats thundered along above the sea and land and people far below, who looked up wondering as the noise rolled overhead. 'Hear how the thunder rumbles!' they said. 'Thor is on a long journey tonight.' And a long journey it was, as the tired goats found before they reached the end.

Thrym heard the sound of their approach, for his ear was eager. 'Hola!' he cried. 'Some one is coming from Asgard, – only one of Odin's children could make a din so fearful. Hasten, men, and see if they are bringing Freyia to be my wife.'

Then the lookout giant stepped down from the top of his mountain, and said that a chariot was bringing two maidens to the door.

'Run, giants, run!' shouted Thrym, in a fever at this news. 'My bride is coming! Put silken cushions on the benches for a great banquet, and make the house beautiful for the fairest maid in all space! Bring in all my golden-horned cows and my coal-black oxen, that she may see how rich I am, and heap all my gold and jewels about to dazzle her sweet eyes! She shall find me richest of the rich; and when I have her, – fairest of the fair, – there will be no treasure that I lack, – not one!'

The chariot stopped at the gate, and out stepped the tall bride, hidden from head to foot, and her handmaiden muffled to the chin. 'How afraid of catching cold they must be!' whispered the giant ladies, who were peering over one another's shoulders to catch a glimpse of the bride, just as the crowd outside the awning does at a wedding nowadays.

Thrym had sent six splendid servants to escort the maidens: these were the Metal Kings, who served him as lord of them all. There was the Gold King, all in cloth of gold, with fringes of yellow bullion, most glittering to see; and there was the Silver King, almost as gorgeous in a suit of spangled white; and side by side bowed the dark Kings of Iron and Lead, the one mighty in black, the other sullen in blue; and after them were the Copper King, gleaming ruddy and brave, and the Tin King, strutting in his trimmings of gaudy tinsel which looked nearly as well as silver but were more economical. And this fine troop of lackey kings most politely led Thor and Loki into the palace, and gave them of the best, for they never suspected who these seeming maidens really were.

And when evening came there was a wonderful banquet to celebrate the wedding. On a golden throne sat Thrym, uglier than ever in his finery of purple and gold. Beside him was the bride, of whose face no one had yet caught even a glimpse; and at Thrym's other hand stood Loki, the waiting-maid, for he wanted to be near to mend the mistakes which Thor might make.

Now the dishes at the feast were served in a huge way, as befitted the table of giants: great beeves roasted whole, on platters as wide across as a ship's deck; plum-puddings as fat as feather-beds, with plums as big as footballs; and a wedding cake like a snow-capped haymow. The giants ate enormously. But to Thor, because they thought him a dainty maiden, they served small bits of everything on a tiny gold dish. Now Thor's long journey had made him very hungry, and through his veil he whispered to Loki, 'I shall starve, Loki! I cannot fare on these nibbles. I must eat a goodly meal as I do at home.' And forthwith he helped himself to such morsels as might satisfy his hunger for a little time. You should have seen the giants stare at the meal which the dainty bride devoured!

For first under the silver veil disappeared by pieces a whole roast ox. Then Thor made eight mouthfuls of eight pink salmon, a dish of which he was very fond. And next he looked about and reached for a platter of cakes and sweetmeats that was set aside at one end of the table for the lady guests, and the bride ate them all. You can fancy how the damsels drew down their mouths and looked at one another when they saw their dessert disappear; and they whispered about the table, 'Alack! if our future mistress is to sup like this day by day, there will be poor cheer for the rest of us!' And to crown it all, Thor was thirsty, as well he might be; and one after another he raised to his lips and emptied three great barrels of mead, the foamy drink of the giants. Then indeed Thrym was amazed, for Thor's giant appetite had beaten that of the giants themselves.

'Never before saw I a bride so hungry,' he cried, 'and never before one half so thirsty!'

But Loki, the waiting-maid, whispered to him softly, 'The truth is, great Thrym, that my dear mistress was almost starved. For eight days Freyia has eaten nothing at all, so eager was she for Jotunheim.'

Then Thrym was delighted, you may be sure. He forgave his hungry bride, and loved her with all his heart. He leaned forward to give her a kiss, raising a corner of her veil; but his hand dropped suddenly, and he started up in terror, for he had caught the angry flash of Thor's eye, which was glaring at him through the bridal veil. Thor was longing for his hammer.

'Why has Freyia so sharp a look?' Thrym cried. 'It pierces like lightning and burns like fire.'

But again the sly waiting-maid whispered timidly, 'Oh, Thrym, be not amazed! The truth is, my poor mistress's eyes are red with wakefulness and bright with longing. For eight nights Freyia has not known a wink of sleep, so eager was she for Jotunheim.'

Then again Thrym was doubly delighted, and he longed to call her his very own dear wife. 'Bring in the wedding gift!' he cried. 'Bring in Thor's hammer, Miolnir, and give it to Freyia, as I promised; for when I have kept my word she will be mine, – all mine!'

Then Thor's big heart laughed under his woman's dress, and his fierce eyes swept eagerly down the hall to meet the servant who was bringing in the hammer on a velvet cushion. Thor's fingers could hardly wait to clutch the stubby handle which they knew so well; but he sat quite still on the throne beside ugly old Thrym, with his hands meekly folded and his head bowed like a bashful bride.

The giant servant drew nearer, nearer, puffing and blowing, strong though he was, beneath the mighty weight. He was about to lay it at Thor's feet (for he thought it so heavy that no maiden could lift it or hold it in her lap), when suddenly Thor's heart swelled, and he gave a most unmaidenly shout of rage and triumph. With one swoop he grasped the hammer in his iron fingers; with the other arm he tore off the veil that hid his terrible face, and trampled it under foot; then he turned to the frightened king, who cowered beside him on the throne.

'Thief!' he cried. 'Freyia sends you this as a wedding gift!' And he whirled the hammer about his head, then hurled it once, twice, thrice, as it rebounded to his hand; and in the first stroke, as of lightning, Thrym rolled dead from his throne; in the second stroke perished the whole giant household, – these ugly enemies of the Aesir; and in the third stroke the palace itself tumbled together and fell to the ground like a toppling play-house of blocks.

But Loki and Thor stood safely among the ruins, dressed in their tattered maiden robes, a quaint and curious sight; and Loki, full of mischief now as ever, burst out laughing.

'Oh, Thor! if you could see' – he began; but Thor held up his hammer and shook it gently as he said:

'Look now, Loki: it was an excellent joke, and so far you have done well, – after your crafty fashion, which likes me not. But now I have my hammer again, and the joke is done. From you, nor from another, I brook no laughter at my expense. Henceforth we will have no mention of this masquerade, nor of these rags which now I throw away. Do you hear, red laugher?'

And Loki heard, with a look of hate, and stifled his laughter as best he could; for it is not good to laugh at him who holds the hammer.

Not once after that was there mention in Asgard of the time when Thor dressed him as a girl and won his bridal gift from Thrym the giant.

But Miolnir was safe once more in Asgard, and you and I know how it came there; so some one must have told. I wonder if red Loki whispered the tale to some outsider, after all? Perhaps it may be so, for now he knew how best to make Thor angry; and from that day when Thor forbade his laughing, Loki hated him with the mean little hatred of a mean little soul.

Thor's Duel

In the days that are past a wonderful race of horses pastured in the meadows of heaven, steeds more beautiful and more swift than any which the world knows today. There was Hrîmfaxi, the black, sleek horse who drew the chariot of Night across the sky and scattered the dew from his foaming bit. There was Glad, behind whose flying heels sped the swift chariot of Day. His mane was yellow with gold, and from it beamed light which made the whole world bright. Then there were the two shining horses of the sun, Arvakur the watchful, and Alsvith the rapid; and the nine fierce battle-chargers of the nine Valkyrs, who bore the bodies of fallen heroes from the field of fight to the blessedness of Valhalla. Each of the gods had his own glorious steed, with such pretty names as Gold-mane and Silver-top, Light-foot and Precious-stone; these galloped with their masters over clouds and through the blue air, blowing flame from their nostrils and glinting sparks from their fiery eyes. The Aesir would have been poor indeed without their faithful mounts, and few would be the stories to tell in which these noble creatures do not bear at least a part.

But best of all the horses of heaven was Sleipnir, the eight-legged steed of Father Odin, who because he was so well supplied with sturdy feet could gallop faster over land and sea than any horse which ever lived. Sleipnir was snow-white and beautiful to see, and Odin was very fond and proud of him, you may be sure. He loved to ride forth upon his good horse's back to meet whatever adventure might be upon the way, and sometimes they had wild times together.

One day Odin galloped off from Asgard upon Sleipnir straight towards Jotunheim and the Land of Giants, for it was long since All-Father had been to the cold country, and he wished to see how its mountains and ice-rivers looked. Now as he galloped along a wild road, he met a huge giant standing beside his giant steed.

'Who goes there?' cried the giant gruffly, blocking the way so that Odin could not pass. 'You with the golden helmet, who are you, who ride so famously through air and water? For I have been watching you from this mountain-top. Truly, that is a fine horse which you bestride.'

'There is no finer horse in all the world,' boasted Odin. 'Have you not heard of Sleipnir, the pride of Asgard? I will match him against any of your big, clumsy giant horses.'

'Ho!' roared the giant angrily, 'an excellent horse he is, your little Sleipnir. But I warrant he is no match for my Gullfaxi here. Come, let us try a race; and at its end I shall pay you for your insult to our horses of Jotunheim.'

So saying, the giant, whose ugly name was Hrungnir, sprang upon his horse and spurred straight at Odin in the narrow way. Odin turned and galloped back towards Asgard with all his might; for not only must he prove his horse's speed, but he must save himself and Sleipnir from the anger of the giant, who was one of the fiercest and wickedest of all his fierce and wicked race.

How the eight slender legs of Sleipnir twinkled through the blue sky! How his nostrils quivered and shot forth fire and smoke! Like a flash of lightning he darted across the sky, and the giant horse rumbled and thumped along close behind like the thunder following the flash.

'Hi, hi!' yelled the giant. 'After them, Gullfaxi! And when we have overtaken the two, we will crush their bones between us!'

'Speed, speed, my Sleipnir!' shouted Odin. 'Speed, good horse, or you will never again feed in the dewy pastures of Asgard with the other horses. Speed, speed, and bring us safe within the gates!'

Well Sleipnir understood what his master said, and well he knew the way. Already the rainbow bridge was in sight, with Heimdall the watchman prepared to let them in. His sharp eyes had spied them afar, and had recognized the flash of Sleipnir's white body and of Odin's golden helmet. Gallop and thud! The twelve hoofs were upon the bridge, the giant horse close behind the other. At last Hrungnir knew where he was, and into what danger he was rushing. He pulled at the reins and tried to stop his great beast. But Gullfaxi was tearing along at too terrible a speed. He could not stop. Heimdall threw open the gates of Asgard, and in galloped Sleipnir with his precious burden, safe. Close upon them bolted in Gullfaxi, bearing his giant master, puffing and purple in the face from hard riding and anger. Cling-clang! Heimdall had shut and barred the gates, and there was the giant prisoned in the castle of his enemies.

Now the Aesir were courteous folk, unlike the giants, and they were not anxious to take advantage of a single enemy thus thrown into their power. They invited him to enter Valhalla with them, to rest and sup before the long journey of his return. Thor was not present, so they filled for the giant the great cups which Thor was wont to drain, for they were nearest to the giant size. But you remember that Thor was famous for his power to drink deep. Hrungnir's head was not so steady; Thor's draught was too much for him. He soon lost his wits, of which he had but few; and a witless giant is a most dreadful creature. He raged like a madman, and threatened to pick up Valhalla like a toy house and carry it home with him to Jotunheim. He said he would pull Asgard to pieces and slay all the gods except Freyia the fair and Sif, the golden-haired wife of Thor, whom he would carry off like little dolls for his toy house.

The Aesir knew not what to do, for Thor and his hammer were not there to protect them, and Asgard seemed in danger with this enemy within its very walls. Hrungnir called for more and more mead, which Freyia alone dared to bring and set before him. And the more he drank the fiercer he became. At last the Aesir could bear no longer his insults and his violence. Besides, they feared that there would be no more mead left for their banquets if this unwelcome visitor should keep Freyia pouring out for him Thor's mighty goblets. They bade Heimdall blow his horn and summon Thor; and this Heimdall did in a trice.

Now rumbling and thundering in his chariot of goats came Thor. He dashed into the hall, hammer in hand, and stared in amazement at the unwieldy guest whom he found there.

'A giant feasting in Asgard hall!' he roared. 'This is a sight which I never saw before. Who gave the insolent fellow leave to sit in my place? And why does fair Freyia wait upon him as if he were some noble guest at a feast of the high gods? I will slay him at once!' and he raised the hammer to keep his word.

Thor's coming had sobered the giant somewhat, for he knew that this was no enemy to be trifled with. He looked at Thor sulkily and said: 'I am Odin's guest. He invited me to this banquet, and therefore I am under his protection.'

'You shall be sorry that you accepted the invitation,' cried Thor, balancing his hammer and looking very fierce; for Sif had sobbed in his ear how the giant had threatened to carry her away.

Hrungnir now rose to his feet and faced Thor boldly, for the sound of Thor's gruff voice had restored his scattered wits. 'I am here alone and without weapons,' he said. 'You would do ill to slay me now. It would be little like the noble Thor, of whom we hear tales, to do such a thing. The world will count you braver if you let me go and meet me later in single combat, when we shall both be fairly armed.'

Thor dropped the hammer to his side. 'Your words are true,' he said, for he was a just and honorable fellow.

'I was foolish to leave my shield and stone club at home,' went on the giant. 'If I had my arms with me, we would fight at this moment. But I name you a coward if you slay me now, an unarmed enemy.'

'Your words are just,' quoth Thor again. 'I have never before been challenged by any foe. I will meet you, Hrungnir, at your Stone City, midway between heaven and earth. And there we will fight a duel to see which of us is the better fellow.'

Hrungnir departed for Stone City in Jotunheim; and great was the excitement of the other giants when they heard of the duel which one of their number was to fight with Thor, the deadliest enemy of their race.

'We must be sure that Hrungnir wins the victory!' they cried. 'It will never do to have Asgard victorious in the first duel that we have fought with her champion. We will make a second hero to aid Hrungnir.'

All the giants set to work with a will. They brought great buckets of moist clay, and heaping them up into a huge mound, moulded the mass with their giant hands as a sculptor does his image, until they had made a man of clay, an immense dummy, nine miles high and three miles wide. 'Now we must make him live; we must put a heart into him!' they cried. But they could find no heart big enough until they thought of taking that of a mare, and that fitted nicely. A mare's heart is the most cowardly one that beats.

Hrungnir's heart was a three-cornered piece of hard stone. His head also was of stone, and likewise the great shield which he held before him when he stood outside of Stone City waiting for Thor to come to the duel. Over his shoulder he carried his club, and that also was of stone, the kind from which whetstones are made, hard and terrible. By his side stood the huge clay man, Mockuralfi, and they were a dreadful sight to see, these two vast bodies whom Thor must encounter.

But at the very first sight of Thor, who came thundering to the place with swift Thialfi his servant, the timid mare's heart in the man of clay throbbed with fear; he trembled so that his knees knocked together, and his nine miles of height rocked unsteadily.

Thialfi ran up to Hrungnir and began to mock him, saying, 'You are careless, giant. I fear you do not know what a mighty enemy has come to fight you. You hold your shield in front of you; but that will serve you nothing. Thor has seen this. He has only to go down into the earth and he can attack you conveniently from beneath your very feet.'

At this terrifying news Hrungnir hastened to throw his shield upon the ground and to stand upon it, so that he might be safe from Thor's under-stroke. He grasped his heavy club with both hands and waited. He had not long to wait. There came a blinding flash of lightning and a peal of crashing thunder. Thor had cast his hammer into space. Hrungnir raised his club with both hands and hurled it against the hammer which he saw flying towards him. The two mighty weapons met in the air with an earsplitting shock. Hard as was the stone of the giant's club, it was like glass against the power of Miolnir. The club was dashed into pieces; some fragments fell upon the earth; and these, they say, are the rocks from which whetstones are made unto this day. They are so hard that men use them to sharpen knives and axes and scythes. One splinter of the hard stone struck Thor himself in the forehead, with so fierce a blow that he fell forward upon the ground, and Thialfi feared that he was killed. But Miolnir, not even stopped in its course by meeting the giant's club, sped straight to Hrungnir and crushed his stony skull, so that he fell forward over Thor, and his foot lay on the fallen hero's neck. And that was the end of the giant whose head and heart were of stone.

Meanwhile Thialfi the swift had fought with the man of clay, and had found little trouble in toppling him to earth. For the mare's cowardly heart in his great body gave him little strength to meet Thor's faithful servant; and the trembling limbs of Mockuralfi soon yielded to Thialfi's hearty blows. He fell like an unsteady tower of blocks, and his brittle bulk shivered into a thousand fragments.

Thialfi ran to his master and tried to raise him. The giant's great foot still rested upon his neck, and all Thialfi's strength could not move it away. Swift as the wind he ran for the other Aesir, and when they heard that great Thor, their champion, had fallen and seemed like one dead, they came rushing to the spot in horror and confusion. Together they all attempted to raise Hrungnir's foot from Thor's neck that they might see whether their hero lived or no. But all their efforts were in vain. The foot was not to be lifted by Aesir-might.

At this moment a second hero appeared upon the scene. It was Magni, the son of Thor himself; Magni, who was but three days old, yet already in his babyhood he was almost as big as a giant and had nearly the strength of his father. This wonderful youngster came running to the place where his father lay surrounded by a group of sad-faced and despairing gods. When Magni saw what the matter was, he seized Hrungnir's enormous foot in both his hands, heaved his broad young shoulders, and in a moment Thor's neck was free of the weight which was crushing it.

Best of all, it proved that Thor was not dead, only stunned by the blow of the giant's club and by his fall. He stirred, sat up painfully, and looked around him at the group of eager friends. 'Who lifted the weight from my neck?' he asked.

'It was I, father,' answered Magni modestly. Thor clasped him in his arms and hugged him tight, beaming with pride and gratitude.

'Truly, you are a fine child!' he cried; 'one to make glad your father's heart. Now as a reward for your first great deed you shall have a gift from me. The swift horse of Hrungnir shall be yours, – that same Gullfaxi who was the beginning of all this trouble. You shall ride Gullfaxi; only a giant steed is strong enough to bear the weight of such an infant prodigy as you, my Magni.'

Now this word did not wholly please Father Odin, for he thought that a horse so excellent ought to belong to him. He took Thor aside and argued that but for him there would have been no duel, no horse to win. Thor answered simply:

'True, Father Odin, you began this trouble. But I have fought your battle, destroyed your enemy, and suffered great pain for you. Surely, I have won the horse fairly and may give it to whom I choose. My son, who has saved me, deserves a horse as good as any. Yet, as you have proved, even Gullfaxi is scarce a match for your Sleipnir. Verily, Father Odin, you should be content with the best.' Odin said no more.

Now Thor went home to his cloud-palace in Thrudvang. And there he was healed of all his hurts except that which the splinter of stone had made in his forehead. For the stone was imbedded so fast that it could not be taken out, and Thor suffered sorely therefor. Sif, his yellow-haired wife, was in despair, knowing not what to do. At last she bethought her of the wise woman, Groa, who had skill in all manner of herbs and witch charms. Sif sent for Groa, who lived all alone and sad because her husband Orvandil had disappeared, she knew not whither. Groa came to Thor and, standing beside his bed while he slept, sang strange songs and gently waved her hands over him. Immediately the stone in his forehead began to loosen, and Thor opened his eyes.

'The stone is loosening, the stone is coming out!' he cried. 'How can I reward you, gentle dame? Prithee, what is your name?'

'My name is Groa,' answered the woman, weeping, 'wife of Orvandil who is lost.'

'Now, then, I can reward you, kind Groa!' cried Thor, 'for I can bring you tidings of your husband. I met him in the cold country, in Jotunheim, the Land of Giants, which you know I sometimes visit for a bit of good hunting. It was by Elivagar's icy river that I met Orvandil, and there was no way for him to cross. So I put him in an iron basket and myself bore him over the flood. Br-r-r! But that is a cold land! His feet stuck out through the meshes of the basket, and when we reached the other side one of his toes was frozen stiff. So I broke it off and tossed it up into the sky that it might become a star. To prove that what I relate is true, Groa, there is the new star shining over us at this very moment. Look! From this day it shall be known to men as Orvandil's Toe. Do not you weep any longer. After all, the loss of a toe is a little thing; and I promise that your husband shall soon return to you, safe and sound, but for that small token of his wanderings in the land where visitors are not welcome.'

At these joyful tidings poor Groa was so overcome that she fainted. And that put an end to the charm which she was weaving to loosen the stone from Thor's forehead. The stone was not yet wholly free, and thenceforth it was in vain to attempt its removal; Thor must always wear the splinter in his forehead. Groa could never forgive herself for the carelessness which had thus made her skill vain to help one to whom she had reason to be so grateful.

Now because of the bit of whetstone in Thor's forehead, folk of olden times were very careful how they used a whetstone; and especially they knew that they must not throw or drop one on the floor. For when they did so, the splinter in Thor's forehead was jarred, and the good Asa suffered great pain.

Maui Snaring the Sun

'Maui became restless and fought the sun
With a noose that he laid.
And winter won the sun,
And summer was won by Maui.'
Queen Liliuokalani's family chant.

MAUI IS A DEMI GOD and may mean 'to live' or 'to subsist' and is recognized as belonging to remote Polynesian antiquity. The Maui story is believed to contain a larger number of unique and ancient myths than that of any other legendary character in the mythology of any nation.

A very unique legend, The story of Maui's 'Snaring the Sun' – as a way to explain the legend of the change from short to long days – was told among the Maoris of New Zealand, the Kanakas of the Hervey and Society Islands, and the ancient natives of Hawaii. The Samoans tell the same story without mentioning the name of Maui. They say that the snare was cast by a child of the sun itself. This legend is a misty memory of some time when the Polynesian people were in contact with the short days of the extreme north or south. It is a very remarkable exposition of a fact of nature perpetuated many centuries in lands absolutely free from such natural phenomena. Some of the legends are as follows:

After Maui had succeeded in throwing the heavens into their place, and fastening them so that they could not fall, he learned that he had opened a way for the sun-god to come up from the lower world and rapidly run across the blue vault. This made two troubles for men – the heat of the sun was very great and the journey too quickly over. Maui planned to capture the sun and punish him for thinking so little about the welfare of mankind.

As Rev. A. O. Forbes, a missionary among the Hawaiians, relates, Maui's mother was troubled very much by the heedless haste of the sun. She had many kapa-cloths to make, for this was the only kind of clothing known in Hawaii, except sometimes a woven mat or a long grass fringe worn as a skirt. This native cloth was made by pounding the fine bark of certain trees with wooden mallets until the fibres were beaten and ground into a wood pulp. Then she pounded the pulp into thin sheets from which the best sleeping mats and clothes could be fashioned. These kapa cloths had to be thoroughly dried, but the days were so short that by the time she had spread out the kapa the sun had heedlessly rushed across the sky and gone down into the under-world, and all the cloth had to be gathered up again and cared for until another day should come. There were other troubles. 'The food could not be prepared and cooked in one day. Even an incantation to the gods could not be chanted through ere they were overtaken by darkness.'

This was very discouraging and caused great suffering, as well as much unnecessary trouble and labor. Many complaints were made against the thoughtless sun.

Maui pitied his mother and determined to make the sun go slower that the days might be long enough to satisfy the needs of men. Therefore, he went over to the northwest of the island on which he lived. This was Mt. Iao, an extinct volcano, in which lies one of the most beautiful and picturesque valleys of the Hawaiian Islands. He climbed the ridges until he could see the course of the sun as it passed over the island. He saw that the sun came up the eastern side of Mt. Haleakala.

He crossed over the plain between the two mountains and climbed to the top of Mt. Haleakala. There he watched the burning sun as it came up from Koolau and passed directly over the top of the mountain. The summit of Haleakala is a great extinct crater twenty miles in circumference, and nearly twenty-five hundred feet in depth. There are two tremendous gaps or chasms in the side of the crater wall, through which in days gone by the massive bowl poured forth its flowing lava. One of these was the Koolau, or eastern gap, in which Maui probably planned to catch the sun.

The Hawaiian legend says Maui was taunted by a man who ridiculed the idea that he could snare the sun, saying, 'You will never catch the sun. You are only an idle nobody.'

Maui replied, 'When I conquer my enemy and my desire is attained, I will be your death.'

After studying the path of the sun, Maui returned to his mother and told her that he would go and cut off the legs of the sun so that he could not run so fast.

His mother said: 'Are you strong enough for this work?' He said, 'Yes.' Then she gave him fifteen strands of well-twisted fiber and told him to go to his grandmother, who lived in the great crater of Haleakala, for the rest of the things in his conflict with the sun. She said: 'You must climb the mountain to the place where a large wiliwili tree is standing. There you will find the place where the sun stops to eat cooked bananas prepared by your grandmother. Stay there until a rooster crows three times; then watch your grandmother go out to make a fire and put on food. You had better take her bananas. She will look for them and find you and ask who you are. Tell her you belong to Hina.'

When she had taught him all these things, he went up the mountain to Kaupo to the place Hina had directed. There was a large wiliwili tree. Here he waited for the rooster to crow. The name of that rooster was Kalauhele-moa. When the rooster had crowed three times, the grandmother came out with a bunch of bananas to cook for the sun. She took off the upper part of the bunch and laid it down. Maui immediately snatched it away. In a moment she turned to pick it up, but could not find it. She was angry and cried out: 'Where are the bananas of the sun?' Then she took off another part of the bunch, and Maui stole that. Thus he did until all the bunch had been taken away. She was almost blind and could not detect him by sight, so she sniffed all around her until she detected the smell of a man. She asked: 'Who are you? To whom do you belong?' Maui replied: 'I belong to Hina.' 'Why have you come?' Maui told her, 'I have come to kill the sun. He goes so fast that he never dries the tapa Hina has beaten out.'

The old woman gave a magic stone for a battle axe and one more rope. She taught him how to catch the sun, saying: 'Make a place to hide here by this large wiliwili tree. When the first leg of the sun comes up, catch it with your first rope, and so on until you have used all your ropes. Fasten them to the tree, then take the stone axe to strike the body of the sun.'

Maui dug a hole among the roots of the tree and concealed himself. Soon the first ray of light – the first leg of the sun – came up along the mountain side. Maui threw his rope and caught it. One by one the legs of the sun came over the edge of the crater's rim and were caught. Only one long leg was still hanging down the side of the mountain. It was hard for the sun to move that leg. It shook and trembled and tried hard to come up. At last it crept over the edge and was caught by Maui with the rope given by his grandmother.

When the sun saw that his sixteen long legs were held fast in the ropes, he began to go back down the mountain side into the sea. Then Maui tied the ropes fast to the tree and pulled until the body of the sun came up again. Brave Maui caught his magic stone club or axe, and began to strike and wound the sun, until he cried: 'Give me my life.' Maui said: 'If you live, you may be a traitor. Perhaps I had better kill you.' But the sun begged for life. After they had conversed a while, they agreed that there should be a regular motion in the journey of the sun. There should be longer days, and yet half the time he might go quickly as in the winter time, but the other half he must move slowly as in summer. Thus men dwelling on the earth should be blessed.

* * *

Another legend says that he made a lasso and climbed to the summit of Mt. Haleakala. He made ready his lasso, so that when the sun came up the mountain side and rose above him he could cast the noose and catch the sun, but he only snared one of the sun's larger rays and broke it off. Again and again he threw the lasso until he had broken off all the strong rays of the sun.

Then he shouted exultantly, 'Thou art my captive; I will kill thee for going so swiftly.'

Then the sun said, 'Let me live and thou shalt see me go more slowly hereafter. Behold, hast thou not broken off all my strong legs and left me only the weak ones?'

So the agreement was made, and Maui permitted the sun to pursue his course, and from that day he went more slowly.

* * *

The legend of the Hervey group of islands says that Maui made six snares and placed them at intervals along the path over which the sun must pass. The sun in the form of a man climbed up from Avaiki (Hawaiki). Maui pulled the first noose, but it slipped down the rising sun until it caught and was pulled tight around his feet.

Maui ran quickly to pull the ropes of the second snare, but that also slipped down, down, until it was tightened around the knees. Then Maui hastened to the third snare, while the sun was trying to rush along on his journey. The third snare caught around the hips. The fourth snare fastened itself around the waist. The fifth slipped under the arms, and yet the sun sped along as if but little inconvenienced by Maui's efforts.

Then Maui caught the last noose and threw it around the neck of the sun, and fastened the rope to a spur of rock. The sun struggled until nearly strangled to death and then gave up, promising Maui that he would go as slowly as was desired. Maui left the snares fastened to the sun to keep him in constant fear.

It has been said that 'These ropes may still be seen hanging from the sun at dawn and stretching into the skies when he descends into the ocean at night. By the assistance of these ropes he is gently let down into Ava-iki in the evening, and also raised up out of shadow-land in the morning.'

* * *

Another legend from the Society Islands is related by Mr. Gill: Maui tried many snares before he could catch the sun. The sun was the Hercules, or the Samson, of the heavens. He broke the strong cords of cocoanut fibre which Maui made and placed around the opening by which the sun climbed out from the under-world. Maui made stronger ropes, but still the sun broke them everyone.

Then Maui thought of his sister's hair, the sister Inaika, whom he cruelly treated in later years. Her hair was long and beautiful. He cut off some of it and made a strong rope. With this he lassoed or rather snared the sun, and caught him around the throat. The sun quickly promised to be more thoughtful of the needs of men and go at a more reasonable pace across the sky.

Leading Ladies & Affairs of the Heart

Introduction

BY DEFINITION TRADITIONAL, myth hasn't generally questioned traditional gender roles. The most obviously bold and swashbuckling heroes have been men. Women have of course inspired heroic deeds with their feminine beauty and their gentle softness, but their courage has largely been shown in quieter ways. Theirs has been by and large a heroism of humility, fidelity and patience; of stoic endurance in the face of pain and loss. And a sense of self-sacrifice that can seem to border on the masochistic. Miao Shan, for instance, in the Chinese buddhist tale. She is cruelly abused by the King her father. But – without hesitation – she allows her hands to be cut off and her eyes gouged out to save his life. However uneasy we may be with the implications of such heroines for gender politics, we should nevertheless recognize their importance in the mythic mix, as embodiments of empathy and love.

A Thousand and One Nights: Storyteller Heroine, Scheherazade

IN THE CHRONICLES OF THE ANCIENT DYNASTY of the Sassanidae, who reigned for about four hundred years, from Persia to the borders of China, beyond the great river Ganges itself, we read the praises of one of the kings of this race, who was said to be the best monarch of his time. His subjects loved him, and his neighbors feared him, and when he died he left his kingdom in a more prosperous and powerful condition than any king had done before him.

The two sons who survived him loved each other tenderly, and it was a real grief to the elder, Schahriar, that the laws of the empire forbade him to share his dominions with his brother Schahzeman. Indeed, after ten years, during which this state of things had not ceased to trouble him, Schahriar cut off the country of Great Tartary from the Persian Empire and made his brother king.

Now the Sultan Schahriar had a wife whom he loved more than all the world, and his greatest happiness was to surround her with splendour, and to give her the finest dresses and the most beautiful jewels. It was therefore with the deepest shame and sorrow that he accidentally discovered, after several years, that she had deceived him completely, and her whole conduct turned out to have been so bad, that he felt himself obliged to carry out the law of the land, and order the grand-vizir to put her to death. The blow was so heavy that his mind almost gave way, and he declared that he was quite sure that at bottom all women were as wicked as the sultana, if you could only find them out, and that the fewer the world contained the better. So every evening he married a fresh wife and had her strangled the following morning before the grand-vizir, whose duty it was to provide these unhappy brides for the Sultan. The poor man fulfilled his task with reluctance, but there was no escape, and every day saw a girl married and a wife dead.

This behaviour caused the greatest horror in the town, where nothing was heard but cries and lamentations. In one house was a father weeping for the loss of his daughter, in another perhaps a mother trembling for the fate of her child; and instead of the blessings that had formerly been heaped on the Sultan's head, the air was now full of curses.

The grand-vizir himself was the father of two daughters, of whom the elder was called Scheherazade, and the younger Dinarzade. Dinarzade had no particular gifts to distinguish her from other girls, but her sister was clever and courageous in the highest degree. Her father had given her the best masters in philosophy, medicine, history and the fine arts, and besides all this, her beauty excelled that of any girl in the kingdom of Persia.

One day, when the grand-vizir was talking to his eldest daughter, who was his delight and pride, Scheherazade said to him, 'Father, I have a favour to ask of you. Will you grant it to me?'

'I can refuse you nothing,' replied he, 'that is just and reasonable.'

'Then listen,' said Scheherazade. 'I am determined to stop this barbarous practice of the Sultan's, and to deliver the girls and mothers from the awful fate that hangs over them.'

'It would be an excellent thing to do,' returned the grand-vizir, 'but how do you propose to accomplish it?'

'My father,' answered Scheherazade, 'it is you who have to provide the Sultan daily with a fresh wife, and I implore you, by all the affection you bear me, to allow the honour to fall upon me.'

'Have you lost your senses?' cried the grand-vizir, starting back in horror. 'What has put such a thing into your head? You ought to know by this time what it means to be the sultan's bride!'

'Yes, my father, I know it well,' replied she, 'and I am not afraid to think of it. If I fail, my death will be a glorious one, and if I succeed I shall have done a great service to my country.'

'It is of no use,' said the grand-vizir, 'I shall never consent. If the Sultan was to order me to plunge a dagger in your heart, I should have to obey. What a task for a father! Ah, if you do not fear death, fear at any rate the anguish you would cause me.'

'Once again, my father,' said Scheherazade, 'will you grant me what I ask?'

'What, are you still so obstinate?' exclaimed the grand-vizir. 'Why are you so resolved upon your own ruin?'

But the maiden absolutely refused to attend to her father's words, and at length, in despair, the grand-vizir was obliged to give way, and went sadly to the palace to tell the Sultan that the following evening he would bring him Scheherazade.

The Sultan received this news with the greatest astonishment.

'How have you made up your mind,' he asked, 'to sacrifice your own daughter to me?'

'Sire,' answered the grand-vizir, 'it is her own wish. Even the sad fate that awaits her could not hold her back.'

'Let there be no mistake, vizir,' said the Sultan. 'Remember you will have to take her life yourself. If you refuse, I swear that your head shall pay forfeit.'

'Sire,' returned the vizir. 'Whatever the cost, I will obey you. Though a father, I am also your subject.' So the Sultan told the grand-vizir he might bring his daughter as soon as he liked.

The vizir took back this news to Scheherazade, who received it as if it had been the most pleasant thing in the world. She thanked her father warmly for yielding to her wishes, and, seeing him still bowed down with grief, told him that she hoped he would never repent having allowed her to marry the Sultan. Then she went to prepare herself for the marriage, and begged that her sister Dinarzade should be sent for to speak to her.

When they were alone, Scheherazade addressed her thus:

'My dear sister; I want your help in a very important affair. My father is going to take me to the palace to celebrate my marriage with the Sultan. When his Highness receives me, I shall beg him, as a last favour, to let you sleep in our chamber, so that I may have your company during the last night I am alive. If, as I hope, he grants me my wish, be sure that you wake me an hour before the dawn, and speak to me in these words: 'My sister, if you are not asleep, I beg you, before the sun rises, to tell me one of your charming stories.' Then I shall begin, and I hope by this means to deliver the people from the terror that reigns over them.' Dinarzade replied that she would do with pleasure what her sister wished.

When the usual hour arrived the grand-vizir conducted Scheherazade to the palace, and left her alone with the Sultan, who bade her raise her veil and was amazed at her beauty. But seeing her eyes full of tears, he asked what was the matter. 'Sire,' replied Scheherazade, 'I have a sister who loves me as tenderly as I love her. Grant me the favour of allowing her to sleep this night in the same room, as it is the last we shall be together.' Schahriar consented to Scheherazade's petition and Dinarzade was sent for.

An hour before daybreak Dinarzade awoke, and exclaimed, as she had promised, 'My dear sister, if you are not asleep, tell me I pray you, before the sun rises, one of your charming stories. It is the last time that I shall have the pleasure of hearing you.'

Scheherazade did not answer her sister, but turned to the Sultan. 'Will your highness permit me to do as my sister asks?' said she.

'Willingly,' he answered. So Scheherazade began...

(Scheherazade of course goes on to captivate the Sultan with her stories, always beginning another as soon as she finishes the preceding one, and this way, since he must hear every story's conclusion, postponing her execution. This continues for a thousand and one nights, during which she gives birth to three children and by the end the Sultan has fallen in love and grants her pardon.)

The Princess of Babylon

AS WITH THOSE OF ANCIENT EGYPT AND GREECE, the cultures and mythologies of ancient Mesopotamia have always held a fascination for writers and artists of the modern world, not least because they remain shrouded in a degree of mystery, which has fostered immense flights of imagination. The tale featured here was written by François-Marie Arouet, a.k.a. Voltaire (1694–1778) in 1768.

Though in fact a philosophical satire of European mores, its use of characters inspired by Babylonian names and gods and its initial setting in the exotic, opulent, romanticized world of ancient Babylon is evidence of the enduring appeal of this venerable land and its society.

Chapter 1: Royal Contest for the Hand of Formosanta

The aged Belus, king of Babylon, thought himself the first man upon earth; for all his courtiers told him so, and his historians proved it. We know that his palace and his park, situated at a few parafangs from Babylon, extended between the Euphrates and the Tigris, which washed those enchanted banks. His vast house, three thousand feet in front, almost reached the clouds. The platform was surrounded with a balustrade of white marble, fifty feet high, which supported colossal statues of all the kings and great men of the empire. This platform, composed of two rows of bricks, covered with a thick surface of lead from one extremity to the other, bore twelve feet of earth; and upon the earth were raised groves of olive, orange, citron, palm, cocoa, and cinnamon trees, and stock gillyflowers, which formed alleys that the rays of the sun could not penetrate.

The waters of the Euphrates running, by the assistance of pumps, in a hundred canals, formed cascades of six thousand feet in length in the park, and a hundred thousand jets d'eau, whose height was scarce perceptible. They afterward flowed into the Euphrates, from whence they came. The gardens of Semiramis, which astonished Asia several ages after, were only a feeble imitation of these ancient prodigies, for in the time of Semiramis, everything began to degenerate amongst men and women.

But what was more admirable in Babylon, and eclipsed everything else, was the only daughter of the king, named Formosanta. It was from her pictures and statues, that in succeeding times Praxiteles sculptured his Aphrodita, and the Venus of Medicis. Heavens! what a difference between the original and the copies! so that king Belus was prouder of his daughter than of his kingdom. She was eighteen years old. It was necessary she should have a husband worthy of her; but where was he to be found? An ancient oracle had ordained, that Formosanta could not belong to any but him who could bend the bow of Nimrod.

This Nimrod, 'a mighty hunter before the Lord,' (Gen. x:9), had left a bow seventeen Babylonian feet in length, made of ebony, harder than the iron of mount Caucasus, which is wrought in the forges of Derbent; and no mortal since Nimrod could bend this astonishing bow.

It was again said, 'that the arm which should bend this bow would kill the most terrible and ferocious lion that should be let loose in the Circus of Babylon.' This was not all. The bender of the bow, and the conquerer of the lion, should overthow all his rivals; but he was above all things to be very sagacious, the most magnificent and most virtuous of men, and possess the greatest curiosity in the whole universe.

Three kings appeared, who were bold enough to claim Formosanta. Pharaoh of Egypt, the Shah of India, and the great Khan of the Scythians. Belus appointed the day and place of combat, which was to be at the extremity of his park, in the vast expanse surrounded by the joint waters of the Euphrates and the Tigris. Round the lists a marble amphitheatre was erected, which might contain five hundred thousand spectators. Opposite the amphitheatre was placed the king's throne. He was to appear with Formosanta, accompanied by the whole court; and on the right and left between the throne and the amphitheatre, there were other thrones and seats for the three kings, and for all the other sovereigns who were desirous to be present at this august ceremony.

The king of Egypt arrived the first, mounted upon the bull Apis, and holding in his hand the cithern of Isis. He was followed by two thousand priests, clad in linen vestments whiter than snow, two thousand eunuchs, two thousand magicians, and two thousand warriors.

The king of India came soon after in a car drawn by twelve elephants. He had a train still more numerous and more brilliant than Pharaoh of Egypt.

The last who appeared was the king of the Scythians. He had none with him but chosen warriors, armed with bows and arrows. He was mounted upon a superb tiger, which he had tamed, and which was as tall as any of the finest Persian horses. The majestic and important mien of this king effaced the appearance of his rivals; his naked arms, as nervous as they were white, seemed already to bend the bow of Nimrod.

These three lovers immediately prostrated themselves before Belus and Formosanta. The king of Egypt presented the princess with two of the finest crocodiles of the Nile, two sea horses, two zebras, two Egyptian rats, and two mummies, with the books of the great Hermes, which he judged to be the scarcest things upon earth.

The king of India offered her a hundred elephants, each bearing a wooden gilt tower, and laid at her feet the vedam, written by the hand of Xaca himself.

The king of the Scythians, who could neither write nor read, presented a hundred warlike horses with black fox skin housings.

The princess appeared with a downcast look before her lovers, and reclined herself with such a grace as was at once modest and noble.

Belus ordered the kings to be conducted to the thrones that were prepared for them. 'Would I had three daughters,' said he to them, 'I should make six people this day happy!' He then made the competitors cast lots which should try Nimrod's bow first. Their names inscribed were put into a golden casque. That of the Egyptian king came out first, then the name of the King of India appeared. The king of Scythia, viewing the bow and his rivals, did not complain at being the third.

Whilst these brilliant trials were preparing, twenty thousand pages and twenty thousand youthful maidens distributed, without any disorder, refreshments to the spectators between the rows of seats. Everyone acknowledged that the gods had instituted kings for no other cause than every day to give festivals, upon condition they should be diversified – that life is too short for any other purpose – that lawsuits, intrigues, wars, the altercations of theologists, which consume human life, are horrible and absurd – that man is born only for happiness that he would not passionately and incessantly pursue pleasure, were he not designed for it – that the essence of human nature is to enjoy ourselves, and all the rest is folly. This excellent moral was never controverted but by facts.

Whilst preparations were making for determining the fate of Formosanta, a young stranger, mounted upon an unicorn, accompanied by his valet, mounted on a like animal, and bearing upon his hand a large bird, appeared at the barrier. The guards were surprised to observe in this equipage, a figure that had an air of divinity. He had, as hath been since related, the face of Adonis upon the body of Hercules; it was majesty accompanied by the graces. His black eye-brows and flowing fair tresses, wore a mixture of beauty unknown at Babylon, and charmed all observers. The whole amphitheatre rose up, the better to view the stranger. All the ladies of the court viewed him with looks of astonishment. Formosanta herself, who had hitherto kept her eyes fixed upon the ground, raised them and blushed. The three kings turned pale. The spectators, in comparing Formosanta with the stranger, cried out, 'There is no other in the world, but this young man, who can be so handsome as the princess.'

The ushers, struck with astonishment, asked him if he was a king? The stranger replied, that he had not that honour, but that he had come from a distant country, excited by curiosity, to see if there were any king worthy of Formosanta. He was introduced into the first row of the amphitheatre, with his valet, his two unicorns, and his bird. He saluted, with great respect, Belus, his daughter, the three kings, and all the assembly. He then took his seat, not without blushing. His two unicorns lay down at his feet; his bird perched upon his shoulder; and his valet, who carried a little bag, placed himself by his side.

The trials began. The bow of Nimrod was taken out of its golden case. The first master of the ceremonies, followed by fifty pages, and preceded by twenty trumpets, presented it to the king of Egypt, who made his priests bless it; and supporting it upon the head of the bull Apis, he did not question his gaining this first victory. He dismounted, and came into the middle of the circus. He tries, exerts all his strength, and makes such ridiculous contortions, that the whole amphitheatre re-echoes with laughter, and Formosanta herself could not help smiling.

His high almoner approached him:

'Let your majesty give up this idle honour, which depends entirely upon the nerves and muscles. You will triumph in everything else. You will conquer the lion, as you are possessed of the favour of Osiris. The Princess of Babylon is to belong to the prince who is most sagacious, and you have solved enigmas. She is to wed the most virtuous: you are such, as you have been educated by the priests of Egypt. The most generous is to marry her, and you have presented her with two of the handsomest crocodiles, and two of the finest rats in all the Delta. You are possessed of the bull Apis, and the books of Hermes, which are the scarcest things in the universe. No one can hope to dispute Formosanta with you.'

'You are in the right,' said the King of Egypt, and resumed his throne.

The bow was then put in the hands of the king of India. It blistered his hands for a fortnight; but he consoled himself in presuming that the Scythian King would not be more fortunate than himself.

The Scythian handled the bow in his turn. He united skill with strength. The bow seemed to have some elasticity in his hands. He bent it a little, but he could not bring it near a curve. The spectators, who had been prejudiced in his favour by his agreeable aspect, lamented his ill success, and concluded that the beautiful princess would never be married.

The unknown youth leaped into the arena and addressing himself to the king of Scythia said:

'Your majesty need not be surprised at not having entirely succeeded. These ebony bows are made in my country. There is a peculiar method in using them. Your merit is greater in having bent it, than if I were to curve it.'

He then took an arrow and placing it upon the string, bent the bow of Nimrod, and shot the arrow beyond the gates. A million hands at once applauded the prodigy. Babylon re-echoed with acclamations; and all the ladies agreed it was fortunate for so handsome a youth to be so strong.

He then took out of his pocket a small ivory tablet, wrote upon it with a golden pencil, fixed the tablet to the bow, and then presented it to the princess with such a grace as charmed every spectator. He then modestly returned to his place between his bird and his valet. All Babylon was in astonishment; the three kings were confounded, whilst the stranger did not seem to pay the least attention to what had happened.

Formosanta was still more surprised to read upon the ivory tablet, tied to the bow, these lines, written in the best Chaldean:

The bow of Nimrod is that of war;
The bow of love is that of happiness
Which you possess. Through you this conquering God
Has become master of the earth.
Three powerful kings, – three rivals now,
Dare aspire to the honour of pleasing you.
I know not whom your heart may prefer,
But the universe will be jealous of him.

This little madrigal did not displease the princess; but it was criticised by some of the lords of the ancient court, who said that, in former times, Belus would have been compared to the sun, and Formosanta to the moon; his neck to a tower, and her breast to a bushel of wheat. They said the stranger had no sort of imagination, and that he had lost sight of the rules of true poetry, but all the ladies thought the verses very gallant. They were astonished that a man who handled a bow so well should have so much wit. The lady of honour to the princess said to her:

'Madam, what great talents are here entirely lost? What benefit will this young man derive from his wit, and his skill with Nimrod's bow?'

'Being admired!' said Formosanta.

'Ah!' said the lady, 'one more madrigal, and he might well be beloved.'

The king of Babylon, having consulted his sages, declared that though none of these kings could bend the bow of Nimrod, yet, nevertheless, his daughter was to be married, and that she should belong to him who could conquer the great lion, which was purposely kept in training in his great menagerie.

The king of Egypt, upon whose education all the wisdom of Egypt had been exhausted, judged it very ridiculous to expose a king to the ferocity of wild beasts in order to be married. He acknowledged that he considered the possession of Formosanta of inestimable value; but he believed that if the lion should strangle him, he could never wed this fair Babylonian. The king of India held similar views to the king of Egypt. They both concluded that the king of Babylon was laughing at them, and that they should send for armies to punish him – that they had many subjects who would think themselves highly honoured to die in the service of their masters, without it costing them a single hair of their sacred heads, – that they could easily dethrone the king of Babylon, and then they would draw lots for the fair Formosanta.

This agreement being made, the two kings sent each an express into his respective country, with orders to assemble three hundred thousand men to carry off Formosanta.

However, the king of Scythia descended alone into the arena, scimitar in hand. He was not distractedly enamored with Formosanta's charms. Glory till then had been his only passion, and it had led him to Babylon. He was willing to show that if the kings of India and Egypt were so prudent as not to tilt with lions, he was courageous enough not to decline the combat, and he would repair the honour of diadems. His uncommon valor would not even allow him to avail himself of the assistance of his tiger. He advanced singly, slightly armed with a shell casque ornamented with gold, and shaded with three horses' tails as white as snow.

One of the most enormous and ferocious lions that fed upon the Antilibanian mountains was let loose upon him. His tremendous paws appeared capable of tearing the three kings to pieces at once, and his gullet to devour them. The two proud champions fled with the utmost precipitancy and in the most rapid manner to each other. The courageous Scythian plunged his sword into the lion's mouth; but the point meeting with one of those thick teeth that nothing can penetrate, was broken; and the monster of the woods, more furious from his wound, had already impressed his fearful claws into the monarch's sides.

The unknown youth, touched with the peril of so brave a prince, leaped into the arena swift as lightning, and cut off the lion's head with as much dexterity as we have lately seen, in our carousals, youthful knights knock off the heads of black images.

Then drawing out a small box, he presented it to the Scythian king, saying to him.

'Your majesty will here find the genuine dittany, which grows in my country. Your glorious wounds will be healed in a moment. Accident alone prevented your triumph over the lion. Your valor is not the less to be admired.'

The Scythian king, animated more with gratitude than jealousy, thanked his benefactor; and, after having tenderly embraced him, returned to his seat to apply the dittany to his wounds.

The stranger gave the lion's head to his valet, who, having washed it at the great fountain which was beneath the amphitheatre, and drained all the blood, took an iron instrument out of his little bag, with which having drawn the lion's forty teeth, he supplied their place with forty diamonds of equal size.

His master, with his usual modesty, returned to his place; he gave the lion's head to his bird: 'Beauteous bird,' said he, 'carry this small homage, and lay it at the feet of Formosanta.'

The bird winged its way with the dreadful triumph in one of its talons, and presented it to the princess; bending with humility his neck, and crouching before her. The sparkling diamonds dazzled the eyes of every beholder. Such magnificence was unknown even in superb Babylon. The emerald, the topaz, the sapphire, and the pyrope, were as yet considered as the most precious ornaments. Belus and the whole court were struck with admiration. The bird which presented this present surprised them still more. It was of the size of an eagle, but its eyes were as soft and tender as those of the eagle are fierce and threatening. Its bill was rose colour, and seemed somewhat to resemble Formosanta's handsome mouth. Its neck represented all the colours of Iris, but still more striking and brilliant. Gold, in a thousand shades, glittered upon its plumage. Its feet resembled a mixture of silver and purple. And the tails of those beautiful birds, which have since drawn Juno's car, did not equal the splendor of this incomparable bird.

The attention, curiosity, astonishment, and ecstasy of the whole court were divided between the jewels and the bird. It had perched upon the balustrade between Belus and his daughter Formosanta. She petted it, caressed it, and kissed it. It seemed to receive her attentions with a mixture of pleasure and respect. When the princess gave the bird a kiss, it returned the embrace, and then looked upon her with languishing eyes. She gave it biscuits and pistachios, which it received in its purple-silvered claw, and carried to its bill with inexpressible grace.

Belus, who had attentively considered the diamonds, concluded that scarce any one of his provinces could repay so valuable a present. He ordered that more magnificent gifts should be prepared for the stranger than those destined for the three monarchs, 'This young man,' said he, 'is doubtless son to the emperor of China; or of that part of the world called Europe, which I have heard spoken of; or of Africa, which is said to be in the vicinity of the kingdom of Egypt.'

He immediately sent his first equerry to compliment the stranger, and ask him whether he was himself the sovereign, or son to the sovereign of one of those empires; and why, being possessed of such surprising treasures, he had come with nothing but his valet and a little bag?

Whilst the equerry advanced toward the amphitheatre to execute his commission, another valet arrived upon an unicorn. This valet, addressing himself to the young man, said. 'Ormar, your father is approaching the end of his life: I am come to acquaint you with it.'

The stranger raised his eyes to heaven, whilst tears streamed from them, and answered only by saying, 'Let us depart.'

The equerry, after having paid Belus's compliments to the conqueror of the lion, to the giver of the forty diamonds, and to the master of the beautiful bird, asked the valet, 'Of what kingdom was the father of this young hero sovereign?'

The valet replied:

'His father is an old shepherd, who is much beloved in his district.'

During this conversation, the stranger had already mounted his unicorn. He said to the equerry:

'My lord, vouchsafe to prostrate me at the feet of King Belus and his daughter. I must entreat her to take particular care of the bird I leave with her, as it is a nonpareil like herself.'

In uttering these last words he set off, and flew like lightning. The two valets followed him, and in an instant he was out of sight.

Formosanta could not refrain from shrieking. The bird, turning toward the amphitheatre where his master had been seated, seemed greatly afflicted to find him gone; then viewing steadfastly the princess, and gently rubbing her beautiful hand with his bill, he seemed to devote himself to her service.

Belus, more astonished than ever, hearing that this very extraordinary young man was the son of a shepherd, could not believe it. He dispatched messengers after him; but they soon returned with the information, that the three unicorns, upon which these men were mounted, could not be overtaken; and that, according to the rate they went, they must go a hundred leagues a day.

Everyone reasoned upon this strange adventure, and wearied themselves with conjectures. How can the son of a shepherd make a present of forty large diamonds? How comes it that he is mounted upon an unicorn? This bewildered them, and Formosanta, whilst she caressed her bird, was sunk into a profound reverie.

Chapter 2: The King of Babylon Convenes His Council, and Consults the Oracle

Princess Aldea, Formosanta's cousin-german, who was very well shaped, and almost as handsome as the King's daughter, said to her:

'Cousin, I know not whether this demi-god be the son of a shepherd, but methinks he has fulfilled all the conditions stipulated for your marriage. He has bent Nimrod's bow; he has conquered the lion; he has a good share of sense, having written for you extempore a very pretty madrigal. After having presented you with forty large diamonds, you cannot deny that he is the most generous of men. In his bird he possessed the most curious thing upon earth. His virtue cannot be equaled, since he departed without hesitation as soon as he learned his father was ill, though he might have remained and enjoyed the pleasure of your society. The oracle is fulfilled in every particular, except that wherein he is to overcome his rivals. But he has done more; he has saved the life of the only competitor he had to fear; and when the object is to surpass the other two, I believe you cannot doubt but that he will easily succeed.'

'All that you say is very true,' replied Formosanta: 'but is it possible that the greatest of men, and perhaps the most amiable too, should be the son of a shepherd?'

The lady of honour, joining in the conversation, said that the title of shepherd was frequently given to kings – that they were called shepherds because they attended very closely to their flocks – that this was doubtless a piece of ill-timed pleasantry in his valet – that this young hero had not come so badly equipped, but to show how much his personal merit alone was above the fastidious parade of kings. The princess made no answer, but in giving her bird a thousand tender kisses.

A great festival was nevertheless prepared for the three kings, and for all the princes who had come to the feast. The king's daughter and niece were to do the honours. The king distributed presents worthy the magnificence of Babylon. Belus, during the time the repast was being served, assembled his council to discuss the marriage of the beautiful Formosanta, and this is the way he delivered himself as a great politician:

'I am old: I know not what is best to do with my daughter, or upon whom to bestow her. He who deserves her is nothing but a mean shepherd. The kings of India and Egypt are cowards. The king of the Scythians would be very agreeable to me, but he has not performed any one of the conditions imposed. I will again consult the oracle. In the meantime, deliberate among you, and we will conclude agreeably to what the oracle says; for a king should follow nothing but the dictates of the immortal gods.'

He then repaired to the temple: the oracle answered in few words according to custom: Thy daughter shall not be married until she hath traversed the globe. In astonishment, Belus returned to the council, and related this answer.

All the ministers had a profound respect for oracles. They therefore all agreed, or at least appeared to agree, that they were the foundation of religion – that reason should be mute before them – that it was by their means that kings reigned over their people – that without oracles there would be neither virtue nor repose upon earth.

At length, after having testified the most profound veneration for them, they almost all concluded that this oracle was impertinent, and should not be obeyed – that nothing could be more indecent for a young woman, and particularly the daughter of the great king of Babylon, than to run about, without any particular destination – that this was the most certain method to prevent her being married, or else engage her in a clandestine, shameful, and ridiculous union that, – in a word, this oracle had not common sense.

The youngest of the ministers, named Onadase, who had more sense than the rest, said that the oracle doubtless meant some pilgrimage of devotion, and offered to be the princess's guide. The council approved of his opinion, but everyone was for being her equerry. The king determined that the princess might go three hundred parasangs upon the road to Arabia, to the temple whose saint had the reputation of procuring young women happy marriages, and that the dean of the council should accompany her. After this determination they went to supper.

Chapter 3: Royal Festival Given in Honour of The Kingly Visitors

In the centre of the gardens, between two cascades, an oval saloon, three hundred feet in diameter was erected, whose azure roof, intersected with golden stars, represented all the constellations and planets, each in its proper station; and this ceiling turned about, as well as the canopy, by machines as invisible as those which direct the celestial spheres. A hundred thousand flambeaux, inclosed in rich crystal cylinders, illuminated the gardens and the dining-hall. A buffet, with steps, contained twenty thousand vases and golden dishes; and opposite the buffet, upon other steps, were seated a great number of musicians. Two other amphitheatres were decked out; the one with the fruits of each season, the other with crystal decanters, that sparkled with the choicest wines.

The guests took their seats round a table divided into compartments that resembled flowers and fruits, all in precious stones. The beautiful Formosanta was placed between the kings of India and Egypt – the amiable Aldea next the king of Scythia. There were about thirty princes, and each was seated next one of the handsomest ladies of the court. The king of Babylon, who was in the middle, opposite his daughter, seemed divided between the chagrin of being yet unable to effect her marriage, and the pleasure of still beholding her. Formosanta asked leave to place her bird upon the table next her; the king approved of it.

The music, which continued during the repast, furnished every prince with an opportunity of conversing with his female neighbour. The festival was as agreeable as it was magnificent. A ragout was served before Formosanta, which her father was very fond of. The princess said it should be carried to his majesty. The bird immediately took hold of it, and carried it in a miraculous manner to the king. Never was any thing more astonishing witnessed. Belus caressed it as much as his daughter had done. The bird afterward took its flight to return to her. It displayed, in flying, so fine a tail, and its extended wings set forth such a variety of brilliant colours – the gold of its plumage made such a dazzling eclat, that all eyes were fixed upon it. All the musicians were struck motionless, and their instruments afforded harmony no longer. None ate, no one spoke, nothing but a buzzing of admiration was to be heard. The Princess of Babylon kissed it during the whole supper, without considering whether there were any kings in the world. Those of India and Egypt felt their spite and indignation rekindle with double force, and they resolved speedily to set their three hundred thousand men in motion to obtain revenge.

As for the king of Scythia, he was engaged in entertaining the beautiful Aldea. His haughty soul despising, without malice, Formosanta's inattention, had conceived for her more indifference than resentment. 'She is handsome,' said he, 'I acknowledge: but she appears to me one of those women who are entirely taken up with their own beauty, and who fancy that mankind are greatly obliged to them when they deign to appear in public. I should prefer an ugly complaisant woman, that exhibited some amiability, to that beautiful statue. You have, madam, as many charms as she possesses, and you, at least, condescend to converse with strangers. I acknowledge to you with the sincerity of a Scythian, that I prefer you to your cousin.'

He was, however, mistaken in regard to the character of Formosanta. She was not so disdainful as she appeared. But his compliments were very well received by the princess Aldea. Their conversation became very interesting. They were well contented, and already certain of one another before they left the table. After supper the guests walked in the groves. The king of Scythia and Aldea did not fail to seek for a place of retreat. Aldea, who was sincerity itself, thus declared herself to the prince:

'I do not hate my cousin, though she be handsomer than myself, and is destined for the throne of Babylon. The honour of pleasing you may very well stand in the stead of charms. I prefer Scythia with you, to the crown of Babylon without you. But this crown belongs to me by right, if there be any right in the world; for I am of the elder branch of the Nimrod family, and Formosanta is only of the younger. Her grandfather dethroned mine, and put him to death.'

'Such, then, are the rights of inheritance in the royal house of Babylon!' said the Scythian. 'What was your grandfather's name?'

'He was called Aldea, like me. My father bore the same name. He was banished to the extremity of the empire with my mother; and Belus, after their death, having nothing to fear from me, was willing to bring me up with his daughter. But he has resolved that I shall never marry.'

'I will avenge the cause of your grandfather – of your father and also your own cause,' said the king of Scythia. 'I am responsible for your being married. I will carry you off the day after to-morrow by day-break – for we must dine to-morrow with the king of Babylon – and I will return and support your rights with three hundred thousand men.'

'I agree to it,' said the beauteous Aldea: and, after having mutually pledged their words of honour, they separated.

The incomparable Formosanta, before retiring to rest, had ordered a small orange tree, in a silver case, to be placed by the side of her bed, that her bird might perch upon it. Her curtains had long been drawn, but she was not in the least disposed to sleep. Her heart was agitated, and her imagination excited. The charming stranger was ever in her thoughts. She fancied she saw him shooting an arrow with Nimrod's bow. She contemplated him in the act of cutting off the lion's head. She repeated his madrigal. At length, she saw him retiring from the crowd upon his unicorn. Tears, sighs, and lamentations overwhelmed her at this reflection. At intervals, she cried out: 'Shall I then never see him more? Will he never return?'

'He will surely return,' replied the bird from the top of the orange tree. 'Can one have seen you once, and not desire to see you again?'

'Heavens! eternal powers! my bird speaks the purest Chaldean.' In uttering these words she drew back the curtain, put out her hand to him, and knelt upon her bed, saying:

'Art thou a god descended upon earth? Art thou the great Oromasdes concealed under this beautiful plumage? If thou art, restore me this charming young man.'

'I am nothing but a winged animal,' replied the bird; 'but I was born at the time when all animals still spoke; when birds, serpents, asses, horses, and griffins, conversed familiarly with man. I would not speak before company, lest your ladies of honour should have taken me for a sorcerer. I would not discover myself to any but you.'

Formosanta was speechless, bewildered, and intoxicated with so many wonders. Desirous of putting a hundred questions to him at once, she at length asked him how old he was.

'Only twenty-seven thousand nine hundred years and six months. I date my age from the little revolution of the equinoxes, and which is accomplished in about twenty-eight thousand of your years. There are revolutions of a much greater extent, so are there beings much older than me. It is twenty-two thousand years since I learnt Chaldean in one of my travels. I have always had a very great taste for the Chaldean language, but my brethren, the other animals, have renounced speaking in your climate.'

'And why so, my divine bird?'

'Alas! because men have accustomed themselves to eat us, instead of conversing and instructing themselves with us. Barbarians! should they not have been convinced, that having the same organs with them, the same sentiments, the same wants, the same desires, we have also what is called a soul, the same as themselves; – that we are their brothers, and that none should be dressed and eaten but the wicked? We are so far your brothers, that the Supreme Being, the Omnipotent and Eternal Being, having made a compact with men, expressly comprehended us in the treaty. He forbade you to nourish yourselves with our blood, and we to suck yours.

'The fables of your ancient Locman, translated into so many languages, will be a testimony eternally subsisting of the happy commerce you formerly carried on with us. They all begin with these words: 'In the time when beasts spoke'. It is true, there are many families among you who keep up an incessant conversation with their dogs; but the dogs have resolved not to answer, since they have been compelled by whipping to go a hunting, and become accomplices in the murder of our ancient and common friends, stags, deers, hares, and partridges.

'You have still some ancient poems in which horses speak, and your coachmen daily address them in words; but in so barbarous a manner, and in uttering such infamous expressions, that horses, though formerly entertaining so great a kindness for you, now detest you.

'The country which is the residence of your charming stranger, the most perfect of men, is the only one in which your species has continued to love ours, and to converse with us; and this is the only country in the world where men are just.'

'And where is the country of my dear incognito? What is the name of his empire? For I will no more believe he is a shepherd than that you are a bat.'

'His country, is that of the Gangarids, a wise, virtuous, and invincible people, who inhabit the eastern shore of the Ganges. The name of my friend is Amazan. He is no king; and I know not whether he would so humble himself as to be one. He has too great a love for his fellow countrymen. He is a shepherd like them. But do not imagine that those shepherds resemble yours; who, covered with rags and tatters, watch their sheep, who are better clad than themselves; who groan under the burden of poverty, and who pay to an extortioner half the miserable stipend of wages which they receive from their masters. The Gangaridian shepherds are all born equal, and own the innumerable herds which cover their vast fields and subsist on the abundant verdure. These flocks are never killed. It is a horrid crime, in that favoured country, to kill and eat a fellow creature. Their wool is finer and more brilliant than the finest silk, and constitutes the greatest traffic of the East. Besides, the land of the Gangarids produces all that can flatter the desires of man. Those large diamonds that Amazan had the honour of presenting you with, are from a mine that belongs to him. An unicorn, on which you saw him mounted, is the usual animal the Gangarids ride upon. It is the finest, the proudest, most terrible, and at the same time most gentle animal that ornaments the earth. A hundred Gangarids, with as many unicorns, would be sufficient to disperse innumerable armies. Two centuries ago, a king of India was mad enough to attempt to conquer this nation. He appeared, followed by ten thousand elephants and a million of warriors. The unicorns pierced the elephants, just as I have seen upon your table beads pierced in golden brochets. The warriors fell under the sabres of the Gangarids like crops of rice mowed by the people of the East. The king was taken prisoner, with upwards of six thousand men. He was bathed in the salutary water of the Ganges, and followed the regimen of the country, which consists only of vegetables, of which nature hath there been amazingly liberal to nourish every breathing creature. Men who are fed with carnivorous aliments, and drenched with spirituous liquors, have a sharp adust blood, which turns their brains a hundred different ways. Their chief rage is a fury to spill their brother's blood, and, laying waste fertile plains, to reign over church-yards. Six full months were taken up in curing the king of India of his disorder. When the physicians judged that his pulse had become natural, they certified this to the council of the Gangarids. The council then followed the advice of the unicorns and humanely sent back the king of India, his silly court, and impotent warriors, to their own country. This lesson made them wise, and from that time the Indians respected the Gangarids, as ignorant men, willing to be instructed, revere the philosophers they cannot equal.

'Apropos, my dear bird,' said the princess to him, 'do the Gangarids profess any religion? have they one?'

'Yes, we meet to return thanks to God on the days of the full moon; the men in a great temple made of cedar, and the women in another, to prevent their devotion being diverted. All the birds assemble in a grove, and the quadrupeds on a fine down. We thank God for all the benefits he has bestowed upon us. We have in particular some parrots that preach wonderfully well.

'Such is the country of my dear Amazan; there I reside. My friendship for him is as great as the love with which he has inspired you. If you will credit me, we will set out together, and you shall pay him a visit.'

'Really, my dear bird, this is a very pretty invitation of yours,' replied the princess smiling, and who flamed with desire to undertake the journey, but did not dare say so.

'I serve my friend,' said the bird; 'and, after the happiness of loving you, the greatest pleasure is to assist you.'

Formosanta was quite fascinated. She fancied herself transported from earth. All she had seen that day, all she then saw, all she heard, and particularly what she felt in her heart, so ravished her as far to surpass what those fortunate muslims now feel, who, disencumbered from their terrestrial ties, find themselves in the ninth heaven in the arms of their Houris, surrounded and penetrated with glory and celestial felicity.

Chapter 4: The Beautiful Bird is Killed by The King of Egypt

Formosanta passed the whole night in speaking of Amazan. She no longer called him any thing but her shepherd; and from this time it was that the names of shepherd and lover were indiscriminately used throughout every nation.

Sometimes she asked the bird whether Amazan had had any other mistresses. It answered, 'No,' and she was at the summit of felicity. Sometimes she asked how he passed his life; and she, with transport, learned, that it was employed in doing good; in cultivating arts, in penetrating into the secrets of nature, and improving himself. She at times wanted to know if the soul of her lover was of the same nature as that of her bird; how it happened that it had lived twenty thousand years, when her lover was not above eighteen or nineteen. She put a hundred such questions, to which the bird replied with such discretion as excited her curiosity. At length sleep closed their eyes, and yielded up Formosanta to the sweet delusion of dreams sent by the gods, which sometimes surpass reality itself, and which all the philosophy of the Chaldeans can scarce explain.

Formosanta did not awaken till very late. The day was far advanced when the king, her father, entered her chamber. The bird received his majesty with respectful politeness, went before him, fluttered his wings, stretched his neck, and then replaced himself upon his orange tree. The king seated himself upon his daughter's bed, whose dreams had made her still more beautiful. His large beard approached her lovely face, and after having embraced her, he spoke to her in these words:

'My dear daughter, you could not yesterday find a husband agreeable to my wishes; you nevertheless must marry; the prosperity of my empire requires it. I have consulted the oracle, which you know never errs, and which directs all my conduct. His commands are, that you should traverse the globe. You must therefore begin your journey.'

'Ah! doubtless to the Gangarids,' said the princess; and in uttering these words, which escaped her, she was sensible of her indiscretion. The king, who was utterly ignorant of geography, asked her what she meant by the Gangarids? She easily diverted the question. The king told her she must go on a pilgrimage, that he had appointed the persons who were to attend her – the dean of the counsellors of state, the high almoner, a lady of honour, a physician, an apothecary, her bird, and all necessary domestics.

Formosanta, who had never been out of her father's palace, and who, till the arrival of the three kings and Amazan, had led a very insipid life, according to the etiquette of rank and the parade of pleasure, was charmed at setting out upon a pilgrimage. 'Who knows,' said she, whispering to her heart, 'if the gods may not inspire Amazan with the like desire of going to the same chapel, and I may have the happiness of again seeing the pilgrim?' She affectionately thanked her father, saying she had always entertained a secret devotion for the saint she was going to visit.

Belus gave an excellent dinner to his guests, who were all men. They formed a very ill assorted company – kings, ministers, princes, pontiffs – all jealous of each other; all weighing their words, and equally embarassed with their neighbours and themselves. The repast was very gloomy, though they drank pretty freely. The princesses remained in their apartments, each meditating upon her respective journey. They dined at their little cover. Formosanta afterward walked in the gardens with her dear bird, which, to amuse her, flew from tree to tree, displaying his superb tail and divine plumage.

The king of Egypt, who was heated with wine, not to say drunk, asked one of his pages for a bow and arrow. This prince was, in truth, the most unskilful archer in his whole kingdom. When he shot at a mark, the place of the greatest safety was generally the spot he aimed at. But the beautiful bird, flying as swiftly as the arrow, seemed to court it, and fell bleeding in the arms of Formosanta. The Egyptian, bursting into a foolish laugh, retired to his place. The princess rent the skies with her moans, melted into tears, tore her hair, and beat her breast. The dying bird said to her, in a low voice:

'Burn me, and fail not to carry my ashes to the east of the ancient city of Aden or Eden, and expose them to the sun upon a little pile of cloves and cinnamon.' After having uttered these words it expired. Formosanta was for a long time in a swoon, and revived again only to burst into sighs and groans. Her father, partaking of her grief, and imprecating the king of Egypt, did not doubt but this accident foretold some fatal event. He immediately went to consult the oracle, which replied: A mixture of everything – life and death, infidelity and constancy, loss and gain, calamities and good fortune. Neither he nor his council could comprehend any meaning in this reply; but, at length, he was satisfied with having fulfilled the duties of devotion.

His daughter was bathed in tears, whilst he consulted the oracle. She paid the funeral obsequies to the bird, which it had directed, and resolved to carry its remains into Arabia at the risk of her life. It was burned in incombustible flax, with the orange-tree on which it used to perch. She gathered up the ashes in a little golden vase, set with rubies, and the diamonds taken from the lion's mouth. Oh! that she could, instead of fulfilling this melancholy duty, have burned alive the detestable king of Egypt! This was her sole wish. She, in spite, put to death the two crocodiles, his two sea horses, his two zebras, his two rats, and had his two mummies thrown into the Euphrates. Had she possessed his bull Apis, she would not have spared him.

The king of Egypt, enraged at this affront, set out immediately to forward his three hundred thousand men. The king of India, seeing his ally depart, set off also on the same day, with a firm intention of joining his three hundred thousand Indians to the Egyptian army, the king of Scythia decamped in the night with the princess Aldea, fully resolved to fight for her at the head of three hundred thousand Scythians, and to restore to her the inheritance of Babylon, which was her right, as she had descended from the elder branch of the Nimrod family.

As for the beautiful Formosanta, she set out at three in the morning with her caravan of pilgrims, flattering herself that she might go into Arabia, and execute the last will of her bird; and that the justice of the gods would restore her the dear Amazan, without whom life had become insupportable.

When the king of Babylon awoke, he found all the company gone.

'How mighty festivals terminate,' said he; 'and what a surprising vacuum they leave when the hurry is over.'

But he was transported with a rage truly royal, when he found that the princess Aldea had been carried off. He ordered all his ministers to be called up, and the council to be convened. Whilst they were dressing, he failed not to consult the oracle; but the only answer he could obtain was in these words, so celebrated since throughout the universe: When girls are not provided for in marriage by their relatives, they marry themselves.

Orders were immediately issued to march three hundred thousand men against the king of Scythia. Thus was the torch of a most dreadful war lighted up, which was caused by the amusements of the finest festival ever given upon earth. Asia was upon the point of being overrun by four armies of three hundred thousand men each. It is plain that the war of Troy, which astonished the world some ages after, was mere child's play in comparison to this; but it should also be considered, that in the Trojans quarrel, the object was nothing more than a very immoral old woman, who had contrived to be twice run away with; whereas, in this case, the cause was tripartite – two girls and a bird.

The king of India went to meet his army upon the large fine road which then led straight to Babylon, at Cachemir. The king of Scythia flew with Aldea by the fine road which led to Mount Imaus. Owing to bad government, all these fine roads have disappeared in the lapse of time. The king of Egypt had marched to the west, along the coast of the little Mediterranean sea, which the ignorant Hebrews have since called the Great Sea.

As to the charming Formosanta, she pursued the road to Bassora, planted with lofty palm trees, which furnished a perpetual shade, and fruit at all seasons. The temple in which she was to perform her devotions, was in Bassora itself. The saint to whom this temple had been dedicated, was somewhat in the style of him who was afterward adored at Lampsacus, and was generally successful in procuring husbands for young ladies. Indeed, he was the holiest saint in all Asia.

Formosanta had no sort of inclination for the saint of Bassora. She only invoked her dear Gangaridian shepherd, her charming Amazan. She proposed embarking at Bassora, and landing in Arabia Felix, to perform what her deceased bird had commanded.

At the third stage, scarce had she entered into a fine inn, where her harbingers had made all the necessary preparations for her, when she learned that the king of Egypt had arrived there also. Informed by his emissaries of the princess's route, he immediately altered his course, followed by a numerous escort. Having alighted, he placed sentinels at all the doors; then repaired to the beautiful Formosanta's apartment, when he addressed her by saying:

'Miss, you are the lady I was in quest of. You paid me very little attention when I was at Babylon. It is just to punish scornful capricious women. You will, if you please, be kind enough to sup with me to-night; and I shall behave to you according as I am satisfied with you.'

Formosanta saw very well that she was not the strongest. She judged that good sense consisted in knowing how to conform to one's situation. She resolved to get rid of the king of Egypt by an innocent stratagem. She looked at him through the corners of her eyes, (which in after ages has been called ogling,) and then she spoke to him, with a modesty, grace, and sweetness, a confusion, and a thousand other charms, which would have made the wisest man a fool, and deceived the most discerning:

'I acknowledge, sir, I always appeared with a downcast look, when you did the king, my father, the honour of visiting him. I had some apprehensions for my heart. I dreaded my too great simplicity. I trembled lest my father and your rivals should observe the preference I gave you, and which you so highly deserved. I can now declare my sentiments. I swear by the bull Apis, which after you is the thing I respect the most in the world, that your proposals have enchanted me. I have already supped with you at my father's, and I will sup with you again, without his being of the party. All that I request of you is, that your high almoner should drink with us. He appeared to me at Babylon to be an excellent guest. I have some Chiras wine remarkably good. I will make you both taste it. I consider you as the greatest of kings, and the most amiable of men.'

This discourse turned the king of Egypt's head. He agreed to have the almoner's company.

'I have another favour to ask of you,' said the princess, 'which is to allow me to speak to my apothecary. Women have always some little ails that require attention, such as vapours in the head, palpitations of the heart, colics, and the like, which often require some assistance. In a word, I at present stand in need of my apothecary, and I hope you will not refuse me this slight testimony of confidence.'

'Miss,' replied the king of Egypt, 'I know life too well to refuse you so just a demand. I will order the apothecary to attend you whilst supper is preparing. I imagine you must be somewhat fatigued by the journey; you will also have occasion for a chambermaid; you may order her you like best to attend you. I will afterward wait your commands and convenience.'

He then retired, and the apothecary and the chambermaid, named Irla, entered. The princess had an entire confidence in her. She ordered her to bring six bottles of Chiras wine for supper, and to make all the sentinels, who had her officers under arrest, drink the same. Then she recommended her apothecary to infuse in all the bottles certain pharmaceutic drugs, which make those who take them sleep twenty-four hours, and with which he was always provided. She was implicitly obeyed. The king returned with his high almoner in about half an hour's time. The conversation at supper was very gay. The king and the priest emptied the six bottles, and acknowledged there was not such good wine in Egypt. The chambermaid was attentive to make the servants in waiting drink. As for the princess, she took great care not to drink any herself, saying that she was ordered by her physician a particular regimen. They were all presently asleep.

The king of Egypt's almoner had one of the finest beards that a man of his rank could wear. Formosanta lopped it off very skillfully; then sewing it to a ribbon, she put it on her own chin. She then dressed herself in the priest's robes, and decked herself in all the marks of his dignity, and her waiting maid clad herself like the sacristan of the goddess Isis. At length, having furnished herself with his urn and jewels, she set out from the inn amidst the sentinels, who were asleep like their master. Her attendant had taken care to have two horses ready at the door. The princess could not take with her any of the officers of her train. They would have been stopped by the great guard.

Formosanta and Irla passed through several ranks of soldiers, who, taking the princess for the high priest, called her, 'My most Reverend Father in God,' and asked his blessing. The two fugitives arrived in twenty-four hours at Bassora, before the king awoke. They then threw off their disguise, which might have created some suspicion. They fitted out with all possible expedition a ship, which carried them, by the Straits of Ormus, to the beautiful banks of Eden in Arabia Felix. This was that Eden, whose gardens were so famous, that they have since been the residence of the best of mankind. They were the model of the Elysian fields, the gardens of the Hesperides, and also those of the Fortunate Islands. In those warm climates men imagined there could be no greater felicity than shades and murmuring brooks. To live eternally in heaven with the Supreme Being, or to walk in the garden of paradise, was the same thing to those who incessantly spoke without understanding one another, and who could scarce have any distinct ideas or just expressions.

As soon as the princess found herself in this land, her first care was to pay her dear bird the funeral obsequies he had required of her. Her beautiful hands prepared a small quantity of cloves and cinnamon. What was her surprise, when, having spread the ashes of the bird upon this funeral pyre, she saw it blaze of itself! All was presently consumed. In the place of the ashes there appeared nothing but a large egg, from whence she saw her bird issue more brilliant than ever. This was one of the most happy moments the princess had ever experienced in her whole life. There was but another that could ever be dearer to her; it was the object of her wishes, but almost beyond her hopes.

'I plainly see,' said she, to the bird, 'you are the phoenix which I have heard so much spoken of. I am almost ready to expire with joy and astonishment. I did not believe in your resurrection; but it is my good fortune to be convinced of it.'

'Resurrection, in fact,' said the phoenix to her, 'is one of the most simple things in the world. There is nothing more in being born twice than once. Everything in this world is the effect of resurrection. Caterpillars are regenerated into butterflies; a kernel put into the earth is regenerated into a tree. All animals buried in the earth regenerate into vegetation, herbs, and plants, and nourish other animals, of which they speedily compose part of the substance. All particles which compose bodies are transformed into different beings. It is true, that I am the only one to whom Oromasdes has granted the favour of regenerating in my own form.'

Formosanta, who from the moment she first saw Amazan and the phoenix, had passed all her time in a round of astonishment, said to him:

'I can easily conceive that the Supreme Being may form out of your ashes a phoenix nearly resembling yourself; but that you should be precisely the same person, that you should have the same soul, is a thing, I acknowledge, I cannot very clearly comprehend. What became of your soul when I carried you in my pocket after your death?'

'Reflect one moment! Is it not as easy for the great Oromasdes to continue action upon a single atom of my being, as to begin afresh this action? He had before granted me sensation, memory, and thought. He grants them to me again. Whether he united this favour to an atom of elementary fire, latent within me, or to the assemblage of my organs, is, in reality, of no consequence. Men, as well as phoenixes, are entirely ignorant how things come to pass, but the greatest favour the Supreme Being has bestowed upon me, is to regenerate me for you. Oh! that I may pass the twenty-eight thousand years which I have still to live before my next resurrection, with you and my dear Amazan.'

'My dear phoenix, remember what you first told me at Babylon, which I shall never forget, and which flattered me with the hope of again seeing my dear shepherd, whom I idolize; 'we must absolutely pay the Gangarids a visit together', and I must carry Amazan back with me to Babylon.'

'This is precisely my design,' said the phoenix. 'There is not a moment to lose. We must go in search of Amazan by the shortest road, that is, through the air. There are in Arabia Felix two griffins, who are my particular friends, and who live only a hundred and fifty thousand leagues from here. I am going to write to them by the pigeon post, and they will be here before night. We shall have time to make you a convenient palankeen, with drawers, in which you may place your provisions. You will be quite at your ease in this vehicle, with your maid. These two griffins are the most vigorous of their kind. Each of them will support one of the poles of the canopy between their claws. But, once for all, time is very precious.'

He instantly went with Formosanta to order the carriage at an upholsterer's of his acquaintance. It was made complete in four hours. In the drawers were placed small fine loaves, biscuits superior to those of Babylon, large lemons, pine-apples, cocoa, and pistachio nuts, Eden wine, which is as superior to that of Chiras, as Chiras is to that of Surinam.

The two griffins arrived at Eden at the appointed time. The vehicle was as light as it was commodious and solid, and Formosanta and Irla placed themselves in it. The two griffins carried it off like a feather. The phoenix sometimes flew after it, and sometimes perched upon its roof. The two griffins winged their way toward the Ganges with the velocity of an arrow which rends the air. They never stopped but a moment at night for the travelers to take some refreshment, and the carriers to take a draught of water.

They at length reached the country of the Gangarids. The princess's heart palpitated with hope, love, and joy. The phoenix stopped the vehicle before Amazan's house; but Amazan had been absent from home three hours, without any one knowing where he had gone.

There are no words, even in the Gangaridian language, that could express Formosanta's extreme despair.

'Alas! this is what I dreaded,' said the phoenix: 'the three hours which you passed at the inn, upon the road to Bassora, with that wretched king of Egypt, have perhaps been at the price of the happiness of your whole life. I very much fear we have lost Amazan, without the possibility of recovering him.'

He then asked the servants if he could salute the mother of Amazan? They answered, that her husband had died only two days before, and she could speak to no one. The phoenix, who was not without influence in the house, introduced the princess of Babylon into a saloon, the walls of which were covered with orange-tree wood inlaid with ivory. The inferior shepherds and shepherdesses, who were dressed in long white garments, with gold coloured trimmings, served up, in a hundred plain porcelain baskets, a hundred various delicacies, amongst which no disguised carcasses were to be seen. They consisted of rice, sago, vermicelli, macaroni, omelets, milk, eggs, cream, cheese, pastry of every kind, vegetables, fruits, peculiarly fragrant and grateful to the taste, of which no idea can be formed in other climates; and they were accompanied with a profusion of refreshing liquors superior to the finest wine.

Whilst the princess regaled herself, seated upon a bed of roses, four peacocks, who were luckily mute, fanned her with their brilliant wings; two hundred birds, one hundred shepherds and shepherdesses, warbled a concert in two different choirs; the nightingales, thistlefinches, linnets, chaffinches, sung the higher notes with the shepherdesses, and the shepherds sung the tenor and bass. The princess acknowledged, that if there was more magnificence at Babylon, nature was infinitely more agreeable among the Gangarids; but whilst this consolatory and voluptuous music was playing, tears flowed from her eyes, whilst she said to the damsel Irla:

'These shepherds and shepherdesses, these nightingales, these linnets, are making love; and for my part, I am deprived of the company of the Gangaridian hero, the worthy object of my most tender thoughts.'

Whilst she was taking this collation, her tears and admiration kept pace with each other, and the phoenix addressed himself to Amazan's mother, saying:

'Madam, you cannot avoid seeing the princess of Babylon; you know –'

'I know everything,' said she, 'even her adventure at the inn, upon the road to Bassora. A blackbird related the whole to me this morning; and this cruel blackbird is the cause of my son's going mad, and leaving his paternal abode.'

'You have not been informed, then, that the princess regenerated me?'

'No, my dear child, the blackbird told me you were dead, and this made me inconsolable. I was so afflicted at this loss, the death of my husband, and the precipitate flight of my son, that I ordered my door to be shut to everyone. But since the princess of Babylon has done me the honour of paying me a visit, I beg she may be immediately introduced. I have matters of great importance to acquaint her with, and I choose you should be present.'

She then went to meet the princess in another saloon. She could not walk very well. This lady was about three hundred years old; but she had still some agreeable vestiges of beauty. It might be conjectured, that about her two hundred and fortieth, or two hundred and fiftieth year, she must have been a most charming woman. She received Formosanta with a respectful nobleness, blended with an air of interest and sorrow, which made a very lively impression upon the princess.

Formosanta immediately paid her the compliments of condolence upon her husband's death.

'Alas!' said the widow, 'you have more reason to lament his death than you imagine.'

'I am, doubtless, greatly afflicted,' said Formosanta; 'he was father to –.' Here a flood of tears prevented her from going on. 'For his sake only I undertook this journey, in which I have so narrowly escaped many dangers. For him I left my father, and the most splendid court in the universe. I was detained by a King of Egypt, whom I detest. Having escaped from this tyrant, I have traversed the air in search of the only man I love. When I arrive, he flies from me!' Here sighs and tears stopped her impassioned harangue.

His mother then said to her:

'When the king of Egypt made you his prisoner, – when you supped with him at an inn upon the road to Bassora, – when your beautiful hands filled him bumpers of Chiras wine, did you observe a blackbird that flew about the room?'

'Yes, really,' said the princess, 'I now recollect there was such a bird, though at that time I did not pay it the least attention. But in collecting my ideas, I now remember well, that at the instant when the king of Egypt rose from the table to give me a kiss, the blackbird flew out at the window giving a loud cry, and never appeared after.'

'Alas! madam,' resumed Amazan's mother, 'this is precisely the cause of all our misfortunes; my son had dispatched this blackbird to gain intelligence of your health, and all that passed at Babylon. He proposed speedily to return, throw himself at your feet, and consecrate to you the remainder of his life. You know not to what a pitch he adores you. All the Gangarids are both loving and faithful; but my son is the most passionate and constant of them all. The blackbird found you at an inn, drinking very cheerfully with the king of Egypt and a vile priest; he afterward saw you give this monarch who had killed the phoenix, – the man my son holds in utter detestation, – a fond embrace. The blackbird, at the sight of this, was seized with a just indignation. He flew away imprecating your fatal error. He returned this day, and has related everything. But, just heaven, at what a juncture! At the very time that my son was deploring with me the loss of his father and that of the wise phoenix, the very instant I had informed him that he was your cousin german –'

'Oh heavens! my cousin, madam, is it possible? How can this be? And am I so happy as to be thus allied to him, and yet so miserable as to have offended him?'

'My son is, I tell you,' said the Gangaridian lady, 'your cousin, and I shall presently convince you of it; but in becoming my relation, you rob me of my son. He cannot survive the grief that the embrace you gave to the king of Egypt has occasioned him.'

'Ah! my dear aunt,' cried the beautiful Formosanta, 'I swear by him and the all-powerful Oromasdes, that this embrace, so far from being criminal, was the strongest proof of love your son could receive from me. I disobeyed my father for his sake. For him I went from the Euphrates to the Ganges. Having fallen into the hands of the worthless Pharaoh of Egypt, I could not escape his clutches but by artifice. I call the ashes and soul of the phoenix, which were then in my pocket, to witness. He can do me justice. But how can your son, born upon the banks of the Ganges, be my cousin? I, whose family have reigned upon the banks of the Euphrates for so many centuries?'

'You know,' said the venerable Gangaridian lady to her, 'that your grand uncle, Aldea, was king of Babylon, and that he was dethroned by Belus's father?'

'Yes, madam.'

'You know that this Aldea had in marriage a daughter named Aldea, brought up in your court? It was this prince, who, being persecuted by your father, took refuge under another name in our happy country. He married me, and is the father of the young prince Aldca Amazan, the most beautiful, the most courageous, the strongest, and most virtuous of mortals; and at this hour the most unhappy. He went to the Babylonian festival upon the credit of your beauty; since that time he idolizes you, and now grieves because he believes that you have proved unfaithful to him. Perhaps I shall never again set eyes upon my dear son.'

She then displayed to the princess all the titles of the house of Aldea. Formosanta scarce deigned to look at them.

'Ah! madam, do we examine what is the object of our desire? My heart sufficiently believes you. But where is Aldea Amazan? Where is my kinsman, my lover, my king? Where is my life? What road has he taken? I will seek for him in every sphere the Eternal Being hath framed, and of which he is the greatest ornament. I will go into the star Canope, into Sheath, into Aldebaran; I will go and tell him of my love and convince him of my innocence.'

The phoenix justified the princess with regard to the crime that was imputed to her by the blackbird, of fondly embracing the king of Egypt; but it was necessary to undeceive Amazan and recall him. Birds were dispatched on every side. Unicorns sent forward in every direction. News at length arrived that Amazan had taken the road toward China.

'Well, then,' said the princess, 'let us set out for China. I will seek him in defiance of both difficulty and danger. The journey is not long, and I hope I shall bring you back your son in a fortnight at farthest.'

At these words tears of affection streamed from his mother's eyes and also from those of the princess. They most tenderly embraced, in the great sensibility of their hearts.

The phoenix immediately ordered a coach with six unicorns. Amazan's mother furnished two thousand horsemen, and made the princess, her niece, a present of some thousands of the finest diamonds of her country. The phoenix, afflicted at the evil occasioned by the blackbird's indiscretion, ordered all the blackbirds to quit the country; and from that time none have been met with upon the banks of the Ganges.

Chapter 5: Formosanta Visits China and Scythia in Search of Amazan

The unicorns, in less than eight days, carried Formosanta, Irla, and the phoenix, to Cambalu, the capital of China. This city was larger than that of Babylon, and in appearance quite different. These fresh objects, these strange manners, would have amused Formosanta could any thing but Amazan have engaged her attention.

As soon as the emperor of China learned that the princess of Babylon was at the city gates, he dispatched four thousand Mandarins in ceremonial robes to receive her. They all prostrated themselves before her, and presented her with an address written in golden letters upon a sheet of purple silk. Formosanta told them, that if she were possessed of four thousand tongues, she would not omit replying immediately to every Mandarin; but that having only one, she hoped they would be satisfied with her general thanks. They conducted her, in a respectful manner, to the emperor.

He was the wisest, most just and benevolent monarch upon earth. It was he who first tilled a small field with his own imperial hands, to make agriculture respectable to his people. Laws in all other countries were shamefully confined to the punishment of crimes: he first allotted premiums to virtue. This emperor had just banished from his dominions a gang of foreign Bonzes, who had come from the extremities of the West, with the frantic hope of compelling all China to think like themselves; and who, under pretence of teaching truths, had already acquired honours and riches. In expelling them, he delivered himself in these words, which are recorded in the annals of the empire:

'You may here do us much harm as you have elsewhere. You have come to preach dogmas of intolerance, to the most tolerant nation upon earth. I send you back, that I may never be compelled to punish you. You will be honourably conducted to my frontiers. You will be furnished with everything necessary to return to the confines of the hemisphere from whence you came. Depart in peace, if you can be at peace, and never return.'

The princess of Babylon heard with pleasure of this speech and determination. She was the more certain of being well received at court, as she was very far from entertaining any dogmas of intolerance. The emperor of China, in dining with her tête-à-tête, had the politeness to banish all disagreeable etiquette. She presented the phoenix to him, who was gently caressed by the emperor, and who perched upon his chair. Formosanta, toward the end of the repast, ingenuously acquainted him with the cause of her journey, and entreated him to search for the beautiful Amazan in the city of Cambalu; and in the meanwhile she acquainted the emperor with her adventures, without concealing the fatal passion with which her heart burned for this youthful hero.

'He did me the honour of coming to my court,' said the emperor of China. 'I was enchanted with this amiable Amazan. It is true that he is deeply afflicted; but his graces are thereby the more affecting. Not one of my favourites has more wit. There is not a gown Mandarin who has more knowledge, – not a military one who has a more martial or heroic air. His extreme youth adds an additional value to all his talents. If I were so unfortunate, so abandoned by the Tien and Changti, as to desire to be a conqueror, I would wish Amazan to put himself at the head of my armies, and I should be sure of conquering the whole universe. It is a great pity that his melancholy sometimes disconcerts him.'

'Ah! sir,' said Formosanta, with much agitation and grief, blended with an air of reproach, 'why did you not request me to dine with him? This is a cruel stroke you have given me. Send for him immediately, I entreat you.'

'He set out this very morning,' replied the emperor, 'without acquainting me with his destination.'

Formosanta, turning toward the phoenix, said to him:

'Did you ever know so unfortunate a damsel as myself?' Then resuming the conversation, she said:

'Sir, how came he to quit in so abrupt a manner, so polite a court, in which, methinks, one might pass one's life?'

'The case was as follows,' said he. 'One of the most amiable of the princesses of the blood, falling desperately in love with him, desired to meet him at noon. He set out at day-break, leaving this billet for my kinswoman, whom it hath cost a deluge of tears:

'Beautiful princess of the mongolian race. You are deserving of a heart that was never offered up at any other altar. I have sworn to the immortal gods never to love any other than Formosanta, princess of Babylon, and to teach her how to conquer one's desires in traveling. She has had the misfortune to yield to a worthless king of Egypt. I am the most unfortunate of men; having lost my father, the phoenix, and the hope of being loved by Formosanta. I left my mother in affliction, forsook my home and country, being unable to live a moment in the place where I learned that Formosanta loved another than me. I swore to traverse the earth, and be faithful. You would despise me, and the gods punish me, if I violated my oath. Choose another lover, madam, and be as faithful as I am.'

'Ah! give me that miraculous letter,' said the beautiful Formosanta; 'it will afford me some consolation. I am happy in the midst of my misfortunes. Amazan loves me! Amazan, for me, renounces the society of the princesses of China. There is no one upon earth but himself endowed with so much fortitude. He sets me a most brilliant example. The phoenix knows I did not stand in need of it. How cruel it is to be deprived of one's lover for the most innocent embrace given through pure fidelity. But, tell me, where has he gone? What road has he taken? Deign to inform me, and I will immediately set out.'

The emperor of China told her, that, according to the reports he had received, her lover had taken the road toward Scythia. The unicorns were immediately harnessed, and the princess, after the most tender compliments, took leave of the emperor, and resumed her journey with the phoenix, her chambermaid Irla, and all her train.

As soon as she arrived in Scythia, she was more convinced than ever how much men and governments differed, and would continue to differ, until noble and enlightened minds should by degrees remove that cloud of darkness which has covered the earth for so many ages; and until there should be found in barbarous climes, heroic souls, who would have strength and perseverance enough to transform brutes into men. There are no cities in Scythia, consequently no agreeable arts. Nothing was to be seen but extensive fields, and whole tribes whose sole habitations were tents and chars. Such an appearance struck her with terror. Formosanta enquired in what tent or char the king was lodged? She was informed that he had set out eight days before with three hundred thousand cavalry to attack the king of Babylon, whose niece, the beautiful princess Aldea, he had carried off.

'What! did he run away with my cousin?' cried Formosanta. 'I could not have imagined such an incident. What! has my cousin, who was too happy in paying her court to me, become a queen, and I am not yet married?' She was immediately conducted, by her desire, to the queen's tent.

Their unexpected meeting in such distant climes – the uncommon occurrences they mutually had to impart to each other, gave such charms to this interview, as made them forget they never loved one another. They saw each other with transport; and a soft illusion supplied the place of real tenderness. They embraced with tears, and there was a cordiality and frankness on each side that could not have taken place in a palace.

Aldea remembered the phoenix and the waiting maid Irla. She presented her cousin with zibelin skins, who in return gave her diamonds. The war between the two kings was spoken of. They deplored the fate of soldiers who were forced into battle, the victims of the caprice of princes, when two honest men might, perhaps, settle the dispute in less than an hour, without a single throat being cut. But the principal topic was the handsome stranger, who had conquered lions, given the largest diamonds in the universe, written madrigals, and had now become the most miserable of men from believing the statements of a blackbird.

'He is my dear brother,' said Aldea. 'He is my lover,' cried Formosanta. 'You have, doubtless, seen him. Is he still here? for, cousin, as he knows he is your brother, he cannot have left you so abruptly as he did the king of China.

'Have I seen him? good heavens! yes. He passed four whole days with me. Ah! cousin, how much my brother is to blame. A false report has absolutely turned his brain. He roams about the world, without knowing to where he is destined. Imagine to yourself his distraction of mind, which is so great, that he has refused to meet the handsomest lady in all Scythia. He set out yesterday, after writing her a letter which has thrown her into despair. As for him, he has gone to visit the Cimmerians.'

'God be thanked!' cried Formosanta, 'another refusal in my favour. My good fortune is beyond my hopes, as my misfortunes surpass my greatest apprehensions. Procure me this charming letter, that I may set out and follow him, loaded with his sacrifices. Farewell, cousin. Amazan is among the Cimmerians, and I fly to meet him.'

Aldea judged that the princess, her cousin, was still more frantic than her brother Amazan. Hut as she had herself been sensible of the effects of this epidemic contagion, having given up the delights and magnificence of Babylon for a king of Scythia; and as the women always excuse those follies that are the effects of love, she felt for Formosanta's affliction, wished her a happy journey, and promised to be her advocate with her brother, if ever she was so fortunate as to see him again.

Chapter 6: The Princess Continues Her Journey

From Scythia the princess of Babylon, with her phoenix, soon arrived at the empire of the Cimmerians, now called Russia; a country indeed much less populous than Scythia, but of far greater extent.

After a few days' journey, she entered a very large city, which has of late been greatly improved by the reigning sovereign. The empress, however, was not there at that time, but was making a journey through her dominions, on the frontiers of Europe and Asia, in order to judge of their state and condition with her own eyes, – to enquire into their grievances, and to provide the proper remedies for them.

The principal magistrate of that ancient capital, as soon as he was informed of the arrival of the Babylonian lady and the phoenix, lost no time in paying her all the honours of his country; being certain that his mistress, the most polite and generous empress in the world, would be extremely well pleased to find that he had received so illustrious a lady with all that respect which she herself, if on the spot, would have shown her.

The princess was lodged in the palace, and entertained with great splendor and elegance. The Cimmerian lord, who was an excellent natural philosopher, diverted himself in conversing with the phoenix, at such times as the princess chose to retire to her own apartment. The phoenix told him, that he had formerly traveled among the Cimmerians, but that he should not have known the country again.

'How comes it,' said he, 'that such prodigious changes have been brought about in so short a time? Formerly, when I was here, about three hundred years ago, I saw nothing but savage nature in all her horrors. At present, I perceive industry, arts, splendor, and politeness.'

'This mighty revolution,' replied the Cimmerian, 'was begun by one man, and is now carried to perfection by one woman; – a woman who is a greater legislator than the Isis of the Egyptians, or the Ceres of the Greeks. Most law-givers have been, unhappily, of a narrow genius and an arbitrary disposition, which conned their views to the countries they governed. Each of them looked upon his own race as the only people existing upon the earth, or as if they ought to be at enmity with all the rest. They formed institutions, introduced customs, and established religions exclusively for themselves. Thus the Egyptians, so famous for those heaps of stones called pyramids, have dishonoured themselves with their barbarous superstitions. They despise all other nations as profane; refuse all manner of intercourse with them; and, excepting those conversant in the court, who now and then rise above the prejudices of the vulgar, there is not an Egyptian who will eat off a plate that has ever been used by a stranger. Their priests are equally cruel and absurd. It were better to have no laws at all, and to follow those notions of right and wrong engraven on our hearts by nature, than to subject society to institutions so inhospitable.

'Our empress has adopted quite a different system. She considers her vast dominions, under which all the meridians on the globe are united, as under an obligation of correspondence with all the nations dwelling under those meridians. The first and most fundamental of her laws, is an universal toleration of all religions, and an unbounded compassion for every error. Her penetrating genius perceives, that though the modes of religious worship differ, yet morality is every where the same. By this principle, she has united her people to all the nations on earth, and the Cimmerians will soon consider the Scandinavians and the Chinese as their brethren. Not satisfied with this, she has resolved to establish this invaluable toleration, the strongest link of society, among her neighbours. By these means, she obtained the title of the parent of her country; and, if she persevere, will acquire that of the benefactress of mankind.

'Before her time, the men, who were unhappily possessed of power, sent out legions of murderers to ravage unknown countries, and to water with the blood of the children the inheritance of their fathers. Those assassins were called heroes, and their robberies accounted glorious achievements. But our sovereign courts another sort of glory. She has sent forth her armies to be the messengers of peace; not only to prevent men from being the destroyers, but to oblige them to be the benefactors of one another. Her standards are the ensigns of public tranquillity.'

The phoenix was quite charmed with what he heard from this nobleman. He told him, that though he had lived twenty-seven thousand nine hundred years and seven months in this world, he had never seen any thing like it. He then enquired after his friend Amazan. The Cimmerian gave the same account of him that the princess had already heard from the Chinese and the Scythians. It was Amazan's constant practice to run away from all the courts he visited, the instant any lady noticed him in particular and seemed anxious to make his acquaintance. The phoenix soon acquainted Formosanta with this fresh instance of Amazan's fidelity – a fidelity so much the more surprising, since he could not imagine his princess would ever hear of it.

Amazan had set out for Scandinavia, where he was entertained with sights still more surprising. In this place, he beheld monarchy and liberty subsisting together in a manner thought incompatible in other states; the laborers of the ground shared in the legislature with the grandees of the realm. In another place he saw what was still more extraordinary; a prince equally remarkable for his extreme youth and uprightness, who possessed a sovereign authority over his country, acquired by a solemn contract with his people.

Amazan beheld a philosopher on the throne of Sarmatia, who might be called a king of anarchy; for he was the chief of a hundred thousand petty kings, one of whom with his single voice could render ineffectual the resolution of all the rest. Eolus had not more difficulty to keep the warring winds within their proper bounds, than this monarch to reconcile the tumultuous discordant spirits of his subjects. He was the master of a ship surrounded with eternal storms. But the vessel did not founder, for he was an excellent pilot.

In traversing those various countries, so different from his own, Amazan persevered in rejecting all the advances made to him by the ladies, though incessantly distracted with the embrace given by Formosanta to the king of Egypt, being resolved to set Formosanta an amazing example of an unshaken and unparalleled fidelity.

The princess of Babylon was constantly close at his heels, and scarcely ever missed of him but by a day or two; without the one being tired of roaming, or the other losing a moment in pursuing him.

Thus he traversed the immense continent of Germany, where he beheld with wonder the progress which reason and philosophy had made in the north. Even their princes were enlightened, and had become the patrons of freedom of thought. Their education had not been trusted to men who had an interest in deceiving them, or who were themselves deceived. They were brought up in the knowledge of universal morality, and in the contempt of superstition.

They had banished from all their estates a senseless custom which had enervated and depopulated the southern countries. This was to bury alive in immense dungeons, infinite numbers of both sexes who were eternally separated from one another, and sworn to have no communication together. This madness had contributed more than the most cruel wars to lay waste and depopulate the earth.

In opposing these barbarous institutions, so inimical to the laws of nature and the best interests of society, the princes of the north had become the benefactors of their race. They had likewise exploded other errors equally absurd and pernicious. In short, men had at last ventured to make use of their reason in those immense regions; whereas it was still believed almost every where else, that they could not be governed but in proportion to their ignorance.

Chapter 7: Amazan Visits Albion

From Germany, Amazan arrived at Batavia; where his perpetual chagrin was in a good measure alleviated, by perceiving among the inhabitants a faint resemblance to his happy countrymen, the Gangarids. There he saw liberty, security, and equality, – with toleration in religion; but the ladies were so indifferent, that none made him any advances; an experience he had not met with before. It is true, however, that had he been inclined to address them, they would not have been offended; though, at the same time, not one would have been the least in love; but he was far from any thoughts of making conquests.

Formosanta had nearly caught him in this insipid nation. He had set out but a moment before her arrival.

Amazan had heard so much among the Batavians in praise of a certain island called Albion, that he was led by curiosity to embark with his unicorns on board a ship, which, with a favourable easterly wind, carried him in a few hours to that celebrated country, more famous than Tyre, or Atlantis.

The beautiful Formosanta, who had followed him, as it were on the scent, to the banks of the Volga, the Vistula, the Elbe, and the Weser, and had never been above a day or two behind him, arrived soon after at the mouth of the Rhine, where it disembogues its waters into the German Ocean.

Here she learned that her beloved Amazan had just set sail for Albion. She thought she saw the vessel on board of which he was, and could not help crying out for joy; at which the Batavian ladies were greatly surprised, not imagining that a young man could possibly occasion so violent a transport. They took, indeed, but little notice of the phoenix, as they reckoned his feathers would not fetch near so good a price as those of their own ducks, and other water fowl. The princess of Babylon hired two vessels to carry herself and her retinue to that happy island, which was soon to possess the only object of her desires, the soul of her life, and the god of her idolatry.

An unpropitious wind from the west suddenly arose, just as the faithful and unhappy Amazan landed on Albion's sea-girt shore, and detained the ships of the Babylonian princess just as they were on the point of sailing. Seized with a deep melancholy, she went to her room, determined to remain there till the wind should change; but it blew for the space of eight days, with an unremitting violence. The princess, during this tedious period, employed her maid of honour,

Irla, in reading romances; which were not indeed written by the Batavians; but as they are the factors of the universe, they traffic in the wit as well as commodities of other nations. The princess purchased of Mark Michael Rey, the bookseller, all the novels which had been written by the Ausonians and the Welch, the sale of which had been wisely prohibited among those nations to enrich their neighbours, the Batavians. She expected to find in those histories some adventure similar to her own, which might alleviate her grief. The maid of honour read, the phoenix made comments, and the princess, finding nothing in the Fortunate Country Maid, in Tansai, or in the Sopha, that had the least resemblance to her own affairs, interrupted the reader every moment, by asking how the wind stood.

Chapter 8: Amazan Leaves Albion to Visit the Land of Saturn

In the mean time, Amazan was on the road to the capital of Albion, in his coach and six unicorns, all his thoughts employed on his dear princess. At a small distance he perceived a carriage overturned in a ditch. The servants had gone in different directions in quest of assistance, but the owner kept his seat, smoking his pipe with great tranquillity, without manifesting the smallest impatience. His name was my lord What-then, in the language from which I translate these memoirs.

Amazan made all the haste possible to help him, and without assistance set the carriage to rights, so much was his strength superior to that of other men. My lord What-then took no other notice of him, than saying, 'a stout fellow, by Jove!' In the meantime the neighbouring people, having arrived, flew into a great passion at being called out to no purpose, and fell upon the stranger. They abused him, called him an outlandish dog, and challenged him to strip and box.

Amazan seized a brace of them in each hand, and threw them twenty paces from him; the rest seeing this, pulled off their hats, and bowing with great respect, asked his honour for something to drink. His honour gave them more money than they had ever seen in their lives before. My lord What-then now expressed great esteem for him, and asked him to dinner at his country house, about three miles off. His invitation being accepted, he went into Amazan's coach, his own being out of order from the accident.

After a quarter of an hour's silence, my lord What-then, looking upon Amazan for a moment, said. 'How d'ye do?' which, by the way, is a phrase without any meaning, adding, 'You have got six fine unicorns there.' After which he continued smoking as usual.

The traveler told him his unicorns were at his service, and that he had brought them from the country of the Gangarids. From thence he took occasion to inform him of his affair with the princess of Babylon, and the unlucky kiss she had given the king of Egypt; to which the other made no reply, being very indifferent whether there were any such people in the world, as a king of Egypt, or a princess of Babylon.

He remained dumb for another quarter of an hour; after which he asked his companion a second time how he did, and whether they had any good roast beef among the Gangarids.

Amazan answered with his wonted politeness, 'that they did not eat their brethren on the banks of the Ganges.' He then explained to him that system which many ages afterward was surnamed the Pythagorean philosophy. But my lord fell asleep in the meantime, and made but one nap of it till he came to his own house.

He was married to a young and charming woman, on whom nature had bestowed a soul as lively and sensible as that of her husband was dull and stupid. A few gentlemen of Albion had that day come to dine with her; among whom there were characters of all sorts; for that country having been almost always under the government of foreigners, the families that had come over with these princes had imported their different manners. There were in this company some persons of an amiable disposition, others of superior genius, and a few of profound learning.

The mistress of the house had none of that awkward stiffness, that false modesty, with which the young ladies of Albion were then reproached. She did not conceal by a scornful look and an affected taciturnity, her deficiency of ideas: and the embarrassing humility of having nothing to say. Never was a woman more engaging. She received Amazan with a grace and politeness that were quite natural to her. The extreme beauty of this young stranger, and the involuntary comparison she could not help making between him and her prosaic husband, did not increase her happiness or content.

Dinner being served, she placed Amazan at her side, and helped him to a variety of puddings, he having informed her that the Gangarids never dined upon any thing which had received from the gods the celestial gift of life. The events of his early life, the manners of the Gangarids, the progress of arts, religion, and government, were the subjects of a conversation equally agreeable and instructive all the time of the entertainment, which lasted till night: during which my lord What-then did nothing but push the bottle about, and call for the toast.

After dinner, while my lady was pouring out the tea, still feeding her eyes on the young stranger, he entered into a long conversation with a member of parliament; for everyone knows that there was, even then, a parliament called Wittenagemot, or the assembly of wise men. Amazan enquired into the constitution, laws, manners, customs, forces, and arts, which made this country so respectable; and the member answered him in the following manner.

'For a long time we went stark naked, though our climate is none of the hottest. We were likewise for a long time enslaved by a people who came from the ancient country of Saturn, watered by the Tiber. But the mischief we have done one another has greatly exceeded all that we ever suffered from our first conquerors. One of our princes carried his superstition to such a pitch, as to declare himself the subject of a priest, who dwells also on the banks of the Tiber, and is called the Old Man of the Seven Mountains. It has been the fate of the seven mountains to domineer over the greatest part of Europe, then inhabited by brutes in human shape.

'To those times of infamy and debasement, succeeded the ages of barbarity and confusion. Our country, more tempestuous than the surrounding ocean, has been ravaged and drenched in blood by our civil discords. Many of our crowned heads have perished by a violent death. Above a hundred princes of the royal blood have ended their days on the scaffold, whilst the hearts of their adherents have been torn from their breasts, and thrown in their faces. In short, it is the province of the hangman to write the history of our island, seeing that this personage has finally determined all our affairs of moment.

'But to crown these horrors, it is not very long since some fellows wearing black mantles, and others who cast white shirts over their jackets, having become aggressive and intolerent, succeeded in communicating their madness to the whole nation. Our country was then divided into two parties, the murderers and the murdered, the executioners and the sufferers, plunderers and slaves; and all in the name of God, and whilst they were seeking the Lord.

'Who would have imagined, that from this horrible abyss, this chaos of dissension, cruelty, ignorance, and fanaticism, a government should at last spring up, the most perfect, it may be said, now in the world; yet such has been the event. A prince, honoured and wealthy, all-powerful to do good, but without power to do evil, is at the head of a free, warlike, commercial, and enlightened nation. The nobles on one hand, and the representatives of the people on the other, share the legislature with the monarch.

'We have seen, by a singular fatality of events, disorder, civil wars, anarchy and wretchedness, lay waste the country, when our kings aimed at arbitrary power: whereas tranquillity, riches, and universal happiness, have only reigned among us, when the prince has remained satisfied with a limited authority. All order had been subverted whilst we were disputing about mysteries, but was re-established the moment we grew wise enough to despise them. Our victorious fleets carry our flag on every ocean; our laws place our lives and fortunes in security; no judge can explain them in an arbitrary manner, and no decision is ever given without the reasons assigned for it. We should punish a judge as an assassin, who should condemn a citizen to death without declaring the evidence which accused him, and the law upon which he was convicted.

'It is true, there are always two parties among us, who are continually writing and intriguing against each other, but they constantly re-unite, whenever it is needful to arm in defence of liberty and our country. These two parties watch over one another, and mutually prevent the violation of the sacred deposit of the laws. They hate one another, but they love the state. They are like those jealous lovers, who pay court to the same mistress, with a spirit of emulation.

'From the same fund of genius by which we discovered and supported the natural rights of mankind, we have carried the sciences to the highest pitch to which they can attain among men. Your Egyptians, who pass for such great mechanics – your Indians, who are believed to be such great philosophers – your Babylonians, who boast of having observed the stars for the course of four hundred and thirty thousand years – the Greeks, who have written so much, and said so little, know in reality nothing in comparison to our inferior scholars, who have studied the discoveries of Our great masters. We have ravished more secrets from nature in the space of an hundred years, that the human species had been able to discover in as many ages.

'This is a true account of our present state. I have concealed from you neither the good nor the bad; neither our shame nor our glory; and I have exaggerated nothing.'

At this discourse Amazan felt a strong desire to be instructed in those sublime sciences his friend had spoken of; and if his passion for the princess of Babylon, his filial duty to his mother whom he had quitted, and his love for his native country, had not made strong remonstrances to his distempered heart, he would willingly have spent the remainder of his life in Albion. But that unfortunate kiss his princess had given the king of Egypt, did not leave his mind at sufficient ease to study the abstruse sciences.

'I confess,' said he, 'having made a solemn vow to roam about the world, and to escape from myself. I have a curiosity to see that ancient land of Saturn – that people of the Tiber and of the Seven Mountains, who have been heretofore your masters. They must undoubtedly be the first people on earth.'

'I advise you by all means,' answered the member, 'to take that journey, if you have the smallest taste for music or painting. Even we ourselves frequently carry our spleen and melancholy to the Seven Mountains. But you will be greatly surprised when you see the descendants of our conquerors.'

This was a long conversation, and Amazan had spoken in so agreeable a manner; his voice was so charming; his whole behavior so noble and engaging, that the mistress of the house could not resist the pleasure of having a little private chat with him in her turn. She accordingly sent him a little billet-doux intimating her wishes in the most agreeable language. Amazan had once more the courage to resist the fascination of female society, and, according to custom, wrote the lady an answer full of respect, – representing to her the sacredness of his oath, and the strict obligation he was under to teach the princess of Babylon to conquer her passions by his example; after which he harnessed his unicorns and departed for Batavia, leaving all the company in deep admiration of him, and the lady in profound astonishment. In her confusion she dropped Amazan's letter. My lord What-then read it next morning:

'D – n it,' said he, shrugging up his shoulders, 'what stuff and nonsense have we got here?' and then rode out a fox hunting with some of his drunken neighbours.

Amazan was already sailing upon the sea, possessed of a geographical chart, with which he had been presented by the learned Albion he had conversed with at lord What-then's. He was extremely astonished to find the greatest part of the earth upon a single sheet of paper.

His eyes and imagination wandered over this little space; he observed the Rhine, the Danube, the Alps of Tyrol, there specified under their different names, and all the countries through which he was to pass before he arrived at the city of the Seven Mountains. But he more particularly fixed his eyes upon the country of the Gangarids, upon Babylon, where he had seen his dear princess, and upon the country of Bassora, where she had given a fatal kiss to the king of Egypt. He sighed, and tears streamed from his eyes at the unhappy remembrance. He agreed with the Albion who had presented him with the universe in epitome, when he averred that the inhabitants of the banks of the Thames were a thousand times better instructed than those upon the banks of the Nile, the Euphrates, and the Ganges.

As he returned into Batavia, Formosanta proceeded toward Albion with her two ships at full sail. Amazan's ship and the princess's crossed one another and almost touched; the two lovers were close to each other, without being conscious of the fact. Ah! had they but known it! But this great consolation tyrannic destiny would not allow.

Chapter 9: Amazan Visits Rome

No sooner had Amazan landed on the flat muddy shore of Batavia, than he immediately set out toward the city of the Seven Mountains. He was obliged to traverse the southern part of Germany. At every four miles he met with a prince and princess, maids of honour, and beggars. He was greatly astonished every where at the coquetries of these ladies and maids of honour, in which they indulged with German good faith. After having cleared the Alps he embarked upon the sea of Dalmatia, and landed in a city that had no resemblance to any thing he had heretofore seen. The sea formed the streets, and the houses were erected in the water. The few public places, with which this city was ornamented, were filled with men and women with double faces – that which nature had bestowed on them, and a pasteboard one, ill painted, with which they covered their natural visage; so that this people seemed composed of spectres. Upon the arrival of strangers in this country, they immediately purchase these visages, in the same manner as people elsewhere furnish themselves with hats and shoes. Amazan despised a fashion so contrary to nature. He appeared just as he was.

Many ladies were introduced, and interested themselves in the handsome Amazan. But he fled with the utmost precipitancy, uttering the name of the incomparable princess of Babylon, and swearing by the immortal gods, that she was far handsomer than the Venetian girls.

'Sublime traitoress,' he cried, in his transports, 'I will teach you to be faithful!'

Now the yellow surges of the Tiber, pestiferous fens, a few pale emaciated inhabitants clothed in tatters which displayed their dry tanned hides, appeared to his sight, and bespoke his arrival at the gate of the city of the Seven Mountains, – that city of heroes and legislators who conquered and polished a great part of the globe.

He expected to have seen at the triumphal gate, five hundred battalions commanded by heroes, and in the senate an assembly of demi-gods giving laws to the earth. But the only army he found consisted of about thirty tatterdemalions, mounting guard with umbrellas for fear of the sun. Having arrived at a temple which appeared to him very fine, but not so magnificent as that of Babylon, he was greatly astonished to hear a concert performed by men with female voices.

'This,' said he, 'is a mighty pleasant country, which was formerly the land of Saturn. I have been in a city where no one showed his own face; here is another where men have neither their own voices nor beards.'

He was told that these eunuchs had been trained from childhood, that they might sing the more agreeably the praises of a great number of persons of merit. Amazan could not comprehend the meaning of this.

They then explained to him very pleasantly, and with many gesticulations, according to the custom of their country, the point in question. Amazan was quite confounded.

'I have traveled a great way,' said he, 'but I never before heard such a whim.'

After they had sung a good while, the Old Man of the Seven Mountains went with great ceremony to the gate of the temple. He cut the air in four parts with his thumb raised, two fingers extended and two bent, in uttering these words in a language no longer spoken: 'To the city and to the universe.' Amazan could not see how two fingers could extend so far.

He presently saw the whole court of the master of the world file off. This court consisted of grave personages, some in scarlet, and others in violet robes. They almost all eyed the handsome Amazan with a tender look; and bowed to him, while commenting upon his personal appearance.

The zealots whose vocation was to show the curiosities of the city to strangers, very eagerly offered to conduct him to several ruins, in which a muleteer would not choose to pass a night, but which were formerly worthy monuments of the grandeur of a royal people. He moreover saw pictures of two hundred years standing, and statues that had remained twenty ages, which appeared to him masterpieces of their kind.

'Can you still produce such work?' said Amazan.

'No, your excellency,' replied one of the zealots; 'but we despise the rest of the earth, because we preserve these rarities. We are a kind of old clothes men, who derive our glory from the cast-off garbs in our warehouses.'

Amazan was willing to see the prince's palace, and he was accordingly conducted thither. He saw men dressed in violet coloured robes, who were reckoning the money of the revenues of the domains of lands, some situated upon the Danube, some upon the Loire, others upon the Guadalquivir, or the Vistula.

'Oh! Oh!' said Amazan, having consulted his geographical map, 'your master, then, possesses all Europe, like those ancient heroes of the Seven Mountains?'

'He should possess the whole universe by divine right,' replied a violet-livery man; 'and there was even a time when his predecessors nearly compassed universal monarchy, but their successors are so good as to content themselves at present with some monies which the kings, their subjects, pay to them in the form of a tribute.'

'Your master is then, in fact, the king of kings. Is that his title?' said Amazan.

'Your excellency, his title is the servant of servants! He was originally a fisherman and porter, wherefore the emblems of his dignity consist of keys and nets; but he at present issues orders to every king in Christendom. It is not a long while since he sent one hundred and one mandates to a king of the Celts, and the king obeyed.'

'Your fisherman must then have sent five or six hundred thousand men to put these orders in execution?'

'Not at all, your excellency. Our holy master is not rich enough to keep ten thousand soldiers on foot: but he has five or six hundred thousand divine prophets dispersed in other countries. These prophets of various colours are, as they ought to be, supported at the expense of the people where they reside. They proclaim, from heaven, that my master may, with his keys, open and shut all locks, and particularly those of strong boxes. A Norman priest, who held the post of confident of this king's thoughts, convinced him he ought to obey, without questioning, the one hundred and one thoughts of my master; for you must know that one of the prerogatives of the Old Man of the Seven Mountains is never to err, whether he deigns to speak or deigns to write.'

'In faith,' said Amazan, 'this is a very singular man; I should be pleased to dine with him.'

'Were your excellency even a king, you could not eat at his table. All that he could do for you, would be to allow you to have one served by the side of his, but smaller and lower. But if you are inclined to have the honour of speaking to him, I will ask an audience for you on condition of the buona mancia, which you will be kind enough to give me.' 'Very readily,' said the Gangarid. The violet-livery man bowed: 'I will introduce you to-morrow,' said he. 'You must make three very low bows, and you must kiss the feet of the Old Man of the Seven Mountains.' At this information Amazan burst into so violent a fit of laughing that he was almost choked; which, however, he surmounted, holding his sides, whilst the violent emotions of the risible muscles forced the tears down his cheeks, till he reached the inn, where the fit still continued upon him.

At dinner, twenty beardless men and twenty violins produced a concert. He received the compliments of the greatest lords of the city during the remainder of the day; but from their extravagant actions, he was strongly tempted to throw two or three of these violet-coloured gentry out of the window. He left with the greatest precipitation this city of the masters of the world, where young men were treated so whimsically, and where he found himself necessitated to kiss an old man's toe, as if his cheek were at the end of his foot.

Chapter 10: An Unfortunate Adventure in Gaul

In all the provinces through which Amazan passed, he remained ever faithful to the princess of Babylon, though incessantly enraged at the king of Egypt. This model of constancy at length arrived at the new capital of the Gauls. This city, like many others, had alternately submitted to barbarity, ignorance, folly, and misery. The first name it bore was Dirt and Mire; it then took that of Isis, from the worship of Isis, which had reached even here. Its first senate consisted of a company of watermen. It had long been in bondage, and submitted to the ravages of the heroes of the Seven Mountains; and some ages after, some other heroic thieves who came from the farther banks of the Rhine, had seized upon its little lands.

Time, which changes all things, had formed it into a city, half of which was very noble and very agreeable, the other half somewhat barbarous and ridiculous. This was the emblem of its inhabitants. There were within its walls at least a hundred thousand people, who had no other employment than play and diversion. These idlers were the judges of those arts which the others cultivated. They were ignorant of all that passed at court; though they were only four short miles distant from it: but it seemed to them at least six hundred thousand miles off. Agreeableness in company, gaiety and frivolty, formed the important and sole considerations of their lives. They were governed like children, who are extravagantly supplied with gewgaws, to prevent their crying. If the horrors were discussed, which two centuries before had laid waste their country, or if those dreadful periods were recalled, when one half of the nation massacred the other for sophisms, they, indeed, said, 'this was not well done;' then, presently, they fell to laughing again, or singing of catches.

In proportion as the idlers were polished, agreeable, and amiable, it was observed that there was a greater and more shocking contrast between them and those who were engaged in business.

Among the latter, or such as pretended so to be, there was a gang of melancholy fanatics, whose absurdity and knavery divided their character, – whose appearance alone diffused misery, – and who would have overturned the world, had they been able to gain a little credit. But the nation of idlers, by dancing and singing, forced them into obscurity in their caverns, as the warbling birds drive the croaking bats back to their holes and ruins.

A smaller number of those who were occupied, were the preservers of ancient barbarous customs, against which nature, terrified, loudly exclaimed. They consulted nothing but their worm-eaten registers. If they there discovered a foolish or horrid custom, they considered it as a sacred law. It was from this vile practice of not daring to think for themselves, but extracting their ideas from the ruins of those times when no one thought at all, that in the metropolis of pleasure there still remained some shocking manners. Hence it was that there was no proportion between crimes and punishments. A thousand deaths were sometimes inflicted upon an innocent victim, to make him acknowledge a crime he had not committed.

The extravagancies of youth were punished with the same severity as murder or parricide. The idlers screamed loudly at these exhibitions, and the next day thought no more about them, but were buried in the contemplation of some new fashion.

This people saw a whole age elapse, in which the fine arts attained a degree of perfection that far surpassed the most sanguine hopes. Foreigners then repaired thither, as they did to Babylon, to admire the great monuments of architecture, the wonders of gardening, the sublime efforts of sculpture and painting. They were charmed with a species of music that reached the heart without astonishing the ears.

True poetry, that is to say, such as is natural and harmonious, that which addresses the heart as well as the mind, was unknown to this nation before this happy period. New kinds of eloquence displayed sublime beauties. The theatres in particular reëchoed with masterpieces that no other nation ever approached. In a word, good taste prevailed in every profession to that degree, that there were even good writers among the Druids.

So many laurels that had branched even to the skies, soon withered in an exhausted soil. There remained but a very small number, whose leaves were of a pale dying verdure. This decay was occasioned by the facility of producing; laziness preventing good productions, and by a satiety of the brilliant, and a taste for the whimsical. Vanity protected arts that brought back times of barbarity; and this same vanity, in persecuting persons of real merit, forced them to quit their country. The hornets banished the bees.

There were scarce any real arts, scarce any real genius, talent now consisted in reasoning right or wrong upon the merit of the last age. The dauber of a sign-post criticised with an air of sagacity the works of the greatest painters; and the blotters of paper disfigured the works of the greatest writers. Ignorance and bad taste had other daubers in their pay. The same things were repeated in a hundred volumes under different titles. Every work was either a dictionary or a pamphlet. A Druid gazetteer wrote twice a week the obscure annals of an unknown people possessed with the devil, and of celestial prodigies operated in garrets by little beggars of both sexes. Other Ex-Druids, dressed in black, ready to die with rage and hunger, set forth their complaints in a hundred different writings, that they were no longer allowed to cheat mankind – this privilege being conferred on some goats clad in grey; and some Arch-Druids were employed in printing defamatory libels.

Amazan was quite ignorant of all this, and even if he had been acquainted with it, he would have given himself very little concern about it, having his head filled with nothing but the princess of Babylon, the king of Egypt, and the inviolable vow he had made to despise all female coquetry in whatever country his despair should drive him.

The gaping ignorant mob, whose curiosity exceeds all the bounds of nature and reason, for a long time thronged about his unicorns. The more sensible women forced open the doors of his hotel to contemplate his person.

He at first testified some desire of visiting the court; but some of the idlers, who constituted good company and casually went thither, informed him that it was quite out of fashion, that times were greatly changed, and that all amusements were confined to the city. He was invited that very night to sup with a lady whose sense and talents had reached foreign climes, and who had traveled in some countries through which Amazan had passed. This lady gave him great pleasure, as well as the society he met at her house. Here reigned a decent liberty, gaiety without tumult, silence without pedantry, and wit without asperity. He found that good company was not quite ideal, though the title was frequently usurped by pretenders. The next day he dined in a society far less amiable, but much more voluptuous. The more he was satisfied with the guests, the more they were pleased with him. He found his soul soften and dissolve, like the aromatics of his country, which gradually melt in a moderate heat, and exhale in delicious perfumes.

After dinner he was conducted to a place of public entertainment which was enchanting; but condemned, however, by the Druids, because it deprived them of their auditors, which, therefore, excited their jealousy. The representation here consisted of agreeable verses, delightful songs, dances which expressed the movements of the soul, and perspectives that charmed the eye in deceiving it. This kind of pastime, which included so many kinds, was known only under a foreign name. It was called an Opera, which formerly signified, in the language of the Seven Mountains, work, care, occupation, industry, enterprise, business. This exhibition enchanted him. A female singer, in particular, charmed him by her melodious voice, and the graces that accompanied her. This child of genius, after the performance, was introduced to him by his new friends. He presented her with a handful of diamonds; for which she was so grateful, that she could not leave him all the rest of the day. He supped with her and her companions, and during the delightful repast he forgot his sobriety, and became heated and oblivious with wine. What an instance of human frailty!

The beautiful princess of Babylon arrived at this juncture, with her phoenix, her chambermaid Irla, and her two hundred Gangaridian cavaliers mounted on their unicorns. It was a long while before the gates were opened. She immediately asked, if the handsomest, the most courageous, the most sensible, and the most faithful of men was still in that city? The magistrates readily concluded that she meant Amazan. She was conducted to his hotel. How great was the palpitation of her heart! – the powerful operation of the tender passion. Her whole soul was penetrated with inexpressible joy, to see once more in her lover the model of constancy. Nothing could prevent her entering his chamber; the curtains were open; and she saw the beautiful Amazan asleep and stupefied with drink.

Formosanta expressed her grief with such screams as made the house echo. She swooned into the arms of Irla. As soon as she had recovered her senses, she retired from this fatal chamber with grief blended with rage.

'Oh! just heaven; oh, powerful Oromasdes!' cried the beautiful princess of Babylon, bathed in tears. 'By whom, and for whom am I thus betrayed? He that could reject for my sake so many princesses, to abandon me for the company of a strolling Gaul! No! I can never survive this affront.'

'This is the disposition of all young people,' said Irla to her, 'from one end of the world to the other. Were they enamoured with a beauty descended from heaven, they would at certain moments forget her entirely.'

'It is done,' said the princess, 'I will never see him again whilst I live. Let us depart this instant, and let the unicorns be harnessed.'

The phoenix conjured her to stay at least till Amazan awoke, that he might speak with him.

'He does not deserve it,' said the princess. 'You would cruelly offend me. He would think that I had desired you to reproach him, and that I am willing to be reconciled to him. If you love me, do not add this injury to the insult he has offered me.'

The phoenix, who after all owed his life to the daughter of the king of Babylon, could not disobey her. She set out with all her attendants.

'Where are you going?' said Irla to her.

'I do not know,' replied the princess; 'we will take the first road we find. Provided I fly from Amazan for ever, I am satisfied.'

The phoenix, who was wiser than Formosanta, because he was divested of passion, consoled her upon the road. He gently insinuated to her that it was shocking to punish one's self for the faults of another; that Amazan had given her proofs sufficiently striking and numerous of his fidelity, so that she should forgive him for having forgotten himself for one moment in social company; that this was the only time in which he had been wanting of the grace of Oromasdes; that it would render him only the more constant in love and virtue for the future; that the desire of expiating his fault would raise him beyond himself; that it would be the means of increasing her happiness; that many great princesses before her had forgiven such slips, and had had no reason to be sorry afterward; and he was so thoroughly possessed of the art of persuasion, that Formosanta's mind grew more calm and peaceable. She was now sorry she had set out so soon. She thought her unicorns went too fast, but she did not dare return. Great was the conflict between her desire of forgiving and that of showing her rage – between her love and vanity. However, her unicorns pursued their pace; and she traversed the world, according to the prediction of her father's oracle.

When Amazan awoke, he was informed of the arrival and departure of Formosanta and the phoenix. He was also told of the rage and distraction of the princess, and that she had sworn never to forgive him.

'Then,' said he, 'there is nothing left for me to do, but follow her, and kill myself at her feet.'

The report of this adventure drew together his festive companions, who all remonstrated with him. They said that he had much better stay with them; that nothing could equal the pleasant life they led in the centre of arts and refined delicate pleasures; that many strangers, and even kings, preferred such an agreeable enchanting repose to their country and their thrones. Moreover, his vehicle was broken, and another was being made for him according to the newest fashion; that the best tailor of the whole city had already cut out for him a dozen suits in the latest style; that the most vivacious, amiable, and fashionable ladies, at whose houses dramatic performances were represented, had each appointed a day to give him a regale. The girl from the opera was in the meanwhile drinking her chocolate, laughing, singing, and ogling the beautiful Amazan – who by this time clearly perceived she had no more sense than a goose.

A sincerity, cordiality, and frankness, as well as magnanimity and courage, constituted the character of this great prince, he related his travels and misfortunes to his friends. They knew that he was cousin-german to the princess. They were informed of the fatal kiss she had given the king of Egypt. 'Such little tricks,' said they, 'are often forgiven between relatives, otherwise one's whole life would pass in perpetual uneasiness.'

Nothing could shake his design of pursuing Formosanta; but his carriage not being ready, he was compelled to remain three days longer among the idlers, who were still feasting and merry-making. He at length took his leave of them, by embracing them and making them accept some of his diamonds that were the best mounted, and recommending to them a constant pursuit of frivolity and pleasure, since they were thereby made more agreeable and happy.

'The Germans,' said he, 'are the greyheads of Europe; the people of Albion are men formed; the inhabitants of Gaul are the children, – and I love to play with children.'

Chapter 11: Amazan and Formosanta Become Reconciled

The guides had no difficulty in following the route the princess had taken. There was nothing else talked of but her and her large bird. All the inhabitants were still in a state of fascination. The banks of the Loire, of the Dordogue – the Garonne, and the Gironde, still echoed with acclamation.

When Amazan reached the foot of the Pyrenees, the magistrates and Druids of the country made him dance, whether he would or not, a Tambourin; but as soon as he cleared the Pyrenees, nothing presented itself that was either gay or joyous. If he here and there heard a peasant sing, it was a doleful ditty. The inhabitants stalked with much gravity, having a few strung beads and a girted poniard. The nation dressed in black, and appeared to be in mourning.

If Amazan's servants asked passengers any questions, they were answered by signs; if they went into an inn, the host acquainted his guests in three words, that there was nothing in the house, but that the things they so pressingly wanted might be found a few miles off.

When these votaries to taciturnity were asked if they had seen the beautiful princess of Babylon pass, they answered with less brevity than usual: 'We have seen her – she is not so handsome – there are no beauties that are not tawny – she displays a bosom of alabaster, which is the most disgusting thing in the world, and which is scarce known in our climate.'

Amazan advanced toward the province watered by the Betis. The Tyrians discovered this country about twelve thousand years ago, about the time they discovered the great Atlantic Isle, inundated so many centuries after. The Tyrians cultivated Betica, which the natives of the country had never done, being of opinion that it was not their place to meddle with anything, and that their neighbours, the Gauls, should come and reap their harvests. The Tyrians had brought with them some Palestines, or Jews, who, from that time, have wandered through every clime where money was to be gained. The Palestines, by extraordinary usury, at fifty per cent., had possessed themselves of almost all the riches of the country. This made the people of Betica imagine the Palestines were sorcerers; and all those who were accused of witchcraft were burnt, without mercy, by a company of Druids, who were called the Inquisitors, or the Anthropokaies. These priests immediately put their victims in a masquerade habit, seized upon their effects, and devoutly repeated the Palestines' own prayers, whilst burning them by a slow fire, por l'amor de Dios.

The princess of Babylon alighted in that city which has since been called Sevilla. Her design was to embark upon the Betis to return by Tyre to Babylon, and see again king Belus, her father; and forget, if possible, her perdious lover – or, at least, to ask him in marriage. She sent for two Palestines, who transacted all the business of the court. They were to furnish her with three ships. The phoenix made all the necessary contracts with them, and settled the price after some little dispute.

The hostess was a great devotee, and her husband, who was no less religious, was a Familiar: that is to say, a spy of the Druid Inquisitors or Anthropokaies.

He failed not to inform them, that in his house was a sorceress and two Palestines, who were entering into a compact with the devil, disguised like a large gilt bird.

The Inquisitors having learned that the lady possessed a large quantity of diamonds, swore point blank that she was a sorceress. They waited till night to imprison the two hundred cavaliers and the unicorns, (which slept in very extensive stables), for the Inquisitors are cowards.

Having strongly barricaded the gates, they seized the princess and Irla; but they could not catch the phoenix, who flew away with great swiftness. He did not doubt of meeting with Amazan upon the road from Gaul to Sevilla.

He met him upon the frontiers of Betica, and acquainted him with the disaster that had befallen the princess.

Amazan was struck speechless with rage. He armed himself with a steel cuirass damasquined with gold, a lance twelve feet long, two javelins, and an edged sword called the Thunderer, which at one single stroke would rend trees, rocks, and Druids. He covered his beautiful head with a golden casque, shaded with heron and ostrich feathers. This was the ancient armor of Magog, which his sister Aldea gave him when upon his journey in Scythia. The few attendants he had with him all mounted their unicorns.

Amazan, in embracing his dear phoenix, uttered only these melancholy expressions: 'I am guilty! Had I not dined with the child of genius from the opera, in the city of the idlers, the princess of Babylon would not have been in this alarming situation. Let us fly to the Anthropokaies.' He presently entered Sevilla. Fifteen hundred Alguazils guarded the gates of the inclosure in which the two hundred Gangarids and their unicorns were shut up, without being allowed anything to eat. Preparations were already made for sacrificing the princess of Babylon, her chambermaid Irla, and the two rich Palestines.

The high Anthropokaie, surrounded by his subaltern Anthropokaies, was already seated upon his sacred tribunal. A crowd of Sevillians, wearing strung beads at their girdles, joined their two hands, without uttering a syllable, when the beautiful Princess, the maid Irla, and the two Palestines were brought forth, with their hands tied behind their backs and dressed in masquerade habits.

The phoenix entered the prison by a dormer window, whilst the Gangarids began to break open the doors. The invincible Amazan shattered them without. They all sallied forth armed, upon their unicorns, and Amazan put himself at their head. He had no difficulty in overthrowing the Alguazils, the Familiars, or the priests called Anthropokaies. Each unicorn pierced dozens at a time. The thundering Amazan cut to pieces all he met. The people in black cloaks and dirty frize ran away, always keeping fast hold of their blest beads, por l'amor de Dios.

Amazan collared the high Inquisitor upon his tribunal, and threw him upon the pile, which was prepared about forty paces distant; and he also cast upon it the other Inquisitors, one after the other. He then prostrated himself at Formosanta's feet. 'Ah! how amiable you are,' said she; 'and how I should adore you, if you had not forsaken me for the company of an opera singer.'

Whilst Amazan was making his peace with the princess, whilst his Gangarids cast upon the pile the bodies of all the Anthropokaies, and the flames ascended to the clouds, Amazan saw an army that approached him at a distance. An aged monarch, with a crown upon his head, advanced upon a car drawn by eight mules harnessed with ropes. An hundred other cars followed. They were accompanied by grave looking men in black cloaks or frize, mounted upon very fine horses. A multitude of people, with greasy hair, followed silently on foot.

Amazan immediately drew up his Gangarids about him, and advanced with his lance couched. As soon as the king perceived him, he took off his crown, alighted from his car, and embraced Amazan's stirrup, saying to him: 'Man sent by the gods, you are the avenger of human kind, the deliverer of my country. These sacred monsters, of which you have purged the earth, were my masters, in the name of the Old Man of the Seven Mountains. I was forced to submit to their criminal power. My people would have deserted me, if I had only been inclined to moderate their abominable crimes. From this moment I breathe, I reign, and am indebted to you for it.'

He afterward respectfully kissed Formosanta's hand, and entreated her to get into his coach (drawn by eight mules) with Amazan, Irla, and the phoenix.

The two Palestine bankers, who still remained prostrate on the ground through fear and terror, now raised their heads. The troop of unicorns followed the king of Betica into his palace.

As the dignity of a king who reigned over a people of characteristic brevity, required that his mules should go at a very slow pace, Amazan and Formosanta had time to relate to him their adventures. He also conversed with the phoenix, admiring and frequently embracing him. He easily comprehended how brutal and barbarous the people of the west should be considered, who ate animals, and did not understand their language; that the Gangarids alone had preserved the nature and dignity of primitive man; but he particularly agreed, that the most barbarous of mortals were the Anthropokaies, of whom Amazan had just purged the earth. He incessantly blessed and thanked him. The beautiful Formosanta had already forgotten the affair in Gaul, and had her soul filled with nothing but the valor of the hero who had preserved her life. Amazan being made acquainted with the innocence of the embrace she had given to the king of Egypt, and being told of the resurrection of the phoenix, tasted the purest joy, and was intoxicated with the most violent love.

They dined at the palace, but had a very indifferent repast. The cooks of Betica were the worst in Europe. Amazan advised the king to send for some from Gaul. The king's musicians performed, during the repast, that celebrated air which has since been called the Follies of Spain. After dinner, matters of business came upon the carpet.

The king enquired of the handsome Amazan, the beautiful Formosanta, and the charming phoenix, what they proposed doing. 'For my part,' said Amazan, 'my intention is to return to Babylon, of which I am the presumptive heir, and to ask of my uncle Belus the hand of my cousin-german, the incomparable Formosanta.'

'My design certainly is,' said the princess, 'never to separate from my cousin-germain. But I imagine he will agree with me, that I should return first to my father, because he only gave me leave to go upon a pilgrimage to Bassora, and I have wandered all over the world.'

'For my part,' said the phoenix, 'I will follow every where these two tender, generous lovers.'

'You are in the right,' said the king of Betica; 'but your return to Babylon is not so easy as you imagine. I receive daily intelligence from that country by Tyrian ships, and my Palestine bankers, who correspond with all the nations of the earth. The people are all in arms toward the Euphrates and the Nile. The king of Scythia claims the inheritance of his wife, at the head of three hundred thousand warriors on horseback. The kings of Egypt and India are also laying waste the banks of the Tygris and the Euphrates, each at the head of three hundred thousand men, to revenge themselves for being laughed at. The king of Ethiopia is ravaging Egypt with three hundred thousand men, whilst the king of Egypt is absent from his country. And the king of Babylon has as yet only six hundred thousand men to defend himself.

'I acknowledge to you,' continued the king, 'when I hear of those prodigious armies which are disembogued from the east, and their astonishing magnificence – when I compare them to my trifling bodies of twenty or thirty thousand soldiers, which it is so difficult to clothe and feed; I am inclined to think the eastern subsisted long before the western hemisphere. It seems as if we sprung only yesterday from chaos and barbarity.'

'Sire,' said Amazan, 'the last comers frequently outstrip those who first began the career. It is thought in my country that man was first created in India; but this I am not certain of.'

'And,' said the king of Betica to the phoenix, 'what do you think?'

'Sire,' replied the phoenix, 'I am as yet too young to have any knowledge concerning antiquity. I have lived only about twenty-seven thousand years; but my father, who had lived five times that age, told me he had learned from his father, that the eastern country had always been more populous and rich than the others. It had been transmitted to him from his ancestors, that the generation of all animals had begun upon the banks of the Ganges. For my part, said he, I have not the vanity to be of this opinion. I cannot believe that the foxes of Albion, the marmots of the Alps, and the wolves of Gaul, are descended from my country. In the like manner, I do not believe that the firs and oaks of your country descended from the palm and cocoa trees of India.'

'But from whence are we descended, then?' said the king.

'I do not know,' said the phoenix; 'all I want to know is, to where the beautiful princess of Babylon and my dear Amazan may repair.'

'I very much question,' said the king, 'whether with his two hundred unicorns he will be able to destroy so many armies of three hundred thousand men each.'

'Why not?' said Amazan. The king of Betica felt the force of this sublime question, 'Why not?' but he imagined sublimity alone was not sufficient against innumerable armies.

'I advise you,' said he, 'to seek the king of Ethiopia. I am related to that black prince through my Palestines. I will give you recommendatory letters to him. As he is at enmity with the king of Egypt, he will be but too happy to be strengthened by your alliance. I can assist you with two thousand sober, brave men; and it will depend upon yourself to engage as many more of the people who reside, or rather skip, about the foot of the Pyrenees, and who are called Vasques or Vascons. Send one of your warriors upon an unicorn, with a few diamonds. There is not a Vascon that will not quit the castle, that is, the thatched cottage of his father, to serve you. They are indefatigable, courageous, and agreeable; and whilst you wait their arrival, we will give you festivals, and prepare your ships. I cannot too much acknowledge the service you have done me.'

Amazan realized the happiness of having recovered Formosanta, and enjoyed in tranquillity her conversation, and all the charms of reconciled love, – which are almost equal to a growing passion.

A troop of proud, joyous Vascons soon arrived, dancing a tambourin. The haughty and grave Betican troops were now ready. The old sun-burnt king tenderly embraced the two lovers. He sent great quantities of arms, beds, chests, boards, black clothes, onions, sheep, fowls, flour, and particularly garlic, on board the ships, and wished them a happy voyage, invariable love, and many victories.

Proud Carthage was not then a sea-port. There were at that time only a few Numidians there, who dried fish in the sun. They coasted along Bizacenes, the Syrthes, the fertile banks where since arose Cyrene and the great Chersonese.

They at length arrived toward the first mouth of the sacred Nile. It was at the extremity of this fertile land that the ships of all commercial nations were already received in the port of Canope, without knowing whether the god Canope had founded this port, or whether the inhabitants had manufactured the god – whether the star Canope had given its name to the city, or whether the city had bestowed it upon the star. All that was known of this matter was, that the city and the star were both very ancient; and this is all that can be known of the origin of things, of what nature soever they may be.

It was here that the king of Ethiopia, having ravaged all Egypt, saw the invincible Amazan and the adorable Formosanta come on shore. He took one for the god of war, and the other for the goddess of beauty. Amazan presented to him the letter of recommendation from the king of Spain. The king of Ethiopia immediately entertained them with some admirable festivals, according to the indispensable custom of heroic times. They then conferred about their expedition to exterminate the three hundred thousand men of the king of Egypt, the three hundred thousand of the emperor of the Indies, and the three hundred thousand of the great Khan of the Scythians, who laid siege to the immense, proud, voluptuous city of Babylon.

The two hundred Spaniards, whom Amazan had brought with him, said that they had nothing to do with the king of Ethiopia's succoring Babylon; that it was sufficient their king had ordered them to go and deliver it; and that they were formidable enough for this expedition.

The Vascons said they had performed many other exploits; that they would alone defeat the Egyptians, the Indians, and the Scythians; and that they would not march unless the Spaniards were placed in the rear-guard.

The two hundred Gangarids could not refrain from laughing at the pretensions of their allies, and they maintained that with only one hundred unicorns, they could put to flight all the kings of the earth. The beautiful Formosanta appeased them by her prudence, and by her enchanting discourse. Amazan introduced to the black monarch his Gangarids, his unicorns, his Spaniards, his Vascons, and his beautiful bird.

Everything was soon ready to march by Memphis, Heliopolis, Arsinoe, Petra, Artemitis, Sora, and Apamens, to attack the three kings, and to prosecute this memorable war, before which all the wars ever waged by man sink into insignificance.

Fame with her hundred tongues has proclaimed the victories Amazan gained over the three kings, with his Spaniards, his Vascons, and his unicorns. He restored the beautiful Formosanta to her father. He set at liberty all his mistress's train, whom the king of Egypt had reduced to slavery. The great Khan of the Scythians declared himself his vassal; and his marriage was confirmed with princess Aldea. The invincible and generous Amazan, was acknowledged the heir to the kingdom of Babylon, and entered the city in triumph with the phoenix, in the presence of a hundred tributary kings. The festival of his marriage far surpassed that which king Belus had given. The bull Apis was served up roasted at table. The kings of Egypt and India were cup-bearers to the married pair; and these nuptials were celebrated by five hundred illustrious poets of Babylon.

Oh, Muses! daughters of heaven, who are constantly invoked at the beginning of a work, I only implore you at the end. It is needless to reproach me with saying grace, without having said benedicite. But, Muses! you will not be less my patronesses. Inspire, I pray you, the Ecclesiastical Gazetteer, the illustrious orator of the Convulsionnaires, to say everything possible against The Princess of Babylon, in order that the work may be condemned by the Sorbonne, and, therefore, be universally read. And prevent, I beseech you, O chaste and noble Muses, any supplemental scribblers spoiling, by their fables, the truths I have taught mortals in this faithful narrative.

Wanjiru, Sacrificed by Her Family

THE SUN BEAT DOWN MERCILESSLY and there was no sign of any rain. This happened one year, and it happened again a second year, and even a third year, so that the crops died and the men, women and children found themselves close to starvation. Finally, the elders of the village called all the people together, and they assembled on the scorched grass at the foot of the hill where they had sung and danced in happier times.

Sick and weary of their miserable plight, they turned to each other and asked helplessly:

"Why is it that the rains do not come?"

Not one among them could find an answer, and so they went to the house of the witch-doctor and put to him the same question:

"Tell us why there is no rain," they wept. "Our crops have failed for a third season and we shall soon die of hunger if things do not change."

The witch-doctor took hold of his gourd, shook it hard, and poured its contents on the ground. After he had done this three times, he spoke gravely:

"There is a young maiden called Wanjiru living among you. If you want the rain to fall, she must be bought by the people of the village. In two days' time you should all return to this place, and every one of you, from the eldest to the youngest, must bring with him a goat for the purchase of the maiden."

And so, on the appointed day, the people gathered together again, each one of them leading a goat to the foot of the hill where the witch-doctor waited to receive them. He ordered the crowd to form a circle and called for Wanjiru to come forward and stand in the middle with her relations to one side of her.

One by one, the people began to move towards Wanjiru's family, leading the goats in payment, and as they approached, the feet of the young girl began to sink into the ground. In an instant, she had sunk up to her knees and she screamed in terror as the soil tugged at her limbs, pulling her closer towards the earth.

Her father and mother saw what was happening and they, too, cried out in fear:

"Our daughter is lost! Our daughter is lost! We must do something to save her."

But the villagers continued to close in around them, each of them handing over their goat until Wanjiru sank deeper to her waist.

"I am lost!" the girl called out, "but much rain will come."

She sank to her breast, and as she did so, heavy black clouds began to gather overhead. She sank even lower, up to her neck, and now the rain started to fall from above in huge drops.

Again, Wanjiru's family attempted to move forward to save her, but yet more people came towards them, pressing them to take goats in payment, and so they stood still, watching as the girl wailed:

"My people have forsaken me! I am undone."

Soon she had vanished from sight. The earth closed over her, the rain poured down in a great deluge and the villagers ran to their huts for shelter without pausing to look back.

Now there was a particular young warrior of fearless reputation among the people who had been in love with Wanjiru ever since childhood. Several weeks had passed since her disappearance, but still he could not reconcile himself to her loss and repeated continually to himself:

"Wanjiru is gone from me and her own people have done this thing to her. But I will find her. I will go to the same place and bring her back."

Taking up his shield and his spear, the young warrior departed his home in search of the girl he loved. For almost a year, he roamed the countryside, but still he could find no trace of her. Weary and dejected, he returned home to the village and stood on the spot where Wanjiru had vanished, allowing his tears to flow freely for the first time.

Suddenly, his feet began to sink into the soil and he sank lower and lower until the ground closed over him and he found himself standing in the middle of a long, winding road beneath the earth's surface. He did not hesitate to follow this road, and after a time, he spotted a figure up ahead of him. He ran towards the figure and saw that it was Wanjiru, even though she was scarcely recognizable in her filthy, tattered clothing.

"You were sacrificed to bring the rain," he spoke tenderly to her, "but now that the rain has come, I shall take you back where you belong."

And he lifted Wanjiru carefully onto his back and carried her, as if she were his own beloved child, along the road he had come by, until they rose together to the open air and their feet touched the ground once more.

"You shall not return to the house of your people," the warrior told Wanjiru, "they have treated you shamefully. I will look after you instead."

So they waited until nightfall, and under cover of darkness, the young warrior took Wanjiru to his mother's house, instructing the old woman to tell no one that the girl had returned.

The months passed by, and Wanjiru lived happily with mother and son. Every day a goat was slaughtered and the meat served to her. The old woman made clothes from the skins and hung beads in the girl's hair so that soon she had regained the healthy glow she once had.

Harvest time was now fast approaching, and a great feast was to be held among the people of the village. The young warrior was one of the first to arrive but Wanjiru waited until the rest of the guests had assembled before she came out of the house to join the festivities. At first, she was not recognized by anyone, but after a time, one of her brothers approached her and cried out:

"Surely that is Wanjiru, the sister we lost when the rains came."

The girl hung her head and gave no answer.

"You sold Wanjiru shamefully," the young warrior intervened, "you do not deserve to have her back."

And he beat off her relatives and took Wanjiru back to his mother's house.

But the next day, her family knocked on his door asking to see the young girl. The warrior refused them once more, but still they came, again and again, until, on the fourth day, the young man relented and said to himself:

"Those are real tears her family shed. Surely now they have proven that they care."

So he invited her father and her mother and her brothers into his home and sat down to fix the bride-price for Wanjiru. And when he had paid it, the young warrior married Wanjiru who had returned to him from the land of shadows beneath the earth.

The End of Troy and the Saving of Helen

FROM THE WALLS THE TROJANS saw the black smoke go up thick into the sky, and the whole fleet of the Greeks sailing out to sea. Never were men so glad, and they armed themselves for fear of an ambush, and went cautiously, sending forth scouts in front of them, down to the seashore. Here they found the huts burned down and the camp deserted, and some of the scouts also caught Sinon, who had hid himself in a place where he was likely to be found. They rushed on him with fierce cries, and bound his hands with a rope, and kicked and dragged him along to the place where Priam and the princes were wondering at the great horse of tree. Sinon looked round upon them, while some were saying that he ought to be tortured with fire to make him tell all the truth about the horse. The chiefs in the horse must have trembled for fear lest torture should wring the truth out of Sinon, for then the Trojans would simply burn the machine and them within it.

But Sinon said: 'Miserable man that I am, whom the Greeks hate and the Trojans are eager to slay!'

When the Trojans heard that the Greeks hated him, they were curious, and asked who he was, and how he came to be there.

'I will tell you all, oh King!' he answered Priam. 'I was a friend and squire of an unhappy chief, Palamedes, whom the wicked Odysseus hated and slew secretly one day, when he found him alone, fishing in the sea. I was angry, and in my folly I did not hide my anger, and my words came to the ears of Odysseus. From that hour he sought occasion to slay me. Then Calchas –' here he stopped, saying: 'But why tell a long tale? If you hate all Greeks alike, then slay me; this is what Agamemnon and Odysseus desire; Menelaus would thank you for my head.'

The Trojans were now more curious than before. They bade him go on, and he said that the Greeks had consulted an Oracle, which advised them to sacrifice one of their army to appease the anger of the Gods and gain a fair wind homewards.

'But who was to be sacrificed?' they asked Calchas, who for fifteen days refused to speak. At last, being bribed by Odysseus, he pointed to me, Sinon, and said that I must be the victim. I was bound and kept in prison, while they built their great horse as a present for Pallas-Athene the Goddess. They made it so large that you Trojans might never be able to drag it into your city; while, if you destroyed it, the Goddess might turn her anger against you. And now they have gone home to bring back the image that fell from heaven, which they had sent to Greece, and to restore it to the Temple of Pallas-Athene, when they have taken your town, for the Goddess is angry with them for that theft of Odysseus.'

The Trojans were foolish enough to believe the story of Sinon, and they pitied him and unbound his hands. Then they tied ropes to the wooden horse, and laid rollers in front of it, like men launching a ship, and they all took turns to drag the horse up to the Scaean gate. Children and women put their hands to the ropes and hauled, and with shouts and dances, and hymns they toiled, till about nightfall the horse stood in the courtyard of the inmost castle.

Then all the people of Troy began to dance, and drink, and sing. Such sentinels as were set at the gates got as drunk as all the rest, who danced about the city till after midnight, and then they went to their homes and slept heavily.

Meanwhile the Greek ships were returning from behind Tenedos as fast as the oarsmen could row them.

One Trojan did not drink or sleep; this was Deiphobus, at whose house Helen was now living. He bade her come with them, for he knew that she was able to speak in the very voice of all men and women whom she had ever seen, and he armed a few of his friends and went with them to the citadel. Then he stood beside the horse, holding Helen's hand, and whispered to her that she must call each of the chiefs in the voice of his wife. She was obliged to obey, and she called Menelaus in her own voice, and Diomede in the voice of his wife, and Odysseus in the very voice of Penelope. Then Menelaus and Diomede were eager to answer, but Odysseus grasped their hands and whispered the word 'Echo!' Then they remembered that this was a name of Helen, because she could speak in all voices, and they were silent; but Anticlus was still eager to answer, till Odysseus held his strong hand over his mouth. There was only silence, and Deiphobus led Helen back to his house. When they had gone away Epeius opened the side of the horse, and all the chiefs let themselves down softly to the ground. Some rushed to the gate, to open it, and they killed the sleeping sentinels and let in the Greeks. Others sped with torches to burn the houses of the Trojan princes, and terrible was the slaughter of men, unarmed and half awake, and loud were the cries of the women. But Odysseus had slipped away at the first, none knew where. Neoptolemus ran to the palace of Priam, who was sitting at the altar in his courtyard, praying vainly to the Gods, for Neoptolemus slew the old man cruelly, and his white hair was dabbled in his blood. All through the city was fighting and slaying; but Menelaus went to the house of Deiphobus, knowing that Helen was there.

In the doorway he found Deiphobus lying dead in all his armour, a spear standing in his breast. There were footprints marked in blood, leading through the portico and into the hall. There Menelaus went, and found Odysseus leaning, wounded, against one of the central pillars of the great chamber, the firelight shining on his armour.

'Why hast thou slain Deiphobus and robbed me of my revenge?' said Menelaus.

'You swore to give me a gift,' said Odysseus, 'and will you keep your oath?'

'Ask what you will,' said Menelaus; 'it is yours and my oath cannot be broken.'

'I ask the life of Helen of the fair hands,' said Odysseus; 'this is my own life-price that I pay back to her, for she saved my life when I took the Luck of Troy, and I swore that hers should be saved.'

Then Helen stole, glimmering in white robes, from a recess in the dark hall, and fell at the feet of Menelaus; her golden hair lay in the dust of the hearth, and her hands moved to touch his knees. His drawn sword fell from the hands of Menelaus, and pity and love came into his heart, and he raised her from the dust and her white arms were round his neck, and they both wept. That night Menelaus fought no more, but they tended the wound of Odysseus, for the sword of Deiphobus had bitten through his helmet.

When dawn came Troy lay in ashes, and the women were being driven with spear shafts to the ships, and the men were left unburied, a prey to dogs and all manner of birds. Thus the grey city fell, that had lorded it for many centuries. All the gold and silver and rich embroideries, and ivory and amber, the horses and chariots, were divided among the army; all but a treasure of silver and gold, hidden in a chest within a hollow of the wall, and this treasure was found, not very many years ago, by men digging deep on the hill where Troy once stood. The women, too, were given to the princes, and Neoptolemus took Andromache to his home in Argos, to draw water from the well and to be the slave of a master, and Agamemnon carried beautiful Cassandra, the daughter of Priam, to his palace in Mycenae, where they were both slain in one night. Only Helen was led with honour to the ship of Menelaus.

The Story of Deirdre

THERE WAS A MAN in Ireland once who was called Malcolm Harper. The man was a right good man, and he had a goodly share of this world's goods. He had a wife, but no family. What did Malcolm hear but that a soothsayer had come home to the place, and as the man was a right good man, he wished that the soothsayer might come near them. Whether it was that he was invited or that he came of himself, the soothsayer came to the house of Malcolm.

'Are you doing any soothsaying?' says Malcolm. 'Yes, I am doing a little. Are you in need of soothsaying?'

'Well, I do not mind taking soothsaying from you, if you had soothsaying for me, and you would be willing to do it.'

'Well, I will do soothsaying for you. What kind of soothsaying do you want?'

'Well, the soothsaying I wanted was that you would tell me my lot or what will happen to me, if you can give me knowledge of it.'

'Well, I am going out, and when I return, I will tell you.' And the soothsayer went forth out of the house and he was not long outside when he returned.

'Well,' said the soothsayer, 'I saw in my second sight that it is on account of a daughter of yours that the greatest amount of blood shall be shed that has ever been shed in Erin since time and race began. And the three most famous heroes that ever were found will lose their heads on her account.'

After a time a daughter was born to Malcolm, he did not allow a living being to come to his house, only himself and the nurse. He asked this woman, 'Will you yourself bring up the child to keep her in hiding far away where eye will not see a sight of her nor ear hear a word about her?'

The woman said she would, so Malcolm got three men, and he took them away to a large mountain, distant and far from reach, without the knowledge or notice of anyone. He caused there a hillock, round and green, to be dug out of the middle, and the hole thus made to be covered carefully over so that a little company could dwell there together. This was done.

Deirdre and her foster-mother dwelt in the bothy mid the hills without the knowledge or the suspicion of any living person about them and without anything occurring, until Deirdre was sixteen years of age. Deirdre grew like the white sapling, straight and trim as the rash on the moss. She was the creature of fairest form, of loveliest aspect, and of gentlest nature that existed between earth and heaven in all Ireland – whatever colour of hue she had before, there was nobody that looked into her face but she would blush fiery red over it.

The woman that had charge of her gave Deirdre every information and skill of which she herself had knowledge and skill. There was not a blade of grass growing from root, nor a bird singing in the wood, nor a star shining from heaven but Deirdre had a name for it. But one thing, she did not wish her to have either part or parley with any single living man of the rest of the world. But on a gloomy winter night, with black, scowling clouds, a hunter of game was wearily travelling the hills, and what happened but that he missed the trail of the hunt, and lost his course and companions. A drowsiness came upon the man as he wearily wandered over the hills, and he lay down by the side of the beautiful green knoll in which Deirdre lived, and he slept. The man was faint from hunger and wandering, and benumbed with cold, and a deep sleep fell upon him. When he lay down beside the green hill where Deirdre was, a troubled dream came to the man, and he thought that he enjoyed the warmth of a fairy broch, the fairies being inside playing music. The hunter shouted out in his dream, if there was anyone in the broch, to let him in for the Holy One's sake. Deirdre heard the voice and said to her foster-mother: 'O foster-mother, what cry is that?'

'It is nothing at all, Deirdre – merely the birds of the air astray and seeking each other. But let them go past to the bosky glade. There is no shelter or house for them here.'

'Oh, foster-mother, the bird asked to get inside for the sake of the God of the Elements, and you yourself tell me that anything that is asked in His name we ought to do. If you will not allow the bird that is being benumbed with cold, and done to death with hunger, to be let in, I do not think much of your language or your faith. But since I give credence to your language and to your faith, which you taught me, I will myself let in the bird.' And Deirdre arose and drew the bolt from the leaf of the door, and she let in the hunter. She placed a seat in the place for sitting, food in the place for eating, and drink in the place for drinking for the man who came to the house. 'Oh, for this life and raiment, you man that came in, keep restraint on your tongue!' said the old woman. 'It is not a great thing for you to keep your mouth shut and your tongue quiet when you get a home and shelter of a hearth on a gloomy winter's night.'

'Well,' said the hunter, 'I may do that – keep my mouth shut and my tongue quiet, since I came to the house and received hospitality from you; but by the hand of thy father and grandfather, and by your own two hands, if some other of the people of the world saw this beauteous creature you have here hid away, they would not long leave her with you, I swear.'

'What men are these you refer to?' said Deirdre.

'Well, I will tell you, young woman,' said the hunter. 'They are Naois, son of Uisnech, and Allen and Arden his two brothers.'

'What like are these men when seen, if we were to see them?' said Deirdre.

'Why, the aspect and form of the men when seen are these,' said the hunter: 'they have the colour of the raven on their hair, their skin like swan on the wave in whiteness, and their cheeks as the blood of the brindled red calf, and their speed and their leap are those of the salmon of the torrent and the deer of the grey mountain side. And Naois is head and shoulders over the rest of the people of Erin.'

However they are,' said the nurse, 'be you off from here and take another road. And, King of Light and Sun! In good sooth and certainty, little are my thanks for yourself or for her that let you in!'

The hunter went away, and went straight to the palace of King Connachar. He sent word in to the king that he wished to speak to him if he pleased. The king answered the message and came out to speak to the man. 'What is the reason of your journey?' said the king to the hunter.

'I have only to tell you, O king,' said the hunter, 'that I saw the fairest creature that ever was born in Erin, and I came to tell you of it.'

'Who is this beauty and where is she to be seen, when she was not seen before till you saw her, if you did see her?'

'Well, I did see her,' said the hunter. 'But, if I did, no man else can see her unless he get directions from me as to where she is dwelling.'

'And will you direct me to where she dwells? And the reward of your directing me will be as good as the reward of your message,' said the king.

'Well, I will direct you, O king, although it is likely that this will not be what they want,' said the hunter.

Connachar, King of Ulster, sent for his nearest kinsmen, and he told them of his intent. Though early rose the song of the birds mid the rocky caves and the music of the birds in the grove, earlier than that did Connachar, King of Ulster, arise, with his little troop of dear friends, in the delightful twilight of the fresh and gentle May; the dew was heavy on each bush and flower and stem, as they went to bring Deirdre forth from the green knoll where she stayed. Many a youth was there who had a lithe leaping and lissom step when they started whose step was faint, failing, and faltering when they reached the bothy on account of the length of the way and roughness of the road.

'Yonder, now, down in the bottom of the glen is the bothy where the woman dwells, but I will not go nearer than this to the old woman,' said the hunter.

Connachar with his band of kinsfolk went down to the green knoll where Deirdre dwelt and he knocked at the door of the bothy. The nurse replied, 'No less than a king's command and a king's army could put me out of my bothy tonight. And I should be obliged to you, were you to tell who it is that wants me to open my bothy door.'

'It is I, Connachar, King of Ulster.' When the poor woman heard who was at the door, she rose with haste and let in the king and all that could get in of his retinue.

When the king saw the woman that was before him that he had been in quest of, he thought he never saw in the course of the day nor in the dream of night a creature so fair as Deirdre and he gave his full heart's weight of love to her. Deirdre was raised on the topmost of the heroes' shoulders and she and her foster-mother were brought to the Court of King Connachar of Ulster.

With the love that Connachar had for her, he wanted to marry Deirdre right off there and then, will she nill she marry him. But she said to him, 'I would be obliged to you if you will give me the respite of a year and a day.' He said 'I will grant you that, hard though it is, if you will give me your unfailing promise that you will marry me at the year's end.' And she gave the promise. Connachar got for her a woman-teacher and merry modest maidens fair that would lie down and rise with her, that would play and speak with her. Deirdre was clever in maidenly duties and wifely understanding, and Connachar thought he never saw with bodily eye a creature that pleased him more.

Deirdre and her women companions were one day out on the hillock behind the house enjoying the scene, and drinking in the sun's heat. What did they see coming but three men a-journeying. Deirdre was looking at the men that were coming, and wondering at them. When the men neared them, Deirdre remembered the language of the huntsman, and she said to herself that these were the three sons of Uisnech, and that this was Naois, he having what was above the bend of the two shoulders above the men of Erin all. The three brothers went past without taking any notice of them, without even glancing at the young girls on the hillock. What happened but that love for Naois struck the heart of Deirdre, so that she could not but follow after him. She girded up her raiment and went after the men that went past the base of the knoll, leaving her women attendants there. Allen and Arden had heard of the woman that Connachar, King of Ulster, had with him, and they thought that, if Naois, their brother, saw her, he would have her himself, more especially as she was not married to the King. They perceived the woman coming, and called on one another to hasten their step as they had a long distance to travel, and the dusk of night was coming on. They did so. She cried: 'Naois, son of Uisnech, will you leave me?'

'What piercing, shrill cry is that – the most melodious my ear ever heard, and the shrillest that ever struck my heart of all the cries I ever heard?'

'It is anything else but the wail of the wave-swans of Connachar,' said his brothers.

'No! Yonder is a woman's cry of distress,' said Naois, and he swore he would not go further until he saw from whom the cry came, and Naois turned back. Naois and Deirdre met, and Deirdre kissed Naois three times, and a kiss each to his brothers. With the confusion that she was in, Deirdre went into a crimson blaze of fire, and her colour came and went as rapidly as the movement of the aspen by the stream side. Naois thought he never saw a fairer creature, and Naois gave Deirdre the love that he never gave to thing, to vision, or to creature but to herself. Then Naois placed Deirdre on the topmost height of his shoulder, and told his brothers to keep up their pace, and they kept up their pace. Naois thought that it would not be well for him to remain in Erin on account of the way in which Connachar, King of Ulster, his uncle's son, had gone against him because of the woman, though he had not married her; and he turned back to Alba, that is, Scotland. He reached the side of Loch-Ness and made his habitation there. He could kill the salmon of the torrent from out his own door, and the deer of the grey gorge from out his window. Naois and Deirdre and Allen and Arden dwelt in a tower, and they were happy so long a time as they were there.

By this time the end of the period came at which Deirdre had to marry Connachar, King of Ulster. Connachar made up his mind to take Deirdre away by the sword whether she was married to Naois or not. So he prepared a great and gleeful feast. He sent word far and wide through Erin all to his kinspeople to come to the feast. Connachar thought to himself that Naois would not come though he should bid him; and the scheme that arose in his mind was to send for his father's brother, Ferchar Mac Ro, and to send him on an embassy to Naois. He did so; and Connachar said to Ferchar, 'Tell Naois, son of Uisnech, that I am setting forth a great and gleeful feast to my friends and kinspeople throughout the wide extent of Erin all, and that I shall not have rest by day nor sleep by night if he and Allen and Arden be not partakers of the feast.'

Ferchar Mac Ro and his three sons went on their journey, and reached the tower where Naois was dwelling by the side of Loch Etive. The sons of Uisnech gave a cordial kindly welcome to Ferchar Mac Ro and his three sons, and asked of him the news of Erin. 'The best news that I have for you,' said the hardy hero, 'is that Connachar, King of Ulster, is setting forth a great sumptuous feast to his friends and kinspeople throughout the wide extent of Erin all, and he has vowed by the earth beneath him, by the high heaven above him, and by the sun that wends to the west, that he will have no rest by day nor sleep by night if the sons of Uisnech, the sons of his own father's brother, will not come back to the land of their home and the soil of their nativity, and to the feast likewise, and he has sent us on embassy to invite you.'

'We will go with you,' said Naois.

'We will,' said his brothers.

But Deirdre did not wish to go with Ferchar Mac Ro, and she tried every prayer to turn Naois from going with him – she said: 'I saw a vision, Naois, and do you interpret it to me,' – then she sang:

'O Naois, son of Uisnech, hear
What was shown in a dream to me.
There came three white doves out of the South
Flying over the sea,
And drops of honey were in their mouth
From the hive of the honey-bee.
O Naois, son of Uisnech, hear,
What was shown in a dream to me.
I saw three grey hawks out of the south
Come flying over the sea,
And the red red drops they bare in their mouth
They were dearer than life to me.'

Said Naois: –

'It is nought but the fear of woman's heart,
And a dream of the night, Deirdre.'

'The day that Connachar sent the invitation to his feast will be unlucky for us if we don't go, O Deirdre.'

'You will go there,' said Ferchar Mac Ro; 'and if Connachar show kindness to you, show ye kindness to him; and if he will display wrath towards you display ye wrath towards him, and I and my three sons will be with you.'

'We will,' said Daring Drop. 'We will,' said Hardy Holly. 'We will,' said Fiallan the Fair.

'I have three sons, and they are three heroes, and in any harm or danger that may befall you, they will be with you, and I myself will be along with them.' And Ferchar Mac Ro gave his vow and his word in presence of his arms that, in any harm or danger that came in the way of the sons of Uisnech, he and his three sons would not leave head on live body in Erin, despite sword or helmet, spear or shield, blade or mail, be they ever so good.

Deirdre was unwilling to leave Alba, but she went with Naois. Deirdre wept tears in showers and she sang:

'Dear is the land, the land over there,
Alba full of woods and lakes;
Bitter to my heart is leaving thee,
But I go away with Naois.'

Ferchar Mac Ro did not stop till he got the sons of Uisnech away with him, despite the suspicion of Deirdre.

The coracle was put to sea,
The sail was hoisted to it;
And the second morrow they arrived
On the white shores of Erin.

As soon as the sons of Uisnech landed in Erin, Ferchar Mac Ro sent word to Connachar, king of Ulster, that the men whom he wanted were come, and let him now show kindness to them. 'Well,' said Connachar, 'I did not expect that the sons of Uisnech would come, though I sent for them, and I am not quite ready to receive them.

But there is a house down yonder where I keep strangers, and let them go down to it today, and my house will be ready before them tomorrow.' But he that was up in the palace felt it long that he was not getting word as to how matters were going on for those down in the house of the strangers.

'Go you, Gelban Grednach, son of Lochlin's King, go you down and bring me information as to whether her former hue and complexion are on Deirdre. If they be, I will take her out with edge of blade and point of sword, and if not, let Naois, son of Uisnech, have her for himself,' said Connachar.

Gelban, the cheering and charming son of Lochlin's King, went down to the place of the strangers, where the sons of Uisnech and Deirdre were staying. He looked in through the bicker-hole on the door-leaf. Now she that he gazed upon used to go into a crimson blaze of blushes when anyone looked at her. Naois looked at Deirdre and knew that someone was looking at her from the back of the door-leaf. He seized one of the dice on the table before him and fired it through the bicker-hole, and knocked the eye out of Gelban Grednach the Cheerful and Charming, right through the back of his head. Gelban returned back to the palace of King Connachar.

'You were cheerful, charming, going away, but you are cheerless, charmless, returning. What has happened to you, Gelban? But have you seen her, and are Deirdre's hue and complexion as before?' said Connachar.

'Well, I have seen Deirdre, and I saw her also truly, and while I was looking at her through the bicker-hole on the door, Naois, son of Uisnech, knocked out my eye with one of the dice in his hand. But of a truth and verity, although he put out even my eye, it were my desire still to remain looking at her with the other eye, were it not for the hurry you told me to be in,' said Gelban.

'That is true,' said Connachar; 'let three hundred bravo heroes go down to the abode of the strangers, and let them bring hither to me Deirdre, and kill the rest.' Connachar ordered three hundred active heroes to go down to the abode of the strangers and to take Deirdre up with them and kill the rest. 'The pursuit is coming,' said Deirdre.

'Yes, but I will myself go out and stop the pursuit,' said Naois.

'It is not you, but we that will go,' said Daring Drop, and Hardy Holly, and Fiallan the Fair; 'it is to us that our father entrusted your defence from harm and danger when he himself left for home.' And the gallant youths, full noble, full manly, full handsome, with beauteous brown locks, went forth girt with battle arms fit for fierce fight and clothed with combat dress for fierce contest fit, which was burnished, bright, brilliant, bladed, blazing, on which were many pictures of beasts and birds and creeping things, lions and lithe-limbed tigers, brown eagle and harrying hawk and adder fierce; and the young heroes laid low three-thirds of the company.

Connachar came out in haste and cried with wrath: 'Who is there on the floor of fight, slaughtering my men?'

'We, the three sons of Ferchar Mac Ro.'

'Well,' said the king, 'I will give a free bridge to your grandfather, a free bridge to your father, and a free bridge each to you three brothers, if you come over to my side tonight.'

'Well, Connachar, we will not accept that offer from you nor thank you for it. Greater by far do we prefer to go home to our father and tell the deeds of heroism we have done, than accept anything on these terms from you. Naois, son of Uisnech, and Allen and Arden are as nearly related to yourself as they are to us, though you are so keen to shed their blood, and you would shed our blood also, Connachar.' And the noble, manly, handsome youths with beauteous, brown locks returned inside. 'We are now,' said they, 'going home to tell our father that you are now safe from the hands of the king.' And the youths all fresh and tall and lithe and beautiful, went home to their father to tell that the sons of Uisnech were safe. This happened at the parting of the day and night in the morning twilight time, and Naois said they must go away, leave that house, and return to Alba.

Naois and Deirdre, Allan and Arden started to return to Alba. Word came to the king that the company he was in pursuit of were gone. The king then sent for Duanan Gacha Druid, the best magician he had, and he spoke to him as follows: – 'Much wealth have I expended on you, Duanan Gacha Druid, to give schooling and learning and magic mystery to you, if these people get away from me today without care, without consideration or regard for me, without chance of overtaking them, and without power to stop them.'

'Well, I will stop them,' said the magician, 'until the company you send in pursuit return.' And the magician placed a wood before them through which no man could go, but the sons of Uisnech marched through the wood without halt or hesitation, and Deirdre held on to Naois's hand. 'What is the good of that? That will not do yet,' said Connachar. 'They are off without bending of their feet or stopping of their step, without heed or respect to me, and I am without power to keep up to them or opportunity to turn them back this night.'

'I will try another plan on them,' said the druid; and he placed before them a grey sea instead of a green plain. The three heroes stripped and tied their clothes behind their heads, and Naois placed Deirdre on the top of his shoulder.

They stretched their sides to the stream,
And sea and land were to them the same,
The rough grey ocean was the same
As meadow-land green and plain.

'Though that be good, O Duanan, it will not make the heroes return,' said Connachar; 'they are gone without regard for me, and without honour to me, and without power on my part to pursue them or to force them to return this night.'

'We shall try another method on them, since yon one did not stop them,' said the druid. And the druid froze the grey ridged sea into hard rocky knobs, the sharpness of sword being on the one edge and the poison power of adders on the other. Then Arden cried that he was getting tired, and nearly giving over. 'Come you, Arden, and sit on my right shoulder,' said Naois. Arden came and sat, on Naois's shoulder. Arden was long in this posture when he died; but though he was dead Naois would not let him go.

Allen then cried out that he was getting faint and nigh-well giving up. When Naois heard his prayer, he gave forth the piercing sigh of death, and asked Allen to lay hold of him and he would bring him to land.

Allen was not long when the weakness of death came on him and his hold failed. Naois looked around, and when he saw his two well-beloved brothers dead, he cared not whether he lived or died, and he gave forth the bitter sigh of death, and his heart burst.

'They are gone,' said Duanan Gacha Druid to the king, 'and I have done what you desired me. The sons of Uisnech are dead and they will trouble you no more; and you have your wife hale and whole to yourself.'

'Blessings for that upon you and may the good results accrue to me, Duanan. I count it no loss what I spent in the schooling and teaching of you. Now dry up the flood, and let me see if I can behold Deirdre,' said Connachar. And Duanan Gacha Druid dried up the flood from the plain and the three sons of Uisnech were lying together dead, without breath of life, side by side on the green meadow plain and Deirdre bending above showering down her tears.

Then Deirdre said this lament: 'Fair one, loved one, flower of beauty; beloved upright and strong; beloved noble and modest warrior. Fair one, blue-eyed, beloved of thy wife; lovely to me at the trysting-place came thy clear voice through the woods of Ireland. I cannot eat or smile henceforth. Break not today, my heart: soon enough shall I lie within my grave. Strong are the waves of sorrow, but stronger is sorrow's self, Connachar.'

The people then gathered round the heroes' bodies and asked Connachar what was to be done with the bodies. The order that he gave was that they should dig a pit and put the three brothers in it side by side. Deirdre kept sitting on the brink of the grave, constantly asking the gravediggers to dig the pit wide and free. When the bodies of the brothers were put in the grave, Deirdre said: –

'Come over hither, Naois, my love,
Let Arden close to Allen lie;
If the dead had any sense to feel,
Ye would have made a place for Deirdre.'

The men did as she told them. She jumped into the grave and lay down by Naois, and she was dead by his side.

The king ordered the body to be raised from out the grave and to be buried on the other side of the loch. It was done as the king bade, and the pit closed. Thereupon a fir shoot grew out of the grave of Deirdre and a fir shoot from the grave of Naois, and the two shoots united in a knot above the loch. The king ordered the shoots to be cut down, and this was done twice, until, at the third time, the wife whom the king had married caused him to stop this work of evil and his vengeance on the remains of the dead.

Tales of the Goddess of Mercy

THE MOST POPULAR Goddess of the Chinese Buddhist faith is the beautiful Kuan Yin, a deity originally represented as a man. This transition from a male deity into a female one seems to have emerged sometime during the Northern Sung Dynasty (ad 960–1126) and is reflected in Kuan Yin's miraculous appearance in human form in the saga of Miao Shan that follows.

According to the ancient myth, Kuan Yin was about to enter Heaven when she heard a cry of anguish from the earth beneath her and could not prevent herself from investigating its source. Hence her name translates as 'one who hears the cries of the world'.

Kuan Yin is the patron saint of Tibetan Buddhism, the patron Goddess of mothers, the guardian of the storm-tossed fisherman and the overall protector of mankind. If, in the midst of a fire she is called upon, the fire ceases to burn. If during a battle her name is called, the sword and spear of the enemy prove harmless. If prone to evil thoughts, the heart is immediately purified when she is summoned. Her image is that of a Madonna figure with a child in her arms. All over China this Goddess is revered and it is this image that appears not only in temples of worship but also in households and other public places.

The Birth of Miao Shan

In the twenty-first year of the reign of Ta Hao (the Great Great One) of the Golden Heavenly Dynasty, a man named P'o Chia, whose first name was Lo Yu – an enterprising kinglet of Hsi Yii – seized the throne for twenty years after fighting a war for three years. His kingdom was known as Hsing Lin and the title of his reign as Miao Chuang.

The kingdom of Hsing Lin was situated between India on the west, the kingdom of T'ien Cheng on the south and the kingdom of Siam on the north. Of this kingdom the two pillars of State were the Grand Minister Chao Chen and the General Ch'u Chieh. The Queen Pao Te, whose maiden name was Po Ya, and the King Miao Chuang had lived nearly half a century without having a son to succeed to the throne. This was a source of great grief to them. Po Ya suggested to the King that the God of Hua Shan, the sacred mountain in the west, had the reputation of being always willing to help; and that if he prayed to him and asked his pardon for having shed so much blood during the wars which preceded his accession to the throne he might obtain an heir.

Welcoming this suggestion, the King sent for Chao Chen and ordered him to dispatch the two Chief Ministers of Ceremonies, Hsi Heng-nan and Chih Tu, to the temple of Hua Shan with instructions to request fifty Buddhist and Taoist priests to pray for seven days and seven nights in order that the King might obtain a son. When that period was over, the King and Queen would go in person to offer sacrifices in the temple.

The envoys took with them many rare and valuable presents and for seven days and seven nights the temple resounded with the sound of drums, bells and all kinds of instruments, intermingled with the voices of the praying priests. On their arrival the King and Queen offered sacrifices to the god of the sacred mountain.

But the God of Hua Shan knew that the King had been deprived of a male heir as a punishment for the extensive loss of life during his three years' war. The priests, however, interceded for him, urging that the King had come in person to offer the sacrifices, so the God could not altogether reject his prayer. So he ordered Ch'ien-li Yen, 'Thousand-li Eye', and Shun-feng Erh, 'Favourable-wind Ear', to go quickly and find out if there were not some worthy person who was on the point of being reincarnated into this world.

The two messengers shortly returned and stated that in India, in the village of Chih-shu Yuan in the Chiu Ling Mountains, there lived a good man named Shih Ch'in-ch'ang whose ancestors had observed all the ascetic rules of the Buddhists for three generations. This man was the father of three children – the eldest Shih Wen, the second Shih Chin and the third Shih Shan – all worthy followers of the great Buddha.

Meanwhile, Wang Che, a bandit chief and thirty of his band of men, finding themselves pursued and harassed by the Indian soldiers, without provisions or shelter and dying of hunger, went to Shih Wen and begged for something to eat. Knowing that they were evildoers, Shih Wen and his two brothers refused to give them anything; if they starved, they said, the peasants would no longer suffer from their attacks. So the robbers decided that it was a case of life for life and broke into the house of a rich family of the name of Tai, burning their home, killing a hundred men, women and children, and carrying off everything they possessed.

The local t'u-ti (or Local God) made a report to Yu Huang at once.

'This Shih family,' replied the god, 'for three generations has given itself up to good works, and certainly the robbers were not deserving of any pity. However, it is impossible to deny that the three brothers Shih, in refusing them food, morally compelled them to loot the Tai family's house, putting all to the sword or flames. Is this not the same as if they had committed the crime themselves? Let them be arrested and put in chains in the celestial prison and let them never see the light of the sun again.'

'Since,' said the messenger to the God of Hua Shan, 'your gratitude toward Miao Chuang compels you to grant him an heir, why not ask Yu Huang to pardon their crime and reincarnate them in the womb of the Queen Po Ya, so that they may begin a new terrestrial existence and give themselves up to good works?' As a result, the God of Hua Shan called the Spirit of the Wind and gave him a message for Yu Huang.

The message was as follows: 'King Miao Chuang has offered sacrifice to me and begged me to grant him an heir. But since by his wars he has caused the deaths of a large number of human beings, he does not deserve to have his request granted. Now these three brothers Shih have offended your Majesty by forcing Wang Che to be guilty of murder and robbery. I pray you to take into account their past good works and pardon their crime, giving them an opportunity of expiating it by causing them all three to be reborn, but of the female sex, in the womb of Po Ya the Queen. In this way they will be able to atone for their crime and save many souls.' Yu Huang was pleased to comply and he ordered the Spirit of the North Pole to release the three captives and take their souls to the palace of King Miao Chuang, where in three years' time they would be changed into females in the womb of Queen Po Ya.

The King, who was anxiously expecting the birth of an heir, was informed one morning that a daughter had been born to him. She was named Miao Ch'ing. A year went by and another daughter was born. This one was named Miao Yin. When, at the end of the third year, another daughter was born, the King, beside himself with rage, called his Grand Minister Chao Chen and said to him, 'I am past fifty, and have no male child to succeed me on the throne. My dynasty will therefore become extinct. Of what use have been all my labours and all my victories?' Chao Chen tried to console him, saying, 'Heaven has granted you three daughters: no human power can change this divine decree. When these princesses have grown up, we will choose three sons-in-law for your Majesty, and you can elect your successor from among them. Who will dare to dispute his right to the throne?'

The King named the third daughter Miao Shan. She became noted for her modesty and many other good qualities and scrupulously observed all the tenets of the Buddhist doctrines. Virtuous living seemed, indeed, to be like second nature.

Miao Shan's Ambition

One day, when the three daughters of King Miao Chuang were playing in the palace garden of Perpetual Spring, Miao Shan said to her sisters, 'Riches and glory are like the rain in spring or the morning dew; a little while, and all is gone. Kings and emperors think to enjoy to the end the good fortune which places them in a rank apart from other human beings; but sickness lays them low in their coffins, and all is over. Where are now all those powerful dynasties which have laid down the law to the world? As for me, I desire nothing more than a peaceful retreat on a lone mountain, there to attempt the attainment of perfection. If someday I can reach a high degree of goodness, then, borne on the clouds of Heaven, I will travel throughout the universe, passing in the twinkling of an eye from east to west. I will rescue my father and mother, and bring them to Heaven; I will save the miserable and afflicted on earth; I will convert the spirits which do evil, and cause them to do good. That is my only ambition.'

No sooner had she finished speaking than a lady of the Court came to announce that the King had found sons-in-law for his two elder daughters. The wedding feast was to be the very next day. 'Be quick,' she added, 'and prepare your presents, your dresses and so forth, for the King's order is imperative.' The husband chosen for Miao Ch'ing was a First Academician named Chao K'uei. His personal name was Te Ta, and he was the son of a celebrated minister of the reigning dynasty. Miao Yin's husband-to-be was a military officer named Ho Feng, whose personal name was Ch'ao Yang. He had passed first in the examination for the Military Doctorate. The marriage ceremonies were magnificent. Festivity followed festivity; the newlyweds were duly installed in their palaces and general happiness prevailed.

There now remained only Miao Shan. The King and Queen wished to find for her a man famous for knowledge and virtue, capable of ruling the kingdom and worthy of being the successor to the throne. So the King called her and explained to her all his plans regarding her and how all his hopes rested on her.

'It is a crime,' she replied, 'for me not to comply with my father's wishes; but you must pardon me if my ideas differ from yours.'

'Tell me what your ideas are,' said the King. 'I do not wish to marry,' she said. 'I wish to attain to perfection and to Buddhahood. Then I promise that I will not be ungrateful to you.'

'Wretch of a daughter,' cried the King in anger, 'you think you can teach me, the head of the State and ruler of so great a people! Has anyone ever known a daughter of a king become a nun? Can a good woman be found in that class? Put aside all these mad ideas of a nunnery and tell me at once if you will marry a First Academician or a Military First Graduate.'

'Who is there,' answered the girl, 'who does not love the royal dignity? What person who does not aspire to the happiness of marriage? However, I wish to become a nun. With respect to the riches and glory of this world, my heart is as cold as a dead cinder and I feel a keen desire to make it ever purer and purer.'

The King was furious and wished to cast her out from his presence. Miao Shan, knowing she could not openly disobey his orders, took another course. 'If you absolutely insist upon my marrying,' she said, 'I will consent; only I must marry a physician.'

'A physician!' growled the King. 'Are men of good family and talents wanting in my kingdom? What an absurd idea, to want to marry a physician!'

'My wish is,' said Miao Shan, 'to heal humanity of all its ills; of cold, heat, lust, old age and all infirmities. I wish to equalize all classes, putting rich and poor on the same footing, to have community of goods, without distinction of persons. If you will grant me my wish, I can still in this way become a Buddha, a Saviour of Mankind. There is no necessity to call in the diviners to choose an auspicious day. I am ready to be married now.'

At these words the King was mad with rage. 'Wicked imbecile!' he cried, 'What diabolical suggestions are these that you dare to make in my presence?' Without further ado he called Ho T'ao, who on that day was officer of the palace guard. When he had arrived and kneeled to receive the King's commands, the latter said: 'This wicked nun dishonours me. Take from her her Court robes and drive her from my presence. Take her to the Queen's garden and let her perish there of cold: that will be one care less for my troubled heart.'

Miao Shan fell on her face and thanked the King. She went with the officer to the Queen's garden, where she began to lead her retired hermit life with the moon for companion and the wind for friend, content to see all obstacles overthrown on her way to Nirvana – the highest state of spiritual bliss – and glad to exchange the pleasures of the palace for the sweetness of solitude.

The Nunnery of The White Bird

After many futile attempts to dissuade Miao Shan from her purpose, one day the King and Queen sent Miao Hung and Ts'ui Hung to make a last attempt to bring their misguided daughter to her senses. Miao Shan, annoyed at this renewed attempt, ordered them never again to come and torment her with their silly prattle. 'I have found out,' she added, 'that there is a well-known temple at Ju Chou in Lung-shu Hsien. This Buddhist temple is known as the Nunnery of the White Bird. In it five hundred nuns give themselves up to the study of the true doctrine and the way of perfection. Go then and ask the Queen to obtain the King's permission for me to retire there. If you can do me this favour, I will not fail to reward you later.'

Miao Chuang summoned the messengers and inquired the result of their efforts. 'She is more unapproachable than ever,' they replied; 'she has even ordered us to ask the Queen to obtain your Majesty's permission to retire to the Nunnery of the White Bird in Lung-shu Hsien.'

The King gave his permission, but sent strict orders to the nunnery instructing the nuns to do all in their power to dissuade the Princess from remaining.

This Nunnery of the White Bird had been built by Huang Ti and the five hundred nuns who lived in it had as Superior a lady named I Yu, who was remarkable for her virtue. On receipt of the royal mandate, she had summoned Cheng Cheng-ch'ang, the choir mistress, and informed her that Princess Miao Shan would shortly arrive at the temple. She requested her to receive the visitor courteously, but at the same time to do all she could to dissuade her from adopting the life of a nun. Having given these instructions, the Superior, accompanied by two novices went to meet Miao Shan at the gate of the temple. On her arrival they saluted her. The Princess returned the salute, but said: 'I have just left the world in order to place myself under your orders: why do you come and salute me on my arrival? I beg you to be so good as to take me into the temple, in order that I may pay my respects to the Buddha.' I Yu led her into the principal hall and instructed the nuns to light incense sticks, ring the bells and beat the drums. The visit to the temple finished, she went into the preaching hall, where she greeted her instructresses. The latter obeyed the King's command and tried to persuade the Princess to return to her home but, as none of their arguments had any effect, they decided to give her a trial. She was to be put in charge of the kitchen, where she could prepare the food for the nunnery and generally be at the service of all. If she did not do a good job, they could dismiss her.

Miao Shan joyfully agreed, and went to make her humble submission to the Buddha. She knelt before Ju Lai and made offering to him, praying: 'Great Buddha, full of goodness and mercy, your humble servant wishes to leave the world. Grant that I may never yield to the temptations which will be sent to try my faith.' Miao Shan further promised to observe all the regulations of the nunnery and to obey the superiors.

This generous self-sacrifice touched the heart of Yu Huang, the Master of Heaven, who summoned the Spirit of the North Star and instructed him as follows:

'Miao Shan, the third daughter of King Miao Chuang, has renounced the world in order to devote herself to the attainment of perfection. Her father has consigned her to the Nunnery of the White Bird. She has happily undertaken the burden of all the work in the nunnery. If she is left without help, who is there who will be willing to adopt the virtuous life? Go quickly and order the Three Agents, the Gods of the Five Sacred Peaks, the Eight Ministers of the Heavenly Dragon, Ch'ieh Lan and the t'u-ti to send her help at once. Tell the Sea Dragon to dig her a well near the kitchen, a tiger to bring her firewood, birds to collect vegetables for the nuns and all the spirits of Heaven to help her in her duties, so that she may give herself up without disturbance to the pursuit of perfection. See that my commands are promptly obeyed.' The Spirit of the North Star complied without delay.

Seeing all these gods arrive to help the novice, the Superior, I Yu, spoke with the choir mistress, saying: 'We assigned to the Princess the burdensome work of the kitchen because she refused to return to the world; but since she began her duties the gods of the eight caves of Heaven have come to offer her fruit, Ch'ieh Lan sweeps the kitchen, the dragon has dug a well, the God of the Hearth and the tiger bring her fuel, birds collect vegetables for her, the nunnery bell every evening at dusk booms of itself, as if struck by some mysterious hand. Obviously miracles are being performed. Hasten and fetch the King and beg his Majesty to recall his daughter.'

Cheng Cheng-ch'ang travelled to the palace and informed the King of all that had happened. The King called Hu Pi-li, the chief of the guard, and ordered him to go the Nunnery of the White Bird and burn it to the ground, together with the nuns. When he reached the place the commander surrounded the nunnery with his soldiers and set fire to it. The five hundred doomed nuns invoked the aid of Heaven and earth, and then, addressing Miao Shan, said: 'It is you who have brought upon us this terrible disaster.'

'It is true,' said Miao Shan. 'I alone am the cause of your destruction.' She then knelt down and prayed to Heaven: 'Great Sovereign of the Universe, your servant is the daughter of King Miao Chuang; you are the grandson of King Lun. Will you not rescue your younger sister? You have left your palace; I also have left mine. You in former times took yourself to the snowy mountains to attain perfection; I came here with the same object. Will you not save us from this fiery destruction?'

Her prayer ended, Miao Shan took a bamboo hairpin from her hair. She pricked the roof of her mouth with it and spat the flowing blood toward Heaven. Immediately great clouds gathered in all parts of the sky and sent down heavy rain, which put out the fire that threatened the nunnery. The nuns threw themselves on their knees and thanked her for having saved their lives.

The Execution of Miao Shan

After witnessing the extraordinary event at the Nunnery of the White Bird, Hu Pi-li rushed back to inform the King. The King was enraged. He ordered Hu Pi-li to go back at once and bring his daughter in chains. He was to behead her on the spot.

But the Queen, who had heard of this new plot, begged the King to grant her daughter one last chance. 'If you will give permission,' she said, 'I will have a magnificent pavilion built at the side of the road where Miao Shan will pass in chains on the way to her execution. We will go there with our two other daughters and our sons-in-law. As she passes we will have music, songs and feasting – everything likely to impress her and make her contrast our luxurious life with her miserable plight. This will surely make her repent.'

'I agree,' said the King, 'to counter-order her execution until your preparations are complete.' Nevertheless, when the time came, Miao Shan showed nothing but disdain for all this worldly show, and to all advances replied only: 'I love not these pompous vanities; I swear that I prefer death to the so-called joys of this world.' She was then led to the place of execution. All the Court was present. Sacrifices were made to her as to one already dead. In the midst of all this the Queen appeared. She ordered the officials to return to their posts, so that she might once more urge her daughter to repent. But Miao Shan only listened in silence with downcast eyes.

The King felt great disgust at the thought of shedding his daughter's blood. He ordered her to be imprisoned in the palace so that he might make a last effort to save her. 'I am the King,' he said; 'my orders cannot be lightly set aside. Disobedience to them involves punishment and in spite of my paternal love for you, if you persist in your present attitude, you will be executed tomorrow in front of the palace gate.'

The t'u-ti, hearing the King's verdict, immediately went to Yu Huang and reported to him the sentence that had been pronounced against Miao Shan. Yu Huang exclaimed: 'Save Buddha, there is none in the west so noble as this Princess. Tomorrow, at the appointed hour, go to the scene of execution, break the swords and splinter the lances they will use to kill her. See that she suffers no pain. At the moment of her death transform yourself into a tiger and bring her body to the pine wood. Having deposited it in a safe place, put a magic pill in her mouth to arrest decay. Her triumphant soul on its return from the lower regions must find it in a perfect state of preservation in order to be able to re-enter it and animate it afresh. After that she must go to Hsiang Shan on P'u T'o Island, where she will reach the highest state of perfection.'

On the appointed day, Commander Hu Pi-li led the condemned Princess to the place of execution. Troops had been stationed there to maintain order. The t'u-ti was in attendance at the palace gates. Miao Shan was radiant with joy. 'Today,' she said, 'I leave the world for a better life. Hasten to take my life, but beware of mutilating my body.'

The King's warrant arrived, and suddenly the sky became overcast and darkness fell upon the earth. A bright light surrounded Miao Shan, and when the sword of the executioner fell upon the neck of the victim it was broken in two. Then they thrust at her with a spear, but the weapon fell to pieces. After that the King ordered that she be strangled with a silken cord. A few moments later a tiger leapt into the execution ground, dispersed the executioners, put the body of Miao Shan on his back and disappeared into the pine forest. Hu Pi-li rushed to the palace. He told the King full all that had happened and received a reward of two ingots of gold.

Meanwhile, Miao Shan's soul, which remained unhurt, was carried on a cloud. She awoke, as from a dream, lifted her head and looked round but she could not see her body. 'My father has just had me strangled,' she sighed. 'How is it that I find myself in this place? Here are neither mountains, nor trees, nor vegetation; no sun, moon, nor stars; no habitation, no sound, no cackling of a fowl nor barking of a dog. How can I live in this desolate region?'

Suddenly a young man appeared carrying a large banner. He was dressed in blue, shining with a brilliant light. He said to her: 'By order of Yen Wang, the King of the Hells, I come to take you to the eighteen infernal regions.'

'What is this cursed place where I am now?' asked Miao Shan.

'This is the lower world, Hell,' he replied. 'Your refusal to marry, and the magnanimity with which you chose death rather than break your resolutions, deserve the recognition of Yu Huang. The ten gods of the lower regions, impressed by your eminent virtue, have sent me to you. Fear nothing and follow me.'

So Miao Shan began her visit to all the infernal regions. The Gods of the Ten Hells came to congratulate her. 'Who am I,' asked Miao Shan, 'that you should take the trouble to show me such respect?'

'We have heard,' they replied, 'that when you recite your prayers all evil disappears as if by magic. We should like to hear you pray.'

'I consent,' replied Miao Shan, 'on condition that all the condemned ones in the ten infernal regions be released from their chains in order to listen to me.'

At the appointed time the condemned were led in by Niu T'ou ('Ox-head') and Ma Mien ('Horse-face'), the two chief constables of Hell, and Miao Shan began her prayers. No sooner had she finished than Hell was suddenly transformed into a paradise of joy, and the instruments of torture into lotus-flowers.

P'an Kuan, the keeper of the Register of the Living and the Dead, presented a memorial to Yen Wang stating that since Miao Shan's arrival there was no more pain in Hell; and all the condemned were beside themselves with happiness. 'Since it has always been decreed,' he added, 'that, in justice, there must be both a Heaven and a Hell, if you do not send this saint back to earth, there will no longer be any Hell, but only a Heaven.'

'Since that is so,' said Yen Wang, 'let forty-eight flag bearers escort her across the Styx Bridge so that she may be taken to the pine forest to re-enter her body and resume her life in the upper world.'

The King of the Hells, having paid his respects to her, asked the youth in blue to take her soul back to her body, which she found lying under a pine tree. Having re-entered it, Miao Shan found herself alive again. A bitter sigh escaped from her lips. 'I remember,' she said, 'all that I saw and heard in Hell. I sigh for the moment which will find me free of all impediments, and yet my soul has re-entered my body. Here, without any lonely mountain on which to give myself up to the pursuit of perfection, what will become of me?' Great tears welled from her eyes.

Just then Ju Lai Buddha appeared. 'Why have you come to this place?' he asked. Miao Shan explained why the King had put her to death and how after her descent into Hell her soul had re-entered her body. 'I greatly pity your misfortune,' Ju Lai said, 'but there is no one to help you. I also am alone. Why should we not marry? We could build ourselves a hut and pass our days in peace. What say you?' 'Sir,' she replied, 'you must not make impossible suggestions. I died and came to life again. How can you speak so lightly? Do me the pleasure of withdrawing from my presence.'

'Well,' said the visitor, 'he to whom you are speaking is no other than the Buddha of the West. I came to test your virtue. This place is not suitable for your devotional exercises; I invite you to come to Hsiang Shan.'

Miao Shan threw herself on her knees and said: 'My bodily eyes deceived me. I never thought that your Majesty would come to a place like this. Pardon my seeming want of respect. Where is this Hsiang Shan?'

'Hsiang Shan is a very old monastery,' Ju Lai replied, 'built in the earliest historical times. It is inhabited by Immortals. It is situated in the sea, on P'u T'o Island. There you will be able to reach the highest perfection.'

'How far off is this island?' Miao Shan asked. 'More than a thousand miles,' Ju Lai replied. 'I fear,' she said, 'I could not bear the fatigue of so long a journey.' 'Calm yourself,' he replied. 'I have brought with me a magic peach, of a kind not to be found in any earthly orchard. Once you have eaten it, you will experience neither hunger nor thirst; old age and death will have no power over you: you will live for ever.'

Miao Shan ate the magic peach, left Ju Lai and started on the way to Hsiang Shan. From the clouds the Spirit of the North Star saw her making her way toward P'u T'o. He called the Guardian of the Soil of Hsiang Shan and said to him: 'Miao Shan is on her way to your country; the way is long and difficult. I ask you take the form of a tiger and carry her to her journey's end.'

The t'u-ti transformed himself into a tiger and stationed himself in the middle of the road along which Miao Shan must pass. As Miao Shan approached the tiger she said, 'I am a poor girl devoid of filial piety. I have disobeyed my father's commands; devour me, and make an end of me.'

The tiger then spoke, saying: 'I am not a real tiger, but the Guardian of the Soil of Hsiang Shan. I have received instructions to carry you there. Get on my back.'

'Since you have received these instructions,' said the girl, 'I will obey, and when I have attained to perfection I will not forget your kindness.'

The tiger went off like a flash of lightning, and in the twinkling of an eye Miao Shan found herself at the foot of the rocky slopes of P'u T'o Island.

Miao Shan Attains Perfection

After nine years in the retreat of P'u T'o Island Miao Shan had reached the pinnacle of perfection. Ti-tsang Wang then came to Hsiang Shan, and was so astonished at her virtue that he inquired of the local t'u-ti as to what had brought about this wonderful result. 'With the exception of Ju Lai, in all the west no one equals her in dignity and perfection. She is the Queen of the three thousand P'u-sa's and of all the beings on earth who have skin and blood. We regard her as our sovereign in all things. Therefore, on the nineteenth day of the eleventh moon we will enthrone her.'

The t'u-ti sent out his invitations for the ceremony. The Dragon king of the Western Sea, the Gods of the Five Sacred Mountains, the one hundred and twenty Emperor saints, the thirty-six officials of the Ministry of Time, the celestial functionaries in charge of wind, rain, thunder and lightning, the Three Causes, the Five Saints, the Eight Immortals, the Ten Kings of the Hells – all were present on the appointed day. Miao Shan took her seat on the lotus throne and the assembled gods proclaimed her sovereign of Heaven and earth and a Buddha. Furthermore, they decided that it was not right that she should remain alone at Hsiang Shan; so they begged her to choose a worthy young man and a virtuous young woman to serve her in the temple.

The t'u-ti was entrusted with the task of finding them. In his search he met a young priest named Shan Ts'ai. After the death of his parents he had become a hermit on Ta-hua Shan and was still a novice in the science of perfection. Miao Shan ordered him to be brought to her. 'Who are you?' she asked.

'I am a poor orphan priest of no merit,' he replied. 'From my earliest youth I have led the life of a hermit. I have been told that your power is equalled only by your goodness, so I have ventured to come to pray you to show me how to attain to perfection.'

'My only fear,' replied Miao Shan, 'is that your desire for perfection may not be sincere.'

'I have now no parents,' the priest continued, 'and I have come a very long way to find you. How can I be wanting in sincerity?'

'What special degree of ability have you attained during your course of perfection?' asked Miao Shan.

'I have no skill,' replied Shan Ts'ai, 'but I rely for everything on your great pity, and under your guidance I hope to reach the required ability.'

'Very well,' said Miao Shan, 'take up your station on the top of yonder peak, and wait till I find a means of transporting you.'

Miao Shan called the t'u-ti and asked him to go and beg all the Immortals to disguise themselves as pirates and to besiege the mountain, waving torches and threatening with swords and spears to kill her. 'Then I will seek refuge on the summit, and will leap over the precipice to prove Shan Ts'ai's fidelity and affection.'

A minute later a ferocious gang of robbers rushed up to the temple of Hsiang Shan. Miao Shan cried for help, rushed up the steep incline, missed her footing and rolled down into the ravine. Shan Ts'ai, seeing her fall into the abyss, without hesitation flung himself after her in order to rescue her. When he reached her, he asked: 'What have you to fear from the robbers? You have nothing for them to steal; why throw yourself over the precipice, exposing yourself to certain death?'

Miao Shan saw that he was weeping, and wept too. 'I must comply with the wish of Heaven,' she said.

Shan Ts'ai, inconsolable, prayed Heaven and earth to save his protectress. Miao Shan said to him: 'You should not have risked your life by throwing yourself over the precipice, I have not yet transformed you. But you did a brave thing and I know that you have a good heart. Now, look down there.' 'Oh,' said he, 'if I am not mistaken, that is a corpse.' 'Yes,' she replied, 'that is your former body. Now you are transformed you can rise at will and fly in the air.' Shan Ts'ai bowed low to thank her. She said to him: 'From now on you must say your prayers by my side and not leave me for a single day.'

'Brother and Sister'

With her spiritual sight Miao Shan perceived at the bottom of the Southern Sea the third son of Lung Wang, who, in carrying out his father's orders, was making his way through the waves in the form of a carp. While doing so, he was caught in a fisherman's net and taken to the market at Yueh Chou where he was offered for sale. Miao Shan at once sent her faithful Shan Ts'ai, disguised as a servant, to buy him. She gave him the money to purchase the fish, which he was to take to the foot of the rocks at P'u T'o and set free in the sea. The son of Lung Wang heartily thanked his deliverer, and on his return to the palace he told his father what had occurred. The King said: 'As a reward, make her a present of a luminous pearl, so that she may recite her prayers by its light at night time.'

Lung Nu, the daughter of Lung Wang's third son, asked her grandfather's permission to take the gift to Miao Shan and beg that she might be allowed to study the doctrine of the sages under her guidance. After having proved her sincerity, she was accepted as a pupil. Shan Ts'ai called her his sister, and Lung Nu reciprocated by calling him her dear brother. Both lived as brother and sister by Miao Shan's side.

The King's Punishment

After King Miao Chuang had burned the Nunnery of the White Bird and killed his daughter, Ch'ieh Lan Buddha presented a petition to Yu Huang praying that the crime be not allowed to go unpunished. Yu Huang, justly irritated, ordered P'an Kuan to consult the Register of the Living and the Dead to see how long this homicidal King had yet to live. P'an Kuan turned over the pages of his register and saw that according to the divine ordinances the King's reign on the throne of Hsing Lin should last for twenty years, but that this period had not yet expired. 'That which has been decreed is unable to be changed,' said Yu Huang, 'but I will punish him by sending him illness.' He called the God of Epidemics, and ordered him to afflict the King's body with ulcers, of a kind which could not be healed except by remedies to be given him by his daughter Miao Shan.

The order was promptly executed and the King could get no rest by day or by night. His two daughters and their husbands spent their time feasting while he tossed about in agony on his sickbed. The most famous physicians were called in but the pain only grew worse. Despair took hold of the patient. He then proclaimed that he would grant the succession to the throne to any person who would provide him with an effectual remedy to restore him to health.

Miao Shan had learnt all that was taking place at the palace. She assumed the form of a priest doctor, clothed herself in a priest's gown and attached to her girdle a gourd containing pills and other medicines. Then she went straight to the palace gate, read the royal edict posted there, and tore it down. Some members of the palace guard seized her, and inquired angrily: 'Who are you that you should dare to tear down the royal proclamation?'

'I, a poor priest, am also a doctor,' she replied. 'I read the edict posted on the palace gates. The King is looking for a doctor who can heal him. I am a doctor of an old cultured family and propose to restore him to health.'

'If you are of a cultured family, why did you become a priest?' they asked. 'Would it not have been better to gain your living honestly in practising your art than to shave your head and go loafing about the world? Besides, all the highest physicians have tried in vain to cure the King; do you imagine that you will be more skilful than all the aged practitioners?'

'Set your minds at ease,' she replied. 'I have received from my ancestors the most effective remedies and I guarantee that I shall restore the King to health,' The palace guard informed the King and in the end the priest was admitted. Having reached the royal bed chamber, he sat still awhile in order to calm himself before feeling the pulse, and to have complete control of all his faculties while examining the King. When he felt quite sure of himself, he approached the King's bed, took the King's hand, felt his pulse, carefully diagnosed the nature of the illness and assured himself that it was easily curable.

One serious difficulty, however, presented itself, and that was that the right medicine was almost impossible to obtain. The King showed his displeasure by saying: 'For every illness there is a medical prescription and for every prescription a specific medicine; how can you say that the diagnosis is easy, but that there is no remedy?'

'Your Majesty,' replied the priest, 'the remedy for your illness is not to be found in any pharmacy, and no one would agree to sell it.'

The King became angry and ordered those about him to drive away the priest, who left smiling.

The following night the King dreamt of an old man who said to him: 'This priest alone can cure your illness and, if you ask him, he himself will give you the right remedy.' The King awoke as soon as these words had been uttered and begged the Queen to recall the priest. When the priest returned the King related his dream and begged him to give him the remedy required. 'What, after all, is this remedy that I must have in order to be cured?' he asked.

'There must be the hand and eye of a living person, from which to compound the ointment which alone can save you,' answered the priest.

The King called out: 'This priest is fooling me! Who would ever give his hand or his eye? Even if anyone would, I could never have the heart to make use of them.'

'Nevertheless,' said the priest, 'there is no other effective remedy.'

'Then where can I obtain this remedy?' asked the King.

'Your Majesty must send your ministers, who must observe the Buddhist rules of abstinence, to Hsiang Shan, where they will be given what is required.'

'Where is Hsiang Shan, and how far from here?'

'About a thousand or more miles, but I myself will indicate the route to be followed. In a very short time they will return.'

The King, who was suffering terribly, was more contented when he heard that the journey could be made quickly. He called his two ministers, Chao Chen and Liu Ch'in, and instructed them to lose no time in starting for Hsiang Shan. They were warned to scrupulously observe the Buddhist rules of abstinence. Meanwhile, the king ordered the Minister of Ceremonies to detain the priest in the palace until their return.

The two sons-in-law of the King, Ho Feng and Chao K'uei, had already made secret preparations to succeed to the throne as soon as the King should breathe his last. They were surprised to learn that the priest had hopes of curing the King's illness and that he was waiting in the palace until the remedy was brought to him. Fearing that they might be disappointed in their ambition, and that after his recovery the King would give the crown to the priest, they entered into a conspiracy with an unscrupulous courtier named Ho Li. They needed to act quickly because the ministers would soon be back. That same night Ho Li was to give to the King a poisoned drink made, he would say, by the priest to numb the King's pain until the return of his two ministers. Shortly after, an assassin, Su Ta, was to murder the priest. Both the King and the priest would meet their death and the kingdom would pass to the King's two sons-in-law.

Miao Shan had returned to Hsiang Shan, leaving the bodily form of the priest in the palace. She saw the two traitors preparing the poison and was aware of their wicked intentions. Calling the spirit Yu I, she told him to fly to the palace and change the poison about to be administered to the King into a harmless soup and to bind the assassin hand and foot.

At midnight Ho Li carried the poisoned drink and knocked at the door of the royal apartment. He said to the Queen that the priest had prepared a soothing potion while waiting for the return of the ministers. 'I come,' he said, 'to offer it to his Majesty.' The Queen took the bowl in her hands and was about to give it to the King, when Yu I arrived unannounced. Quickly he snatched the bowl from the Queen and poured the contents on the ground; at the same moment he knocked over those present in the room, so that they all rolled on the floor.

At the same time, the assassin Su Ta entered the priest's room and struck him with his sword. Instantly the assassin, without knowing how, found himself wrapped up in the priest's robe and thrown to the ground. He struggled and tried to free himself but found that his hands had been rendered useless by some mysterious power and that there was no escape. The spirit Yu I then returned to Hsiang Shan and reported to Miao Shan.

The next morning, the two sons-in-law of the King heard of the turn things had taken during the night. The whole palace was in a state of great confusion.

When he was informed that the priest had been killed, the King called Ch'u Ting-lieh and ordered him to have the murderer arrested. Su Ta was tortured and confessed all that he knew. Together with Ho Li he was condemned to be cut into a thousand pieces.

The two sons-in-law were seized and executed. It was only through the Queen's intervention that their wives were spared. The infuriated King, however, ordered that his two daughters should be imprisoned in the palace.

In the meantime, Chao Chen and Liu Ch'in had reached Hsiang Shan. When they were brought to Miao Shan the ministers took out the King's letter and read it to her.

'I, Miao Chuang, King of Hsing Lin, have learned that there dwells at Hsiang Shan an Immortal whose power and compassion have no equal in the whole world. I have passed my fiftieth year, and am afflicted with ulcers that all remedies have failed to cure. Today a priest has assured me that at Hsiang Shan I can obtain the hand and eye of a living person, with which he will prepare an ointment able to restore me to health. Relying on his word and on the goodness of the Immortal to whom he has directed me, I venture to beg that those two parts of a living body necessary to heal my ulcers be sent to me. I assure you of my everlasting gratitude, fully confident that my request will not be refused.'

The next morning Miao Shan urged the ministers to take a knife and cut off her left hand and gouge out her left eye. Liu Ch'in took the knife but did not dare to obey the order. 'Be quick,' urged the Immortal; 'you have been commanded to return as soon as possible; why do you hesitate as if you were a young girl?' Liu Ch'in was forced to do it. He plunged in the knife, and the red blood flooded the ground, spreading an odour like sweet incense. The hand and eye were placed on a golden plate, and, having paid their grateful respects to the Immortal, the envoys left.

After they had gone, Miao Shan – who had transformed herself in order to allow the envoys to remove her hand and eye – told Shan Ts'ai that she was now going to prepare the ointment that would cure the King. 'Should the Queen,' she added, 'send for another eye and hand, I will transform myself again and you can give them to her.' No sooner had she finished speaking than she mounted a cloud and disappeared in space. The two ministers reached the palace and presented the Queen with the gruesome remedy. She wept, overcome with gratitude and emotion. 'What Immortal,' she asked, 'can have been so charitable as to sacrifice a hand and eye for the King's benefit?' Then suddenly she uttered a great cry, as she recognized the hand of her daughter.

'Who else, in fact, but his child,' she continued amid her sobs, 'could have had the courage to give her hand to save her father's life?' 'What are you saying?' said the King. 'In the world there are many hands like this.' Just then the priest entered the King's apartment. 'This great Immortal has long devoted herself to the attainment of perfection,' he said. 'She has healed a great many people. Give me the hand and eye.' He took them and quickly produced an ointment which, he told the King, was to be applied to his left side. No sooner had it touched his skin than the pain on his left side disappeared as if by magic; no sign of ulcers was to be seen on that side, but his right side remained as swollen and painful as before.

'Why is it,' asked the King, 'that this remedy, which is so effective for the left side, should not be applied to the right?' 'Because,' replied the priest, 'the left hand and eye of the saint cures only the left side. If you wish to be completely cured, you must send your officers to obtain the right eye and right hand also.' The King accordingly dispatched his envoys again with a letter of thanks, and begging as a further favour that the cure should be completed by the healing of his right side.

On the arrival of the envoys Shan Ts'ai met them in the mutilated form of Miao Shan. He told them to cut off his right hand, pluck out his right eye and put them on a plate. At the sight of the four bleeding wounds, Liu Ch'in could not stop himself from calling out indignantly: 'This priest is a wicked man to make a martyr of a woman in order to obtain the succession!'

Having said this, he left with his companion for the kingdom of Hsing Lin. On their return the King was overwhelmed with joy. The priest quickly prepared the ointment, and the King applied it to his right side. At once the ulcers disappeared like the darkness of night before the rising sun. The whole Court congratulated the King and praised the priest. The King gave the latter the title Priest of the Brilliant Eye. He fell on his face to return thanks and added: 'I, a poor priest, have left the world, and have only one wish, namely, that your Majesty should govern your subjects with justice and sympathy and that all the officials of the realm should prove themselves men of integrity. As for me, I am used to roaming about. I have no desire for any royal estate. My happiness exceeds all earthly joys.'

The priest then waved the sleeve of his cloak and a cloud descended from Heaven. Seating himself on it, the priest disappeared in the sky. From the cloud a note containing the following words was seen to fall: 'I am one of the Teachers of the West. I came to cure the King's illness, and so to glorify the True Doctrine.'

All who witnessed this miracle exclaimed with one voice: 'This priest is the Living Buddha, who is going back to Heaven!' The note was taken to King Miao Chuang, who exclaimed: 'Who am I that I should deserve that one of the rulers of Heaven should deign to descend and cure me by the sacrifice of hands and eyes?'

'What was the face of the saintly person like who gave you the remedy?' he then asked Chao Chen.

'It was like that of your deceased daughter, Miao Shan,' he replied.

'When you removed her hands and eyes did she seem to suffer?'

'I saw a great flow of blood, and my heart failed, but the face of the victim seemed radiant with happiness.'

'This certainly must be my daughter Miao Shan, who has attained to perfection,' said the King. 'Who but she would have given hands and eyes? Purify yourselves and observe the rules of abstinence. Go quickly to Hsiang Shan to return thanks to the saint for this favour. I myself will soon make a pilgrimage there to return thanks in person.'

The King's Repentance

Three years later the King and Queen, with the noblemen of their Court, set out to visit Hsiang Shan. On the way the monarchs were captured by the Green Lion, or God of Fire, and the White Elephant, or Spirit of the Water – the two guardians of the Temple of Buddha – who transported them to a dark cavern in the mountains. A terrific battle then took place between the evil spirits on the one side and some hosts of heavenly genii, who had been summoned to the rescue, on the other. While its issue was still uncertain, reinforcements under the Red Child Devil, who could resist fire, and the Dragon king of the Eastern Sea, who could subdue water, finally defeated the enemy and the prisoners were released.

The King and Queen now resumed their pilgrimage, and Miao Shan instructed Shan Ts'ai to receive the monarchs when they arrived to offer incense. She herself took up her place on the altar, her eyes torn out, her hands cut off and her wrists all dripping with blood. The King recognized his daughter and bitterly reproached himself; the Queen fell swooning at her feet. Miao Shan then spoke and tried to comfort them. She told them of all that she had experienced since the day when she had been executed and how she had attained to immortal perfection. She then went on: 'In order to punish you for having caused the deaths of all those who perished in the wars preceding your accession to the throne and also to avenge the burning of the Nunnery of the White Bird, Yu Huang afflicted you with those terrible ulcers. It was then that I changed myself into a priest in order to heal you and gave my eyes and hands, with which I prepared the ointment that cured you. It was I, moreover, who secured your liberty from Buddha when you were imprisoned in the cave by the Green Lion and the White Elephant.'

At these words the King threw himself with his face on the ground, offered incense, worshipped Heaven, earth, the sun and the moon, saying with a voice broken by sobs: 'I committed a great crime in killing my daughter, who has sacrificed her eyes and hands in order to cure my sickness.'

No sooner were these words uttered than Miao Shan reassumed her normal form and, descending from the altar, approached her parents and sisters. Her body had again its original completeness; and in the presence of its perfect beauty and finding themselves reunited as one family, all wept for joy.

'Well,' said Miao Shan to her father, 'will you now force me to marry and prevent my devoting myself to the attainment of perfection?'

'Speak no more of that,' replied the King. 'I was in the wrong. If you had not reached perfection, I should not now be alive. I have made up my mind to exchange my sceptre for the pursuit of the perfect life, which I wish to lead together with you.'

Then he addressed his Grand Minister Chao Chen, saying: 'Your devotion to the service of the State has rendered you worthy to wear the crown: I surrender it to you.' The Court proclaimed Chao Chen King of Hsing Lin, said farewell to Miao Chuang and set out for their kingdom accompanied by their new sovereign.

Buddha had summoned the White Elephant and the Green Lion, and was on the point of sentencing them to eternal damnation when the compassionate Miao Shan interceded for them. 'Certainly you deserve no forgiveness,' he said, 'but I cannot refuse a request made by Miao Shan, whose clemency is without limit. I give you over to her, to serve and obey her in everything. Follow her.'

Miao Shan Becomes a Buddha

The guardian spirit on duty that day then announced the arrival of a messenger from Yu Huang. It was T'ai-po Chin-hsing, who was the bearer of a divine decree, which he handed to Miao Shan. It read as follows: 'I, the august Emperor, make known to you this decree: Miao Chuang, King of Hsing Lin, forgetful alike of Heaven and Hell, the six virtues, and metempsychosis, has led a blameworthy life; but your nine years of penitence, the filial piety which caused you to sacrifice your own body to effect his cure, in short, all your virtues, have redeemed his faults. Your eyes can see and your ears can hear all the good and bad deeds and words of men. You are the object of my especial regard. Therefore I make proclamation of this decree of canonization.

'Miao Shan will have the title of Very Merciful and Very Compassionate P'u-sa, Saviour of the Afflicted, Miraculous and Always Helpful Protectress of Mortals. On your lofty precious lotus-flower throne, you will be the Sovereign of the Southern Seas and of P'u T'o Isle. Your two sisters, until now tainted with earthly pleasures, will gradually progress till they reach true perfection. Miao Ch'ing will have the title of Very Virtuous P'u-sa, the Completely Beautiful, Rider of the Green Lion. Miao Yin will be honoured with the title of Very Virtuous and Completely Resplendent P'u-sa, Rider of the White Elephant. King Miao Chuang is raised to the dignity of Virtuous Conquering P'u-sa, Surveyor of Mortals. Queen Po Ya receives the title of P'u-sa of Ten Thousand Virtues, Surveyor of Famous Women. Shan Ts'ai has the title of Golden Youth. Lung Nu has the title of Jade Maiden.' Finally he said, 'During all time incense is to be burned before all the members of this canonized group.'

The Bamboo Cutter and the Moon Maiden

LONG AGO THERE LIVED an old bamboo-cutter by the name of Sanugi no Miyakko. One day, while he was busy with his hatchet in a grove of bamboos, he suddenly perceived a miraculous light, and on closer inspection discovered in the heart of a reed a very small creature of exquisite beauty. He gently picked up the tiny girl, only about four inches in height, and carried her home to his wife. So delicate was this little maiden that she had to be reared in a basket.

Now it happened that the Bamboo Cutter continued to set about his business, and night and day, as he cut down the reeds, he found gold, and, once poor, he now amassed a considerable fortune.

The child, after she had been but three months with these simple country folk, suddenly grew in stature to that of a full-grown maid; and in order that she should be in keeping with such a pleasing, if surprising, event, her hair, hitherto allowed to flow in long tresses about her shoulders, was now fastened in a knot on her head. In due season the Bamboo Cutter named the girl the Lady Kaguya, or 'Precious-Slender-Bamboo-of-the-Field-of-Autumn'. When she had been named a great feast was held, in which all the neighbours participated.

The Wooing of the 'Precious-Slender-Bamboo-of-the-Field-of-Autumn'

Now the Lady Kaguya was of all women the most beautiful, and immediately after the feast the fame of her beauty spread throughout the land. Would-be lovers gathered around the fence and lingered in the porch with the hope of at least getting a glimpse of this lovely maiden. Night and day these forlorn suitors waited, but in vain. Those who were of humble origin gradually began to recognise that their love-making was useless. But five wealthy suitors still persisted, and would not relax their efforts. They were Prince Ishizukuri and Prince Kuramochi, the Sadaijin Dainagon Abe no Miushi, the Chiunagon Otomo no Miyuki, and Morotada, the Lord of Iso. These ardent lovers bore 'the ice and snow of winter and the thunderous heats of midsummer with equal fortitude.' When these lords finally asked the Bamboo Cutter to bestow his daughter upon one of them, the old man politely explained that the maiden was not really his daughter, and as that was so she could not be compelled to obey his own wishes in the matter.

At last the lords returned to their mansions, but still continued to make their supplications more persistently than ever. Even the kindly Bamboo Cutter began to remonstrate with the Lady Kaguya, and to point out that it was becoming for so handsome a maid to marry, and that among the five noble suitors she could surely make a very good match. To this the wise Kaguya replied: 'Not so fair am I that I may be certain of a man's faith, and were I to mate with one whose heart proved fickle what a miserable fate were mine! Noble lords, without doubt, are these of whom thou speakest, but I would not wed a man whose heart should be all untried and unknown.'

It was finally arranged that Kaguya should marry the suitor who proved himself the most worthy. This news brought momentary hope to the five great lords, and when night came they assembled before the house where the maiden dwelt 'with flute music and with singing, with chanting to accompaniments and piping, with cadenced tap and clap of fan.' Only the Bamboo Cutter went out to thank the lords for their serenading. When he had come into the house again, Kaguya thus set forth her plan to test the suitors:

'In Tenjiku (Northern India) is a beggar's bowl of stone, which of old the Buddha himself bore, in quest whereof let Prince Ishizukuri depart and bring me the same. And on the mountain Horai, that towers over the Eastern ocean, grows a tree with roots of silver and trunk of gold and fruitage of pure white jade, and I bid Prince Kuramochi fare thither and break off and bring me a branch thereof. Again, in the land of Morokoshi men fashion fur-robes of the pelt of the Flame-proof Rat, and I pray the Dainagon to find me one such. Then of the Chiunagon I require the rainbow-hued jewel that hides its sparkle deep in the dragon's head; and from the hands of the Lord Iso would I fain receive the cowry-shell that the swallow brings hither over the broad sea-plain.'

The Begging-bowl of the Lord Buddha

The Prince Ishizukuri, after pondering over the matter of going to distant Tenjiku in search of the Lord Buddha's begging-bowl, came to the conclusion that such a proceeding would be futile. He decided, therefore, to counterfeit the bowl in question. He laid his plans cunningly, and took good care that the Lady Kaguya was informed that he had actually undertaken the journey. As a matter of fact this artful suitor hid in Yamato for three years, and after that time discovered in a hill-monastery in Tochi a bowl of extreme age resting upon an altar of Binzuru (the Succourer in Sickness). This bowl he took away with him, and wrapped it in brocade, and attached to the gift an artificial branch of blossom.

When the Lady Kaguya looked upon the bowl she found inside a scroll containing the following:

'Over seas, over hills
hath thy servant fared, and weary
and wayworn he perisheth:
O what tears hath cost this
bowl of stone,
what floods of streaming tears!'

But when the Lady Kaguya perceived that no light shone from the vessel she at once knew that it had never belonged to the Lord Buddha. She accordingly sent back the bowl with the following verse:

'Of the hanging dewdrop
not even the passing sheen
dwells herein:
On the Hill of Darkness, the Hill
of Ogura,
what couldest thou hope to find?'

The Prince, having thrown away the bowl, sought to turn the above remonstrance into a compliment to the lady who wrote it.

'Nay, on the Hill of Brightness
what splendour
will not pale?
Would that away from the light
of thy beauty
the sheen of yonder Bowl might
prove me true!'

It was a prettily turned compliment by a suitor who was an utter humbug. This latest poetical sally availed nothing, and the Prince sadly departed.

The Jewel-bearing Branch of Mount Horai

Prince Kuramochi, like his predecessor, was equally wily, and made it generally known that he was setting out on a journey to the land of Tsukushi in quest of the Jewel-bearing Branch. What he actually did was to employ six men of the Uchimaro family, celebrated craftsmen, and secure for them a dwelling hidden from the haunts of men, where he himself abode, for the purpose of instructing the craftsmen as to how they were to make a Jewel-bearing Branch identical with the one described by the Lady Kaguya.

When the Jewel-bearing Branch was finished, he set out to wait upon the Lady Kaguya, who read the following verse attached to the gift:

'Though it were at the peril
of my very life,
without the Jewel-laden Branch
in my hands never again
would I have dared to return!'

The Lady Kaguya looked sadly upon this glittering branch, and listened without interest to the Prince's purely imaginative story of his adventures. The Prince dwelt upon the terrors of the sea, of strange monsters, of acute hunger, of disease, which were their trials upon the ocean. Then this incorrigible story-teller went on to describe how they came to a high mountain rising out of the sea, where they were greeted by a woman bearing a silver vessel which she filled with water. On the mountain were wonderful flowers and trees, and a stream 'rainbow-hued, yellow as gold, white as silver, blue as precious *ruri* (lapis lazuli); and the stream was spanned by bridges built up of divers gems, and by it grew trees laden with dazzling jewels, and from one of these I broke off the branch which I venture now to offer to the Lady Kaguya.'

No doubt the Lady Kaguya would have been forced to believe this ingenious tale had not at that very moment the six craftsmen appeared on the scene, and by loudly demanding payment for the ready-made Jewel-Branch, exposed the treachery of the Prince, who made a hasty retreat. The Lady Kaguya herself rewarded the craftsmen, happy, no doubt, to escape so easily.

The Flameproof Fur-Robe

The Sadaijin (Left Great Minister) Abe no Miushi commissioned a merchant, by the name of Wokei, to obtain for him a fur-robe made from the Flame-proof Rat, and when the merchant's ship had returned from the land of Morokoshi it bore a fur-robe, which the sanguine Sadaijin imagined to be the very object of his desire. The Fur-Robe rested in a casket, and the Sadaijin, believing in the honesty of the merchant, described it as being 'of a sea-green colour, the hairs tipped with shining gold, a treasure indeed of incomparable loveliness, more to be admired for its pure excellence than even for its virtue in resisting the flame of fire.'

The Sadaijin, assured of success in his wooing, gaily set out to present his gift to the Lady Kaguya, offering in addition the following verse:

'Endless are the fires of love
that consume me, yet unconsumed
is the Robe of Fur:
dry at last are my sleeves,
for shall I not see her face this day!'

At last the Sadaijin was able to present his gift to the Lady Kaguya. Thus she addressed the Bamboo Cutter, who always seems to have been conveniently on the scene at such times: 'If this Robe be thrown amid the flames and be not burnt up, I shall know it is in very truth the Flame-proof Robe, and may no longer refuse this lord's suit.' A fire was lighted, and the Robe thrown into the flames, where it perished immediately. 'When the Sadaijin saw this his face grew green as grass, and he stood there astonished.' But the Lady Kaguya discreetly rejoiced, and returned the casket with the following verse:

'Without a vestige even left
thus to burn utterly away,
had I dreamt it of this Robe of Fur.
Alas the pretty thing! far otherwise
would I have dealt with it.'

The Jewel in the Dragon's Head

The Chiunagon Otomo no Miyuki assembled his household and informed his retainers that he desired them to bring him the Jewel in the Dragon's head.

After some demur they pretended to set off on this quest. In the meantime the Chiunagon was so sure of his servants' success that he had his house lavishly adorned throughout with exquisite lacquer-work, in gold and silver. Every room was hung with brocade, the panels rich with pictures, and over the roof were silken cloths.

Weary of waiting, the Chiunagon after a time journeyed to Naniwa and questioned the inhabitants if any of his servants had taken boat in quest of the Dragon. The Chiunagon learnt that none of his men had come to Naniwa, and, considerably displeased at the news, he himself embarked with a helmsman.

Now it happened that the Thunder God was angry and the sea ran high. After many days the storm grew so severe and the boat was so near sinking that the helmsman ventured to remark: 'The howling of the wind and the raging of the waves and the mighty roar of the thunder are signs of the wrath of the God whom my lord offends, who would slay the Dragon of the deep, for through the Dragon is the storm raised, and well it were if my lord offered a prayer.'

As the Chiunagon had been seized with a terrible sickness, it is not surprising to find that he readily took the helmsman's advice. He prayed no less than a thousand times, enlarging on his folly in attempting to slay the Dragon, and solemnly vowed that he would leave the Ruler of the deep in peace.

The thunder ceased and the clouds dispersed, but the wind was as fierce and strong as ever. The helmsman, however, told his master that it was a fair wind and blew towards their own land.

At last they reached the strand of Akashi, in Harima. But the Chiunagon, still ill and mightily frightened, vowed that they had been driven upon a savage shore, and lay full length in the boat, panting heavily, and refusing to rise when the governor of the district presented himself.

When the Chiunagon at last realised that they had not been blown upon some savage shore he consented to land. No wonder the governor smiled when he saw the wretched appearance of the discomfited lord, chilled to the very bone, with swollen belly and eyes lustreless as sloes.

At length the Chiunagon was carried in a litter to his own home. When he had arrived his cunning servants humbly told their master how they had failed in the quest. Thus the Chiunagon greeted them: 'Ye have done well to return empty-handed. Yonder Dragon, assuredly, has kinship with the Thunder God, and whoever shall lay hands on him to take the jewel that gleams in his head shall find himself in peril. Myself am sore spent with toil and hardship, and no guerdon have I won. A thief of men's souls and a destroyer of their bodies is the Lady Kaguya, nor ever will I seek her abode again, nor ever bend ye your steps thitherward.'

When the women of his household heard of their lord's adventure they laughed till their sides were sore, while the silken cloths he had caused to be drawn over the roof of his mansion were carried away, thread by thread, by the crows to line their nests with.

The Royal Hunt

Now the fame of the Lady Kaguya's beauty reached the court, and the Mikado, anxious to gaze upon her, sent one of his palace ladies, Fusago, to go and see the Bamboo Cutter's daughter, and to report to his Majesty of her excellences.

However, when Fusago reached the Bamboo Cutter's house the Lady Kaguya refused to see her. So the palace lady returned to court and reported the matter to the Mikado. His Majesty, not a little displeased, sent for the Bamboo Cutter, and made him bring the Lady Kaguya to court that he might see her, adding: 'A hat of nobility, perchance, shall be her father's reward.'

The old Bamboo Cutter was an admirable soul, and mildly discountenanced his daughter's extraordinary behaviour. Although he loved court favours and probably hankered after so distinguished a hat, it must be said of him that he was first of all true to his duty as a father.

When, on returning to his home, he discussed the matter with the Lady Kaguya, she informed the old man that if she were compelled to go to court it would certainly cause her death, adding: 'The price of my father's hat of nobility will be the destruction of his child.'

The Bamboo Cutter was deeply affected by these words, and once more set out on a journey to the court, where he humbly made known his daughter's decision.

The Mikado, not to be denied even by an extraordinarily beautiful woman, hit on the ingenious plan of ordering a Royal Hunt, so arranged that he might unexpectedly arrive at the Bamboo Cutter's dwelling, and perchance see the lady who could set at defiance the desires of an emperor.

On the day appointed for the Royal Hunt, therefore, the Mikado entered the Bamboo Cutter's house. He had no sooner done so than he was surprised to see in the room in which he stood a wonderful light, and in the light none other than the Lady Kaguya.

His Majesty advanced and touched the maiden's sleeve, whereupon she hid her face, but not before the Mikado had caught a glimpse of her beauty. Amazed by her extreme loveliness, and taking no notice of her protests, he ordered a palace litter to be brought; but on its arrival the Lady Kaguya suddenly vanished. The Emperor, perceiving that he was dealing with no mortal maid, exclaimed: 'It shall be as thou desirest, maiden; but 'Tis prayed that thou resume thy form, that once more thy beauty may be seen.'

So the Lady Kaguya resumed her fair form again. As his Majesty was about to be borne away he composed the following verse:

'Mournful the return
of the Royal Hunt,
and full of sorrow the
brooding heart;
for she resists and stays behind,
the Lady Kaguya!'

The Lady Kaguya thus made answer:

'Under the roof o'ergrown
with hopbine
long were the years
she passed.
How may she dare to look upon
The Palace of Precious Jade?'

The Celestial Robe of Feathers

In the third year after the Royal Hunt, and in the spring-time, the Lady Kaguya continually gazed at the moon. On the seventh month, when the moon was full, the Lady Kaguya's sorrow increased so that her weeping distressed the maidens who served her. At last they came to the Bamboo Cutter, and said: 'Long has the Lady Kaguya watched the moon, waxing in melancholy with the waxing thereof, and her woe now passes all measure, and sorely she weeps and wails; wherefore we counsel thee to speak with her.'

When the Bamboo Cutter communed with his daughter, he requested that she should tell him the cause of her sorrow, and was informed that the sight of the moon caused her to reflect upon the wretchedness of the world.

During the eighth month the Lady Kaguya explained to her maids that she was no ordinary mortal, but that her birthplace was the Capital of Moonland, and that the time was now at hand when she was destined to leave the world and return to her old home.

Not only was the Bamboo Cutter heart-broken at this sorrowful news, but the Mikado also was considerably troubled when he heard of the proposed departure of the Lady Kaguya. His Majesty was informed that at the next full moon a company would be sent down from that shining orb to take this beautiful lady away, whereupon he determined to put a check upon this celestial invasion. He ordered that a guard of soldiers should be stationed about the Bamboo

Cutter's house, armed and prepared, if need be, to shoot their arrows upon those Moonfolk, who would fain take the beautiful Lady Kaguya away.

The old Bamboo Cutter naturally thought that with such a guard to protect his daughter the invasion from the moon would prove utterly futile. The Lady Kaguya attempted to correct the old man's ideas on the subject, saying: 'Ye cannot prevail over the folk of yonder land, nor will your artillery harm them nor your defences avail against them, for every door will fly open at their approach, nor may your valour help, for be ye never so stout-hearted, when the Moonfolk come vain will be your struggle with them.' These remarks made the Bamboo Cutter exceedingly angry. He asserted that his nails would turn into talons – in short, that he would completely annihilate such impudent visitors from the moon.

Now while the royal guard was stationed about the Bamboo Cutter's house, on the roof and in every direction, the night wore away. At the hour of the Rata great glory, exceeding the splendour of the moon and stars, shone around. While the light still continued a strange cloud approached, bearing upon it a company of Moonfolk. The cloud slowly descended until it came near to the ground, and the Moonfolk assembled themselves in order. When the royal guard perceived them every soldier grew afraid at the strange spectacle; but at length some of their number summoned up sufficient courage to bend their bows and send their arrows flying; but all their shafts went astray.

On the cloud there rested a canopied car, resplendent with curtains of finest woollen fabric, and from out the car a mighty voice sounded, saying: 'Come thou forth, Miyakko Maro!'

The Bamboo Cutter tottered forth to obey the summons, and received for his pains an address from the chief of the Moonfolk commencing with, 'Thou fool,' and ending up with a command that the Lady Kaguya should be given up without further delay.

The car floated upward upon the cloud till it hovered over the roof. Once again the same mighty voice shouted: 'Ho there, Kaguya! How long wouldst thou tarry in this sorry place?'

Immediately the outer door of the storehouse and the inner lattice-work were opened by the power of the Moonfolk, and revealed the Lady Kaguya and her women gathered about her.

The Lady Kaguya, before taking her departure, greeted the prostrate Bamboo Cutter and gave him a scroll bearing these words: 'Had I been born in this land, never should I have quitted it until the time came for my father to suffer no sorrow for his child; but now, on the contrary, must I pass beyond the boundaries of this world, though sorely against my will. My silken mantle I leave behind me as a memorial, and when the moon lights up the night let my father gaze upon it. Now my eyes must take their last look and I must mount to yonder sky, whence I fain would fall, meteorwise, to earth.'

Now the Moonfolk had brought with them, in a coffer, a Celestial Feather Robe and a few drops of the Elixir of Life. One of them said to the Lady Kaguya: 'Taste, I pray you, of this Elixir, for soiled has your spirit become with the grossnesses of this filthy world.'

The Lady Kaguya, after tasting the Elixir, was about to wrap up some in the mantle she was leaving behind for the benefit of the old Bamboo Cutter, who had loved her so well, when one of the Moonfolk prevented her, and attempted to throw over her shoulders the Celestial Robe, when the Lady Kaguya exclaimed: 'Have patience yet awhile; who dons yonder robe changes his heart, and I have still somewhat to say ere I depart.' Then she proceeded to write the following to the Mikado:

'Your Majesty deigned to send a host to protect your servant, but it was not to be, and now is the misery at hand of departing with those who have come to bear her away with them. Not permitted was it to her to serve your Majesty, and despite her will was it that she yielded not obedience to the Royal command, and wrung with grief is her heart thereat, and perchance your Majesty may have thought the Royal will was not understood, and was opposed by her, and so will she appear to your Majesty lacking in good manners, which she would not your Majesty deemed her to be, and therefore humbly she lays this writing at the Royal Feet. And now must she don the Feather Robe and mournfully bid her lord farewell.'

Having delivered this scroll into the hands of the captain of the host, together with a bamboo joint containing the Elixir, the Feather Robe was thrown over her, and in a moment all memory of her earthly existence departed.

Then the Lady Kaguya entered the car, surrounded by the company of Moonfolk, and the cloud rapidly rose skyward till it was lost to sight.

The sorrow of the Bamboo Cutter and of the Mikado knew no bounds. The latter held a Grand Council, and inquired which was the highest mountain in the land. One of the councillors answered: 'In Suruga stands a mountain, not remote from the capital, that towers highest towards heaven among all the mountains of the land.' Whereupon his Majesty composed the following verse:

'Never more to see her!
Tears of grief overwhelm me,
and as for me,
with the Elixir of Life
what have I to do?'

Then the scroll, which the Lady Kaguya had written, together with the Elixir, was given to Tsuki no Iwakasa. These he was commanded to take to the summit of the highest mountain in Suruga, and, standing upon the highest peak, to burn the scroll and the Elixir of Life.

So Tsuki no Iwakasa heard humbly the Royal command, and took with him a company of warriors, and climbed the mountain and did as he was bidden. And it was from that time forth that the name of Fuji (*Fuji-yama*, 'Never Dying') was given to yonder mountain, and men say that the smoke of that burning still curls from its high peak to mingle with the clouds of heaven.

The Maiden with the Wooden Bowl

IN ANCIENT DAYS there lived an old couple with their only child, a girl of remarkable charm and beauty. When the old man fell sick and died his widow became more and more concerned for her daughter's future welfare.

One day she called her child to her, and said: 'Little one, your father lies in yonder cemetery, and I, being old and feeble, must needs follow him soon. The thought of leaving you alone in the world troubles me much, for you are beautiful, and beauty is a temptation and a snare to men. Not all the purity of a white flower can prevent it from being plucked and dragged down in the mire. My child, your face is all too fair. It must be hidden from the eager eyes of men, lest it cause you to fall from your good and simple life to one of shame.'

Having said these words, she placed a lacquered bowl upon the maiden's head, so that it veiled her attractions. 'Always wear it, little one,' said the mother, 'for it will protect you when I am gone.'

Shortly after this loving deed had been performed the old woman died, and the maiden was forced to earn her living by working in the rice-fields. It was hard, weary work, but the girl kept a brave heart and toiled from dawn to sunset without a murmur. Over and over again her strange appearance created considerable comment, and she was known throughout the country as the 'Maiden with the Bowl on her Head.' Young men laughed at her and tried to peep under the vessel, and not a few endeavoured to pull off the wooden covering; but it could not be removed, and laughing and jesting, the young men had to be content with a glimpse of the lower part of the fair maiden's face. The poor girl bore this rude treatment with a patient but heavy heart, believing that out of her mother's love and wisdom would come some day a joy that would more than compensate for all her sorrow.

One day a rich farmer watched the maiden working in his rice-fields. He was struck by her diligence and the quick and excellent way she performed her tasks. He was pleased with that bent and busy little figure, and did not laugh at the wooden bowl on her head. After observing her for some time, he came to the maiden, and said: 'You work well and do not chatter to your companions. I wish you to labour in my rice-fields until the end of the harvest.'

When the rice harvest had been gathered and winter had come the wealthy farmer, still more favourably impressed with the maiden, and anxious to do her a service, bade her become an inmate of his house. 'My wife is ill,' he added, 'and I should like you to nurse her for me.'

The maiden gratefully accepted this welcome offer. She tended the sick woman with every care, for the same quiet diligence she displayed in the rice-fields was characteristic of her gentle labour in the sick-room. As the farmer and his wife had no daughter they took very kindly to this orphan and regarded her as a child of their own.

At length the farmer's eldest son returned to his old home. He was a wise young man who had studied much in gay Kyoto, and was weary of a merry life of feasting and frivolous pleasure. His father and mother expected that their son would soon grow tired of his father's house and its quiet surroundings, and every day they feared that he would come to them, bid farewell, and return once more to the city of the Mikado. But to the surprise of all the farmer's son expressed no desire to leave his old home.

One day the young man came to his father, and said: 'Who is this maiden in our house, and why does she wear an ugly black bowl upon her head?'

When the farmer had told the sad story of the maiden his son was deeply moved; but, nevertheless, he could not refrain from laughing a little at the bowl. The young man's laughter, however, did not last long. Day by day the maiden became more fascinating to him. Now and again he peeped at the girl's half-hidden face, and became more and more impressed by her gentleness of manner and her nobility of nature. It was not long before his admiration turned into love, and he resolved that he would marry the Maiden with the Bowl on her Head. Most of his relations were opposed to the union. They said: 'She is all very well in her way, but she is only a common servant. She wears that bowl in order to captivate the unwary, and we do not think it hides beauty, but rather ugliness. Seek a wife elsewhere, for we will not tolerate this ambitious and scheming maiden.'

From that hour the maiden suffered much. Bitter and spiteful things were said to her, and even her mistress, once so good and kind, turned against her. But the farmer did not change his opinion. He still liked the girl, and was quite willing that she should become his son's wife, but, owing to the heated remarks of his wife and relations, he dared not reveal his wishes in the matter.

All the opposition, none too kindly expressed, only made the young man more desirous to achieve his purpose. At length his mother and relations, seeing that their wishes were useless, consented to the marriage, but with a very bad grace.

The young man, believing that all difficulties had been removed, joyfully went to the Maiden with the Bowl on her Head, and said: 'All troublesome opposition is at an end, and now nothing prevents us from getting married.'

'No,' replied the poor maiden, weeping bitterly, 'I cannot marry you. I am only a servant in your father's house, and therefore it would be unseemly for me to become your bride.'

The young man spoke gently to her. He expressed his ardent love over and over again, he argued, he begged; but the maiden would not change her mind. Her attitude made the relations extremely angry. They said that the woman had made fools of them all, little knowing that she dearly loved the farmer's son, and believed, in her loyal heart, that marriage could only bring discord in the home that had sheltered her in her poverty.

That night the poor girl cried herself to sleep, and in a dream her mother came to her, and said: 'My dear child, let your good heart be troubled no more. Marry the farmer's son and all will be well again.' The maiden woke next morning full of joy, and when her lover came to her and asked once more if she would become his bride, she yielded with a gracious smile.

Great preparations were made for the wedding, and when the company assembled, it was deemed high time to remove the maiden's wooden bowl. She herself tried to take it off, but it remained firmly fixed to her head. When some of the relations, with not a few unkind remarks, came to her assistance, the bowl uttered strange cries and groans. At length the bridegroom approached the maiden, and said: 'Do not let this treatment distress you. You are just as dear to me with or without the bowl,' and having said these words, he commanded that the ceremony should proceed.

Then the wine-cups were brought into the crowded apartment and, according to custom, the bride and bridegroom were expected to drink together the 'Three times three' in token of their union. Just as the maiden put the wine-cup to her lips the bowl on her head broke with a great noise, and from it fell gold and silver and all manner of precious stones, so that the maiden who had once been a beggar now had her marriage portion. The guests were amazed as they looked upon the heap of shining jewels and gold and silver, but they were still more surprised when they chanced to look up and see that the bride was the most beautiful woman in all Japan.

The Loves of Gompachi and Komurasaki

ABOUT TWO HUNDRED AND THIRTY YEARS AGO there lived in the service of a daimyo of the province of Inaba a young man, called Shirai Gompachi, who, when he was but sixteen years of age, had already won a name for his personal beauty and valour, and for his skill in the use of arms. Now it happened that one day a dog belonging to him fought with another dog belonging to a fellow-clansman, and the two masters, being both passionate youths, disputing as to whose dog had had the best of the fight, quarrelled and came to blows, and Gompachi slew his adversary; and in consequence of this he was obliged to flee from his country, and make his escape to Edo.

And so Gompachi set out on his travels.

One night, weary and footsore, he entered what appeared to him to be a roadside inn, ordered some refreshment, and went to bed, little thinking of the danger that menaced him: for as luck would have it, this inn turned out to be the trysting-place of a gang of robbers, into whose clutches he had thus unwittingly fallen. To be sure, Gompachi's purse was but scantily furnished, but his sword and dirk were worth some three hundred ounces of silver, and upon these the robbers (of whom there were ten) had cast envious eyes, and had determined to kill the owner for their sake; but he, all unsuspicious, slept on in fancied security.

In the middle of the night he was startled from his deep slumbers by someone stealthily opening the sliding door which led into his room, and rousing himself with an effort, he beheld a beautiful young girl, fifteen years of age, who, making signs to him not to stir, came up to his bedside, and said to him in a whisper:

'Sir, the master of this house is the chief of a gang of robbers, who have been plotting to murder you this night for the sake of your clothes and your sword. As for me, I am the daughter of a rich merchant in Mikawa: last year the robbers came to our house, and carried off my father's treasure and myself. I pray you, sir, take me with you, and let us fly from this dreadful place.'

She wept as she spoke, and Gompachi was at first too much startled to answer; but being a youth of high courage and a cunning fencer to boot, he soon recovered his presence of mind, and determined to kill the robbers, and to deliver the girl out of their hands. So he replied:

'Since you say so, I will kill these thieves, and rescue you this very night; only do you, when I begin the fight, run outside the house, that you may be out of harm's way, and remain in hiding until I join you.'

Upon this understanding the maiden left him, and went her way. But he lay awake, holding his breath and watching; and when the thieves crept noiselessly into the room, where they supposed him to be fast asleep, he cut down the first man that entered, and stretched him dead at his feet. The other nine, seeing this, laid about them with their drawn swords, but Gompachi, fighting with desperation, mastered them at last, and slew them. After thus ridding himself of his enemies, he went outside the house and called to the girl, who came running to his side, and joyfully travelled on with him to Mikawa, where her father dwelt; and when they reached Mikawa, he took the maiden to the old man's house, and told him how, when he had fallen among thieves, his daughter had come to him in his hour of peril, and saved him out of her great pity; and how he, in return, rescuing her from her servitude, had brought her back to her home. When the old folks saw their daughter whom they had lost restored to them, they were beside themselves with joy, and shed tears for very happiness; and, in their gratitude, they pressed Gompachi to remain with them, and they prepared feasts for him, and entertained him hospitably: but their daughter, who had fallen in love with him for his beauty and knightly valour, spent her days in thinking of him, and of him alone. The young man, however, in spite of the kindness of the old merchant, who wished to adopt him as his son, and tried hard to persuade him to consent to this, was fretting to go to Edo and take service as an officer in the household of some noble lord; so he resisted the entreaties of the father and the soft speeches of the daughter, and made ready to start on his journey; and the old merchant, seeing that he would not be turned from his purpose, gave him a parting gift of two hundred ounces of silver, and sorrowfully bade him farewell.

But alas for the grief of the maiden, who sat sobbing her heart out and mourning over her lover's departure! He, all the while thinking more of ambition than of love, went to her and comforted her, and said: 'Dry your eyes, sweetheart, and weep no more, for I shall soon come back to you. Do you, in the meanwhile, be faithful and true to me, and tend your parents with filial piety.'

So she wiped away her tears and smiled again, when she heard him promise that he would soon return to her. And Gompachi went his way, and in due time came near to Edo.

But his dangers were not yet over; for late one night, arriving at a place called Suzugamori, in the neighbourhood of Edo, he fell in with six highwaymen, who attacked him, thinking to make short work of killing and robbing him. Nothing daunted, he drew his sword, and dispatched two out of the six; but, being weary and worn out with his long journey, he was sorely pressed, and the struggle was going hard with him, when a wardsman, who happened to pass that way riding in a chair, seeing the affray, jumped down from his chair and drawing his dirk came to the rescue, and between them they put the robbers to flight.

Now it turned out that this kind tradesman, who had so happily come to the assistance of Gompachi, was no other than Chobei of Bandzuin, the chief of the *Otokodate*, or Friendly Society of the wardsmen of Edo – a man famous in the annals of the city, whose life, exploits, and adventures are recited to this day, and form the subject of another tale.

When the highwaymen had disappeared, Gompachi, turning to his deliverer, said:

'I know not who you may be, sir, but I have to thank you for rescuing me from a great danger.'

And as he proceeded to express his gratitude, Chobei replied:

'I am but a poor wardsman, a humble man in my way, sir; and if the robbers ran away, it was more by good luck than owing to any merit of mine. But I am filled with admiration at the way you fought; you displayed a courage and a skill that were beyond your years, sir.'

'Indeed,' said the young man, smiling with pleasure at hearing himself praised; 'I am still young and inexperienced, and am quite ashamed of my bungling style of fencing.'

'And now may I ask you, sir, whither you are bound?'

'That is almost more than I know myself, for I am a *ronin,* and have no fixed purpose in view.›

'That is a bad job,' said Chobei, who felt pity for the lad. 'However, if you will excuse my boldness in making such an offer, being but a wardsman, until you shall have taken service I would fain place my poor house at your disposal.'

Gompachi accepted the offer of his new but trusty friend with thanks; so Chobei led him to his house, where he lodged him and hospitably entertained him for some months. And now Gompachi, being idle and having nothing to care for, fell into bad ways, and began to lead a dissolute life, thinking of nothing but gratifying his whims and passions; he took to frequenting the Yoshiwara, the quarter of the town which is set aside for tea-houses and other haunts of wild young men, where his handsome face and figure attracted attention, and soon made him a great favourite with all the beauties of the neighbourhood.

About this time men began to speak loud in praise of the charms of Komurasaki, or 'Little Purple', a young girl who had recently come to the Yoshiwara, and who in beauty and accomplishments outshone all her rivals. Gompachi, like the rest of the world, heard so much of her fame that he determined to go to the house where she dwelt, at the sign of 'The Three Sea-coasts', and judge for himself whether she deserved all that men said of her. Accordingly he set out one day, and having arrived at 'The Three Sea-coasts', asked to see Komurasaki; and being shown into the room where she was sitting, advanced towards her; but when their eyes met, they both started back with a cry of astonishment, for this Komurasaki, the famous beauty of the Yoshiwara, proved to be the very girl whom several months before Gompachi had rescued from the robbers' den, and restored to her parents in Mikawa. He had left her in prosperity and affluence, the darling child of a rich father, when they had exchanged vows of love and fidelity; and now they met in a common stew in Edo. What a change! what a contrast! How had the riches turned to rust, the vows to lies!

'What is this?' cried Gompachi, when he had recovered from his surprise. 'How is it that I find you here pursuing this vile calling, in the Yoshiwara? Pray explain this to me, for there is some mystery beneath all this which I do not understand.'

But Komurasaki – who, having thus unexpectedly fallen in with her lover that she had yearned for, was divided between joy and shame – answered, weeping:

'Alas! my tale is a sad one, and would be long to tell. After you left us last year, calamity and reverses fell upon our house; and when my parents became poverty-stricken, I was at my wits' end to know how to support them: so I sold this wretched body of mine to the master of this house, and sent the money to my father and mother; but, in spite of this, troubles and misfortunes multiplied upon them, and now, at last, they have died of misery and grief. And, oh! lives there in this wide world so unhappy a wretch as I! But now that I have met you again – you who are so strong – help me who am weak. You saved me once – do not, I implore you, desert me now!!' and as she told her piteous tale the tears streamed from her eyes.

'This is, indeed, a sad story,' replied Gompachi, much affected by the recital. 'There must have been a wonderful run of bad luck to bring such misfortune upon your house, which but a little while ago I recollect so prosperous. However, mourn no more, for I will not forsake you. It is true that I am too poor to redeem you from your servitude, but at any rate I will contrive so that you shall be tormented no more. Love me, therefore, and put your trust in me.' When she heard him speak so kindly she was comforted, and wept no more, but poured out her whole heart to him, and forgot her past sorrows in the great joy of meeting him again.

When it became time for them to separate, he embraced her tenderly and returned to Chobei's house; but he could not banish Komurasaki from his mind, and all day long he thought of her alone; and so it came about that he went daily to the Yoshiwara to see her, and if any accident detained him, she, missing the accustomed visit, would become anxious and write to him to inquire the cause of his absence. At last, pursuing this course of life, his stock of money ran short, and as, being a *ronin* and without any fixed employment, he had no means of renewing his supplies, he was ashamed of showing himself penniless at 'The Three Sea-coasts'. Then it was that a wicked spirit arose within him, and he went out and murdered a man, and having robbed him of his money carried it to the Yoshiwara.

From bad to worse is an easy step, and the tiger that has once tasted blood is dangerous. Blinded and infatuated by his excessive love, Gompachi kept on slaying and robbing, so that, while his outer man was fair to look upon, the heart within him was that of a hideous devil. At last his friend Chobei could no longer endure the sight of him, and turned him out of his house; and as, sooner or later, virtue and vice meet with their reward, it came to pass that Gompachi's crimes became notorious, and the Government having set spies upon his track, he was caught red-handed and arrested; and his evil deeds having been fully proved against him, he was carried off to the execution ground at Suzugamori, the 'Bell Grove', and beheaded as a common male-factor.

Now when Gompachi was dead, Chobei's old affection for the young man returned, and, being a kind and pious man, he went and claimed his body and head, and buried him at Meguro, in the grounds of the Temple called Boronji.

When Komurasaki heard the people at Yoshiwara gossiping about her lover's end, her grief knew no bounds, so she fled secretly from 'The Three Sea-coasts', and came to Meguro and threw herself upon the newly-made grave. Long she prayed and bitterly she wept over the tomb of him whom, with all his faults, she had loved so well, and then, drawing a dagger from her girdle, she plunged it in her breast and died. The priests of the temple, when they saw what had happened, wondered greatly and were astonished at the loving faithfulness of this beautiful girl, and taking compassion on her, they laid her side by side with Gompachi in one grave, and over the grave they placed a stone which remains to this day, bearing the inscription 'The Tomb of the Shiyoku'. And still the people of Edo visit the place, and still they praise the beauty of Gompachi and the filial piety and fidelity of Komurasaki.

The Outcast Maiden and the Hatamoto

ONCE UPON A TIME, some two hundred years ago, there lived at a place called Honjo, in Edo, a Hatamoto named Takoji Genzaburo; his age was about twenty-four or twenty-five, and he was of extraordinary personal beauty. His official duties made it incumbent on him to go to the Castle by way of the Adzuma Bridge, and here it was that a strange adventure befel him. There was a certain Outcast, who used to earn his living by going out every day to the Adzuma Bridge, and mending the sandals of the passers-by. Whenever Genzaburo crossed the bridge, the Outcast used always to bow to him. This struck him as rather strange; but one day when Genzaburo was out alone, without any retainers following him, and was passing the Adzuma Bridge, the thong of his sandal suddenly broke: this annoyed him very much; however, he recollected the Outcast cobbler who always used to bow to him so regularly, so he went to the place where he usually sat, and ordered him to mend his sandal, saying to him: 'Tell me why it is that every time that I pass by this bridge, you salute me so respectfully.'

When the Outcast heard this, he was put out of countenance, and for a while he remained silent; but at last taking courage, he said to Genzaburo, 'Sir, having been honoured with your commands, I am quite put to shame. I was originally a gardener, and used to go to your honour's house and lend a hand in trimming up the garden. In those days your honour was very young, and I myself little better than a child; and so I used to play with your honour, and received many kindnesses at your hands. My name, sir, is Chokichi. Since those days I have fallen by degrees info dissolute habits, and little by little have sunk to be the vile thing that you now see me.'

When Genzaburo heard this he was very much surprised, and, recollecting his old friendship for his playmate, was filled with pity, and said, 'Surely, surely, you have fallen very low. Now all you have to do is to presevere and use your utmost endeavours to find a means of escape from the class into which you have fallen, and become a wardsman again. Take this sum: small as it is, let it be a foundation for more to you.' And with these words he took ten riyos out of his pouch and handed them to Chokichi, who at first refused to accept the present, but, when it was pressed upon him, received it with thanks. Genzaburo was leaving him to go home, when two wandering singing-girls came up and spoke to Chokichi; so Genzaburo looked to see what the two women were like. One was a woman of some twenty years of age, and the other was a peerlessly beautiful girl of sixteen; she was neither too fat nor too thin, neither too tall nor too short; her face was oval, like a melon-seed, and her complexion fair and white; her eyes were narrow and bright, her teeth small and even; her nose was aquiline, and her mouth delicately formed, with lovely red lips; her eyebrows were long and fine; she had a profusion of long black hair; she spoke modestly, with a soft sweet voice; and when she smiled, two lovely dimples appeared in her cheeks; in all her movements she was gentle and refined. Genzaburo fell in love with her at first sight; and she, seeing what a handsome man he was, equally fell in love with him; so that the woman that was with her, perceiving that they were struck with one another, led her away as fast as possible.

Genzaburo remained as one stupefied, and, turning to Chokichi, said, 'Are you acquainted with those two women who came up just now?'

'Sir,' replied Chokichi, 'those are two women of our people. The elder woman is called O Kuma, and the girl, who is only sixteen years old, is named O Koyo. She is the daughter of one Kihachi, a chief of the Outcasts. She is a very gentle girl, besides being so exceedingly pretty; and all our people are loud in her praise.'

When he heard this, Genzaburo remained lost in thought for a while, and then said to Chokichi, 'I want you to do something for me. Are you prepared to serve me in whatever respect I may require you?'

Chokichi answered that he was prepared to do anything in his power to oblige his honour. Upon this Genzaburo smiled and said, 'Well, then, I am willing to employ you in a certain matter; but as there are a great number of passers-by here, I will go and wait for you in a tea-house at Hanakawado; and when you have finished your business here, you can join me, and I will speak to you.' With these words Genzaburo left him, and went off to the tea-house.

When Chokichi had finished his work, he changed his clothes, and, hurrying to the tea-house, inquired for Genzaburo, who was waiting for him upstairs. Chokichi went up to him, and began to thank him for the money which he had bestowed upon him. Genzaburo smiled, and handed him a wine-cup, inviting him to drink, and said:

'I will tell you the service upon which I wish to employ you. I have set my heart upon that girl O Koyo, whom I met today upon the Adzuma Bridge, and you must arrange a meeting between us.'

When Chokichi heard these words, he was amazed and frightened, and for a while he made no answer. At last he said:

'Sir, there is nothing that I would not do for you after the favours that I have received from you. If this girl were the daughter of any ordinary man, I would move heaven and earth to comply with your wishes; but for your honour, a handsome and noble Hatamoto, to take for his concubine the daughter of an Outcast is a great mistake. By giving a little money you can get the handsomest woman in the town. Pray, sir, abandon the idea.'

Upon this Genzaburo was offended, and said:

'This is no matter for you to give advice in. I have told you to get me the girl, and you must obey.'

Chokichi, seeing that all that he could say would be of no avail, thought over in his mind how to bring about a meeting between Genzaburo and O Koyo, and replied:

'Sir, I am afraid when I think of the liberty that I have taken. I will go to Kihachi's house, and will use my best endeavours with him that I may bring the girl to you. But for today, it is getting late, and night is coming on; so I will go and speak to her father tomorrow.'

Genzaburo was delighted to find Chokichi willing to serve him.

'Well,' said he, 'the day after tomorrow I will await you at the tea-house at Oji, and you can bring O Koyo there. Take this present, small as it is, and do your best for me.'

With this he pulled out three riyos from his pocket and handed them to Chokichi. who declined the money with thanks, saying that he had already received too much, and could accept no more; but Genzaburo pressed him, adding, that if the wish of his heart were accomplished he would do still more for him. So Chokichi, in great glee at the good luck which had befallen him, began to revolve all sorts of schemes in his mind; and the two parted.

But O Koyo, who had fallen in love at first sight with Genzaburo on the Adzuma Bridge, went home and could think of nothing but him. Sad and melancholy she sat, and her friend O Kuma tried to comfort her in various ways; but O Koyo yearned, with all her heart, for Genzaburo; and the more she thought over the matter, the better she perceived that she, as the daughter of an Outcast, was no match for a noble Hatamoto. And yet, in spite of this, she pined for him, and bewailed her own vile condition.

Now it happened that her friend O Kuma was in love with Chokichi, and only cared for thinking and speaking of him; one day, when Chokichi went to pay a visit at the house of Kihachi the Outcast chief, O Kuma, seeing him come, was highly delighted, and received him very politely; and Chokichi, interrupting her, said:

'O Kuma, I want you to answer me a question: where has O Koyo gone to amuse herself today?'

'Oh, you know the gentleman who was talking with you the other day, at the Adzuma Bridge? Well, O Koyo has fallen desperately in love with him, and she says that she is too low-spirited and out of sorts to get up yet.'

Chokichi was greatly pleased to hear this, and said to O Kuma:

'How delightful! Why, O Koyo has fallen in love with the very gentleman who is burning with passion for her, and who has employed me to help him in the matter. However, as he is a noble Hatamoto, and his whole family would be ruined if the affair became known to the world, we must endeavour to keep it as secret as possible.'

'Dear me!' replied O Kuma; 'when O Koyo hears this, how happy she will be, to be sure! I must go and tell her at once.'

'Stop!' said Chokichi, detaining her; 'if her father, Master Kihachi, is willing, we will tell O Koyo directly. You had better wait here a little until I have consulted him;' and with this he went into an inner chamber to see Kihachi; and, after talking over the news of the day, told him how Genzaburo had fallen passionately in love with O Koyo, and had employed him as a go-between. Then he described how he had received kindness at the hands of Genzaburo when he was in better circumstances, dwelt on the wonderful personal beauty of his lordship, and upon the lucky chance by which he and O Koyo had come to meet each other.

When Kihachi heard this story, he was greatly flattered, and said:

'I am sure I am very much obliged to you. For one of our daughters, whom even the common people despise and shun as a pollution, to be chosen as the concubine of a noble Hatamoto – what could be a greater matter for congratulation!'

So he prepared a feast for Chokichi, and went off at once to tell O Koyo the news. As for the maiden, who had fallen over head and ears in love, there was no difficulty in obtaining her consent to all that was asked of her.

Accordingly Chokichi, having arranged to bring the lovers together on the following day at Oji, was preparing to go and report the glad tidings to Genzaburo; but O Koyo, who knew that her friend O Kuma was in love with Chokichi, and thought that if she could throw them into one another's arms, they, on their side, would tell no tales about herself and Genzaburo, worked to such good purpose that she gained her point. At last Chokichi, tearing himself from the embraces of O Kuma, returned to Genzaburo, and told him how he had laid his plans so as, without fail, to bring O Koyo to him, the following day, at Oji, and Genzaburo, beside himself with impatience, waited for the morrow.

The next day Genzaburo, having made his preparations, and taking Chokichi with him, went to the tea-house at Oji, and sat drinking wine, waiting for his sweetheart to come.

As for O Koyo, who was half in ecstasies, and half shy at the idea of meeting on this day the man of her heart's desire, she put on her holiday clothes, and went with O Kuma to Oji; and as they went out together, her natural beauty being enhanced by her smart dress, all the people turned round to look at her, and praise her pretty face. And so after a while, they arrived at Oji, and went into the tea-house that had been agreed upon; and Chokichi, going out to meet them, exclaimed:

'Dear me, Miss O Koyo, his lordship has been all impatience waiting for you: pray make haste and come in.'

But, in spite of what he said, O Koyo, on account of her virgin modesty, would not go in. O Kuma, however, who was not quite so particular, cried out:

'Why, what is the meaning of this? As you've come here, O Koyo, it's a little late for you to be making a fuss about being shy. Don't be a little fool, but come in with me at once.' And with these words she caught fast hold of O Koyo's hand, and, pulling her by force into the room, made her sit down by Genzaburo.

When Genzaburo saw how modest she was, he reassured her, saying:

'Come, what is there to be so shy about? Come a little nearer to me, pray.'

'Thank you, sir. How could I, who am such a vile thing, pollute your nobility by sitting by your side?' And, as she spoke, the blushes mantled over her face; and the more Genzaburo looked at her, the more beautiful she appeared in his eyes, and the more deeply he became enamoured of her charms. In the meanwhile he called for wine and fish, and all four together made a feast of it. When Chokichi and O Kuma saw how the land lay, they retired discreetly into another chamber, and Genzaburo and O Koyo were left alone together, looking at one another.

'Come,' said Genzaburo, smiling, 'hadn't you better sit a little closer to me?'

'Thank you, sir; really I'm afraid.'

But Genzaburo, laughing at her for her idle fears, said:

'Don't behave as if you hated me.'

'Oh, dear! I'm sure I don't hate you, sir. That would be very rude; and, indeed, it's not the case. I loved you when I first saw you at the Adzuma Bridge, and longed for you with all my heart; but I knew what a despised race I belonged to, and that I was no fitting match for you, and so I tried to be resigned. But I am very young and inexperienced, and so I could not help thinking of you, and you alone; and then Chokichi came, and when I heard what you had said about me, I thought, in the joy of my heart, that it must be a dream of happiness.'

And as she spoke these words, blushing timidly, Genzaburo was dazzled with her beauty, and said:

'Well, you're a clever child. I'm sure, now, you must have some handsome young lover of your own, and that is why you don't care to come and drink wine and sit by me. Am I not right, eh?'

'Ah, sir, a nobleman like you is sure to have a beautiful wife at home; and then you are so handsome that, of course, all the pretty young ladies are in love with you.'

'Nonsense! Why, how clever you are at flattering and paying compliments! A pretty little creature like you was just made to turn all the men's heads – a little witch.'

'Ah! those are hard things to say of a poor girl! Who could think of falling in love with such a wretch as I am? Now, pray tell me all about your own sweetheart: I do so long to hear about her.'

'Silly child! I'm not the sort of man to put thoughts into the heads of fair ladies. However, it is quite true that there is someone whom I want to marry.'

At this O Koyo began to feel jealous.

'Ah!' said she, 'how happy that someone must be! Do, pray, tell me the whole story.' And a feeling of jealous spite came over her, and made her quite unhappy.

Genzaburo laughed as he answered:

'Well, that someone is yourself, and nobody else. There!' and as he spoke, he gently tapped the dimple on her cheek with his finger; and O Koyo's heart beat so, for very joy, that, for a little while, she remained speechless. At last she turned her face towards Genzaburo, and said:

'Alas! your lordship is only trifling with me, when you know that what you have just been pleased to propose is the darling wish of my heart. Would that I could only go into your house as a maid-servant, in any capacity, however mean, that I might daily feast my eyes on your handsome face!'

'Ah! I see that you think yourself very clever at hoaxing men, and so you must needs tease me a little;' and, as he spoke, he took her hand, and drew her close up to him, and she, blushing again, cried:

'Oh! pray wait a moment, while I shut the sliding-doors.'

'Listen to me, O Koyo! I am not going to forget the promise which I made you just now; nor need you be afraid of my harming you; but take care that you do not deceive me.'

'Indeed, sir, the fear is rather that you should set your heart on others; but, although I am no fashionable lady, take pity on me, and love me well and long.'

'Of course! I shall never care for another woman but you.'

'Pray, pray, never forget those words that you have just spoken.'

'And now,' replied Genzaburo, 'the night is advancing, and, for today, we must part; but we will arrange matters, so as to meet again in this tea-house. But, as people would make remarks if we left the tea-house together, I will go out first.'

And so, much against their will, they tore themselves from one another, Genzaburo returning to his house, and O Koyo going home, her heart filled with joy at having found the man for whom she had pined; and from that day forth they used constantly to meet in secret at the tea-house; and Genzaburo, in his infatuation, never thought that the matter must surely become notorious after a while, and that he himself would be banished, and his family ruined: he only took care for the pleasure of the moment.

Now Chokichi, who had brought about the meeting between Genzaburo and his love, used to go every day to the tea-house at Oji, taking with him O Koyo; and Genzaburo neglected all his duties for the pleasure of these secret meetings. Chokichi saw this with great regret, and thought to himself that if Genzaburo gave himself up entirely to pleasure, and laid aside his duties, the secret would certainly be made public, and Genzaburo would bring ruin on himself and his family; so he began to devise some plan by which he might separate them, and plotted as eagerly to estrange them as he had formerly done to introduce them to one another.

At last he hit upon a device which satisfied him. Accordingly one day he went to O Koyo's house, and, meeting her father Kihachi, said to him:

'I've got a sad piece of news to tell you. The family of my lord Genzaburo have been complaining bitterly of his conduct in carrying on his relationship with your daughter, and of the ruin which exposure would bring upon the whole house; so they have been using their influence to persuade him to hear reason, and give up the connection. Now his lordship feels deeply for the damsel, and yet he cannot sacrifice his family for her sake. For the first time, he has become alive to the folly of which he has been guilty, and, full of remorse, he has commissioned me to devise some stratagem to break off the affair. Of course, this has taken me by surprise; but as there is no gainsaying the right of the case, I have had no option but to promise obedience: this promise I have come to redeem; and now, pray, advise your daughter to think no more of his lordship.'

When Kihachi heard this he was surprised and distressed, and told O Koyo immediately; and she, grieving over the sad news, took no thought either of eating or drinking, but remained gloomy and desolate.

In the meanwhile, Chokichi went off to Genzaburo's house, and told him that O Koyo had been taken suddenly ill, and could not go to meet him, and begged him to wait patiently until she should send to tell him of her recovery. Genzaburo, never suspecting the story to be false, waited for thirty days, and still Chokichi brought him no tidings of O Koyo. At last he met Chokichi, and besought him to arrange a meeting for him with O Koyo.

'Sir,' replied Chokichi, 'she is not yet recovered; so it would be difficult to bring her to see your honour. But I have been thinking much about this affair, sir. If it becomes public, your honour's family will be plunged in ruin. I pray you, sir, to forget all about O Koyo.'

'It's all very well for you to give me advice,' answered Genzaburo, surprised; 'but, having once bound myself to O Koyo, it would be a pitiful thing to desert her; I therefore implore you once more to arrange that I may meet her.'

However, he would not consent upon any account; so Genzaburo returned home, and, from that time forth, daily entreated Chokichi to bring O Koyo to him, and, receiving nothing but advice from him in return, was very sad and lonely.

One day Genzaburo, intent on ridding himself of the grief he felt at his separation from O Koyo, went to the Yoshiwara, and, going into a house of entertainment, ordered a feast to be prepared, but, in the midst of gaiety, his heart yearned all the while for his lost love, and his merriment was but mourning in disguise. At last the night wore on; and as he was retiring along the corridor, he saw a man of about forty years of age, with long hair, coming towards him, who, when he saw Genzaburo, cried out, 'Dear me! why this must be my young lord Genzaburo who has come out to enjoy himself.'

Genzaburo thought this rather strange; but, looking at the man attentively, recognized him as a retainer whom he had had in his employ the year before, and said:

'This is a curious meeting: pray, what have you been about since you left my service? At any rate, I may congratulate you on being well and strong. Where are you living now?'

'Well, sir, since I parted from you I have been earning a living as a fortune-teller at Kanda, and have changed my name to Kaji Sazen. I am living in a poor and humble house; but if your lordship, at your leisure, would honour me with a visit –'

'Well, it's a lucky chance that has brought us together, and I certainly will go and see you; besides, I want you to do something for me. Shall you be at home the day after tomorrow?'

'Certainly, sir, I shall make a point of being at home.'

'Very well, then, the day after tomorrow I will go to your house.'

'I shall be at your service, sir. And now, as it is getting late, I will take my leave for tonight.'

'Good night, then. We shall meet the day after tomorrow.' And so the two parted, and went their several ways to rest.

On the appointed day Genzaburo made his preparations, and went in disguise, without any retainers, to call upon Sazen, who met him at the porch of his house, and said, 'This is a great honour! My lord Genzaburo is indeed welcome. My house is very mean, but let me invite your lordship to come into an inner chamber.'

'Pray,' replied Genzaburo, 'don't make any ceremony for me. Don't put yourself to any trouble on my account.'

And so he passed in, and Sazen called to his wife to prepare wine and condiments; and they began to feast. At last Genzaburo, looking Sazen in the face, said, 'There is a service which I want you to render me – a very secret service; but as if you were to refuse me, I should be put to shame, before I tell you what that service is, I must know whether you are willing to assist me in anything that I may require of you.'

'Yes; if it is anything that is within my powcr, I am at your disposal.'

'Well, then,' said Genzaburo, greatly pleased, and drawing ten riyos from his bosom, 'this is but a small present to make to you on my first visit, but pray accept it.'

'No, indeed! I don't know what your lordship wishes of me; but, at any rate, I cannot receive this money. I really must beg your lordship to take it back again.'

But Genzaburo pressed it upon him by force, and at last he was obliged to accept the money. Then Genzaburo told him the whole story of his loves with O Koyo – how he had first met her and fallen in love with her at the Adzuma Bridge; how Chokichi had introduced her to him at the tea-house at Oji, and then when she fell ill, and he wanted to see her again, instead of bringing her to him, had only given him good advice; and so Genzaburo drew a lamentable picture of his state of despair.

Sazen listened patiently to his story, and, after reflecting for a while, replied, 'Well, sir, it's not a difficult matter to set right: and yet it will require some little management. However, if your lordship will do me the honour of coming to see me again the day after tomorrow, I will cast about me in the meanwhile, and will let you know then the result of my deliberations.'

When Genzaburo heard this he felt greatly relieved, and, recommending Sazen to do his best in the matter, took his leave and returned home. That very night Sazen, after thinking over all that Genzaburo had told him, laid his plans accordingly, and went off to the house of Kihachi, the Outcast chief, and told him the commission with which he had been entrusted.

Kihachi was of course greatly astonished, and said, 'Some time ago, sir, Chokichi came here and said that my lord Genzaburo, having been rebuked by his family for his profligate behaviour, had determined to break off his connection with my daughter. Of course I knew that the daughter of an Outcast was no fitting match for a nobleman; so when Chokichi came and told me the errand upon which he had been sent, I had no alternative but to announce to my daughter that she must give up all thought of his lordship. Since that time she has been fretting and pining and starving for love. But when I tell her what you have just said, how glad and happy she will be! Let me go and talk to her at once.' And with these words, he went to O Koyo's room; and when he looked upon her thin wasted face, and saw how sad she was, he felt more and more pity for her, and said, 'Well, O Koyo, are you in better spirits today? Would you like something to eat?'

'Thank you, I have no appetite.'

'Well, at any rate, I have some news for you that will make you happy. A messenger has come from my lord Genzaburo, for whom your heart yearns.'

At this O Koyo, who had been crouching down like a drooping flower, gave a great start, and cried out, 'Is that really true? Pray tell me all about it as quickly as possible.'

'The story which Chokichi came and told us, that his lordship wished to break off the connection, was all an invention. He has all along been wishing to meet you, and constantly urged Chokichi to bring you a message from him. It is Chokichi who has been throwing obstacles in the way. At last his lordship has secretly sent a man, called Kaji Sazen, a fortune-teller, to arrange an interview between you. So now, my child, you may cheer up, and go to meet your lover as soon as you please.'

When O Koyo heard this, she was so happy that she thought it must all be a dream, and doubted her own senses.

Kihachi in the meanwhile rejoined Sazen in the other room, and, after telling him of the joy with which his daughter had heard the news, put before him wine and other delicacies. 'I think,' said Sazen, 'that the best way would be for O Koyo to live secretly in my lord Genzaburo's house; but as it will never do for all the world to know of it, it must be managed very quietly; and further, when I get home, I must think out some plan to lull the suspicions of that fellow Chokichi, and let you know my idea by letter. Meanwhile O Koyo had better come home with me tonight: although she is so terribly out of spirits now, she shall meet Genzaburo the day after tomorrow.'

Kihachi reported this to O Koyo; and as her pining for Genzaburo was the only cause of her sickness, she recovered her spirits at once, and, saying that she would go with Sazen immediately, joyfully made her preparations. Then Sazen, having once more warned Kihachi to keep the matter secret from Chokichi, and to act upon the letter which he should send him, returned home, taking with him O Koyo; and after O Koyo had bathed and dressed her hair, and painted herself and put on beautiful clothes, she came out looking so lovely that no princess in the land could vie with her; and Sazen, when he saw her, said to himself that it was no wonder that Genzaburo had fallen in love with her; then, as it was getting late, he advised her to go to rest, and, after showing her to her apartments, went to his own room and wrote his letter to Kihachi, containing the scheme which he had devised. When Kihachi received his instructions, he was filled with admiration at Sazen's ingenuity, and, putting on an appearance of great alarm and agitation, went off immediately to call on Chokichi, and said to him:

'Oh, Master Chokichi, such a terrible thing has happened! Pray, let me tell you all about it.'

'Indeed! what can it be?'

'Oh! sir,' answered Kihachi, pretending to wipe away his tears, 'my daughter O Koyo, mourning over her separation from my lord Genzaburo, at first refused all sustenance, and remained nursing her sorrows until, last night, her woman's heart failing to bear up against her great grief, she drowned herself in the river, leaving behind her a paper on which she had written her intention.'

When Chokichi heard this, he was thunderstruck, and exclaimed, 'Can this really be true! And when I think that it was I who first introduced her to my lord, I am ashamed to look you in the face.'

'Oh, say not so: misfortunes are the punishment due for our misdeeds in a former state of existence. I bear you no ill-will. This money which I hold in my hand was my daughter's; and in her last instructions she wrote to beg that it might be given, after her death, to you, through whose intervention she became allied with a nobleman: so please accept it as my daughter's legacy to you;' and as he spoke, he offered him three riyos.

'You amaze me!' replied the other. 'How could I, above all men, who have so much to reproach myself with in my conduct towards you, accept this money?'

'Nay; it was my dead daughter's wish. But since you reproach yourself in the matter when you think of her, I will beg you to put up a prayer and to cause masses to be said for her.'

At last, Chokichi, after much persuasion, and greatly to his own distress, was obliged to accept the money; and when Kihachi had carried out all Sazen's instructions, he returned home, laughing in his sleeve.

Chokichi was sorely grieved to hear of O Koyo's death, and remained thinking over the sad news; when all of a sudden looking about him, he saw something like a letter lying on the spot where Kihachi had been sitting, so he picked it up and read it; and, as luck would have it, it was the very letter which contained Sazen's instructions to Kihachi, and in which the whole story which had just affected him so much was made up. When he perceived the trick that had been played upon him, he was very angry, and exclaimed, 'To think that I should have been so hoaxed by that hateful old dotard, and such a fellow as Sazen! And Genzaburo, too! – out of gratitude for the favours which I had received from him in old days, I faithfully gave him good advice, and all in vain. Well, they've gulled me once; but I'll be even with them yet, and hinder their game before it is played out!' And so he worked himself up into a fury, and went off secretly to prowl about Sazen's house to watch for O Koyo, determined to pay off Genzaburo and Sazen for their conduct to him.

In the meanwhile Sazen, who did not for a moment suspect what had happened, when the day which had been fixed upon by him and Genzaburo arrived, made O Koyo put on her best clothes, smartened up his house, and got ready a feast against Genzaburo's arrival. The latter came punctually to his time, and, going in at once, said to the fortune-teller, 'Well, have you succeeded in the commission with which I entrusted you?'

At first Sazen pretended to be vexed at the question, and said, 'Well, sir, I've done my best; but it's not a matter which can be settled in a hurry. However, there's a young lady of high birth and wonderful beauty upstairs, who has come here secretly to have her fortune told; and if your lordship would like to come with me and see her, you can do so.'

But Genzaburo, when he heard that he was not to meet O Koyo, lost heart entirely, and made up his mind to go home again. Sazen, however, pressed him so eagerly, that at last he went upstairs to see this vaunted beauty; and Sazen, drawing aside a screen, showed him O Koyo, who was sitting there. Genzaburo gave a great start, and, turning to Sazen, said, 'Well, you certainly are a first-rate hand at keeping up a hoax. However, I cannot sufficiently praise the way in which you have carried out my instructions.'

'Pray, don't mention it, sir. But as it is a long time since you have met the young lady, you must have a great deal to say to one another; so I will go downstairs, and, if you want anything, pray call me.' And so he went downstairs and left them.

Then Genzaburo, addressing O Koyo, said, 'Ah! it is indeed a long time since we met. How happy it makes me to see you again! Why, your face has grown quite thin. Poor thing! have you been unhappy?' And O Koyo, with the tears starting from her eyes for joy, hid her face; and her heart was so full that she could not speak. But Genzaburo, passing his hand gently over her head and back, and comforting her, said, 'Come, sweetheart, there is no need to sob so. Talk to me a little, and let me hear your voice.'

At last O Koyo raised her head and said, 'Ah! when I was separated from you by the tricks of Chokichi, and thought that I should never meet you again, how tenderly I thought of you! I thought I should have died, and waited for my hour to come, pining all the while for you. And when at last, as I lay between life and death, Sazen came with a message from you, I thought it was all a dream.' And as she spoke, she bent her head and sobbed again; and in Genzaburo's eyes she seemed more beautiful than ever, with her pale, delicate face; and he loved her better than before. Then she said, 'If I were to tell you all I have suffered until today, I should never stop.'

'Yes,' replied Genzaburo, 'I too have suffered much;' and so they told one another their mutual griefs, and from that day forth they constantly met at Sazen's house.

One day, as they were feasting and enjoying themselves in an upper storey in Sazen's house, Chokichi came to the house and said, 'I beg pardon; but does one Master Sazen live here?'

'Certainly, sir: I am Sazen, at your service. Pray where are you from?'

'Well, sir, I have a little business to transact with you. May I make so bold as to go in?' And with these words, he entered the house.

'But who and what are you?' said Sazen.

'Sir, I am an Outcast; and my name is Chokichi. I beg to bespeak your goodwill for myself: I hope we may be friends.'

Sazen was not a little taken aback at this; however, he put on an innocent face, as though he had never heard of Chokichi before, and said, 'I never heard of such a thing! Why, I thought you were some respectable person; and you have the impudence to tell me that your name is Chokichi, and that you're one of those accursed Outcasts. To think of such a shameless villain coming and asking to be friends with me, forsooth! Get you gone! – the quicker, the better: your presence pollutes the house.'

Chokichi smiled contemptuously, as he answered, 'So you deem the presence of an Outcast in your house a pollution – eh? Why, I thought you must be one of us.'

'Insolent knave! Begone as fast as possible.'

'Well, since you say that I defile your house, you had better get rid of O Koyo as well. I suppose she must equally be a pollution to it.'

This put Sazen rather in a dilemma; however, he made up his mind not to show any hesitation, and said, 'What are you talking about? There is no O Koyo here; and I never saw such a person in my life.'

Chokichi quietly drew out of the bosom of his dress the letter from Sazen to Kihachi, which he had picked up a few days before, and, showing it to Sazen, replied, 'If you wish to dispute the genuineness of this paper, I will report the whole matter to the Governor of Edo; and Genzaburo's family will be ruined, and the rest of you who are parties in this affair will come in for your share of trouble. Just wait a little.'

And as he pretended to leave the house, Sazen, at his wits' end, cried out, 'Stop! stop! I want to speak to you. Pray, stop and listen quietly. It is quite true, as you said, that O Koyo is in my house; and really your indignation is perfectly just. Come! let us talk over matters a little. Now you yourself were originally a respectable man; and although you have fallen in life, there is no reason why your disgrace should last for ever. All that you want in order to enable you to escape out of this fraternity of Outcasts is a little money. Why should you not get this from Genzaburo, who is very anxious to keep his intrigue with O Koyo secret?'

Chokichi laughed disdainfully. 'I am ready to talk with you; but I don't want any money. All I want is to report the affair to the authorities, in order that I may be revenged for the fraud that was put upon me.'

'Won't you accept twenty-five riyos?'

'Twenty-five riyos! No, indeed! I will not take a fraction less than a hundred; and if I cannot get them I will report the whole matter at once.'

Sazen, after a moment's consideration, hit upon a scheme, and answered, smiling, 'Well, Master Chokichi, you're a fine fellow, and I admire your spirit. You shall have the hundred riyos you ask for; but, as I have not so much money by me at present, I will go to Genzaburo's house and fetch it. It's getting dark now, but it's not very late; so I'll trouble you to come with me, and then I can give you the money tonight.'

Chokichi consenting to this, the pair left the house together.

Now Sazen, who as a Ronin wore a long dirk in his girdle, kept looking out for a moment when Chokichi should be off his guard, in order to kill him; but Chokichi kept his eyes open, and did not give Sazen a chance. At last Chokichi, as ill-luck would have it, stumbled against a stone and fell; and Sazen, profiting by the chance, drew his dirk and stabbed him in the side; and as Chokichi, taken by surprise, tried to get up, he cut him severely over the head, until at last he fell dead. Sazen then looking around him, and seeing, to his great delight, that there was no one near, returned home. The following day, Chokichi's body was found by the police; and when they examined it, they found nothing upon it save a paper, which they read, and which proved to be the very letter which Sazen had sent to Kihachi, and which Chokichi had picked up. The matter was immediately reported to the governor, and, Sazen having been summoned, an investigation was held. Sazen, cunning and bold murderer as he was, lost his self-possession when he saw what a fool he had been not to get back from Chokichi the letter which he had written, and, when he was put to a rigid examination under torture, confessed that he had hidden O Koyo at Genzaburo's instigation, and then killed Chokichi, who had found out the secret. Upon this the governor, after consulting about Genzaburo's case, decided that, as he had disgraced his position as a Hatamoto by contracting an alliance with the daughter of an Outcast, his property should be confiscated, his family blotted out, and himself banished. As for Kihachi, the Outcast chief, and his daughter O Koyo, they were handed over for punishment to the chief of the Outcasts, and by him they too were banished; while Sazen, against whom the murder of Chokichi had been fully proved, was executed according to law.

The Story of Princess Hase

MANY, MANY YEARS AGO there lived in Nara, the ancient Capital of Japan, a wise State minister, by name Prince Toyonari Fujiwara. His wife was a noble, good, and beautiful woman called Princess Murasaki (Violet). They had been married by their respective families according to Japanese custom when very young, and had lived together happily ever since. They had, however, one cause for great sorrow, for as the years went by no child was born to them. This made them very unhappy, for they both longed to see a child of their own who would grow up to gladden their old age, carry on the family name, and keep up the ancestral rites when they were dead. The Prince and his lovely wife, after long consultation and much thought, determined to make a pilgrimage to the temple of Hase-no-Kwannon (Goddess of Mercy at Hase), for they believed, according to the beautiful tradition of their religion, that the Mother of Mercy, Kwannon, comes to answer the prayers of mortals in the form that they need the most. Surely after all these years of prayer she would come to them in the form of a beloved child in answer to their special pilgrimage, for that was the greatest need of their two lives. Everything else they had that this life could give them, but it was all as nothing because the cry of their hearts was unsatisfied.

So the Prince Toyonari and his wife went to the temple of Kwannon at Hase and stayed there for a long time, both daily offering incense and praying to Kwannon, the Heavenly Mother, to grant them the desire of their whole lives. And their prayer was answered.

A daughter was born at last to the Princess Murasaki, and great was the joy of her heart. On presenting the child to her husband, they both decided to call her Hase-Hime, or the Princess of Hase, because she was the gift of the Kwannon at that place. They both reared her with great care and tenderness, and the child grew in strength and beauty.

When the little girl was five years old her mother fell dangerously ill and all the doctors and their medicines could not save her. A little before she breathed her last she called her daughter to her, and gently stroking her head, said:

'Hase-Hime, do you know that your mother cannot live any longer? Though I die, you must grow up a good girl. Do your best not to give trouble to your nurse or any other of your family. Perhaps your father will marry again and someone will fill my place as your mother. If so do not grieve for me, but look upon your father's second wife as your true mother, and be obedient and filial to both her and your father. Remember when you are grown up to be submissive to those who are your superiors, and to be kind to all those who are under you. Don't forget this. I die with the hope that you will grow up a model woman.'

Hase-Hime listened in an attitude of respect while her mother spoke, and promised to do all that she was told. There is a proverb which says 'As the soul is at three so it is at one hundred,' and so Hase-Hime grew up as her mother had wished, a good and obedient little Princess, though she was now too young to understand how great was the loss of her mother.

Not long after the death of his first wife, Prince Toyonari married again, a lady of noble birth named Princess Terute. Very different in character, alas! to the good and wise Princess Murasaki, this woman had a cruel, bad heart. She did not love her step-daughter at all, and was often very unkind to the little motherless girl, saying to herself:

'This is not my child! this is not my child!'

But Hase-Hime bore every unkindness with patience, and even waited upon her step-mother kindly and obeyed her in every way and never gave any trouble, just as she had been trained by her own good mother, so that the Lady Terute had no cause for complaint against her.

The little Princess was very diligent, and her favourite studies were music and poetry. She would spend several hours practicing every day, and her father had the most proficient of masters he could find to teach her the koto (Japanese harp), the art of writing letters and verse. When she was twelve years of age she could play so beautifully that she and her step-mother were summoned to the Palace to perform before the Emperor.

It was the Festival of the Cherry Flowers, and there were great festivities at the Court. The Emperor threw himself into the enjoyment of the season, and commanded that Princess Hase should perform before him on the koto, and that her mother Princess Terute should accompany her on the flute.

The Emperor sat on a raised dais, before which was hung a curtain of finely-sliced bamboo and purple tassels, so that His Majesty might see all and not be seen, for no ordinary subject was allowed to look upon his sacred face.

Hase-Hime was a skilled musician though so young, and often astonished her masters by her wonderful memory and talent. On this momentous occasion she played well. But Princess Terute, her step-mother, who was a lazy woman and never took the trouble to practice daily, broke down in her accompaniment and had to request one of the Court ladies to take her place. This was a great disgrace, and she was furiously jealous to think that she had failed where her step-daughter succeeded; and to make matters worse the Emperor sent many beautiful gifts to the little Princess to reward her for playing so well at the Palace.

There was also now another reason why Princess Terute hated her step-daughter, for she had had the good fortune to have a son born to her, and in her inmost heart she kept saying:

'If only Hase-Hime were not here, my son would have all the love of his father.'

And never having learned to control herself, she allowed this wicked thought to grow into the awful desire of taking her step-daughter's life.

So one day she secretly ordered some poison and poisoned some sweet wine. This poisoned wine she put into a bottle. Into another similar bottle she poured some good wine. It was the occasion of the Boys' Festival on the fifth of May, and Hase-Hime was playing with her little brother. All his toys of warriors and heroes were spread out and she was telling him wonderful stories about each of them. They were both enjoying themselves and laughing merrily with their attendants when his mother entered with the two bottles of wine and some delicious cakes.

'You are both so good and happy.' said the wicked Princess Terute with a smile, 'that I have brought you some sweet wine as a reward – and here are some nice cakes for my good children.'

And she filled two cups from the different bottles.

Hase-Hime, never dreaming of the dreadful part her step-mother was acting, took one of the cups of wine and gave to her little step brother the other that had been poured out for him.

The wicked woman had carefully marked the poisoned bottle, but on coming into the room she had grown nervous, and pouring out the wine hurriedly had unconsciously given the poisoned cup to her own child. All this time she was anxiously watching the little Princess, but to her amazement no change whatever took place in the young girl's face. Suddenly the little boy screamed and threw himself on the floor, doubled up with pain. His mother flew to him, taking the precaution to upset the two tiny jars of wine which she had brought into the room, and lifted him up. The attendants rushed for the doctor, but nothing could save the child – he died within the hour in his mother's arms. Doctors did not know much in those ancient times, and it was thought that the wine had disagreed with the boy, causing convulsions of which he died.

Thus was the wicked woman punished in losing her own child when she had tried to do away with her step-daughter; but instead of blaming herself she began to hate Hase-Hime more than ever in the bitterness and wretchedness of her own heart, and she eagerly watched for an opportunity to do her harm, which was, however, long in coming.

When Hase-Hime was thirteen years of age, she had already become mentioned as a poetess of some merit. This was an accomplishment very much cultivated by the women of old Japan and one held in high esteem.

It was the rainy season at Nara, and floods were reported every day as doing damage in the neighbourhood. The river Tatsuta, which flowed through the Imperial Palace grounds, was swollen to the top of its banks, and the roaring of the torrents of water rushing along a narrow bed so disturbed the Emperor's rest day and night, that a serious nervous disorder was the result. An Imperial Edict was sent forth to all the Buddhist temples commanding the priests to offer up continuous prayers to Heaven to stop the noise of the flood. But this was of no avail.

Then it was whispered in Court circles that the Princess Hase, the daughter of Prince Toyonari Fujiwara, second minister at Court, was the most gifted poetess of the day, though still so young, and her masters confirmed the report. Long ago, a beautiful and gifted maiden-poetess had moved Heaven by praying in verse, had brought down rain upon a land famished with drought – so said the ancient biographers of the poetess Ono-no-Komachi.

If the Princess Hase were to write a poem and offer it in prayer, might it not stop the noise of the rushing river and remove the cause of the Imperial illness? What the Court said at last reached the ears of the Emperor himself, and he sent an order to the minister Prince Toyonari to this effect.

Great indeed was Hase-Hime's fear and astonishment when her father sent for her and told her what was required of her. Heavy, indeed, was the duty that was laid on her young shoulders – that of saving the Emperor's life by the merit of her verse.

At last the day came and her poem was finished. It was written on a leaflet of paper heavily flecked with gold-dust. With her father and attendants and some of the Court officials, she proceeded to the bank of the roaring torrent and raising up her heart to Heaven, she read the poem she had composed, aloud, lifting it heavenwards in her two hands.

Strange indeed it seemed to all those standing round. The waters ceased their roaring, and the river was quiet in direct answer to her prayer. After this the Emperor soon recovered his health.

His Majesty was highly pleased, and sent for her to the Palace and rewarded her with the rank of Chinjo – that of Lieutenant-General – to distinguish her. From that time she was called Chinjo-hime, or the Lieutenant-General Princess, and respected and loved by all.

There was only one person who was not pleased at Hase-Hime's success. That one was her stepmother. Forever brooding over the death of her own child whom she had killed when trying to poison her step-daughter, she had the mortification of seeing her rise to power and honour, marked by Imperial favour and the admiration of the whole Court. Her envy and jealousy burned in her heart like fire. Many were the lies she carried to her husband about Hase-Hime, but all to no purpose. He would listen to none of her tales, telling her sharply that she was quite mistaken.

At last the step-mother, seizing the opportunity of her husband's absence, ordered one of her old servants to take the innocent girl to the Hibari Mountains, the wildest part of the country, and to kill her there. She invented a dreadful story about the little Princess, saying that this was the only way to prevent disgrace falling upon the family – by killing her.

Katoda, her vassal, was bound to obey his mistress. Anyhow, he saw that it would be the wisest plan to pretend obedience in the absence of the girl's father, so he placed Hase-Hime in a palanquin and accompanied her to the most solitary place he could find in the wild district. The poor child knew there was no good in protesting to her unkind step-mother at being sent away in this strange manner, so she went as she was told.

But the old servant knew that the young Princess was quite innocent of all the things her step-mother had invented to him as reasons for her outrageous orders, and he determined to save her life. Unless he killed her, however, he could not return to his cruel task-mistress, so he decided to stay out in the wilderness. With the help of some peasants he soon built a little cottage, and having sent secretly for his wife to come, these two good old people did all in their power to take care of the now unfortunate Princess. She all the time trusted in her father, knowing that as soon as he returned home and found her absent, he would search for her.

Prince Toyonari, after some weeks, came home, and was told by his wife that his daughter Hime had done something wrong and had run away for fear of being punished. He was nearly ill with anxiety. Everyone in the house told the same story – that Hase-Hime had suddenly disappeared, none of them knew why or whither. For fear of scandal he kept the matter quiet and searched everywhere he could think of, but all to no purpose.

One day, trying to forget his terrible worry, he called all his men together and told them to make ready for a several days' hunt in the mountains. They were soon ready and mounted, waiting at the gate for their lord. He rode hard and fast to the district of the Hibari Mountains, a great company following him. He was soon far ahead of everyone, and at last found himself in a narrow picturesque valley.

Looking round and admiring the scenery, he noticed a tiny house on one of the hills quite near, and then he distinctly heard a beautiful clear voice reading aloud. Seized with curiosity as to who could be studying so diligently in such a lonely spot, he dismounted, and leaving his horse to his groom, he walked up the hillside and approached the cottage. As he drew nearer his surprise increased, for he could see that the reader was a beautiful girl. The cottage was wide open and she was sitting facing the view. Listening attentively, he heard her reading the Buddhist scriptures with great devotion. More and more curious, he hurried on to the tiny gate and entered the little garden, and looking up beheld his lost daughter Hase-Hime. She was so intent on what she was saying that she neither heard nor saw her father till he spoke.

'Hase-Hime!' he cried, 'it is you, my Hase-Hime!'

Taken by surprise, she could hardly realize that it was her own dear father who was calling her, and for a moment she was utterly bereft of the power to speak or move.

'My father, my father! It is indeed you – oh, my father!' was all she could say, and running to him she caught hold of his thick sleeve, and burying her face burst into a passion of tears.

Her father stroked her dark hair, asking her gently to tell him all that had happened, but she only wept on, and he wondered if he were not really dreaming.

Then the faithful old servant Katoda came out, and bowing himself to the ground before his master, poured out the long tale of wrong, telling him all that had happened, and how it was that he found his daughter in such a wild and desolate spot with only two old servants to take care of her.

The Prince's astonishment and indignation knew no bounds. He gave up the hunt at once and hurried home with his daughter. One of the company galloped ahead to inform the household of the glad news, and the step-mother hearing what had happened, and fearful of meeting her husband now that her wickedness was discovered, fled from the house and returned in disgrace to her father's roof, and nothing more was heard of her.

The old servant Katoda was rewarded with the highest promotion in his master's service, and lived happily to the end of his days, devoted to the little Princess, who never forgot that she owed her life to this faithful retainer. She was no longer troubled by an unkind step-mother, and her days passed happily and quietly with her father.

As Prince Toyonari had no son, he adopted a younger son of one of the Court nobles to be his heir, and to marry his daughter Hase-Hime, and in a few years the marriage took place. Hase-Hime lived to a good old age, and all said that she was the wisest, most devout, and most beautiful mistress that had ever reigned in Prince Toyonari's ancient house. She had the joy of presenting her son, the future lord of the family, to her father just before he retired from active life.

To this day there is preserved a piece of needle-work in one of the Buddhist temples of Kyoto. It is a beautiful piece of tapestry, with the figure of Buddha embroidered in the silky threads drawn from the stem of the lotus. This is said to have been the work of the hands of the good Princess Hase.

Text Sources & Biographies

The stories in this book derive from a multitude of original sources, often from the nineteenth century and often based on the writer's first-hand accounts of tales narrated to them by natives, while others are their own retellings of traditional tales. Authors, works and contributors to this book include:

George W. Bateman

George W. Bateman (1850–1940) was the British-born author of the famous *Zanzibar Tales: Told by Natives of the East Coast of Africa* (1901), in which he presented stories, 'translated from the Original Swahili', told to him in Zanzibar, by locals 'whose ancestors told them to them, who had received them from *their* ancestors, and so back.' Reportedly many of these tales were the inspiration for several Disney films such as *Bambi*, *The Lion King* and so on.

Abbie Farwell Brown

American author Abbie Farwell Brown (1871–1927) was born in Boston and attended the Girls' Latin School. While attending school she set up a school newspaper and also contributed articles to other magazines. Brown's books were most often retellings of old tales for children such as in *The Book of Saints* and *Friendly Beasts*. She also published a collection of tales from Norse mythology, *In the Days of Giants*, which became the common text held by many libraries for several generations.

Sarah Peverley

(Text on *Le Morte d'Arthur*)

Sarah Peverley is an award winning medievalist, cultural historian and BBC New Generation Thinker. As Professor of English at the University of Liverpool, she teaches and researches medieval literature and history. She also directs The Liverpool Players, a performance group specialising in early literature and drama. Her current research focuses on literature produced during the Wars of the Roses and the cultural history of mermaids. As an expert on the Middle Ages, Sarah regularly contributes to television documentaries, broadcasts on BBC Radio, and gives public talks at festivals and heritage events. For more information visit her website at www.sarahpeverley.com.

W.H.I. Bleek

Wilhelm Heinrich Immanuel Bleek (1827–75) was a German linguist and philologist. He participated in projects in Niger and Natal before becoming Sir George Grey's official interpreter, cataloguer and curator. Bleek conducted research and contributed to publications, collecting examples of African literature from missionaries and travellers. He wrote regularly for the newspaper *Het Volksblad*, and published his *A Comparative Grammar of South African Languages* in two parts in 1862 and 1869. Together with Lucy Lloyd, he met and interviewed members of the San people in order to research and record linguistic, anthropological, ethnographic and cultural information, leading to 'The Bleek and Lloyd Archive' of |Xam and !Kung texts. Examples from this were collated into a printed book called *Specimens of Bushman Folklore* (1911).

James S. de Benneville

James Seguin de Benneville was a nineteenth-century author whose writings concerning Japan include *The Fruit of the Tree* ('travel notes on thoughts and things Japanese, experienced during a four years' sojourn in the country'), *Tales of the Wars of the Gempei* ('being the story of the lives and adventures of Iyo-no-Kami Minamoto Kurō Yoshitsune and Saitō Musashi-Bō Benkei the Warrior Monk), *Tales of the Samurai* ('being the story of the lives, the adventures, and the misadventures of the Hangwan-dai Kojirō Sukéshigé and Ternte-hime, his wife) and his *Tales of the Tokugawa* – in two volumes (1917 and 1921) and 'retold from the Japanese originals': *The Yotsuya Kwaidan; Or O'Iwa Inari* and *Bakémono Yashiki (The Haunted House)*, the latter including the *Bancho Sarayashiki*.

F. Hadland Davis

Frederick Hadland Davis was a writer and a historian – author of *The Land of the Yellow Spring and Other Japanese Stories* (1910) and *The Persian Mystics* (1908 and 1920). His books describe these cultures to the western world and tell stories of ghosts, creation, mystical creatures and more. He is best known for his book *Myths and Legends of Japan* (1912).

Elphinstone Dayrell

Dayrell (1869–1917) collected his tales after hearing many first-hand from the Efik and Ibibio peoples of Southeastern Nigeria when he was District Commissioner of South Nigeria. His collections of folklore include *Folk Stories From southern Nigeria* (1910) and *Ikom Folk Stories From southern Nigeria*, the latter published by the Royal Anthropological Institute of Great Britain and Ireland in 1913.

Herbert A. Giles

Herbert Allen Giles (1845–1935) was a British diplomat and sinologist, working in Mawei, Shanghai, Tamsui and finally as British Consul at Ningpo. In 1897 he became professor of Chinese language at Cambridge University, a post that lasted for 35 years. He published many writings on Chinese language, as well as on literature and religion, such as his *Chinese-English Dictionary* (1891), and several translations of classic Chinese tales, including Pu Songling's *Strange Stories from a Chinese Studio* (1880).

William Elliot Griffis

Born in Philadelphia, William Elliot Griffis (1843–1928) went on to serve as a corporal during the American Civil War. He studied at Rutgers University after the war and graduated in 1869. He tutored Latin and English to a samurai from Fukui and then travelled around Europe for a year prior to studying at what is now known as the New Brunswick Theological Seminary. In 1870, Griffis went to Japan and became Superintendent of Education in the province of Echizen because of his organisation of schools there. During the 1870s, Griffis and his sister taught at many different institutes and he wrote for many newspapers and magazines. In 1872 he prepared the *New Japan Series of Reading and Spelling Books* and left Japan in 1874, having made many connections and friendships with Japan's future leaders. On returning to the United States he worked in several churches on the east coast but retired in 1903 to write. With the help of his extensive knowledge of Japanese and European culture, he produced a number of books, such as *Japanese Fairy World* (1880), *The Fire-fly's Lovers and Other Fairy Tales of Old Japan* (1908), *Japanese Fairy Tales* (1922), *Korean Fairy Tales* (1922), *Belgian Fairy Tales* (1919) and many more.

H.A. Guerber

Hélène Adeline Guerber (1859–1929) was a British historian who published a large number of works, largely focused on myths and legends. Guerber's most famous publication is *Myths of the Norsemen: From the Eddas and Sagas*, a history of Germanic mythology. Her works continue to be published today and include *The Myths of Greece and Rome*, *The Story of the Greeks* and *Legends of the Middle Ages*.

Lafcadio Hearn

After being abandoned by both of his parents, Lafcadio Hearn (1850–1904) was sent from Greece to Ireland and later to the United States where he became a newspaper reporter in Cincinnati and later New Orleans where he contributed translations of French authors to the *Times Democrat*. His wandering life led him eventually to Japan where he spent the rest of his life finding inspiration from the country and, especially, its legends and ghost stories. Hearn published many books in his lifetime, informative on aspects of Japanese custom, culture and religion and which influenced future folklorists and writers whose writings feature in this collection – standout examples of Hearn's output include *Glimpses of Unfamiliar Japan* (1894), *Kokoro: Hints and Echoes of Japanese Inner Life* (1896), *Japanese Fairy Tales* (1898, and sequels), *Shadowings* (1900), *Kottō: Being Japanese Curios, with Sundry Cobwebs* (1902) and *Kwaidan: Stories and Studies of Strange Things* (1903). In 1891 Hearn married and had four children but later died of heart failure in Tokyo in 1904.

Stephen Hodge

(Introductory material on Japanese Mythology)

A linguist in Japanese and an author with a specialist knowledge of Japanese culture, oriental religions and theology, Stephen Hodge (b. 1947) graduated from the School of Oriental and African Studies, did MA research in Japan and taught at the University of London.

James A. Honeij, M.D.

Dr James Albert Burnside Honeij (1880–1924) was born in Bloemfontein in Free State, South Africa, but worked and died in Cambridge, Massachusetts. Though a doctor, he had an apparent interest in folklore, publishing a collection of *South-African Folk-Tales* (1910) for an American audience, stating that many of them have 'appeared among English collections previous to 1880, others have been translated from the Dutch, and a few have been written from childhood remembrance.

Joseph Jacobs

Joseph Jacobs (1854–1916) was born in Australia and settled in New York. He is most famous for his collections of English folklore and fairytales including 'Jack and the Beanstalk' and 'The Three Little Pigs'. He also published Celtic, Jewish and Indian fairytales during his career. Jacobs was an editor for books and journals centered on folklore and a member of The Folklore Society in England.

Michael Kerrigan

(Introductory material)

Michael Kerrigan has written on the history, mythology, arts and culture of many different countries, from India to Ireland and from Mongolia to Peru. His abridgements of *The Journals of Lewis and Clark* (2004) and Charles Darwin's *Voyage of the Beagle:*

The Journals that Revealed Nature's Grand Plan (2005) presented the explorers' own journals, in their own words, for modern readers. A longstanding contributor to the *Times Literary Supplement*, he lives with his family in Edinburgh.

Andrew Lang

Poet, novelist and anthropologist Andrew Lang (1844–1912) was born in Selkirk, Scotland. He is now best known for his collections of fairy stories and publications on folklore, mythology and religion. Inspired by the traditional folklore tales of his home on the English-Scottish border, Lang complied twelve coloured fairy books which collected 798 stories from French, Danish, Russian and Romanian sources, amongst others. *The Grey Fairy Book* (1900) contains a lone African-inspired story of 'The Jackal and the Spring'. This hugely successful series further encouraged the increasing popularity of fairy tales in children's literature

Davide Latini

Davide Latini is currently a PhD student at SOAS. He obtained his BA in Foreign Cultures and Languages at Carlo Bo University of Urbino, and focused on classical Chinese studies during his MA at Ca' Foscari University of Venice. His field of research revolves around the symbology of ancient Chinese mythology and its relationship with the ideological and textual context in which the narratives are inserted.

L.C. Lloyd

Lucy Catherine Lloyd (1834–1914) worked with W.H.I. Bleek to create 'The Bleek and Lloyd Archive' of of |Xam and !Kung texts which led to *Specimens of Bushman Folklore* (1911), which she edited. When the first |Xam speakers arrived to live with them at their house in Mowbray, she became responsible for recording two thirds of the texts collected, and continued the work alone after Bleek's death, assuming the curatorship of the Grey Collection and maintaining her own research. Lucy also played an important role in the founding of both the South African Folklore Society and, in 1879, the *Folklore Journal*. In 1913 Lloyd became the first woman in South Africa to receive an Honorary Doctorate from the University of the Cape of Good Hope in recognition of her contribution to research.

Eirikr Magnusson

Eirikr Magnusson (1833–1913) was an Icelandic scholar who worked during his life as a librarian at Cambridge University. He arrived in England in 1862 after being sent by the Icelandic Bible Society to translate Christian texts. Magnusson's most notable work was his teaching of Old Norse to William Morris and their collaborations on translations. Together they published numerous Icelandic sagas including *The Story of Grettir the Strong*, *Volsunga Saga* and *Heimskringl*. Magnusson and Morris also spent time traveling around Iceland to visit places which were of significance to the Icelandic sagas they translated.

Minnie Martin

Minnie Martin was the wife of a government official, who arrived in South Africa in 1891 and settled in Lesotho (at that time Basutoland). In her preface to *Basutoland: Its Legends and Customs* (1903) she explains that 'We both liked the country from the first, and I soon became interested in the people. To enable myself to understand them better, I began to study the language, which I can now speak fairly well.' And thus she wrote this work, at the suggestion of a friend. Despite the inaccuracies pointed out by E. Sidney Hartland in his review of her book, he deemed the work 'an unpretentious, popular account of a most interesting branch of the Southern Bantus and the country they live in.'

Frederick H. Martens

Frederick Herman Martens (1874–1932) was an author, lyricist and translator, whose work includes a translation of Pietro Yon's 1917 Christmas carol 'Gesu Bambino', a biography of the musician A.E. Uhe (1922), *A Thousand and One Nights of Opera* (1926), *Violin Mastery* (*Talks with Master Violinists and Teachers*) (1919), and fairy-tale translations in *The Chinese Fairy Book* (ed. Dr. R. Wilhelm).

Norman Hinsdale Pitman

Norman Hinsdale Pitman (1876–1925) was an author and educator, born in Lamont, Michigan. His works include: *The Lady Elect: A Chinese Romance* (1913), *A Chinese Wonder Book* (1919), *Chinese Fairy Tales* (1924) and *Dragon Lure: A Romance of Peking* (1925).

A.B. Mitford, Lord Redesdale

Algernon Bertram Freeman-Mitford, 1st Baron Redesdale (1837–1916), was a writer, collector and British diplomat. He was educated at Eton and at Oxford University, and later went to Japan as second secretary of the British Legation. His stay in Japan and his meeting Ernest Satow inspired the writing of *Tales of Old Japan* (1871). The book allowed several Japanese classics to be exposed to the Western world.

William Morris

Textile designer, poet, novelist and translator William Morris (1834–96) was born in Essex and studied at Oxford University. Morris is best known for his textiles work as he created designs for wallpaper, stained glass windows and embroideries that are enduringly popular. Alongside this, Morris wrote poetry, fiction and essays and after befriending Eirikr Magnusson he helped to translate many Icelandic tales. In his final years Morris published fantasy fiction including *The Wood Beyond the World* and *The Well at the World's End* and these were the first fantasy books to be set in an imaginary world. His legacy is an important one as he was a major contributor to both textile arts and literature.

Ovid

A contemporary of Virgil and Horace and alongside them ranked as one of the three canonical poets of Latin literature, Publius Ovidius Naso (43 BC–17/18 AD) was a Roman poet during the reign of Augustus and is best known for his *Metamorphoses*, an epic narrative poem dealing with the transformations of characters from Greco-Roman myth.

Yei Theodora Ozaki

The translations of Japanese stories and fairy tales by Yei Theodora Ozaki (1871–1932) were, by her own admission, fairly liberal ('I have followed my fancy in adding such touches of local colour or description as they seemed to need or as pleased me'), and yet proved popular. They include *Japanese Fairy Tales* (1908), 'translated from the modern version written by Sadanami Sanjin', and *Warriors of Old Japan, and Other Stories* (1909).

Professor James Riordan
James Riordan (1936–2012) was Emeritus Professor at the University of Surrey and Honorary Professor at both Stirling and Hong Kong Universities. He published several books on myths and folklore, including Heracles and Jason and the Argonauts from Ancient Greece, and Yoruba myths from Africa. He also gathered tales among the natives of North America and Siberia.

Pu Songling
Pu Songling (1640–1715) was a private tutor and writer in Qing Dynasty China, best known as the author of *Strange Stories from a Chinese Studio* (*Liaozhai Zhiyi*), a collection of classical Chinese stories often of a fantastical or supernatural character which implicitly criticise contemporary societal issues.

Henry M. Stanley
'Dr Livingstone, I presume?' Welshman Sir Henry Morton Stanley (1841–1904) is probably most famous for a line he may or may not have uttered, on encountering the missionary and explorer he had been sent to locate in Africa. He was also an ex-soldier who fought for the Confederate Army, the Union Army, and the Union Navy before becoming a journalist and explorer of central Africa. He joined Livingstone in the search for the source of the Nile and worked for King Leopold II of Belgium in the latter's mission to conquer the Congo basin. His works include *How I Found Livingstone* (1872), *Through the Dark Continent* (1878), *The Congo and the Founding of Its Free State* (1885), *In Darkest Africa* (1890) and *My Dark Companions* (1893).

Capt. C.H. Stigand
Chauncey Hugh Stigand (1877–1919) was a British army officer, colonial administrator and big game hunter who served in Burma, British Somaliland and British East Africa. He was in charge of the Kajo Kaji district of what is now South Sudan, and was later made governor of the Upper Nile province and then Mongalla Province before being killed during a 1919 uprising of the Aliab Dinka people. During his time in Africa he managed to write prolifically, from *Central African Game and its Spoor* (1906), through *Black Tales for White Children* (1914), to *A Nuer-English Vocabulary*, published posthumously in 1923.

Maria Tatar
(Foreword)
Maria Tatar is the John L. Loeb Research Professor of Germanic Languages & Literatures and Folklore & Mythology at Harvard University, where she is also a Senior Fellow at the Society of Fellows. Her books include *Enchanted Hunters: The Power of Stories in Childhood* and *The Annotated Brothers Grimm*.

Virgil
(*The Aeneid,* text translated by J.W. Mackail)
Publius Virgilius Maro (70–19 BC) was a Roman poet during the reign of Augustus. Virgil is best-known for his epic poem the *Aeneid,* modelled on the great epics of Homer, in which he describes the adventures of the Trojan hero Aeneas as he abandons Troy after the Greeks win the war and seeks a new home in Italy. Aeneas is the ancestor of Romulus and Remus, who eventually found Rome itself. Virgil's other

major works were the *Eclogues*, which explore the theme of revolutionary change; and the *Georgics*, which are ostensibly about agriculture but contain many other underlying themes.

Alice Werner

Alice Werner (1859–1935) was a writer, poet and professor of Swahili and Bantu languages. She travelled widely in her early life but by 1894 had focused her writing on African culture and language, and later joined the School of Oriental Studies, working her way up from lecturer to professor. *Myths and Legends of the Bantu* (1933) was her last main work, but others on African topics include *The Language Families of Africa* (1915), *Introductory Sketch of the Bantu Languages* (1919), *The Swahili Saga of Liongo Fumo* (1926), *A First Swahili Book* (1927), *Swahili Tales* (1929), *Structure and Relationship of African Languages* (1930) and *The Story of Miqdad and Mayasa* (1932).

E.T.C. Werner

Edward Theodore Chalmers Werner (1864–1954) was a sinologist specialising in Chinese superstition, myths and magic. He worked as a British diplomat in China during the final imperial dynasty, working his way up to British Consul-General in 1911. Being posted to all four corners of China encouraged Werner's interest in the mythological culture of the land, and after retirement he was able to concentrate on his sinological studies, of which *Myths & Legends of China* (1922) was one result.

Dr R. Wilhelm

Richard Wilhelm (1873–1930) was a German theologian, missionary and sinologist. He is best known for his works of translations of philosophical works from Chinese into German, including his translation of the *I Ching* and *The Secret of the Golden Flower*. He also edited *The Chinese Fairy Book* (1921).

W.B. Yeats

William Butler Yeats (1865–1939) was an Irish poet and is considered one of the greatest writers from the twentieth century. He played an important role in the Celtic Twilight, a revival of Irish literature focused on Gaelic heritage and Irish nationalism. Yeats was fascinated by Irish legends, including many Irish heroes in his works and focusing his poetry on Irish folklore. Alongside his poetry he is famous for writing short stories and plays. Yeats set up the Abbey Theatre in 1899 which held Irish and Celtic performances. In recognition of Yeats' important work he received a Nobel Prize in 1923.

FLAME TREE PUBLISHING
Epic, Dark, Thrilling & Gothic

New & Classic Writing

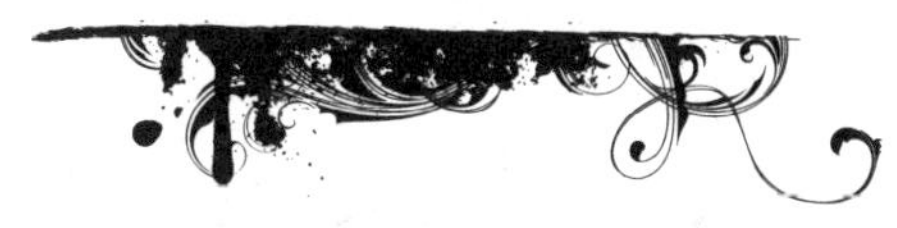

Flame Tree's Gothic Fantasy books offer a carefully curated series of new titles, each with combinations of original and classic writing:

Chilling Horror • *Chilling Ghost* • *Science Fiction*
Murder Mayhem • *Crime & Mystery* • *Swords & Steam*
Dystopia Utopia • *Supernatural Horror* • *Lost Worlds*
Time Travel • *Heroic Fantasy* • *Pirates & Ghosts* • *Agents & Spies*
Endless Apocalypse • *Alien Invasion* • *Robots & AI* • *Lost Souls*
Haunted House • *Cosy Crime* • *American Gothic*
Urban Crime • *Epic Fantasy* • *Detective Mysteries*

Also, new companion titles offer rich collections of classic fiction, myths and tales in the gothic fantasy tradition:

H.G. Wells • *Lovecraft* • *Sherlock Holmes*
Edgar Allan Poe • *Bram Stoker* • *Mary Shelley*
African Myths & Tales • *Celtic Myths & Tales* • *Greek Myths & Tales*
Norse Myths & Tales • *Chinese Myths & Tales* • *Japanese Myths & Tales*
Irish Fairy Tales • *King Arthur & The Knights of the Round Table*
Alice's Adventures in Wonderland • *The Divine Comedy*
Hans Christian Andersen Fairy Tales • *Brothers Grimm*
The Wonderful Wizard of Oz • *The Age of Queen Victoria*

Available from all good bookstores, worldwide, and online at
flametreepublishing.com

See our new fiction imprint
FLAME TREE PRESS | FICTION WITHOUT FRONTIERS
New and original writing in Horror, Crime, SF and Fantasy

And join our monthly newsletter with offers and more stories:
FLAME TREE FICTION NEWSLETTER
flametreepress.com

GOTHIC FANTASY